V

MW01234423

Hearts

a 4-in-1 Anthology

Marianne Evans

*'includes all three Woodland Church novels
and the Contest-winning novella that started it all.'*

Hearts Crossing
Hearts Surrender
Hearts Communion
Hearts Key

This is a work of fiction. Names, characters, places, and incidents either are the product of the author's imagination or are used fictitiously, and any resemblance to actual persons living or dead, business establishments, events, or locales, is entirely coincidental.

Woodland Hearts: A 4-in-1 Anthology

COPYRIGHT 2010, 2011, 2016 by Marianne Evans

Contact Information: titleadmin@pelicanbookgroup.com

All scripture quotations, unless otherwise indicated, are taken from the Holy Bible, New International Version(R), NIV(R), Copyright 1973, 1978, 1984, 2011 by Biblica, Inc.™ Used by permission of Zondervan. All rights reserved worldwide. www.zondervan.com

Cover Art by *Nicola Martinez*

White Rose Publishing, a division of Pelican Ventures, LLC
www.pelicanbookgroup.com PO Box 1738 *Aztec, NM * 87410

White Rose Publishing Circle and Rosebud logo is a trademark of Pelican Ventures, LLC

Publishing History
First White Rose Edition, 2016
Paperback Edition ISBN 978-1-61116-873-0
Electronic Edition ISBN 978-1-61116-872-3
Published in the United States of America

What People are Saying

Hearts Crossing is a Gayle Wilson Award of Excellence finalist for Best Novella of 2010 Southern Magic, the Birmingham Alabama Chapter of RWA

…a realistic look at Christians without being preachy or over-the-top. I know anyone who reads this book will love it. In fact, I hope there is a sequel. ~ 5-Hearts / Brenda Talley, The Romance Studio on Hearts Crossing

Both Daveny and Collin are wonderful characters who have a delightful relationship. I enjoyed the path to Collin's returning faith and the sweetness of Hearts Crossing. ~ 4.5 Books Top Pick / Silvermage, Night Owl Reviews on Hearts Crossing

Ms. Evans has once again delivered a book which I could not put down…I cannot wait for the rest of this series. If possible, it just got better than the first book. ~ 5 Hearts—Book of the Week, Brenda Talley, The Romance Studio on Hearts Surrender

Hearts Surrender is a satisfying, feel good romance that goes beyond mere happy endings…I can't wait for the next Woodland book to be published! ~ 5 Klovers— Recommended Read, Crystal, Kwips & Kritiques

Hearts Crossing

Hearts Crossing Dedication

Beth—Thank you, thank you for brainstorming this with me! I owe you, honey. Dan & Mary—you both mean the world to me. Having you at my side when I found out about this book's publication is a memory I'll forever treasure.

Prologue

Collin Edwards stood before the funeral assembly.

Nervous heat crawled up his body and settled in. He clutched the edges of the podium where he stood and softly cleared his throat. The gesture was in vain. His throat constricted so much it hurt. Before the altar, just to the right, rested a flag-draped casket.

Collin looked down at a piece of paper upon which he had crafted the words to a eulogy. The words had refused to pour forth until just after three in the morning, not that he had slept much over the past few days.

He glanced at the cheat sheet. Tears built and stung. The white paper, the black scribblings blurred together into a hideous shade of gray.

"He took the bullet," Collin began in a voice that felt far removed and tight, yet shockingly calm. "He answered the call to serve and protect, and he took the bullet. He helped a woman in need, a woman threatened by the man she loved, and he took the bullet. He was the oldest of our family, our leader and compass. And he took the bullet. He lived a life meant to enforce the law and the idea that we must do what's right. And he took the bullet. Lance Edwards was my big brother, my benchmark. Our family now bears a tremendous hole. Because he took the bullet."

Only then did Collin take a conscious breath. Only then did he release his death grip on the podium. He slid the paper into a crumpled clutch and walked quickly to the first pew.

He didn't notice much right away. He didn't search out individual faces. The only image that immediately clung to Collin's consciousness was that of his mother, her head bowed, her shoulders shaking as she wiped her eyes free of the tears that simply kept coming.

He bit the inside of his cheek. Hard.

The service continued. Now, despite an odd form of detachment, images and sensations became a flood, spinning into place like the ever-shifting patterns of a kaleidoscope. Sunlight split into prisms by vibrant stained glass; the aroma of lilies, roses and carnations; the gleaming brass cross suspended above the altar, above them all.

The cross.

It offered Collin no comfort now. In fact, it felt foreign. Senseless. Pain roiled then overwhelmed him. Pain turned to resentment. Resentment bloomed into fury.

Where are You? He screamed in silence. *Where* were *You?*

This was Your plan? This was Your purpose for Lance's life? Obviously the answer is yes, so obviously You're a God of waste and pain.

Don't ever speak to me again about being loving and providential and merciful.

Just like that, a switch in his heart clicked from on to off, in his mind and his soul. Darkness rode in, and he embraced it. To do so was so much easier than dealing with the pain he felt, the guilt, the agony of losing hope and the innocent joy of faith.

Never again.

Collin looked around, deliberately taking stock of Woodland Church of Christ. He captured everything in a definitive moment of resolution and life change.

Never again will I return to the home of a supposed Lord and Savior who would allow such a thing. It'll be better for me to stay away now, right, God?

Well don't worry. Never again will I darken the door of a church. And You keep as far away from me as possible, too. I want nothing more to do with You.

Ever.

1

Five Years Later

"Daveny, don't rush off. I want to talk to you."

Daveny Montgomery squirmed inwardly but hid the reaction. Ten o'clock services at Woodland Church were freshly concluded. The narthex was filling rapidly with bodies in motion and the chatter of voices as greetings were exchanged and parishioners mixed and mingled for a bit before leaving. Children dodged through the maze of people, happily calling out to one another.

The summons of Pastor Kenneth Lucerne stalled Daveny's retreat to the parking lot. Hoping to make an unobtrusive exit from church, she quickly moved herself into a more welcoming mindset.

Pastor Ken had been part of her faith life for well over five years now, ever since the end of her college years. She adored him.

Crowds gradually thinned to small clusters; then Pastor Ken was able to give Daveny his full attention.

"So how you doing, kiddo?" he greeted.

Daveny stepped into a hug and gave him a smile. "I'm good, thanks."

He chuckled, tucking her hand into the crook of

his arm. They walked outside to the expansive, if barren, entryway of the church building. Sunshine warmed the air even as soft, cool breezes curved inward through budding tree branches, making them chatter.

"Spring is here," Pastor Ken observed. "Finally. You'll be stepping into high gear over the next few months, huh?"

"I'm happy to say Montgomery Landscaping already has two big assignments lined up—one for a health club in Grosse Pointe and another for a loft development in downtown Detroit."

"That's my girl." He complimented her, but cast her a sly grin. "Perhaps that's why I'm not seeing you around quite so often these days?"

Daveny wilted, leaning on him in exaggerated physical apology. "Convicted. Sorry."

He gave her hand a squeeze as they wandered the perimeter of the church building. "Apology accepted. You haven't been gone *that* often, but I miss you when you're not at service. Keep up the fight, Daveny. You're needed."

"Yes, sir," she replied and meant it.

Daveny loved the Woodland church community, the faith life she had built here. Recently though, she found herself falling flat spiritually. She considered that fact as they continued to stroll. The setting was gorgeous. Towering pines and thick old maples filled a rolling tract of land just starting to wake up following a long, typically brutal, Michigan winter. Like her faith walk at the moment, it did its job, and was pleasantly utilitarian—but the grounds lacked zest. Spark. They needed an uplift.

"Did you hear about Jim Cavanaugh's passing?"

Pastor Ken asked.

Sadness trickled downward from her head to her heart. "Yeah, Sarah Miles told me. He was a total sweetheart and a tremendous volunteer."

"He'll be deeply missed, not just because he was an active member of our church, but because of who he was as a person." Pastor Ken laughed, the sound warm and tender. "I'll always think of his homemade pasties each year when we have the International Dinner."

"They were my favorite."

"A taste of Northern Michigan for the down-staters," they said in unison, recalling one of Jim's favorite quotes.

"He was the kindest greeter," Daveny added. "People flocked to him when they entered church every week just to be able to shake his hand and get a smile and that big, boisterous greeting."

Daveny waited. Judging by the way Pastor Ken let the conversation dangle, it seemed he was about to elaborate. He bent, picking at weeds, dead leaves and a bit of overgrowth that spilled over the small black rubber edging of the narrow flowerbeds. Effective border shaping, but not at all picturesque, Daveny thought. Not at all what this church deserved.

Reviewing the grounds through the eyes of her chosen profession—a landscape architect—Daveny uncovered incredible potential.

A cross-tipped spire stretched into a cobalt sky devoid of clouds. Adding much to the setting was the fact that directly across Jefferson Avenue was Lake Saint Clair, a wide, sparkling blue jewel that dominated the horizon and added a gentle rumble of water life and boat sound to the air; especially on a restful and gorgeous Sunday morning like this.

"Jim had no children," Pastor Ken continued. "He had an older brother and a younger sister, both of whom passed on before him. I think that's part of what led him to be such a vital component of our church family." He stole a glance toward Daveny. "I can only assume that's why Woodland was named a beneficiary in his will."

Their meandering ended. Pastor Ken turned to face her fully. Daveny went into landscape design mode once again, thinking about how wonderful a wrought iron bench would be right now, a few of them perhaps, along the curved edges of the sidewalk that skirted the church. That way they could sit and be comfortable.

Pastor Ken continued. "He designated fifty thousand dollars toward restoration and beautification of the church."

Daveny's jaw dropped. She froze, staring at Pastor Ken. He simply smiled and nodded, saying, "I see you can already tell where I'm headed with this."

"Oh...ah...gosh..."

His laughter filled the rapidly warming air. Bird song and the light aroma of lily of the valley and hyacinth flowed into the atmosphere.

"You're an incredible designer and a remarkable woman. God needs to use that. Frankly, there's no one I'd trust more to make this project work. I discussed the idea with church council last week, and they're behind it one hundred percent. Contracts will have to be put together, as well as timing and fee schedules of course, but we want you to design and execute the exterior development." He paused just long enough to give her a kind and challenging look. "Can I count you in?"

"Count me in? It would be an honor. Just try to keep me away."

Delighted, with seeds of vigor taking root, Daveny squeezed his hand as they sealed the deal.

2

"Mom, *please*. You're pushing. *Again*."

Collin stood firm, steady and unaffected when his mom, Elise, clucked her tongue. She turned from her salad-building exercise to give him a glare. She was a tad put-out, despite the fact that his reprimand had been quietly spoken. That settled his disquiet to simmer instead of boil.

"Collin Alexander Edwards, I'm not asking you to do anything but deliver paver bricks and some bags of mulch to the church. Just drop it and leave. The landscape company is going to be on site today and tomorrow so they need the materials as soon as possible."

"And since I happen to have a truck..."

"And since you happen to live in the area..." She paused from her lunch creation once again; this time she beamed at him.

Yep, Collin thought in resignation, *I'm toast. Hooked right in.* He couldn't hold out against his mom. Not when she smiled like that. Plus, like she said, he wasn't attending services or anything. This was simply a delivery job. Nothing to it. And it would help her out.

Collin relented and walked to the kitchen counter where she stood, timeless as a precious memory with her sweatshirt, blue jeans and page-boy style hair of silver. Though he had already eaten lunch, he swiped a few slices of celery. A baby tomato. She slapped his hand and sighed.

"Do I get dinner tonight if I say yes?" he asked.

"A bribing mercenary," she muttered, continuing her salad creation. "I raised a bribing mercenary."

Collin pecked her cheek. "Where are the supplies I need to take?"

"The mulch is in the garage. On the cork board behind you is the receipt to pick up the pavers we bought the other day to donate to the cause."

He found and removed the receipt in question. Framed by a picture window overlooking the freshly mowed back yard, his mother paused to give Collin a final smile. "I appreciate this, and I'm counting on you for dinner. Love you, sweetheart."

He winked at her. "Thanks, Mom. I love you, too."

Marching orders in place, Collin turned to leave behind the sunny, airy kitchen of his parent's home.

∼✦∽

The closer he got to Woodland Church, the more Collin's tension increased. He faced that fact without flinching and without apologizing.

He couldn't help the sense of anger he felt whenever he considered matters of faith and the topic of God's goodness, so he didn't try to stem the tide. Helping his mom is what mattered, and the thought kept Collin centered as he turned off Jefferson Avenue and into the church parking lot.

"Wow."

The single word exclamation was Collin's instinctive reaction upon seeing the church. Grounds were torn up in large spots and contractors worked at the open sores. Collin slowed his truck to a stop next to a series of graders, haulers, and a semi that were presently swarmed by what he assumed were church volunteers.

He hopped down from the cab of his pickup and released the back latch, looking around for a person who might be deemed the leader of this renovation project.

And a project is exactly what this was. Major league. A sizable chunk of land to the rear of the facility was torn up as well. There, a hauler and backhoe were being put to use. Field stones and flat limestone pieces were positioned, ready for placement, and it looked as though some kind of water supply system was being put into place.

A pond perhaps?

Flower beds were being expanded and upgraded across the front and sides of the church. Bushes and trees stood in waiting, roots wrapped and tied in protective burlap. The grounds were a transitory mess.

The fact that he stopped to stare drew the attention of a passerby, an older, friendly looking man who called affably, "Need some help?"

Collin gave him a nod. "Delivery. Can you point me to the right person?"

"You bet. That'd be Daveny. She'll get you taken care of. Follow me over."

"Thanks."

They crossed the lot and closed in on a cluster of folks who were in scrubby clothes, water bottles and gardening tools in hand. At the center of it all was a slender, petite woman wearing jeans and a lime green t-shirt. They stepped up, and Collin realized she was in the process of assigning volunteers to designated sections of the church grounds, occasionally consulting an overview spec sheet of the project spread out across a picnic table and secured at each end by a pair of weighty rocks.

During a pause in the delegation efforts, Collin's escort spoke up.

"Daveny, this gentleman brought us some supplies. Looks like the brick borders and mulch have arrived."

"Perfect. Thanks, Gabe."

She turned.

Her gaze lifted to his in greeting.

Collin's world tilted.

Something—something overwhelming and instantly captivating swept through him like wind song when she smiled. The gesture was radiant and warm, straight from the heart.

"Hi, I'm Daveny Montgomery."

Collin, meanwhile, stumbled over his own name, mentally stalling out while he stared at her. There was a purity he sensed, elusive and instantly haunting.

"Collin Edwards," he finally managed, taking hold of her extended hand. Firm grip, he noted. Skin, soft as silk. Nice.

"Glad to meet you—wait—*Edwards*. You must be one of Elise and Ben's sons."

Collin focused on a faint, fresh smudge of dirt on her cheek. The sight made his fingertips twitch with a longing to stroke it gently away. "Guilty as charged."

"They're amazing." Daveny's compliment was stated with a flat out degree of conviction. Something flickered through her eyes though, confusion it seemed. "You live around here?"

"Just a couple miles away."

"Oh. I thought I had met all of the family." Her confusion fell away, replaced by acceptance and kindness. "Let me recruit some volunteers to help unload."

"OK."

With a nod, she headed to a group of men who were ripping out a series of disintegrating rounded rubber boarder frames. As they ripped, they tossed the refuse into a rapidly growing discard pile.

Daveny wore a gray baseball cap that featured the green and white Spartan logo of Michigan State University. Her long brown hair was fashioned into a straight, shiny ponytail that she had tucked through the back end of her cap. The ponytail bounced in time to her movements, and Collin found himself smiling, strangely fixated.

Daveny Montgomery. Pretty name...

Then it occurred to him. Suddenly Collin understood why she seemed somewhat flummoxed by his arrival. Every week, the entire Edwards family made it a practice to attend ten o'clock services together at Woodland.

Everyone except Collin.

She probably wondered why he wasn't in the pews along with his obviously loving and close-knit clan—especially if he lived nearby.

The realization fell on Collin's heart as Daveny gathered their reinforcements. The weight was unpleasant, but it burned off nicely in the face of his bitterness. No matter Daveny's brightness and appeal, he refused to feel bad about leaving church life, and God, behind.

The unloading process didn't take long, but the

bricks were gritty and cumbersome. At the end, Daveny turned to him, wiping her hands on her jeans. "Thanks again for providing shuttle service, Collin. We really appreciate it."

There it was again. That flash of heat and promise she could inspire by simply looking at him and speaking his name out loud.

He didn't want to leave. Not quite yet anyway.

As that realization took hold, Collin glanced around, looking for a means by which he might be useful. He had a few hours to spare before dinner, and it wouldn't hurt to lend this lovely lady some assistance. A group of people were gathered by that sizable hole in the ground at the rear of the property. A variety of tools and materials were spread out across the grass, along with a light blue-colored skin of plastic.

"You're creating a pond?"

"Yep. If it turns out the way I hope, it'll be the showpiece of the entire renovation."

"Can I help?"

Daveny turned to him with wide-eyed gratitude. "Are you kidding? We'd love it. You can help stretch and place the pond liner, or you could help lay and spread pea gravel for the overflow channel. Check in with Jim Sauser. He's the one with the bright orange cap—and our head contractor. He'll get you hooked up."

But where will you be?

That's the question Collin most wanted to ask, but refrained. For now it would be enough to just work near her, and watch—gain familiarity by absorbing her mannerisms.

"Sounds good. I'll go see what they need."

Her gaze lingered, as did her smile. "Thank you, Collin. Really. This is a big help."

"No problem."

3

Collin Edwards certainly didn't seem to mind hard work.

Daveny watched the newcomer and appreciated his easy demeanor with the crew to which she had assigned him, the efficient, vital aura he projected.

Intermittent spurts of joking and laughter spurred on the team as they stretched and placed the lining of the pond, settling it into place on the freshly graded ground. Next would be the rock placement and construction of the spill channel.

"I don't blame you. He's *hot!*"

Jerking free of her revelry Daveny turned to her right-hand colleague and up-and-coming designer in her own right, Kiara Jordan. She looked like a movie star, tall and willowy, with a big, gorgeous smile and an ocean of straight honey blonde hair that fell just past her shoulders. A pair of oversize sunglasses temporarily masked her wide, green eyes but accentuated high cheekbones and flawless olive skin.

"The new guy. He's hot," Kiara reiterated, nudging Daveny for unneeded emphasis. "Tell you what. While you enjoy the view, I'm off to rescue him with a bottle of cold water."

Daveny swatted her arm. "Oh, no you're not. I am."

Kiara lifted a bottle from the large iron tub full of

ice and beverages, chuckling when she handed it over.

"Reverse psychology. Works every time. Go. Give him a break." She slid down her glasses and peeked at Daveny over the rims. "While you're at it? Give yourself one, too."

Daveny issued a sigh of exasperation and eternal martyrdom. "Wench."

"Whatever gets the job done," Kiara quipped right back.

Daveny walked toward Collin with a bit of a huff to her attitude, purely for Kiara's benefit. When she neared the pond area, that sense of bravado slipped to tentative and shy.

Get over it, Montgomery. It's just attraction.

Broad shoulders worked against the cotton fabric of his white t-shirt. His biceps flexed, sinewy forearms went taut and lax as he lifted bags of gravel in tandem with the rest of his team.

Tall and lean, Collin looked great in his worn jeans and untucked, loose fitting shirt. Short brown hair had gone a bit damp while he worked and exertion added a touch of ruddy color to his face.

That focus drew Daveny's attention to deep-set eyes of sapphire framed by thick lashes and crowned by well-shaped brows. A bit of sweat glistened there, and she felt an even stronger compulsion to see to his comfort.

He turned away from her full view, which helped calm her nerves and that sudden, potent sizzle of masculine appeal.

But then he turned, as if sensing her approach. The impact of his gaze sent Daveny's just restored sense of calm into extinction.

"Hey," he greeted softly.

"Hey." She fidgeted with her delivery for a second before offering over the chilled plastic bottle, its surface already coated with condensation that trickled over her fingers, then his, as he took custody. "Pretty rude of me to put you to work without even a cold drink."

"Read minds in your spare time? This is great. Thank you very much."

He twisted the lid and Daveny watched him swig back a healthy swallow. Dangerous, since watching him quench his thirst made her mouth go dry.

"You're welcome." She took a deep, fortifying breath, preparing herself. Then the words came, without any type of filter or fore-planning. "The hired contractors are getting paid by the hour, and the volunteers are here for the benefit of our church. The least I can do after assigning you to hard labor is treat you to a cup of coffee or something when we finish up."

As soon as the words were out, Daveny realized how much she hoped he would say yes. She blushed, surprised at herself for even asking. She fell back on a touch of humor, adding, "That is, if you don't mind how I look at the moment."

"Daveny, you look just fine." There he paused for a moment, watching her intently. "I'd love it."

The pleasure Daveny saw in his eyes was more than enough of a reward for being so bold. The compliment helped tremendously as well.

She nodded and turned to rejoin Kiara, knowing her friend would just love this development. "I'll catch up with you later then?"

"That'd be great."

Collin left the restaurant choice to Daveny, so she picked The Java Hut, a lakeside establishment located just a few miles away from Woodland. Before leaving church, she had freshened up, unbinding her hair from its utilitarian ponytail. Collin now wore a new shirt he had grabbed from the cab of his truck. Free of project buffers, Daveny couldn't escape the intensity of his effect on her expectant, stuttering heart. From across the table she took in his fresh scrubbed skin and re-styled hair. Warm, tingling magnetism went to work on her senses all over again.

She ordered iced coffee, heavy on the whipped cream, and Collin did the same, adding a blueberry scone for them to divide and share.

Patio seating afforded an uninterrupted view of the sparkling blue waters of Lake Saint Clair, the vista dotted by brightly-colored sailboats, jet skis and a sky full of cottony clouds and squawking, wheeling gulls.

"A high school English teacher? I give you tremendous credit, Collin." Daveny sipped her bittersweet beverage and savored the chill. "Have you always loved writing and language?"

"I'm the classic book nerd. I'll tell you all of my awkward and sad junior high and high school stories some day."

They laughed together.

"All present evidence to the contrary." *Where in heaven's name is this flirty behavior coming from?* Daveny wondered, not that Collin seemed to mind.

"Being the youngest of eight left me in the position of observer. I always watched the other seven, as well as everything around us. I guess I've always been a watcher, chronicling my view of the world. Helping my students reach more fully into theirs, and express it, is something I love. There's such a beauty to well crafted writing and expression."

"Like I said, I admire you. It can't be easy teaching teenagers." But then Daveny did the math. "Eight children? I thought Elise and Ben had six—well seven—counting you."

That stilled him and sent the moment into a stilted pause.

"We, ah, lost my oldest brother. He died in the line of duty. He was a police officer."

"I'm so sorry." Daveny imagined it would be like losing a piece of your heart forever. "When did it happen?"

Collin sighed. He fingered a piece of scone, but then left it on his plate. "Five years, three months, fourteen days."

The murmured response, his downcast eyes, broke her heart. Even after this amount of time, he seemed raw. In deference to his comfort, Daveny revisited their earlier topic, his job.

"So, back to me admiring your patience and stamina…" She warmed the words with a smile she hoped would pave the way to their earlier ease.

"I figure it's worth the struggle. Books, words, thoughts and ideas, they intrigue me, and I tend to lose myself in the places and people I find in what they create."

His comfort returned. Mission accomplished. A soft, cool breeze skimmed in over the water, kissing Daveny's skin, inspiring her to close her eyes and sigh happily.

"You, Daveny Montgomery, are most definitely a nature girl."

Her eyes came open when he spoke, and she found her attention fixed on his face. A squared jaw was traced by a bit of stubble. Once again the clarity and depth of his eyes reached into her like a feathery caress that was brief but seductive when she realized he had observed her enjoyment of the elements.

"From the time I was little."

"Tell me your story. What led you to become a landscape architect?"

"Flowers."

They laughed at Daveny's simplistic overview then she relented with a smile and looked out at the waves that crested on the nearby curve of sandy beach. "I can't say for sure, although I remember, vividly, the year my parents completely reconstructed their yard." She looked back at Collin for a moment. "I was maybe nine or ten, and since I was an only child, and both my parents made good livings, we had a bit of extra money to do things like house renovations, gardening and landscaping. Anyway, our back yard was huge, and my mom helped oversee its creation from a typical yard in suburbia to an oasis. I think watching that process, seeing how beautiful it came to be, left me intrigued. I've always loved gardens." Daveny downed a chunk of scone and let it dissolve on her tongue. "I love the idea of making my mark."

"Like at Woodland."

She nodded. "The project is very special to me. My favorite part of it is what you were working on today. The pond. When we're finished, the narrow end of the pond will be surrounded by those flat limestone rocks you helped move. They'll form steps of a sort leading to a wooden bridge that spans the water. The church is sponsoring a fundraiser so parishioners can have their name, or the names of their loved ones, engraved on each plank. We look at it as a kind of footbridge for God, created by His people."

Once again Collin went mysteriously silent and unreadable. He fiddled with his knife. To fill the silence Daveny continued. "I needed this, to be honest. Lately I've found it to be way too easy to slip away from my faith; well, no more. This project has been my wake-up call."

They ordered a second scone, but the silence returned, and with it, that niggling degree of disquiet.

"Did I say something wrong?" she finally asked, puzzled.

"No. Nothing wrong." He smiled at her, but the smile was a bit strained at the edges. "Your conviction is wonderful, and completely sincere."

"Yes, it is."

He paused, but Daveny didn't step in again. This time she wanted him to continue and urged him to do so by staying quiet. A thread was being developed here, winding between them in a tentative, promising connection.

"I just—it's been a long time since I've been anywhere near Woodland. I don't feel the same way about God that you do."

"How *do* you feel about God?" she asked gently.

"I *don't*," he replied. But then he softened, and gave her an apologetic look. "For now, if you don't mind, can we leave it at that?"

The answer, coupled with accompanying pain she sensed, left her wanting to press. She wanted to comfort and assure, but she didn't. She didn't want to intrude where she didn't belong. After all, they were just getting to know one another.

"OK, I will. For now. Just one question though. Is that why you don't attend church with the rest of your family?"

Again, like something divinely inspired, the words escaped before she could even consider them or hold them in check. All Collin did was nod.

The reactions, his character, intrigued her tremendously because he seemed a genuinely wonderful person. Daveny sensed as much in the way he behaved and the vibration of goodness he gave off.

Yet he seemed lost, too.

Perhaps God had more in store for her than renovating Woodland. Maybe there was a way she might touch his heart, and his faith light. She had wondered, just a short time ago, how to re-find her fire for God. It seemed He was answering her prayers in abundance.

They chatted a bit longer and finished their treat. When the waitress delivered their bill their hands bumped, then connected when they simultaneously reached for it.

"My treat, remember?" Daveny said. "Easing my guilty conscience for putting you to work so shamelessly."

Collin looked into her eyes and a sensation of warmth slid right through her. He took her hand in his and gave it a squeeze.

"I want to. Really. If you hadn't asked me, I promise you this: I would have."

Daveny absorbed that comment in a moment of silence. Collin didn't release his hold on her hand. In fact, he stroked her wrist with the light, automatic touch of his thumb. Tingles, like soft sparkles, danced against her skin.

"When can I see you again? I've got dinner with my family tonight, but..."

"I've got a movie night planned with girlfriends. Sunday is church, and then we're taking advantage of the weather and continuing our landscaping job Monday and Tuesday night."

"Maybe I could come back. Help out."

"Oh...I get it now. You're a glutton for punishment." He didn't swallow the humor. Instead his regard was intent. Serious. "If you're sure you're game, I'd certainly love the help. And your company."

His answering smile picked up the pace of Daveny's pulse.

"Consider it done."

He slid the bill from her grasp, taking possession.

4

Dinner with the family was always noisy, crazy, boisterous...and fun.

Collin loved spoiling the kids, and being the youngest, and probably youngest at heart because of his job and single status, he wore the mantle of favored uncle with pleasure.

He ate perfectly prepared pork loin accompanied by fruit salad, biscuits and corn. When his parents put on a feast, they left no base uncovered—right up to the New York style cheese cake for desert.

After that came a baseball game played in the back yard, then Collin watched NBA playoff action with the guys while the women gathered in the kitchen and chatted.

His mom had plenty to chew on after asking him earlier about his supply delivery to the church. As soon as Collin mentioned staying for a few hours to help, she had jumped all over the topic, grilling him like a Marine sergeant. His three sisters were then just as bad, quizzing him endlessly on things like "chemistry" and "interest" and "potentiality" with regard to a certain landscape architect.

So, walking into his ranch-style condo after all was said and done felt like entering a soft cocoon full of peace and quiet. Collin toed off his sneakers and nudged them to the edge of the entryway, sighing with happiness to be home and able to fall flat on his back and rest.

My back.

The thought left him taking stock of his body. Ibuprofen. He needed ibuprofen. Desperately. Collin padded to the master bath that adjoined his bedroom and swallowed back the pain reliever, inwardly sighing over the fact that as he let himself relax and slow down, his body reacted with muscles that now screamed. In a few days, he was in for more of the same.

Pain or not, the idea left him smiling, but first things first. Rest and recovery were in order. He clicked off the lights after performing a cursory check of snail- and e-mail. Bed called, and he was exhausted.

∂∽

"Seriously? You want to do a ride-along?"

"Absolutely! It's for that senior level sociology class I'm taking. We're supposed to interact with caregivers or service providers, and study their relationship to the world around them. It'll be great because of the extraordinary circumstances you come across. Would it be OK?"

Lance sat behind the scarred wooden desk of the squad room. Collin loved seeing him here. It was late afternoon, but his blue uniform still looked neatly pressed, so official. Collin was insanely proud of him. The sergeant's insignia and silver badge hadn't come easy, but for Lance, his life as a police officer was a vocation. Collin waited, earnest and enthusiastic about seeing his brother on the job, and chronicling what he saw.

Lance grinned at him and Collin knew he had won. He

started to grin, too.

"Well, first of all, my job is far from extraordinary there, Joe College," Lance said. "Plus, there's waivers and releases, and not to mention the fact that Mom would kill me, kill me, then do some serious harm if anything happened to you. Then there's Sandy, who I'm quite sure hopes you survive long enough to graduate and make good on that ring you put on her finger."

Joe College. For three years running, ever since Collin started attending Oakland University, it was Lance's favorite nickname for him. Collin loved it, though of course he'd never let Lance know that. Collin realized the endearment stemmed from pride.

"Don't worry about either issue, bro. Didn't you just say how far from extraordinary your job is? It'll be no problem."

Collin's shot at sarcasm and needling did the job. Lance stood, adjusting the belt at his waist, which held a night stick, cuffs, pepper spray, and his gun. He was thick muscled and tended toward stocky, but only because he was built like a solid wall. Thick brown hair was worn regulation short, and his hazel eyes—like their dad's—were dark and intent, except when in the company of his family. Then they sparkled with mischief and life—vitality. Affection deeper than an ocean.

He was Collin's hero. Period.

"You'll be bored outta your mind," he warned. But at the same time he grinned. Lance left his desk behind, saying over his shoulder, "Hang tight a sec. Lemme get the forms. I assume since you're sitting here with a notebook you want to go tonight."

"May as well get it over with, right?" Collin replied, heavy on the bland and bored.

Lance just laughed.

A half hour later they were on the road, Collin riding shotgun, Lance at the wheel of a St. Clair Shores patrol car, taking in everything around them with a gaze that never rested for long. Collin stood by as Lance answered a robbery call at a gas station, settled an escalating bar fight at a somewhat seedy-looking bar. But the time passed mostly in the squad car, and that was fine. Collin talked and joked with his brother like always. Still, Lance's vigilance while on patrol was absolute, and impressive. He was a protector in its truest sense.

Humm...good observation. Collin jotted it down in his notebook and looked at the darkened, empty streets, trying hard to see it through Lance's eyes.

Meanwhile Lance explained the radio connection both in the car, and on the shoulder unit clipped near his right ear. Collin was confused by the verbiage.

"What's that mean? That Ten-Seven code?"

"Returning to the station. That's Tim Thompson. He's ending his tour for the night."

Collin nodded, jotting notes.

"And the other one that came in right after that from someone else? Ten-Eight?"

Lance chuckled, still watchful and vigilant. "Means he's back on duty. Ready for the next call." He reached to the storage compartment at Collin's knees and clicked it open, quipping, "Rookies. Take out that top laminated card. Keep it. I've got more."

It gave a run down of 10-Code and its translation.

"Cool," Collin replied, studying it.

"Pretty dull night. Not much for you to go on for your paper."

Collin shrugged, sidled him a look. "I could always come back."

Lance gave him a glance. "Yeah. You could I suppose.

Rookie."

The radio crackled and dispatch came through. "Unit 23, 415 in progress, 824 Lattimore."

Lance picked up the receiver and clicked on. "Ten-Four. 824 Lattimore."

"Four-Fifteen?" Collin asked.

Lance went all business, his eyes glinting hard, his jaw line set, but he answered: "Domestic disturbance."

Lance picked up the pace, moving the car smoothly and quickly to a quiet neighborhood, most of its lights gone dark for the night. Not this house though. He parked in front of an older, time-worn bungalow with lights ablaze. As soon as Lance opened the car door, Collin could hear the shouting, the crash and bang of a heated fight taking place.

"Stay put. Pay attention and keep your head down if anyone comes out. Hear me?"

Collin nodded, going tense inside.

Lance shut the door soundly and moved to the doorway with a brisk, authoritative stride. Collin cracked the window open a couple inches.

"Saint Clair Shores PD. Open the door." He spoke into the radio as he waited, a hand resting lightly on the butt of his gun. Collin watched, engrossed. No one answered, so this time Lance banged hard on the door. The cacophony of sound just increased. "Police. Open up." He cast a quick glance back at the car then Collin saw him glance up and down the street and speak into the radio again.

He trotted back to the car, opening the door. "I've got a bad feeling about this. I'm calling for back up." Lance was laser focused. "Stay where you are, and keep alert."

"Yeah. Got it." Collin frowned as Lance barked into the car radio for backup and activated the roof top light bars. He left the car to return to the front door.

This time his pounding was answered. The door was

yanked open, and a hulking, angry man filled the entrance.

"Step outside, sir." Lance directed, hand at the butt of his gun.

Instead of answering the man pushed open the screen door and in the process shoved Lance out of his way. He took off.

Lance shouted, giving chase.

What passed through Collin in that instant was an instinct driven desire to help his brother. To help put away a bad guy. That instinct overrode any safety concern as well as common sense. The man closed in on where the car was parked, cursing as he attempted evasion and escape.

Something small and silver glinted in his hand.

A gun.

Collin opened the car door, intending to slam it into the guy.

Lance tore toward him, shouting. "Get in the car. Stay down!"

Both men were now distracted. Lance had focused on Collin, worry creasing his face. The man looked back at Lance…and he stumbled.

The gun went off, its report filling the air like a lethal lightning circuit.

The man tumbled to the ground and cop cars began to squeal and peel, sirens flashing, strobe light filling the air. Lance went down like he'd been flattened.

Responding officers swarmed the scene quickly, cuffing the perpetrator and pulling him into a patrol car.

"Lance! Lance!"

Collin fell to Lance's side. Responding officers called frantically, "Ten-Double-Zero! Ten-Double-Zero…"

There was a hole in Lance's crisp blue shirt. Right at the heart. Collin stared at the ripped opening, a red stain coloring the fabric.

Lance's eyes fluttered. He focused on Collin for a moment and tried hard to speak but all that came out was wheezing. He fought for breath.

Unintelligible words faded into a gurgling whisper. His eyes faded and closed. Collin's stomach rolled and pitched and he felt his chest heave as his lungs clutched for air, trying to drag in enough oxygen to remain conscious while the rest of the world spun wildly out of control. A horrible, wailing cry split through him, straight from the depths of his heart.

"Lance! No!"

"Officer down. Ten-Double-Zero. 824 Lattimore. Officer down."

The words echoed, searing through Collin like a knife. He pressed his hands down tight against the wound, but Lance's blood tracked steadily against Collin's fingers. He sobbed so hard his entire body shook and trembled.

Officers pulled him away, settling him into a squad car as freshly arrived paramedics went to work, but only one truth remained, one unalterable fact.

Collin had distracted them both. He had gotten in the way—against Lance's orders.

It was all his fault. Shaking horribly, he looked down, and came upon the sight of his tightly clenched fists. Once more his stomach threatened to revolt.

Literally and figuratively, Lance's blood was on his hands.

❧❦

Collin awoke in a tangle of bed sheets, his body coated by a sheen of sweat, his breathing labored and rough.

He scrubbed a hand over his face, assuring himself

of substance and a return to reality.

Uttering a soft curse, he climbed out of bed and raked his hands through still-damp hair. In the bathroom he clicked on a light. Light helped push away the remnants of the dream.

In a pounding silence, Collin considered the matter. He hadn't had the nightmare about Lance's death in probably a year. Ghosts had haunted his mind frequently in the first year or so afterward. Of late, though, Collin had pushed, fought and bullied them into remission. It had to have been prompted by the conversation with Daveny.

This episode had been bad, though. Horrifically vivid.

He gulped down some water.

Coming upon his reflection in the mirror gave Collin pause—haunted, red touched eyes and pallid skin.

No one, not even the members of his family, knew he had interfered. No one but Collin knew he was the one to blame for Lance looking away, for the reaction of the man who had stumbled and fired off the weapon. Foolish folly and bravado on Collin's part had ended with Lance's death.

The burden rested with him always, and Collin had compensated for its weight in ways both emotional and spiritual. Oh, everyone knew he had been there, but no one knew the depth and degree of culpability—and the resulting responsibility he assumed.

Different memories crashed in, sucking him back into a vortex.

The eternal ride to the hospital. The smell of the police car he rode in—a subtle but permanent combination of mustiness, cigarettes, sweat and years of grime. The overly bright lights of the ER at St. John's Hospital. The nurses who helped calm the entire gathered family as doctors went to work trying to save Lance's life.

In the end, it had all been futile.

Collin gripped the metal basin of the sink so hard his knuckles turned white.

Despite our best efforts…

A one in a million shot…

The blood loss and muscle damage were severe, and irreparable…

Those memory-bound images were followed promptly by thoughts of Sandy.

Collin turned away from the mirror and doused the light. The return to darkness was welcome. He went back to bed, sinking into it with a groan.

Sandy had remained his fiancée until after a graduation delayed by a semester. Separate lives and a failed commuter relationship left them deciding to end the engagement in a civil if not overly friendly manner. The situation had hurt Sandy, and Collin knew it. Trouble was, he had no ability whatsoever to see to her well-being.

He couldn't even see to his own.

At that desolate realization, Collin settled an arm over his eyes. Behind closed lids swirled a new image—radiant and refreshing as cool, flowing water in a desert. Daveny. Clear as a high resolution photograph Collin saw her smiling in warm, happy welcome. The thought of her stilled his jangled nerves and soothed his soul.

That's when he recognized the most startling fact of all: He wanted to see more of her. He longed for her tenderness and innate sense of care. She had awakened something dormant inside of him.

And so, with her smile as an accompaniment, he drifted back to rest and peace.

5

Daveny's back was to Collin. Hedge trimmer in hand, she stood before a tall, somewhat rounded burning bush at the entrance of Woodland. She presented a petite, jean-clad counterpoint to its lush, overgrown state. The dichotomy of the image struck home and rendered Collin stationary for a moment inside the cab of his truck.

Grooming didn't take her long. While he watched, Daveny trimmed branches, smoothing and shaping until wild became spectacular, until untended turned into polished enhancement, health and beauty revived by the removal of overgrowth and excess.

Branches fell to the ground at her feet. Galvanized, Collin left his observations behind and joined her. A tall paper recycle bag stood nearby, and he stepped up to help, sliding on heavy duty work gloves. At first Daveny didn't seem to register his arrival. She wore protective ear plugs and moved through the task efficiently. Her smooth grace and confidence left him focused on the motion of her slender arms, the movement of her legs, her hips, the tiny waist he longed to span with his hands so he could draw her tenderly close.

Collin blinked free of those sensual imaginings and dumped a load of branches into the refuse bag. It was then that he must have entered her peripheral vision. Daveny turned off the trimmer and focused on him with the same kind of large, warm smile that had soothed his recent dreamscape.

"Hi there," she called.

"Hey."

Why did her instant openness, that simple but profound happiness, set off a trigger in his heart? In truth, he knew the answer, but quelled the idea of confronting it head on. He reacted the way he did because every moment spent in her company left him keenly aware of a soul-deep thirst that she brought to life, and then quenched, with no effort whatsoever. In her presence, Collin literally felt his emotional defenses slide away.

"If you keep pruning I'll bat clean-up," he offered, struggling to remain steady.

"That'd be perfect. Thanks, Collin."

Again with that radiant smile. Yet there were no wiles in her disposition. Her personality flowed naturally from her core—engaging, charming and lovely.

They took a break about an hour later, sitting side by side on the warm, soft grass. In near unison, they removed their baseball caps and sunglasses. When Collin got up to find some water and snacks to tide them over for the rest of the session, he watched Daveny stretch out on the grass, extending her ponytail behind her. She crossed her ankles and sighed with delight.

When he returned she sat up once again, tucking her sunglasses into place and accepting a couple packets of cheese and crackers as well as a dripping wet but suitably chilled bottle of water. "You're awesome. Thank you!"

"My pleasure." And he meant it.

While she ate, she looked around, taking in the grounds. Contentment rolled off her, toward Collin, a compelling, saturating sensation.

"This makes me feel so good."

"It should. Your company has done an outstanding job."

She shook her head. "We just designed. The contractors are the ones who do the heavy lifting." She shrugged. "Besides, that's not quite what I meant. It's just that this place? It's special to me. I've always loved the grounds here. They're peaceful and beautiful. A perfect setting for a church. I've always imagined what it might be like to make it, I don't know, I guess the word is *worthy* of Woodland."

Her comment held Collin's attention.

"I want people to find peace and tranquility here. I want the grounds to be inviting." Again she shrugged, stating simply, "This church is important."

For so long, before the world had crashed in around him, Collin would have felt the same way. Not any longer. But he didn't need to go down that road—especially with this spirited, idealistic woman. Instead he delivered a smile and a nod of agreement while internally he worked toward evasion of the subject.

Her attitude touched upon a soft spot in his heart, though, and that truth couldn't be denied. Rebuked, yes. Denied, no.

He took stock of the freshly soiled flower beds along the stone wall of the church front. "I think there are some plants with our names on them over there."

She groaned, but the verbal protest lacked authentic heat. She handed him a second packet of

Marianne Evans

crackers and delivered a wink as well. "Keep your strength up, hear?"

Collin unwrapped the snack, and teased, "I have to, in order to keep up with you."

She sashayed away, looking back over her shoulder in playful challenge.

Right behind you, he found himself thinking.

This woman possessed bottled-up charisma and the stunning beauty of a lightning bolt.

❧❧

"Oh, man! Ow!"

Daveny's startled exclamation left Collin turning her way. He had become so involved in the layout of the front border of annuals that he jumped a bit when she yelped. Daveny shook out her hand, yanking off her thin, latex glove

"Dang it! Serves me right!"

Collin went to her side immediately, motivated by the sight of a red stain on her hand and on the glove she held.

"What happened?" He took her hand and glided a gentle touch against the side of her index finger. Bearing a neat, shallow slice the digit bled steadily.

"I need to—I should probably clean it up," she murmured in a thick tone, looking into his eyes.

"What happened?" he repeated, holding her in place without even being conscious of the gesture. Automatically, he took the edge of his T-shirt and wrapped it around her finger so pressure could be applied.

Daveny watched in horror. "Don't do that, you'll ruin…"

"Stop," he interrupted succinctly. "What happened? And bear in mind, I hope the third time is a charm."

She rolled her eyes at that, but Collin just grinned.

Daveny answered, "I should have worn heavy duty gloves like everyone else, but sometimes I just hate them. You can't really feel the dirt, and the roots and stems, and—" She sighed in resignation. "I dug the spade in deep and way too close to my finger. My own dumb fault. I'll be fine."

With a bit more insistence this time she moved free of Collin's shirt bandage and started toward the church interior. He let her go, but followed.

"There's a kitchen area in the activity center with a shelf of supplies," she said, squeezing her finger and wincing. "I think I saw a medical kit there once. The facility is right over here."

"I remember the center."

"You remember?" They entered the building and Daveny paused in her trek down the common hallway. "So once upon a time you *did* attend church here."

"Once upon a time I was a regular here. Like the rest of my family." And now he wanted to shift emphasis. Fast. "There's the kit."

He nodded toward a shelf above a large, double sink and they walked to it. Collin pulled down the small metal box. Opening the lid he fished for disinfectant and band aids. This area of the church didn't bother him nearly as much as the church proper, and with Daveny hurting, no way would he allow emotional responses to get in the way of helping her.

The air was refreshingly cool indoors, but a tempting drizzle of perspiration tracked down Daveny's neck as he ministered to her cuts. The scent of her drifted against his senses, evoking a primitive, possessive response. She embodied spice and sweet florals, and Collin could all but taste the flavor of her, carried by those small beads of moisture that now disappeared beneath the neckline of her shirt. He stared, hard-pressed to keep steady.

"You know," he began, "whenever I got hurt, my mom had a rule."

"What's that?" She didn't conceal a grimace when he poured a bit of peroxide across the gash, then dabbed it dry with paper towel.

"Well, when I got hurt—and it wasn't because of torturing my siblings, which didn't happen very often anyway, since I was the baby and all—"

"Yeah?" She bit her lip while he finished cleaning the wound.

"I got a treat. My favorite ice cream." Collin blew very lightly on the cut and looked into her eyes as he wound a band aid around her finger. "What's your favorite flavor?"

"Butterscotch," she whispered, not blinking, her persona soft and beckoning, enchanting to him by sheer virtue of its brightness and appeal.

"Done. Under one condition."

"Conditions? Hey, mister, I'm the injured party here, remember?" The words were playful, an attempt at humor, but they came out sounding husky and affected.

"Dinner's included. Would tomorrow night work?"

"I'd love it." She surveyed the repair job he had performed on her finger then looked into his eyes once more, seeming shy—but grateful. "Thanks, Collin."

All he could do was nod.

❧❧

Daveny opened her front door and for a few precious pulse beats of time Collin simply stared.

Gorgeous.

Gone were grub clothes, the ponytail and baseball cap. Dirt debris and smudges were long gone as well, replaced by lightly made up skin and a perfume that reminded him of jasmine and vanilla. Large green eyes and her heart-shaped face were framed by a gently waved fall of dark brown hair that danced around her shoulders as she moved.

He wasn't accustomed to needs this potent.

"Uhm..." She stammered a bit shyly and blushed, gesturing toward the bouquet of gerbera daisies he carried. "Thank you. Those are lovely. Come on in for a second so I can put them in water."

Collin followed her into her modest but beautifully maintained ranch house, still speechless and reeling. Finally, he managed a quietly heartfelt, "You look amazing."

Daveny reached to open a cupboard that was a bit too high for her. His comment caused her to pause and blink, and afforded him the opportunity to be of help.

"Vases up here?" he asked, opening the door above her refrigerator.

"Yeah..."

He selected a tall one, rectangular in shape, and filled it with water while she unwrapped and trimmed the stems.

"You look pretty amazing yourself," she finally replied, her voice soft, her eyes deflected.

A simple suit coat and tie were hardly what Collin

would call dazzling, but Daveny's reaction was authentic and appreciated.

"Nice change of pace from old worn jeans and shirts, huh?"

"Absolutely," she replied, giving a light chuckle.

She cast a few furtive glances his way, and Collin realized they both felt the intensity—the pull of a tender magnet. Something about the two of them being on a level field gave him comfort.

Still, she knocked him out.

Collin handed her the full vase and their fingertips brushed when she took custody and arranged the daisies. A mauve silk sheath shimmered as she moved, and from the knee on down he couldn't help savoring the vision of her bare, tanned legs, supple and smooth.

She finished with the flowers, and an impulse swelled, then took over. He couldn't resist touching her. He skimmed the back of his fingertips, light as a feather, down her sun-kissed arm. A slight tremble and the bloom of goose flesh were his reward as he took her hand and placed a kiss upon its back. She was satin and cashmere combined, and she tasted like a moonlit midnight.

"We ready?" he asked.

She nodded, her eyes luminous and seeking. "Let's go."

6

"Collin, I love this place!"

He turned his pickup into the parking lot of Frank's Trattoria, and it was packed.

"After our visit to The Java Hut, I could tell you enjoy waterfront dining."

"Very true, but the food here, it's some of the best Italian I've ever had."

"I know the owners. They're old family friends. Comes from living in The Shores for so long."

A long, shady overhang surrounded the gray clapboard style restaurant. Hydrangea bushes in purples, pinks and whites surrounded the building's exterior. To the rear, scrub grass and sandy beach met the silvery blue waters of Lake Saint Clair.

"Stay put. I'll get your door."

Chivalry. Once again Daveny was touched by the natural way he displayed attentiveness and a sense of caring that went beyond mere words and straight into deeds.

Collin took her hand and lent support while she stepped from the cab of the truck; then he kept a gentle, guiding touch at her back as they walked inside.

Frank's Trattoria was a restaurant full of lovely, romantic atmosphere, and Daveny absorbed it with pleasure. Fine white linens adorned intimately positioned tables. On the tables and windowsills, votive candles burned in brightly hued crystal holders, casting flickering light across surfaces accented by deep blue stoneware and gleaming silver. Aromas tempted her appetite and senses—simmering tomato, sautéing meats, baking bread and coffee. Everything mingled perfectly with the sound of dish-chimes, soft music and low conversations.

They were led past an open set of French doors to a table located outside on a wooden deck that overlooked the water. The sun dipped low, preparing for its daily explosion of farewell across the far horizon. Though wide open, the space featured rails and columns that enclosed them, fostering an unexpected and welcome sense of affinity. They placed an order for mozzarella cheese sticks as an appetizer along with wine, and both were delivered promptly.

"There's just one tiny flaw in this fantastic itinerary of yours, Collin."

"What would that be?"

Daveny shrugged, all wide-eyed innocence. "No butterscotch ice cream."

"Oh, but you underestimate me." He pointed toward a space just over Daveny's shoulder; she turned in response. "Do you see that wooden kiosk over there?"

"Yes."

"Ice cream vendor. I know from experience he carries butterscotch."

She burst out laughing and turned back. "You win."

"Maybe." He smiled and toasted her with his wine goblet, which was half full of the house Chianti. She tinked her own against his in reply.

Dinner consisted of linguine in clam sauce, fragrant, fresh from the oven garlic bread. Daveny's favorite moment came when Michael, the head chef and owner, prepared a table-side Caesar salad for Collin and her to share.

Meanwhile, the sun sank below the horizon, burnishing the sparkling waters of Lake Saint Clair a deep gold, painting the sky pink, orange and a velvety pale blue.

"Why did you decide to go out with me, Daveny? I mean, aside from my medic-in–shining-armor episode, why did you say yes?"

His question was tentatively spoken and completely unexpected. Daveny paused in the midst of twirling a forkful of pasta. Despite the temperate humor, Collin waited on her answer seeming puzzled somehow, as though he couldn't quite figure out the wheres and whys. Daveny took a sip of wine, buying enough time to think her words through. "Well, beyond those supreme bandaging capabilities, I've seen that you're kind hearted. You're giving and genuine. What's not to like?"

In slow, steady measure they were moving forward, so she added, "I have to admit, I'm curious about your relationship to Woodland though." Instantly his shoulders tensed, and he studied the swirl of wine in his goblet as he moved the stem between his fingers. Undaunted by the reaction, Daveny continued gently. "What happened, Collin? You're the only one in your family who doesn't attend services—yet you've been an incredible volunteer, and I get the feeling..."

"If only life were uncomplicated. Straight and easy," he interrupted quietly.

"It's not."

He looked Daveny square in the eye, and she nearly flinched at the pain she saw. "Most definitely. Maybe that's what draws me to you so strongly. I like the way you nurture. I like how free and idealistic you are. You bring environments to life; you know how to create beauty from the barren. Lay down roots and watch them bloom. That's a remarkable gift."

Daveny took in his comment, completely enchanted. Collin wasn't flattering her on purpose. His genuine tone left her deeply affected.

"But what happened, Collin? Did something turn you away or hurt you?"

"I know it's asking a lot, but can you give me a little more time?"

Ripples of water sparkled like diamonds, lapping and hissing a constant rhythm against the nearby sand. Around them darkness drifted in and became a soft cloak, the lake fading to nothing more than the pulse beat of waves cut through by the silvery white glow of a half moon.

"Is it that bad?" Daveny gave him a playful look. Inwardly though she tensed, steeling against what he might reveal.

"It is to me, but finding a way to tell you, to explain...it's a struggle."

"I've hit too close to home."

"For now, yes." But, as though as assurance, he tucked his fingertips beneath hers on the table and met her gaze directly. "I'm not trying to hide anything from you, but I *am* trying to reconcile the fact that you seem to be of one belief about God, and I come from somewhere totally different."

That definitive statement left her heart aching.

"But you didn't used to."

White twinkle lights came on, illuminating the space with cozy warmth. The lights were wound along the rails, the columns and the potted shrubbery, casting a saffron glow across the deck.

Not sure how to proceed with the conversation, wondering whether she even should, Daveny watched a band set up on the nearby stage, preparing to play.

"Dance with me?" he queried.

She shook free of her distractions and looked into Collin's eyes. Sank into them. They were soft, warm and beautiful.

"I'd love to."

He reached up to stroke her cheek then took hold of her hand. The simple gestures were more than enough to make her nerve endings sing. Her hand fit into his perfectly. The sensation of his skin sliding against hers did provocative things to her senses, warming her with longing as her heart performed a softly cushioned tumble.

They walked to the empty dance floor in front of the band's dais. Collin wrapped his arm around her waist, bringing the hand he held to rest against his chest. Jazz music turned into an alluring wash of sound that drew Daveny away from the fact that they were all alone on the floor and settled her instead into a world with Collin alone.

A soft hum of pleasure escaped her. It felt so good to be held close, to experience the solid strength of his arms. She looked up at Collin as they swayed together, moving in a slow, artful pattern. Collin rested her hand on his chest just long enough to slide his fingers through her hair, twisting an end softly around his fingers before releasing the strands. Daveny shivered with pleasure.

She tucked her head against his shoulder when he reclaimed her hand. She wanted to capture and isolate each one of the feelings he released, so she closed her eyes, savoring.

Daveny felt cherished and utterly content—as though her soul were melding into place with its perfect mate.

❧

"Two single scoops of butterscotch coming right up."

"Thank you," Collin replied, paying for the treat.

Daveny claimed her cup and added spoons to both servings. "I didn't know your favorite was butterscotch, too."

"Kind of spooky, isn't it?"

"A *Twilight Zone* moment."

They meandered along the waterfront while they ate. Daveny went barefoot, her sandals dangling from a fingertip. The sand still felt warm beneath her feet, retaining the last of the day's heat. Occasionally she strayed just close enough to the breaking water to douse her feet.

"There's a bench up ahead. We can sit down to eat if you'd like."

Daveny nodded in reply to Collin's offer, following his lead and sitting next to him. Lights rimmed the water to the left and right. A foghorn sounded periodically, its pitch low and mournful. They finished their ice cream in silence.

"I've really enjoyed this Collin. Thank you so much."

"You're welcome." He focused on the cup he held. "I've had a great time."

"I want to thank you for something else, too."

"What's that?" He looked at her, outwardly puzzled.

"Thank you for making me feel so special."

He deferred his attention and shrugged, but Daveny intended to make her point. Collin set aside his ice cream cup, and she did likewise.

"You've found dozens of little ways to show that you care. That you're thoughtful. I want you to know I've noticed every gesture, and those actions tell me a lot about who you are."

He shrugged again. "I didn't do anything out of the ordinary, Daveny."

"You're right. It's part of who you are. You're wonderful, Collin."

He leaned in and claimed her lips so quickly, with such breathless need, Daveny was swept away then pulled under before she could even blink. She sighed out an exclamation and the mingling of their breath created sweetness—longing.

She reached out, holding on to him, trying to ground herself amidst delicious, spinning desire—an onrushing wave of need that went far beyond the mere physical, for Collin reached out emotionally as well, wrapping himself around her heart and mind.

"Daveny," he whispered at last, "you make me come so close to believing that statement."

She held his face between her hands and searched his shadowed features beneath the milky white glow of the moon.

"Believe it, Collin," she urged stridently. "Please. *Believe it.*"

7

Late Thursday morning, Daveny sat in her office and worked on freshly negotiated landscaping plans for a Grosse Pointe Woods home that skirted the shores of the Detroit River. Photos, documents and overview sheets covered the gleaming surface of her pride and joy—a Victorian style desk of maple, complete with a brass desk lamp, presently turned on to warm the area with needed light and emphasis. Outside, rain spattered against the window display of a world colored gray.

The stately, 1920's masterpiece of pale cream stucco featured wide and deep grounds that sloped gently toward the river. That would be her canvas. Plans came to life in her mind, and she began to work in earnest, losing all track of time until the soft electronic chime of an e-mail delivery alert brought her back to reality.

"How brave are you?" Daveny puzzled aloud over the subject line as she clicked it open. It was from Collin.

To: Daveny.Montgomery@Montgomerylandscape1.com
From: CEdwards@stclairschools.org
Subject: How brave are you?

Our conversation at dinner the other night left me

thinking about your job—and gave me an idea. Since I've gotten to see you at work in your natural habitat, I'd like to return the favor. If you're interested, I'd love to have you talk to my English class about putting yourself into nature and making it come alive. You game? I'll give you more details if you aren't scared off.

Collin

Daveny smiled to herself; she nibbled on her lower lip. If she breathed in just deeply enough, she experienced him in phantom, tasted his skin, felt his touch.

He was a special man; she only hoped he would find a way to reconcile himself to his faith and the spirit of God. Daveny couldn't imagine a relationship without that most vital component. So, despite a lurching fear of speaking in front of gatherings, she clicked on the reply toggle and began to type:

To: CEdwards@stclairschools.org
From: Daveny.Montgomery@Montgomerylandscape1.com
Subject: Re: How brave are you?

I have to admit, I'm more than a little intimidated by your request, but if you let me know what you're after, I guess I can somehow dissolve that big lump of fear in my throat and say yes.

Let me know the date and time. Call me. Hope you're surviving the end of the school year...I'm looking forward to seeing you.

Daveny

Anticipation over seeing him again and pleasure at his continued connection stirred a sparkle against her nerve endings.

"Earth to Dav!"

Daveny jumped when Kiara made an abrupt motion in front of her eyes. The imp just grinned when Daveny glowered at her.

"Distracted?" she queried sweetly, batting her lashes in a coy way as she settled into the chair across from Daveny's desk. Kiara crossed her long legs, gracefully arranging her skirt. "Late night with the beau?"

Her words, though light and teasing, struck home. A floodgate released, a realization and recognition.

"Kiara," Daveny replied in all seriousness, "I'm in trouble."

Daveny's partner and the Jane-of-all-trades for Montgomery Landscaping waited attentively while Daveny nipped at a thumb nail. At length, Kiara prompted, "What's wrong?"

"It's Collin. I swear I can't get him out of my mind." Issuing a frustrated sigh, Daveny started to reorganize project papers and photos, hoping the effort would help her re-center and focus.

"Dinner was fun, huh?"

"Very."

Kiara arched a brow. Waited.

"He's amazing. Sweet and strong, and heaven knows he's attractive—to a degree that leaves me..."

"Flushed? Like you are right now?"

"I am not..." Oh, yes she was. Daveny's overly warm cheeks were a dead giveaway. "There's something about him that's remote though. Barricaded in a way."

Kiara just shrugged. "So bust down the walls."

"Oh, OK. Thanks. Wish I'd have thought of that myself. Have a nice day now."

"You're prickly today. Feeling a little tense?" Kiara teased, unaffected by Daveny's half-hearted snipe. "Listen, if anyone can entice a soul to trust and openness, it's you. The quality is built into your DNA. It's how you're wired. People *relate* to you."

"Thanks for the vote of confidence, but I think it goes deeper than trust. Maybe I feel this weird disquiet because of his stand on God."

"Which is?"

"He doesn't stand for God at all. That's huge for me. A deal breaker." But then Daveny considered that statement. "He wasn't always that way. He told me he used to be a regular at Woodland." Then his brother died. Loss and pain ensued. Daveny began to connect the puzzle pieces to form a somewhat clearer picture.

"Dav, hear me out about something before you fire me."

Daveny narrowed her eyes for show, restraining an affectionate grin. "Go on. Carefully."

"Well, maybe you're *meant* to help him..."

"Oh, no." Daveny rebuked that conclusion, lifting both hands to ward it off. "I'm nobody's reformer. Faith comes from within."

"Very true, but look at what's been accomplished already. Look what's come to be between the two of you. Maybe God is taking a hand in both your lives. I'm not talking about reforming him—I'm talking about continuing to be exactly who and what you are. I believe he'll come around."

Daveny digested that summation for a moment. The point was valid. Besides, what was the rush and urgency? There were no time clocks here, nor schedules with which to adhere.

"Is he worth it?" Kiara asked in conclusion.

"Worth what?"

"Worth waiting for. Working for?"

Daveny took a deep breath before replying from the heart. "Yes. I believe he is."

Kiara's smile dawned, slow and sure.

∂∾

"It's not that big a deal. Promise."

Daveny snorted softly, twirling the phone cord around her finger as she chatted with Collin a few hours later. "Yeah. Isn't that what the crew of Titanic said right after spotting that big ol' chunk of ice in the middle of the ocean?"

He ignored that quip. "Here's the drill. You come in, take your assigned position on a stool at the front of my class, and talk about the beauty to be found in nature. Describe it all—the colors, the scents, the tapestry you create. Explain how you see it evolve in your mind."

Daveny arched a brow. "You've nailed it already. I nominate you to do the talk instead."

Collin just laughed. "They hear me talk all the time. Besides, you'll make them see the world through *your* eyes. I've had three other guest speakers, you're number four. My goal is to spur them into new perceptions of ordinary things. C'mon, relax. It'll be great."

"How long do I have to speak?"

"Not more than 20 minutes."

She stifled a surge of energy, trying not to go taut with nervousness. "You'll be right there, cheering me on even if I start to blather, correct?"

"Absolutely." His low, appreciative chuckle slid through the phone line, tickled her inner ear. "Your hesitance is showing, and it's charming as all get out."

"Trouble maker," Daveny muttered, but the pulse beat at her throat went heavy and rapid. Collin's words had already triggered ideas about what she could say, and even a few visual aids she could bring along as enticements to help his students soak in the beauty of the world around them. In fact, she had an easel as well as a number of over-sized photographs that would help emphasize her points.

"The last week of school is week after next," Collin continued. "Your presentation is part of a pre-finals, de-stress initiative of mine. Don't do it for me. Do it for the kids."

Daveny sighed dramatically at his blatant manipulation, swiveling in her desk chair. "When do you want me to present?"

"How about Monday?"

"Ah…gosh…that's soon…"

"Dinner afterward, if that sweetens the deal for you."

Indeed it did. In fact, his offer had her pushing back against fear and nodding as she replied, "OK, OK. Since it's for the kids."

Once again his low, rich laughter tingled in her ear.

8

"Good afternoon, everyone. Let's get seated and get focused."

The senior level English Comp class began to assemble, complying with Collin's request.

"Welcome to the final installment of Visionaries on Parade, subtitled The Last Days of Freedom before cramming for finals."

A chorus of groans rose up, and he smiled and lifted his hands to quell the uproar. "As you know," he went on, recapturing the attention of the class, "the point of this exercise is to introduce you to a number of people who challenge us to see the world from a new and different point of view. Today's topic is involving yourself in the world around us very directly and powerfully. Few people I've met accomplish this goal as well as Daveny Montgomery. Daveny is a landscape architect who will talk about quite literally getting in touch with the earth and how working with the resources we're given—nature—can enlighten our view not just of nature, but of our place within it as well."

Daveny stepped to the forefront, and Collin moved to the rear of the room, intending to enjoy unobtrusively watching her.

Daveny settled onto a stool she had positioned

next to an easel where she had positioned a trio of matted photographs face down on its shelf. "Mr. Edwards asked me to talk to you about my job, but in a different context than I've ever tried to describe it before, so I have to give him a nod of appreciation for making me take a look at my work from a whole new point of view."

They exchanged a smile. Beneath the surface, Collin experienced its ulterior sense of knowing.

"His job is teaching you how to express your thoughts and ideas—your perceptions. My job today is to help that process along by letting you know how I see the world I've chosen, landscape design and creation." She engaged the students with eye contact and warm charm. "To start I'm going to give you two diametrically opposed ideas and then show how they're actually woven very tightly together. I call it variety through consistence."

Daveny paused there, giving the class time to consider the idea. She stood and lifted the top photo from the easel and turned it over. She adjusted the lapel of her dark blue blazer, which matched the slacks she wore. Professional, but not prim. So far the students responded, watching her intently.

"Point one: Variety." She gestured toward the picture. It featured some lucky soul's perfectly laid out and spacious backyard with a raised stone garden, sculpted shrubs that framed the edges of the ground floor windows, perfectly matched color schemes in the flowers and a thick, dark carpet of grass you could all but touch. "What does this say to you?"

Answers came fast from her audience: "Organized." "Themed." "Detailed."

"Next," she continued. "What about this?" She

turned over photograph number two and set it into place. This photo revealed the rolling terrain of a golf course with wild, Scottish-style heather bushes and tufts of tallish scrub grass. Flaming orange day lilies, natural tree lines and a sparing use of organized and plotted annuals formed the features of this particular canvas.

Students replied: "Natural." "Lush." "Wild."

"Great answers; and all of them are correct. Variety. Different settings, different textures, different requirements are needed for both. But it's all held together by what?"

Silence followed, as did a few shrugs and puzzled looks.

Daveny smiled and Collin's heart reacted with an eager pounding.

"All of this variety is dependent upon the constant and never ending cycle of time. Years pass, seasons change one to the next. Time and the importance of each of its seasons moves through both of these environments. Frost comes in the fall, deadening the growth, winter covers the ground like a blanket, then spring brings it all to life again and summer bursts into fullness in the flowers that saturate these places with color and vitality."

The deeper meaning of her words carried to Collin, hitting home in ways for which he was completely unprepared.

"Shoots uncoil into the soil, seeking and receiving nourishment. The plants grow, the blooms unfold in time to the cycle of creation. Consistency forms variety in a cycle that can't be rushed; it can't be bullied. Nature has to emerge and evolve. Sounds kind of like life as well, right?"

With that Daveny turned over the last photo on the easel, unveiling it at last.

The vibrant bend of a rainbow split the dark blue clouds of a sky just starting to welcome sunlight after the breaking of a storm. Dewy green grass rolled on and on in a meadow carpeted by wildflowers in a myriad of colors. A small lake, banked by field stones, pine trees and ferns completed the composition. In essence, it depicted the perfect blending of the organized versus the wild.

Meanwhile, Collin stood by, stunned. In words and visuals Daveny spoke directly to every wound and pierce mark in his heart. Evolution. Change. The passing of time and perception fulfilling life's needs despite outside influence and elements. Like death—and sorrow.

He felt grateful to remain in the corner, tucked away for the moment. Meanwhile, Daveny absolutely owned the classroom. The coup de gras? At the end of her presentation, she gave each student a laminated, trading card sized copy of her concluding photograph. When the student closest to him received her copy, Collin studied the piece, noting the phrase Daveny included on its plain white back:

A season and a time to every purpose under heaven.

By the time class ended, closing out school for the day, Collin's emotions were pulled taut, trembling in a form of suspense. The room slowly emptied of students. Daveny packed up, taking her time about the task, lingering but content in the silence as he gathered up items of his own and prepared to call it a day.

Meanwhile, a ripple slid against his senses, pulling him relentlessly forward. To Daveny—and much, much more.

"Can I walk you to your car?"

Collin's offer had her looking over her shoulder with a nod as she crouched to pick up a carry-all for her props. Open toed heels afforded a peek of pink-tipped nails. Well-tailored slacks snugged and released against her body as she moved.

Daveny stowed everything except a few extras of the cards she had handed out at the end of her presentation. With a look that touched Collin intimately she stepped up and gave him one.

"For you. Keep it close."

Collin fingered the gift, drawn to the words and image all over again. Because of Daveny and a heart he could all but feel beginning to shift and change.

God was showing up in his life, whether he wanted Him to or not. Hope built, despite Collin's most stalwart efforts to tamp it down.

But what was he supposed to do with that recognition?

Typically graceful, Daveny didn't intrude upon his introspection. They walked to her car, one of the few left in a parking lot that tended to empty faster and faster as summer swept in and the end of the school year quirked its finger like a temptress to students and faculty alike.

She loaded her car and opened the driver's side door. Collin stepped into the space before her and murmured, "Daveny, come here."

He skimmed his fingers light and slow down the length of her slender throat, and then kissed and nuzzled, capturing her scent by breathing in deep. Need became a craving that battled to override restraint.

Her head tilted back in welcome; fragrant strands

of her hair, tossed by a gentle breeze, slid across Collin's face as his explorations continued along her cheek, then found her waiting, trembling mouth. He kissed, provoked, enticed.

Dipping her head, she slid her fingertips along his forearm, the affection ripe with promise and longings potent enough to leave Collin's equilibrium in shambles. Reluctantly, he pulled back. "I wish you could stay," he remarked quietly.

"Me, too. I've got to get back to the office though." She looked up, eyes luminous and seeking.

"I'll call you later about dinner."

She nodded, and he kissed her one last time, their lips gliding together in a natural, satiny dance. They parted slowly, with reluctance. Once Daveny was in the car, Collin closed the door but leaned in through the window she opened.

"By the way—you were fantastic. Thank you."

"Thanks for asking me to present. To be honest, I was flattered. Despite the bout of nerves, I enjoyed it, too."

Her smile accompanied that comment; its power left him temporarily unable to draw a normal breath. A few seconds later she was gone, and Collin's mind promptly went on a timer of sorts, ticking off the minutes until he'd see her again.

9

A few days later, Collin went back to work on the Woodland project. The grounds swarmed as final plantings and polishing touches took place. Seemingly, the entire parish showed up to help and partake in a final work-a-thon and food-fest. Antonio's Brasserie catered the burgers, hot dogs and fries—the scent of which began to fill the air with appetite enticing aromas.

Stationed at the pond, Daveny saw to the final placement of trees and shrubs. Collin knelt at the flowerbeds, his usual spot, digging holes for a batch of multi-colored snap dragons set to be placed.

"Hey, Col—just to give you warning—Sandy's back in town."

Collin's brother Marty stepped up and spoke the jarring words. Collin was so focused on Daveny that hearing Sandy's name was, in a way, like trying to work through a foreign translation.

"She's back, meaning?"

"She's back...meaning heads up, bro, your ex-fiancée is standing right over there, with Pastor Ken, by that WWJ News van."

Collin turned to verify; the spade he held fell from his grasp.

"What the..."

"Also meaning she's back in Detroit permanently. Stephanie and I ran into her at a friend's house this past weekend at a barbecue. She's working at WWJ radio now."

Collin's heart raced, not out of pleasure or anticipation, but anxiety. "And WWJ is interested in Woodland because we're so incredibly newsworthy?"

We. He had said *we*. Where exactly had *that* inclusive statement come from?

Fortunately, Marty didn't comment on that but instead replied, "Sandy's started attending services here again. So, she's gotten wind of the fact that all of this improvement comes as the result of a parishioner leaving the bulk of his estate to the benefit of his church. She took that story back to the station, and the rest is apparently history. Now WWJ is doing a story on Woodland for their Community Focus program. Sandy's its director now."

At present, Sandy was hidden from view by a production crew and Pastor Ken who led her away, taking her on a walk around the grounds. While Collin watched in trepidation, Marty squatted next to him in front of the brick lined edge of the flowerbeds that lined the church entry. In an assembly line of sorts Marty tilled, Collin dug holes, and the following team planted flowers.

Taller perennials were placed to the back, shorter, sturdy annuals to the front. Collin didn't know phlox from rocks, but the end result transformed barren grounds into a riot of perfume and color. Another group filled large brown terracotta tubs at each side of the church entrance with petunias in all sorts of pastel shades interspersed with white.

Every once in a while Collin hazarded a glance

over his shoulder, but Sandy's back remained to him. Despite two years apart he easily recognized the gentle wave of red hair. She still wore it shoulder length. Slim, jean clad, of average build but dynamic, appealing features, Sandy turned to profile as she and Pastor Ken began to walk in tandem. Nope. She hadn't changed much at all.

They were headed straight to Daveny, which made perfect sense, but Collin's pulse went haywire.

When they stepped up, Daveny concluded a conversation with the head of the team commissioned to complete the wood engravings now that the bridge was in place over the pond. Introductions were exchanged and Collin's panic index went off the charts.

Returning his efforts to the job at hand, Collin did his best not to overreact, but the effort was futile. The final group of helpers in his group gently laid and smoothed a layer of protective wood chips.

Marty continued the thread of their conversation. "Apparently, Mom saw her at services this past weekend."

Sandy and Collin had attended church here before...well, *before*.

Inwardly he sighed. "Really? Well, I'm sure she's glad to be back home." Collin hoped the finality of his tone would guide Marty toward a new topic of conversation.

No such luck.

"Col, you should at least *talk* to her. Mom said Sandy seems kinda lost. No, unsettled. Yeah, that was the word she used. Unsettled."

Perfect. Just what Collin needed. Guilt with a side of well-intended, conscience-provoking motherly influence.

Jeremy, the family's second-to–the-youngest, stepped up. He looked over Collin's shoulder and checked his progress. "Marty, stop gossip-mongering. Sheesh."

Collin grinned to himself, grateful beyond measure for Jeremy's timely arrival and interruption. "Hey, JB. The lilac tree looks great."

Freshly planted with his help, it resided just to the right of the bridge. It would take a year or so for the fragrant blooms to burst free, but it would be a perfect augment to the gently arched structure. The pine bore that fresh, bright sheen of un-scarred wood, light and glowing beneath the midday sun. That was the trouble with wood, and life, however. Sooner or later chips, creases and wear marks would develop. An overall dimming.

"Food's on," Jeremy elaborated needlessly, since the aroma of grilling hot dogs and hamburgers permeated the air. "C'mon. Let's eat. I'm starved."

"Like that's news?" Marty quipped, though he dumped his work supplies and stood to stretch.

But Collin remained lost to his thoughts, watching Sandy and Daveny as Pastor Ken took his leave from the freshly completed pond area. And a memory took hold.

"It's almost finished now, and I'm so excited! It's being called Parishioner's Bridge." Daveny lingered over dessert and coffee after the dinner following the class presentation. She took delight in the idea. "Everyone seems to have taken to the idea we have of the bridge being a physical testimony to the impact of those who worship at Woodland, past and present, which is everything I had hoped for when we came up with the idea for it."

Hope. God. Her belief in both lit Daveny from the

inside out. Collin wondered, not for the first time since being in her company, what it would feel like to once again capture that kind of conviction for himself. Out of habit, he shook off the silky promise of that idea.

Instead, he stood and made his way to the area of the grounds where a barbecue was underway and attracting volunteers in droves. Tables were set up and stocked with things like fruit salad, veggies and dip, cookies and chips.

He needed to clean up before eating, though. He turned back and followed a group of people inside to wash up. He blew out a puff of air, rolling his shoulders, a sense of internal pressure on the rise. It was time for him to explain—everything—to Daveny. Circumstances seemed to be converging on him all at once and needed to be dealt with: the advent of a lovely, wonderful woman in his life; Sandy's return to Detroit; Woodland's renovation and all of its emotional ties to Lance; and, by far, the worst moment of Collin's life.

Once in the main building, the entrance to the church itself caused him to pause. The double wooden doors were open, as if in welcome or perhaps a predestined invitation.

Since all the activity was happening outside, the church proper was empty and dimly illuminated. Backlit by the afternoon sun, the rich hues of the stained glass glowed, casting patterns on the dark gray carpeting.

Collin walked inside without being fully conscious of it until he started to tremble. The nearer he got to the altar, the more his knees threatened to weaken and give way. He made it about halfway down the rows of pews before figuring he'd come close enough.

He slid into place and sat, looking around. So much was the same. To welcome summer, flowers adorned the altar, lending a subtle scent to the air. The colorful bouquets lent a contrast of vibrant color to the simple white walls.

"Collin. How are you?"

Collin closed his eyes and drew a fortifying breath. Despite years of distance, he knew that voice.

"Hi, Pastor Ken."

"I'll leave you to prayer or meditation if you'd like."

Pastor Ken started to turn, but before doing so he gave Collin a welcoming smile. He offered nothing beyond that simple greeting.

Therefore, Collin could only assume he had picked up on the underlying current of disquiet in his salutation. That made Collin feel bad. After all, his problems weren't Pastor Ken's fault. "I don't mind. How...ah...how are you?"

"I'm well. Excited about the improvements, obviously."

Pastor Ken's smile was as warm and compelling as ever. The church leader had been a tremendous source of support to Collin's family at the time of Lance's death, onward to this day—but Collin had stepped away. He had seen no other path to take. What would this man of God make of that?

The wooden pew creaked comfortably when Pastor Ken sat next to him. Black attire, white collar, kind, inquiring eyes—everything about him spoke of approachability and kindness. "I'll be glad when the project is finished. Being in limbo is never fun."

"Yeah. I can imagine." Awkwardness skittered through Collin, but Pastor Ken seemed content and at ease.

"I notice you've been pitching in over the past few weeks, Collin. We appreciate it. It's been nice to see you around."

Was there underlying sentiment to that comment? Collin looked briefly into the pastor's eyes and found nothing but sincerity, no calculating judgments or pressure. "I've enjoyed it."

"Daveny is a remarkable talent when it comes to stuff like this. Me? I don't know potting soil from mulch."

That left Collin laughing spontaneously since he could completely relate. "I'm the same way, but I had some muscle that could be put to good use. No big deal."

"It is to her, and it is to us." Pastor Ken started to stand, and the oddest compulsion took over Collin. A compulsion to confession.

"Sorry I haven't been around, it's...it's not about you or Woodland itself."

Pastor Ken sat back down. "I realize that Collin. You need to make peace. In your own time and in your own way."

"You're not...angry?"

"How could I be? What you feel, what you go through, is between you and God. I'd never force the issue. Though I will say I've put considerable prayer time into your name, my friend."

Somehow, for some reason, that left Collin feeling good.

"If...if I told you..." Collin stopped right there. This wasn't a good time to approach Pastor Ken, to follow through on this sudden and startling need to come clean. Pastor Ken was busy; the church was bustling and Collin felt sure any number of people needed his counsel and assistance at the moment. "Never mind." This time Collin stood to leave.

Pastor Ken stretched out his long, lean legs and settled an arm along the back of the pew. And he waited.

"I have all the time in the world, Collin. I hope...I *really* hope you can find the strength to finally stop running."

His words packed enough power to sink Collin back to the seat.

"I need to know...if I say something...I mean, I know this isn't a confessional, but..."

"It's just as sacred. If you want assurances that I won't divulge anything you say to me in confidence, I can offer that to you without hesitation." For emphasis, and most likely to offer Collin a bit of time to gather his thoughts, Pastor Ken went to the doors and pulled them quietly closed.

After that, Collin's words poured out freely into the Pastor's safekeeping.

Collin told him everything—his responsibility with regard to Lance, the pain he felt over hiding the truth from his family and regret over hurting Sandy and leaving her to feel withdrawn in her own place of worship. Collin even talked about his burgeoning feelings for Daveny.

"You fear Daveny's disappointment?"

Pastor Ken sounded genuinely surprised, so Collin enlightened him. "I could never—ever—stand the idea of Daveny looking at me through different eyes— through eyes that see my scars and my worst possible elements. Same holds true with my family, to be honest."

"You feel that strongly about her."

It wasn't a question. It didn't need to be framed as such.

So Collin nodded, but he felt lost within that admission.

"Collin, do you see that perhaps that degree of feeling is also part of the reason why you turned away from God? You were scared of the scars?"

No censure or reprimand could be detected in that statement—try, though Collin might. Then it would be easy to retreat and refocus himself on bitterness and regret and that soul-tying shame. But, he did find enough ire to say, "I turned away from God because He turned away from me first. He's shown me clearly that He doesn't need Collin Edwards. I'm insignificant. God ignored me. God allowed that horrible wrong, that waste! Furthermore, the reasons for it fall squarely on my stupidity, my lack of…of…"

"Collin, stand back far enough, with enough clarity of mind to grant another truth—the truth that your heart was in the right place. You meant no harm! You wanted good. You wanted to help. That needs to count somewhere in your scale of justice."

"Not given the end result. Instead of good, I caused nothing but disaster. Why have faith after that? Why hope for goodness? Where was my faithful God? Why didn't He intervene? Why didn't He see fit to keep Lance alive? It's left such a hole in our family, in…in…"

"In your heart."

"Yes." No way would Collin ever deny that fact. "And I want it to go away, Pastor Ken, but it never does."

Those last whispered words faded to silence and

Collin rested his head in the open cup of his hands. He felt completely drained.

"Has it occurred to you that perhaps Daveny has become the answer to that plea? That God sent her to you for just that purpose?"

"But she's...she's like...like an ideal to me. She's what I'd strive for, if only I didn't, or hadn't..."

"Please stop. Right there." Pastor Ken earned Collin's full gaze and attention. And he wasn't doing the warm and fuzzy any longer. "Don't put her into a category she can never live up to or you'll both end up disappointed. Don't make her more than she is. She's a human being with the same hopes and fears and dreams and scars as everyone else. But at the same time, recognize her impact on your life. You need to let her in, and you need to let your family in or this will keep eating you alive."

Collin thought about that for a moment. "I know they'll change toward me. Once they know about my part in Lance's death, things will change. I don't want that! As for Daveny, I'm not saying she'd back away, or not feel compassion. She's too full of love and optimism and hope for such a thing. The same holds true for my whole family. In a way, I feel trapped. That night damaged me. My family would ultimately rally around me, I know that. But Daveny? She possesses too much brightness for someone like me to drag her down. I can't seem to reconcile myself."

"Then you grossly underestimate her, and your own goodness. That's a grave disservice to you both. Look what she's done for you already. Do you honestly think that will end? Or change? I don't, because I know Daveny well enough to realize she doesn't give her heart away unless it's completely and with one hundred percent conviction to go along with it. I see it in church nearly every week. And I'll warn you again not to hold her up to idealism. She struggles, too, Collin."

A pause settled between them for a time. Collin absorbed that silence, letting it balm his jangled nerves. "I feel so much. I feel anger, bitterness, love, loss, guilt. Shame most of all…"

"That's a lot of negativity pushing at you. *Let it go.*"

"I've done so well 'til now keeping it at bay."

"Do you think? I'm not so sure."

Collin speared Pastor Ken with a wry look. Pastor Ken just grinned.

"She's opening you up, Collin. She's setting you free. That's God at work. Don't fight it. You can't run or hide from Him, so stop trying. Instead, turn to the love you'll find. God is, and always will be, right there waiting for you."

His definitive inflection won Collin's attention once more. The words of Daveny's presentation, of time and seasons and circumstances not being bullied, played through his mind.

"Let your family help heal you, and let Daveny have your heart. You won't regret it."

That was a step forward Collin couldn't quite make. Not yet. He couldn't face the guilt he felt; the anger and bitterness still tasted powerful enough to cling to. After all, its pattern was familiar.

Collin didn't mean to be rude, but he needed to leave. Suddenly the church interior felt claustrophobic and overly warm. He stood somewhat abruptly and nodded at Pastor Ken, who watched him in a steady, unresisting manner.

"Thanks, Pastor Ken. I...I should be going, but...thanks. I appreciate hearing what you have to say."

Without waiting for a reply Collin walked up the main aisle and out the doors into a blinding, bright sunlit day.

Good. He could blame stinging, watery eyes on the elements.

10

To be completely honest, despite back-breaking work, Daveny couldn't help cracking up, and Kiara joined right in. What a pair of planting pros. *Not.*

"Forget the manicure for five minutes and push down, Kiara! The roots need to be buried deep!"

Daveny bullied the trunk of a rose bush while Kiara exerted pressure, wedging the roots securely and as far down into the dirt as possible.

Sandy Pierson stepped up, offering readily, "Let me help."

After performing introductions, Pastor Ken had left the group a few minutes ago, and to her credit, the WWJ Radio personality, having finished mingling with the volunteers, launched into action and chipped right in. Daveny liked her already. What wasn't to love about a media person who was willing to give the Woodland project free publicity plus a day's worth of work?

Crouching, utilizing her shoulder as a brace, Sandy helped Daveny prop and position the trunk. Then she reached down to help Kiara bury the roots.

"Thanks." Daveny encouraged, "Teamwork saves the day."

Sandy smiled up at her. "You're welcome. Learned long ago that authentic story coverage requires a bit of dirt and sweat."

"No doubt," Kiara quipped, giving their new teammate a grin.

Church members dug shovels deep into a pile of planting soil to the left, filling in the ground and mounding the dirt to a soft rise soon to be polished off by a perimeter of fieldstones.

"I started attending church here again a few weeks ago. I remember Jim Cavanaugh. When I heard he bequeathed part of his estate to Woodland, I wanted his story to be told," Sandy said.

Daveny helped her wriggle and till and bury.

"The segment I imagine will be a two minute overview, with interviews. I'd love your help with that, as well as Pastor Ken's, and some of the volunteers, too."

"What a great gesture to the church, Sandy," Daveny replied, thinking, *Impressive. So, Sandy has a history here.* Daveny looked at Kiara and received her agreeing nod. "We're on board if you need anything."

"Thanks. This particular Spotlight feature might be a *bit* biased, but that can't be helped. This was my church home for years before I moved to Chicago. It feels good to be back."

Her eyes strayed. Her attention moved to the front of the church. A short time ago, when the flowerbeds were being finished off by Collin and his brothers, Daveny had noticed the way Sandy watched. Collin had gone inside briefly but had returned now to join his family for a meal break; once again Sandy focused on him. The entire Edwards clan was freshly seated on and around a vivid gingham blanket set with food and beverages.

Daveny intended to join them, so she offered, "Let's break for lunch. We can work on the rock border afterward."

Sandy turned as though abruptly jarred from her revelry. "Ah...sure. That'd be great. I'm supposed to meet up with Pastor Ken."

She'd answered, somewhat quickly Daveny felt, especially when she noticed the way Sandy continued to study Collin and his family. Her actions left Daveny puzzled enough to inquire: "Do you know the Edwards family?"

Sandy shrugged, nearly accomplishing a posture of nonchalance. "They're regulars here. A long-time part of Woodland. I might interview them."

Sandy's attitude was almost businesslike, but Daveny noticed her dark hazel eyes were vulnerable and guarded. Intuition told Daveny that Sandy possessed an affiliation to the Edwards family. But how?

"I want to interview you and Kiara as well. After all, you're the architects of this masterpiece."

They took off for the food line. But Daveny couldn't help noticing two things. First, Sandy hadn't answered her question. Second, in passing the Edwards' spot on the lawn, Sandy gave them a wide berth.

ॐ

Something rode beneath the surface of Collin's mood. A subtle degree of tension rolled off him, sliding over Daveny. Lunchtime brought them together after working apart for the bulk of the morning. He remained pleasant and warm, but a layer of disquiet that Daveny could all but feel worked like static against her nerves.

Sandy, Kiara and Pastor Ken linked up with a group of volunteers not far away. Daveny noticed his furtive glances, the subtle squeeze of tension between his brows when he looked at Sandy. He chatted with Daveny, with his brothers and sisters; he horsed around with the myriad of nieces and nephews who toppled all over him. But eyes mirrored the soul—and those mirrors kept track of Sandy—his mouth uncharacteristically set into a tight, straight line.

Being welcomed so warmly into the fold of the Edwards family helped redirect her thoughts, though. Daveny enjoyed getting to know the extended family a bit better, but bodily refreshment barely kicked in before work called once more.

During lunch Daveny had idly mentioned needing some spare muscle to place and secure the circle of perimeter stones by the bridge. Collin didn't say much in reply, but when the break finished, he trailed Daveny to the freshly planted rose bush, which gave her a needed psychological boost.

They went to work, Collin settling the weighty stones firmly into place. Daveny knelt next to him and preceded his efforts by grooming the ground then digging out suitable space within which to nestle the rocks. They created the circle in silence, conversations humming around them, laughter and the dash and squeal of playing children a soothing backdrop.

After a time, the sun became scorching, so she plucked two water bottles from a passing volunteer. Daveny handed one to Collin, finally venturing, "You're working like a man on a mission. Wish I had more of a reward for you."

The water bottle traveled from her grip to his and he drank deeply.

"No problem. Besides, good works are a reward unto themselves, right?"

His tone and attitude verified her suspicion that he was troubled. His words provided the perfect opening to conduct just a bit of probing. "Is that what you believe?"

At first he just shrugged, but then he went back to work. Briskly. "It's easier to believe in the tangible results of good works, even punishment for bad ones, than it is to believe in the unseen and unheard."

Daveny settled onto her knees, cushioned from the ground by a protective pad. Almost like a plea she asked, "What happened to make you feel that way, Collin?"

"Some day I'll tell you."

"But not today?"

His shoulders sagged as if burdened by a weight he could hardly bear.

"I'm a little raw today, so this probably isn't the best time to delve deep." He looked at her in earnest. "Daveny, it's not you. Honestly, it's not." There he paused, seeming to consider. He examined the soil, running his gloved hand over its base. "I know what I'm saying may sound overly dramatic; I don't mean for it to. I feel like I'm at a complete crossroads right now." Daveny moved to speak, but he held up a hand to stave off further questioning. "I'll work it out, but for now I'm trying to sort things out. I'm just in a funk, I guess. Sorry for not being better company."

The admission made her bold. She didn't hesitate. She kissed his cheek, her lashes fluttering closed against his skin as she did so. The pleasant scent of male musk, the tang of salt from his sweat-touched skin skimmed through her. The essence of him remained on Daveny's lips as she moved slowly away.

"You're fine company, Collin."

The expression he wore when she looked at him put her heart to work in double time, her pulse racing in syncopation to its beat. Heat flushed through her system when she saw the need, the undisguised hope and openness in his eyes.

Looking at him this way left Daveny with the strangest feeling that those were emotions he didn't allow himself to feel, or reveal, very often.

If ever there was someone in need of God's loving embrace, and a renewed faith, Collin, it's you.

I don't know all the details. I don't need *to know all the details yet. I simply need to reach out to a questing soul and maybe help you find your way back home.*

The words seeped into Daveny's mind as though spoken aloud and directly.

Will of God? *A purpose?*

Her teeth sank gently into her lower lip when she found herself lost within his eyes and saturated by the pleasure she felt in simply being near him.

Collin called to a longing in her heart; he elicited patterns in Daveny's soul that left her yearning and wistful. She wanted a man like Collin Edwards in her life. She craved his intimacy, a connection both physical and emotional.

In that moment she leaned close once more, the space between them closing slowly but surely; at the last second Daveny blinked and took a deep breath— trembling.

"I want you to know something," she said. "It's OK if you don't open up to me today or in a week or even a month. I just hope you do so at some point. I'd feel honored by that degree of trust and faith. 'Til then,

I promise I won't push. The ball is in your court, OK?"

Something about the statement left his eyes seeming haunted.

But he nodded—and that was enough. For now.

They resumed their task, and Daveny mulled over the circumstances.

Sandy was a member of the media. As such, Daveny could probably perform an Internet search and gain some unobtrusive history simply by virtue of her stature. Something in her arrival and the currents she stirred piqued Daveny's curiosity.

11

Tuesday morning dawned with sunshine, sweet air, and soft breezes. Collin carried his golf clubs out of the garage, settling them next to his truck.

C'mon, Edwards. This is no big deal. Explain everything to Daveny. Move forward. Move forward or you'll regret it.

That truth didn't make his present reality any easier. Sandy's reemergence gave Collin much to think about—not because of harbored feelings, but because the situation treaded fine lines both in his relationship with Daveny and the very real, very passionate feelings he maintained about his faith life.

Bottom line? Big deal or no big deal, Daveny Montgomery infiltrated a part of his heart he had deliberately and resolutely nailed shut. Something about her compelled Collin toward the truth, and into a more objective, distanced view of the guilt and shame he still had difficulty releasing.

"Hello, Collin."

A beat of silence passed as Collin absorbed the greeting of a familiar female voice.

Well, he thought wryly, *she hasn't forgotten the way to my condo.*

"Hi, Sandy. How are you?"

His tentative greeting faded to nature noise,

billowing breezes and more distant traffic sounds. Collin hoisted and stored his clubs, closing the back latch of his truck. Then he turned to face the inevitable.

"I'm OK," she replied. "I saw you the other day and wanted to say hello, but—"

"Yeah, I saw you and your crew from WWJ."

"But you didn't stop by either."

Her eyes teased, but he read between the lines. *We saw each other and practiced avoidance.*

"I didn't want to get in the way," he said, extricating himself as best he could.

She offered a shrug and a gracious degree of understanding. Pulling a hair tie from her pocket, she threaded fiery hued curls into a ponytail. "I'm glad to see you helping out. It's actually why I'm here."

"Oh?"

"Can you spare a few minutes to talk before pulling out?"

Briefly she glanced at the golf clubs. Due to finals scheduling, Collin didn't have to report to school until after lunch so he was on his way to a morning session at the driving range with Marty and Jeremy.

"I've got a few minutes before I have to leave. Come on back and I'll get us some lemonade."

Collin led her to the backyard patio and extended the table umbrella to afford them a bit of shade.

"I'm actually here in an official capacity, in case you're worried," she informed.

About to walk inside, Collin turned and met her gaze squarely. "I'm not worried, Sandy. You and I have been through more than enough. We don't have anything between us that should cause any more worry or pain. Right?"

All she did was nod.

Minutes later they sat comfortably, sipping the iced, sweet beverage. "Daveny tells me you and your family have been active supporters of the beautification."

Hooked into church, back where he had started and ended. The panic inside Collin began to swell. On the heels of his conversation with Pastor Ken at the picnic, then Daveny thereafter, this meeting with Sandy hit on a number of nerves.

"I don't know, Sandy. I mean, my mom and dad, Marty and JB, they're a lot more involved in the activities at Woodland than me. They know more about—"

"But I'd like to talk to *you*."

The interruption was quietly firm—gentle, but insistent. Rife with double meaning.

Temporarily delaying plans to practice his golf swing, Collin settled back and nodded in invitation.

"You've changed," she observed. "You've started to reemerge. Finally."

The last part sounded a bit like a dig—until he looked into her vulnerable eyes.

Make it right, came an instinctive prompting, a voice from within.

"The project has helped."

"Church helped, or the renovations helped?"

"One step at a time," he answered, offering an intent look. "I still haven't braved services; I'm just not *there* yet." Discomfort prompted him to shift topics. "The exposure you're going to give the church through Community Spotlight is a huge benefit. Thank you for that."

"It's my church, too," she replied simply.

"It hasn't been my church in a long time; coming

back though, even as a grounds worker, somehow feels like a homecoming. I never expected that. The prodigal, I suppose."

She thought about that for a moment, and then admitted in a torn voice, "I miss you, Collin."

He kept quiet at that comment but watched her steadily. *Make it right...*

"I didn't want to leave," she continued, "but—"

"But I didn't give you much of a choice did I?"

To that, she didn't reply. "Seeing you at Woodland the other day, remembering the plans we made, it brought back a lot of happy memories I have of you." She shrugged lightly. "Of the two of us. And there were a lot of them. I may have tried to forget, but that doesn't change the truth."

"There were a lot of good things we gave each other, Sandy. I wouldn't be who I am without what you brought to my life. I haven't forgotten that, and I never will."

"But?"

"*But.*" Collin regarded her steadily; the image of Daveny danced against the edges of his mind, settled richly into his soul.

Sandy finished her lemonade and stood to leave. "I'm glad I stopped by. Hope you don't mind. I had to at least...at least talk to you."

She started to turn, not quite meeting Collin's eyes; he couldn't allow the retreat. Not on those terms. Gently he took hold of her hand until their eyes met.

Collin gave her a smile that came right from his heart. "Thanks, Sandy. You're a special lady."

Her eyes filled, but she smiled back. "That road goes both ways, Collin. I think I'll give your mom a call and see if she's game for a radio interview."

"Knowing Mom, she'll be thrilled."

"See you."

He nodded, watching her leave. In doing so, the oddest thing happened. He bid an internal farewell to sores that had truly healed and were returning to normalcy as the result of nothing more than acceptance and the power of loving care.

The realization left Collin straightening, staring straight ahead as he realized what else needed to be done.

Promptly.

12

Tuesday afternoon Daveny sat in her office. Stewing.

Curiosity about Sandy Pierson dominated her thoughts and overrode restraint. Compelled by the need to know more about her, Daveny hesitantly logged onto Google. Within the search engine, she typed Sandy's name and slowly clicked her way forward.

Kiara entered Daveny's office with her typical burst of energy and chic verve.

Daveny grinned at her. "Have you recovered yet?" she asked, discreetly checking the results on her screen. There were a number of entries, thanks to Sandy's stature as a member of the media.

Putting on a pout, Kiara held up her hands so Daveny could see her fingernails. Sure enough. Two of them were now shorter than the rest. "Oh, what I sacrifice for my job!"

Her theatrical moanings caused Daveny to laugh. "Don't be such a sissy. Take it like a woman."

"Uh-huh." Kiara settled into the chair before Daveny's desk.

"And remember, the help you've provided is for the greater good."

"Uh-huh, part two."

They shared a laugh, and then surprisingly, Kiara went shy. She studied her hands. "Actually I don't mind the battered nails much. Besides, I think Pastor Ken is incredible, Dav. I got to spend some time talking to him during the picnic, and I have to say, he hardly seems like a stodgy, stern man of the cloth type guy. I like his attitude." Daveny ignored incoming search results and focused instead on her colleague. There was a thread of irrefutable longing in Kiara's tone that left Daveny plagued by sadness. Kiara was a fantastic individual, inside and out.

"But, typical to the story of my life, the third finger of the left hand is a dead giveaway. Story of *my* life—the good ones are always taken. Like, say, Collin for example. He's hooked on you, Dav."

That comment snapped Daveny free of introspection. Another of Kiara's formidable talents? Expert table turning.

"Some day," she concluded quietly, "I want a man to look at me the way Collin looks at you."

"Honey, they *do* look at you that way."

An unexpected degree of melancholy crossed Kiara's features. "Maybe, but not for the same reason."

Daveny's thoughts crashed on a wave of guilt. Now it seemed sneaky to Net search a woman who, it seemed, carried ties to Collin's family. Still, her gaze strayed to the flat screen; she itched to explore the items on display.

Soon Kiara leaned forward, waving a hand in front of Daveny's eyes.

"You still with me?"

"Sorry. Lost in thought."

"Obviously. Humm. Happened the minute I mentioned Collin. You guys getting together again any time soon?"

Daveny cleared her throat and shrugged. "I don't know. He didn't have much to say the other day."

"What would you think of me joining your church, Dav? I know it may sound corny and all, but it feels like family. I want to start going to church again."

Daveny gave her an emphatic nod and relaxed against her chair. "Seriously? I think that'd be great. Come to services on Sunday. They're at ten o'clock. We can sit together if you want."

"That'd be perfect." Kiara lifted out of the chair. "For now, I'm headed back to the grindstone."

When she left, Daveny turned back to her computer, greedily clicking through the search results.

❧❦

Neighbors In The News

Terrance and Claire Pierson of Shelby Township are pleased to announce the engagement of their daughter, Sandy Pierson, to Collin Edwards, son of Benjamin and Elise Edwards of Saint Clair Shores.

Pierson and Edwards, soon to graduate from Oakland University, intend a wedding ceremony late next year at Woodland Church of Christ.

The Internet tidbit, gleaned from an archive of news stories at the Saint Clair Shores Observer, was the fourth item down on the list. Accompanying the blurb? A beautiful picture of a smiling couple—Collin and Sandy—with the entire future ahead.

Daveny stared ahead blindly, drumming her fingertips along the edge of the desk, trying hard to remain neutral. Reasonable.

The effort was in vain. Why did it wrinkle a piece of Daveny's heart to confront the fact that Collin had been engaged before? That the engagement had ended?

Though stunned, her heart ached for him—losing a brother, ending a seriously committed relationship.

Daveny read the news release about Sandy's new position at WWJ then clicked off the Internet.

A chime sounded when the main door to the office opened and someone walked in.

A few seconds later, Kiara ducked her head in the doorway, her eyes sparkling like sunshine on water.

"You have a guest, Dav."

Puzzling, Daveny stared after Kiara who simply turned away in a smooth maneuver and left.

In the lobby stood Collin Edwards, and the sight of him made Daveny's heart leap.

"Hi there!"

"Hi," he replied, welcoming her with a smile that warmed her blood. She stepped into his open arms for a hug and pecked his cheek in a lingering way. Breathing in the scent of him was like capturing a beautiful memory and holding it close to heart. When Daveny began to pull back, his mouth found hers and closed in with smooth, warm finesse.

"Sorry for just dropping in." He seemed uncertain.

Once she caught her breath, Daveny went about reassuring him. "Don't apologize. I'm glad to see you."

"Do you have a few minutes? Maybe time for a quick walk?"

She checked her watch. It was just after four o'clock and a break sounded great—especially one spent in the company of Collin Edwards. "Absolutely."

Collin thrust his hands into the pockets of his jeans, looking around. Kiara could be seen just inside her office, diagramming on an easel. Her office, which was right next to Daveny's, along with an open, comfortably appointed seating area for clients, comprised the domicile of Montgomery Landscaping.

"You're sure you don't mind me just showing up?"

To answer, Daveny simply looked into his eyes, took his arm and led the way outside.

Her firm was housed in a single story strip of stylishly turned out brick buildings that framed the east and west sides of Old Woodward in downtown Birmingham. Central to all of Detroit's most robust suburbs, Birmingham featured a bevy of shops to explore, restaurants to sample, and any variety of high-end establishments all within walking distance, places that were perfect to explore during moments like this.

So they strolled along the picturesque street in a companionable silence. Since this visit was Collin's idea, she let him take the lead and didn't push. It turned out she didn't need to.

"There's something I wanted to talk to you about, to tell you."

"OK."

"The trouble is—it's something I can't easily bring myself to face off against and confront."

"Until now?"

"Now I can't seem to avoid it. I just…I hope…"

It was time to stop talking in circles. Daveny ventured, "Collin, it's fine to hope, but hope can always use vindication, right? Open up to me. Trust me."

She placed slight emphasis on the last two words though she had no idea what the trouble might be. In the end, she simply wanted him to grasp the fact that problems or not, she wanted to be present to him. A source of help, and beneath that wish, perhaps even more.

They walked past clusters of people who milled about and window-shopped the boutiques. Collin picked up the pace a bit. It seemed as if he quite literally longed to outrun something. So Daveny touched his arm and stood still. "Let's sit. And talk." She lifted her face to the warmth of sunlight and still summer air, sidling him a glance. "I hear an orange smoothie calling."

Soon they were seated at a white metal bistro table, beneath a green and white striped restaurant awning. They nursed their drinks companionably, but Collin's disquiet seemed to rise.

"I wonder where I can even start."

The murmured question was a rhetorical, not meant to be answered. Daveny waited, leaning back against the wrought iron chair, letting the day's warmth touch a piece of her body gone chilly with trepidation.

At last he sighed and scrubbed a hand over his face. "Oh, who am I kidding? I know right where to start. The beginning."

Again, Daveny simply waited and watched.

"Five years ago I was exactly where I wanted to be. I was happy. I was a semester away from graduating college with my teaching degree. I was engaged." There he paused and looked at her. She didn't flinch, and the tension in his shoulders and the lines of doubt on his face eased. But Daveny knew what would help even more. She had to tell him.

"Collin, will it make this easier if I tell you I know

about the engagement?"

He looked at her for the longest time—studious at first, then with a smile that dawned slowly but with breathtaking impact. The moment stretched. Daveny blushed furiously beneath his intense regard and finally shrugged. "The Internet. God's little miracle. I wondered about her. About her affect on you, and her reaction to your family."

The admission came freely once she found her equilibrium.

Collin's smile warmed again, turning into an invitation that slid against her heart, and turned her logic into nothing more than dizzy, sweet longing.

Collin leaned across the small table and Daveny found out that, oh yes, this moment, this vibration and pull, was *well* worth fighting for. His lips touched hers; then he moved in possessively, claiming her mouth with firm, but tender purpose. Perfectly attuned to the give and take of hers, his kiss, poured heat through Daveny—bone melting, pure and lush. Intoxicating in the very best sense of the word.

Extraction required a mutual and supreme act of will, but Collin slowed the exchange and moved carefully away. The troubled expression on his face shook Daveny back to reality. She didn't understand that reaction at all.

"Daveny, I wish an engagement were the only issue."

"Then what is? Please trust me, and have faith enough to…"

He cut her off sharply. "That's the issue. Faith. Hope. Goodness. God and mercy and all the platitudes you hear preached from the pulpit every Sunday."

"Collin, what *ended* it for you? What *happened*? Tell

me."

"Death happened. Aggravated Manslaughter, or so it's called in a court of law. Scales of justice. What a joke. What a sick, pathetic joke."

Collin seemed far removed from her now, lost in a world only he truly saw and felt. All Daveny saw was that whatever circumstance he visited tore him apart.

He told her the story of Lance's last moments, relived the funeral, tasted the bitterness of anger he turned upon a God he no longer understood nor tolerated. She could feel the dam breaking free around his heart but at the same time witnessed his controlled fury and his pain.

"So you've taken the blame and believe that because of your intervention God didn't protect Lance from what happened—*well-intended as it was*? You've decided to simply get out of God's way and leave Him alone?"

"That sums it up. Yes."

"Then it seems to me you're expecting life to be perfect for believers in God. You're trying to reconcile pure goodness into a world that contains the knowledge of good and evil, Collin. It's never going to happen. *Faith* has to enter into the equation somewhere along the line."

Daveny had his attention so she didn't relent. This was far too important—for both their sakes. "It may seem trite and simplistic to cling to the truth that God is there anyway—that God will never, ever leave us, and in fact will heal us of the pain we feel. If we let Him. It's about free will, Collin. We have to choose Him. He can't exist where He isn't allowed or invited. Let yourself believe again, and miracles happen. I promise you that. It's guaranteed in God's word. You may have left Him alone, but He's never left you alone. If you need intrinsic proof, look at what you've done for Woodland. And look at what you've done for me."

"What have I truly done in either instance?"

"Oh, I was hoping you'd ask." She paused, snaring his full attention. "You've helped give new life to a parish in need of tender loving care. You did it by lending time and talent to the renovation project. What you've done for me is help recharge my faith. The project invigorated my faith, but you helped me rediscover all over again how unexpected and how absolutely beautiful God's grace is. Especially when it's revealed through love."

In his eyes, Daveny caught a glimpse of his hope and a contradictory fear.

"I can't even find words to describe the feeling I have when I'm around you, Daveny. I've been without it for so long."

The words, the feeling behind them, were all she had ever dreamed of, but she wasn't satisfied. Not quite. Daveny knew he was at a crossroads and needed to make his own choices about where to go next.

"I appreciate that more than you'll ever know, Collin, but you need to come to terms. Your soul needs peace, and I can't give you that. Only God can. I should get back to work, but take this thought with you: God is *good*. *Always*. Only those who know they have been loved beyond all deserving can begin to understand the possibility of loving others in the same generous way. I want that kind of love, Collin. With a man of exceptional heart and faith. Is that you?"

13

That night Collin engaged his cell phone and auto dialed his folks' number.

"Collin!" his mom greeted enthusiastically. "How are you?"

He smiled deeply and automatically. "Hey, Mom. I'm good." He paused, stalling for a few seconds. "Ah...I know it's a weekday and all, and we usually do dinner on Sundays, but—"

"Yes?"

The single word was spoken in a leading way, with anticipation he could all but taste. "Well, I was wondering if I could stop by. I know Dad's been wanting help fixing the lattice on the deck. If it sweetens the deal, I'll be bringing a guest. One I think you'll approve of."

"What time would you and Daveny like to eat?"

He sputtered his way into a laugh. "Six thirty works. I'll bring steaks for the grill."

"What a treat! That sounds wonderful, sweetheart. Can't way to see you both."

He flipped the cell closed and grinned. It didn't surprise him any that his mom had connect the dots between him and Daveny.

His contentment faded. Of course he wanted to mix Daveny into the composition of his family. The

Marianne Evans

other purpose of his visit was much more difficult. Collin breathed in, breathed out, steadied himself.

Revelation needed to come full circle. Daveny would be at his side, though. That helped immeasurably. That fact, plus the renewal of hope she inspired, just might make all the difference.

৵৽৽

Collin held Daveny's hand tight, bringing it to rest on the seat divider.

"No need for this to be a big production, right?" he murmured, focused on the road ahead, his left hand gripped tight on the wheel. "I'll help with the deck then I'll talk to them both."

"Collin?" She didn't continue until he glanced at her. In her eyes was a light that, like a sunbeam, worked right through him. She possessed the most reassuring serenity of spirit and calmness. "It's going to be OK."

When they arrived, Ben was already prepped with hammers, nails and pre-measured wood pieces. Before exiting the cab of Collin's truck, Daveny stayed his leaving by placing a hand on his arm.

"Hey." She moved a bit closer.

She opened herself to him in a kiss ripe and giving. Collin claimed the offering, mindless to all but her taste, the love that poured forward from her being into his starved, eager soul. Want, elemental and primitive, mixed with an emotion so sacred, so rich in flavor he could summon no resistance.

At last, he traced a fingertip against the line of her jaw and looked into her eyes, hoping she could feel the passion and gratitude that filled him.

"You talk to Ben," she urged. "I'm going to go inside and see if I can help Elise. There's something I want to talk to her about anyway. Church stuff."

Collin arched a brow, teasing, "Oh? Secrets already?"

"Maybe," she taunted in a saucy manner, giving him a last, lingering kiss before leaving the cab.

From behind the seat, she gently lifted out a freshly purchased ice cream cake—pralines and cream—his parent's favorite.

"Collin?" He turned back as they went their separate ways. "Rest easy."

He nodded, truly trying to heed her advice.

⟡

Sweat beaded Collin's hairline. The trickle of it slid down his neck and back. From his prone position on the patio he spaced and held in place small, angled wood pieces and then secured them with nails. Squatting next to him at the edge of the deck, his father handed him supplies while Collin fixed an open hole in the ground level lattice work.

Collin cleared his throat, and ventured forward cautiously. "You know, I've been thinking a lot since I started helping out at Woodland."

"Yeah." With a steady hand his father lined up the next angled wood slice. Collin proceeded to hammer.

"Working there brings some stuff back. I can't help but think—think about—"

"Lance," his father filled in easily, nodding as he studied the results of their work so far. "I can imagine." He held the position of the next crisscrossing segment of wood while Collin nailed. "You've been OK with it? With working at the church? Seems to me you've enjoyed it."

Collin glanced up just in time to catch sight of his father's pleased, knowing grin.

"Yeah. Daveny is incredible, so I've enjoyed the project and getting to know her, but—"

"But you never wanted to go back."

Condemnation couldn't be found. Nor could any other form of judgment. It was simple statement of fact.

"True."

"Pain runs deep, Collin. We understand that, but we keep hoping."

Collin half laughed, half sighed in reply to that not-surprising admission. "You, Mom and everyone else, it seems."

They continued repairs—wood overlaying wood, secured by nails—and the job was nearly finished, the lattice work refurbished and filled in perfectly once more.

"Dad, I..." *Let it go.* The words rang through Collin, powerful and promising. "I realize I've had a lot of trouble moving ahead since Lance's death."

"It was a gut-punch to all of us. You especially. You saw it happen. I know that added a huge weight for you to carry, son."

"But Dad it goes beyond that. It goes *way* beyond that—into responsibility and even involvement." Deliberately Collin drew out the last word, willing his dad to pick up on its meaning.

His father paused, swiped a short sleeve across his sweat-stained face, and then sat back on his heels, finally asking, "What do you mean by involvement?" He focused on Collin exclusively, directing them to the nearby wooden steps of the deck. They settled there side by side.

"I tried, Dad. I *tried* to help." Collin's words were a choked whisper. Rather than look his father in the eye, he looked straight ahead, to a yard dotted by large, old trees and enlivened by dashing black and brown squirrels, birds and swaying branches.

After a pause, Collin went on. "I wanted to help him. And in the end, the guy? He tripped over himself. The gun went off, and Lance ended up shot, and killed. Lance had told me to stay put. I ignored him, Dad. Like some kind of a stupid naïve wanna-be hero, I jumped into a situation where I had no business. But all I wanted to do was *protect* him. Instead...Instead I..."

Collin felt a hand on his arm, strong, calloused and warm.

"Son." Collin stopped talking and finally braved a look at his father. "Son, is this why? My God, you didn't think we *knew*? Collin, we knew what happened all along. We knew you were in the thick of it. Doug Kennal was a first responder. He spoke to the wife of the perp. She saw everything. We knew you tried to look out for your brother and help. Yes, he asked you to stay put. Rightfully so. But you acted on pure, loving instinct. Do you honestly believe there's fault to be found in that? Did you think we wouldn't understand? Is that what drove you into—into"—he gestured flatly with outspread hands—"spiritual seclusion?"

Collin's heart thundered against his ribs, freedom setting its pace. Freedom, hope and a promise trying desperately to take root and come to life.

"So you knew? Mom and everybody—you knew?"

"Yes, Collin."

"I had no idea."

"Do you think we'd want to open up sores, revisit that awful night by bringing back something that wounded you so deeply?" He blew out through pursed lips, seeming to consider everything. "Maybe we were wrong to try to shield you from that pain. It might have helped you let go of your troubles a lot sooner."

"I'm just as guilty on that count, Dad."

His father placed an arm around Collin's shoulders, nodding toward the work they had finished. He breathed out a satisfied sound. "Repair jobs. They're hard, sweaty work, you know? No arguing with the results though. Sometimes you just need to hunker down and start again. Right?"

Yes, Collin knew what he was saying. But was he ready for that last, fateful step?

Honestly, right now, he just didn't know.

14

Collin sighed, nervously twitching at his tie. Blasted thing refused to lie correctly. Loosening the knot, he worked at it all over again. His reflection in the bathroom mirror was somewhat comforting. White dress shirt in place. Khaki slacks, too. A blue blazer hung on the back of the door, ready to be worn.

And a confounded tie of royal blue silk that possessed a will of its own.

The third time was a charm, and his stalling ended. Collin slid the sport coat on. With an attitude of resolution he left his home behind beneath gray skies that foreshadowed a soft summer rain. Climbing into his truck, Collin trembled as he started the engine and pulled out—turning right onto Jefferson Avenue.

Toward Sunday services at Woodland Church of Christ.

❧❧

If walking into Woodland a week ago had been accomplished on shaky legs, this time they felt like overcooked spaghetti.

Collin looked around, feeling such familiarity, yet such a sense of disconnect. So many people wandered past—so many faces with a light he could only attribute to an aura fostered by God. By a commitment to faith and hope.

It would take time for him to reach that point again; there remained a strong willed, stubborn part of his heart that felt like he was giving in and surrendering to something he promised never to revisit. But then he thought of Daveny, who had instigated a domino-style chain reaction in his life that culminated right here—in this moment of returning.

Those thoughts so enveloped Collin he made it to the halfway point of the main aisle without fully realizing it. To the right, as always, a pew full of Edwardses were in attendance.

He paused by his family, but only for a moment. When Collin looked into his mom's eyes, he could have sworn they sparkled and filled, but it may have been a trick of the light slanting in through the stained glass windows.

She held out a hand but followed the track of Collin's gaze, seeming to realize he was headed to a pew a few rows ahead. That's where Daveny sat, unaware of his arrival, chatting amiably with her seatmate, Kiara.

Collin held and squeezed his mom's hand then kissed the back. He felt sure she sensed his wariness, even before he quietly disclaimed, "Don't make a big deal out of this, OK?"

"Out of what?" she retorted. "You're where you're supposed to be. See you after services."

Collin forced down the fear and continued on. Thank God—and that was the first time he'd had *that* thought in a very long while—the second spot next to Daveny remained empty. He tucked into place, touching her shoulder lightly.

"Collin!"

His name came out as a murmured exclamation of delight and welcome.

She gave him a quick, tight hug then Pastor Ken began worship, precluding further conversation.

∂∽

After services his mother stepped up to Daveny. "You know, it's far past time we had you over for a full-blown Sunday dinner. It's the very least we can do after all the work you and Collin have put in here at Woodland. Can you join us?"

Standing in the narthex after church, Collin looked over Daveny's head and rolled his eyes at his mother. Romantic machinations dispensed with, his mother just smiled serenely.

"How sweet," Daveny replied. "I'd love it—but first can I steal him away for a minute?"

"Absolutely. We'll see you at the house later?"

Daveny nodded and linked her arm though Collin's. Her happiness enveloped him in a sensation so absolute it sucked him in like a thirsty soul questing for water.

"Come here," she beckoned. "I want to show you something."

When Collin nodded, Daveny led him outside.

To the bridge.

Rain drizzled, gliding down the umbrella she extended, making it gleam. For now, Collin stood just outside the edge of its shelter. He preferred the cool wetness on his skin. Rain dampened clothes were the least of his concerns. Like a baptism of sorts, he felt reborn.

"Pastor Ken still knows how to deliver a great sermon," he observed. In fact, Collin wondered if the entire sermon had been directed to him. Pastor Ken had used the example of Parishioner's Bridge to illustrate the power of God's people in action and to address the pain and loss of releasing loved ones from an earthly existence while still maintaining a loving remembrance.

Through God, Collin discovered anew, love lives on in a timeless cycle of variety and consistency—just like Daveny had observed in her presentation.

The flat rocks positioned around the pond looked like stepping-stones; they shimmered with moist gloss. The sky featured luminous, blue-gray cloud cover. The church grounds were deep green beneath a bank of fat, low-rolling clouds. Bright flowers, the heightened finish of the bright pine wood, combined into a softly focused glow that took Collin's breath away despite the rain.

Daveny had shown him the beauty to behold in God's creation. No longer would he run and hide, blind to that truth. Everything led to one place. God's kingdom. Now, Collin decided firmly, it was time to get busy *living* that truth.

With Daveny at his side.

"Here it is," she said at last, leading Collin to the midpoint of the bridge's subtle arch.

"I wanted you to see this. Privately. I hope you don't mind it's me showing you this rather than your entire family."

Daveny's fingertips stroked slow and confident along the deeply etched, black letters of a name engraved into the hand rail.

Sergeant Lance Maxwell Edwards.

Collin's throat constricted. He knew, somehow, that Lance would be commemorated here. Lance had loved his faith walk and Woodland. Collin wasn't surprised by the sight of his brother's name inscribed as one of the memorialized parishioners.

Still, his eyes stung. Heat clawed at him, pushing for release—so reminiscent of the day of Lance's burial—and yet leagues different as well.

"I wanted him here. For you. I asked your parents if they'd mind me making the donation to include his name on the bridge. I figured if he was here, you just might keep coming here as well." Now tears filled her eyes, too. "You don't have to do anything more than just stand here, remember him, and love him like you always have and always will. Just as he loved you." She dashed the moisture from her cheeks and turned to face Collin directly. "That love goes on *forever*. But I guarantee you something else, too. God loves *you*. God will bring you what you need the most if you just listen, and love him, and let him."

Now Collin traced the letters of Lance's name—slowly—with reverence. "I want to try, Daveny. I'm here because I want to try. I want to come home to God and my faith again." His tone went almost fierce—emphatic. "But I have to warn you, I may stumble, and I may fail."

"We all do, Collin. We all will. That doesn't scare me. What scares me is loving a man who rebukes God. Giving up scares me. Rejecting His mercy scares me, too, because doing so goes against everything I hold most important."

Daveny's words were strong, but her demeanor was calm, typically generous. She retracted her umbrella and rain instantly kissed her skin, slicked her hair and cheeks.

But she remained resolute. "Let's make a go of this, Collin. Together."

How much good fortune, how much happiness, could one person be granted? Collin paid fleeting thought to the idea then dismissed it, letting it fall away. "Do you think you could love me that much?"

"I can, and I do. May I ask you the same thing?" she teased gently, seeking a connection by sliding her fingertips against his, lacing their two hands snugly together.

"I want to marry you, Daveny. I love you completely. Nothing means more to me than being right here, with you, and realizing where that love comes from. It comes from God. We're meant to be. I knew it from the moment I saw you."

With trembling lips, Daveny nodded. Collin pulled her close and initiated a hard, deep kiss. Sweet rain and salty tears mixed together. Moisture cooled flushed skin; a floral tinged scent of summer surrounded him. He sighed, dissolving into the moment, desperately craving oxygen. Daveny's breath moved into his mouth and worked through him, filling one craving, stirring millions more that were new and thrilling.

Against his mouth she replied softly, "We're going to create one heck of a love story together."

He kept right on kissing her, but couldn't restrain a rumbling, pleasured chuckle. "Daveny? I think we already have."

Hearts
Surrender

Hearts Surrender Dedication

To my church family at Guardian Angels. You're an inspiration to me in so many ways - and an ever-present reminder of God's community of love. Thank you for the blessing of your friendship and faith life. To Denise Ficorelli in particular, thanks for your help with the mission trip information and research questions. The youth of Guardian Angels are so blessed by your service!

1

Kenneth Lucerne donned a weighty, calf-length vestment, the white, gold-trimmed mantle of his calling. In the seclusion of his pastoral office at Woodland Church, he adjusted its fit and fall.

Something in his spirit tried to ignite…and failed.

A centering breath later, he closed his eyes, and prayed. *God, grace me with the strength to fulfill the mission You have entrusted to my care. Grant me the heart and wisdom to share Your mercy, Your love, and Your truth. Please be with me, in Jesus' name. Amen.*

Beyond the partially-opened door came the gradually building noise from the narthex as parishioners arrived for ten o'clock services.

Ken opened his eyes slowly, seeing and absorbing. First thing that hit him? Naturally, it was the brass framed photograph of his wife, Barb. He firmed his heart against a familiar onslaught of pain as his thoughts performed an auto correct: His *late* wife, Barb.

Outside the office, Ken heard the Edwards family arrive. Their voices stood out—won his interest by virtue of familiarity and deep affection. Exuberant conversations and laughter, so typical to the clan, were interrupted suddenly by the sharp, plaintive cry of a baby. A unison chorus of tender assurances followed, so too, a smattering of gentle coos.

A smile tugged against the corners of his mouth.

Today, Woodland would welcome in baptism the soul of two-month-old Jeffrey Lance Edwards, son of Collin and Daveny Edwards.

He attempted spiritual ignition once again and came closer this time.

Still, a void yawned before him, widened by the prospect of a loving family gathering. Moments like this intensified that deep, almost breath-stealing sense of loss, but he tried not to dwell on that fact. He couldn't afford to think of Barb, of losing the most precious person in his life. Not in a moment so full of God's joy and light.

Determination rode in, heightening his resolve to leave melancholy behind and meet God's present moment head-on, in his role as Pastor.

His heart's ignition switch flickered, sparked hot, and then fired to life.

Leaving the office, he walked a short corridor leading to the church proper.

"Have you ever seen such a perfectly shaped mouth in your *life*?" Collin Edwards asked the family assemblage.

Stepping up from behind, Ken stifled a laugh. Collin fit the stereotypical role of proud father to a 'T', but the emotion behind his comment was authentic and warming.

"Yes, I have," said Collin's wife, Daveny. "Every time I look at you."

Amidst laughter, and a few groans from Collin's brothers, Ken entered the circle of the Edwards family and clapped a hand against Collin's shoulder. "Have you ever seen such a proud *father* in your life?"

Through the enthusiastic welcome he received, through the teasing that ensued, Ken searched...and found. *Kiara Jordan.*

He knew she'd be front and center. Daveny's best friend and business partner wasn't part of the Edwards family by blood, but rather by unanimous consent.

She gently lifted Jeffrey from Daveny's arms and brought the baby into a close tuck. She nuzzled his plump, pink cheek. The fall of Kiara's straight, honey-colored hair danced like a curtain around her shoulders, the satin of which Ken could nearly feel. For a moment, he just stared, taking his fill of a beautiful woman cradling an innocent baby.

"He is, without question, the *cutest* baby *ever*," Kiara said.

"Absolutely," concurred Elise Edwards, the equally proud grandmother.

Ken noticed the somewhat aged christening blanket draped over Kiara's arm. She would be up front with the whole family during the baptism, standing next to the gray and white marble font during the ceremony. Made sense. Daveny Montgomery Edwards, an only child, considered Kiara a surrogate sister.

"You want to see Pastor Ken, Jeffrey?" Kiara murmured, stepping close. She focused her gaze on his, her emerald eyes alive and sparkling. When she handed Jeffrey over, the light scent of a floral perfume drifted up. Like the woman who wore it, the aroma was evocative.

"How are you?" Ken asked quietly, unwilling to relinquish her gaze.

"Good. I'm sure glad to see *you* again. Welcome back." Her smile bloomed, large and beautiful—engaging. It took a few seconds for Ken to find his equilibrium.

"Thanks. It's good to be back."

"How was the mission trip?"

While Ken cuddled Jeffrey, Kiara rubbed the baby's back. The motion left him keenly aware of the connection between the three of them. "It was hard work—but very rewarding."

"You were in Louisiana, right? Just outside of New Orleans? Habitat for Humanity?"

"Exactly." The knowledge that this compelling woman had tracked his absence sent pleasure seeping through his bloodstream. Within her observations, though, Ken sensed an underlying current, one that traveled beyond simple interest. She cared about the answer. So he elaborated. "There's a world of great work being done down there. We helped build new houses, even assisted in improving dilapidated structures inside and out. We fed masses of homeless people, too. In fact, the whole program left me wanting to get members of our youth group motivated to donate some time and muscle to a mission trip of our own—maybe sometime this fall."

Jeffrey's back rub ended when Kiara went still, though her hand remained in place while she looked into Ken's eyes. Almost instantly, the baby started a restless squirm. "Really? What an amazing experience that would be." She retreated a bit, breaking the connection to Jeffrey. She looked down as she ran her fingertips against the tassels that edged the christening blanket. She looked up once more. "You must have enjoyed being a source of help and benefit. I give you a lot of credit."

Ken could tell her comment didn't stem from polite conversation or small talk. Images from the trip came to him, click-by-click, like a slideshow display.

He had witnessed helplessness, poverty, the destitute living conditions of over-burdened families. But he had also witnessed transformation—hope and rebirth delivered by hard working hands and giving hearts.

Giving hearts like Kiara's.

Not for the first time in the years since they had met, Ken sensed within her a quest, a longing for self-discovery. Trouble was, she fought that instinct, too.

So he challenged. "Maybe you can find out." He studied her for a moment. "I have a good memory. I'll remember this conversation if we end up putting the mission trip together. You may become one of my first adult recruits."

She blushed, looking away shyly while she shook her head. Her pattern, he knew, might be to step aside, but her heart turned her toward service—service that could be put to miraculous use.

Magnetized, Ken could have studied her features, that delicate flush of reaction, for much longer; however, family conversations, plans and questions took her away from his direct focus. Besides, more and more parishioners filtered in, sweeping him into his role as Pastor.

Ken tried not to be blatant about watching Kiara, but following their conversation, he had time to consider the ideas he had about crafting a mission trip that involved Woodland Church. In fact, the seeds of that plan took root and bloomed into a flare of color and life that was instantaneous. While he watched her move through the church, mixing with people and chatting, Ken knew he wanted Kiara involved—and he felt confident he could convince her to participate.

That fact alone provided a spurring push of motivation.

2

Even before they met in the common area of Woodland Church, Kiara knew Pastor Ken was back in town, following a month-long sabbatical to participate in a Christian outreach and mission program.

He'd been doing such things a lot during the past couple years—ever since his wife Barb passed away. He had spent weeks in the far reaches of Michigan's upper peninsula working with impoverished families and assisting their far-removed charitable organizations. During the winter months, he had spent countless hours at homeless shelters and soup kitchens around metro Detroit.

This past excursion had been his longest yet, however—a full month away from Woodland. Associate Pastor Ben McCallum always performed admirably, but the heart of Woodland Church beat strongest within the soul of its Pastor, Kenneth Lucerne. For almost a dozen years now—ever since his ordination, according to Daveny—Woodland was his home. Kiara often wondered if that wasn't the reason why in recent times being at the helm of the church seemed difficult for him. After all, at thirty-five, he was far too young to have suffered through the terrible life-quake of becoming a widower.

Despite it all, Kiara gave him tremendous credit for natural charisma, and nothing lessened the impact of being in his presence once again.

Short brown hair, softly waved, framed a face that featured a strong, squared jaw and a pair of warm brown eyes that searched the faces of today's attendees, drawing them in one by one as he preached.

Kiara included.

Before she knew it, his gaze tagged hers. A slight quirk of his lips let her know she'd been busted for staring.

"Where there's love, there is self-sacrifice," Ken said, walking the length of the front line of pews. Kiara shook free of distraction and listened. "There's a giving over, one to the other. A surrender. By that I don't just mean the surrender of time, or of giving up a few hours...right now probably *more* than a few hours...of sleep to soothe the cries of a newborn baby." Ken smiled at Daveny and Collin who sat next to her. He slid his hand tenderly against Jeffrey's cheek. "What I mean by surrender is sacrifice. Love can't grow into place without self-surrender. If either withholds the self, love cannot exist."

Ken continued. "You know what? Sacrifice gets a bad rap. Sacrifice evokes the image and emotion of denial, of setting aside something we wish for. That's not the case here. When we speak of sacrifice in this instance, it involves nurturing and seeing to the needs of a newborn, sometimes as we set aside our own wants and needs. It's selfless. We give and teach as a baby becomes a toddler, and yet again, as that child grows to adulthood beneath the protective wings of a loving parent and family. Furthermore, those sacrifices aren't without benefit. For example? What a blessing, to witness the good that comes from watching a newborn grow into a self-sufficient being who remains, always, a part of our hearts and lives. Ultimately though, our children reach independence. When that happens, a different kind of surrender takes place. A release of the ones we love to the fullness of life—knowing in our hearts that the unchanging truth of God's ultimate shepherding always stays in place."

The sermon concluded a short time later, and Ken invited the Edwards family to gather around a baptismal font stationed to the right of the altar. Kiara followed behind Daveny. Once everyone was in place, Jeffrey's christening blanket was removed. Then, clothed only in a cloth diaper, he was handed to Pastor Ken.

Ken offered introductory blessings and a prayer before holding him over the warmed, gurgling water of the font. "Jeffrey Lance Edwards, the Christian community of Woodland welcomes you with great joy. I baptize you in the name of the Father, and of the Son, and of the Holy Spirit. Amen."

As he spoke, Pastor Ken dipped Jeffrey into the water three times. The family gathered in close and a few flashes went off, recording the moment. Swaddling Jeffrey in fresh, white linen adorned by a vivid red cross, and lifting the baby carefully, Pastor Ken walked the main aisle of the church in a ceremonious presentation to the parish of its newest member. Chills of pure joy skimmed against Kiara's skin as piano music swelled and the congregation chimed in with a sung chorus of "Alleluia."

Tears filled her eyes and spilled slowly down her cheeks. She looked over at Daveny, who watched the proceedings and glowed with happiness; her eyes sparkled with moisture as well and Collin tucked his arm around her waist, drawing her tight to his side.

They both looked so proud, so fulfilled. Kiara rejoiced deeply for her dearest friends and their newborn son—named in part for Collin's late brother.

When Ken returned to the baptismal font, he handed Jeffrey to Daveny, but his gaze settled on Kiara's at the moment a fresh trickle of tears fell free. She dashed them away fast. It was time to leave services temporarily so that Jeffrey could be dressed in his baptismal garments.

Before returning to the proceedings, however, Ken passed by and discreetly pressed an item into her right hand. A soft, snow-white handkerchief. He touched her with a smile that made her muscles go weak.

∂∾∾

Seeking a few moments of peaceful meditation following services, Kiara ducked back into the church. It would take a while for the crowds to thin, for the Edwards family to accept the multitude of congratulations and admiring comments.

The idea prompted a smile and a sense of contentment on behalf of her friends. Daveny and Collin could make even the most jaded person believe in the power of love all over again.

Which became part of Kiara's quandary at the moment.

She longed to taste that kind of happiness, but trying to find it always seemed to end her up in tight, complex emotional tangles. Like the situation she faced right now with her most current male admirer…

"You coming, Kiara?"

The summons startled her. Kiara turned when she felt Daveny's hand come to rest on her shoulder. She hadn't even heard her friend approach—testimony to the degree of distraction she fought. "Yeah, I am. Sorry."

"No worries, sweetie. Just wondered about you is all." Daveny sat next to her with a sigh. "OK, so the pudgy ankles are gone, the waistline is starting to resemble that of a normal human being again, but I'm here to tell you; Ken wasn't kidding. *Boy*, does sleep deprivation take it out of you."

Kiara grinned. "I slept in until eight thirty this morning."

"Wench."

"Stop snarling. I may have slept through the night, but I don't have a beautiful baby boy to tend to. And I certainly didn't wake up next to a man the likes of Collin Edwards."

"Was it Andrew, perhaps?" Daveny asked tentatively.

"No." The reply was flat and lifeless.

Daveny paused. "Have you decided?"

On the inside, Kiara cringed. On the inside, she braced against…everything. Right versus wrong. God versus the devil in her soul.

In an instant, Kiara found herself thousands of miles away. She traversed the narrow, cobbled streets of Paris, hand in hand with a sexy, and admittedly, besotted suitor, her world painted a soft, dusky shade of rose. In her mind's eye, she saw the Eiffel Tower framed in the window of a five-star hotel where she lounged on a balcony overlooking the ancient, gorgeous city. She could almost feel a cool evening breeze ripple the glossy fabric of a satin robe and negligee against her skin.

Beyond the set of double French doors at her back?

Andrew—dark haired, olive skinned, a bewitching specimen—stretched out upon a king-sized bed, tangled up in its sheets, half covered by a plush down comforter…

"Kiara?"

Jarred back to reality by Daveny's voice, Kiara took a deep breath and spoke from the heart. "I realize my 'No' should be automatic. It's wrong. His offer to take me to France for a romantic getaway feels too much like a deliberate ploy. A blatant seduction. Payment for services rendered."

Daveny didn't agree, or disagree. But then, she didn't need to. Like a good friend, she waited and allowed Kiara to come to terms.

"Why does it appeal to me so strongly?" Kiara wondered aloud. "Why is it so hard to just refuse and move on?"

"Because he's attractive. He's successful, and he's absolutely enchanted by you, Kiara. He has been from the start of our landscaping project for his company. He's offering you a trip that's certainly a fantasy come true. Once in a lifetime."

Daveny was correct. First class flight, the Ritz Hotel, a week of…

Surrender to mutual attraction.

But was it mutual? Was it *right*?

Kiara studied the simple altar illuminated by vibrant stained glass windows that framed its perimeter. She wondered. Did her longing to agree to this trip stem from feelings she harbored for Andrew, or from the fact that she felt increasingly lonely? After all, what woman wouldn't enjoy being sought after by a well-to-do, sexy man who wanted to treat her like a princess?

"However," Daveny continued, "let me be clear about something. When all is said and done? You deserve *much* more than a seductive interlude, Kiara. You deserve a man, a relationship, of substance and honor. Don't lose sight of that. Is this developing relationship playing to your heart? Do you really even know him?"

Kiara shrugged. "Well, that's kind of the point. To escape together, to find our footing—"

"Really?"

Kiara heard and understood the skeptical tone—and found no fault with the mild reprimand that rode beneath its surface. "Well, no. It's about...well—"

Chuckling wryly, Daveny bumped Kiara's shoulder with hers. "I know, I know."

A frail sense of self, a near life-long quest for affirmation, clawed at Kiara's chest. By careful design, that fact might surprise most people who knew her. She wore a Donna Karan ensemble from Saks, a new pair of Jimmy Choos. Perfectly styled hair and an expert application of makeup downplayed every flaw and up-played every attribute like a protective shield. Her smile lit up, her bubbly personality engaged...

But the demons she fought were over 25-years-old, and they were relentless.

She stood and sighed through the smile. "I'm going to say no. I know you're right. I know I deserve more, I know what God would want, but so far, the best offers I get come from men who are attracted to this face, this figure, and not much more. To be honest, I've played to that truth for so long, I'm not so sure about finding a way out." She shrugged. "Trapped in my own cage, I guess."

Daveny watched her for a few moments then took

her hand in a firm squeeze. "Don't *ever* sell yourself short like that, Kiara. You're anything but shallow—or immoral. You'll find the one—the one who will give you so much more than you've gotten so far. God's preparing you, honey. And when you're ready, I promise, He'll send you a man who looks deep and long at *who* you are, not just the gorgeous cover-work."

Too serious. Too close to home. Kiara forced herself into an easy-going demeanor, re-sealing her heart as they left the serenity of the church. She tossed Daveny a saucy look, and then linked their arms together. "By the time that happens, I'll be ninety-something, but hope does indeed spring eternal. Come on. The family's waiting."

In the narthex, Pastor Ken stood amidst the Edwards family, temporary custodian of Jeffrey, who gurgled and squiggled. A cloth had been draped over Ken's shoulder to protect his vestment. He cuddled Jeffrey against it and rubbed the infant's back, swaying just a bit, in time to music only the two of them could hear. Kiara's forward progress halted while she absorbed more of the scene—his soft, assuring hum of sound, the tender way he held Jeffrey close.

Thoughts of Andrew left her empty. Instead, she made a wish, then and there, that a man who possessed the tenderness and charisma of Ken Lucerne might be out there for her...somewhere.

3

Early summer breezes set pastel-hued tablecloths rippling. Contentment filled Ken as he absorbed the musk of flowers and the spice of cooking meat that flavored the air. A dozen or so picnic tables filled the space of Daveny and Collin's backyard. Inside their house, he passed through the kitchen where clusters of friends and family bustled, preparing the fixings for brunch following Jeffrey's baptism.

"Hey, Pastor Ken," Kiara called when he walked by. "Can you please grab that platter of biscuits? The one right there next to the stove?"

"Sure."

Flushed and in her glory, Kiara hoisted pitchers of lemonade and water from inside the refrigerator and made ready to return to the backyard. He followed, carrying the requested tray.

"Hey, Kiara?"

"Um-hm?" She turned and her hair slid against her shoulders and shimmered in a way that tantalized his senses.

"Let me promise you something."

"What's that?" Already she grinned, seeming to decipher the mischievous tone of his voice.

He lowered his voice to a whisper and leaned close. "God won't stir up an earthquake or a volcano or anything if you should happen to call me *Ken*."

The pink tinge on her cheeks intensified. He moved by her with a wink, delighted at catching her off guard.

"What about Kenny?" she sassed right back. "Will that suffice?"

He laughed at the rejoinder while they continued through the yard and placed their items on the food table. "Not if you expect to live to tell about it."

"Spoken like a true man of God, *Ken*." Kiara turned back toward the house. Before leaving, she cast a deliberate look over her shoulder and delivered a playful grin.

He watched her disappear inside, enjoying how easily they fell into affectionate teasing. At the heart of the matter, though, he wanted and hoped for her to think of him in terms that weren't strictly related to his role as a pastor. Of late, despite an abundance of people in his life, he felt desperately short of friends and the intimate tapestry of close relationships. Marriage to Barb had helped insulate him from the sensation of being isolated and somehow set apart from the world-at-large. Now, as a widowed pastor, rules and perceptions had definitely changed.

He lingered at the table and a short time later Kiara returned, this time carrying a large platter of fluffy scrambled eggs. Ken decided to go back to the house as well, wanting to see what else might be needed. When she smiled in passing, when their shoulders brushed, warmth bloomed outward from his midsection.

Before long, the table overflowed with food. Fragrant bacon and sausage links were left to warm on an electric tray. French toast and a towering stack of pancakes had been added to the mix as well. Ken delivered plates and cutlery, wanting to make a last trip to the kitchen for two carafes of coffee.

All the while, the yard filled with people who arrived for the day's celebration.

That's when he came up short; an unfamiliar man entered the backyard. Kiara moved toward the new arrival, dodging a few colorful balloons that had been tied to the ends of the tables and bobbed in the air.

"Andrew!" she greeted happily, stepping into his offered hug.

"Hey, sweetheart."

He nuzzled her cheek just before they exchanged a quick kiss. Kiara slid her arm through his, giving it a squeeze and sending him one of those smiles that now hit Ken's system like lightening fire.

Meanwhile, Andrew looked left and right, taking in the party scene, shifting in an uncomfortable way while Kiara enthused: "Drew, the ceremony was just *amazing*. It literally left me in tears. Jeffrey was such a good baby, too. He—"

"It's OK that I didn't go, right? I mean, I'm anxious to meet all your friends, but I'm not family after all, and…well…I'm not too comfortable about the whole church thing."

Ken heard Andrew's dismissive words and sank on the inside.

"Give that time. I'm just glad you're here now." Kiara walked him through the maze of tables and people "C'mon. I want you to say hello to Collin and Dav. They've been asking about you."

She led him toward the spot where Daveny and Collin stood. Their conversation faded with distance. A sense of alarm crept through Ken. He centered his attention on the pair and kept it there. He watched as

Andrew's expression softened to congenial, warm lines and he seemed to react kindly to the family. In fact, he seemed to say something that made the group around them laugh merrily. Kiara kept her supportive physical connection in place as they visited for a bit, then wandered toward the display of food.

Don't reject his comments about God's church so easily, Kiara. The thought crashed in, prompting Ken's protective desire to somehow move between them. *Don't compromise the faith-walk you're starting.*

The party progressed and after a time, the celebratory tone of the day displaced all else. He mingled from table to table, enjoying the company of a number of familiar faces from Woodland. He paused from conversations for a moment, stepping over to the food table so he could replenish his mug of coffee. Daveny joined him, linking her arm through his.

"Hello there." She rose on tiptoe to peck his cheek. That made him smile. Ken adored this long-time, spirited member of his congregation. She lived and breathed the spirit of God. With tender love, and leading by example, she had not only won Collin's heart, she had also inspired Collin, once so disillusioned and embattled with God, to return to his faith. "You having fun?"

"I am. You've done a beautiful job, kiddo." With a glance, Ken indicated the festive décor, the tables packed with people that spread across the entirety of their spacious backyard.

"Thanks. I had a ton of help, though. Yours included. Thanks, Ken, for everything you've done. I really feel like Jeffrey became part of God's family today—and you're the conduit."

That analogy Ken couldn't quite accept. "The

community is the conduit. You and Collin are the conduit. Not me."

She shrugged. "OK. Not you alone, but you importantly."

Laughing, he kissed her cheek. "OK, OK. You win. I know better than to argue with a new, likely sleep-deprived, mom."

"You've always been a smart man." She looked around the yard, picking up a celery stick from the vegetable tray and taking a bite. "Have you seen Kiara?"

"Not in the last few minutes. Why?"

"She brought a fruit and cheese tray and I think we should probably bring it out now."

"Yeah, there's actually room for it on the table now," Ken teased, picking up a few stray plates that had been left behind. He stashed them on top of a pair of empty serving platters. "I'll take these in. Let me get the fruit for you."

"Are you sure?"

"Absolutely. Now get back to the party."

Before she could argue, he turned away, retreating to the kitchen. Dishes filled the sink. Paper debris, bows and discarded wrapping paper covered the counter tops and breakfast table. Sunlight streamed in through an oversized window above the sink and silence enveloped and soothed him for a time.

Until he heard voices. A conversation drifted to him from the next room over, the dining room, which adjoined the kitchen via a swinging door.

"So?" This from a male voice he couldn't readily identify.

"So?" That was Kiara.

Her companion—had to be Andrew—chuckled.

"*So* have you decided?"

"Paris."

"Mmmm...Paris."

Ken heard what sounded like a kiss, then Kiara's shy laughter.

His stomach fell away as he realized the implications of their private moment. He felt like a voyeur. He tried not to listen, but their voices carried regardless of his will.

"First class flight," Andrew continued. "Top of the line accommodations; a week of *Europe*, Kiara. Just the two of us. *Imagine it!*"

"I know, I know. It's exotic, and thrilling. Still, something about all of this makes me feel like a kept woman."

Ken heard Andrew sigh.

"Well it shouldn't. This is something I want to do for you." Andrew paused. "You know something? I mean it when I say I've never ever met anyone like you, Kiara. I promise you that. You're all I think about. All I can focus on."

Andrew's voice had softened to velvet. Ken closed his eyes, battling the urge to wince. He wanted to leave. *Knew* he should leave. His feet stayed rooted to the spot.

"Drew—"

"No. *Please.* Hear me out." Silence followed. "I've loved having you work on the landscaping project at my office, but...but...it's over now, and I *hate* that. I want to keep seeing you. I want to *be* with you."

"I've enjoyed it too, but this is so sudden, so fast."

In each syllable of those simple words, Ken heard her longing, her questioning.

Kiara continued. "I...I just...I don't know what to

say to all this. I'm dazzled and amazed, of course, but—but I *can't!*"

"No buts, sweetheart. OK? Yes, you *can*. Just say *yes*. Just trust me. Trust *us*. I want to do this for you. I want you dazzled and amazed, because you dazzle and amaze *me*. Turnabout's fair play, Kiara. I want to take you to one of the most fantastic places in the world, and I don't want you to have to think about a thing except being with me, about where we can go together as a couple—"

"That's just it, Drew. I *have* imagined those things. I've thought about them just as much as you." Her soft, pleading tone dissipated on air that turned muggy with the first signs of an encroaching summer afternoon. Ken felt each notch upward in the temperature with a startling intensity that had nothing at all to do with the weather.

"Don't deny us this chance," Andrew whispered. "I want this so much. I want *you* so much. You and I walking through the streets, hand in hand, kissing under *le Tour Eiffel*—"

"I have to get back to the party," she interrupted, sounding breathless. Even at a distance, Ken detected the underlying desperation in her tone. He went taut against the temptation he knew she faced, trying hard to rebuke it on her behalf.

"Anyway, you're not being fair," she teased. "I can't think straight when you're like this."

"Good. There's nothing wrong with being off balance. Besides, that'd make two of us. This outfit you're wearing is making me crazy. You look gorgeous."

Ken's reaction was instinctive—couldn't be helped. Andrew's comment left him envisioning the way she looked. A white lace skirt edged by blue satin, a sea-blue shell that, in church, had been discreetly covered by a matching cardigan. For the party, the sweater had been removed to reveal dewy soft skin just hinting at the start of a rich, summer tan. Ken pictured the strappy white sandals on her feet, the dancing line of her skirt as it skimmed against her ankles.

And the images didn't just flow; they flooded him. He felt like he had been pulled under by a warm, swift current. Yes, just looking at her, and absorbing her, was plenty enough to intoxicate a man. He couldn't fault Drew for that.

"Thank you for the compliment," she concluded. "Now unhand me, you beast."

"Not...quite...yet."

Ken didn't need to see the kisses they shared. What he heard provided more than enough entrée into the private moment.

"Six short days, Kiara. Think about it. The plane leaves Saturday at 7 p.m. *Please* say you're going to be there."

Ken didn't wait on Kiara's reply. He didn't want to hear it. Nor did he want to intrude any longer. Still, his heart sank. He grabbed the tray filled with cheese and a variety of fruits then headed outside to dodge the possibility of being discovered. Besides, he needed to regain his composure.

But his legs felt like lead.

4

The following Sunday Ken's psyche morphed into radio receiver mode. He prepared for services, yet all the while, he twisted and tuned an internal dial, seeking Kiara, hoping she'd show up and wondering what she chose to do about Andrew's scintillating offer. When she walked through the double doors and entered the narthex, a sense of relief slid so powerfully through his body that it rendered him dissolved. The relief he'd expected, the degree of near euphoria that accompanied, however, took him by surprise.

After church, he found her sitting in the deserted sanctuary, head bowed, hands folded, eyes closed. He couldn't walk away. For a few unobserved moments, he watched her through the etched glass of the main doors to the sanctuary, riveted in place. Reaching forward, he grasped the cool chrome handle and slowly pulled it open.

Quiet footsteps led him to her pew. "Hey, Kiara."

"Hi, Pas...Ken."

He laughed and gave her shoulder a squeeze. "You're getting better." He sat down.

"Old habits and all."

"Am I interrupting?"

"Not at all." She looked at him with an eagerness that reassured. "I'm glad to see you. It's just...well, it's not often I get a chance to absorb the silence and just be still. I sat here, just like this, after the baptism last weekend, and it really helped me find my center."

"Prayer time always does. Really, I don't mean to be rude. I can leave…"

Kiara pondered that statement for a moment, and watched him steadily. "Please don't. It's not so much that I'm even praying; I just take everything in, if that makes any sense." She shrugged shyly and went quiet, as though a bit discomfited by the topic of prayer and her spirit life. Ken, on the other hand, took in her every nuance and revelation.

"For me those are the moments when God speaks loudest," he offered. "Even silence is a prayer."

"Like we're listening instead of monopolizing."

"Exactly. But there's nothing wrong with *petitioning*," he amended. "Either way, I think God just wants us to be with him."

Kiara looked up at him and smiled. His blood pounded thick and heavy.

"I never got a chance to tell you what a beautiful job you did with the baptism." Her eyes went wide and she gasped, cutting off any kind of response he might offer. "Shoot! That reminds me. I forgot your handkerchief at home. I meant to bring it back to you today."

Her chagrin caused him to chuckle. "Don't worry about it." Crazy, yes, but for some reason Ken liked the fact that she had something of his. So instead of dwelling, he switched topics. "Collin's the picture of contentment and pleased fatherhood, isn't he? Plus, over two years after the wedding, I still see Daveny's glow."

Kiara went unusually still, looking toward a large vibrant floral arrangement at the center of the altar.

"They deserve it. They're very special people."

Wistfulness coated her every word. Her tone and posture left Ken more curious than ever as to why she had refused Andrew's extraordinary invitation to jet off to Europe.

"So are you, Kiara."

She shrugged in too dismissive a way.

"I'm glad to see you here today."

"Where else would I…" The words, and her puzzled expression, faded away. She studied him for a long moment, and then her eyes went wide as the broader implication of his comment sank in. Ken regarded her calmly, remaining steady so she could come forward and feel safe about it. "Oh." She blinked. "Oh, my goodness." She enunciated each word and her shoulders drooped beneath a figurative weight. "You *know*? How could you have known…*Daveny*."

"*No*. Daveny would never betray a confidence. I overheard you and your boyfriend talking about Europe. It was at the Christening party. I was in the kitchen getting food. You and Andrew were in the other room talking. I'm sorry. I didn't mean to pry."

Kiara wilted further. She tilted her head back and groaned. "*Great*. To have someone I respect, my Pastor of all people, think of me as a woman of loose morals. That's just *great*."

On the inside Ken froze. *My Pastor. Respect.* Not bad things, to be sure, but those terms defined the parameters of her feelings. Her perceptions. He didn't come away feeling altogether flattered.

He stood in an abrupt motion. "Thanks for the confidence, Kiara. I only brought it up because I thought you might have some faith in my care and friendship." He snapped the words and moved toward the aisle. Her eyes revealed she was stricken. Too bad. Simplicity turned complex with regard to her presence in his life these days.

But then she stopped him with a restraining hand. "I said no to him. Obviously. I'm here. I didn't end up going."

"That's between the two of you," Ken concluded more gently this time. He didn't sit quite yet. He felt raw, his vulnerabilities exposed.

"I'm so sorry," she whispered. She sounded miserable. He sat, and let her continue. "I'm so sorry you heard that conversation, and I'm sorrier still for what you must think of me because of it."

Once more with what other people thought. Ken wanted to cringe. "Does the opinion of others matter that much to you, Kiara?" He sighed, agonized over an onrush of want. He'd always admired her tender, energetic spirit. Now, however, he had no idea what to do with a desire that intensified each time he saw her. "Let me assure you. I'm nobody's judge. That's not what I'm about, and judgment is certainly not part of my job description."

"I didn't mean it that way! Still, I can't help caring about what you think. I value your opinion because I care about *you*."

The admission stopped him short, flowed against his unsettled heart like a softly curving breeze. "So you want to know what *I* think?"

She nodded. Her eyes remained turbulent, though.

He gathered in a breath, ached to reach for her hands, which still lay folded in her lap. He couldn't cross that physical line right now though, so he held back. "I think you displayed a lot of fortitude and strength turning down what must have seemed like a wonderful opportunity. Fortunately, you realized to do so would surrender a part of your soul. I'm gratified you didn't. It says a lot to me about who you are."

She nipped at her lower lip. Released it. "Don't hold me up to that kind of an ideal, Pastor Ken. Please. Trust me; I'm nobody's moral barometer."

He shook his head. Restraining the connection to her vanished. He stroked her cheek with a light touch. "Funny. Neither were any of the apostles, the saints, right on back to King David." He shrugged. "We're all flawed, Kiara, so it seems to me you're in good company."

She looked at him, her wide eyes reflecting the patterns and uncertainty of a questing soul.

For now, those words had to be Ken's final say on the subject. He hoped—prayed, in fact—that his words might be enough to spur her onward. He stood and slid from the pew, stepping resolutely into the main aisle. He retreated, seeking the safe haven of his office.

There he could find respite from a woman who played through his heart like a sweet, promising song.

Sitting behind his desk, Ken decided to bury himself in fiscal bureaucracy. It was preliminary budget time, and number crunching would put an end to any kind of romantic revelry. Though he loathed the annual numbers process, he couldn't avoid the matter, so he opened up last year's manila file folder and slid it into place, determined to make progress on the upcoming model.

He pulled open the top drawer of his desk, sifting through clutter in search of a red pen. There, almost hidden beneath a box of paperclips and a square of yellow sticky notes rested a single rectangular admittance ticket, dated just about two years ago.

Woodland Church — Autumn Fest

The sight of it stilled Ken's hand at once. He carefully drew out the ticket, and then stretched back in his chair to study it for a moment. Like a port-key, the small piece of pumpkin colored cardstock sent him reeling backward in time, awash in memories both painful and beautiful. Unable to focus on the here and now, Ken allowed himself to drift.

He sank into the moment completely, reliving that fateful night, and its aftermath, all over again.

In a figurative sense, Barb had twisted his arm to attend the event. She seemed to have recovered well from her two-days-ago chemo treatment and was eager to participate in the festival. It's not that he didn't support and appreciate the event. Instead, Barb's continuing battle with stomach cancer pinned his focus to the exclusion of everything else.

New this time was a parade of costumes. Parishioners, young and old alike, would strut a catwalk that cut through the center of the church activity center.

Committee member Kiara Jordan had coordinated that aspect of the proceedings while Daveny and Elise Edwards championed the music and food/beverage offerings respectively. The event promised to be a huge success, but in truth, Ken had paid attention with only half a heart.

He worried about Barb overdoing it, but had no strength to argue against her wishes. Not after everything she had been through during the past eight months.

"This is just what I need tonight, Ken," she said as they walked into the already crowded hall.

He kissed her cool, pale cheek, smiling down at

her. "I know, so I promise not to be a pest as long as you—"

"Promise to let you know if I start to get tired," she finished, rolling her eyes.

They laughed and she squeezed his arm, her weight transferring to him bit by bit as they neared a table. *Small steps*, he thought. *The treatments mean she'll tire easily, and rebound faster if I let her rest in spells.*

Ken seated her at a table that included the Edwards family so she could visit with friends while he dispensed with some mandatory mingling, and searched for Kiara. During the course of planning meetings, she had worked enough magic to convince Ken to emcee the costume display, so he needed the order of participants and accompanying descriptions.

"Want some pop?" he asked Barb. "There's also some veggies and fruit at the food table, pumpkin bread, too."

"Sure, that'd be great. Thank you."

"Be right back."

He glanced up, at a raised runway, which was the focal point of the room. Tables and chairs surrounded the platform. Behind the runway he saw a curtained off staging area. The curtain, of orange, yellow and deep red, featured an overlay of white netting plastered by vivid colored leaves that had just fallen across the grounds of Woodland. Under Kiara's supervision, the youth group had raked, then created, the display. Further enhancement came in the form of a dozen or so cut outs of pumpkins, cornucopias and shimmery red apples. Cornucopias and a few small pumpkins also served as table highlights.

Ken grinned. Kiara's touch again. She had mobilized the youth group into a decorating frenzy and come up with terrific results. He enjoyed the atmosphere while he stood in line and prepared Barb's soft drink and food plate. He greeted a few parishioners then returned to Barb briefly before leaving to find out more about his emcee duties.

Figuring he'd find Kiara in the staging area, Ken ducked behind the black curtain where fashion show participants had already started to gather. Kiara stood at the center of the crowd, clipboard in hand. She gave him a smile of such warmth and vitality its impact stroked against an unexpected, vibrating spot and brought it to life.

She sported the attire of a woman on safari, right down to the tan colored jacket and matching calf-length shorts. A safari hat rested atop hair plaited into twin braids. Binoculars, of course, dangled from her neck.

"You look great," Ken said when he joined her.

"Our master of ceremonies is here! Hey, Pastor Ken. And don't you look every inch the dashing emcee." She reached up to fuss with the black bow tie at his throat. "Let me guess—you're the groom at the top of a wedding cake?"

He laughed. "Close, but not quite. The tuxedo might lead you to that conclusion, but I'm not a groom—although this is a dual costume with my bride."

"Oh?" She waited on elaboration.

He gave her a sheepish look. "Think about it, Kiara. Barbie and –"

She burst into laughter. "Ken! I love it! I can't wait to see Barb all done up." The jovial moment stilled. "How's she doing?"

Ken couldn't—wouldn't—slide into sadness. Not

right now. "She's fighting hard. She'll love seeing you. She says she's feeling good, but she gets tired fast."

Kiara reached for his hand and gave it a squeeze then offered an ease-restoring grin. "Is she in pink, I hope?"

"Oceans of it, in satin of course, along with a gleaming, way-too-perfect blonde wig." That covers steadily thinning hair, he added in silence. "It's a hoot. She's having fun with it."

"Tell her I'll see her right after the show."

"I will."

From beneath the clip of the board she held, Kiara slipped free a stack of note cards. "Here's your script, in order."

"Thanks."

A young boy with eyes full of moisture and lips quivering stepped up and tugged on Kiara's cropped jacket.

"Miss Kiara, my tail fell off!"

Dejected, this young Mustafa the Lion King offered up a long brown snake of cloth with a fuzzed, fluffy tip. A tear made its way down his plump cheek. Above the boy's head, Kiara gave Ken a quick look before taking her charge by the hand, saying, "No worries. I can fix it. Your costume will be just fine."

"Really?"

"Promise. So, no tears, OK? Remember, you're going to be on stage soon!"

Kiara's excitement turned the tide. Ken watched them walk away while crowds pressed in, increasing the noise level as well as an air of backstage anticipation.

Elise Edwards came charging into the cordoned off space, expelling a huge sigh of relief when she caught sight of him. "Ken. Ken, you need to come with me. Now."

The concerned look on her face prompted him to move fast. She pressed a hand against her chest as they trotted out the doors of the activity center. "Barb had to leave, to go to the ladies room. When she didn't come back right away, I went to check on her. Well…"

Oh no.

Ken pushed into the lavatory without hearing anything else Elise said.

"Barb?" He called with studied calm. He crumbled on the inside when he saw waves of pink satin on the floor of the second stall. She breathed hard, and he could hear her crying. "Barb, honey. Let me in."

"No."

"Sweetheart, please. Let me in."

She didn't reply. A series of tense, silent seconds beat past, but at last the door latch slid slowly free. She didn't rise from her kneeling position on the floor. Ken moved in carefully while she flushed the toilet then wiped a shaky hand across her damp mouth. She began to sob uncontrollably, then choked, "Can you take me home?" She pulled the shimmering wig from her head, leaning her elbows on the bowl. She didn't make eye contact of any kind, she looked shamed, and beyond that, devastated.

"You bet. Come here." Ken lifted her up, alarmed anew by how light she felt, even at a near dead weight.

"I'm sorry, Ken. I'm so sorry."

"Shhh. You have nothing at all to be sorry for."

"I thought I could do this. Honestly I felt fine until I ate."

"I know you did. Don't worry. It's OK now. We'll get you home, you'll get a good night's rest and you'll rebound. Don't worry about it."

He set her gently on her feet, holding her snug to his side. He guided her outside the building, into cool, reviving air.

"Oh, Ken." She paused after whispering the words, breathing deep. "Thank you. This helps a lot. I got so hot, and it hit me so fast."

Despite renewed comfort, Barb's skin remained splotched by the red stains of a blood rush that contrasted violently against the milk-white tone of her skin. He captured her face gently between his hands and looked into eyes that were still too bright.

"Thank you," he said quietly.

"For?"

"For keeping your promise."

He watched her throat work as she swallowed hard. Her eyes filled. "So have you, Ken. You always do. I love you for that, and for so much more."

He touched her cheek, so soft despite her physical battle against illness. "That road works both ways. I love you, too."

He drove the few short blocks home. Barb's head lolled against the seat and she sighed. When they arrived, he nearly called Collin to take his place as emcee, but Barb wouldn't allow it. She needed rest and peace, so he didn't push. Instead, he brewed a mug of green tea for her.

Just looking at her, Ken knew she fought valiantly to keep down the offering, but minutes after settling into place, she calmed. She laid on the couch, beneath a quilt she had made years ago during a church sponsored quilting bee. She looked frail and pale to the point of translucence.

"It's bad this time," she murmured. "I just want to

rest." Tears beaded on her lashes. "I hate that I don't have energy anymore. That I'm not even strong enough to move around. This is horrible."

"I want to stay with you."

"No. Ken, you need to go back to church. They're counting on you."

"So are you. And you're more important than anything else. Period."

She touched his face. When she reached up, he noticed how elongated and too thin her fingers had become. "Will you pray with me, Ken?"

The request melted his soul, poured it free. "Of course."

They joined hands and bowed heads; a fine tremor translated from her hands to his, further depleting his control mechanisms. He closed his eyes, fighting to find the ability to persevere. "Lord Jesus, we pray for the touch of Your healing, for the merciful grace of Your comfort through each and every cell of Barb's body. Give her rest. Bless her with peace and calm in the midst of the storm she faces. Assure her of Your steadfast, faithful love and provision."

"And dear Lord," Barb continued softly, "I pray Your peace and comfort on Ken as he sees to my needs, his own needs, and the needs of Woodland Church. Guide, guard and bless him, dear Lord. He needs Your strength as much as I do."

Ken looked into her eyes as they finished in unison: "In Jesus' name we pray. Amen."

Barb squeezed her lips tight and dashed away the moisture that sparkled at the edges of her eyes. "Now get out of here. Go back to the festival. I can rest now, and it'll do you good to get out for a while. I'll be fine...and you're just a cell call away."

Ken obeyed. Her tired eyes left him no choice.

As ever, especially these days, Woodland and its circle of faith brought him a much-needed sense of normalcy. He still visualized Barb back home, but gradually allowed himself to get into the spirit of the event. In fact, it wasn't long before Kiara peeked out from behind the stage curtain and signaled Ken to start the proceedings.

Amazing to think that only about forty-five minutes had passed since the time they had greeted one another.

Ken gave her a nod. He walked to a podium set up to the right of the catwalk and picked up the microphone. "Welcome to Woodland Autumn Fest, everyone." It was then that he remembered: He had completely lost track of his note cards. He froze for a few seconds—seconds that felt like hours—then did the only thing he could. He began to wing it. "Our charity this year is the Macomb County Shelter, MCS for short. The winter months are coming, and the funds being raised tonight will warm literally hundreds of stranded, displaced homeless people. Thank you for that blessing to our community."

The lights dimmed and the stage became illuminated. He floundered internally but moved on. "So, without further ado, please join me in viewing the very latest in what the best dressed autumn reveler will be wearing this year. It's no trick, just a treat, no matter what your age."

A round of applause gave him time to make eye contact with Kiara. Busy with a hundred details of her own, she had no clue about what had happened to Barb; nor did she realize he had forgotten the note cards. She gave him a thumbs-up and an encouraging nod before sending the first runway participant into the spotlight.

Ken was eternally grateful for the fact that God graced him with a close-knit parish family. He knew, by name, each of the twenty-five participants. As to the costume descriptions, he did the best he could, improvising on the fly. A few times, he caught sight of Kiara in his peripheral vision, watching in puzzlement as he continued. He'd have to explain later.

The last two on parade were Mustafa the Lion, little Jimmy Ginion, and Kiara. Jimmy had re-found his outgoing demeanor now that his tail was back in place; Kiara, meanwhile, vamped like a long-time owner of the runway, watching Mustafa through her binoculars, posing playfully, even cringing when he turned toward her and growled.

Ken continued emceeing. "Last but not least, we have the lovely Kiara Jordan, enjoying a safari-side view of the king of the African plains: Mustafa the Lion."

At the end of the runway, Kiara lifted Jimmy into her arms and paused so they could both acknowledge the applauding crowd. She encouraged Jimmy's enthusiastic waves and they blew kisses toward the audience. The duo left everyone, Ken included, laughing, rejoicing in pure, sweet innocence.

"Kiara, is it smart for safari participants to play with the animals?" Ken couldn't help but tease.

She looked over her shoulder at him and replied handily, "You bet it is, Pastor Ken."

More laughter followed, and applause reached a crescendo while they returned to the staging area. As fast as Ken's energy level had peaked, motivating him to get through the show, it evaporated. He exited the podium as fast as he could, leaning against a check-in table behind the curtain.

Thank you, Lord Jesus. Thank you. I needed you so much, and as always, you faithfully lift me up. Thank you. The prayer sang through his blood stream and soothed a depleted spirit, a tense body.

"Ken?" Very quietly Kiara spoke, stepping up from the buzzing crowd to touch his arm. She smiled, but hesitance shadowed her eyes. "That was quite a show. You were awesome."

He didn't answer. He didn't know what to say.

"What happened?" she asked.

"Lost my note cards."

She didn't take her hand from his arm. The assurance of connecting to someone helped steady him further. Ken breathed deep and could have sworn he came upon her scent—roses, and an undercurrent of vanilla.

"Something happened," she said.

He nodded. "Barb. She got sick a little while after we arrived. I had to get her home, and I just...I...I lost track of everything to be honest. Everything but her."

Kiara looked into his eyes, and her own went full, sparkling in the soft white light coming from overhead. "Which is just as it should be. And P.S.? You were amazing. Tonight shows how connected you are to your church, Ken. You knew every person by name. You brought everyone into the mood and fun, and all the while—all the while you—" Her words softened to nothing more than a whisper as she continued to look at him.

"Don't look at me like that. I just did what I had to do. What she asked me—actually what she forced me to do."

"Ken."

She spoke his name on a breath. She gave him a tight, lingering hug then stepped back, brushing tears from her lashes. Meanwhile, he experienced a delayed reaction. He received and accepted her affection, of course, but the essence of her lingered. Surrounded.

Penetrated.

Ken stared at her, not really seeing—only feeling—a spark of life and heat filling his heart.

Kiara continued. "Tell Barb I'm going to stop by. I really did miss seeing her tonight. Would that be OK?"

He found his voice just fast enough to reply, "That would be very OK."

"I'll call first, and make sure she's up to it."

"If she's able, she'll love it."

She nodded. "I'll be there."

After that, it didn't take long for her to get swept into the congratulations and camaraderie of the people who put on the Autumn Fest. Ken, meanwhile, moved quietly, slowly away.

But Kiara didn't make idle offers and let them vanish. The next day, after the promised phone call, she showed up at the front door, arms laden by a white wicker basket overflowing with multi-colored, fall-hued mums.

Ken appreciated the way Kiara focused on Barb, her affection plain as the two women chatted over the steaming mugs of the jasmine tea he prepared. They talked about Kiara's job, happenings at Woodland, they even joked about Barbie attire and platinum blonde wigs. There was no awkwardness Ken could discern, not even at the mention of Autumn Fest. All that flowed between them was easy friendship. The relaxed way Barb related to Kiara assured him that the visit wasn't just welcome, but enjoyed as well.

When Kiara left an hour or so later, he walked her outside, to where her car was parked in the driveway.

"Thanks for coming over," he said. A cool breeze, spiced by the aroma of nearby burning leaves, slid against his face. "The flowers are beautiful. You didn't have to do that."

"I wanted to do that," Kiara answered, sliding a set of keys from her purse and settling the strap on her shoulder. She unlocked the car with a blip of her key-fob then opened the door. When she turned toward him, her lower lip disappeared beneath the press of her teeth. A second later, tears sprang to her eyes and a few of them overflowed. "I don't want her to suffer. She's such a sweetheart."

Her reaction cut Ken to the quick, lancing straight through to the very heart of every fear, every anxiety he possessed. He stuffed his hands into the pockets of his slacks, willing himself not to weaken. Not to crumble like a too-brittle reed.

The effort was wasted.

He pulled his hands free, gathered Kiara into his arms and held on fast. She answered the gesture with equal force and need for support. Ken could summon no resistance to the truth that her touch, the connection they shared, felt beautiful.

Into the moment had ridden a tension-relieving sensation of affirmation and comfort that had played in perfect contradiction to his embroiled spirit.

Leaving memories behind, Ken shook his head and rubbed his eyes. His fingertips came away damp with a few tears that had squeezed free. He sighed, blinking until his vision cleared and the ticket he held came back into focus. His earlier plan to escape Kiara's impact had utterly backfired.

He needed…

One last escape from home—one last respite from the non-stop battle he fought against a loneliness that periodically pervaded and choked his life. He wanted to channel negativity into something positive, a blessing to those in need.

He re-stowed the ticket and straightened, resolved to move forward with a plan that had been percolating in his mind for a few weeks now. He'd conduct a mission trip this coming autumn. Preliminary research had already been completed. The mountains of Pennsylvania called with a need for service, and he wanted Woodland Church to help answer the summons.

Kiara seemed intent on growing her faith walk and relationship with God. If she could help out, so much the better. It might be just the needed way forward—for both of them.

5

To: Kiara.Jordan@Montgomerylandscape1.com;
Daveny.MontgomeryEdwards@Montgomerylands
cape1.com
From: Lucerne@WoodlandCC.com
Subject: Lunch?

Do you crave sustenance? Let me know if the two of you can get together for lunch at some point this week. I'll come to Birmingham to make things easier logistically. I'd love to see you, and brainstorm an idea I want to explore…(Are you intrigued yet?)

Ken

Kiara re-read the e-mail from Ken then beelined to Daveny's office. Standing at the threshold, she asked, "Did you see the e-mail from—"

Daveny studied her flat-screen. She chuckled quietly then looked up. "Ken, right?"

"Ah—*yeah*."

Daveny shrugged, but her eyes sparkled, which further unsettled Kiara's nervous system.

"A warning, my friend," Daveny said. "Take it from someone who knows first hand—Ken Lucerne possesses the gift of sneak-attack."

No kidding. Kiara's heart trip hammered.

"Something's brewing—and he knows just how to draw people in. So beware, my dear."

Fabulous. This was precisely what Kiara needed to hear when just the thought of him made her nerves shiver. "Well it seems, *my dear*, that his e-mail was directed to *both* of us."

Daveny just kept on grinning. "What day works best for you? I'm open this week." Kiara set her jaw, tension and anticipation rolling off her in waves. Meanwhile Daveny waited, calm and unaffected. Further, she arched a brow, prodding. "Well?"

Kiara huffed at her friend's demure posture then muttered, "Thursday."

Daveny nodded. "Thursday it is."

Turning on her heel, Kiara exited the doorway. Daveny's accompanying laughter did nothing at all to sooth Kiara's stirred up senses.

Daveny called sweetly: "Hey, Miss Agitated, shall you reply, or shall I?"

"I'll do it," Kiara cringed because her sharp reply would do nothing but confirm nervousness at spending time with Ken outside the comfort zone of Woodland Church.

"Touchy, touchy," Daveny replied. "By the way? A bistro table in the courtyard at 220 Merrill sounds wonderful…"

A deliberately appealing and relaxing restaurant choice—idyllic in a way—which only worsened Kiara's escalating tensions. With fierce keystrokes, she hit the reply toggle and began to type. She could have left the task of responding to Daveny, but didn't want to. *She* wanted to be the one to connect to him. *She* wanted to see him. But facing that realization scared her to bits at the moment, because in reality the anticipation of seeing Ken outside of church overrode everything else. Pushed. Magnetized. Provoked.

Attracted.

Lord was she was in trouble. Hence, she felt like a trapped grizzly bear.

∂∞∂

Daveny looked crestfallen. "You're leaving? *Again*?"

Ken nodded. "Yes, but only for a week, and this time it involves Woodland. After this mission, I promise, I'm staying put."

"A week in Appalachia." Kiara continued to listen, and watch him. Her words came out as a statement, not a question.

Ken looked at her, and his gaze stayed put for a moment. "With the STAGE group."

Woodland's teen-based service organization. Kiara nodded, still wondering why he needed Daveny's input, or hers. It seemed all systems were go. Why did Ken urge the lunch they now shared? They had claimed a small metal table on the outside patio at 220 Merrill, a favored hot-spot in the heart of a very busy, summer-kissed downtown Birmingham.

Ken continued, his gaze now including Daveny. "Here's where I could use your help. I need volunteers. Daveny, can you help me recruit a few adult chaperones?" While Daveny thought that over, his focus returned to Kiara. "And actually, Kiara, I was hoping you might be able to join the trip."

At that moment, their food arrived—thank

goodness. While the server placed platters, shock swept in. Kiara swallowed hard, staring down at her corned beef on rye.

"Told you I'd remember," Ken said. The soft tone of his voice bore undercurrents of an intimacy that her heart welcomed, even if her head resisted. Heat moved through her body in a rush, speeding upward from her toes straight on through to her dizzying head.

A week. With Ken.

She couldn't quite move past the fact. Meantime, he kept quiet, taking his time about unwrapping cutlery and spreading a linen napkin across his lap. Dressed in crisply pressed tan slacks and a simple blue shirt that he wore un-tucked over a loose white t-shirt, he looked a far cry from the role of preacher. Everything about him spoke of approachability—and male appeal.

Daveny perched her chin on folded hands. "I think I know of a couple people we could approach."

"There'll probably be a dozen or so kids—evenly divided into performance teams—so the way I figure it we need a couple men and a couple women to help oversee everything. Maggie Voorhees, our secretary and youth group director, already signed on."

"So," Daveny said, "you'd be looking for one more woman and two men, right?"

"Yep." He sidled Kiara a look, but that was it.

Shell shocked, Kiara remained a silent observer. She ate, watched and listened, until Daveny slid her cell phone from the pocket of her blazer, checking its face.

"Dang," she muttered. "I've gotta head back to the office."

Kiara snapped to, and her heart leapt into

overdrive. "What? There's nothing on the schedule—"

Daveny grabbed her purse from the spot at her feet and pecked Ken's cheek in passing. "Just came up. Ken, can you take Kiara back to the office?"

"Sure."

"Thanks. Talk to you later. Take your time, though, OK?"

Daveny vanished and Kiara couldn't help being bewildered. A strand of hair rippled across her face. Nervous and shy, she tucked it behind her ear. She tried to focus on lunch, but her appetite no longer existed.

"So," Ken murmured, his focus on his plate. He picked up a section of his turkey club, but didn't bite in right away. He looked uncomfortable as well, and in fairness, Kiara realized she wasn't helping matters by acting like a bewitched teenager.

So she reigned in her poise and pushed disquiet to the side. She gave him a smile. "So."

"I honestly didn't mean for this lunch to turn into an ambush, Kiara." His gaze lifted to hers, and her heart stuttered. That fact she knew without being told.

Conciliatory, she touched his arm. "I'm surprised by the suggestion, but I don't feel ambushed. Please don't worry about that. It does give me a lot to think about, though."

"You came to mind immediately when I planned this trip."

"Really?" She honestly couldn't figure out why that might be, but felt flattered he thought of her.

"Yes, *really*. To me, it's obvious."

Kiara puzzled, and waited on elaboration. Realizing that, Ken's smile dawned as warm as spring sunlight.

"Kiara, stop being the deer that's caught in the headlights. You're a natural to work with. You'll be more than able to guide and engage a group of teenagers. Remember how well you handled preps for Autumn Fest?"

Her heart went light at his praise; at the same time, a lance of painful memory pierced her spirit. *Barb*. "That was years ago, and…and, that was *easy*."

He gave her a pointed look. "Do you think so?"

To fill time, Kiara broke their visual connection and munched on a chip. She hoped to disguise her turmoil and deflect the power of his appeal. Being attracted to him, considering the prospect of intense, out-of-church interaction, left her with a mid-section full of tickling, dancing butterfly wings.

The idea tempted, but at the same time, the thought of participating in a Christian service mission removed her far—make that *very* far—from her comfort zone. Still, she melted into a form of mental surrender. Mission work would fill an empty spot in her spirit, a need and a call to do something *more*. Most likely, Ken sensed that fact as well—he was as perceptive as he was caring. Dogging Kiara's heels of late nipped the feeling that her life lacked merit beyond that of being arm candy for sexy, successful men. A chic fashionista. Didn't she feel increasing unease about being seen as nothing more than a honey-blonde who could attract attention as easily as nectar attracted bees?

The life she embraced up to now left her empty, and wanting. Had for years. Ever since meeting Ken— ever since joining Woodland Church—she had discovered a world outside her heretofore narrow focus.

As though reading her mind, he leaned forward, closing their slight physical distance. He was intent and *enthused*. That snared her heart like nothing else could, and filled Kiara with longing. In the end, she wanted to live up to the promise Ken saw inside her.

"I've participated in a few missions recently. I know what I'm doing. You're a special lady. I'd love for you to participate, and get a sense of what these trips accomplish. The joy and hope and freedom a little help from people like us can give to these people is amazing. One week away from everything you know, and all that's familiar, is going to bring you to a place in your life and your walk with God that nothing else can match." His eyes fixed on Kiara, drawing her in—a most seductive impetus. "It'll be a gift, Kiara. In so many ways…"

His full lips, the tumbled wavy brown hair that danced in a gentle breeze, left her transfixed. Wistful— *in so many ways.*

"Do me a favor?" He asked.

She nodded numbly.

"Will you *consider* it? I understand it's a lot to ask. I know being a part of this trip would mean sacrificing a week of vacation time from your job, but…"

His voice trailed off. The impact of his gaze did not. Like she could refuse satiny eyes of chocolate brown—

She caught her breath. "Of course I'll think about it. The offer has taken me by surprise, that's all."

They concluded their lunch companionably, and she had to admit that once she moved past the initial bout of giddiness Ken's presence stirred, the surprise generated by his mission suggestion, she found it easy to settle into a comfortable rhythm. They caught up with one another and enjoyed lunching outdoors on a gorgeous afternoon.

Much as she hated for the interlude to end, soon enough work schedules called and Ken accompanied her back to the office.

There, Daveny waited.

And there certainly didn't seem to be a work-related fire going on that Kiara could detect.

She deposited her purse in a desk drawer then paid her partner and best friend a visit in her office. True to sassy form, Daveny wasted no time on preamble. "When do you leave for Pennsylvania?"

"As soon as I find out about the big corporate emergency you're taking care of," Kiara shot back.

Daveny just blinked prettily. "Emergency? What emergency?"

Kiara's jaw dropped. "Daveny Montgomery Edwards. Are you attempting a set up?"

"Everyone needs a hobby."

Kiara sank into the chair before Daveny's desk, expelling a hard, tense breath. "Do you realize this would mean *six* hours. In a *van*." *In close, intimate proximity,* she neglected to add. "What in the world am I going to talk about with him? What'll we say?"

"First off, let me enlighten you. I've helped Collin out in his high school English classes from time to time, doing organizational things and the like. I've gotten to know teenagers. Therefore, I can assure you, conversation will be the least of your worries. This trip to the Appalachians is going to be anything but *quiet.* Furthermore, I think you realize that fact without being told. Since that's the case, I have to ask, Kiara, what's scaring you?" Daveny's eyes narrowed. "Because quite frankly, I'm *stunned*. When have you ever—I repeat—

ever been timid about making conversation with a man?"

Kiara's cheeks stung and prickled, the first alert of a dawning blush. "Dav, come on. You know what I mean. I'll be with Pastor Ken."

"Oh. I see. And as opposed to being a man, Ken's a *zombie,* is that the issue?"

"*Pastor* Ken," Kiara corrected. A touch of something sensuous and enticing skirted her nerve endings.

"*Ken.*" Daveny answered right back. "And he's just a man."

"Thanks for illuminating, but that's not my point. I'm just not sure what we're going to have to say to each other during the course of this proposed mission. We're so *different.*"

"Nice try, but I'm not buying. Kiara, you're afraid of him."

"Am not!"

"I don't mean afraid like Jack-the-Ripper afraid, I mean afraid in a completely different way, and I think you know exactly what I'm talking about." Kiara moved hastily to cut her off, but Daveny quelled a reply by simply lifting her hands. "Proof? Allow me to take you back a few years. You and I were neck deep in a church renovation, remember?'

Kiara remained still, but inwardly fought against the sensation of being cornered by her own heart.

"You sat in that very chair, telling me how much you enjoyed Ken's company, how much you liked him and wished the quote-unquote *good ones* like him weren't already taken."

Kiara squirmed but Daveny kept going. "You longed for a connection to him, but he was married.

Off limits." Shaking her head vigorously, staring into Kiara's eyes, Daveny concluded firmly. "Well he's not off limits anymore."

Like a temptation, that idea dangled before Kiara's thirsty, wanting heart.

And Daveny went on. "He's a man of meaning, a man of depth and substance. He's exactly the kind of man you know you want and need, yet for some reason his attainability has you running for cover." Daveny relented, leaning back once again. "I won't put you on the spot and ask you for reasons why; your face alone tells me I've hit the mark. What I'm saying, sweetie, is that you need to look at that fact more closely. You need to ask yourself why that's the case. Are you afraid of a genuine commitment from a genuine man? Before you answer, I have to I warn you, he'll want it all. He's not after a trophy girl, or instant gratification, but is instead searching for a woman who possesses equal parts substance and beauty. Someone just like you."

"Daveny, he's clergy! He's a man of God. I'm…I'm…Cosmo's with my girlfriends after work. I've had a few casual relationships based on sex appeal and charisma…and…and…" At last, Kiara came out with what she considered the deepest problem. "Dav, the point is, I'd be no good for him. I could never make him happy. Not over the long term. You talk about his substance, and that's exactly what draws me to him. I'll admit that freely. But I'm sorely lacking in the things he needs most."

"Bull!"

"It's true. I'm these looks, and this body, and I've let myself be taken in by flash too many times to ever believe a man like *Ken* could find me suitable. Come on. Seriously. Me? The paramour of a preacher?"

Undeterred Daveny just shrugged. "Why not, Kiara? Why not?"

And one thing was for certain. Mona Lisa's enigmatic turn of lips had nothing on the smile currently displayed on the face of Kiara's best friend.

∂∾∾

Nervousness got the better of her. Kiara could own that fact. She could deal with it. She closed and locked the door of her apartment then trotted to her car. Once there she realized she had forgotten her notebook. Checking her watch, she took in how close she cut her arrival time. She didn't want to be late to the mission trip orientation meeting, but ran back to retrieve the notebook, anyway.

The four-mile drive to Woodland turned into an exercise in finding every red light and slow-moving vehicle in the city of St. Clair Shores, which meant there was too much time to think about Ken, and the idea of actually participating.

With *him*.

The thought followed her to the church parking lot. Kiara left her car and then remembered the notebook still rode shotgun. What was the message here? There had to be a message.

Maybe: *Don't even try.* Or perhaps: *Don't worry about notes, be more concerned with what's written on your heart.*

She mentally admitted her betting money went on the latter option. Still, after an exasperated sigh, she retrieved the wire-bound source of her aggravation and marched through the entrance of Woodland.

Resolute—defiant in fact—Kiara walked the long, narrow corridor to the left of the narthex. Along the way, she passed a number of darkened classrooms and conference rooms. She found her way to the brightly lit gathering spot indicated on Ken's e-mail: Conference Room 1D.

And the most amazing thing happened.

Peace flooded her, unstoppable because it took her by such surprise. Calming peace and a soothing sense of assurance wrapped around her like a tender hug. She absorbed Woodland's familiar flower and must scent, the stillness and quiet of the building. The moment did what nothing else could right now— telegraphed God's presence.

In that instant, she stopped fighting herself.

After signing in, she looked around, cataloguing attendees. A dozen or so teens buzzed amongst themselves, a tight knit group huddled at the long table up front. Talk about multi-tasking—most of them sent text messages, laughed, talked, carried on phone conversations and picked at one another simultaneously. Kiara smiled at the exuberant behavior.

Pastor Ken stood at the head of the teen table, somehow able to focus despite the relentless clamor. The sight of him stalled her at the welcome desk. She noticed the way he gnawed on the end of a pen, reading a paper he held.

"Kiara, are you set?"

"What?" She turned to look at Margaret Voorhees, Woodland's church secretary, who also coordinated youth group activities and had helped implement the upcoming mission trip. Since attendance was completed, Margaret watched her curiously. "Oh.

Yeah. I'm fine, thanks."

Kiara moved away, taking note of a white vinyl banner that covered the wall to her right. Painted a variety of bright colors, the sign read: WELCOME TO THE STAGE!

She stepped up to the table where Ken stood.

"Hi," she greeted tentatively. And she couldn't help wondering where the fluttery, bashful vibe of hers was coming from these days. The look in Ken's eyes warmed her senses, set assurance and welcome sailing through her body.

"Hey! I'm glad you're here. Take the seat by me."

"OK." Kiara returned his smile, but looked away shyly, reacting instantly to his warm kindness. She deposited her notebook and trip materials on the table then checked out the sign a bit more closely, reading its subtext aloud: "Super Teen Angels Go Evangelize."

Ken glanced over his shoulder and looked at the sign as well. He nodded. "STAGE. It's our name, and our mantra. Plus, they're at such a formative age. When necessary, the STAGE name makes it easier for them to talk about meetings and group events without risking stigma."

That kind of pressure Kiara understood. "I can imagine."

"Especially for teenagers dealing with their peers, and type-casting, it's important to live their Christian faith, not lose confidence as they're teased about church related meetings and being part of a youth ministry."

"Like that old saying: Live the Gospel—use words only if necessary."

"Exactly." He filled two Styrofoam cups with ice water and handed her one. She accepted his thoughtful gesture with a smile; her fingertips trailed against his, drawing their eyes into a brief, stirring connection before he walked away.

Ken crossed the room, calling for everyone's attention and quiet. Kiara took her seat as he clicked off the overhead lights. A laptop was set up at his spot on the table. When Ken returned, he began the proceedings. "Meet the Kidwell family."

Click by click, he took the potential attendees through a computerized slideshow presenting each needy family member. First came the young mother, Casey; then Phillip, the oldest boy and freshly minted teenager who smiled shyly for the camera. Next came six-year-old twins, Amber and Alyssa, who both possessed such sparkle and spunk their images leapt from the display screen.

In conclusion, however, he returned to the image of Casey Kidwell. Long brown hair was tied into a simple ponytail. Her fair features were plain, but clear and clean. Jeans and a t-shirt were nondescript, but her eyes were large and wide, retaining an innocence that left Kiara moved.

Pastor Ken continued. "Casey struggles to make ends meet. Her sense of hope? It gets trampled on every day because, as her application states, she feels all alone in the fight to keep her family safe and well provided for."

Silence filled the room as he continued. "This trip is about service, and it's about helping a struggling family find hope, but as many of you know, lately I've spent a lot of time lending assistance to missions very similar to the one I propose to you right now. So let me assure you of something." He paused strategically and performed a slow, deliberate survey of the posture, faces and eyes of the dozen or so teens and the sprinkling of adults who gathered. "Beyond heeding God's call to uplift those who need it the most, this trip will transform you. It's as much about evolution, and advancing your own spiritual walk, as it is about applying fresh layers of paint, cleaning, or planting trees. You'll be the face of Christ to our needy brothers and sisters, but don't expect to walk away from the experience without being changed."

A murmur of acceptance and agreement circuited the room.

"So…details about the mission. If you open your folders, you'll find an itinerary that outlines the details and goals of the program. We're headed to Zion Grove, in the Appalachian Mountains."

Kiara followed along, reviewing statistics and overall program information.

Ken went on. "A community of nine families is living below poverty levels and has been identified by the Christian Youth Outreach Program. What that means is we won't be alone in this. Nine other church-based teams are headed to Pennsylvania to help refurbish homes and reestablish these individuals into lives restored by hard work and a helping hand."

"Where are we going to be staying, Pastor Ken?"

Kiara looked down the table, at the bright-eyed, blonde-haired teen who asked the question. Amy, her nametag read. Ken lifted a color brochure from inside his folder and held it up. "If you pull out this flyer about Red Ridge Lake, I think your questions will be answered. The program we're participating in will take over a small campground. The Woodland team will be responsible for our own meals, cooking and cleanup, but we'll share ministry with the other attendees. We'll be in cabins, four volunteers and one chaperone to each. My hope is to take a dozen members of STAGE and recruit four adult volunteers."

"I don't know anything about, like, home repairs and stuff. What about that?"

Kiara smiled at the second teen who spoke up, a lanky, sandy-haired boy seated next to Amy. Tyler was his name. Kiara readily understood his eager, if somewhat intimidated demeanor.

"Contracted professionals who donate their time will oversee the heavy lifting—stuff like drywall, carpeting and cabinetry. You'll be helping, not supervising, so no worries. You'll get training and tools without a problem."

Questions continued and more details were ironed out while the meeting progressed.

Slowly, Kiara was drawn into the idea of being a part of it all. A tremor from within brought her to the realization that walking away from this opportunity wouldn't be an option. The faces of the Kidwell family, freeze-framed on the wall to her left, pulled at a need in her heart to help. To be present.

At the end of the meeting she hung back, not eager to leave Ken's company. Here she felt assured. Here she felt affirmed and cared for.

The room emptied, and she helped disconnect and store computer parts, then stack up extra information packets while Ken said goodnight to Maggie Voorhees.

When he turned back and saw the results of Kiara's work, he looked pleasantly surprised. "Wow. Thanks."

"No problem."

"Seriously, I appreciate it."

He tossed cups and napkins into the trash. "So

what did you think?" He lingered as well, taking his time about packing supplies into his carryall.

"Well, I think this is a departure for me. It's service, and of course I like that, but it's not like anything I've ever done before."

"Service is what you've provided to Woodland ever since you joined us, Kiara. This trip isn't much different from that."

He nodded toward the chairs they had occupied during the meeting and Kiara made herself comfortable at the table. "But the service you're talking about was provided on a much smaller scale, Pastor Ken." At last she came out with the truth—her biggest fear. "It's intimidating. Am I really up to this? Am I qualified? I'm just not sure, and I don't want to mess things up." She watched for any telltale reactions, but his presence soothed, a gentle oasis in the desert of her unease. "Really. Think about it. Who do I think I am, being a mission participant for heaven's sake?"

"For heaven's sake indeed," Ken quipped in turn.

He looked down at his folded hands. They rested close to Kiara's, and she tingled with a need to touch him. She didn't. Again and again she kept thinking, Pastor. Modernista. Conservative. Contempo. Oil. Water.

Disquiet simmered though her bloodstream, but combating that onslaught rushed a longing that poured through her thick and warm, a quest for…for *something*. Something more than the world, the time and place she currently inhabited. To share an experience like this with Ken? Her mind raced even faster.

"You're stepping off a ledge, Kiara. I understand that. Just remember; the hardest part is letting go."

Their gazes aligned and Ken slid her notebook out of the way. Leaning close he tucked his hand over hers on the tabletop. Her mouth went dry, and she fought hard to focus. "Look at this as an opportunity. I've pushed you. Maybe I shouldn't have. The thing is, though, ever since I've met you, it seems you've been moving into something larger than yourself. You attend church here regularly, but beyond being a *worshiper*, you've *contributed*. I'd love to see that continue. It's been beautiful to watch."

In a perfectly sequenced activation process, his words slid into her then through her. She caught her breath, looking into eyes of deep, velvety brown, falling headfirst. She allowed herself to enjoy the luxury of their soft tenderness.

"This isn't just about opportunity. It's about *ability*. Abilities you possess, Kiara. You're a natural motivator, and the kids love you." He lifted his hand from hers and ticked off a couple more attributes on his fingers. "You magnetize, and you galvanize. You have more energy, spirit and enthusiasm than most people I know. Plus, you draw people in. You can lead."

Silence held sway. She couldn't help thinking about the fact that every word he spoke worked through the spots in her psyche that most craved affirmation and the knowledge that her life, her actions, could have meaning. And, to be validated by a man of such…

Substance and honor.

Daveny's words came back to haunt Kiara—circling around to the one who sat before her, calm and confident, charismatic in his own powerful right. But he was a *pastor*—a chief custodian of God's mission on earth. Her more secular, world-driven life contradicted that pathway. What could ever come to be between the two of them?

It would never work.

Still, her heart swelled, lessening the impact of that thought. Her skin warmed.

Nonplussed by her silence, he continued. "Your instinct may be to step back, and then away, thinking this may be more than you want to take on. I'd only ask you set those feelings aside and take a hard look at the good you'll do. The benefit you'll provide to this family. Think it over. Give it some serious prayer time. If your answer is no after that, then please know I understand. I just don't want you to reject it out of hand because it's something so new, and different for you—or worse yet because you're afraid of a faith jump. You've come so far, so quickly. You're on an important mission, Kiara, whether you join us in Pennsylvania or not. OK?"

She diverted her attention and reclaimed the information folder, fiddling with its edges while silence played out. His words, his spirit loosened her control grips, and left her wanting to fly. "I'm serious about this, Pastor Ken, and I do promise to think everything over very carefully. I just...is it wrong of me to want a little time? A few days maybe? I know my yes should be automatic."

As automatic as my 'No' should have been to Andrew and his offering of a sensual odyssey to Europe. Being a mixed-up mess, spiritually speaking, seemed par for the course these days.

Ken didn't seem to mind. He just nodded and said, "Take what time you need, Kiara. I'll be here."

6

"OK, gang," Ken called. "Let's gather up and finish check-in. We need to hit the road."

Duffle bags decorated the asphalt in front of two vans parked before the entrance of Woodland. He surveyed the milling group of slouching, subdued teenagers dressed in blue jeans, t-shirts and hoodies. There were sixteen in all—yawning and murmuring to one another as dawn crept across the sky. Pale blue turned to mauve, turned to orange then pink behind clouds skirting inland over the horizon of Lake Saint Clair. He leaned against the front of the church's old, reliable standby—an F-250 van—consulting a clipboard of attendees. Dressed in jeans as well, sporting a sweatshirt from his alma mater of Wayne State University, he began to account for staff and teen volunteers.

Daveny drove up, and his focus zipped far from registrations and attendance; Kiara rode shotgun. The car rounded into the lot where Daveny parked then popped the trunk. Kiara climbed out and for a moment, he stood transfixed. Forcing himself forward, Ken moved toward the two women. Kiara tucked a pair of oversized black sunglasses on top of her head. Her eyes roved the assemblage. She nibbled her lower lip, a tiny furrow appearing above her brows while she looked around.

Kiara Jordan, the quintessence of feminine confidence, gave every indication of being tentative. *Beguilingly* tentative, he amended with a push to his heart that enlivened his spirit.

A week—in service with Kiara. The push exploded into a heady rush of anticipation, and joy.

"Hey." He stepped forward, taking the suitcase from Kiara's hand to lighten her load. Her grip was tight, though, and his action took her by surprise judging by the way her gaze lifted to his. She cleared her throat softly and relaxed a bit, surrendering the luggage.

Daveny gave Ken a knowing glance; she hugged Kiara and delivered a wax-coated bakery sack into Kiara's custody. "Don't forget this. Have fun, girlie."

Kiara nodded, continuing to study her surroundings. Ken longed to assure, to draw her in. He understood her reaction. His first few mission trips had featured just such nervousness. Stepping into the unknown never came easy, so all he could do for now was lead her away from Daveny's safe zone.

Daveny, meanwhile, returned to her car and drove away. Distraction might do the trick, Ken figured. So he started to fill in details to help set Kiara's mind at ease. "We've got a two van convoy." A vague gesture indicated both vehicles. "Maggie and her husband are in charge of the second vehicle. I figure you and I will take charge of this one." He patted the engine hood of the Woodland van, and she looked it over.

"Just tell me what I need to do." The words came out heavy, and uncharacteristically shy.

He set her suitcase aside to take her hands, stilling her progress toward check in. "First?" He waited 'til she made eye contact. "What I need you to do is rest easy. OK?"

A pause fell between them. She looked down, seeming embarrassed. Ken quirked a finger beneath her chin and drew her gaze to his once more. "Let go of everything else and embrace the opportunity." He couldn't fight the tremors being near her stirred, nor the hot, dissolving sensation that moved through his body when he took a tumble into her clear, green eyes. "I'm not used to you being unsettled. Relax, Kiara." An intent interlude passed before he concluded, "Here's the itinerary." He handed her a folder, which accepted with a nod. Her attention reverted to the van. Ken embraced the opening. "Don't worry about her. She's still got plenty of life left where it counts."

Kiara smiled. *Really* smiled. "I'm not worried. I trust the mechanic."

Her glance swept over him in a visual caress, gliding down the front of his sweatshirt, causing an electric circuit to zing to completion. He now realized a smudge of oil residue dotted the bottom edge of the shirt from when he had double-checked engine and fluid levels a few minutes ago.

His tone went huskier than usual. "We don't have the money for a new vehicle, so I work on it, and keep it in shape. Hones my mechanical skills and gives me a sense of accomplishment. So far, so good."

Kiara fumbled a bit with the folded edges of the baker's bag she held. Meanwhile, he retrieved her suitcase and stowed it in the back.

"So," she said, "are you hungry?"

"Always." Ken accepted the bag she offered and opened it wide. Swirls of warmth, and the aroma of cinnamon and apple, wafted upward on a tempting cloud of steam. He peeked inside, marveling. "Fresh apple fritters? Kiara, you're amazing."

She laughed. "Yeah. Shopping at a store for baked goods puts me right up there with the saints."

"In my eyes it does."

Ken leaned down and slid his lips against her cheek, ending the connection in a kiss that lingered too long—yet not long enough. He pulled back and her widened eyes struck a chord in his soul. He stroked the skin he had just kissed with a trailing fingertip then tore off a piece of fritter and ate. The confection melted on his tongue, melting into tasty sweetness.

Kiara followed his lead.

"There's a thermos of Italian roast between the front seats. Coffee is the only way I knew I'd survive," he told her.

"That goes for me, too. Thanks for thinking of it."

He continued to eat while she spoke.

"I wish…"

She came up short. Curious, Ken prodded. "What do you wish?"

"I wish…I wish I didn't feel so much like a fish out of water."

He returned the bag to Kiara so she could eat the second fritter. When she tried to take the bag from his grip, Ken held fast until he won her full focus. "If it helps, remember you're surrounded by friends, and you're doing something miraculous. Further? The kids will adore you."

Deflecting her gaze, Kiara murmured, "How do you *do* that?"

"Do what?"

"I swear, it's a gift, the way you can look into a person and see exactly what they're feeling."

Her words struck home, glided against him like a

provocative ripple of silk. Pleasure sizzled through his body. "It's a job hazard—part of what I do." Beauty and grace, sweetness—all of the most attractive elements of her personality combined to leave him bold, and intrigued enough to say, "Besides, Kiara, everything you are is right there—in your eyes, and on your face. Open book. It's not hard to see what you're feeling. I like that about you." Ken took a meaningful pause. "Here's what else I do."

Ken took her free hand in his. With a nod and a gentle tug, he walked her toward a secluded spot on the other side of the van. Wearing a puzzled expression, Kiara glanced around for a moment—at the quiet roadway, at the fragrant, shimmering grass kissed by morning dew, and the waking shoreline of Lake Saint Clair.

It was perfect.

Ken kept hold of her hand, and said in a whisper, "Pray with me? Privately? Before we do so with the others?"

Her hold on his hand weakened, but not in refusal. Her eyes, wide and wistful, touched on his; she seemed eager to share the moment, and Ken realized the weakness wasn't weakness at all. It was a melting. A surrender to something powerful, intimate, and graced. In silence, she nodded.

He bowed his head, murmuring into the quiet air, "Lord, you've granted us an opportunity to serve You, to lend assistance to the most needy of our brothers and sisters. Keep us strong. Keep us centered in your will, your plans and provision. Lord, in a special way, please bless Kiara as she reaches out in mission for the first time. Show her Your calm and love. Keep us all safe. In Jesus' name we pray."

"Amen," came the unison conclusion. Birds began chirping, starting to arise from towering tree branches that rustled in the building breeze. Ken released her hand, but glided a touch upward, against her arm. "So about that feeling of intimidation? It's God's now. Leave it right here in the parking lot. You're not going to regret this, I promise. And you're most certainly not alone."

He continued to look into her eyes, lingering over a final peaceful moment. Her answering nod and the squeeze of her hand against his arm reassured.

"Ken?" Maggie Voorhees stepped up, her brows knit as she studied them. It occurred to Ken that he stood very close to Kiara, his arm nearly around her, their eyes connected, their posture eloquent in its intimacy. "Everyone's here and supplies are loaded. We're ready for the group send-off and prayer."

"Exactly what I was thinking," Ken replied. Reluctant to end the moment, he knew he had to turn away. Praying with Kiara had been spontaneous and stirring, but the team needed to get going. Besides, he'd have hours of travel time with her, and for now, he wanted to stymie the inquisitive, darkened expression on Maggie's face.

❧❧

The mission squad barely crossed the state line of Ohio before debate broke out over potential movies to watch.

"Little Women? No *way*! That movie is so *lame*!" Charlie, one of the teen volunteers spoke up first—and with emphasis.

"You get to pick the next movie," said Amy, the

spokeswoman for the women. "We're going to be here for a while, guys. Compromise, right? And PS? Deal with it. It's a good movie."

"C'mon, it'll be fine," said Tyler quietly. Tyler was one of the shyer members of the posse.

"Whatever," groused Alex, another of the Woodland teens.

"Groan!" said David. "Never have I been so grateful for an iPod."

Kiara looked over her shoulder to monitor the crew. Ken glanced into the rearview mirror just in time to see David tune out, white ear buds stuffed into place. The youth fingered his iPod, then closed his eyes and settled in for a doze. The other guys in the group pretty much followed suit.

Amy, Carlie, Liz and Jen—the ladies of the van— shared a grin at their victory. Amy pushed the DVD into a portable player. The foursome shifted seats until they were tucked together to watch. When the movie began to play, Ken shared a wry look with Kiara, and a grin.

Tyler remained quiet thereafter, seeming immune to the teen-style negotiation process. Instead of an iPod connection, he opted to page through a guitar magazine. Ken kept tabs on him and Amy because there seemed to be undercurrents flowing between the two. Well, on Tyler's part anyway. Ken noticed the way Tyler sat to the side and periodically watched the bubbly, blonde.

That in mind, Ken looked sidelong at the gorgeous woman who rode next to him and found he could completely relate to the longing he detected in Tyler's eyes.

They rumbled along, and the movie played.

Dialogue drifted through the vehicle. On screen, Meg had just returned to her loving, though humble home following a society coming out party. Meg conversed with Marmee about its aftermath:

"I liked to be praised and admired," Meg said. "I couldn't help but like it."

"Of course not," Marmee answered. "I only care what you think of yourself. If you feel your value lies in being merely decorative I fear that someday you might find yourself thinking that's all you really are. Time erodes all such beauty. What it cannot diminish are the wonderful workings of your mind. Your humor, your kindness, your moral courage, those are the things I so admire in you."

Kiara sat quietly and listened, but Ken noticed a turnabout in her mood. Her effervescence dimmed over the next long stretch of highway. Intending to call her out, he reached behind the seat and secured a pair of cups. Next, he lifted the thermos of coffee. "Interested?"

She nodded and smiled. But the quick gesture struck him as false. "Thanks. Here, let me pour."

"You got quiet all of a sudden."

"Yeah. I suppose I did."

The soft-spoken words did nothing to remedy his concern. Neither did the manner in which she turned her head after settling his cup into the holder between them. Looking out the window, she sipped her coffee.

Rather than press, he watched her, indulging a desire to soak her in. The details of her captivated him. A windbreaker, worn to ward off the morning chill, now resided over the back of her seat. She paired a sleeveless, sunshine yellow blouse with tan Capri's. A yellow ribbon wound through the French braid of her hair, securing its end and trailing loose a few inches beyond.

The accessory intrigued him. Considering what it would feel like to slide that piece of satin ribbon free came at him hard, prompting him to look elsewhere in a denial both physical and emotional.

The trip progressed in a mix of movie dialogue, chatter, and an underlying buzz of music from MP3 devices played at decibels only the young could tolerate. Soon the massive state of Pennsylvania welcomed the caravan. The road turned hilly, punctuated by deep, picturesque valleys. Lush green land was dotted by homes and white, clapboard churches became focal points with steeples that soared skyward. Around the valleys rose a rim of mountains skirted by the tree-lined highway.

That's when Ken proposed a 'getting to know you' exercise.

"Kiara," he began, "make a list of five items you see somewhere in the vehicle. It can be anything, but it has to be something here with us."

Everyone started to look around and chatter. Kiara asked, "Can I get some help from the team?"

"Absolutely."

For the next few minutes, the kids called out things they saw and Kiara drafted a list.

"Crayons, from the gift basket we made for the family."

"Bottled water."

"A hoodie!"

"Pop!"

"There's a box of rubber bands back here."

Ken glanced back for a second. "I wondered where those ended up. Thought I had left them at the store."

Seeming puzzled, Kiara kept sidling him glances;

Ken remained silent.

"We're all set," Kiara said. "Now what?"

"Write one of our names by each item, starting with mine and yours."

She scribbled, looking more confused than ever. He grinned—and relented. "Let me show you how the game is played. Kiara, what's the item by your name?"

"Pop."

Ken nodded, and thought about pop for a minute. "How is Kiara like pop?"

Everyone burst out laughing. "Seriously?" One of the mission members asked. "We're comparing ourselves to the things on the list?"

"No. Starting with me, the person sitting next to you is." He began again. "Kiara is like pop because she's bubbly. Just like pop, when you take her in, her spirit sparkles through you."

She turned to listen, leaning her back against the door. Ken's words caused her to stare, her lips slightly parted. Luminous eyes drew him in, just like when they had prayed. That particular recollection causing a spark—like sweet, cool pop—and Ken knew he needed to move things along, fast, before the kids caught on.

"I'm next, right?" Ken asked.

Kiara blinked. "Ah...yeah."

"What item did you assign to me?"

She toyed with the edges of the paper she held, the list on her lap now of paramount importance. "Bottled water."

"OK. How am I like bottled water?"

She blew out a breath, shrugged shyly, and fidgeted with the pen she held. "Pastor Ken is like bottled water because he's...he's clear. And pure. He has a kindness that's thirst-quenching and a heart that gives to others and refreshes. Just like water."

She never glanced his way. She didn't need to. The words spoke strong, and the heat index shot upward. He realized for certain this woman was unaccustomed to being out of her comfort zone with a man.

She recovered fast though, turning to Tyler. "You're next, and you're talking about Amy. Amy's name is by crayons."

Chortles filled the air, prompting Kiara to retort, "Yuck it up for now, hot-shots, but you're all going to have a turn."

He marveled anew at her ease with the teens and kept tabs via the rearview mirror, noting the way Tyler looked at Amy with surprising steadiness. Amy, meanwhile, watched him right back and waited, sliding a strand of hair behind her ear.

Following a brief pause, he answered the question. "Amy is like a box of crayons because she's bright and she has lots of different parts to her personality—like crayon colors. You can use them to crate artwork, and things that are beautiful. When you open a box of crayons, it's kind of like seeing a rainbow."

That shut up the raucous comments, and Amy looked a little breathless. Kiara, fortunately, kept matters going. "OK, Amy, you're up. How is Tyler like…a rubber band?"

Amy groaned and Tyler rolled his eyes, seeming to expect the worst.

"Well," she began in a tentative voice, "I think Tyler is kinda like a rubber band 'cause rubber bands are flexible. They expand when they need to, and they're resilient. They're dependable in that they always go back to what they were once you're done." Then she really warmed up, looking him straight in the eye. "Plus, when you pluck a rubber band after you've pulled it tight, it makes *music*."

Amy's final comment caused Tyler to look at her in sharp surprise. Amy just arched a brow, an all-knowing look in her eyes.

"Carlie," Kiara said, helping move past Amy and Tyler's interlude. "You're up next..."

సౌఫ్

A narrow gravel road led uphill to a series of small, mom-and-pop owned stores along with a dozen or so homes. This wasn't a neatly organized setting, however. The area was time worn and suffered from a state of near-terminal neglect. The neglect, Ken knew from research, didn't stem from uncaring inhabitants, but rather a lack of funds, time and ability. So, mission teams from across the country converged on this tiny, poverty-stricken village to lend assistance. A few vans similar to those from Woodland were parked in the street and clusters of people walked about exploring.

Ken pulled the van to a stop in front of the dilapidated structure owned by Casey Kidwell. For a time, silence reigned within the vehicle. Everyone looked outside, surveying the scene. Clapboard siding was separated in spots to show gaping holes. The roof sagged, and a corner of it looked to be missing completely. Overgrown shrubs and plant life masked a porch that also sagged and featured rotted openings in spots—the product of neglect.

Woodland's arrival prompted the Kidwell family to emerge from inside. Volunteers exited the van and Amy lifted the gift basked into her arms. Amy hesitated at the family's enthusiastic onrush. "Gee, it's like an episode of that home makeover show or something," she said.

True enough. The entire team soon found itself engulfed by hugs, and Casey Kidwell's grateful tears punctuated her appreciation. Amy handed the gift basket to Casey, who let the two youngest kids dive into the contents. The twin girls tugged Amy right down on the front yard grass and pulled her in to explore; the rest of the team joined in on a celebration that looked more like Christmas than the offering of a simple gift basket.

Ken kept an eye on the proceedings and then followed Casey into the house, with Kiara at his side. Soon he discovered just how big a task lay ahead.

Casey, a shy and diminutive woman, ushered them across the threshold, but her demeanor struck him as weighted, and oppressed. "I just want you to know; I'm embarrassed to show you how we've been living. I'm so ashamed, but there hasn't been any other way, and all we wanted to do was stay in our home—such as it is."

Ken rested an arm around her shoulder. "Please don't be uncomfortable. We understand where you're coming from; that's why we want to help."

She looked at him in silence then nodded, leading the way through the house. The tour didn't take long, considering its small size and shotgun style composition. Brief discussions ensued amongst the team members who filtered in. Ken listened, but paid particular attention to the way Kiara absorbed the scene. She trailed fingertips against a patchwork quilt drawn between the kitchen and living room as a makeshift door. She looked out windows covered by cloudy, scarred sheets of plastic designed to add protection from the outside elements. Living room furniture, spare to say the least, had passed the "timeworn" mark long ago. A stale, musty smell permeated the house.

Kiara's eyes went somber, her demeanor subdued.

Two tiny bedrooms skirted a narrow hallway of barren, distressed wood. The bathroom clung to usefulness by virtue of nothing more than heavy globs of caulk and duct tape. Chips and stains dotted the tub, sink and walls.

When they returned outside, Ken made sure to pass by Kiara. Shell shocked, eyes wide, she scanned the scene, her lips down turned. He gave her hand a discreet, understanding squeeze.

In reply to the gesture she firmed her chin and stated quietly, "I can't wait to get started."

The comment warmed his blood. Supermodel looks and her chic style and attractive persona, amounted to nothing compared to the determination and compassion he saw in the depths of her eyes.

7

Red Ridge Lake featured the type of commonplace camping facilities that called to Kiara's memories of summer camp, and rustic vacations with her family. Pleasantly weathered plank-wood cabins featured step-up porches with wrap around awnings. Amenities included a store, a long, narrow recreational/mess hall and a pair of male and female bath facilities. Trees burnished by the vibrant, fiery birth of autumn rimmed a wide calm lake that perfectly reflected the colors, the puffy white clouds and surrounding mountain peaks. Wood and pine spiced air assailed her senses.

She helped unpack the two vans, then the group broke off into four teams of five and they trekked to their cabins.

Following a quick settling in period, Kiara wandered toward the lake. Canoes were neatly stacked near the shoreline. A sturdy looking dock extended several feet into the water. Plastic chairs surrounded a deep, rock-lined fire pit. Next to that resided an endearingly timeworn swing set.

The wooden structure, with thick chain links and a pair of wooden seats, called to a child-like part of her soul. Besides, after the non-stop cacophony of traveling for hours with teenagers, a touch of solitude is exactly what her spinning mind needed in order to reboot.

So Kiara sat down at the swing and pushed off.

Delighted, she pumped her legs and the lake climbed toward her then filled her vision, receding when momentum sent her backwards. The freefall flipped her stomach lightly and tickled her insides. A cool wind kissed against her skin.

She slowed when footsteps crunched on the leaf and needle strewn path of gravel behind her. She turned and butterflies erupted when Ken approached.

A whole different type of freefall took place.

"I wanted to make sure you hadn't run away," he greeted, a teasing smile curving his lips.

She tried not to stare at that perfect, tempting mouth and instead, feigned offense. "You have that little faith in me, eh?"

He stepped into the scuffed and worn spot of dirt behind her and settled his hand against the small of her back. She nibbled on her lower lip as he gave her a push.

The motion sent her gently forward, and then she glided right back to him. He pushed again.

"I have faith in you." He left it at that. "The sundry shop is still open for business in case you're hungry."

Kiara chuckled. "After all the junk food we consumed during the trip? I won't be hungry for days."

She soared back to him, close enough that their gazes met when she turned to look at him. Close enough that she could glean the flecks of gold that highlighted his dark brown eyes.

He pushed; Kiara flew.

"This is a gorgeous setting," she offered starting to tingle, and tremble.

"Um-hmm. Lakes and swim-time never fail to get kids to sign up for mission trips. They don't care how cold the water is."

"Not me. I'm not a fan of ice-swimming."

"When you see the shower facilities, you might change your mind."

Kiara swung a bit more. Sunlight burnished the world to a molten hue of gold. Rich shades of green, red and orange illuminated the waving scrub grass and surrounding trees.

"Can I ask you a question?" he asked.

"Sure."

"I noticed the point in Little Women when you turned inward. You stopped bubbling the minute Marmee March told Meg not to worry so much about being the belle of the ball as maintaining her strength of character. Do you mind my asking why that scene in particular seemed to hit you so hard?"

His question struck against the crux of Kiara's deepest inner-dilemma—one she tried desperately to avoid confronting. To compensate for self-doubt and insecurity, Kiara took comfort in control, especially with regard to relationships. She called the shots with men who fell into easy admiration. Right now though, she depended on Ken, on winning his interest, and not just physically. She wanted something *more*. Something he offered that left her feeling not just beautiful, but fulfilled.

This means something, a voice inside her said, *but you're not the one in control. Neither is Ken. It's out of both your hands. Instead, your fate resides in the steady possession of a loving, heavenly Father. Rest easy in that truth.*

Kiara swung her legs slower and slower,

decreasing her levitation, but continuing to swing.

"The scene kind of hits home," she finally said. "Especially as I find myself mixing and mingling with teenagers."

"Why's that?"

She came to rest, but Ken pushed her just slightly, giving her the freedom of flight, of movement, while she considered how to answer.

"I've been Meg. I've been the wallflower who bloomed. But Meg believed in herself enough to give up fancy trappings and rely instead on her strength of character. I'm not sure I possess that kind of courage. I've clung to vanity-centered ideals for too long, I suppose. I've worked hard to fit in, and finally I succeeded. Problem is that kind of success is a double-edged sword. That pathway, once you start to follow it, is hard to leave."

In an unexpected, graceful motion, Ken caught her swing by the chains. He held her in place, suspended backward, with nothing but a cushion of air between them. All at once Kiara went dizzy and hyper-focused, tempted once more by that full, supple mouth, and the satiny-looking fall of his thick brown hair as he leaned over her. He was close enough to touch. In this moment, she wanted nothing more than to do just that.

"Some time, at some point, I'd like to hear more about that, Kiara. I'd like very much to know how you became the woman you are."

She looked at him steadily. "I'd bore you to tears. It's nothing extraordinary."

"All present evidence to the contrary." He set her gliding once again and Kiara's stomach performed a sparkling fall-away. She delighted in his words but forced herself to brush them aside before they could take root and sway her into believing he saw richness to her spirit. After all, it was part of Ken's persona to be gracious and encouraging.

But he continued, and those arguments splintered to shards when he said, "You're moving forward in directions that are not only admirable, but eye-opening—not just for you, most likely, but to everyone who's part of your life—don't hold to what other people see, or expect of you. Be who you are. And while you're at it, create the best version of yourself you can imagine. The only question, with the only relevance that matters, is this, Kiara: Who are you *now*?"

When she sailed back his way, he caught the chains of her swing once again and whispered in her ear, "I believe in you."

With that, he released her on a push, sending her on another dizzying spin of sensation. He walked away, retracing his steps up the path to the cabins and mess hall. She swung to a stop then sat in silence for long moments after he left, absorbing, shivering in a way that had nothing at all to do with the cool of the encroaching night.

❧

Since the Woodland team ate dinner on the road, Kiara didn't have to worry about food—or cooking and cleaning—once they settled into camp. To finish off day one, the entire troop met in the recreation hall, which doubled as the eating area. The building featured a huge kitchen and lines of cafeteria-style tables. While Ken conducted a brief info-session to map out tomorrow's schedule and the KP itineraries,

Kiara noticed even the most energetic teens leaned their heads and elbows on the tabletops and yawned frequently.

In conclusion, they toured the campgrounds and became familiar with its layout. They entered the bathhouse en masse to check out the facilities, which were empty for now. The kids performed a unilateral grumble when viewing the space. Sure enough, Kiara found out Ken's earlier comments about the condition of the showers hit the mark.

Sliding back a white vinyl curtain Amy poked her head into a stall. Kiara peeked in along with her, and cringed. Couldn't help it.

Amy said it for them both: "OK, seriously? This is so far beyond the word gross."

Peripherally Kiara noticed Ken standing in the doorway, watching; he seemed to be waiting on her reaction.

In honesty, she tended to agree with Amy, who made a valid point. To her credit, though, Amy didn't whine. She made her comment, and then shrugged, looking at Kiara for reaction as well.

Attempting stalwart behavior despite black mildew splotches on the yellowed calking, despite the peeling floor and chipped wall tiles Kiara said, "Yeah. Gross covers it pretty well." A clean-looking plastic floor mat hung on the wall next to the stall. Kiara unhooked it and dropped it to the floor inside the shower. "This will help. Besides—at least it's a shower, with hot water. We're staying in a cabin with beds and clean linens. For now, we're a few steps ahead of the family we're here to help, right? And for us, it's temporary. For them, it's constant."

Just like that, she found herself the center of

attention. Mere words stirred comprehension of what they were there for, along with a renewed perspective. Amy's eyes brightened. She nodded and pulled the curtain back into place, saying, "Yep. You're right."

A few more murmurs of reluctant agreement followed as they gathered outside. When Kiara passed Ken, leading her four lady delegates to their assigned cabin, he slid his hand against hers and he gave it a squeeze. His smile spread slow and sure, like sunlight breaking through a thick bank of clouds.

"And to think you were once intimidated," he said.

8

Sunlight beat onto Kiara's exposed neck, the air thick, laden by an unusual degree of humidity. She yanked away an obstructing line of overgrowth and bramble that lined and overcrowded the front of the Kidwell residence.

"This is gonna take forever," Amy muttered.

"Yeah—but it'll make dinner and shower time feel that much better," Tyler said, ever present and encouraging. Kneeling next to Amy, he pulled weeds as well. Kiara swiped her brow with the back of her hand and watched the twosome move in a neat tandem down the wood-beam border that had just been installed to frame in a small flowerbed.

Kiara smiled at the way Tyler looked at Amy, quietly enamored. Pretty similar, she imagined, to the way she looked at Ken. The thought left her searching for him. Ken stood atop a nearby ladder propped against the roofline, handing up equipment and supplies to a crew that replaced disintegrated tiles.

"It's not that I don't want to help, but, *dang*!" Punctuating her statement, Amy grabbed a handful of tall, leafy sprigs and yanked them free. "This thing is a mini *tree*!"

Tyler gave her shoulder a shove and they laughed.

Kiara piped in, picking up a pair of gardening shears and giving her all to trimming bushes. "I hear that, Amy." Minutes later, she gathered up discarded branches. "Maybe you can think about it this way: Consider the fact that everything we do right now is one less thing Casey has to worry about. Plus, it's not like she has any extra money to spend. She can't repair the roof, or replace those rotted floorboards in the porch. She can't replace kitchen cabinets and lay new flooring. The elbow grease is tough, and sweaty, but it's why we're here, right?"

"Well said, Kiara."

She froze, her arms chock-full of thick, prickly tree branches. A recycle bag stood nearby, tall and half full—completely ignored when she turned, and faced Ken.

"She's brilliant," Amy deduced, not even looking their way while she continued to tug at the weeds and wrinkle her nose at the muddy debris. Her unguarded praise made Kiara's skin flame, because it only served to expand Ken's smile.

She faced him like a statue, roughened bark and pungent leaves punctuating her senses of touch and smell. Ken stepped close and removed the refuse from her grasp. "Let's dispose of these before they end up back on the ground."

Ken stuffed the branches into the recycling bag, then took Kiara's arm and led her away from the activities of the landscaping detail. He walked toward a stack of boxed up shingles that stood on the porch. "Can you help me with some supplies over here on the porch? The contractors need more materials. I was thinking you could hand them up to me while I'm on the ladder."

"Sure," she answered quickly, glad to divert from the fact that she had openly gawked at the man.

"We're nearing the end of the day ahead of schedule." He looked over his shoulder at Tyler, Amy and Carlie. Kiara puzzled over the way he paused. He seemed to be buying time while he retrieved roofing nails, a short-stack of shingles and water to replenish the crew. He gathered the supplies rather than handing them over. At length he said, "Kiara, have you ever thought about joining the youth group ministry as a team leader?"

Kiara blinked a few times. "Ah. No."

"You should."

"Me?"

"You."

Flattered by his confidence, she tried to clear her head, and think. Ken's idea took strong, unexpected root, weaving through her mind, thriving, enlivening her spirit. She stammered a bit then tried to call him out on the suggestion, probing his seriousness. "Trust me, I'm nobody's theologian. I can't quote scripture verse for verse, or lead discussions on doctrine, or—"

"Who says you have to? Who says that's even necessary? Knowing the Bible is important, of course, but more important to these kids is someone who leads by example."

That ideal crashed in, obliterating her fast-breaking happiness. "That's definitely not me. I'm the Cosmo girl, remember?" He looked at her for a long, intent moment. Kiara's automatic, teasing smile weakened a bit under his regard.

"I tend to look a bit deeper than that, Kiara. In you, I see much more than a Cosmo girl and a beautiful face. Personally? I think STAGE was tailor-made for you."

OK, that was the last thing she expected to hear.

Really? She wanted to ask.

"Ken...I—"

"These kids need engaging. Someone they want to relate to," he continued, cutting off her disquieted protest. "Someone they admire. Someone who leads them to Christ in the manner by which they live, not just in their words, but in their actions as well. Look around you, Kiara, at what you've helped create. That's *you*. And you have a history of success."

"But...*Ken*..."

Her breath hitched and held somewhere deep in her chest. Kiara's heart thundered; her bones turned fluid. *Because, dang it, the idea pulled at her. Tempted. He honestly thought she was worthy and capable of such a challenge.*

Never had a man made her feel so precious and important. Ken seemed to believe she could be much more in this life than a trophy, a woman to be shown off and admired, yet never taken to heart with true relevance.

Kiara didn't realize she was staring at him, absorbing his words, until Ken leaned in with that mind-dizzying smile, and kissed her cheek. "By the way?" he murmured, "You might want to be careful."

Careful? Huh? His voice, low and smooth, danced across her skin in a flutter of sensation.

"The way you said my name just now? Hit me harder than a long, deep look into your eyes. Thanks for leaving *Pastor* off this time."

Before Kiara could stammer out a response, he turned, making ready to rejoin the rooftop crew. Kiara floundered, in a number of ways. "Ah, didn't you need my help?"

Ken looked over his shoulder. "Nah. That was a

diversionary tactic. I just wanted to talk to you alone for a minute."

He moved back, leaving her to stare, and melt, and *wonder*.

Late that afternoon everyone returned to camp. Taking a break before dinner preparations, individual teams adjourned to their cabins. Finally, Kiara's spotty cell phone reception decided to play nice, and she received a series of delayed text messages. The first one came from Daveny, just wanting to check in. That left Kiara smiling as she tumbled flat into bed with a delicious sigh, letting the girls blow off steam. Giggles echoed off the walls, and a pillow fight ensued—as did a simultaneous session of the Scoop, Info and Gossip Society.

Content, thoroughly happy, Kiara tuned out the chatter and paged through a couple more messages from friends, then a final, more surprising entry from Drew.

Miss u. Hear thru the grapevine u left 4 a church trip? Is that 4 real? Mission work over Paris? Whats up w/that? LOL. Fill me in. Ur silent these days. Why?

Interested in deflecting the skeptical undercurrent of Drew's missive, she decided to fill him in promptly. Ignoring the other messages, she started to type a reply.

Dont b so surprised! Our pastor knows how to motivate. Hes awesome n experienced w/ projects like this. Im in PA w/the youth group helping a family of four get back on their feet. Doing landscape and basic home repair. Great program! Im inspired! TTY when I get back.

A stuffed yellow duck whizzed through the air, zipping across Kiara's prone form. The unfortunate, battered toy was the object of a game of keep-away.

Squeals filled the air, followed by a chase full of thunder-feet. Did these kids *ever* get tired? Increasingly able to deflect the ruckus of exuberant teenage girls, Kiara clicked send, and her lips quirked into a private grin.

Don't be so surprised I'm on a mission. I'm inspired. He's awesome...

One thing was certain: Her eyes were opening up to a whole new world, and her joy and contentment within that world, while startling, could not be denied.

9

An hour later, as dinnertime approached, Ken came upon Kiara in the mess hall. Alone, she prepped the evening's entrée. The sight of her made him smile.

Standing in profile, she laid out defrosted Tilapia in a line. Before her were three bowls. Her motions as expert as any New York sous chef, she coated the fish in egg, dipped the piece into flour until it was dusted white, then flipped it repeatedly and methodically until bread crumbs formed a light coating. Setting the complete section of fish on a baking tray she hummed and swayed, unaware of his presence.

Deliberately covert, he moved to join her. Ken realized now why she didn't hear him, and why her body moved in time to a beat. She tuned into an iPod, a set of telltale white ear buds tucked into place. Ken wondered. Was he now, officially, the only person on the planet without one?

He wanted to touch her. He wanted connection. He craved her attention and the return of affection that rose up fast and overwhelmed him—but what about *her*? A feminine mystique enveloped her, and enticed.

She turned her back for a moment, dialing the oven to 350 degrees. That's when he stepped up and checked out the meal progression. By design, when she returned to the counter, she came up against his solid, waiting form. She yelped in surprise.

Ken settled his hands on her shoulders, and came upon skin so dewy soft he found himself looking at her bare arms, savoring their warmth and supple texture. Moisturizer. Of course she would moisturize her skin. The thought of massaging cream onto her arms, her shoulders and legs, left him decidedly lax in the concentration and focus department.

"Ken…ah…hello there…"

Her voice, the perfect combination of smoke satin that haunted his mind, took on a new measure of huskiness. Her smile trembled a bit—just like his fingertips, which twitched in a longing to skate against her arms, and caress her.

Thus, his plan to take her by surprise utterly backfired. Now he was the one who came away jostled and hot-wired. It was one thing to have the goal of getting under her skin. It would be quite another figuring out what to do once he got there. *If* he got there. Why did he brave this exercise? Why did he long so urgently to move into her life?

Because within her he sensed passion for life—joy and most important of all, an authentic heart.

"Tilapia happens to be a favorite of mine," he finally said.

She looked down quickly, her cheeks an appealing hue of pink. "Glad to hear that."

Ken felt the way her body tightened, hated the way her eyes shuttered and her focus remained on everything else but him. In a way, he understood her shy avoidance—heady atmosphere ranged around them, intensifying each time they came together.

So he couldn't resist. He grazed his knuckles against her cheek and came away aching. Cheeks of satin—just like the skin of her arms. "Relax, Kiara."

"Easier said than done," she murmured.

Curious he lifted her iPod from where she had resettled it on the counter. He cycled through her play list and hummed with approval.

"One Republic, Creed, David Gray, Mercy Me, Coldplay—" She blushed further and tried to swat his hand away but he dodged the effort and continued reciting: "The Fray, Five for Fighting…they're *great* by the way."

"You *know* them?"

Kiara's surprise ignited a nipping bite of frustration. She was surprised because he knew and enjoyed current music as well as Christian offerings. In a way, she reflected the attitude of most of his parishioners, especially since Barb's death. They saw him as something beyond a man with standard, relatable likes and dislikes, pains and joys.

And needs.

Ken stilled and fought back that dose of negativity by taking in a breath and observing a silence that caused Kiara's brows to pucker. He took a chance on revelation. "I don't know why it surprises people so much that I'm a part of the world I live in. Part of its culture." Absent of forethought he fingered the electronic device. He waited, hoping she might be curious enough—and *care* enough—to pick up the threads he laid out. He wished she would pursue a more personal, more meaningful conversation.

"I didn't mean to offend you." Earnest eyes and genuine regret shaded her words. Ken shook his head and returned the iPod, wanting to rail at how formal, how forced her words sounded.

He kept quiet and started to turn away but fought the leaving. He longed for her to somehow understand

198

him and his life. Was that even a possibility?

She touched his arm. "You wanted to say something. I wish you would."

Her gesture stayed Ken's exit. He expelled a breath. "Oh, boy."

He looked her straight in the eye, thinking, *you wanted her unguarded, right? That's what appealed to you most about this moment, right?* Well, apparently this was his chance, the answer to a prayer.

"Are you sure?" he asked.

She took a moment. Ken watched as she steeled herself a bit. But she nodded.

He kept his tone low. Soft. "First of all, you didn't offend. You reacted in a way that made me want to make something clear, that's all."

"What's that?"

He moved very close. Perhaps leading her forward based on his own strident emotions was just this side of aggressive, but Ken didn't want to fight himself any more. God's hand was here; he just needed to take hold, and have faith.

So he invaded her space to such a degree that she had to look up. Her eyes were wide—and alluring. She didn't step back, or away, so neither did he.

"I believe in being an engaged part of the world around me, Kiara. In fact, I enjoy it. John Muir once wrote that we should be in the world, not just on it. That philosophy hit home with me. I believe that's what God wants for all of us. No matter what our calling. After all, that's why we're here, right?"

Her mouth opened, as if she wanted to respond, but she remained silent, looking at him intently. He reached out, stroked a fingertip against her cheek once more. He couldn't get enough of the sensation that slid through his body when he touched her.

"Secondly I want you to think about something for me."

"What's that?"

The cadence of her voice ignited a dance of sparks through his bloodstream. Ken looked nowhere else but her eyes. "Think about finding a way to see past me being a pastor and understand there's more to me than church leadership. That would mean a lot, Kiara."

Not waiting on an answer, he ended the moment. "I'm going to rally our crew to start helping set up for dinner. The food looks great."

"It certainly does," came the voice of Maggie Voorhees. She stood at the entry of the mess hall, and moved slowly forward. "I wanted to be sure Kiara found everything she needed to cook the fish. Everything okay?"

Startled, a shower of cold, prickling ice danced through Ken's body. Openly curious, openly suspicious of the blatantly cozy stance he presently shared with Kiara, Maggie joined them, but quickly moved her features into smoother, friendlier lines.

"Can I help with veggies? Or some rice, maybe?"

Kiara drifted, as unobtrusively as possible, back toward the baking tray. "That'd be great. Perfect timing, actually. I'm sure the oven has preheated by now, and these won't take long to cook."

Ken prepared to take his leave, figuring it would be for the best. They shared a lingering look before he turned away, and he swore he could feel her eyes on his back when he pushed open the squeaky screen door and walked outside.

The following day, Kiara yanked weeds. She chopped back excess evergreen branches. She worked herself to a wicked extreme, consumed by her thoughts.

Of *course* Pastor Ken—*Ken*, she corrected firmly—possessed a multitude of facets and layers as a person. He was obviously more than a pastor, active and attuned to his time and place in *culture*. Of *course* she realized that truth.

A convicting voice spoke up, though: *Then why is it so difficult for you to call him Ken? Why is it so uncomfortable for you to let this wonderful, textured person into your heart—not as a preacher, but as a man?*

She knelt in the front yard, before the Kidwell's freshly soiled flowerbed. Day two was on the wane, and niggling thoughts kept playing and replaying through her mind. She dove into hard labor and the process of planting a variety of annuals and perennials. She paused to swipe beads of sweat from her forehead while she studied the gradually improving grounds.

Kiara answered that inner voice while she resumed working. *The situation with* Ken *is difficult because letting him inside my life would open up an even more personal channel between the two of us at a point when I don't know if I'm* right *for him. Plus, I've just uncovered a whole new element to exploring a relationship with him—parishioner response. Oh, she played silent and uninvolved while we finished up dinner preps last night, but Maggie's intrigue and almost disapproving suspicions only affirm the fact that there are members of Woodland Church who would be disconcerted by romantic developments in the life of their shepherd—no matter how innocent or above-board.*

Especially with a woman like me.

Stop trying to handle *this, Kiara,* came that irritatingly irrefutable voice of reason.

She'd always been attracted to Ken, ever since meeting him years ago at the church renovation project. Married at the time, he became a safe point—a man she could admire from afar, and even learn from, without risking her heart.

Or so she had thought.

Times had changed. His single status left Kiara floundering now—to the point of being uncharacteristically on edge. Acutely aware. Thing was, he knew it. She recognized as much by the way he kept tabs, and stayed near—but not *too* near. He paid close attention, stoked a fever then slid tantalizingly back, allowing her to absorb. Beneath it all simmered heat. Desire. An inviting, although unnerving, degree of tension.

Kiara's volunteer team continued to focus on landscaping. The roof now restored, Ken's team focused on interior renovations side by side with a crew of contractors from local businesses and churches who donated their time. Margaret Voorhees and her husband led Woodland's third and fourth teams in reshaping the backyard.

A hand glided against Kiara's shoulder, warm and large, stirring a jolt. She knew it was him. She recognized his touch.

"You doing OK?" Ken asked. He didn't look at her. He looked instead at a freshly prepped flowerbed now set for flowers.

"Great," she answered—too quickly.

He grinned at Amy who pulled off her work gloves and paused for a long gulp of bottled water. Ken directed his next comment to her, not Kiara. "Well,

I'm not one for micro-managing so I'll leave you to it, but I wanted to say it looks really good out here. I'm headed back inside."

"See ya, Pastor Ken," Amy answered breezily, recapping her drink. She continued to pull away the last of the overgrowth.

Kiara returned to work as well, but hang it all, Ken had her chasing after her tail these days.

"Miss Kiara?" A pair of identical twin pixies, Casey Kidwell's twin daughters, stepped up and stood near her side.

"Hi, Amber! Hi, Alyssa!" Matching, gap-toothed smiles were her return greeting. "How are you?"

"Good," came the unison answer. The little girls shared a quick glance then Alyssa spoke. "Can you and Miss Amy come to our room for a sec? We got somethin' to show you."

Amy looked up, and Kiara gave a slight shrug and nodded. Amy replied, "Sure, guys. What's up?"

"Nothin.' Just a surprise," answered Amber. She pulled Kiara's hand while Alyssa grabbed Amy by the arm.

Inside, at the far end of the hallway, plastic sheeting trapped the dust and floating debris where the more substantial outer wall demolition was taking place. Soon this area would become a third bedroom for the house. Presently, a second bedroom was shared by the three children, the space divided in half by a colorful if threadbare quilt to give the oldest child, Phil some semblance of privacy. Before the week was out, though, Phil would have his own room. The girls would continue to share, following an upgrade and proper maintenance to the room where they now stood. Ken worked outside the doorway, pulling down drywall and hauling away litter.

Oblivious to the construction chaos, Amber said, "It's right in here. C'mere."

Kiara shared an expectant look with Amy, waiting while the girls dug through a large plastic tub where they stored a few of their possessions during this temporary displacement.

At last, they pulled out two small, cloth pouches and handed one to Kiara, and one to Amy. Puzzled, Kiara opened the one from Amber. She tipped the contents into her palm and out tumbled a colorful, beaded bracelet. The beads were the kind of tiny, rainbow colored trinkets to be found in any dime-store jewelry making kit, and her throat swelled. Alyssa tended to Amy; Amber, meanwhile, took custody of Kiara's bracelet, pulling the elastic band just wide enough to slip it onto her wrist.

"We made 'em on our own. It was fun." Amber turned Kiara's wrist this way and that, studying the placement and shine of the piece. "Lots of stuff is fun now. Mommy smiles all the time now. She hasn't done that in a long, long time. It's because of you guys—we just know it. This is a gift. It's to say thank you. OK?"

Kiara bit her trembling lower lip. No use. Tears still filled her eyes, and she tried to blink them back so as not to embarrass the little girls. Meanwhile, the twins waited and watched them with expectant eyes, smiling with the humble joy of giving someone a present.

Thank God for Amy, who, though choked up as well, chimed right in. "You guys are awesome. This is gorgeous. I'm not taking it off."

"Me either. And you certainly don't need to do this to thank us, but we'll treasure these bracelets.

Always. Thank you."

Kiara and Amy scooped them into hugs, and shared a happy laugh as the foursome tumbled into a bit of a heap on the floor. From the corner of her eye, while Amber and Alyssa trounced and giggled, Kiara caught sight of Ken who hefted several large chunks of busted up drywall and dumped them into a nearby wheelbarrow. He looked keenly into her eyes, and then the corners of his mouth lifted, forming into a smile that heated her body—and her soul.

A short time later Kiara returned outside, seeking a private spot where she could release some small portion of the emotions that roiled through her system. At the edge of the backyard, she found what she sought—peace and sanctuary. She leaned against the thick trunk of a ripe-leafed maple tree and tears fell unheeded down her cheeks. She closed her eyes and lifted her face to the sun, letting its warmth bathe her dampened cheeks, her neck and arms.

From behind, a tender touch slid along the length of Kiara's shoulder. This time she didn't even flinch. She didn't even open her eyes. Dang it. Why did the man always happen upon her when she was most exposed? In general, she didn't cry—now it seemed that crying was a way of life. She willed herself to remain lax. Ken stepped close and stroked an errant tear onto his fingertip. "Amy was getting ready to send out a search party. She was pretty emotional, too."

Kiara's senses swirled. She couldn't find her focus or get to a safe, even center. Did she even want to? Kiara looked up, and came upon Ken's warm, penetrating gaze. With a quirk of his lips, he handed her a handkerchief, which caused her to laugh in a shaky manner and inform, "This makes two. I never returned…"

"Never mind that," he interrupted.

She wiped her eyes and absorbed the vibration of intimacy they shared. "I just need a minute."

Silence fell while a breeze set branches chattering. "I saw what happened—what the girls did for you and Amy." Ken held her shoulders, furthering a connection that pulled her irrevocably forward, yet scared her as well. She wrapped her arms against her midsection, bracing against tremulous and varied emotions— gratitude, humility, and beyond all else, a longing that flowed straight from the core of her to Ken in wave after wave.

"Stop fighting so hard," he whispered. "I warned you this trip would stir up changes. That statement wasn't just directed at the kids."

He drew her in and rubbed her back, swaying a bit as he held her close. The tears stopped, but Kiara dissolved on a sigh of pure contentment. Something foreign and completely unexpected broke free inside of her, and then took over. "Those little girls have nothing, but they made gifts. And here's the thing— they didn't say they were grateful for *things*—for their new, improved room, a prettier house, or a better way of life. They never once even mentioned those things. They made these bracelets because they were grateful to us for making their mom smile again. They did it for what we've done for Casey, not what we're doing for them. Destitute as they are, that's where their heart is. That selflessness did something to me, Ken. It makes me feel so ashamed for all the times I've been me-centered, or greedy."

The words poured out of her; emotions worked free and untangled into a fluid, silky sensation of connection between her, and the man who held her steady—and strong.

"Kiara?" he murmured gently, after a stilling, calm silence moved past.

"Yes?" She happily savored the beat of his heart beneath her cheek. Reluctantly she lifted her head and looked into his eyes. The peace, the all-encompassing love that defined his nature was all right there, in a sea of rich brown that penetrated, and aroused. Her pulse started to race.

"Welcome to God's mission on Earth, angel."

They separated, just as footfalls could be heard from the left. Maggie called out rather stridently, "Ken, you're needed inside…"

Kiara couldn't stifle a sigh, nor avoid the pin-pricks of her own self-doubt.

10

That night, after dinner, the kids settled in their cabins, hooked into handheld games, iPods and portable DVD players. Ken, meanwhile, embraced the idea of giving them a few hours of independence and opted for a peaceful, nighttime walk along the shores of Red Ridge Lake.

He had a lot to think about.

Granted, he had asked God for a way into Kiara's heart, but what he'd neglected to consider were the ramifications of what he'd do if ever allowed to inhabit that space.

Ken breathed deep of cool air laced by wood smoke from a blooming campfire. He soothed himself by closing his eyes, and turning his world to black. Instantly, an image of Kiara came to life—vivid green eyes, gorgeous, sexy and charismatic; a devastating smile, willowy stature softened by gentle curves…

And an enormous heart in the process of a God-inspired transformation.

Two very intriguing and appealing sides to a coin. But questions plagued him. Could she be satisfied with him in the long term? Could the woman who inspired offers of jet-set trips to Europe, who enjoyed a glittery lifestyle and active social circle, be content with a minister? A missionary with a quiet, modest life? Kiara was a woman accustomed to successful men of means.

His own success was notable, to be sure, but not on an intrinsic level, or in ways modern culture would embrace.

Demons of doubt had crept into his soul without Ken fully realizing it until now.

The encroaching night dimmed his world as he resumed walking. A half-moon became more vivid with the passing minutes, lending milky light to the surroundings. Lost in thought, he moved along the edge of the shoreline, continuing to ponder. Muffled voices from the fire pit echoed through the quiet atmosphere. Trees stood in inky silhouette. Meanwhile, his heart thudded, a deflated feeling taking charge of his mind while he studied the angles of building a long-term relationship with Kiara.

His pace picked up in response to the disquiet that surged, leading him to…

A sensual shockwave.

Nearing a dock, he came upon Kiara, and his footsteps literally stuttered until he stood at its edge, frozen still, studying her dimly-illuminated outline. She sat at the end of the structure, unguarded and unaware, dipping her feet into the water. She braced on her hands, leaning back to study the star-dusted bowl of a sky.

Ken stepped onto the back end of the dock and moved toward her. The creak of a wooden board beneath his feet alerted her to his approach and she turned. Her smile of welcome eased any hesitance he would have felt at interrupting her solitude. In fact, the power of it slid warm through his turbulent, yearning heart.

"This feels good," she remarked.

"I can imagine." He paused about mid-way down

the dock. "You probably don't want me to interrupt."

"Please do. No worries."

He hesitated, part out of shyness, part out of an honest desire to simply leave her to her thoughts, and the peace of the night. So he fell back onto a touch of humor. "OK, but I might be tempted to continue my recruitment efforts on behalf of Woodland." He stuffed his hands into the pockets of his jeans, wondering why the compulsion to reach out to her hit him with such conquering force.

"I'm up to the challenge." She moved over a tad—just enough to make room for him at the end of the dock.

And God help him through complicated emotions, he literally ached to join her. Ken's steps forward were tentative, but his heart most definitely was not.

"If you're sure…"

"Ken, I'm positive."

Ken. Not *Pastor* Ken. Formalities between them eased day by day, and that fact pleased and assured him.

So he settled next to her, shoulder to shoulder. Her skin was warm, and soft. He looked down at her as she watched the rippling waters of the lake and the silvery moonbeams that sparkled on its surface, reflecting back on her features with an ethereal glow. He slipped off his sandals and set them on the dock, dipping his feet into the lake as well.

"So."

Kiara laughed. "So."

He sidled her a mischievous look. "So I slid a sleeping pill into Maggie's coffee tonight. Hopefully that'll put her out for a couple of hours…"

She spun toward him, obviously shocked. Then

she started to laugh, hard. "I can't believe you just said that!"

"I've known and worked with her for well over a decade. I'm allowed. I honestly adore the woman, but…"

The dangling sentence spurred her on. "But she's protective," Kiara observed, a gentle kindness in her tone.

"Yes she is. Seeing the way you and I interact obviously has her radar working overtime. It's not you; it's the situation. Nonetheless, I'm not going to apologize to anyone for taking the time to be with you."

Kiara tilted her head, watching, and despite the darkness, Ken could almost see the wheels turning in her mind. Whether his words comforted or disquieted, he couldn't quite tell.

"I'm flattered, by the way," she finally said.

The statement came at him out of nowhere, so he drew back from a world of black cashmere and focused instead on reality.

"What?"

She looked his way. "I want you to know I'm flattered by the idea that you think I'm capable of working in the youth ministry."

Ken looked after her, wishing he had a clearer read on her facial features at the moment. "From where I sit, it's obvious. And this wouldn't be *working*. It would be *leading*." She attempted to laugh that comment aside, but he didn't let her. "Remember when we first toured the camp, and saw the bathroom facilities? You aced that tricky situation like a champ. And don't even get me started on the way you've helped unite our group to hard physical labor." He paused. "That said, I'll now officially let the topic rest."

"Promise?" She teased, arching a brow. In the half-light of the moon, her eyes sparkled.

Ken busted her chops right back. "I promise. *Except…*"

"*Except?*"

"Except that watching you and Amy makes me think of what you must have been like at her age. Popular and sparkling—the belle of the ball."

That stilled their sense of levity. Kiara kept smiling, but something in the air between them went taut. Ken wasn't sure what to make of it until Kiara replied quietly. "Nope. Not even close."

"Would you care to elaborate?"

She hesitated for a moment or two, and then shrugged. "Actually, I was the high school wall flower."

Truly surprised, he shook his head. "Sorry. Not buying that one at all."

"It's true. I was a total plain-Jane."

"I can't even imagine."

Kiara nodded. "I lived in Grosse Pointe but what most people don't realize when they hear the words *Grosse Pointe* is that there's a layer of people who don't live the so called luxury, high-end Grosse Pointe lifestyle. There are thousands of families who want the address, the school system, but aren't wealthy, or at all upwardly mobile. That's my story."

He watched her, silent and enthralled.

"My mom and dad moved there for my benefit, and my younger brother's benefit, but we had a modest home. Actually, we had a slightly below modest home, to be honest. The school system opened up opportunities, but as I'm sure you've seen in working with kids, there's a clique culture when it comes to adolescence, and there are perceptions that escalate out of all proportion."

"You weren't the cheerleader? The girl voted most likely to..."

Kiara interrupted with haste. "No. Not in the least. I buried myself in academics. I fought, scraped and bled for any scholarship I could find and ended up at Michigan State. With Daveny. I couldn't afford designer labels, or drive an expensive car like a lot of my classmates. I was beneath notice, so I became invisible. High school was a lonely experience, but that loneliness paid off. It gave me the motivation to get good grades, and get a college education."

"Still—forgive me, Kiara, but—I can't even picture it," he said. "You're certainly not invisible anymore. What changed?"

Water flowed around his feet and calves, silky and softly enticing. An inner heat pushed outward to do battle with the chill of soft breezes and cooling night air.

The woman to whom he attributed the bloom of warmth continued. "Going to college helped open me up. It leveled the playing field, you know? I met all kinds of interesting people, but by the same token, I have to admit to going a little shallow in the process."

They swished their feet and let them float. Occasional fish-jumps in the water beyond added noise to a near perfect silence. Kiara continued. "I started taking my looks more seriously. I worked every second I could to earn enough money to be able to—well I'm ashamed to admit this, especially to you—"

Her words caused him to interrupt. "Why not *me*, especially?"

She looked Ken straight in the eye. Even in the deepening black, he could feel her earnestness, her hesitance. "Because I don't want you to think any the less of me."

"You don't have to worry about that, Kiara. I promise."

She waited a moment before speaking. "Well, I wanted to know what it felt like to fit in. To be a part of the 'A' crowd. I didn't mind working myself into exhaustion if at the end of the rainbow I might be able to pay for the perfect haircut and color—or maybe a bar night with my sorority sisters, or a manicure and pedicure. I studied, I learned, I copied whatever 'hot' styles I could, until ultimately I transformed."

"And people noticed," Ken concluded unnecessarily. After all, how could they not? This woman was exquisite.

Kiara gave him a quick glance then looked away. "I suppose so, yes. But the capper happened when some girlfriends and I, on a total lark, and probably after a couple too many beers at PT O'Malley's, decided to take a flirting class. I found my calling." She laughed; it was the bubbly, appealing laugh that resonated with beauty and all things genuine. "Don't take that completely the wrong way. I wasn't trying to be a diva, but I found the experience to be a way to open up. Lo and behold, I found out I had a personality. After being part of the woodwork for so long, I discovered friends, and socializing. I found if I took care of myself, I wasn't the ghost I had always felt like while I grew up. Thing is, the changes I experienced kind of took hold. I started to appreciate fine things, and fine men, more than I probably should have."

"It's only human to want to be affirmed, Kiara, and—"

"It's a double edged sword." She shook her head. Silvery light shimmered off her smooth, glossy hair, causing Ken to lose focus for a moment. "Once I made a conscious effort to fit in, to mix with people, my life changed—in some ways for the better, but in many ways I lost sight of the things that bring meaning to life. I turned into that stereotypical person who gives more credence to instant gratification and easy, convenient relationships than things that are more substantial." Her sadness caused him to snap-to.

As a pastor, and friend, Ken was compelled to speak up on her behalf. "That's precisely why you're here. Now you're working yourself to exhaustion not for notoriety, or labels and haircuts, but for the betterment of a family that had lost hope. That says just as much about you as anything from your past. OK?"

She went still, and when she looked into his eyes, searching, he felt swept away.

"I went without affirmation for so long that I get sucked in by the attention I'm given. It feels good to be liked by women…desired by men. It's flattering to a hungry spirit like mine. Just like Meg in Little Women."

He moved as close as propriety would allow, wanting only to give her as much support and connected-warmth as possible.

Kiara continued, her voice husky and low. "I realize, probably too late, that I've given away parts of myself that I wish I hadn't. I had no idea how precious the waiting, and the finding, can be. I didn't have faith. I didn't believe I'd ever find a relationship that was strong, and right."

Like this? Ken longed to ask. *Like I feel whenever I'm near you?* He swallowed and grasped just enough of his role as a pastor to say, "I believe we're the composition of *all* the things we experience in the life God gives us."

"But I've been tempted to do things that aren't right, Ken. You've seen that first hand, unfortunately. I've made some stupid choices."

"Welcome to humanity, Kiara Jordan," he teased lightly, giving her a nudge. "And remember, you've grown from what you've experienced. Remember, too, that being *tempted* is worlds away from *surrender*. If you don't believe me, check out that part in the Bible where Jesus is alone in the desert with the Devil himself."

They shared a smile at that.

"What I'm getting at," he continued, "is that the person you are is the result of everything you experience—the good and the bad. Life is about what you do with what you learn and the circumstances God gives you. Have you grown? Have you learned and evolved? As far as I can see, the answer to all those questions is yes." He touched her cheek. "Stop carrying the weight and accept the forgiveness you're given, Kiara. Then, ask yourself this: What would you allow yourself to write on a completely clean slate?"

Her steady gaze stayed with his. Ken tucked an arm around her waist to both build a connection and lend her warmth and support.

Comfort and ease settled between them for a time, until Kiara said quietly, "OK. Your turn."

"My turn?"

"Yep. I want to know how you've managed to keep your life, your church, and your heart together after losing Barb. I think that's an amazing accomplishment."

Ken could only shake his head. "That's a God thing." She waited on him in silence. The quiet wasn't disconcerting, though. Instead, it soothed, and gave him a chance to evaluate, analyze. "Don't doubt for a moment that the loneliness stings."

"I'm sure. Besides, you're preaching to the choir, Pastor." She gazed toward the heavens and he felt her shrug beneath the hold of his arm. "But look at it this way: At least you've known a deep, abiding love. I'm starting to wonder if I ever will. Maybe I'm just not wired to—"

"Nuh-uh. No. Stop that line of thinking, OK? It's just…well…you need to be *ready* for it. I think God's preparing you for that step. You have to be discerning enough to recognize what will, and what *won't* bring you happiness."

"Like Drew," she said.

In the deepest reaches of her reply, he discerned shame; he saw her struggles and wishes, her passions.

"You know, Daveny made an interesting comment at the party after Jeffrey's baptism. She called me the conduit between Jeffrey and God."

"She's right. In that case, she was absolutely right."

Ken gave her an appreciative squeeze, soaking in her loyalty and absolute conviction of heart. "Thanks— but not completely. Remember who else gathered around that baptismal font? A family. A community. That's the conduit to God. You're a very important part of that, Kiara. Daveny's comment was given with the best of intentions, but, well, do you know what it did? It made me realize, not for the first time lately, that there's a distance between me and the people I serve.

Separation. I can't say as I like that."

She turned, waiting on more. Most likely without even realizing it, she came to lean against him a bit more.

Ken continued. "Barb and I were a somewhat insulated pair, not too dissimilar from most married couples, I suppose. Losing her left so many parts of my life empty." He shrugged. "In a way, I realize that's what I've been trying to escape from lately. The missions were, and are, a part of the healing process for me. The missions are vital, and provide for so much good, but by the same token, I can't keep avoiding the life I built at Woodland. I can't avoid God's calling because of a void."

Kiara sighed. "You really did hit the jackpot with Barb."

"I won't deny that. But, to be honest, I have to admit to being naïve about the whole thing."

"How so?"

His shoulder connected to hers briefly when he shifted to watch a night bird cut across the moon. "I've been a part of Woodland ever since I was ordained. First as Associate, then pastor. I was married the whole time, so I guess I've never felt the distance, the intimidation factor. The title of pastor can close people off just as often as it helps to lend comfort and assistance. I always had Barb at my side, though, an anchor and a buffer against feeling like an outsider."

She nodded, obviously waiting for him to continue. Ken gave up a momentary study of the sky to look down at her. *So close,* he thought. And he fought off a strong inner tremble.

"Do you feel like an outsider now?" She finally asked.

"Right this second? No." Frog voices filled the silence. A steady hum of insect life buzzed in his ears. She didn't look away, and neither did he. "Stewardship is the life I'm called to. The mission I've been given not just as a job, but as a calling from God. I'm happy in it. I love what I do."

"It shows. Believe me. It's compelling to watch you in your element."

"Thanks." He paused there, because he wanted her to absorb the genuine appreciation he felt at her compliment. "Still, my position creates barriers of a sort, and I...it..."

She watched intently, waiting. Her curiosity all but engulfed him, but he couldn't quite complete the thought the way he wanted.

Not yet, anyway.

So he concluded, "It dawns on me more and more that the time for mourning, for retreat, is over. God is showing me that truth with increasing frequency."

Unaware of the underlying current of that statement, Kiara replied with a simple and emphatic, "*Good*."

Ken nodded. "I move on, and I cope. That's what Barb would expect, and want. But...it's hard."

He swished his feet slowly across the surface of the water, raising ripples and mild agitation. The mirrored motion of her feet drew his attention, held it fast, left his throat parched, his soul needy.

Parts of me still ache when her birthday comes around each year, or our anniversary, or when I officiate at baptisms for the babies we welcome into our parish. I banked on more years with her than what we were given, but our lives are in God's hands. I'm at peace with that truth, but that peace, that faith, doesn't mean I don't face an ongoing adjustment, or that there isn't pain involved, and questions as to why I had to watch her wither—leaving me, and this world, piece by piece."

He choked up, taking a couple deep breaths to restore himself. Innocently their legs slid against one another, his roughened a touch by coarse hair, hers silky and infinitely smooth. His senses tingled and sparked. He came alive.

"I want that kind of love."

Her words hit Ken like a thunderbolt. He traced his fingertips against her cheeks, then her jaw, murmuring, "You deserve that kind of love, Kiara, so please, don't ever sell yourself short."

Her breathing went unsteady, and he saw her firm up her jaw and blink a couple of times, her eyes flashing even more vividly as moisture built, and receded. Quickly, he shifted emphasis, wanting to give her some comfort and equilibrium. "Right now, the thing I pray for most is that even a trace of the transformations I'm able to help bring about in others rubs off on me, too. God knows I need that mercy."

Silence returned, near perfect, holy in a way. No light pollution hazed the bowl of black above them. No clouds or dimming atmospheric properties spoiled this perfect slice of the stars, moon, galaxies and even the occasional slow-moving satellite and plane. Against the dock, a gentle lapping of water was accompanied by nocturnal life and the rush and rustle of tree leaves and grass reeds. The sounds soothed and calmed. Lent a bit of finality to the night's revelations.

"We should get back to the cabins," he ventured at last. He extended his hand and she accepted the connection. With a gentle tug, Ken helped her stand.

There was just a hairbreadth of air between them, then none at all. Their bodies brushed, their gazes connected. "Just remember that there's beauty in the simplest things, Kiara. Just open yourself up to it, and receive."

11

The walk back was quiet, but unhurried.

Meandering left Kiara with time to think. In fact, almost *too* much time…

Something about Ken's demeanor caused questions to flow, accompanied by a sense of anxiety she couldn't deny, or escape. This moment between them felt unfinished. She sensed hanging threads and wanted them tied up. Resolved.

So, deliberately she slowed her pace. "Ken?" He turned, waiting. "Was there something more you wanted to say to me? Back at the dock?" Kiara waited, hoping for more from him—for anything that might connect her to him more fully.

"No…not really."

On the inside, she wilted. Looking up she did her best to study his shadowed features and came away unfulfilled. A tree-hidden moon shrouded them in a deep black, and she wondered about his true reactions. The only giveaway she could detect was the quick way he averted his gaze.

That prompted her to push. "Please tell me what's bothering you." She wanted to reach out, the urge so strident her body yearned. "Something's on your mind. Maybe I can help. You're always present to everyone else. I'd be honored to be the one to listen and lend support if you need it."

For some reason, Kiara could tell her offer didn't hit the right mark. She realized the fact instantly when Ken sighed, then closed his eyes for a moment, almost as though in prayer. The dim, sporadic light of the night had made them sparkle. She missed that instantly.

Maybe that was part of the problem. Kiara wanted this man—very much—and in the here and now of performing side-by-side mission work, everything between them felt right—uncomplicated and united. Ultimately, though, they would have to return to the world of reality. Kiara, the quintessence of flirt and playful, modern femininity. Ken, the traditionalist, pastor—a man of calling and humble service.

Maggie Voorhees came to mind, and all of a sudden Kiara's mind's eye conjured the image of oil forming a shimmering, but tarnishing rainbow over a surface of pristine water. Dramatic, yes, but a proper mix would never be accomplished. Attraction could provide a lovely sheen of various colors, but over the long haul she'd end up heartbroken when she disappointed him, and he found it necessary to move away.

Insecurity pinned her within a world of doubt. They were simply too different.

A lengthening moment passed in stillness then they cleared the tree line. He stopped short. He nodded in the direction of a nearby birch and they moved toward it, standing beneath its cover of branches. In fact, Kiara was close enough to the trunk that her back came up against the slightly rough bark. He stood before her, tall and lithe. Broad shoulders blocked out starlight and leaves; his features were inked out, but she didn't need light to gather the image of a squared jaw, deep-set eyes brimming with affection, and compassion, the thick tussle of dark brown hair that waved against the back of his neck. Ken was...was...she wanted to use the word seductive—but the words seductive and preacher? Kiara shivered.

At last, he said, "I don't want to leave you with the feeling that I don't appreciate your support."

"I didn't think that." Well, not *exactly*, she added in silence.

"You possess the sweetest heart, Kiara. But, to you I'm a pastor, and you're my parishioner. There's a divide. It's like I was saying. I'm not good at divides. I haven't faced them very often, that is, until—" The words *Barb passed away* went unspoken, but understood. "I feel a distance, a guardedness in the way you talk to me sometimes, the way you intensify, and go formal when I try to reach out. Please, just keep in mind that I'm only a man. I have a vocation, true, but that makes me no different from everyone else."

This was her fault, just as she feared. She would let him down; she would fail him, and he deserved the very best. Even though she didn't think that person would ever be her, Kiara couldn't stop from asking, "What do you need? What is it you're looking for? Please tell me. Not as a pastor. I care about you above and beyond that title. So many people do. You shouldn't feel alone in this."

Ken clenched his jaw. She saw the taut line bloom, even in the moonlight. She was maintaining the divide, and she knew it. But, she felt terrified to step over that final threshold and lose her heart for good.

"You're not *everyone*, Kiara. Not to me."

Confusion and uncertainty started to clear because Ken's words forced her to connect a few emotional dots. There was something unique and powerful about the two of them, and the bonds they discovered. Ken was sounding her out about that fact. In a round-about manner, true, but nonetheless he tried.

She pondered that fact until Ken asked quietly, "Kiara do you trust me enough to let me try something?"

The way he asked the question made her throat go dry. Her pulse raced and a dizzy, wonderful ache slid straight through her, rendering her completely open and receptive. "How could I not?"

He slid his fingers slowly through the length of her hair. Velvety warmth coasted in on the heels of that stirring ache. He brushed his fingertips against her neck and cheeks, cupping her face. She felt vulnerable, but weakness dissolved her bones, melding her spirit neatly to his.

"Close your eyes."

His request, a mere whisper, left her swallowing cotton. He waited on her compliance, his gaze on her face. Even in the night air, she felt the warmth of his eyes, the patience and care that always seemed to motivate him. Her eyes fluttered closed and she tried desperately to remember how to breathe.

A petal-soft whisper of air slid against her mouth an instant before his lips claimed hers. Moist as dew, as silky and sensuous as the night that cocooned them, his kiss caused her head to spin, left her pliant. A pleasured exclamation left her. Just like that, the sense of drifting to the conclusion of this evening without a completed circle—a sense of fulfillment—evaporated into the air, lifting high and away.

He drew her into his arms, but didn't press further. Instead, he simply fed her—passion for passion, intimacy for intimacy—in kiss after warm, giving kiss. The beauty and mastery he poured into the connection knocked any other emotion and memory Kiara associated with love and physicality into total oblivion.

She held fast to his forearms, clung to him. It was either that or she would literally sink to the bramble-and-brush-covered floor of the woods. She could lose herself in him so easily, and so willingly.

The kiss intensified as they fell into the moment, the act deep and exploratory, provocative and open. Their embrace turned radiant and strangely encapsulating. The crackle of a branch jarred them back to reality and the possibility of being discovered. Nothing else moved around them except a soft, cooling stroke of air as they parted.

Wordless, suffering from what seemed to be a mutual case of shell-shock, they left privacy and seclusion behind. They closed the distance to her cabin and Ken tucked her hand securely in his, caressing the back with his thumb.

Once they reached the steps leading up to the door, she kept hold of his hand to halt his leaving and said, "I want you to know something." He waited and she shored up her courage and unshielded her heart just far enough to take a risk. "Ken, I think of you as being much more than just the head of my church. You're a wonderful pastor, yes, but you're a wonderful man as well."

He stepped close and used a slow finger stroke to tuck her hair back. He leaned in close to nuzzle her neck, then her cheek. "Good night, Kiara." He kissed her cheek then moved away. "And thank you." There was such earnestness to the tone of those final words.

"See you in the morning."

"I hope you have sweet dreams."

He turned back in mid-stride. Beneath the yellow light of a nearby security lamp that illuminated the sandy pathway between cabins, she saw him smile, and her chest swelled with happiness. "I think, tonight, that's pretty much a given. You rest well, too, angel."

He disappeared into the night and Kiara stood at the doorway of the cabin, stupefied. Her mouth tingled. She touched it with shaky hands, ran her tongue slowly against her lower lip. She breathed in deep and he surrounded her—scent, warmth and an ache ripe with longing.

As quietly as she could, she pushed open the door and caught herself in a mindless stumble when her sneaker caught on the edging of the threshold. She cringed, waiting for one of the slumbering girls to awaken. Kiara nearly laughed out loud. Her cabin mates rested in silence. Thank goodness.

Well, so much for being the sexy sophisticate. She was transported, operating completely outside of herself. She felt as giddy as any one of the teens with whom she presently kept company. She smiled the whole time she sneaked beneath the covers and tucked in for the night. Over and over again, she played out the kiss. *Their* kiss.

Ken.

He pulsed through her heart like a living thing. She closed her eyes and he was there. And he was in no way, shape or form simply a preacher any longer. She was in love. The return to reality she had been concerned with earlier seemed suddenly distant and misty. She snuggled beneath the blankets trying to make a restless body go still and comfortable.

Ken Lucerne left her believing she had more to offer this world than the male-enchanting looks and willowy, curved frame, which heretofore had been her claim to fame. The idea of such strength of belief thrilled her—but scared her to bits as well.

A fear of heartbreak loomed—so mist-blanketed fears resurfaced, but only for a moment.

Ken longed, and he ached. At the same time, he struck her as being so strong, so sufficient. So Godly.

He's just a man, Kiara.

Daveny's words echoed, helping her grasp anew the truth that Pastor Ken—*Ken*—experienced needs and pains, joys and triumphs like everyone else. He succeeded and failed like everyone else.

The night rang with a silence broken only by the steady breathing of her bunkies. Ken's words rang through her, body and soul.

"Ask yourself this: What would you allow yourself to write on a completely clean slate?"

She already knew the answer. She'd write his name upon it and guard that slate with the entirety of her heart.

At last she dozed, a smile playing on her lips as she drifted off to a deep, thoroughly restful night's sleep.

12

"Kiara, you are *so* cool."

Kiara couldn't hold back an affectionate laugh at Amy's pronouncement. "Takes one to know one, Miss Thing."

Amy dipped a spoon into the potato salad Kiara was creating and scooped out a sample, devouring it with a sigh. "I'm serious. You even make cooking seem chic. Where did you get your top? I love it."

Kiara burst out laughing again at Amy's CD-skip style conversation. "Amy, the next time I'm feeling down in the dregs, I'm calling you, and you're ordered to say exactly those words to me over and over again." With a downward glance, Kiara paid regard to the sleeveless pink microfiber athletic shirt she wore. "I got this at a running shop in Sterling Heights. I'll take you there some time."

"Deal. Seriously, I'd so love to go shopping with you."

The fourth day of the mission trip was drawing to a close. They were past the midway point and the results were remarkable. Backbreaking, but remarkable. Enough camaraderie and trust had been established, enough observations made, for Kiara to comfortably remark, "You know, Tyler sure is enchanted by you. Bonus? He's such a great guy."

Amy shrugged. "He's really nice. I like how he

treats me."

"You should. Believe me when I say that's the whole ballgame," Wanting to pass along as much wisdom as possible to this younger version of herself, Kiara didn't shy away from the role of mentor.

"I feel bad around him though."

"Why's that?"

"Because I know he likes me, and honest, I like him too. I like him just fine. But..." She paused and watched Kiara dice a bit more onion and celery into the mix. "Need more milk?"

"Yeah. Just a little. The secret is making it creamy, and using enough eggs."

Amy poured, and then Kiara mixed.

"You were saying?"

Amy leaned on her elbows, watching the motion of the spoon in the bowl instead of meeting Kiara's eyes. Kiara didn't know much about young adults, but the body language spoke loud and clear. Amy wanted to confess but wasn't sure what to admit, so she diverted parts of herself—like a gaze that would reveal too much.

"It's just that there's this other guy. Mark Samuels. He's kind of, like, spectacular, Kiara." She grinned. "The type of guy I bet you'd have gone for big time back in high school. He's so handsome, and funny, and he's a total jock—captain of the basketball team. He's awesome. Everybody wants to be around him, and, well, he likes me. I even think he's going to ask me to Homecoming."

Dreamy preoccupation left Amy neglecting Kiara's reaction. Thank God. Amy's words convicted Kiara in the worst way. Amy's ideas, and ideals, were carbon copies of Kiara—once upon a time—until Woodland,

and Ken's presence in her life. In an effort to find conformity, acceptance and, yes, pleasure, Kiara knew she had gone shallow in spots, and this conversation with Amy served to amplify that fact.

So Kiara continued the process of transforming. "Amy, if Tyler treats you well, and he cares about you, and you like him, why wait around for a different guy just because he's popular, or a handsome jock? You've got so much to offer, and to match up with someone who recognizes how special you are, is an amazing blessing."

Kiara turned to put a cover on top of the potato salad then walked to the fridge to store it.

"Like you and Pastor Ken?" Dishware bobbled, but Kiara executed a fast recovery, trembling as she safely shelved the salad then turned back around.

There was a deliberate watchful manner to Amy's posture, and then she said, "I'm sorry. I don't mean to be nosy or anything, it's just that I figured since I'm confessing to you, you might want to do the same."

"Pastor Ken?" The words were nothing but a stall maneuver. She didn't know how to react, or what to say to this insightful, keen-eyed young lady.

Amy elaborated. "Last night. The trees."

Kiara's heart lurched. "Yeah."

"I had to go to the bathroom, and the night was so pretty. There were billions of stars. I wanted to go see the lake. I started down the path through the woods, and I, well, I'm sorry, but I saw you and Pastor Ken."

Kiara didn't know what to say.

"Kissing," Amy clarified.

"Oh."

They eyed one another, mutually unsure how to proceed. Kiara felt trapped by the shared knowledge of an event that she had hoped would remain private.

"You really like him," Amy continued. "I could tell that before I saw what I did."

"Amy, I need to ask you, please, to be discreet about what you saw. It was just a kiss, and it was completely innocent, so I don't want gossip to build, not around Pastor Ken. OK? Can I trust you?"

Her expression turned instantly affronted. "I wouldn't hurt you guys. I didn't tell anyone, Kiara. And I won't. I promise. I really like you both."

Kiara crossed through the kitchen and sat down on the stool next to Amy's. Amy flipped her hair over her shoulder and fingered the spoon she still held, studying it. Kiara settled her hand over Amy's to still the nervous fidgeting.

Amy's features went soft. "I went back to bed and you came in a few minutes later. I could tell by your breathing that you couldn't get to sleep right away. Truth is? I envy you finding that kind of a moment. It seemed so perfect, and wonderful."

"Life isn't ever idyllic, OK? Understand that Ken misses his wife very, very much. And, in truth, I don't know that I'm the best person to fill that kind of a role in his life."

"Kiara?" she paused. "You're awesome. How can you doubt that? Like, *ever*?"

Quite easily, she wanted to say, but Amy's plaintive, emphatic decree softened Kiara's heart and her determination to turn away from the onslaught of emotion Ken stirred.

The screen door of the mess hall squeaked open, and the guys stormed in, laughing boisterously, colliding with one another on purpose, and preparing to toss a football across the kitchen area, until...

"Guys—food. Don't mess around the food."

Ken entered the hall and herded the gang to a seating area where they were scheduled to reconfirm the delegation of table set up and cleaning assignments for the following day. Kiara spared him a grateful look for his intervention, and he gave her an understanding nod. Kiara tucked a piece of aluminum foil across the top of a tray full of fruit selections she had cleaned and arranged just before her conversation with Amy had begun.

Understanding the need for their interlude to conclude, Amy left the stool and stretched, making a happy sound as she sifted her fingers through her hair. "I call shower!" she sang.

Kiara launched into action; nightmares that featured icy jets of water danced through her head. She gave her newfound confidante a mock glower and literally jogged toward the exit. "Think again, Miss Thing. I'm pulling rank. I crave hot water. For five measly seconds I need hot water! I'll be out in a flash. You can even time me."

"Kiara!" Amy bellowed, chasing after her at full-bore. "No fair!"

The sound of Ken's laughter tickled the skin along the back of Kiara's neck, and danced against her senses as she and Amy charged from the mess hall.

13

The mission trip didn't conclude with a big-reveal style television moment; however, the community reactions, the humble, overwhelming gratitude, remained just as powerful, and just as touching to Kiara.

A farewell breakfast concluded the agenda in Pennsylvania. Afterwards, no sooner did a round of hugs from the Kidwell family end, than they started all over again. Everyone seemed reluctant to part. A new circle of love began with each communion; the Kidwell's happiness turned into a blanket that wrapped around the entire mission team just as tight and warm as their arms. In particular, Casey Kidwell's voice quavered with emotion that laced her repeated words of thanks and praise, not just to the workers, but to the God who had brought everyone together.

On departure, a quiet, somewhat somber mindset colored Kiara's world. The Woodland team began its return trip to Michigan with everyone tired, quiet, and introspective. Still overcome by the outpouring, the teen volunteers spent a good portion of the drive home in what she felt sure was a prayerful, thoughtful silence.

Attempting subtlety, she glanced over at Ken. One hand rested on the steering wheel, the other rested on the divider between them. Kiara was sorely tempted by the image of strong, perfectly muscled forearms lightly dusted by hair that she now knew by touch was as soft as satin. She longed to reach out, to touch him and reconnect. Instead, she held back. Discretion kept her in place, but yearning remained a persistent ting that struck against her heightened nerve endings.

One by one, Ken dropped off their travel companions. When they reached Kiara's apartment, he parked the van, turning to her. They were alone now, confined within the intimate space of the vehicle, surrounded by warmth, dim light and the vibrating purr of the engine.

"I miss you already," he said.

The heartfelt words emboldened her to take the initiative and move forward. She touched his face, her fingertips memorizing each subtle curve, dip and plane. She glided her hand against his neck and drew him close, seeking to indulge a need which had consumed her from the start of the voyage home. Understanding at once, he wrapped an arm around her and she sank into a kiss so sweet, so potent, she went pliant against him.

"I know how you feel. Will we see each other soon? When we…I mean…what will happen…?" Kiara couldn't meet the power of his eyes when she felt such uncertainty. She didn't want to see anything within their depths that might warn of hesitance, or worse yet, doubt. "I wanted—and waited for—this moment for the entire trip."

Even in the darkness, his smile could be discerned. "Me, too. And it was well worth the wait."

Kiara looked up at him shyly, but ventured forth into trickier territory. "Please know that I don't want to make anything awkward for you or uncomfortable at

Woodland."

"Kiara, it's fine. Let's just take it step-by-step as far as revealing ourselves goes. There's no reason to think people won't be thrilled for us."

"Day by day."

He nodded. "Day by day."

She paused, burdened by the secret she knew she needed to share—especially given this conversation. "I have to tell you—"

"What?"

Kiara paused again. "Amy saw us."

"The kiss. In the woods."

She nodded. "Remember that branch that snapped and popped?"

Ken ducked his head in a gesture both endearing and boyish. "I remember." Then his gaze returned to hers, full of heated intensity. "In fact, I remember everything about that moment, angel. Everything."

"You're not worried."

"Not a bit. First, I think Amy'll keep quiet. She looks up to you and wouldn't hurt you."

"Or you," Kiara assured further.

"Come here."

He didn't wait for her to comply. Instead, Ken drew her snug against his hard, warm chest. With restrained hunger, his mouth claimed hers and she gave herself over to a moment of loving joy. She trusted him completely, so she tucked her head into the crook of his shoulder, cradled safe and perfect into a spot of his body and soul that felt like it had been designed for her by God.

Instead of an abrupt, jarring break, Ken ended their connection by soothing degrees. Kiara's heart raced as his lips moved from her mouth to glide smoothly against both cheeks, then to trail against her neck until at last they shared one last, lingering kiss.

With typical, thoughtful chivalry, he hauled her suitcase out of the rear storage area of the van then carried it into the entryway of her apartment. He turned to say goodbye. Before leaving, though, he enfolded her in a hug so snug and eloquent Kiara wanted to sink into the sensation for good.

"Thank you for being the face of Christ to the Kidwells', Kiara. In word and in deed. Your commitment made a huge difference in their lives." He traced a lone fingertip against the underside of her chin, using the subtle gesture to lift her gaze to his. "I'll see you at services tomorrow."

She nodded. Along came an impulse she couldn't possibly ignore. She lifted her hand and allowed her touch to linger against his cheek, then his strong, square jaw. A silence lingered between them before she concluded strongly, "I'll see you then."

❧❧

"Hey! Welcome back, stranger! I missed you!"

"Me, too, Dav! I looked for you at church yesterday."

Kiara hugged her best friend tight. Daveny, meanwhile, all but thrust her through the doorway of her office and into the chair in front of her desk. Kiara was starting to actually harbor a fear of that hideously innocent-looking chair.

"I know, right? Jeffrey and Collin are both under the weather. I had to pull nursing duty, times two, and I'm awfully afraid I'm on borrowed health time." They shared a grin. "So! Tell me all about it!"

Kiara snorted. "Not until I decompress. I swear, teenagers have more energy and stamina, and exist on less sleep, than any living organism I know of!"

Daveny chuckled. "When did you get in?"

"Saturday night. I literally dumped my suitcase in the laundry room of my apartment, still stuffed with grimy, smelly clothes, then I showered—in *hot* water, praise God—for almost a half hour before collapsing into bed. I didn't wake up until the alarm rang. I rolled into church, on time—will miracles never cease—and then returned home for another lengthy sleep session that ended with me waking up just in time to get to work. How's that for a hero's return home?"

Daveny laughed with what Kiara felt was just a bit too much glee. "I take it you're exhausted?"

"Times ten, yes, but in the best way. It was awesome, Dav. I can't get over how much a week of our time helped these people—and gave them a new lease on life. To see their faces, to see the hope our work left behind, makes every ache and every lost hour of rest *so* worth it."

Let that be enough, Kiara thought in a rush. She even started to stand, knowing full well that a bevy of work awaited. Perfect excuse to retreat—er—leave.

Please, oh, please, don't ask about Ken, she pled in silence. *I'm so drained and vulnerable right now I have no defenses left against what I feel. Don't ask about Ken. Don't ask about Ken.*

"And how did my favorite pastor hold up?"

Dang. She asked. And just hearing his name, just thinking about him, betrayed Kiara to her best friend. In an instant, she knew Daveny registered her reaction—the flight of heat that slid smooth and fast up her neck, and cheeks. Kiara diverted her softened eyes, knowing evasion was in vain.

As expected, Daveny wasted no time calling her out, either. *Figured.* Kiara had done the same thing to Daveny a time or two during the course of their friendship—especially when Daveny fell hard, and irrevocably, for Collin Edwards.

"Are you going to sit back down, or do I need to get the restraints?"

Kiara glared. Daveny shrugged. Then, she even *grinned.*

Relenting, Daveny leaned forward, ignoring the photos and layout plans covering her desk. "Consider this a 'me returning the favor' moment. After all, you've done the same for me, now haven't you?"

Kiara sank into the chair and sighed. Every bit of bravado evaporated from her blood stream.

"I'm in trouble."

"Honey? I figured that one out solo. *Talk* to me."

Where to start? What to say? At length, Kiara figured the truth might serve her well.

"OK. You want flat out? I'll *give* you flat out. Daveny, no man has ever impacted my waking thoughts, my dreams. No man has ever forced me to look so long, and so hard, at who I am, and who I want to become. No man's touch has ever worked me over like this. You know me. I can take or leave an attractive man, and I've done both on more occasions that I'd care to admit anymore. Well this isn't casual. This isn't something frivolous, or something to fill time. This is real. This is leagues different from anything I've ever felt before, and it's miles away from my comfort zone. He fills a hunger I didn't even know I had."

The words spilled free. She couldn't stop them. Didn't want to any longer. Kiara lost the will to fight.

Meanwhile, Daveny listened; she nodded, seeming to know exactly what Kiara meant.

"He fills your spirit," Daveny said at last. "Ken brings you close to himself, and close to a God you're beginning to relate to on a much more personal level, Kiara. He's helping you discover the very best of yourself. That's a beautiful thing. Embrace it."

"Until he leaves me, or realizes our two-plus-two doesn't exactly make four when it comes to the two of us becoming a couple."

Daveny reared back. "What on earth do you mean by that?"

"Oh, come on. Do the math! When the equation of Kiara plus Ken patterns down to its conclusion, I just don't see a way for a man like him, and a woman like me, to make a relationship work." Daveny seemed about to speak up, but Kiara shook her head in a silent request for Daveny to hear her out. "I'm way too different from him. Most of all, I'm not *Barb*. I could never fill her role. She was tender and soft—a born nurturer. I'm the sassy, playful modernista."

Daveny studied her for a long, hard moment. Seemed a perfect point in the conversation for Kiara to execute a swift change of subject. "Anyway, enough of all that. Tell me about Sir Jeffrey. How's my baby boy been, other than recovering from a bug?"

That did the trick. In an instant Daveny turned completely maternal—all happy, proud and glowing. Vicariously Kiara shared her joy. "Oh, he's up to his usual tricks—sleeping, eating, and cooing. C'mere. Let me show you the latest pictures."

Truly eager to catch up, she stood behind Daveny's shoulder and viewed Jeffrey's latest portfolio. One image in particular caught Kiara's attention. The picture was beautifully lit and framed. In it, Daveny and Collin held Jeffrey between them in a gesture both loving and protective. "You're so blessed. What a beautiful family."

"Tired, but blessed, yes." She sidled Kiara a look. "Which reminds me. Will you be seeing Ken in the next few days?"

"Not sure. Why?"

"Oh, nothing. No big deal."

Kiara gave her shoulder a nudge. "C'mon. What's up?"

"Well, there's prep material Collin wanted to deliver to him before the next Parish Council meeting. I'd love to keep close to home these days, at least until everyone is feeling better and I'm certain I've dodged the flu bullet. I only thought if you might be seeing him…"

"Stop being silly. I'd be happy to deliver it for you. I'll drop it by the church. No problem."

Oh, heavens, Kiara thought in a prompt back-pedal. *I leaped at that opportunity now didn't I?* Which was exactly why Daveny had floated the idea. Her knowing grin confirmed Kiara's assumption. "Are you sure?"

"Yeah. Really, it's no biggie." Acting casual, Kiara took possession of the large white envelope Daveny offered.

"Thanks, Kiara. I really appreciate it. Tell Ken I'll see him Sunday—good Lord willing."

14

Day one back on the job edged toward a close.

Ken sat across from Maggie Voorhees at a small conference table tucked into the far corner of his office. After straightening the pages of the most current edition of the budget and tucking them away inside a folder, Maggie leaned back in her chair. She struck Ken as being restless, tapping her pen on top of the legal pad upon which she had prioritized action items for the coming week.

Patiently he waited; he knew Maggie well enough to realize she'd express herself when she was ready.

"So, the word's getting out," she said at last.

Already starting to realign some financial allocations, Ken looked up from the spreadsheet he studied. "Hmm? Word?"

Maggie nodded, but chewed on the corner of her lip in a nervous habit of hers. It seemed she wanted very much to say something, but hesitated. Red flag number one lifted up and rippled. "Talk is going on about you. And Kiara."

Hello, red flag number two. Ken nearly sighed, but didn't. After all, gossip was a part of the human condition, and Woodland was far from exempt. "What about me and Kiara?"

"Well, the trip back was pretty illuminating, I have to say. Some of the kids from the youth group were talking in whispers during the trip home, and…"

The sentence trailed off, but Ken easily polished it off. Maggie and her husband had overheard. Amy, who had witnessed the kiss with Kiara, hadn't been able to resist the siren call of informing her friends about what had happened in the woods. The intent wasn't malicious or mean-spirited at all. Ken knew that without question. Still, Amy had figuratively spilled the beans about him and Kiara. From there, he felt sure a few friends had told a few more friends, until before long the eyes and ears of the Woodland Church community would rest upon their comings and goings—every look, touch, and communication.

Stemming from simple curiosity, the scrutiny would be harmless for the most part, but unnerving nonetheless.

Then, Maggie blew that piece of naïveté to bits. "Isn't she a little…I don't know…high-brow…for the kind of life you lead, Ken?"

"What?" Astounded by her unexpected and brazen comment, he could only stammer his way across the word.

"Look, don't get me wrong, I adore Kiara—she's been a God-send to Woodland, but she's hardly a staid, calming influence. And she's so different from Barb."

"Yes, she is, but that fact has no bearing on anything. That's not good or bad. A large part of what draws me to her is the fact that she's lively. She has passion and drive. She's spirited. She's also—and I can say this with one hundred percent conviction after spending an entire week on mission with her—completely devoted to her relationship with Woodland, and with God. What more would a person need?"

"Ken, I don't mean to offend. It's just that I can't see her settling for—" Maggie coughed quick and performed a fast edit of her words. "—settling *into* a life with a pastor. Honestly. Can you? I don't want her to hurt you, and I don't want her hurt either. It doesn't quite gel for me."

"Well fortunately, you're not the one it needs to *gel* for. Furthermore, this discussion of my life, and Kiara's, is now bordering on inappropriate."

Her eyes went wide. "Funny. I thought I was talking to a *friend* right now. I thought I was talking to someone who's been with me through good times and bad—and vice versa, for well over a decade now. I'm not talking to a pastor. I'm talking to the man I've known, who's been a friend to me, ever since he walked in the door. We've always had each other's backs."

He nodded. "True. But never once have we tried to tell one another what was right or wrong in our lives."

She regarded Ken in silence for a time, her lips a tight line. He could almost see the wheels turning—responses forming and vanishing. "Just be careful. Understandably, losing Barb put you in a spiral. In a completely different way, I worry that Kiara could do the very same thing."

In a ruffled, hot silence, they turned to leave the conference table. Ken's gaze traveled to the office doorway. That's when he heard Maggie draw a sharp breath, and he nearly dropped his paper-stuffed file folder.

Kiara stood framed in the threshold, an envelope in hand. Her expression was smooth, but her eyes were veiled. How much had she heard? Ken's chest felt constricted and his heart pounded.

"Ken, I have a delivery from Collin. Daveny gave it to me at work today. It's for the council meeting next week." She stepped inside as graceful as a movie star, gave him the envelope without missing a beat and even offered up a smile to Maggie. "How are you?"

"I'm good. Recovering, finally." Maggie's answer was friendly and warm, but she shuffled from foot to foot. All Ken wanted to do was fold Kiara into a tight hug. Other than slightly heightened skin, Kiara gave no indication whatsoever of having heard a word that had been exchanged.

Just looking at her, though, and knowing her the way he did, Ken didn't doubt she had heard the conversation. And if she hadn't heard all of it, she had heard more than enough to be upset—though in stalwart fashion, she hid that fact well. Ken realized he was probably one of the few who knew just how easily, and just how well, she could mask the hurt of being degraded.

"Returning to normal sleep patterns is a good thing, isn't it?" Kiara remarked with an almost too-bright tone. "Well, I'll see you both on Sunday. G'night, guys."

Turning away, her body language typically graceful and smooth, she left, but her pace was a bit quicker than Ken would have expected under normal circumstances.

"Maggie, I'll talk to you later."

He moved in haste and didn't stop until he caught up with Kiara. She had already made it to her car, and was currently wrestling with an un-giving door handle. He moved in fast behind her and slid his hands against hers until she went still. She didn't look at him.

He maneuvered her grasp away from the door handle and she froze in place. She squeezed her hands into fists.

"Come inside," he beckoned quietly. "Talk to me."

She did a good job of shrugging off his urging touch against her back, resuming her battle with a key fob that wouldn't unlock her door, and a door handle that refused to open. He felt like saying, *Kiara, sweetheart, take the hint.*

This time he took hold of both her hands and turned her fully away from the car. "Please come back inside."

"Don't, Ken. Not right now."

"Yes, now. Period. Come with me."

On the way in, they crossed paths with Maggie who was just leaving. Maggie issued a quick goodnight, and scurried to her car. Kiara sighed. "It sure didn't take long, now did it? I don't know why I feel angry at Maggie. Her heart's in the right place, even if her words stung. I have to give her snaps for being brave enough to say what everyone else is going to be thinking."

Heat boiled through his blood. "Don't do this Kiara. Don't get all wrapped up in other people. That's a pattern you need to break, isn't it?" She turned her head and glared at him. Ken pressed on, undeterred. "It's hard enough venturing into a new relationship under the best of circumstances, but…"

"But *what*?" Her barking retort, her blazing eyes left something inside him crumbling. Into those fissures and cracks came demons, lapping up his anxieties and doubts and fertilizing them deeply.

They finally reached the sanctuary of his office. Ken shut the door and turned, facing her eye to eye.

This was a matter they needed to resolve. Now.

"How much did you overhear?"

She pretended to ponder for a moment, tilting her head and pursing her lips. "I believe it started with something to the effect of me being a bit...what was the phrase? *High-brow* to ever settle for a life with a pastor."

With that, the worst-case scenario came to be. She had heard it all, a silent witness to someone knocking them down at a most fragile and vulnerable point in time.

He sighed heavily and sat on the front edge of his desk. He leaned forward, clasping his hands between his legs, inching as near to Kiara as he dared. She stood, stiff and apart from him, her arms folded protectively against her midsection.

He started to reach out, wanting to eliminate the distance between them, but she backed away a step. That riled his anger. "Kiara, do you think you're the only one who suffers from self-doubts here?"

"What do you mean by that? Are you lending credence to what Maggie had to say?"

Ken blew out a breath. After that came a pounding, redolent silence. "The point can be made that, that you and I...that elements of, of..."

"Out with it," she demanded. "Respect me enough to come clean. What's at the bottom of this, Ken? Tell me."

"OK." He paused, and looked at her steadily. "First of all, realize something important. Maggie wasn't criticizing *you*. She wasn't judging *you*. She was looking at a mix. A mix of your life with mine. I admit it. I've asked myself lately, what do I bring to you? How does my world enhance yours? My life is modest.

Simple. It's fulfilling to me, it's rewarding, and I treasure every moment of it, but I'm not meant to embrace the grand scale in ways that you have, in ways that you transformed yourself in order to find. How can I compete? How can I fulfill the part of your soul that longs for so much more than I can give?" This time he took hold of her hands and squeezed tight. "That's not a criticism, by the way. It's part of who you are. It's beautiful. *You're* beautiful. You're charming, you sparkle and you possess such vitality. But will we be *right*? Would you be happy? The only life I know is that of a pastor. A missionary. Is that your calling? Is it what's meant to be for you?"

By the end of Ken's speech, her eyes had filled, sparkling with tears. Her hands went limp and lifeless in his. Then, tears fell, and he felt powerless to do anything but go silent, and stare. Meanwhile, she watched him right back.

He had hurt her. Badly. A blade slid neat and deep against his heart. She swiped away the moisture, murmuring, "I understand. I get it." Her lips trembled. She firmed her jaw, but a pair of tears became a glimmering track against her fair, flawless skin. Kiara turned away by a fraction and pressed her fingertips against the bridge of her nose. "But I always thought actions spoke louder than words. I thought I had come so far, and shown you how much…"

At that point, her words ceased and she made a low, frustrated sound in her throat. When she looked into Ken's eyes, her pain transformed the blade cut into sharp, sizzling heat.

"What you just said," she whispered, "It confirms the worst fears I ever entertained about my feelings for you. And that rips my heart to pieces, Ken. I let myself believe. But I'll tell you what else," she continued, her voice now strong and steady despite the telling line of moisture shimmering on her cheeks. "I've grown. And I've changed." Ken moved to automatically cut in and agree with her. She sliced that action short with an abrupt motion of her hand and plowed ahead. "When we were in Pennsylvania, you told me you have faith in me. You told me you believe in me. Well do you, or don't you? You asked me to find out who I am. You urged me to become the best possible version of myself. Well that's what I've done. That's what I'm going to continue to do, no matter what. Not for you, not for me, but for the person I want to be before God. What you're saying right now is hurtful. It cuts away at that foundation I'm building, but I won't let it hurt me anymore. Maybe that's something else I needed to learn—that I have to fight for what I want, and who I am, and who I want to be. Well, don't ever get in the way of that again. I deserve better, and now I won't accept anything less." She straightened and looked at him with narrowed eyes. Strength of conviction rolled off her in waves, creating a God-made masterpiece, a formidable woman, inside and out. "Talk to me again once you've sorted that out."

Chin up, her eyes now blinked clear, Kiara spun, striding out of his office before he could even begin to recover from the staggering blow of hurt he had unwittingly inflicted—on both of them.

15

"Hey, Ken. These are for you, from Amy. She dropped them by the office the other day." The Parish Council meeting was about to begin. Maggie Voorhees approached in the posture of one who sought to make amends, with caution and penitence. Like a peace offering, she handed him an envelope full of photos.

"Thanks, Maggie." He capped the words with a warm smile, hoping to reestablish comfort. She had been an ace in the office, as usual, but since the episode with Kiara, she had avoided prolonged conversations, which was highly unusual for the two of them. He felt grateful for forward progress.

With Maggie, anyhow. Kiara remained a different, and difficult, matter all together.

He had a minute to spare before the meeting was called to order. Curious, he lifted the flap and inside found a neatly printed note from Amy:

Hi, Pastor Ken! I hope you like these. I think they came out pretty good! There are two sets—one for you, and one for Kiara. Can you please give them to her? You'll probably see her before I do. Thanks, and I'll see you in church! Amy

His lips quirked and his heart filled. It seemed Maggie wasn't the only one wanting to reaffirm friendship and care.

Members of the council took their seats. As people settled in, Ken shuffled through the pictures. A group shot taken on the last day rested on top, an instant source of bittersweet nostalgia. He missed…

Kiara.

He missed seeing her daily. He missed the passion and intensity they poured into the mission, and into discovering each other. Why did that realization leave him so conflicted? The love he felt for her was genuine, so why did the arguments he had made to her days ago still resound? Had he, without ever consciously meaning to, led her on? On one hand, was he *ready* for a deep-seated relationship? On the other, could he exist in happiness any longer without her?

He didn't think so. The more time that passed without her, the more his entire being seemed to ache, consumed by need and emptiness. Somehow, he had bungled and fallen. Somehow, he had refused delivery on a gift from God Himself. Kiara filled him. Ken couldn't escape that truth.

Still, there was a flip side he had to explore and resolve. Maggie had observed Kiara's vibrancy and enchanting charm. The statement was true, but guilt came into play whenever he considered the fact that while Barb's life had drifted away from him, Kiara's had swirled inexorably toward, pushing him into life and away from grief. Kiara inspired feelings he feared to face because even now, two years after Barb's death, entertaining the idea of a full and loving relationship with Kiara felt like a betrayal. Ken hadn't lied when he told Kiara he longed for much more time with Barb than they had been given. But his responses to Kiara—in body, heart and spirit—weren't a lie, either.

Despite the tumult, Kiara filled him with hope; her essence and life slid against his senses, enticed his soul to a place so beautiful it defied description.

Ken cleared his throat of a sudden tightness and kept thumbing through the images, continuing to drift away from reality. Now he studied a shot of Kiara and the kids, all in a row, securing landscape borders, then planting flowers and shrubs. Interior shots came after that. There was one of Ken perched on a ladder with a paint roller in hand, surrounded by members of the youth group. Then there was another of a crew of teens and contractors installing drywall and cabinetry.

The final two shots, however, commanded his total focus. First, a picture of him and Kiara. They wore large smiles, their arms around each other. Behind them stood the refurbished home of Casey Kidwell.

The last image featured the two of them on a wooden bench by the lake. Before them crackled a vibrant campfire. Kids encircled the dancing flames and dusk painted the photo in hues of rich blue. Kiara's legs were tucked beneath her, her body turned toward Ken's. In the photograph, he looked away from her, watching Tyler who could be seen strumming his beloved guitar.

What captured Ken about this moment in time was the way Kiara looked at him. Her eyes were unguarded, the dawn of a smile just beginning to curve her lips. Affection well beyond the superficial, and unseen by Ken at the time, telegraphed straight from the image to his heart.

A woman so beautiful, so full of magnetism, looked at him like that? Ken's world rolled over neatly then wobbled slowly back into place. He separated the two pictures, studying them for a few seconds longer before setting them on top of the pack. They were awesome.

"Ken? Ah—*Ken*…" Collin's summons broke

through Ken's fog-veiled mind. Ken snapped to attention and Collin waited for a moment, until he realized Ken was completely lost. "Are you ready to deliver the opening prayer?"

"Yes. Absolutely. I'm sorry for being distracted."

Ken tucked the photos beneath his agenda folder. The meeting moved forward from there and he paid much closer attention. Collin, however, kept tabs. He sent a couple covert glances Ken's way as Woodland's governing body hashed out church business.

Afterward Collin hung back while Ken exchanged good-byes and some final comments with those who departed. Curious about why Collin remained seated and made slow work of gathering paperwork, Ken bussed the table, depositing napkins and Styrofoam cups into a nearby trash can.

At last Collin stood. He took Ken by surprise when he asked, "You in the mood for a beer?"

Ken stopped his cleaning duties to look at him. "I could be talked into it—so long as I don't end up getting in trouble with Daveny."

Collin grinned. "I sent her a text right after we adjourned. Jeffrey's sound asleep so I'm in the clear for an hour or so. Does Grissom's Pub sound good?"

Ken nodded. "Done. I didn't get dinner. I'm starving."

స్త్రౌ

A Wednesday edition of Sports Center played in the background. Ken followed Collin to a table toward the rear of Grissom's where they could talk at reasonable decibels yet at the same time monitor the latest news from the NFL. Ken ordered the house special—burger, fries and a brew. Collin followed suit.

"Those were some great pictures," Collin commented right off the bat. "Especially the ones of you and Kiara at the end. Tell me about the trip."

Uh-oh. I'm in for it. Disconnected from his surroundings at the start of the Parish Council meeting, Ken hadn't realized until now just how close Collin had been watching.

"It was great," he said and cut it off right there. He focused on the plasma screen above them. The smack of pool balls added occasional punctuation to the atmosphere.

"If you think you're getting off that easy, think again, pal."

Their waitress delivered a pair of longnecks, giving Ken just enough time to put up a wall of defense. "Is this an inquisition, or are we going to enjoy having a beer?" Ken tempered the words with a grin then took a swallow of his brew.

Collin followed suit as he pretended to think about that question for a second. "I vote for both." He hit Ken with a probing look. "It's payback time."

Ken couldn't help laughing. Payback indeed.

"You remember my anger at God. You helped me destroy that wall I had around my heart after Lance was killed. You lost your wife. I lost my oldest brother. When I clawed my way back, it was Daveny, and you, who threw me lifelines. You helped me find my way back to faith, to Christ."

Ken had a part to play in that redemptive process, sure, but God worked the miracle. God's faithfulness astounded Ken anew each time he recognized the active, caring role Collin now assumed with his faith and Woodland. For a number of years, until he met

Daveny, Collin had full-out rebuked God. Now he not only attended church, he took on an active role as a newly elected Parish Council member.

In the process of Collin's struggle, Ken had welcomed him back to church, and even challenged him to leave behind emptiness so he could embrace a new point of view with regard to his spirit-life and his relationship with God. It seemed Collin had learned his lessons well.

Collin continued, echoing Ken's thought pattern. "You helped me find my footing. Let me return the favor."

To stall, he took another pull on his beer. Instinct left Ken wanting to step neatly to the side, shrug off what he felt. He didn't want to bring people into his personal turmoil. Dealing with Barb's illness had made him somewhat of a pro at that maneuver. Tonight, however, he shunted that instinct and instead moved toward Collin's offer of friendship.

"OK. I'll cut to the chase for you. She's fantastic, obviously. But I could never keep her interested, Collin. Mine isn't the kind of life she's been looking for. My life is simple. It's about church guidance, serving God, and being present to the members of my parish. It's about church events and budgetary red ink. Meanwhile, Kiara receives offers to jet away to Europe."

"Which she turned down, remember."

Ken shrugged. "Point taken. True. But the fact remains, her life features excitement and adventure. An excitement and adventure she craves."

"Act for one hot second like that isn't exactly what draws you to her."

Hmmm. So Collin wanted to play hardball. Ken

battled right back. "It is. I won't deny it, but therein lies the rub. She's all about embracing new experiences with the people she draws into her life with nothing more than that smile of hers and the easy, attractive way she just *is*. I'm nobody's sophisticate. I'm not electric like she is."

"Oh yes you are," Collin said definitively. "Every time you step up to proclaim God's word, or deliver a sermon, you capture people. It's all in a matter of what you're passionate *about*. It's all in the matter of what God calls you to *do*. You found your calling and embraced it from the get-go. You settled in nicely with Barb. Then, a seismic change occurred. You've had to reevaluate your entire life.

"Now go the other way. Take a good look at Kiara. At her spirit. What does it tell you? Ken, she's doing exactly the same thing you are! She's looking for her calling. She's stepping away from the life she thought she wanted, with all of its temptations and allure, and she's looking for something Godly. Something to fill her soul. She's finding God, and in the process, she's finding *you*. Take the hint." Ken stared, swept into Collin's words and struck silent.

"What I'm saying is, be ready for the chance God's giving you to be a partner to a woman who wants, and *needs*, someone just like *you*. Not to satisfy who she *was*, but who she's *becoming*."

Ken ran his thumb along the cold, moist surface of the bottle he held. "You make it sound so easy."

"It's not."

Ken appreciated that comment and gave Collin a quick glance. "I suppose it's easy for some people to write off the confusion I feel, or just not understand it. Get over it, some may say. Barb's gone. Move on."

Collin gaped. "I'd personally deal with anyone who was that cold about the relationship you had with Barb." He gave Ken a sheepish look. "Forgive the impulse toward violence."

Ken laughed, fingering the cocktail napkin beneath his beer. "Forgiven. Thing is? I can't seem to reconcile myself to let go. On one level, I'm giving over to Kiara. It's like I can't even *help* it. On another, I *want* to hold back. I feel guilty, and definitely afraid. I want to be everything to her, and I know I can't be."

"Let me ask you something."

"Yeah?"

"Is guilt and fear what you were thinking about when you looked at those pictures?"

Ken nodded then sheepishly came clean. "And more."

"I figured out the *and more* part solo." He gave Ken a wry grin, and then continued. "Look, seriously, I'm not belittling what you've said. I'm only asking so you can think about things. What is it about the situation with Kiara that's giving you so much guilt? Is there something about her, or you, that makes you feel this way? As Barb's illness progressed, Kiara's presence in your life sharpened focus. There's no shame in that."

"Not from where I sit," Ken murmured.

Their food arrived, steaming and fragrant, along with a second round of beers. They gave thanks and dug in.

"You know? Really? All I ever wanted was to live my life in guidance of Woodland, happily married to a wonderful woman—a woman I treasure and cherish. Someone to create a family with."

"That's still a possibility. In fact, it would seem to be a very *good* possibility."

"Maybe, Collin, but…but I just can't—dive in to Kiara."

"You're forgetting something." Collin tipped back his beer then downed a trio of fries. "I watched you tonight. Your face tells me the truth that your words won't. I'd say the dive you're talking about already happened; you just need to face it."

Ken stared. Collin's verdict left him no escape hatch. Ken couldn't deny the comment, but he couldn't move forward yet, either. "Know what I feel like?"

"What?"

"A teenager. A teenager with a raging crush. I feel like the high-school geek who's fallen hard for the homecoming queen."

Collin feasted on his burger, and so did Ken.

"You know," Collin said at length, "Kiara would absolutely, without a question or a doubt, *hate* that analogy."

"I know. I'd never say anything like that to her directly, but I can't help how I feel—"

Collin cut him off. "Back up a sec. I'm lost. When exactly did you become the *geek* in this story?"

Ken laughed. "OK, OK. I'm not a geek, but in so many ways it's a similar situation." He turned, squaring off directly with his friend. "Let me clarify the point I'm trying to make—and I can absolutely, without a question or a doubt guarantee that Kiara would agree with what I'm about to say."

Collin smirked at Ken's parroting job, but he listened.

"Kiara's told me herself that she sees me as something up here." Ken held his hand shoulder high. "I'm a pastor, which means—"

"Oh, man, which means you definitely shouldn't

be at a local watering hole tossing back a couple brews with a parish member. Cripe. Gimme that beer right now before you lose your preaching license or something—"

"Collin, you're a jerk. As I was saying, I'm up here, while the rest of mere mortal humanity lies somewhere down here." His hand lowered to almost brush the wood tabletop. "I'm different. Set apart. So you see, while I may not be a geek, it's the same difference." He pointed at Collin. "And the results are just the same, too. Know what I mean?"

"Well, maybe that's because you met and married Barb before you became a full-blown church leader. A comfort zone had already been established, right?"

"Yeah."

"Could that be part of what's upsetting the balance for you and Kiara? That the *comfort zone* just isn't there for Kiara? Yet?"

"Yet?"

"*Yet*. Because it seems to me that during the mission trip, you came down from the mountain a bit, and Kiara found her way upward. Judging by the sapped-out look on your face when you thumbed through those pictures, progress was made. And progress is progress. In fact, I'll bet she's *counting* on you. So don't let her down, and don't you dare give up." Collin sent a direct, penetrating look in Ken's direction. "You gonna give up?"

Collin's words struck him like a bell being chimed. Ken *had* let her down. He had told her not to worry. He had told her they would make it through. But then he had performed an abrupt and shattering back pedal. Out of fear.

Out of a lack of faith.

Lights in Ken's heart clicked on, illuminating a few of his more unsettling errors in judgment. He gave Collin the most honest, bare-bones answer he could. "I can't give up. To do that would be impossible."

Collin stretched back and spread his hands wide, seeming to claim victory. Before digging in to his food again, he lifted his beer bottle and *thunked* it against Ken's. They swallowed a tandem swig then Collin grinned at him, "Then go get her—and my work here is finished."

Ken made plans. He'd talk to her after church this weekend. He'd take her home and make her breakfast after services. They'd talk—really talk—about a future. Together.

The idea left Ken smiling, and Collin just looked at him with a knowing smirk. Ken snapped to proper attention and they continued their meal companionably before Collin remarked, "So—now to the stuff that's *really* important."

Ken chuckled, weights unbuckling from his heart, allowing it to rise. "Which is?"

After wiping his mouth on a napkin, Collin munched on a French fry and looked up at the television screen, promptly losing himself in Sports Center. "Do you think the Lions are *ever* gonna climb out of the NFL cellar?"

16

Kiara immersed herself deep within the landscape design for a law firm in Bloomfield Hills. Thus settled, she only vaguely registered the tinkling alert of an incoming text message to her cell phone. Next came a more persistent vibration that sent the device skittering across the surface of her desk until it bumped and stalled against an open folder of renderings and lay-out plans.

Concentration shattered, her thoughts turned instantly to Ken. She fought the urge to growl. Growling wouldn't do when she wore her professional demeanor—but plenty times of late she growled, stammered her way through ineffective mutterings, unanswered prayers, shivers of loneliness, and a pervasive, overriding need that rolled through her over and over and over again. Especially in the night. Especially when her body and mind sought refuge, rest and peace from loving him so much. The silence permeated her world. Obviously, Ken had written off their relationship as mutually unsuitable.

Days had passed since she stumbled upon the exchange between Ken and Maggie, and the lack of communication left her roiling. What was Ken thinking? Going through? Granted, she had turned away, but by the same token, Ken hadn't reached out either. That spoke volumes.

A headache bloomed. Not an uncommon development these days. She worked her fingertips fruitlessly against a tight knot of tension that ran a circuit from her neck to her shoulders straight on down to her back. With stubbornness of will, she refused delivery and acknowledgement of her pain—again—and forced Ken Lucerne to a locked chamber of her heart.

Once again, she hunkered down with layout plans for the sweeping roll of land upon which rested the stately, Colonial designed headquarters of Stuart and Littleson, Attorneys at Law. She lost herself in work, mapped out bush and tree possibilities. She plotted the perfect display and color scheme of annuals, perennials, and accents like ultra-fine gravel in glimmering shades of pearl, or perhaps a more dramatic red stone border frame…

She pushed and pushed, relentless and hyper focused. She wanted—she needed—anything that would take her thoughts, and heart, far from an image that kept crowding her brain. The image came to her regardless. Spirit enticing warmth, flowing straight out from clear brown eyes, a wide smile framed by soft, full lips—lips she could now taste and feel…a rich, deep voice, a commanding, compelling personality.

Kiara straightened in her chair. She pinched the bridge of her nose and rolled her shoulders, finally picking up the cell phone, which, though silent, now flashed a tiny red attention light. Apparently, she was such a mess she now needed a distraction from distraction. She needed to keep herself from holding on so tightly to someone who, by virtue of their final words and a building silence, wanted nothing more to do with her.

She opened the text message, from a girlfriend, Anne Marie, who tended to coordinate group gatherings.

220 Merrill
Sunday @ 10 am
Brunch w/the gang
Bacon, eggs n gossip
U in?

The invite left her with mixed emotions. Once-upon-a-Kiara would have been filled with the happy expectation of a high-end meal with friends. But she was starting to wonder. Were these really her friends? Did they have her heart, and did she have theirs? Were they all simply convenient counterparts, possessing similar goals and life points, staving off an ever-present void by pushing one another with the goal of professional and material success?

Quite frankly, her time with Ken left Kiara questioning everything. Pastor Ken Lucerne had opened her heart and filled it up with God's promise and grace, and the power of love. For a time, she had actually tasted fulfillment, experienced a sense of spiritual growth that made her happier than anything else she could remember.

She missed him so much she literally ached—especially in those moments when she found herself most alone, when vulnerability climbed to its highest peak—when dreams and memories turned into a tantalizing swirl.

Now only emptiness remained.

Pain twisted its way through a deep, heretofore impenetrable area of Kiara's spirit. She reviewed the invitation to 220—a favorite restaurant of hers in downtown Birmingham. Ten o'clock in the morning on a Sunday. That would mean missing church.

And for some odd reason, that realization caused her worst, most painful memory to descend...her final words to Ken.

"You told me you have faith in me. That you believe in me. Well do you, or don't you? You asked me to find out who I am. You urged me to become the best possible version of myself. Well that's what I've done. That's what I'm going to continue to do, no matter what. Not for you, not for me, but for the person I want to be before God."

Noble? Sure. Meant it whole-heartedly? At the time, absolutely. But now Kiara felt weak. Her strength waned, siphoned pint by pint and replaced by overwhelming pain and need. Did anything really make a difference? And honestly—would missing a Sunday service truly matter? She needed a taste of her old life—of the old Kiara.

Pain continued to grow, blooming into a debilitating burn. She went tense, jiggling her crossed leg nervously. She clenched the cell phone tight and started to rapid-fire click the keys. With a resolute push of the "send" button, she returned a simple, three word reply:

Count me in.

༄༅

"We're here today," Anna Marie began, "to toast the end of an era. To mourn the death of manslayer supreme, Kiara Jordan, who is a newly sanctified Holy Roller and mission worker. So, tell us about the trip."

Anna Marie lifted her flute of orange juice and the half-dozen people gathered at their table followed suit. Kiara's beverage remained untouched. She couldn't bring herself to join in the chortles. The way Anna Marie emphasized the words *Holy Roller* rankled her nerves something fierce.

Yep—this brunch date was one colossal mistake.

Sharing a meal at 220 Merrill with the gang didn't sit well with her today. Elements of this get together rubbed her in places which were already raw and aggravated. Well, she supposed, this kind of newness, this revised perception, shouldn't be shocking. She had changed a great deal recently.

So Kiara glowered at Anna Marie, delivering a tight, unfeeling grin. "Thanks so much for the eulogy, Anna Marie. Really. That's so nice."

The group laughed and teased as Kiara rolled her eyes and finally sipped her drink. But she didn't chink glasses with everyone else. At one time, perhaps the guffaws and bawdy comments that followed her comment would have seemed harmless—nothing more than good-natured fun and one-upmanship.

Not anymore.

Reaching beneath the surface of this group revealed much more. The mention of God's power and mission taken out of proper context hit Kiara first; then the lack of sensitivity hit her heart. The joking session left her aching instead of laughing. No one asked about the truth of her mission trip, or its impact on her heart. Truthfully, they didn't care. That was fair enough. What she disliked was the fact that she was being torn down and mocked based on conviction of belief.

Kiara had slipped into her former role for this gathering. It was comfortable to her right now. Familiar. She wore a Michael Kors cashmere twin set of delicate pink, and the cardigan presently rested on the chair behind her. A slim cut, royal blue skirt of silk was paired with leg flattering high-heeled pumps crafted by Ferragamo. The hair and makeup were perfect, but the needs of her soul beat relentlessly against her heart, refusing to be still, or quiet, any longer.

She glanced at the slim gold bangle watch on her wrist. It was almost eleven. Right about now, services at Woodland would be winding down. Ken would be doing everything in his power to wrap the church in God's embrace—though preaching and presence.

She bit her lips together to ward off the pain, the ache of longing. Her counterparts didn't even notice the fact that she'd retreated, inch by inch, during the course of the meal. They were so wrapped up in their own worlds they didn't focus outward. Meanwhile, Kiara picked at her mandarin salad and did her best to simply endure.

Conversation ebbed and flowed while she faded into the background and discreetly checked her watch again. She could make a getaway soon. A beautiful Sunday called, and she longed to spend it in a more productive, contented way.

If only, if only, if only…

"Hey, Kiara."

The summons came from behind and she braced against the sound of a deep, perfectly modulated voice. Kiara stifled a cringe, but it took tremendous effort. Andrew. Perfect. Her day glided into an even steeper downward angle. She wanted to scream she felt so displaced and sad. Now, on top of it all, *Drew*. She did the best and only thing she could. She surrendered herself for a few precious seconds, and prayed:

Lord Jesus, please help me. I miss Ken so much. I miss the constancy of our connection during the mission trip. I miss the love we shared in furthering Your kingdom, and discovering one another. Lord, please help us and guide us according to Your will. I promise to try to trust You even more. I can't fight any longer. Forgive me for even trying. I'm tired and I feel broken. Ease this ache, this longing that keeps tearing away at my spirit.

Polite behavior dictated she turn and greet Drew, so that's what she did, but all Kiara really wanted to do was leave. She wanted Ken.

"Hi, Drew. How are you?"

"Good." He quickly scanned the faces of the people at the table. "Ah, if you have a few minutes, I'd like to talk to you."

Kiara's mind raced through the scenario, and within it, she sensed an escape hatch. She could dismiss herself from the table, spend a moment or two with Drew, then leave. The promise of an imminent exit from 220 beckoned to her like beautiful music.

So after a quick goodbye, a couple of air kisses to her girlfriends and empty-sounding promises of outings to come, Kiara shouldered her purse. She hitched her sweater from the chair and followed Drew to a couple of empty stools at the nearby bar where they settled.

"Want a drink or anything?"

"No thanks, I'm good."

Drew just nodded. Kiara waited, and resisted the urge to check her watch for what had to be the dozenth time.

"Welcome back," he offered.

Drew's hesitance softened Kiara's heart, and she smiled at him. "Thanks. It's good to be home, but I'll be honest. I miss the Kidwells already. I love what we were able to accomplish for them. It was the best—we helped fixed a roof, built a bedroom addition, landsca—"

Drew wasn't really listening. His attention was focused elsewhere. As her words trailed off, he reached out to touch Kiara's wrist. Brows knit, he studied the simple and precious bracelet that had not left her possession since Amber settled it into place.

"What's this?" he asked.

His interruption struck her as rude, and his tone felt accusing. In counterpoint, she kept her reply smooth. "A gift from the family we helped out. It was made for me by one of the kids."

Andrew shrugged, and made a noncommittal sound. Meanwhile Kiara touched the beads, absorbing the memory of faith and love, the gratitude built in to each one. Her focus rested on the piece as a memory slid against her like satin.

"Thank you—for being the face of Christ to these people, Kiara, in word and in deed. Your commitment has made a huge difference in their lives."

Ken's words sang through her mind, a source of reassurance. In phantom, she felt his kiss, his tender touch. Most of all, though, his powerful example lent her fledgling spirit some much-needed strength of resolve, as well as the assurance of God's unconditional love.

Andrew interrupted those thoughts. "You know? I have to say, I just don't get it. Frankly, I'm shocked that someone as worldly as you would get pulled in by a program like that. I mean, they're fine enough I suppose, but at the end of the day—"

"They're fine enough? Someone as worldly as me? Gee. Thanks for the show of support, Drew. This was, and is, important to me."

His eyes widened with surprise. "OK. I get it."

She sighed inwardly, saying, "I wish you did. What about the equation of me helping people and committing myself to God, doesn't make sense, Drew?"

For a moment, he just looked uncomfortable. He shrugged again, and astonishment flooded her. To think, just a short time ago she had been tempted to abandon her core dreams and beliefs in favor of a sensual odyssey with this man. Paris had called, as had the fleeting promise, and arms, of a successful, sexy man who, at his center, remained woefully empty.

It occurred to Kiara that chasing a placebo to loneliness might very well have been her undoing. Self-doubt may have cost her one of the most precious relationships God could provide.

Images skimmed and weaved through her mind, then clicked into focus like a high-res digital photo display: Amy and Tyler's playful sparring, Ken leading a campfire bonding session, the simple and breathtaking beauty of a country lake, its surrounding woods and the stars sparkling above, a grateful, jubilant family.

But it was Ken's image that repeated most often. The most powerful recollection was not of his pastoral uniform—the crisp black suit and white collar—nor his formal vestments. Instead, she recalled him decked out in an old WSU sweatshirt speckled by a trace of grease. Her heart held fast to the way he kept an ancient van in shape because it ran great, shuttled batches of kids efficiently, and remained reliable and performance-ready by virtue of his caring hand and commitment.

Even in loneliness and longing, Kiara treasured the time she had spent working side by side with him, helping a destitute family struggling to overcome life's harshest blows. Her heart swelled, filled by a love deeper, richer and more intoxicating than any emotion she had ever known.

At last, Drew continued. "You asked why this doesn't make sense to me. You want my answer? Seriously?"

"Yes."

"Good, because in all honesty it's the reason why I want to talk to you."

Kiara waited. Meanwhile, Drew shifted in his seat. His disquiet seemed to grow. "I guess I'm more than a little surprised."

"At?"

"At *you*." He faced her fully now, and the look on his face made her bristle. There was dark challenge in his eyes. Big-time skepticism. "I have to admit, it surprises me that the modern-thinking, enlightened woman I know and wanted to get to know even better, has turned into a Jesus freak all because her pastor is some kind of an idealistic do-gooder."

How Kiara kept from gasping aloud would remain a forever mystery, attributable only to years of well-practiced control and emotional shielding. She blinked a few times. She leaned back and away from the close proximity of their shared space at the bar. Her voice, however, she regulated to low and even. "Ken Lucerne isn't a do-gooder. He lends a helping hand to those in need. Yes, that's idealistic. But my question to you is: when did that become something negative?"

"Maybe it's a jealousy factor," he retorted hotly. "Maybe I'm being negative because all you've been doing lately is singing his praises. If I didn't know any better, I'd think you were going all warm and cozy for your *religion* and a man of the *cloth* who's transforming you into something you're really *not*.. You—one of the most cosmopolitan people I know. I mean, Jes—"

"Stop it right there. And while we're at it, stop thinking you know me well enough to make any kind of informed judgments about my life."

"You mean to tell me you intend to waste that beauty," he gestured at her expansively, "that body," he gestured again. "And that sex appeal of yours? Get serious, Kiara!" With that, he sank against the edge of the bar and just stared.

Each word he spoke socked into her stomach like a fist, robbing her of precious air. She looked at him for an open-mouthed second and Andrew continued hotly. "Oh, come on! Are you surprised I feel this way? You're too intelligent and too vibrant a woman to waste time on the moral opiate of religion. That's not what life's about."

This time her breath caught. "Wow," she whispered. She shook her head, feeling hot and dizzy. "Just...wow." Kiara's breaking point came and went. "Let me make something clear to you, Drew. In my world, the sacrifice and love of my Lord and Savior isn't a moral opiate; it's the entire universe." She stood abruptly and hoisted her purse from the next seat. She yanked her sweater from its spot on the bar ledge and balled it in her fist. *To heck with cashmere*. "All I'm going to add is this: If being a *Jesus Freak* kept me from making the mistake of taking a hedonistic voyage with you to Europe, and kept me from a relationship that would have ended in emptiness and disaster, then I say more power to Him."

Kiara spun away; Andrew grabbed her hand. She jerked free of his touch, but stayed put while he said, "This kind of overreaction is *exactly* what I'm talking about. Sit down and stop acting so offended!"

She'd thought she couldn't be any more shocked. She was woefully wrong. "You ridicule my beliefs, mock a part of my life that's increasingly important to me, a part of my life I'm exploring, and growing into, yet you tell me to not act offended? Well here's a clue, Drew, I'm not *acting*."

His gaze darted left and right, no doubt checking for eavesdroppers and the attention of nearby patrons. "Would you *lighten up?* Seriously, do you see yourself as being that, I don't know, holy? Or righteous?" His tone made it sound like the terms *holy* and *righteous* were a bad thing. Thank God she had learned differently.

There was no need for more. Kiara shook her head, giving him a long, last look. "Goodbye, Drew."

Without another word, she left the restaurant. Her eyes stung, yet remained miraculously dry. She gasped a bit, struggling to still herself and just breathe as she strode to the nearby public lot where she had parked her car. She slid behind the wheel and started to drive. Tears built, periodically blurring her vision. Once they fell, Kiara dashed them away with a careless swipe; anger burbled through her bloodstream until she thought she would overflow with a blend of sadness and rage.

Not fully realizing her intent, not even aware of the direction she took, Kiara pulled into the parking lot at Woodland and stopped. There she sat in the car, resting her head on the steering wheel, finally letting the sobs overwhelm.

Nobody would understand her now. No one would recognize the impact of God's presence, or the turning of her heart toward service and faith rather than self-centered pursuits. But that was OK.

Because God does. Because, no matter what comes to be between the two of us, Ken does, too.

Right now, she wanted Woodland's sanctuary. She wanted Ken's presence, his tenderness, so desperately. At the same time, she heard the echo of Andrew's every word. The conversation brought her worst fears and self-doubts into a sharp and unforgiving focus. She wasn't worthy. She didn't deserve a man like Ken. Her life, to the point of meeting him, had been too vivid a compilation of unsuccessful relationships and selfish pursuits, the pain of which she masked with empty moments in dimly lit clubs and bars, competitive professional pursuits. The resulting circle of friends, save a few, weren't truly friends, for they didn't know her in the least. Hers was a quest for fulfillment. Yet the closer she came to authentic contentment, the more those around her watched in confusion.

Everyone except Ken. He thoroughly understood her evolution as a Christian; he encouraged her attempts and saw past her failures at faith building. Furthermore, in his hands rested the unquestioned key to her heart and happiness.

Dear Jesus, she prayed in silence, *please help me. I'm trying. I want to be worthy of You. I want to be worthy of a man who carries Your word and mission and truth into the world. I feel inadequate, and unfit to travel the pathway You're opening up in my heart, yet it answers every longing I have. I want to serve You, and I want to fulfill that role at Ken's side. Is that Your will? Is that Your plan? I just don't know. I'm not sure of anything anymore. I leave everything to You in surrender and trust. I want to give more of myself to You, Lord. Please give me the chance. Please help me."*

In the calm, pervasive stillness that filled the car,

Kiara fought to regain control. She grabbed a couple tissues from the storage compartment next to her seat. She dabbed her eyes, and cleared her runny nose. Steadying her trembles, she exited the car, considering a plan. She'd go inside and pray. She'd rest for a time inside the church.

That's when she surveyed the grounds of Woodland…

And there he was.

17

Ken walked the perimeter of the pond, tossing bread bits to the newest members of Woodland's family—a flock of Canadian geese. Kiara's heart performed a somersault, expanding with an emotion so powerful, so perfect it could only be captured in one small word. Love.

So this is what it felt like to leave behind a world full of haze and smoggy pollution to come upon fresh air, warmth and a tender, perfect light.

Overwhelmed once more, tears filled her eyes. She didn't even care. Need spurred her forward. She left the car behind and literally ran to him.

When he heard her footfalls, he turned, an expression of curiosity transforming immediately to concern when he saw her face. He didn't speak, and either did Kiara. She didn't want to talk. She wanted...she wanted...

At that exact moment, he opened his arms.

Kiara tumbled into his embrace and Ken held her steady and sure. He rubbed her back, and silently squeezed her tight.

Home. Her soul came to sureness and rest. *This is home.*

A sigh passed through her body, exiting on a soft release of air as she tried to wipe away tears. Ken still wore his pastoral uniform—the black slacks and shirt—the white collar and black suit coat. Her tears fell and she tried to pull away so she wouldn't make a mess of him, but he held her fast. Kiara rejoiced. Laying her head on his shoulder, she snuggled close and slid her fingertips beneath the lapel of his jacket, breathing in the sandalwood scent of him. "I'm blubbering all over you."

"It's OK. I missed you at services today. Very much. It was like a piece of me went missing."

Urgency coated his words. She knew the feeling well, so she opened herself and responded from the heart. "I'm so sorry for not being here. You have no idea what a mistake I made. But I learned something important today, if that's any consolation."

Ken swayed slightly, taking her with him on a subtle dance. "What's that?"

"It seems God can teach me a lesson whether I attended church or not." She leaned back, wanting to look into his eyes. She absolutely loved those sparkling, gentle eyes. "You're still dressed for work," she observed lamely. "Am I interrupting?"

He visually puzzled while studying her face. "Not at all. I'm headed to St. John's Hospital in a couple hours. I found out Pat Dunleavy is having an emergency heart cath procedure, so I want to visit him."

Typical. Did he have any clue at all what a miracle he was? Probably not. Meanwhile his warm, calloused fingertips slid against her cheek. He looked into her eyes, waiting on explanations. Kiara felt her eyes fill again, whether from gratitude for his presence or gratitude for peace and joy, she couldn't quite tell anymore. Cushioned within the haven of Ken's arms, she didn't even care.

"Come here, angel." He led her to a metal bench positioned at the edge of a pathway that cut through the lush grounds of the church. There they sat. Before them rolled a deep green carpet of grass that was pleasingly damp and dewy smelling. A few hearty, last-of-summer blooms colored the scene. Old trees with thick trunks held leaves bursting with fiery color. The pond and its geese, the arch of Parishoner's Bridge spanning its width, formed a lovely scene.

Ken fingered back the fall of her hair and slid it over her shoulder. He settled his arm along the curved back of the bench, opening himself, encouraging her close. She tucked in gratefully at his side.

"Can you tell me what happened?" he asked.

This wasn't a pastor asking a church member. This was man to woman. The difference was distinct, and bone melting. *Lord,* she beseeched, *please, please let there be love here. Deep, holy, abiding love…*

The instant his arm slid against her shoulder, the moment he drew her into the warm, solid wall of his body, Kiara wanted nothing but to dissolve into the respite he offered.

"Just for now, can explanations wait? Can I please just rest here? With you? It's all I want."

"Take all the time you need."

Kiara tucked her head into the crook of his shoulder and closed her eyes, doing just as she wished, and dreamed. She allowed herself to melt away and go absolutely calm, thinking: *If I could only have this for a lifetime…*

"Why is it I get so emotional around you?" she asked. "Why do all my emotions rise to the surface and spill over, whenever I'm with you?"

"Because you're safe. I promise that. I'll try not to

hurt you, or ever judge."

Kiara dipped her head, wiping her eyes with fingertips that were already moist. On cue, Ken handed her a handkerchief. Accepting the offering, she gave him a watery laugh. "I still have the one you gave me at Jeffrey's baptism, plus the one from Pennsylvania. My collection seems to be growing. I should get them back to you, but I keep forgetting."

Ken leaned in and dotted her nose with a lingering kiss. "Don't worry about that." He paused for a beat. "What happened, Kiara?"

It was time. It was time for the ultimate heart gambit—with God guiding the way. In His hands, no matter what the outcome, she knew without question she'd find a way to goodness, and grace. Such was her newfound faith.

So, Kiara took a deep breath. She looked out, at the waterline of Lake Saint Clair across the horizon, at the fiery tree leaves that heralded autumn in Michigan. Sunlight danced in and out of large, gray puffs of pure white clouds, painting the world around them in vivid, tantalizing colors.

"I think I started to answer a few questions today."

"About?"

She couldn't quite bring herself to say the words *Is my love for you what brings me to God, or is my love for God sufficient enough?* Instead, she replied, "Is my faith in God strong? Is it focused where it should be? I've discovered the answer is yes. To both."

Tired and spent, she luxuriated in the sensation of resting against him, though she finally detailed the episode that had taken place at 220 Merrill just a short time ago. Patient and steady, he watched after her, held her close, and listened.

"My friends refuse to see me in the framework of a Christian spirit; especially Drew. He couldn't see me living up to Christian principles. He said I was too enlightened and too intelligent to be drawn in by something as intangible as religion and faith. Ken, I got so mad at him, and I felt so hurt. It raised insecurities I have about my relationship with God. Stuff I need to really work on."

"Like what? What's holding you back?"

Not being good enough for the man I love so dearly.

That truth stalled in her throat. "I just...I can't quite bring myself to believe I'm worthwhile. Am I qualified to be a part of His mission?" *With you...?*

Yet again, that addenda item remained frozen inside her.

Ken quirked a finger beneath Kiara's chin and directed her gaze up to his. "Kiara, you answered that question as well. Take a close look at the past two months. Review what you intend to do from this point on, then answer that question for me. Right now. Honestly. From the gut. I want to hear you say it. *Are you qualified?*"

She could literally feel herself drift into his warmth. And he was right—despite everything between them, and despite everything rocking her world—she felt safe enough, and confident enough, to say, "Yes. Yes, I am."

Ken smiled and her heart took flight.

"Good answer," he said, stroking her cheek, causing her eyes to flutter closed on a flood of contentment. "You're human. Kiara. You'll succeed. You'll fail. The only guarantee is an imperfect trying, and that God loves each and every effort we make. Don't feel doubt because of someone else's misperceptions. Don't give other people that kind of power. That kind of thinking has been a weight on your shoulders for far too long."

"I know." She watched, enrapt, as the stroke of his hand against her neck, and shoulders, emphasized his point. Quietly, she continued. "He made me so angry. I left him feeling shocked at how angry and hurt I felt about the way he attacked people who believe in God, people who have faith."

"But you stood up to him. When you turned the tables on him, you did so by standing on your own two feet, and by relying on your own belief system rather than someone else's influence. I'd call that God inspired."

Brightness took root, expelling all else, warming her through. "Exactly. Dang but you're good, *Pastor* Ken."

"*Ken*," he corrected with a grin and a sparkle in his eyes that she loved. She wanted to just sink into him, to stay in this moment, this connectedness, forever. "In the end, no matter who, no matter what, no single person is ever going to fulfill you. At some point, we're all going to fail one another. We're going to fall short, no matter how good our intentions." He paused. "Even me."

That opened the doorway to all that lay between them—compatibility, mutual faith and trust. Love.

Kiara decided it was time to move forward, saying, "I was stubborn, and it was wrong of me to walk away from you the way I did."

"You were justified, because you were hurt. But please know, I never meant to—"

She silenced him by reaching up to stroke his lips closed. "That doesn't even need to be said," she whispered. "I know that without being told, Ken. It just...it *hit* me. Everything seemed to pile up on me, and open up old sores. My issue. Not yours. I know you were defending me—"

"Us," he clarified.

Us. The simple, two letter word slipped through her like a sweet, tempting breeze.

Ken continued. "But I blew it afterwards by showing I didn't have the kind of faith I urge everyone else to hold on to. I was going to talk with you after services today, and when you didn't show up, I honestly felt something inside me crumble. I wanted to take you home, make you breakfast, and at least *try* to explain myself. All I could think about the past couple days was having the chance to just be together outside of everything, and everyone, but each other."

Meanwhile she had suffered through that horrendous brunch. Kiara sighed out loud, sad for the emptiness they had both endured, but so very eager to make up for lost time, to build goodness anew. She sifted her fingertips through his hair and the subtle earth spice aroma of his shampoo was released. The scent tickled her nose, most intriguing...

"We need this, Kiara."

The tenor of his voice was promising, deep and rich. The power behind that statement filled her with delicious tingles. Just as quickly as it had been born, that biting ache of need she carried died in the arms of hope, and joy.

"But you have to go to the hospital."

Ken slid his fingers against hers, linking their hands together. "Not for a while yet. Will you come home with me?"

She nodded. He drew Kiara to her feet, and she

felt so light she wondered if she couldn't actually float away on the wind. Ironically, a punctuating breeze drifted against them, lifting her hair, causing a few strands to dance across her face. The look in Ken's eyes, when he reached up, and slid them back into place, made her shiver. She reached up, caressing his forearm, moving her touch up to his shoulder. She stepped close, feeling bold now about taking custody of God's gifts, and plans. So she curved a hand around his neck, drawing him down, initiating a kiss that was open, mutually receptive, moist and warm.

They sighed in unison, a pleasured punctuation mark to what Kiara considered a distinct, treasured moment of homecoming.

એન્≪

Ken hadn't even thought about the bouquet. The fact that it was the first thing Kiara's attention fixed upon when she entered his home, however, left him keenly aware. Her focus on the item opened up his portion of some of the things that needed to be said between them, for the bouquet was a silk flower replica of the arrangement Kiara had given to Barb following Woodland's Autumn Fest years ago. In fact, it resided in the same low, expansive white wicker basket, at the center of Ken's living room coffee table.

Her eyes widened in instant recognition.

Ken tried not to feel sheepish and embarrassed; he tried to maintain balance when he had been caught in a gesture of a secret homage to Barb—and to Kiara.

Her gaze darted away from the now conspicuous display. In a shy, somewhat nervous gesture, she tucked a slice of hair behind her ear and moved inside.

Grace and poise back in place, she set her purse on the floor and sat down on the couch—but after a brief look into his eyes, she reached out to touch a rust colored mum.

"This is beautiful."

Her questioning glance left Ken, a wizened 30-something, at the precipice of a blush. But he was ready for the challenge now, and he gave her a nod, meeting her gaze head-on. "It honors two of the most spectacular women I've ever known." His voice went low. "But something tells me you already know that."

Kiara blew out a soft puff of air, and diverted her eyes. "When did you make this?"

"At the end of last year." Ken joined her on the couch. This time he was the one to reach out, and he stroked the petals of a vibrant, yellow bloom. "I finally felt ready to box up a few things, and donate them to charity. I came across the basket in a storage closet."

She listened intently, watching him. Ken continued. "Barb meant to do something with the basket, but—"

"But she died a month after my visit," Kiara murmured.

Ken nodded sadly. "She ran out of time." He sighed and scrubbed a hand across his face. Exploring the memory of Barb's last days wasn't the way he would have orchestrated this particular conversation, but things needed to be said, and understood, between him and Kiara. God would do the rest. So he simply let go and released himself into the moment.

"Time came, last fall, that I started to move forward," Ken said. "I packed things away and organized my life. I tried to go on."

"You did her proud."

Ken didn't agree or disagree. Instead, he *felt*; he embraced his emotions and strove to keep his voice from wavering. "I was boxing and sorting, wanting to finally, and fully, deal with the aftershocks of her death. That's when I found the basket." He paused.

Kiara nodded.

"It brought so many things to light. I remembered how your visit touched Barb—and me. How a simple, thoughtful gesture, in the form of a fall bouquet, lifted her spirits. It made me think about you. The effortless, instant way you touch people. It's an amazing gift, Kiara." He shrugged, wondering if anything he said made much sense. Judging by the soft, tender radiance of her eyes, she understood. "In that instant, in that moment of memory and perception, I woke up again. My heart, my focus, turned to you, and all the wonderful things that you are."

"So you recreated the bouquet."

"Symbolic—and safe enough a gesture to reemerging, I suppose, since it remained private. Until now."

Kiara shook her head, looking into his eyes with an expression he could only describe as amazement. "Ken, you never, ever fail to slide into my soul like a piece of velvet."

"What a coincidence," he replied, skimming a fingertip against the outline of her jaw, then her chin. "I could say the same thing to you."

A silence stretched between them before Ken picked up the conversational ball once more. "Love is about the process of surrendering just enough of yourself to say you want to grow in unison with someone else. It's not easy, but it's real, and it fills a part of your soul, and it lasts. If you let yourself find it and if you make that surrender it return."

"I think I understand that now. Better than I ever have," Kiara answered. "I don't control this, Ken. God does. *We* do. Give me the chance. Please? Have faith and let me follow His lead and be the person I want most to be. With you."

In the pause that followed Ken's heart stuttered, then began to pound.

"You've shown me possibilities. You've helped me remember how wonderful innocence is. I've been without that kind of purity for a long, long time. You helped me realize I haven't lost it for good. You showed me the way to a God who loves me, flaws and all. I suppose I thought I could hide those blemishes from the world at large. With God, with you. I can't. And what's more? I don't have to.

"I've worn armor all my life, of one sort or another. The right look, the right persona, the right way of life, but it wasn't truly me. It wasn't real. You saw through to the heart of me; then God entered in and did the rest. He transformed me into someone different. I thought you saw that end result. I thought you believed in my strength of conviction—my rebirth. If you need assurance, let me say this: I can't—I won't put on that armor ever again. It doesn't fit anymore. It doesn't protect me at all. It never did. I want to share who I am now, with you. But you need to make that step forward as well. You need to show me I matter, and that I have a place in God's plan for your life—if you think that's even the case."

He tucked her hands into his, looking straight and deep into her eyes when he whispered, "My turn now." He paused. "Kiara, nothing you do, nothing you've done is going to change what Christ did for you. You've been influenced by the people in your life, parents who pushed you past what they felt was a meager upbringing. Your beauty, internal and external, draws people in. Your personality warms hearts and opens them wide. Your taste for beauty, in all its forms, is paramount to your job and the success you've found. You say you've made mistakes, veered off the path, let yourself be won over by glamour and material things. Name me one prophet who didn't stumble. Name one person who hasn't been tempted to do something they wouldn't ordinarily even consider."

"That's part of my point. You know my secrets, and my failings. What are yours?"

Ken shook his head. He focused on the bouquet for a moment, then on their joined hands. "The situation I've had to reason through and come to terms with is *you*, Kiara. And when I say that, I want you to take it very seriously. Don't brush it aside or ignore its impact on me. I want you to put yourself into the following scene and live it with me."

Ken focused on her intently. She watched, and waited.

"Over the past couple of years, as I got to know you, you pulled me in deeper and deeper. You enchanted me, Kiara." In an instant her face transformed from questioning to stormy. He hastened to add, "I mean that in the best possible way. Meanwhile, my wife, whom I loved beyond measure, the woman I pledged my whole life to, who possessed such beauty and such strength, began to fade. Her life dimmed as yours brightened. You filled me with vibrancy and laughter—with passion and hope. You brought me everything I most needed. I clung to every second I had with you, just as strongly as I held on to my wife as she died. Can you understand how guilty I felt? I never, ever imagined my life without her. I wanted my fifty or more years with her. I wanted a lifetime. I wanted kids, and grandkids, but that wasn't God's plan. I got angry with that at times. Anyone would. When I saw her suffering, it shattered me. I needed to find a way to deal with losing her, while at the same time, reconcile myself to the betrayal I felt in being so...so...*pulled* to you while Barb fought with every inch of her being to keep on living.

"Still, I met you and you entered my bloodstream. I haven't been the same since. I agonized over Barb. I watched her suffer and endure so much. I loved her. I *still* love her. But at the same time, I'd go to church, and I'd see you. Your vitality, your heart and your spirit—reached out and filled me up."

"I never knew. Not even for an instant—"

"How desperate I felt? How drawn I am to you?" he concluded for her.

Kiara nodded.

"Good. You weren't meant to. I hid as best I could. Then, when she died, I prayed for hours about what I felt was my heart betraying itself. That's when God provided me with the answer I sought."

"Which is?"

For emphasis he kept quiet, studying each curve and line of her face, saturating his needy heart with her beauty and soft tenderness of her jade colored eyes until he was certain he had her full focus. "He was preparing my heart, and my life, for *you*. It was Barb's time, but it wasn't *mine*. And God prepared me for you perfectly. He led you to my church where I got to know you, and understand the myriad of gifts you possess, the joy you give. No one prompted, no one pushed, you were *eager* to be part of the church. That passion made you part of my life in a very personal way. I let you in—couldn't help it. We worked side by side, and grew closer through every project we tackled. The church renovation. Working on church activities. The mission trip to Pennsylvania. You've become a partner, Kiara. Your spirit and love feeds mine. You're part of me now. No matter what's happened in either of our lives, Jesus' plan remains. That plan is *us*, Kiara. *Together*. And I promise you that we go forward together with every bit of love I have to give. It's yours. Forever."

EPILOGUE

Six Months Later

Sea waves tumbled and rumbled, a rhythmic punctuation that added life to the steamy, sun-drenched atmosphere that swept gradually through the interior of the hotel suite. Salt-tanged air swirled, tickling Kiara's senses alert, coming from the beach just beyond a set of wide open terrace doors.

Reluctantly she stirred, leaving slumber behind. She instantly found herself pulled backwards, drawn up tight against the long line of a strong, warm body. A low growl of approval came from the spot next to her in bed, as did a huskily spoken: "Good morning, Mrs. Lucerne."

She turned, sliding against Ken. She beamed when she came upon sleep-weighted, cocoa-colored eyes, a tumble of thick brown hair, and a smile of greeting that melted every bone in her body.

"Good morning," she replied, snuggling against him.

Ken lifted up to glance at the clock. "Unreal. It's already eleven o'clock in the morning? That's *not* possible. I'm completely losing track of time."

Kiara stroked her fingertips against the mild, abrasive stubble that shadowed his chin. "That's what the island of St. Thomas is for. Besides, sleeping in from time to time is a supreme indulgence and luxury. Don't knock it."

They drew together in a slow, rich kiss that went on and on and on and moved inexorably from lazy ease to fire and electricity. Kiara continued to melt, and she sighed, surrendering her all to the arms and heart of the man who rolled above her. He moved just far enough away to stroke back her hair, and study her eyes.

"Speaking of indulgence and luxury," he said, "we owe them."

"*Them* meaning Daveny and Collin."

Ken nodded.

Kiara giggled. "Yep. We sure do. They're experts at pampering."

A wooden ceiling fan spun lazily above them stirring air that already leaned toward pleasantly humid. Light increased, beaming chunky, thick rays that angled inward through the open doorway and the window above their bed. Sunshine glinted upon a band of yellow gold on the third finger of Kiara's left hand and her soul spun in a timeless dance of joy. Opting away from a traditional engagement ring and diamond, she told Ken what she wanted most were simple, matching wedding bands bearing a subtle, geometric design. Inside, both were inscribed: Ken & Kiara, April 3, United by God—in love.

Kiara's contentment lifted, growing until it was off the record charts. She studied the piece for, oh, about the millionth time since Ken had placed it on her finger during a candlelight ceremony held amidst a bevy of family and friends at Woodland Church just a few days ago.

Picking up the thread of their conversation, Kiara

continued. "I still can't believe they did this for us. I mean, all expenses paid? For a *week*? In the *Caribbean*?"

"Quite the honeymoon," Ken remarked huskily, his voice rough and sexy. When he nibbled on her neck, and shoulders, his warm breath gliding against her skin, Kiara went so brainless she nearly forgot what in the world they were talking about…

She murmured, through shivers, "All Daveny said is, *'I never had a sister, 'til I had you. You're my family. We just want you to enjoy it.'* I think we're fulfilling our part of the bargain."

Ken just laughed at that woeful understatement, continuing his nuzzling explorations. At present, he focused on her jaw. Next came the ticklish underside of her chin. Kiara closed her eyes, lifted to him, and sighed with delight.

"I'd have to agree with that assessment," he finally murmured.

They kissed once more and his flavor filled her; his textures and tastes blended with her own, becoming a whole unit—a spirit of one. Never had she experienced such pure and undiluted happiness.

Sliding way, Ken exclaimed, "Uh-oh…I almost forgot. I have a final wedding gift for my bride."

His bride. His. She'd never tire of that moniker. Kiara smiled with expectation, drawing the pale blue cotton sheet against her body as she sat up, and watched him root through his suitcase. From within he pulled out a small, soft-sided package wrapped in white and gold complete with a frilly wedding-esque bow. When he slipped back into bed and handed her the gift, Kiara just looked at him, knowing her happiness telegraphed straight through from her heart, to her eyes, to him. She nibbled on her lower lip, hiding an inner bout of laughter—because she had one last secret gift for him stashed away in her luggage as well.

Tearing into the wrapping, giving an appropriate 'Oooh' and 'Ahhh' to the packaging, she stopped short, silent and stunned when she saw what resided within the folds of paper.

It was a six pack of handkerchiefs, complete with monogram: *KAJL*

Kiara gaped, covering her trembling mouth. Obviously puzzled, Ken watched her. In confusion, he started to reach out, seeming to want to question her reaction, and perhaps reassure—but Kiara dashed out of bed before he could take hold of her hand, or get a word out. She tossed on a satin robe that was part of her wedding trousseau and made for her suitcase, moving fast to pull out a wrapped gift of her own that featured a small note card on top that was addressed to Ken.

Her husband.

The reality still caused her lips to tremble, her eyes to fill...

Wordless, she offered it to him—a smaller, soft-sided package quite similar to his.

Ken already smiled, pulling on her hand until she was back in bed with him. He sat up and propped his back against the headboard, watching her with teasing suspicion. "Is this what I think it is?"

Kiara couldn't hazard a reply. Her heart was too full, her throat too tight. A haze of tears blurred his image, but never, ever eradicated it completely. First, he opened and read the card. Then, his eyes went to smoke and silk, all things attractively, protectively, lovingly male... Message read, he looked into her eyes;

she was sure they sparkled with tears, and he simply nodded his agreement to the words she had inscribed within.

'Ken — my heart is yours. In happiness and in tears. All my love always — Kiara'

He pulled off wrapping paper, adding it to the pile that now decorated their puffy, down comforter of pale green. His smile spread fast and strong at what he found. "How appropriate," he murmured, watching Kiara slide a fingertip quickly beneath her eyes. Inside rested three handkerchiefs, complete with monogram: *KJL*

"I finally remembered to return them," she whispered, moved and overcome.

"So," Ken said, lifting up the one on top and holding it out to her. "Yours or mine?"

Kiara moved close and wrapped herself around him contentedly. In decision, she chose the top one from the package that had come from Ken — then accepted the one he offered as well — the one of his which she had just returned. "How about *both*?"

Ken laughed, and held her tight. "Sounds perfect to me, angel. Just perfect."

Hearts
Communion

Hearts Communion Dedication

This book is dedicated to the grace of God that is
revealed through one simple, yet powerful gift: the gift
of family.

1

Jeremy Edwards's cell phone came to life. A vibration sizzled against his hip, and as he unclipped his BlackBerry, the display screen lit up with an incoming text:

HELP! Ur nephew is raging with 101 fever. Can u pick him up from daycare n keep him 4 a while? Txt, don't call. Im in class. DESPERATE! APPRECIATE! C

Jeremy, JB to everyone who knew him best, re-read the missive from his brother, Collin. Collin's wife, Daveny, was out of town, pitching a corporate landscaping project in southern Ohio. Collin would be teaching his high school English class for another— Jeremy flicked his wrist and quick-checked his watch— two hours or so, depending on student demands.

So he stopped painting freshly installed drywall and stepped off the ladder, calling out to one of the crewmen at work on the task. "Greg, I'm gone for a couple hours. Tell Mindy I'll be back later tonight to install the dishwasher for her."

"Will do. See ya, JB."

Gotta love flexibility, Jeremy thought with honest gratitude. Leaving behind a living room buzzing with remodeling activity, he went to the kitchen of the modest, three-bedroom bungalow his construction company was helping to renovate. *Gratis*. There he grabbed his leather jacket from the spot where he had draped it over a chair at the dining table. After sliding it on, he texted his "yes" to Collin's request and hit the send button.

The project he currently spearheaded was part of an effort to give back to his hometown, especially as summer construction activity slowed down and a fiery Michigan autumn bent toward winter. That fact drove itself home as soon as Jeremy stepped out the back door of the kitchen and found himself buffeted by a stiff, biting wind. He stuffed his hands in his coat pockets, lowering his head as he jogged to his pickup truck.

He auto-started the vehicle, then his thoughts zeroed in on Jeffrey, his nearly three-year-old nephew. Jeremy grinned to himself. He was happy to help Collin. After all, Jeremy absolutely doted on his nephew—and everyone else in his family.

Climbing into the cab of his truck was a welcome relief from the elements. Before leaving, he pulled out his phone once again and performed a location search on Sunny Horizons Day Care Center. He had a vague idea of where the facility was located, but had never been there.

Navigation in place, he backed down the bumpy driveway of Mindy Nather's home, frowning at the cracks he saw in the asphalt.

"Needs work," he muttered, driving toward the business district of Saint Clair Shores. Meanwhile, he mentally mapped out crews, supplies and the time necessary to repair the driveway, tacking that aspect of the job onto the living room and dining room renovations, which were nearly complete. He used downtime at a stoplight to open up a pack of cashews and pour a few into his mouth.

Crunching the snack, he shook out some more and moved forward, following traffic to an area of the city that featured a number of stand-alone retail buildings. Behind them were neighborhoods full of nice homes, still-green grass and trees gone spindly and barren. JB munched on more cashews, chewing while he kept watch for the address of Jeffrey's daycare center. According to technology, he was getting close.

Sure enough, a minute or two later he spotted a wooden sign featuring a rainbow, a large sun full of rays, and the words *Sunny Horizons* painted in a variety of bold, primary colors. The moniker resided on a patch of grass in front of a well-maintained ranch-style home crafted of red brick that had been converted to commercial use.

Finishing up his get-me-through-to-a-late-dinner protein boost, Jeremy tossed the wrapper into a cup holder and turned into the parking lot. He brought the truck to a stop, thinking about his nephew. Poor Jeffrey. He'd take him straight home to Collin's place where the boy could rest up and recover in his own bed.

But what, exactly, should somebody give a sick two-year-old? How much of that liquid medicine stuff would Jeffrey need? While he considered, and made plans to call Collin on that count, JB walked past the window line of the facility and glanced inside

That's when his focus sharpened on the scene inside, and his footsteps came to an abrupt halt. A thought slipped into place with compelling impact: *What a gorgeous woman.* Long blonde hair fell forward in layers, framing a face that featured fair skin and expressive, baby-blue eyes. The straight, thick strands swung as she moved from place to place, spotting pre-school kids currently playing Twister, which caused his insides to spark. Jeans and an aqua colored sweater showed off a trim figure. She laughed easily, talking the kids through difficult moves and exclaiming when players tumbled and fell.

Quick as a blink he watched the lovely lady shift focus. She turned away from the Twister competition and whisked up one of the smaller toddlers who lingered shyly near her legs. Lovely Lady stepped into a clear space. Face alight with pleasure, she spun the toddler, who seemed to laugh and enjoy it just as much as her female charge.

In fact, the sensation was contagious. Jeremy smiled in response to the pair.

And I'm still riveted to the sidewalk. He silently chastised himself, performing a mental shake that jostled him back to the moment at hand. *Stay on point, JB! Jeffrey. Nephew. Sick kid in need of help.*

He approached the entryway and stepped inside. But rescue mission or not, he looked forward to meeting the woman.

2

Monica Kittelski moved with long-honed ease through a sea of bustling children. She automatically dodged bodies, an obstacle course of shoes, socks, toys, even spinner boards that were being used to aid in a raucous game of Twister. Unaffected by the stream of movement and cacophony, she made her way toward the man who had just entered the lobby.

Jeremy, she thought. *Jeremy Edwards. This must be Jeffrey's uncle.* Collin had called a few minutes ago saying his brother would be picking up the sick toddler.

The noise level was off the charts, but the racket didn't even make him blink. Stepping up, already extending her hand, she gave him an inner nod of respect for that fact. He accepted the gesture, and Monica found herself pleased by the calloused texture and warmth of his skin against hers.

"I'm Jeremy Edwards."

She squelched a grin. "And I'm impressed." He simply arched a brow and waited, looking around, likely for his nephew. "You haven't even cringed yet."

His focus zeroed in on her, and Monica was caught off-guard by the sly, playful curve of his lips — the sparkle in his eyes that ticked against her nerve endings. The lips were full and expressive. *Nice.* Her heart rate shot up, and a fluttery, tingling sensation washed through her body.

"No worries. I'm not *quite* a rookie."

Monica smiled, and so did he. "I've seen many a man stagger to their knees upon entering the bedlam of afternoon game time. I'm Monica Kittelski. The owner."

"Hello, Monica Kittelski. Daveny raves about you. And I won't be staggering any time soon. I'm used to kid chaos, so I guess I'm not just *any* man."

"Guess not," she sassed right back. "Thanks for getting here so quickly."

"Not a problem. Glad I could help out."

The playful spice of his personality dissolved into familial love and protection when he caught sight of little Jeffrey shuffling out of Monica's office, holding hands with Deborah Nielson, the co-owner and facility director.

Jeremy knelt to Jeffrey's level and opened his arms. "Come here, Chief."

It was those little things that told the full story here—the way Jeremy embraced Jeffrey—fevered kid or not—and the low, tender tone of voice.

Listless, Jeffrey snuffled, his chin trembling as he sank into his uncle's embrace. Jeremy lifted him up, and then turned his attention back to Monica. Residual tenderness lived in his eyes.

"Chief?" Monica asked, charmed by the nickname.

Jeremy nuzzled Jeffrey's plump, overly red cheek. Jeffrey seemed to fight tears, but a few spilled nonetheless, trailing against his skin. "Oh, man, buddy, you're on broil. Let's get you home." He peered up at Monica. "It's kind of a long story." Over Jeffrey's head, he delivered a lingering, steady look. "I'll have to tell you about it some time."

She could only hope. "I'd like that."

Jeremy made to leave, moving between the two plastic floor mats where kids currently called out and contorted like pretzels. He carefully stepped his way toward a low-slung wooden coat rack with small, square storage cubbies on top.

"Twister gives them the chance to learn colors, flexibility and left versus right. It's the best of all worlds." The teacher in Monica came to the fore as she led the way, or, maybe it was a touch of nervous chatter meant to deflect her intuitive reaction to the man. Monica pushed that idea aside for later consideration.

He glanced over his shoulder and their eyes tagged. "Best of all worlds is also that spinning session I watched you perform through the window a few minutes ago. Wish I'd've had more teachers like you growing up."

Monica's poised, smooth footsteps nearly ended in a tumble at his comment. Her heart actually stuttered.

"I'll just get his coat," Jeremy said, evidently unfazed by her startled silence and affected reaction.

"There's a plastic tub as well, right above it, with his afternoon snack." Monica glided a gentle hand against Jeffrey's back. The toddler took a deep, shaky breath and stuffed his thumb in his mouth, closing his eyes. "Poor pumpkin. He sure seems relieved to see you. He's been hit pretty hard. Here, don't disturb him. You're just taking him to the car." Monica pulled down his coat and went to work. "We'll tuck this around him nice and snug."

She lifted the hood up and over his head for additional protection. As she ministered, Jeremy's eyes went wide. "Houston? We have a problem."

Monica looked up at him. Boy, did he have great—no, make that *awesome*—dark brown eyes. "What's that?"

"I don't have a car seat. Oh, man. Guess I bragged too soon. I *am* a kid rookie."

More like a deer caught in the headlights, Monica thought with compassion. He started to look around a bit frantically, so she didn't wait long before coming to the rescue. "Know why they pay me the big bucks?"

He chuckled. "You know? I'd love to knock that one right out of the ballpark, but I'll refrain."

She rolled her eyes, but didn't restrain a grin. He was cute—in so many ways. "Because I'm prepared. Stay here. I'll be right back."

Monica went to her office and opened a spacious utility closet where she stored any number of odds and ends—among them a couple of ready-to-roll car seats. It paid to think ahead; in her line of business, stuff like this happened all the time. She lifted one and rejoined Jeremy, who looked at her as though she had transformed into Houdini himself.

"You just earned every word of praise Daveny ever spoke about you."

"Charmer." Monica scanned the activities taking place in the great room. Satisfied the kids were adequately supervised by Deborah and a trio of teachers, she gestured toward the exit. "I'll help you buckle it in. You just take care of the bambino."

"Thanks. Really."

Stepping outside, a brisk wind cut straight through her. Fall, she realized with chagrin, was giving way to winter without much of a fight. Jeremy unlocked his pickup with the keyless entry and auto-started the engine. Monica prepped the car seat. Fortunately he stood behind her, with Jeffrey snuggled in his arms, and he blocked the wind.

That is, until she straightened and turned around. A large chunk of hair skittered straight across her face. She reached up to slide it out of the way and immediately noticed she held Jeremy's full attention. The smoky heat of his gaze did delicious things to her insides; suddenly it didn't feel quite so cold anymore.

"All set," she said. "Just settle him in and drop the safety bar into place. It'll lock right up, and he should be good to go."

Jeremy didn't move right away. He gave a tiny, almost imperceptible shake of his head. "I'll bring this back tomorrow. Seriously, I owe you. I got the call from Collin and just took off. Didn't even think about how I'd get him home."

"No problem at all; that's what I keep this around for. I'll see you tomorrow."

Those deep-set, mahogany eyes fixed on her. When he smiled, it felt like the first rays of sun at daybreak. She took a deep breath and turned, hugging her arms to her midsection as he moved to leave. The wind blasted against her once again.

"Count on it, Monica." The chattering branches of nearby trees and tumbling leaf noise nearly drowned out his answer, but her name on his lips warmed her insides once more.

3

The next morning, Jeremy climbed into his truck and shut the door. Glancing to the right, he caught sight of the car seat that rode shotgun. He grinned like a fool, starting the engine and cranking the heat.

His timing, admittedly, was deliberate. At just after 10 AM, he wouldn't be missed at the project site for another hour or so. He had a bit of that precious autumn-into-winter flextime to spare. Meanwhile, the morning rush of parents dropping off their kids at Sunny Horizons would most likely have dwindled by now. He hoped he might be able to take advantage of some additional one-on-one time with Monica Kittelski when he returned her gear. The idea left him buoyed.

Sure enough, when he arrived, the semi-circle drive leading to the facility was empty, with a handful of cars lined up neatly in a lot to the rear. Jeremy parked and walked inside, car seat in tow. He was greeted promptly by the smiling staff member who had brought Jeffrey out of Monica's office yesterday. What was her name again…?

"Mr. Edwards, right?"

She offered her hand, and he shifted the car seat to accept the gesture. "Hi. Jeremy, please."

"Jeremy, I'm Deborah. Nice to meet you."

"Same here." Deborah was tall and slim, with

short, curly salt-and-pepper hair—maybe in her late forties. She seemed, by nature, a bubbly and warm-hearted woman. He couldn't help but return her positive energy, though as discreetly as possible, he searched for Monica.

"I'm sure Monica will appreciate the quick return. I'll let her know you're here."

"That'd be great. I'd like to thank her." He paused a beat. "Ah, for the loaner."

Was he just imagining Deborah's sly grin, those knowing eyes? She turned and walked away—headed to a doorway on the left of a short hallway. Moments later, out came Monica. Seeing her again hit him just as hard today as it had yesterday. Sunshine hair was held back by a brown clip, which naturally drew his eye to her slender neck, to the soft angles of her face. She entered the room, full of supple, alluring grace, and her energy instantly filled the space. Those clear, blue eyes brimmed with warmth. Jeremy took her in, and savored, enrapt.

"Jeremy. Hi."

"Hi, Monica." He indicated his delivery. "Where can I put this for you?"

She gestured in the direction of her office. "Right over here. Come on back."

He followed her.

"Are you in a hurry? Can I offer you a cup of coffee?"

An excuse to stay for a bit? You bet. "I'm in no rush. Coffee'd be nice."

"Least I can do since you returned the car seat so fast."

"Trust me—the speed of return is fear-induced."

"Oh? How's that?"

"Frankly, I couldn't stand the idea of someone getting stuck like I almost did. You really came to the rescue yesterday. I appreciate it."

"No thanks necessary. It's my pleasure."

Monica took the seat from his custody and settled it on the floor of the storage closet. That accomplished, she moved to a coffeemaker on the credenza behind her desk, but not before giving him a look that pushed heat and adrenaline through his heart. Once again, her sense of innate grace piqued his interest, and admiration. The moment between them lingered a bit. "How do you like your coffee?"

"Black is good. Thanks."

Jeremy settled on a small, brown leather couch positioned beneath the window. The window was closed in deference to a chilly autumn morning, but sunlight dappled the space of her office. As Monica poured two cups of coffee, he paid attention. Third finger, left hand, no ring. A vibration of satisfaction skimmed against his insides.

After passing him a rich-smelling mug, she sat down behind her desk. "So Jeffrey is still under the weather, I hear."

"Yeah. The fever broke last night, but Collin's not taking any chances. He took the day off to be home with him since Dav's still out of town."

While they talked, a myriad of items captured his attention, filling in bits and pieces about the woman before him. First came the framed photograph on her desk of Monica, surrounded by a group of people he assumed were her family. Next, there was a small, crystal bowl full of colorful jellybeans that rested on the corner of her desk. Nearby, her steaming mug declared: *Teaching: It ain't for sissies*. Jeremy nearly laughed aloud.

In juxtaposition, and curiously enough, a porcelain rendering of a ballerina, *en pointe*, claimed center stage of her credenza, just to the right of the coffee machine. The art piece drew his steady focus. It was intricate and compelling in its detail. On the wall behind the piece hung a framed print of a ballet scene, identified at the bottom as *The Dance Class* by Edgar Degas.

Hmm. So, family was important enough for memorializing, and dance was a reoccurring theme. Interesting. Monica tracked the direction of his gaze, turning in her chair to join his study of the classic painting.

"I got that at the Detroit Institute of Arts a few years back, when they had an exhibition of his work."

"I gather you're a fan of art and ballet?"

"You might say."

Jeremy's eyes narrowed in speculation at her evasive reply and the deflective posture she presented. Deflection didn't sit well with him when this pervasive longing to get to know her better reached in so far, and so deep. So he kept the thread moving. "The ballet part's not surprising to me."

"Oh? Why would that be?"

"Because I've been sitting here, watching you, and noticing the way you move." Her attention pinged to him, and froze. "You're effortless."

"That's very kind of you to say." Her fingertips, now resting against the handle of her mug, trembled just a tad. She looked down, her eyes veiled; the gesture struck him as charmingly shy.

"That's very kind of me to *mean*." He sipped from his mug to give her time to recover from being startled. And provoked. Color heightened her cheeks. Jeremy sipped deep, his lips curving against the edge of his mug.

Monica straightened, regrouping. "You know, at this point, I think turnabout is only fair play."

"Meaning?"

"Meaning you've figured out a few things about me. It's my turn to find out a few things about you."

Jeremy knew his answering look was wolfish—and teasing—but he couldn't help it. Inexplicably, he longed to nudge at her a bit. Push. "What would you like to know, Monica?"

She leaned back in her chair, her brows lifted in challenge. She was undeterred, and back to center. All Jeremy could think is: *Wow. This is fun.*

"You have the ability to be pretty flexible with the work schedule. What do you do, Jeremy Edwards?"

He relented, setting his mug aside for the moment. "First off, my friends call me JB. I own and run a construction company."

"Really. Wow."

"It's not any more of a 'wow' than what you've created right here." But, he did appreciate her sincerity. "I'm entering the slow season—which allows me a bit of freedom. In the spring and summer, I never would have been able to pull off what I did yesterday. Anything else?"

"Yep. What does the 'B' in JB stand for?"

"Blaise. My middle name."

No mask fell into place; no guard shaded her eyes. Intrigue and interest sparked to life. "That's a really great middle name."

"You think so?"

She nodded readily.

"I always hated it. Too stuffy."

"Not in the least, though I think JB fits you better."

"Yeah?"

"Yeah. It's catchy. More fun."

There is so *much potential here, so much more I'd love to explore.* But Jeremy wasn't inclined to move forward too quickly, and risk halting their forward progress, despite rampant chemistry. Besides, sadly, it was time to get to work. He stood, and Monica followed suit. "I've got a jobsite calling, so I'd better hit the road." He took note of her silence, the discreet way she studied him. She followed him to the exit. Before leaving, Jeremy faced her, itching to reach out, to touch her. "But, if you don't mind, I'll be seeing you again soon, Monica."

All she did was smile; the launch of it was slow and tempting. That alone gave Jeremy plenty of motivation to follow through.

❧❦

As if he needed motivation.

He secured wood molding along the ceiling line of Nather's living room, worked with installation crews who laid new flooring in the kitchen—a cream-colored, shiny ceramic—and he helped measure and cut floorboard trim. All the while his mind drifted. Thoughts of Monica filled him, a breeze of sorts— unseen, but powerful. He fielded calls and arranged details to line up a contract crew to repair the driveway, and she even invaded that simple task. She worked on him like an angel's call.

Late in the afternoon, his cell phone rang. He glanced at the caller ID display. Collin. "How's the Chief?" Jeremy greeted without preamble.

"On the mend, big time. In fact, and I say this with all the love I have for my son, I need a break, bro. One hour—two max. Basketball. Tonight. You in?"

"Seriously? I'd love to, but who's going to take care of—"

"Lemme head you off at the pass, Bro. Our beloved sister, Caroline, is sitting with Jeffrey." Collin snorted. "Trust me. She made it abundantly clear I owe her big time for a simple, yet mandatory, two hour window of sanity. Sisters. You know I love 'em."

JB kept from laughing, but it was a difficult proposition. Collin's tone was desperate. He seemed pretty frazzled by assuming the role of Mr. Mom, but that didn't keep Jeremy from wanting to needle his brother. "You're being a snark. About our sibling, no less."

"My *snark*, as you so *aptly* put it, is *justified*. Caroline's at the control switch, and she's lovin' it. I took Jeffrey out to get a hamburger. I figured a lunch together would be fun, since he felt great and had so much energy to spare. Big mistake. I swear, by the end of the meal we had the wait staff cringing and twitching with nerves because he was so rambunctious."

That only caused Jeremy to grin. "You're embellishing. To get your way. It's working, too."

"Four on four, JB," he growled. "The school gym's available tonight, and everyone else can make it. So, last chance and final answer before I move up the family ladder and ask Marty or Phil. You interested in a basketball sweat-fest?"

Jeremy's introspective, muddled mood perked up fast. He could use the time with Collin to perform additional reconnaissance on Monica. Jarred by the thought, Jeremy's brows pulled together, and his grip on the phone tightened. This was ridiculous. He was rapidly becoming obsessed. "Yeah, sure. I'm in. When?"

"Seven?"

"See you at the gym."

∂∾∽

The shoe-squeaks, basketball dribbling and game-chatter that took place in the middle of the Saint Clair High School gym vied for Jeremy's wavering focus. Distractions moved against him continuously in the form of soft, fluid images. And those images created a reoccurring theme—the face of a lovely, blonde-haired lady with luminous eyes.

In fact, he didn't even pay attention to—

The basketball smacked him right in the stomach, his fumbling catch completely out of character. Generally, he cleaned up the floorboards with these guys. Collin, his teammate who lobbed the pass, now called time out.

"Hey, bro," he said on approach, "here's some advice: How about putting some D in defense instead of distraction?"

During the pause, they went to their duffle bags and pulled out water bottles. Collin sat on the bleachers, and Jeremy followed suit.

Collin leaned on his knees and turned to his brother. "What's up with you tonight?"

Jeremy ignored the question. "What's the intel on Monica Kittelski?"

Collin looked at him with drawn brows, and he shrugged. In tandem, they downed some water before

Collin answered. "She's great at her job. Beyond that I don't know a whole lot. Why?"

Jeremy grinned.

Collin groaned. "No. No, no and no. Really?"

Jeremy tossed back another deep swig of water. He grinned again.

Collin openly stared.

"I enjoyed the rescue operation, and not just because it took care of the Chief, and not just because it left you owing me. By the way, boy are you ever racking up the family debts, pal."

"Like I'm afraid of *that* development. And?"

"And she's cute. She's sassy. I like her. Plus, she's got that whole Reese Witherspoon thing going on, which is enough to make any man—"

"Aw, JB! Back it up a second. You're talking like that about my son's daycare provider for heaven's sake. You get that, right?" But then the mano-a-mano teasing ended. Collin paused, seeming to test out the flavor of this conversation.

Jeremy waited. And waited.

"I can only add this." Collin rested his elbows on his knees and faced Jeremy directly. "She's pretty much married to Sunny Horizons. It's her baby in a way. Her world."

"I can relate."

"Yeah. You can. You created and built Edwards Construction from the ground up. You sweat the details, and the quality you provide, just like she does."

"Nothing wrong with that."

"Nope. Not a thing. Unless it's the *only* thing." Collin ended there, pointedly. "For her, it might be."

Jeremy studied his brother, pondering that

statement. "Can I take Jeffrey to daycare tomorrow?"

"Oh, man." Collin shook his head; a huge grin spread across his face. "You've got it bad, JB."

"Hey, maybe I'm just magnanimous. Maybe I just want to help out my brother while his wife's out of town. I'm awesome like that."

Collin snorted. "Yeah? Keep sellin' that line. You might get a taker."

"I'm serious about taking him in."

Collin paused. "Sure. If you want to." Another pause ticked past. "But Daveny comes back tomorrow night. What'll ya' do then, with no more Uncle-JB-to-the-rescue cards to play?"

Nonplussed, Jeremy lifted a shoulder and tossed his water bottle back into his duffle bag, reclaiming the basketball so they could resume the game. "I'm good at improvising, Coll. Always have been. I think on the fly."

Collin swiped the ball from his grasp. "Yeah? Then fly *this*." He heaved the ball—but this time, Jeremy snatched it out of the air like a pro and hit the court.

Head and heart now firmly engaged in the basketball game, Jeremy came alive. Team Edwards ended the night victorious by a score of twenty-one to fourteen.

4

Monica's evening ended at eight o'clock when little Tracey Michael bounded up to her at the conclusion of the weekly dance class that Monica taught for preschoolers at the Saint Clair Shores Community Center.

"Bye-bye, Miss Monica! See you next week!" Red curls bouncing, the effervescent four-year-old hugged Monica's legs and Monica chuckled, rubbing Tracey's back gently. The aspiring ballerina wore a pink one-piece, pink tights, and pink ballet slippers. Monica dressed much the same, except in a shade of pale blue.

"Your timing was awesome today. You were on the mark, honey. Keep up the great work, OK?"

Tracey beamed at the praise, and left Monica feeling like a million bucks.

Tracey skipped to her waiting mom, who waved goodbye to Monica as she linked hands with her daughter, and they left the building. Almost immediately, silence rode in.

Always the silence.

Monica sighed, but bullied her outlook into more positive territory.

After all, the kids might not be hers, but the life she crafted brought her close enough. No mistake, this could never be as fulfilling, never as important and satisfying as having her own children might have been, but this was close enough.

It had to be.

"Stop," she muttered sharply. Resolved, she pushed through the blackness, the longing, and forced herself forward. By now, this was standard operating procedure. She gathered her stereo and a white canvas carryall. Emblazoned on the front was the word *Dance*, crafted of carefully stitched, multi-colored sequins. The bag was a gift from a student she had taught years ago named Kim Chavis. Kim would probably be in 7th or 8th grade by now.

Sighing at the thought, Monica walked outside and took in a deep, satisfying breath. Fireplace smoke added zesty spice to the air; stars laced the ink-black sky above. Night wrapped around her, and she felt soothed.

Until she thought of Jeremy.

Monica stashed her dance class supplies in the trunk of her car and climbed in, starting the drive home. *What a great guy*, she thought. He was spirited, flirtatious, and handsome in that strong, provocative construction-worker way of his. His foundation? Family. That much she knew from her interactions with Daveny. The Edwards's family was large, and extremely close-knit.

Large.

Monica drove, and tried to ignore the bite of longing one small word could inspire when coupled with a second small word: *family*.

She pressed her lips together, opting to crank up the radio rather than continue that train of thought. Minutes later, she coasted her car to a stop in the driveway that led to her ranch-style home. She unlocked the trunk, smiling at the happy whoops and barking that came from inside.

"Coming, Toby," she said on a laugh, her arms full of gear once more. She fumbled a bit to unlock the back door then slipped inside. She barely had time to safely settle the stereo. Toby, her chocolate lab, was all over her, bounding and bouncing, sniffing and making all kinds of low, throaty noises while he circled her and reared up to gain attention.

"OK, OK! Let me get into the house, you goon!"

As if he cared. He head-butted, he licked, and Monica loved every second of his attention. Toby did a decent job of keeping that deafening silence, the sad bitterness, at bay. Dogs were great like that. All they needed, and wanted, was *you*.

Monica walked through her darkened house, flipping on lights as she went. She loved living here but, particularly at night, shadows crept in from all around. Emptiness filled the space like a haunting refrain. At that point, Toby's companionship and unconditional affection touched her heart, and kept her from wallowing.

Toby followed, still nudging and pushing. Monica knew the drill. A dog walk called. Immediately, in fact. So she didn't bother changing out of her dance ensemble. On dance nights, a neighbor walked Toby at lunchtime, but once she got home, late hour or not, Monica didn't mind the time spent in his company.

She remained bundled within a heavy, soft wool coat and grabbed Toby's leash. The instant he heard the jingle, he charged for the back door. Once he was next to her, he sat like a perfect, begging gentleman, ready and waiting.

Monica sneered at him, scratching his head, giving

his sides a firm, loving rub. "Yeah. Like I believe this attitude."

She latched him up, grabbed a plastic bag from her back-door stash and began their walk around the block of homes that made up her quiet, well-tended neighborhood.

The rhythm of walking gave her time to think and reason things through.

She was filled with longings. On a number of levels. Jeremy touched off a domino reaction in her heart and in her mind. Some of the energy generated from those falling chips elicited red flags. Danger warnings.

Strangely enough, despite their brief interactions, she couldn't form a retreat. She didn't want to. Getting to know Jeremy would be fun. Crisp air, steady motion and time to think helped her sort that one right out. Yep. There was absolutely no harm to be found in exploring a mutually pleasing relationship.

That is, if Jeremy followed through on that tempting promise from earlier in the day.

❧

Boy, did he.

The next morning Jeremy entered the facility, with a fully recovered Jeffrey in custody.

"Hey there, JB," she greeted.

He sidled her a look. The quirk of his lips let her know clearly he enjoyed her use of the nickname. He helped Jeffrey out of his coat. "Hey yourself, Jellybean."

She laughed, taken aback by the slightly audacious reply. "Wait a minute. Jellybean?"

Jeffrey tended to, JB reached inside the pocket of that same, supple, somewhat distressed leather jacket from yesterday and pulled out a bag of the candy. It was her very favorite. He stepped close and handed it over. "I noticed the supply on your desk yesterday. Figured you might enjoy a refill."

"Well you get big points for continuing to be an awfully good charmer. Jellybeans are my weakness, I admit it."

"Want to know what mine is?"

That playful spark, the absurdly tempting magnetism he displayed had her skin tingling, her tummy fluttering. "I shudder to think."

"Coffee, of course. Charm, by the way, is the blessing and the curse of the Irish, land of my ancestors."

"So's blarney," Monica retorted, which made Jeremy laugh deeply. "Feel free to have a seat in my office. I'll be right there after I help Deborah set up some art supplies for the kids."

"You sure I'm not keeping you?"

"Positive. Go on in. Make yourself comfortable."

Monica walked to a supply cabinet in the main room. She pulled out a stack of paper, and several plastic containers of water-based paints. She carried the supplies to a group of long tables and set them out, energized by the idea of spending some time with Jeremy before they had to move forward into the day. In passing, Deborah caught her eye and had no problem addressing Monica with a satisfied smirk, and an arched brow. Monica clucked her tongue and laid out materials so the kids could paint. But she blushed, too, muttering, "Oh, grow up."

"You first," Deborah retorted, off to start ushering

the pre-K kids into place.

Monica returned to her office, and, bless his heart, Jeremy had already poured them cups of coffee.

"So. You've already pegged me as the charming Irishman who's full of blarney, eh?"

"The evidence doesn't lie." She absorbed his interested gaze with a smooth smile that belied the way his attention worked through her system. "But, since I'm Polish, I'm bowing out of the whole ethic stereotype and mythology thing."

His brows went up. The two mugs remained suspended in his grip. "That does it."

"Does what?"

"Polish. Don't bow out quite yet. We have to go to Polonia. We *have* to."

"Since we've just met, and I highly doubt you're offering me a trip to my motherland, I can only assume you mean the restaurant. The one in Hamtramck." Eagerly he nodded. Monica didn't fight a laugh. "I'm Hamtramck born and raised. That place is an institution in my family."

"When's the last time you were there? What did you get?"

He was enthralled. He was salivating. He was the epitome of winsome appeal. Plus, there was something irresistible about watching a well-sculpted man doing battle with his stomach. For a precious moment, Monica savored having the upper hand, and she smirked at him. "Stop it. You're seriously about to drool."

"Yeah, I am. So what? Quit stalling and spill. What'd you have?"

"I had Polish smoked sausage and kraut." Then, she became just as distracted. In fact, she quickly warmed to the topic. "Oh! And I had that really great appetizer they serve—the cucumbers, onion and dill in sour cream. Do you know the one I mean?"

Jeremy was the one who smirked now. He set the mugs aside then stepped in close. He reached up and lightly stroked the corner of her mouth, and all things cool and temperate went up in smoke. "Careful. You're seriously about to drool."

Monica was lost. Suddenly she was assaulted by cravings—for food—for surcease to the hungers she felt—especially her hunger to build on this wild, heady connection to Jeremy Blaise Edwards...

"I think we have to go there. Together."

His statement left her silent, and blinking. "Ah."

"Get back to me on that. You're lost at the moment."

"Lost in a world of food." She longed to moisten her lips without being obvious about, well, moistening her lips. Attraction had completely taken over, but she shouldered that reaction to the side and met him in the middle of the field, saying, "I could be cajoled. I suppose, though, I should complete the tale by letting you know my last Polonia dining experience came about as the result of what turned into a monumentally unsuccessful blind date. How about you?"

Jeremy didn't move away by a single trace, not even a fraction of a millimeter. That fact left Monica swept through by a tantalizing, melting *pull*.

"I was there for a friend's birthday celebration. I had their beef and cheese pierogies. Like you, I indulged in that wickedly good cucumber dish. So, all things considered, I'm thinking we're more than compatible. In fact, I'd be about willing to bet tonight's friendly poker pot that our first date would be far from unsuccessful."

His smile lit her nerve endings and set them on fire. So she shored up her wiles. "Careful, there, hotshot. You're making some pretty strong assumptions. After all, I haven't even accepted yet."

He gave her a mischievous grin that made her shiver. "Maybe. But you will. I have faith." He sealed the deal by gliding his hand against hers, and taking hold. Teasing ended. He went serious, but just as intense, and ten times as provocative. "Are we on, Monica? You game?"

Oh yes. Yes, indeed. But she schooled her features into calm, unruffled lines. Just barely. "I guess that'd be fun. When?"

"Friday?"

She didn't even look at her calendar. In fact, her gaze didn't leave his. "Let me get you my address."

∂∾∽

It only took about ten seconds past Jeremy's departure. Monica clocked it on her wristwatch, stretching back in her chair as Deborah stormed the gate—or office threshold as it were.

"OK, day three with Adonis. I want information, Monica." To emphasize her point, she propped her hip against the corner of Monica's desk. She folded her arms and drum-tapped impatient fingers on her arms, clearly going nowhere until answers were delivered.

Demure and nonplussed, Monica simply looked up, and blinked prettily. "Information? About what? The uncle of a student? Nothing much to—"

"Oh, no. No dice. Kittelski, you fail to heed a pair of key points." Deborah lifted a finger. "First of all, I saw you when he came in the other day. Sparks flew like pyrotechnics around here." Up came finger number two. "Second of all, he couldn't wait to return that car seat and see you today." Then a third. "Now that I've witnessed round three today, I have but one observation. It's a good one, too."

Monica rolled her eyes, forcing herself to act bored. "Then by all means, don't keep me in suspense. I can hardly wait."

"You two are off the barometer."

Monica burst out laughing. "Barometer? What barometer?"

"The flirt and play barometer. Surely you've heard of it." She waggled her brows. "Seriously. You guys are completely off the scale. To kick things off there's the whole 'Jellybean' nickname thing. Then, you bat those obscenely thick lashes of yours and mention Polonia?" She shrugged widely. "Yeah, I heard that part of the conversation when I walked past the door. You'll *so* have a dinner date before this day is done."

Monica's throat went dry. Was this whole playful affection and discovery thing with Jeremy headed to those danger levels she sensed yesterday? Monica gulped, but gulping didn't help much. This was just harmless fun. Good-natured man and woman playfulness, with a date or two on the side.

Right?

"We've already…umm…" Monica was too taken aback by now to finish the sentence.

Deborah, however, whooped it up, then concluded for her: "You've already *made* a date, right?" Numb and wide-eyed, Monica could only nod. Deborah just rejoiced all the more, chortling. "Ha! *I win*!"

5

In a gesture that Monica found both protective and stimulating, Jeremy tucked his arm around her waist as they followed the hostess to a quiet, corner booth at Polonia. There he settled her comfortably before taking his seat.

Monica adjusted the fall of her dress, leaning back against the chair as she opened the wide, plastic menu and began to study the selections. Her mouth already watered.

Until…"Ew."

Jeremy lowered his own menu and looked at her in question. "Hmm?"

"Ew. I can't help it. I always react that way to the only two words on this menu that I just can't tolerate."

"Which are?"

She offered an exaggerated wince. "Blood sausage."

Jeremy laughed, and nodded. "I have to agree. Not one of my favorites, either. My brother Marty, on the other hand, absolutely loves it."

Monica cringed, but gave Jeremy a teasing wink, which, as she intended, made him smile. She resumed the task of narrowing her food choices, but Jeremy's gaze slid against her like a piece of silk. Behind the cover of her menu, Monica nearly sighed, flattered to be the center of this man's exclusive attention. His reactions made her glad she had opted for a decidedly feminine, flowing dress of deep green knit and simple, but tall, black leather heels. Yeah. She was on a mission to win, and maintain, his interest. No doubt about it.

But Jeremy kept pace with her easily. He possessed the kind of frame she loved best in a man—broad of shoulder, lean, and long of leg, strongly muscled, but not to excess. On top of it all, he wore a gray wool suit and vivid, burgundy tie with total flair.

He leaned close, closing the space between them. "You look fantastic, Monica. Absolutely fantastic. The ankle bracelet, in particular, is very eye-catching."

Monica nearly dropped her menu. He had noticed that small of a detail? Jeremy's voice was low and come-hither, but completely sincere as well. Granted, she had chosen her ensemble with care—right down to the drape of a few thin silver chains, matching earrings, and yes, even the thin, shimmering ankle bracelet that decorated her right leg. Still. Wow. "You make me very glad I chose the accessory."

"Good."

Her insides danced, but she ducked behind the menu, her pretense of dinner selection lasting just a few minutes longer. Soon their waitress checked in and they placed an appetizer order of pierogies to share. Monica added a glass of merlot to the mix; Jeremy chose a pint of beer. The selections arrived shortly thereafter.

He unfolded his dinner napkin and spread it across his lap. "I want your story. All of it. Then to now." A sense of quiet intensity wrapped around Monica's heart like velvet, almost protective enough to muffle the undercurrent of edginess his request stirred.

"Leave out nothing." But then he sipped from his drink and reconsidered. "Hang on. I take that back. Hairstyles, fashions and any kind of girl drama can be edited."

She forced a laugh. Despite the warm atmosphere, despite a call to relax her guard, alarm bells sounded. Sure, the warning chimes were just an undercurrent for the moment, but Jeremy's request triggered a tense internal circuit.

I want your story. Would he like it? She didn't think so, all things considered.

So, in motions that were well-practiced to the point of being instinctive, she executed a diversion. "Sorry. Yours comes first. You promised me a story of your own, remember?"

He paused for a few seconds, glanced down at the table. "Chief."

"Chief."

Jeremy nodded, albeit with trace levels of disquiet, and reservation. "OK. But I warn you now, it's not a happy story—"

"Not to worry. I have a few 'not happy stories' of my own. Still, I'd love for you to share it with me."

An intimate, testing silence fell between them before Jeremy nodded. "I only ask one thing in return." Monica leaned into the conversation at hand and urged him to continue with a look and a nod. Those eyes of his—eyes she could easily sink into—narrowed slightly. "Reciprocation."

She nearly flinched, but held her ground. She nodded once more. "Agreed."

Jeremy settled for that answer by softening, and relaxing once more. "I come from a family of eight— well—we *used* to be eight. Five boys, three girls. A total handful for my parents, but they somehow manage to see the best in us anyway."

"Gotta love parents. What happened to the eight?"

Jeremy flexed his jaw, deflected his eyes. "Eight became seven."

A sensation took over, akin to ice sliding down her spirit; the chill built, but then came a tender warmth. "I'm so sorry, Jeremy. How?"

He gathered a breath, blew it out. "We lost my oldest brother in the line of duty. He was an officer with the St. Clair Shores PD."

He paused there, and Monica drifted with the silence. It wasn't uncomfortable or awkward, but rather, a seek-and-find.

"You know," he continued quietly, looking at a spot beyond her, "there are things that happen in life that change you forever, no matter who, no matter what. Kind of like the gut-punch you never see coming. This was one of those moments for us. All of us were shocked and stunned when he was killed."

Sudden memories flashed through her mind—the recollection of news reports about a police sergeant who had been killed in the midst of a domestic dispute. "Lance Edwards—your brother was Lance Edwards."

Jeremy nodded.

"I was fairly new to The Shores at that point, which is probably why it stuck with me—I remember the media coverage."

"It hit my brother Collin the hardest, I think. You see, he was doing a ride-along that night, and he witnessed the whole thing. He even tried to help stop the perp—but Lance—well, obviously he didn't make it—and Collin wrestled with a lot of ghosts and negativity afterward."

Monica listened, enrapt.

"When he met Daveny, he found his way back—back to God, back to his faith—and he found the most incredible woman—a woman who's tailor-made for him."

Monica smiled at the romance of the words, the simple joy of them.

"When Jeffrey was born, I don't even remember quite how it happened, but the guys in our family started calling him Chief. We talked about it at Sunday dinner one time, asking ourselves why the nickname even began. That's when Collin piped in and put it in stone." Jeremy grinned, but a sadness lingered, etched around the corners of his mouth. "It's probably just family pride and all, but we decided, if Lance had survived, he'd've easily made police chief someday. Since Jeffrey's middle name is Lance, after our brother, we figured the nickname should stick."

Family love. Legacies. Children.

Monica's heart lurched. A sharp pang, accompanied by a lump that formed hard and fast in her throat, threatened to break her. She responded to an influx of emotion—emotion that had nothing to do with Jeremy's story, and everything to do with her own.

As ever, though, she pushed on, rebuking her feelings and shoving them away.

"I still remember every word of Collin's eulogy," Jeremy continued, unaware of her discomfort. "Collin is a born writer—a teacher of the language. He did a fantastic job. Me, I'm no wordsmith."

Safe ground. Internally Monica eased up a bit, feeling relieved. She slid into a shared moment of warm, meat-spiced air, soft dinner sounds, flickering candlelight and charming, checkered-cloth table linens that spoke not of ritzy elegance, but rather all things homey, comforting and *good.* The centering interlude helped.

"So how did *you* cope?"

Jeremy shrugged. "I swing hammers. I build. I get physical. What I went through with Lance is what brought me to where I am today. I work hard, I give thanks, and I give back by helping people in need." For a moment he toyed with the flatware next to his plate; the unsettled motion drew Monica's attention to the glimmer of soft candlelight against the toughness of silver. The parallel to Jeremy softened her heart, but shored her resolve to not let him in too fast—nor too deep. "He died in late autumn. My workload was slowing down for the season, and that's the last thing I needed at that point. So, I looked for opportunities to help some people in my community who needed construction assistance—fix-ups, repairs, that kind of thing. There was a lot I knew I could do, and I wanted to be busy. I wanted work. Work helped me think, and sort things through."

"So you volunteered your time with what? Community agencies and such?"

"I got more work than I could handle just by talking to my Pastor."

"Really." She took in yet another facet of his character and came away increasingly intrigued, and that lovely little pull kept coaxing her toward him. In fact, the strength of it increased exponentially. *Careful, Monica,* she thought in a building panic. *Proceed with extreme caution. This is enjoyable, but it can never, ever work. Not over the long haul. Not with everything you lack.* She cleared her throat, and found a smile. "Where do you attend services?"

"Woodland Church. I'm a lifelong member. I'm an usher, and actually just found myself appointed to the worship commission."

"Congratulations—I think that's wonderful. Your place of worship means a lot to you."

"God—Christ—means a lot to me," he amended. "Always has. Always will."

She didn't have much time to admire that conviction, that absolute faith, and recognize the empty void that loomed in her own heart. For in the passing of a heartbeat, his playful smile dawned, and it hit her hard, making her smile in turn, for no other reason than she simply had to respond to him. Add in those sparkling eyes, and she was swept away.

"Do you know what else?"

"What?"

"You, Jellybean, are one smooth customer."

"Well thanks for noticing, but where does that comment fit into our lovely dinner conversation? Not that I'm complaining, mind you—"

Jeremy laughed. "With an expert's precision you have absolutely and shamelessly allowed me to dominate this chat session."

"Chat session? Gee. I thought you and I were on a date."

He didn't allow that mischievous jab to gain traction. "C'mon. It's your turn. And then some. Can I have your story now?"

Monica lifted her glass and sipped—stalling, thinking, considering. Mostly she wondered: *How can I dodge the question? How can I dodge this man?*

The answer came in short order. She couldn't. She wasn't even sure she wanted to—baggage and all.

"If it helps any," he said, "I'll freely admit to the fact that you fascinate me. I'm not asking out of casual interest."

The intoxicating smile that accompanied that whammy left Monica dizzy, deliciously carried away. "What's behind this?" she whispered. "Don't you wonder about that a little, JB? Where's this...this *stuff* between us *coming* from?"

He leaned forward and distance evaporated. Firelight burnished the angles of his face. "Call it chemical. Call it magnetism. I don't know—but I'm on board. You fascinate me."

She let the words sink in and the flutters die down. She watched him across the small table, wrapped up by soothing, courting atmosphere and flirty sensation. The silence lingered, and lingered ... but that was completely OK.

Jeremy softened, went tender. In his eyes alone, she found warm protection, safety and care. *So tempting,* she thought. *Such a call forward into every wish, every dream I've ever held.* "So. Jellybean. What about your story?"

On the inside, deep at her core, Monica began to shake, tremors working through her system in subtle, but unstoppable ripples. Soon, her hands would be trembling and he'd see much more than she cared to reveal. "Well. You already know I own and operate Sunny Horizons." Nerves got the better of her. She slid a lock of hair behind her ear, clearing her throat to steady her voice.

"Yeah. It's amazing. I give you credit. The place bustles like mad. Seems like a happy place, too. Can't be easy."

"Never," she agreed.

"Know what I wonder?"

"What's that?"

"What on Earth do you do when you have a headache?"

Monica's laugh bubbled.

"I'm not kidding! I can't imagine that level of activity, noise and the degree of focus you have to maintain. What happens when you're not functioning at one-hundred percent?"

"Believe me, I understand what you're getting at." She shrugged. "When you get hit, all you can do is survive. I suppose it helps that I pay attention to being healthy, and fit. I teach ballet once a week, so that keeps me in shape."

Jeremy gave a victorious nod. "I knew it. You're a dancer."

"I used to be. Especially in high school and college. I love it."

"OK, then, I have a stumper for you."

"What's that?"

"Tell me about your favorite moment on stage."

The question caused Monica to sit back, and ponder for a moment. He seemed so comfortable in his own skin that he inspired that same level of comfort from the people around him. It was a formidable attribute, especially when Monica considered how to continue avoiding the one, key topic that left her reeling with literal emptiness. Disconcerted by her natural guard and reserve being tipped upside-down, she was grateful when their waitress approached the table.

Jeremy welcomed their entrée of grilled sausage, steamed potatoes and the cucumber, dill and onion salad they both favored. They promptly dug in.

"I'd have to say it was when I competed in a state-wide competition for classic ballet my senior year of college. It was Christmas, and I danced to Beethoven's Ode to Joy. I took second, and never dreamed I'd get that far. It was amazing."

Jeremy stopped eating. He paused, fork in hand, and watched her with genuine admiration. "That's incredible." A momentary pause moved past, and he shook his head. "I'd love to see you dance."

How long had it been since a man made her blush? Ages. Jeremy inspired the reaction without breaking a sweat—mostly because his manner was so heartfelt. So *real*.

"So you teach." He had just finished a bite of food; he wiped his mouth and resettled his napkin. "That means you love dancing enough that you're still active. I think that's great."

Monica nodded, loving the mix of flavors that burst on her tongue when she crunched into a chilly, crisp cucumber, mixed with sour cream and a tangy slice of onion. "I teach pre-school ballet at the Saint Clair Shores Community Center. We have two recitals a year, one at Christmas and one in the spring. It keeps me in practice."

They ate for a bit in silence.

"So, kids. They're certainly center stage in your life." Jeremy winced. "Pardon the pun."

Monica laughed, but the sound came out false, and she knew it. Her hands clenched in reflex. She held her fork way too tightly and fought hard against the fear of turning him off, of losing his interest by virtue of being an incomplete woman. "Yes. I graduated from Central Michigan with a degree in child development. You might say it's my calling."

"Sounds to me like you'll make a great mother someday, Monica. Seriously."

Oh, dear Lord above, if only that could be true. A boulder rolled straight over her heart and pressed it down. Unwittingly, Jeremy had struck the bulls-eye.

Monica bit her lip so hard she could have sworn she tasted blood. She needed to call a halt to this conversation. Pronto. He had moved, swift and clean, past every single one of her defensive barriers. *How?* The one-word question raced through her mind.

She struggled, inside and out; this time she couldn't hide that fact. Somehow, Jeremy had worked his way inside chambers she had left barricaded. She tried to eat another forkful of their perfectly prepared meal, but the food tasted like sawdust now. She even tried to garner a casual, agreeing smile, but failed miserably.

"Hey...you OK?" Of course, he'd picked up on her mood; this man was both keen and caring.

"Sure I am. Yeah."

"Liar," he teased, smiling gently to temper that mild reproach. They eyed each other in momentary suspense. "I'm really sorry if I said something wrong, Monica."

She found her hand swallowed up by his; he held on, bringing their joined hands to rest on the tabletop. In an automatic way, he began to thumb-stroke her wrist in light, feathery strokes that made the flutters and tingles go crazy all over again. This man possessed just enough strength of heart, just enough appeal, to make her want to believe again. A night in his company left her wanting, desperately in fact, to leave fears and misgivings behind.

Almost...but not quite.

So Monica fell back on poise, and the veneer of a half-truth. "You didn't say anything wrong."

"Well, just for the record? The questions, the interest, aren't just superficial. This isn't causal first date stuff, Monica. I think I've made that clear. I like you. I already know I want this to be the first of many dinner dates. So have faith. Relax." He gave her hand a squeeze. "Don't be afraid."

Looking into his eyes, absorbing the satiny tenor of his voice, Monica allowed herself the luxury of sinking in and enjoying. She used her free hand to lift the goblet of ruby-red merlot and she took a deep sip.

Jeremy Edwards went to her head far more quickly, and efficiently—and with more real impact—than anything she had ever known, and she needed to find a way to move forward in a manner she could control and be comfortable with. After all, Jeremy was solid electricity to her, a heart-call she couldn't resist.

She definitely wanted more of him, so, she silently vowed to come up with a way to shore up her guard—to shield her own 'unhappy stories' and at the same time keep his interest and build on this budding—in fact flourishing—relationship.

6

Jeremy whistled a tune as he unlocked the front door of his townhome. He grabbed the day's mail, paging through a couple of bills and store ads. Then, he spied something a lot more interesting—a large, cream-colored vellum envelope with the return address of Grand Haven, Michigan. Rebecca Tomblin's wedding. Jeremy smiled to himself. His cousin. And she was a sweetheart. Last year had been a blockbuster for her: a move to the west side of the state, a meeting, courtship, and engagement to an up-and-coming executive at a pharmaceutical firm located in Grand Rapids. Now came the wedding, and it promised to be a blast.

After hanging up his coat, he tore into the envelope and pulled out the invitation. For the time being, he stood in the entryway. Just as he started to peruse the details of the event, his cell phone went off.

His smile only increased when he checked caller ID. "Hey, Mom." He could swear the woman had radar when it came to her kids.

"I miss you."

"Opening salvo delivered, and duly noted. PS? I miss you, too."

"Ahhh, but do you miss me enough to stop by the house so I can feed you? I'm sure you're starving."

"Me? Starving? Never."

His mom snorted. "OK. Where is my son, and what have you done with him?"

"You planning a get-together?" Jeremy walked into the kitchen and set the mail aside. Propping a hip against the long, main counter of green-and-white-veined marble, he opened the stainless fridge and pulled out some ground beef. For dinner, he'd throw a couple burgers on the stovetop grill and boil up some fresh frozen corn his sister-in-law, Stephanie, had given him a while back. One of the perks of being the only remaining bachelor in his family—he was pampered by the women.

"That's part of why I'm calling. Sunday dinner this weekend. Can you make it?"

The question caused wheels to spin in Jeremy's mind.

"I'm also wondering if you got the invite to Becky's wedding, yet."

The wheels clicked into position and began to hum in a smooth, promising motion. "Yeah, I can make it to dinner on Sunday, and yeah, I got the invitation just now. In fact, I'm looking at it as we speak." He picked it up once more. There were directions, an RSVP card and an information sheet on the venue for the reception, complete with photos.

"Small affair, at a gorgeous-looking Victorian-style bed and breakfast that's right on the shoreline of Lake Michigan. Should be lovely."

The descriptors were received, and then promptly discarded. Instead, he changed the subject. "Hey, Mom, can I bring a guest on Sunday?"

"Of course. At their own risk, naturally…"

Now it was Jeremy's turn to give a growling laugh. "Naturally. Edwards's clan gatherings do tend to be overwhelming."

"Anyone we know?"

"Sort of, yes. Monica Kittelski."

"She owns the daycare center that Jeffrey goes to."

Jeremy nodded. Another thing about Elise Edwards? Nothing slid past her notice when it came to her beloved grandkids. "That's the one." Dead silence greeted that confirmation. Jeremy could all but see the calculations taking place in a little cartoon bubble positioned right over his mom's head.

"Are Daveny and Collin aware of your…interest?"

"Collin is, so, by the de facto truth of pillow talk, I'm sure Daveny is aware, as well. I haven't heard about anyone leaping out of tall buildings, yet."

"Jeremy!"

"I'm just kidding, Mom."

"I think it'd be wonderful! If she's brave enough, we'd love to have her join the insanity."

Expectant warmth did a neat little slide through his body. "Great. I appreciate it."

"This is turning into a real party! Ken and Kiara are joining us as well."

Even better, Jeremy thought. The pastor of Woodland Church and his bride of almost two years were extended family to begin with. Secondary to that, introducing Monica to his family, and the importance of his church life, would continue forward motion in the relationship department—something Jeremy wanted to encourage.

"Sounds perfect. Thanks for letting me include her. My needling aside, Mom, she's a sweetheart. I'm enjoying getting to know her. I want you guys to meet her, too. I think the admiration society will definitely be mutual."

"Wow. This *must* be serious. You haven't wanted to include a significant other at a family meal in ages."

"Family dinners are reserved for only a few."

"In your case, *very* few. That makes me proud. You're not cavalier where your emotions are concerned. I think that's commendable. We need more JB's on the planet."

"That's a completely scary thought, Mom. Really." He pulled a batch of romaine lettuce from the vegetable crisper and set it on an inlayed cutting board. Next, he grabbed a knife. "Think about it. I'm the one who paid the most visits to the hospital growing up, and I probably pushed boundaries more than the rest."

"Perhaps, but character tells the tale, honey, and you've got it."

Jeremy squirmed as he began to dice up lettuce, but deep inside, the praise vindicated his decisions and way of life. Praise, or disappointment, from the parents was more than enough to lift him high, or chop him at the knees. "Thanks, Mom. My love to you and Dad. See you Sunday."

"Love you back, and I can't wait."

Jeremy ended the call, lost in thought for a bit while he completed his salad. His gaze settled upon the elegant invitation with its raised, scripted black lettering. He picked it up, tapping it against the palm of his hand. The inner envelope was addressed to Jeremy Edwards and guest. The wedding was six weeks away. Plenty of time to get a more definitive handle on this lightning strike of a situation with Monica.

Promptly her face came to life in his mind—and heart. There was that sassy, girl-power posture, her natural glow, those sparkling, warm blue eyes. And her smile—her smile alone packed enough power to send his pulse into overdrive.

I'm hooked, Jeremy thought, without a trace of chagrin. *I want to bring her to Sunday dinner and have her meet the family. I want to take her to Becky's wedding. I want to keep moving forward with her.*

His mom's comment was true—he enjoyed dating, but didn't allow many women into the sanctuary of his deepest heart, where his strongest emotions, his most precious beliefs, and his family, resided. The way he looked at it, some places in the soul were simply too precious to share in an arbitrary manner.

He whipped up dinner, ate, then toyed with a bit of romantic strategy while he unwound from the workday to the strains of ESPN. How best to ask Monica to a family dinner? The thought of dinner had his gaze tracking to the kitchen.

Hmm. Maybe that was it. Maybe he could test the waters by making her a dinner of his own.

❧

Rule one of courtship and male-female interaction: women love flowers. That in mind, Jeremy purchased a bouquet of white, pink-tipped roses. While the store clerk wrapped them in green tissue paper and boxed them perfectly, Jeremy penned a card.

Monica:

I hope you enjoy the enclosed. These flowers are meant to be an enticement to madness, chaos, and fun. Call me if you're at all intrigued.

JB

Directing delivery to Sunny Horizons, Jeremy could now do nothing but wait for her response.

During the next several hours, he lost himself in work. Easy enough, because today's assignment was a kitchen remodel in Grosse Pointe Woods that featured high-end materials, a tight deadline, and a high-maintenance client who lived in a massive, white brick number positioned along the banks of the Detroit River.

"Thanksgiving will be here before you know it! I'm opening my home to the entire family, and they're so particular. It's my first big holiday gathering, and all I see right now is chaos. It'll be complete, right? I have your word, right? You did promise—"

"The ceramic floor tiles will be installed today," JB assured her. "Once that's situated, we'll install the wall and base cabinets and the island, all of which arrived yesterday and are set to go. When that phase is completed, all that's left is placing the appliances. Those are shipping out the middle of next week, to conclude the project. We're operating on schedule, so I don't want you to worry." Calm and confident, Jeremy set about reassuring the nervous young wife of his client.

"My in-laws are lovely people, but they're so used to perfection, and the best of the best." Still obviously nervous, she looked around skeptically. "I never should have taken this on right now. I'll let everyone down."

Her slender form sagged a bit as she eyed tarps covered by dust, and workmen bustling through a large space that suddenly went small when equipment and supplies rolled in. Jeremy felt sympathy for this society darling. Obviously, she carried a heavy burden, and he wished he could find a way to help her see past outward appearances to the simple joy of hosting a family holiday celebration.

"I know remodels look messy, and we're at the point right now where you may feel like the dust will never settle, but we're in great shape, Mrs. Whittmore. We'll be done in plenty of time. You have my word."

Morning passed to afternoon. Despite pleasing progress on the remodel, Jeremy became increasingly edgy, waiting for a reply from Monica. When lunch break ended, he decided to check the delivery tracking information he had been given along with his order receipt. It was then that Monica's call came in.

"Hey, Jellybean," he teased. Her laughter tickled his senses, left him smiling, and relieved. *Connected*. "What's up?"

"What's up? Well, right now about two-dozen gorgeous looking, long-stemmed roses. In a vase. On my desk. And I've been presented with somewhat of a riddle."

"Really? Do tell. Perhaps I can help you solve it."

"Bet you can."

Jeremy grinned, strolling slowly into the welcome silence and privacy of a massive, perfectly appointed dining room.

"It seems," Monica continued, "I've been invited to—now how did your note put it? Madness, chaos and fun. No further elaboration, though."

"I wanted you to be tantalized."

"You've succeeded."

He pictured her, behind her desk, stretched back in her chair, looking out the window, perhaps, seeing the same rain pattern drumming against her windows as drummed against the large bay before him. He tracked the streaks of water that turned the pearly gray world outside to a wavering, shimmery shade of silver. "I want to cook you dinner tonight, if you're free. And I have a question to ask, about this weekend. But more on that, later."

"You're not going to give me the full scoop, are you, JB?"

"Nope. Not until you accept my dinner invitation."

"One of my many weaknesses as a human being is that I detest the task of cooking dinner every night. Therefore, I guess I better concede this match. I accept."

"Terrific. Come by whenever you're done at work." He gave her his address, and they concluded their call a short time later.

Returning to the kitchen, Jeremy looked at his watch. Anticipation curled through his body. Only three hours to go.

7

The front door to the daycare center came open, forcing Monica away from her present world of daydreams about Jeremy, and that breathtaking, unexpected delivery of roses. She heard the door buzz and left her office behind, coming upon a woman who looked around as though a bit lost.

"Hi," Monica greeted. "Can I help you?"

"I'm looking for Monica. Monica Kittelski."

"I'm Monica."

"Hi. I called earlier today about the possibility of enrolling my daughter at your daycare center."

Nodding with recognition, Monica stepped forward and extended her hand. "You must be Mrs. Carter."

The woman shook Monica's hand. "Yes."

"Come on back to my office and let's talk. It's a pleasure to meet you."

Business claimed her focus, but, once again, so did Jeremy. The image of him skimmed through her mind, and caused her lips to curve as she walked the narrow hallway with Caroline close behind. Monica pictured him, hard at work, in a gutted-out home, coordinating crews, swinging a hammer, getting physical in the way he had described so well at dinner. Once they entered the office, she closed the door and sat down at her desk, relegating Jeremy to the back of her mind. For now.

Mrs. Carter took the chair across from Monica, her posture hesitant. "Actually, I prefer Caroline Dempsey. I'm in the process of a name change. My husband and I are divorcing, and I'll be going by my maiden name. But, please, call me Caroline."

"Caroline Dempsey it is. I remember you saying you have a four-year-old."

Caroline visibly relaxed a bit, warming up as Monica recalled their conversation. "Her name is Jessica. She'll be five in a few months. She's been in daycare for a year now, but I need to change centers because I'm moving from Detroit. Until I find an apartment nearby, I'll be living with my parents here in Saint Clair Shores."

"So she's familiar with the routine of going to pre-school. That will make adjusting to a new center much easier, for both of you."

The comment seemed to set Caroline further at ease, and she smiled for the first time. "I hope so. I want to do everything I can for her. She's confused about all the conflict going on at home, and I'm not sure how she'll handle all the changes. I'm being even more cautious than usual about the facility I choose."

"No problem at all. We'll come back here and talk after I give you a tour of the school. If you'll follow me, I'll explain our pre-K programs and introduce you to our teachers."

Monica took Caroline through the main room. "Aside from being the lobby, this is also where we set up tables for group art projects, or floor games and such. As you can see, we have easels and paints, magazines and all kinds of cardboard and construction paper for the children to use."

Along the far side of the lobby, glass windows and doors lined the wall, revealing rooms that were sectioned off for each group of children—infants, toddlers, and preschoolers. Monica explained the workings of each class, then showed Caroline to the pre-school room where her daughter would spend the most time.

Once the door swung open, voices that had been muffled turned up full blast. Inside were about twenty kids, divided into groups for free play, reading and puzzle works. Four teachers provided supervision, moving from spot to spot when kids needed support, or questions came up.

As always, Monica's entrance was marked by shouts for attention. Two or three youngsters came up to her straight away and waited for a hug. She greeted them all, then picked up the last one in line, a shy newcomer named Joshua who beamed at her, but looked at Caroline in question.

"Hi, Josh." Monica gave him a squeeze and walked Caroline through the room, taking Joshua along on automatic. The only thought that crossed her mind beyond touring a prospect through her school was the idea of Jeremy, and kids, and how much family meant to him. By sheer dent of will, Monica refused to let the thought take root. JB had delivered roses and ready affection. *Fun and easy,* she told herself. *It's still just fun and easy. We'll keep it that way.* She refused to let sadness and trepidation diminish her pleasure.

Caroline looked through the windows of this classroom, into a wide open, large space, which once again, was full of kids. Monica laughed at Caroline's wide-eyed reaction, keying in on her guest once more.

"I call that the rumpus room. It's a real blessing on rainy days like this. As you can see, we have a small jungle gym, floor cushions for exercising, and foam balls to toss and kick around."

Letting Joshua run off to color, Monica picked up strewn toys and automatically stored them while Caroline looked around. The woman seemed pleased. "I like the art work."

She referred to a selection of drawings and paintings that covered a nearby wall. "We put paintings everywhere. My center is a showcase for budding artistic talent."

Caroline's eyes went distant, and troubled, as she watched the children play. "Everything here is so innocent. Carefree. That's what I want Jessica to have. I like your center, Miss Kittelski."

Absorbing Caroline's vibration of sadness stirred empathy, and Monica's encouraging smile. "It's Monica, please."

"Monica. I like it very much. Can I talk with you about some things in private?"

"Of course. Let's go back to my office and sit down."

When they returned, Caroline sat down while Monica moved to her side of the desk.

Caroline picked up a nearby paperclip and started to twist it nervously. "Monica," she began softly, not looking up from her fidgeting hands, "the most important thing in the world to me right now is knowing that my daughter will be well cared for and protected while I'm at work during the day."

"Protected?" The distinction took Monica by surprise, and her brows pulled together.

"Yes. Protected." Dropping the mangled

paperclip, Caroline finally looked at Monica directly. "I'm enduring a bitter divorce from my husband David, and I don't trust him. In fact, I wouldn't put it past him to try and take Jessica away from me. I have legal custody, but...well, especially lately, he can be volatile. If he got hold of her, he'd take her away, I just know it! I can't let that happen. I'm already at my wit's end. If he reentered the picture, I know I'd fall apart."

In a professional sense, Monica had faced this kind of situation before—a divorced parent, emotions taxed to the maximum, trying to look out for the best interests of their child. It left her heartsick on behalf of the entire wounded family—but most especially the innocent, unsuspecting child.

Leaning forward, Monica hastened to assure by carefully emphasizing her next words. "I have strict guidelines about who can and cannot take the children from my facility. When you enroll Jessica, you'll fill out a standard form that gives me the names of people you want Jessica to be released to should you be unable to pick her up for some reason. If they're not on the list, they're not allowed access."

"And that system works? I mean, I'm not trying to question you, or the rules you have in place, but I just—I need to be sure."

"Don't worry about asking tough questions. I understand. I'm very protective of the children I care for. I'm trusted to act on the parent's behalf during the day, and I take that fact very seriously. I have to." She reached across the desk and gave Caroline's arm a gentle, reassuring squeeze. "As we can't foresee every possible scenario, there are never guarantees, but we'll take good care of Jessica for you."

Caroline eased into a more relaxed posture.

"Thank you. I'd like to fill out the paperwork. I'd like her to start school here next week if possible."

Opening a desk drawer, Monica extracted a packet of enrollment forms and slid them toward Caroline, along with a pen. She debated for only a second or two before adding, "If you and Jessica are new to living in the Shores, I have a suggestion that might help her fit in and adjust even more."

"What's that?" Caroline looked up with interest, her pen now still.

"Wednesday evenings I teach youth dance classes at the Community Center. Jessica could begin in the pre-ballet class if you think she'd be interested. We're only a few weeks into the fall term, so she hasn't missed much."

"Dance." Approval marked her smile and sparkling eyes. "I'm sure she'd love it. You must really be dedicated to children. I admire your involvement with them."

Monica's gaze strayed to the stunning bouquet of roses. She breathed in the subtle, yet intoxicating aroma. In an instant, longing pervaded her spirit. *Kids. Jeremy.* She firmed her lips and blinked free of hope. Rather than elaborate on the thread of Caroline's conversation, Monica smiled, her hands going tense around a mug of cooled coffee from earlier. "Can I offer you something to drink? Some coffee or tea?"

"I'd love some tea, if it isn't much trouble. Thank you. And how do I go about signing her up for dance?"

Monica refreshed her mug and filled another with hot water for Caroline. Next to her jellybean bowl was a small tea caddy, which she opened and offered to Caroline for selection.

"The program is wonderful. It places no pressure

on the girls. They have a lot of fun learning and dancing for their friends and relatives. We have a recital in just a few months."

"A taste of show-biz. Jessica would love it, and she deserves the fun."

"I can get you those forms as well. They're right over here."

While Caroline continued to sign up for Sunny Horizons, Monica went to the black leather satchel she carried with her to work each day and sifted through its contents until she found a registration form for the Community Center dance program. "Here you go."

Caroline sighed, looking into Monica's eyes with heart-tugging gratitude. "A half-hour with you, and I feel like I just might get a handle on my life with Jessica after all."

The compliment provided a needed boost to Monica's outlook and helped her find an even center. "Thank you, Caroline. I'm looking forward to meeting your daughter."

8

"JB, your place is beautiful."

Taking Monica's coat and hanging it in the entryway closet, Jeremy absorbed the details of his home, seeing it through her eyes.

Granted, he injected a lot of TLC into the place, but that was half the fun. He loved open, airy spaces, so the cathedral ceilings, recessed lights and skylights suited him. He was also a fan of the polish and durability of ceramic, so the entryway and the nearby kitchen featured a smoky, salmon hue that offered up a visual of the warm welcome he carried internally.

Slow, but not shy, Monica moved forward, looking around with curiosity. He watched, and a mysterious emotion went to work in his heart. He found pleasure and a cozy sense of comfort at seeing her in his space, at watching her acclimate, and better yet, enjoying his home.

But Monica didn't fail him. She was also all about spunk, and sass. When she strolled into the living room, she tossed him an over-the-shoulder look that gave him a delicious heat rush. "You are *such* a guy," she muttered affectionately.

"Thanks for noticing."

"Seriously. The bigger the plasma, the better the man, right?"

"That's always been *my* mantra."

She laughed, taking note of little things. She paused by pictures of his family, slid her fingertips against fat candles in hurricane holders that were placed upon the mantle above a crackling fire in the fireplace. From a nearby coffee table, she picked up the remote and aimed it at the television screen. But she didn't activate it quite yet. "I'm making you a bet."

"Which is?"

"ESPN, ESPN 2 or, outside money riding on the NFL network. May I?"

"I'm up for the challenge. Go for it." Jeremy waited; in fact, he even arched a brow. Her eyes narrowed, revealing the fact that her confidence was wavering just a trace. He had set her a touch off balance. And he loved it.

She turned on the TV and was rewarded by…Fox News.

Monica sighed. She nodded in solemn defeat then turned to him. "I'm officially impressed."

"Like I told you when we met, I'm not just *any* man."

"Guess I should have paid better attention," she quipped, then turned off the TV and rejoined him.

"Actually, I did the whole man-versus-ESPN thing before turning in last night. Watched Fox before leaving for work this morning. So, to be fair, you almost had me busted."

"Your honesty is commendable. Regardless, you're a well-balanced individual. I like that about you."

That did it. Jeremy wrapped an arm around her waist and drew her in for a snug, warm hug that she returned eagerly. The moment ended with both of them sighing happily. As they parted, he leaned down, capturing her chin gently in his hand so he could prompt a subtle tilt to her head and kiss her cheek. He lingered a bit over their contact. Monica's eyes closed, he noticed, and her body softened. Welcomed.

"Are you hungry?"

"That's a loaded question." Her husky voice brought him back around, and made him realize the double meaning behind that question. They both burst out laughing.

"C'mon. Let's get cooking."

Monica gave his shoulder a shove. "Well, aren't *you* on a *roll* tonight?"

"That one was deliberate." He led her to the kitchen, guiding her by a touch to the small of her back. She was such a dynamo. He marveled over the fact, crediting her anew for the aspects of her personality that were so magnetic and appealing. In deference to her job with the kids, she wore dress slacks and comfortable, stylish blouses for the most part. Today's gray pants and softly draped, silk blouse of peach were both feminine and functional.

She happened to catch his perusal and looked at him with a surprising degree of shyness. "What?"

Jeremy touched her cheek in passing, making his way to the cabinet for cookware. "Nothing. Just thinking."

"About?"

"About the fact that I'm not the only one in this room who's a well-balanced individual." Monica looked down for a second, re-gathering herself, he imagined. Jeremy let her, and continued on. "Can I interest you in something to drink?"

"That'd be nice. Thanks. Today was kind of a tense one at work, and that weather's giving me a chill, too.

Do you happen to have any tea?"

"Absolutely. Name your herbal combo."

Monica giggled, and her blush slipped through his soul like the softest of caresses. "You crack me up."

"You're surprised. Again."

"Yep."

Jeremy clucked his tongue, and shook his head. "I beat you at the man versus TV game, and then you doubt my tea-making capabilities? I'm born and raised by an Irish mother who swears by a hot cup of tea." He pointed toward a nearby tea caddy. "I'll heat some water. Help yourself to whatever sounds good...and fill me in about that tough day at work."

For the next several minutes, Jeremy focused on Monica's description of her day, and, in particular, the episode with a new enrollee at Sunny Horizons. She kept specifics, like names and such, out of their conversation, but she appeared to be upset by the issues facing this single-working-mom. He retrieved a bistro mug from the cabinet above his built-in microwave and went to work preparing tea. She chose a version of green tea with jasmine.

When brewing finished, Monica accepted the offering with a grateful look. "You should have seen this woman, JB. She was desperate. She was completely at the end of her rope as a woman and mother contending with a bitter divorce. Furthermore, I have to say, I just don't get it." She watched as he began food preparations. "Can I help?"

"Sure." Jeremy handed her a wrapped package of ground beef and a frying pan. "This can be browned up, if you're sure you don't mind."

"Not at all." Monica lifted an apron from a nearby wall peg and slipped it on.

"So, what don't you get?"

She kicked on the stove heat, grabbed a spatula, and went to work. "I don't get people."

"People?"

"Splintered families, acrimonious divorces. It always tears me up inside to hear about kids caught in the middle of bad circumstances over which they have absolutely no control. It makes me angry. It's such a waste!" She blew out a stream of air, clearing her throat. She sipped from her tea, stirred the sizzling mix of meat and added some of the onion and garlic spices Jeremy offered. "And since I find myself on a soapbox, I'll end my venting session right there."

He watched, taking her in. "No need to do that. I don't mind your soapbox, or your venting." He paused. "You know—it sounds to me like she's trying hard to do the right thing. Maybe she just needs a hand. You've given her that."

"To a degree. It's like you volunteering, though. You always end up wishing you could do more, right?"

He loved her giving, tender heart. Propping a hip against the counter, he looked into her sparkling, beautiful blue eyes and went warm inside. "You bet. I wonder if she belongs to a church community that might help her out. If not, I'd be happy to pass along the name and number of my church's pastor. He's very keyed into the local organizations that lend assistance to people."

He watched as Monica steeled her spine, though she kept her voice neutral and kind when she replied. "That's really sweet. I'll keep it in mind, but I hardly know her at this point. I only know her side of a messy child custody situation. And her desperation. She wants good things for her daughter. I *so* understand that need, and desire. I gave her information about the dance classes I teach at the Community Center, and she's going to enroll her daughter, so that'll help, I think. No innocent child of four years old should *ever* be—" She groaned.

Jeremy glimpsed her discomfort, her realization that, once again, she was being awfully emphatic.

"Look. Never mind me. Let's give it a rest for now. I just want to relax, and enjoy being with you." She looked up into his eyes and smiled—truly smiled.

That made Jeremy feel better, but he kept Pastor Ken Lucerne in the back of his mind. He'd raise the topic once again, at a less vulnerable moment, and re-take Monica's temperature on the idea of connecting the two.

From there, meal creation continued. On the evening's menu—shepherd's pie. For the next half-hour or so, they danced around one another in the kitchen, and Jeremy enjoyed their natural, effortless timing. She stirred and stewed meat. He forked boiling potatoes to check for readiness. She sipped from her tea, then resettled the mug; feeling playful, he picked it up and tossed back a swallow of his own; he smiled when he set the mug back down and caught sight of her arched brow.

Reclaiming the mug, she met his gaze and took a calculated sip of her own. Jeremy watched, captivated. "Know what? Here's the thing."

"Oh, please don't keep me waiting, JB. I'm all about 'the thing.'" She offered a teasing grin, and oddly enough, it struck him that she even knew how to make a simple white apron look appealing. She wiped her hands on a nearby towel and continued to stir.

Jeremy drained potatoes and used a mixer to mash them.

"Do you know what this is—what we're doing here?"

"I guess I'd refer to it as dinner prep, with a side-order of tea commando."

He laughed, from deep in his chest, genuine in his enjoyment of her. Of *them*. "The thing is this: you and me. Now don't get freaked out or anything, but..." At that point, just to play torturer, Jeremy paused. He reclaimed her mug and lifted back a share. She waited, watching him. Whether she realized it or not, she was keenly interested. Aware. Intrigued.

Good.

"You officially owe me a refill." He nodded. "Tonight feels excellent. It's like you and I are a long-time couple. I like it. A lot."

Monica drained the meat, added it to the vegetable mix and stirred it well. Jeremy topped the ensemble with the mashed potatoes then put the metal baking tin in the oven. In unison, they began to tear lettuce into bite-sized pieces, but not before Jeremy caught wind of another subtle shift in her teasing spark, their light-hearted play. He prepared her a second cup of tea, and he realized that something akin to uncertainty creased her brow.

Testing a tad, he added further punch to his statement. "Additionally? My family's gonna go nuts for ya,' Jellybean. You're halfway there already, what with Dav and Collin already being fans."

"Yeah. Eventually." She cast him a quick, flirty glance, but it didn't reach beneath the surface. It didn't hit her eyes, or her heart. He recognized that fact immediately.

So, he sneaked up on her from behind and skimmed his arms around her waist, drawing her against him, snug and true. He nuzzled her neck and breathed deep—instantly assailed by the soft, tantalizing aroma of jasmine, lily, and *Monica*. She went lax, leaning against him. Her eyes fluttered closed.

"Actually, I want you to meet them. This weekend. Mom's assembling the whole motley crew for dinner. I want you to be part of it, if you're game."

Her breathing went shallow. He saw her pulse dance at her throat. "Really?"

"Yes. Does that work for you?"

"Are you sure that would be for the best? Do you really think that you, that I...I mean...I'm positive your family is great, and I'm excited to meet them and everything, but...I..."

She was speed talking. Charmed by that nervous reaction, Jeremy gave her a final squeeze and stepped away. "I'm sure. But more to the point of this conversation, are *you*?"

Monica untied her apron and slid it away. "I suppose—if they're brave enough to take me on, I'm sporting enough to return the favor."

Her voice was quiet. Her eyes were wide, deep and clear. She took hold of his arm, and stepped into him, a request for an embrace that Jeremy readily answered. Arms around one another, they stood in contented silence for a moment.

But layered just beneath that contentment he felt tension in her shoulders, in her arms and across the taut line of her back. She needed this physical gesture of support.

He attributed those undercurrents to the prospect

of meeting his large, exuberant family, and he let it go,
hoping that's all there was to it.

9

Monica didn't get nervous about having dinner with Jeremy's family until she watched him pull up in front of her home. Only then did butterflies go wild in her stomach. Only then did her legs turn to rubber. Pushing those reactions into remission, she steeled her spine and welcomed him with deceptive calm.

"Be prepared for a spread," he warned once they were on the road. "My family does nothing halfway. Especially when it comes to Sunday dinner."

The trip took just minutes. When Jeremy entered a neighborhood of large, newer homes nestled upon rolling tracts of land, she gave him a look. "Success seems to be a genetic trait."

"Dad made a good life for us working for Ford. He didn't fall into this; he busted his back for it."

She studied his profile, feeling proud of the man at her side. "Like you."

Jeremy shrugged. "I suppose. Thing is, my folks give to their kids the way I want to give to my own kids someday. Not in things, and possessions, but in outlook, and character." He turned into the driveway of a gray brick, two-story home. There were already several cars lined up before his.

"So that's why you're so driven. To leave a legacy for your kids?"

"You bet. That, and to make use of the gifts I've been given. I figure that's my responsibility in this life. Know what I mean?"

He paused deliberately, waiting on her, she knew. But Monica couldn't speak. A choking silence forbade comment. That nasty, familiar boulder came back, landing once again at the dead center of her chest, crushing the hope in her heart. Giving up on further discussion, Jeremy leaned in to give her cheek a lingering kiss, then exited the vehicle. After opening her door, he helped her out. Monica trembled. *This exercise is going to be a piece of heaven—and hell.*

They walked through a lacey curtain of snowfall, approaching the front door. They didn't need to ring the bell. The door came open almost immediately by the hand of an attractive, bubbly woman in her mid-sixties. Jeremy quipped in a low voice, "Mom. She sensed our arrival, I swear. She has a kid-detection radar system that never fails."

"Here you are! Come in, come in!" Following her greeting, Jeremy's mom took custody of the coats they peeled off. Jeremy performed introductions and Monica took an appreciative sniff of the air. Already the aroma of slow-cooking meat, onions and pepper, filled the house.

"Something smells delicious," Monica said, following Elise's lead to the living room. There, seating was at a premium, especially for the guys, because the wall-mounted plasma screen flashed through sports reports and the Detroit Lions's pre-game show.

"We're having London broil, garlic potatoes, coleslaw and corn."

"Sounds wonderful," Monica replied, a sense of being overwhelmed sneaking over her.

"Ben, come say hello to Monica and JB."

Ben Edwards, the clan patriarch, rose from the couch, a twinkle in his eyes and laughter on his lips. "I tell you true, if it hasn't moved, Elise cooked it. She goes crazy for family get-togethers."

"Oh, please ignore him," Elise implored. "I simply enjoy gathering the troops. We're about ready to have some appetizers, but let's introduce you around first."

From there, the world of greetings and introductions became a whirlwind and a deluge. Front of the line was Collin Edwards, who gave Monica an understanding smile and a quick hug. "Daveny and Kiara are in the kitchen," he informed, "along with Caroline, Steph, Georgia and Kim." Monica felt her eyes go wide. This was a houseful. Especially when one factored in the numerous youngsters who presently dashed from room to room in a playful game of chase.

Family. It was such an enormous foundation for Jeremy—and such an empty, gaping hole in her life. Melancholy settled over Monica's spirit. She sank into herself, and hated the reaction, but all things considered, fighting inner demons became unavoidable. Following more introductions, they made their way to the kitchen. The Edwards's home was large and graciously appointed. Wood-trimmed stairwells, plush carpeting and crystal light sconces enhanced a formal, but not stuffy tone. Cathedral ceilings lent an airy sense of space and light to the atmosphere, and Monica couldn't help thinking of the similarities, the continuity, expressed in Jeremy's living space.

Jeremy kept hold of her hand the whole time, offering unspoken support as she was inundated by new names and faces. And charming, precocious kid after charming, precocious kid.

A kitchenette played host to the female members of the family as well as a few others. The sight of Daveny Edwards was a welcome delight. Fresh, vibrant and full of a joyful spirit, Daveny enfolded Monica in a tight hug of greeting, whispering in her ear, "You'll muddle through. Promise. The numbers aren't nearly as intimidating once you settle in."

Monica tried to laugh, but she felt hollow inside, especially when she noticed the way the nieces and nephews climbed all over Jeremy, showering him with hugs and hellos. She shifted focus, wanting diversion. That answer came in the form of an absolutely gorgeous woman who sat next to Daveny. This woman kept her eye on a man standing next to Elise; presently he helped prepare a tray of cheese, crackers and veggies.

"Monica Kittelski," Daveny said, "meet Kiara Lucerne. Kiara's my partner at Montgomery Landscaping."

They exchanged handshakes and smiles. Kiara gestured to the nearest empty chair. "Daveny has so many nice things to say about your day care center, Monica. I'd love to hear about it."

Monica watched Daveny stifle a grin and tuck a wave of chocolate-colored hair behind her ear. "Indeed she would," Daveny muttered.

Beneath the table, Monica felt a slight whoosh of air and motion. Judging by Daveny's sudden wince, it seemed Kiara performed a shin-kick to her friend beneath the table.

"Like I'm the only one with secrets," Kiara whispered. The two women shared a knowing look, then focused on Monica. "How long have you owned the facility?"

"For about five years now. It was in place before I purchased it, but the woman who owned it previously decided it was time to retire."

"Well I say God bless anyone who has the patience and stamina to educate and care for children the way you do, Monica." Up to their table stepped the tall, handsome man who'd helped Elise with food preparations. Dressed in a polo shirt and jeans, he radiated warmth and appeal. He sat and slid his hand against Kiara's shoulder in a gesture of quiet intimacy. *This must be the pastor,* Monica thought. *The one who heads the church Jeremy attends.*

The man offered his hand. "Hi, I'm Ken Lucerne."

"It's a pleasure to meet you. Jeremy's told me so many nice things about you. About *all* of you," she amended, taking in the table at large.

Conversations took off from there and Monica sat back, observing. Elise had silver hair, styled into a soft, neat bob around her chin. Dressed in black jeans and a bulky, cream-colored sweater, she looked far younger than she must be to have mothered all of JB's siblings.

Collin entered the kitchen and retrieved a couple of sodas from the refrigerator. He was, Monica now realized, so similar to his brothers in the eyes and face, and in physical stature, but the soft waves of lighter colored hair, almost blond in fact, and the green rather than brown eyes spoke strongly of his mother's heredity.

Then there were the kids. Of various ages and sizes, Monica quickly lost track. They clamored for attention, especially from Elise. Jeremy hiked one in on his back. Not surprisingly, both nephew and uncle were on the hunt for food. When he looked at Monica, Jeremy lowered the youngster. "Go see what Grandma's got stashed on the counter over there, Tommy. Looks like your fave—cheese and crackers."

Jeremy stepped up to Monica from behind, and she calmed instantly when he settled a hand on her shoulder. His other slid neatly beneath her hair, and he massaged her neck, kneading her skin with slow, gentle strokes. Heat bloomed at the center of her body and rose with shimmering intensity to the surface of her skin.

But the connection they shared didn't completely dispel an inner chill. She thought she had been prepared for this gathering. She was woefully mistaken; a sense of inadequacy played havoc against edgy nerves and refused her any semblance of peace.

"How many grandkids are there?" she asked Elise, who lowered the snack tray for Tommy's eager fingers as he danced from foot to foot. He snatched a snack, and off he ran.

"Say thank you to Grandma," came Jeremy's admonishment.

"Thank you, Grandma!" he called over his shoulder, not breaking stride.

Elise watched after her grandson with a happy expression on her face. "We have six grandchildren. And I'd take six more, thank you."

Elise set the tray on the table, and once again Kiara and Daveny shared a puzzling look. Ken ducked his gaze, reaching for the freshly positioned food offering in a manner that seemed more diversionary than anything else. An odd, unexpected sense of foreshadowing crept through her system. Out of her element, starting to tremble on the inside, Monica receded further and further to the background.

Chatter ebbed and flowed through the room, through the entire household, really. Jeremy took Monica on a brief tour of the place where he had grown up. At the conclusion, they met up with Tommy once again. This time, Tommy was trailed by Jeffrey, who hurtled into Monica and hugged her legs tight. "Miss Monica!"

She tried hard not to flinch. She tried hard not to stiffen. She tried hard not to back off when one of the nieces joined in as well, charging forward to join their little group. Tommy bounced up and down. "Uncle JB, come play a game with me and Katie."

"I pway! I pway! I wan' Miss Monica, too," little Jeffrey declared, not releasing his hold.

"She can come, too," Tommy appeased.

The trio of children waited expectantly. Jeremy looked at Monica. She wanted to offer the genuine smile for which he waited. She tried to nod in agreement. Instead, she froze. She longed for an escape hatch—a release from the pressure-cooker sensation that settled around her body and squeezed out every good emotion she should have been feeling right now. Kids and family were a huge equation in Jeremy's life. That didn't bode well for their future. Not from Monica's perspective.

Kid-play just wasn't in her right now.

"Tell you what, Uncle JB, you hit the game room. I'm going to visit the kitchen and see if Elise needs any help."

She ignored Jeffrey's disappointed expression, Jeremy's silent surprise. She turned fast toward the kitchen just in time to see Elise at the threshold of the family room. Jeremy's mom witnessed the exchange and watched in dark puzzlement.

"Actually, I'm all set," Elise said. "You and Jeremy should just relax and enjoy yourselves. Really, go along and have fun."

Monica pressed her lips together, looking away. Defeated on a number of levels, she nodded, pasted on a smile, and followed slowly after Jeremy and the kids. But she couldn't help noticing Elise's expression had gone sharper still. Speculative.

After the board game came a bracing, exuberant game of soccer in the backyard that teamed adults against the kids. Once again, Monica tried to step to the sidelines but Jeremy would have none of that. He brought her in full-bore until Monica was dashing across the lawn along with everyone else, chasing after the black and white striped Spaulding in family-friendly competition. Still, she caught the vibration of puzzlement escalating on behalf of both Jeremy and Elise.

The weather was cold, accented by an on-and-off sputtering of snowflakes, so it was a short match, designed to allow the kids to blow off a bit of cabin fever and build an appetite for dinner. Monica's attempts at play were halfhearted at best—until, at one point, little Jeffrey looked over at her from across the expanse of the backyard. He smiled greatly, and wiggled his fingers. A lump, inspired by longing, expanded in Monica's throat. Stinging, cold wind bit through her, so if anyone noticed that her eyes filled, she could blame it on anything but the ache in her heart. She blew Jeffrey a little kiss and wiggled her fingers right back.

After the match, Jeffrey dashed straight for her. "Miss Monica, you good! Fun, huh? I good, too!"

Monica was so wrapped up in the goings on of her heart, so troubled by thoughts of the family that bounded in and out of focus, she found herself at a loss when the youngster settled warmly against the side of her leg. Jeffrey looked up at her, eager and waiting. Monica realized he probably expected the comfort and familiarity of the way she treated him at Sunny Horizons.

There, in her own environment, she wouldn't hesitate to swing him into the air, or carry him along on her hip as she walked through the center. She could claim temporary possession when she was at Sunny Horizons. To coddle and "parent" him there was as natural as breathing.

But right now Monica was galaxies away from her carefully cultivated element. Jeffrey was centered within the heart of his family. *Jeremy's* family. At this moment, everything she longed for the most remained painfully out of reach, yet at the same time, it was on display before her like an explosion of glitter dust floating on the air—breathtakingly beautiful, yet impossible to claim as her own.

So, Monica couldn't muster much of a reaction to his arrival other than a wan smile. "I did see you play. You're outstanding. Are you having fun with all your cousins and aunts and uncles?"

"Mm-hmm. I like food."

Spoken like a true Edwards. Monica couldn't help melting just a trace; she even chuckled. "Me, too."

"Is it fun? Are you fun, like me?" He tilted his head. "You look sad."

Taken thoroughly aback, Monica opened her mouth, intending to answer, somehow. Words stalled. She looked at Jeffrey and her mind went blank. Early on in her career, Monica had learned absolutely nothing escaped the notice of a child. She should have remembered that axiom.

Jeffrey's brows pulled together until they puckered with curiosity. "Wanna pway again? I pway a game wif Uncle Marty." He pointed toward a nearby gathering. "You pway good games. C'mon!"

The youngster smiled; Monica ached. "No thank you, Jeffrey. I'm going to go back inside and warm up for a little bit."

He surrendered with a nod, but watched her in continuing bewilderment. "'Kay."

After Jeffrey scampered off, things progressed a bit more comfortably until dinner ended. Elsie went about taking meal-concluding coffee orders.

"Decaf, please," came Daveny's surprisingly chipper request.

Kiara spoke up, sounding equally cheerful. "Since misery loves company, I'll go for some decaf as well, Elise. If it's not too much trouble."

Jeremy rolled his eyes. "Oh, come on. Seriously? Decaf? After a dinner like this? You two need to learn how to drink coffee."

As realization dawned in Monica, the table at large shared a round of laughter at Jeremy's oblivious words. Elise, frozen in place, simply stood at the counter, a coffee pot suspended in her grip. She stared at the two women; she began to smile, and glow. Tears filled her eyes.

"Sorry to humiliate you, JB," Daveny said, "but I'm on decaf for at least the next six months."

"Hmm. More like five for me," Kiara chimed in.

Ken couldn't seem to resist. He slid the thick fall of Kiara's dark blonde hair over her shoulder and nuzzled her neck. He rested a protective hand against her abdomen.

Jeremy eyes widened as he finally caught the gist of their interplay. "We're pregnant?"

Daveny and Kiara cracked up, and the Edwards family erupted with congratulations and delighted, happy shouts. "We're pregnant," the women said in unison.

"I refer to it as an abundance of blessings," Ken concluded, keeping loving hold of his wife.

It took every ounce of willpower and grace Monica possessed to keep from running out of the room in tears. She only hoped the assemblage would blame her flushed cheeks and moist eyes on the news of the day and nothing else.

In truth, her heart was shattered.

∂∞

The congratulatory hubbub slowly died down. As quickly as tact and discretion allowed, Monica intended to head outside for a spell of cold, reviving air. Respite became paramount.

An abundance of blessings. Ken had put it so well.

But what about the other side of that coin? Monica wondered, ceding a mite to the devil's temptation. *What would the good pastor have to say about a* denial *of blessings? What about trampled hopes? What about a literal and figurative emptiness?*

Resentment pushed into her heart. Bitterness cut a deep line into her spirit and moved right in. Trying hard to outrun her feelings, Monica walked through the kitchen. A set of sliding glass doors led outside like a portal to salvation.

"Monica?"

She froze and winced at the summons that came to her from behind. Her hands trembled, but she steadied herself and turned toward Jeremy's mother, schooling agitation from her features as best she could. "Yes?" She forced a smile and bullied herself to be carefree and calm. The attempt failed abysmally, and she knew it.

"You seem…" Elise stumbled over her words. She frowned and lowered her gaze briefly. When she looked up again, it was plain to see she was fighting a battle against interfering and pushing at her son's girlfriend.

They were both walking on eggshells, Monica realized.

"You've seemed troubled throughout the day today, and…I wonder why. I just want to know if everything is OK." Elise, who was probably a gregarious, outgoing woman by nature, right now, struck Monica as completely uncertain, and stilted. Monica's heart thundered and a lump formed in her throat. But no way could she—or would she—open up. Not even a trace. Cracks in her weakening control system would explode beneath an onslaught of once tightly held emotion. Emotion Elise Edwards would never understand.

So, in essence, Monica ducked for cover. "Please don't worry," she said too brightly. "I'm just fine. I only wanted to…" She looked almost desperately toward the sanctuary of the deck. "Uh…"

Elise didn't bother stifling a sigh. Obviously disappointed, she shook her head. "Let me know if you need anything. Will we see you back at the table shortly?"

"Of course."

With that assurance, Elise left for the kitchen, but Monica wilted.

What a horrible way of reacting to the woman's hospitality, Monica thought, shamed and regretful at once. She had to escape—just for a minute, long enough to recapture her equilibrium. She moved quickly. Unlatching and opening the doors, she embraced the instant sense of peace and solitude. The spacious deck was empty now, cleared of furniture and accessories as winter dawned.

Don't be this way, she chided herself. *It's wrong. Self-pity won't change anything. Daveny and Kiara have every right to be thrilled. Furthermore, to do anything less than celebrate would hurt them and hurt Jeremy. He brought you here today for a reason. He wants you to become a deeper part of his life. It's an honor. Don't blow it!*

But the battle was like trying to beat back the whirling vortex of a tornado with nothing but smoke and mirrors.

She sank onto a set of steps that led to the backyard. She couldn't help admiring the gorgeous landscaping. Had to be the doing of both Elise and Daveny. Though winter rode in fast, groupings of hearty, large-headed mums still spotted the grounds with autumnal color. The grass remained thick and well-tended, a deep hue of green. Monica lost herself to the scent of burning wood that came from the chimney, the bracing chill of the wind. She quieted her mind. For about two or three seconds.

Why were others so abundantly blessed, as Ken put it, when by contradiction, her lot in this life was empty and barren in more ways than one? Why did others have it so easy—the relationships, the kids, the fulfilled lives, when that very destiny, the one she craved above all others, would never be hers to claim?

It was so easy to believe in God, and His blessings and grace, when your prayers were answered.

Dimly conscious of warm moisture on her cheeks, Monica blinked rapidly, aware now that tears fell from her eyes.

God, I hate feeling this way. It never ends, though. It never goes away. You don't seem to let it. Instead You always seem to narrow my world into a hyper-focus that leaves me seeing nothing else but what I lack, and everything I want so much but will never be able to have. Why?

Not much of a prayer, but right now, Monica didn't feel like God was much in the mood for listening—or answering her plea.

"Hey there, Jellybean. I thought this might come in handy right about now."

Jeremy.

Monica ducked her head and swiped fast at her cheeks. Meanwhile, from behind, he handed her a large, bistro mug of coffee. The warmth against her cold fingertips, and the fragrance, took a bit of the edge off her mood almost immediately.

Jeremy sat down next to her, silent, looking out upon the barren, wavering tree branches, the cloud-thickened sky. Monica stole a glance at him. A loose oxford shirt, comfortable jeans, lent him an air of casual appeal. Jeremy Blaise Edwards was impossibly handsome, but beyond that, he was finely attuned to the ones he loved, and he possessed a heart full of compassion and tenderness. Consequently, his presence in her life seemed yet another way God was letting her down.

Sure, she thought. *Show me the love, and promise, of a*

man like this. Tempt me with everything I want but can never possibly hold on to…then take it all away because I can never, ever be what he wants, and needs, the most.

"Thank you," she replied belatedly, but with genuine gratitude.

He looked into her eyes with that tantalizing quirk of a smile. The man left her aching, longing. Generally, she called the shots, and could perform breezy, graceful steps back when things got this complicated with a man. Not this time, though. *Why, why, why?*

"You're welcome, but I caught the vibe, Monica. I want to know what happened. Can you talk to me about whatever it is that's been bothering you today?"

She sighed out a puff of air. "JB, some things you can't change, or help with, no matter how much you may want to." She chewed on her lower lip and looked away.

"No," he murmured. "Not this time." Jeremy tucked a finger beneath her chin and tilted her head, directing her gaze to his. "Keep it right here." He stroked her cheek softly.

Such tenderness, so much caring. Every bit of the world she wanted was captured deep within his dark brown eyes. Those eyes were her undoing, and she backpedaled in fear. "I just needed some air. Really. No big deal, I promise."

"And that would be strike two, Monica." His irritation grew. She heard as much in his tone, and in the fact that Jellybean had reverted to Monica. "That makes twice you've backed away from me. Twice you've flat-out lied about something you're going through that's troubling. You did it at *Polonia*, and you're doing it now. Well, I'm right here, and I'm not going anywhere. Talk to me."

Her heart dissolved. Desire flowed hot, strong and tempting. But rationality entered the fray as well. "Not right now, OK? Not right this second. Not when your family is in the middle of a wonderful, happy celebration. I need to keep it together. Please understand."

"Fine. But, when I take you home tonight, we're going to talk." There was no room for negotiation. She breathed out heavily, and she stood, but Jeremy caught her hand and held it tight. From his perch on the deck stairs, he looked up at her while he caressed the back of her hand with his thumb. "Don't shut down. Not with me, and not with them." He indicated the people inside with a nod toward the house. "Share this with us. It's important. Because *you're* important."

Her chin quivered at his words. "Thanks. I appreciate it."

"Then like I said—don't close off." He stood smoothly, keeping her hand in his when they walked back inside.

10

While Jeremy focused on the drive to Monica's place, she shrank into the far side of the passenger seat and closed her eyes. Bracing herself, she prepared for the emotional blow she knew was coming. After all, following today's events, he had every right to be put out by her standoffish behavior. "Jeremy," she began timidly, "I'm so sorry I let you down."

No JB. No flirty sass. Instead, she stared straight ahead, into a curving roadway sided by towering trees. Homes, occasional stores, and strip malls flashed past. Silence pressed in on her from all sides, oppressive and nearly claustrophobic.

Sorry I let you down. Those five small words formed a haunting refrain, followed by the main verse: *And this is only the beginning.*

Jeremy turned into the entrance of Monica's subdivision. "I just don't get it. Kids are your passion. They're the largest part of your life. You love them. But today, with my family, and especially when Dav and Kiara made their announcements, when I figured you'd be one of the largest parts of the cheering section, you vanished. You sparkle, and you're so easy to be with, and enjoy. But today you backed yourself into a corner and not only did you refuse to leave that corner behind, you came off seeming—" He paused.

Shrugged. "Distant. You were defensive. For the life of me, I don't understand why."

His tone, laced by frustration, seeped into her system like some kind of slow-acting, destructive poison. The only anti-venom? Revelation.

They reached her home. When Jeremy parked, Monica looked straight ahead. "I didn't mean to be rude," she began, quietly. "I didn't want to feel the way I did today, Jeremy. I couldn't help it. I couldn't stop what came over me. I try, and I try…but…"

Jeremy touched her shoulder. His eyes glittered in the dim illumination of her neighbor's garage light. "Monica, what is it? Please tell me what's going on."

She squeezed her hands into tight fists. Before he could turn the tables, and gain an upper hand in this conversation, an upper hand she was in desperate need of maintaining, Monica exited his truck and walked into her home. Jeremy followed while she flicked on a couple lights and greeted Toby. After Toby leaped around Jeremy's legs, familiarizing himself with this intriguing stranger, and after the dog received a series of hearty pets and greetings, Monica released him into the backyard for a late-night romp so she could talk to Jeremy in peace.

As they sat on the couch in her living room, she began anew. "About today. First and foremost, let me repeat the fact that I'm sorry. Please know I didn't mean to hurt you, or anyone else."

"Apology accepted, Monica, but that's not even the issue for me right now. Not anymore. *You're* the issue. Something hurt you, and I want to know what it is. It's as simple as that."

"And as complicated," she whispered, blowing out a breath she held too tight in her chest. She spoke up louder now. "Actually I had a good time, but…"

Jeremy cut in. "But. *That's* the issue. Talk to me about *but*."

Instinctively she looked up, searching his eyes. The degree of emotion she found there hit her senses, struck heat to her soul. The feelings between them had deepened with such heady speed. That fact alone wouldn't alarm her, but so much stood between them. All would be lost once he knew the truth about her, and that made everything about this day painful, and bittersweet.

"OK, let me try to get this out," she murmured, more to herself than Jeremy. She stood to pace the living room. In counterpoint, Jeremy remained seated. He seemed so calm. So rock steady.

"I enjoyed your family very much. They're funny and warm and loving. They're a symbol to me of everything you deserve, and probably long for in a family of your own. You told me yourself that you're mapping out a legacy. You want to keep tradition, and a family's love, alive in everything that you do. That's a beautiful thing."

"Monica, where is all of this coming from?" When she didn't answer right away, Jeremy persisted. "Let me in. Show me that you trust me."

She wrapped her arms around her waist, trying desperately to hold herself together while she took a sledgehammer to their relationship, a relationship she would have loved embracing. "You want children and a family more than anything, right?"

"Ultimately, yes. Absolutely."

"So do I." She spun toward him, desperate to avoid the fateful blow, but unable to stop it.

Jeremy waited, obviously not yet understanding

where the conversation was headed.

"But I can't be what you want. I'm not able. I can never get pregnant. I can never have children. I can't. I can't ever fill that part of your life—or my own. Your family is wonderful. That's honestly how I feel, even if I showed it poorly today. And family is of vital importance to you, Jeremy. That truth colored my entire time with them, and with you. It shredded a part of my heart, and my hopes for you and me."

His brows pulled together. He shook his head slightly and gave her a startled look. "What are you saying?"

"I'm infertile. The medical term for my condition is endometriosis. My case is severe enough that ultimately I may even require a hysterectomy."

His silence, hers coupled with it, allowed the charged air between them to settle a bit. Monica forced herself to take a few deep breaths to re-steady her trembling legs and hands.

She waited on him, stiff tension climbing up her back inch by fateful inch as the silence continued. She watched Jeremy blink free of his thoughts and lock focus on her face, then her eyes. "Wh…when? How did you find out? I mean—"

Monica stood stock still, facing him as straight as she could manage. "It's a long story."

"I've got time."

She remained frozen in place, in time. "It's got a lot of detail you may not want to hear."

"This is your life, right? The battle you're fighting?"

She nodded.

"Then don't cushion me. Or us. There's nothing about you that I *don't* want to hear about, or know about. Believe that."

The *us* portion of that sentence sounded so good. In fact, it skimmed against her skin like the stroke of a sable brush.

"OK. For better or worse." She paused. "When I"—she shrugged delicately—"came of age physically, I had issues from day one. Symptoms started small, but built, year-by-year, until by the time I was halfway through college, I had it all. The swollen stomach. Nausea. Blinding headaches. Excessive bleeding. To cap it all off, the middle of every blessed month was an odyssey of pain." Memories crashed in—leaving her feeling so bereft. So unfeminine, and immodest. That's why she could discuss the condition with Jeremy now. She had been forced to become clinical about it all. Detached. Except when in the company of large, loving families. Expanding families. Being with the Edwards's today filled her with an ache so acute, so pervasive, it knocked the very breath right out of her.

But she had to tell him everything. She could accept no other option but complete honesty. "My condition became severe enough that I finally sought help. I went to specialists. For months, I lived an honest-to-goodness nightmare when it came to my health. I won't go into the ways in which I felt like a guinea pig, or like I was nothing more than a test specimen. At the end of almost a year, after blood tests, hormone treatments, a laparoscopy, and at last, full-blown surgery, the best they could come up with was that I suffered from ovarian cysts which I had a possibility of outgrowing at some point in the future."

Monica paced, unable to meet his gaze right now. "The process was humiliating, but I was young and figured I had hope. In the meantime, I found my calling with early childhood education. Maybe something inside my head was getting the message my heart refused to accept—that I better prepare myself for life without kids of my own by building my life around those I *could* help, and teach and engage."

Jeremy stood, and he did the pacing now. "Are you sure kids are out of the question? From what very little I know about endometriosis, it's inconsistent, isn't it? Women can still get pregnant, still have happy, healthy babies—right?"

The longing in his voice was a near perfect echo of her own. She understood completely because she lived those desires day by day, month after month, until hope became exhausted. She didn't even try to cushion her answer. "Not this time. Not for me."

Those six quietly spoken words hung in the air.

"You can't hold any illusions about me, Jeremy. I'm beaten, and I'm scared, and I'm angry. I don't even feel…" She shrugged and looked up at the ceiling to blink her blurred vision clear of moisture. "I don't even feel feminine sometimes." She faced him squarely. "I've been told in counseling that that may be part of why I focus on dance and physical expression—to affirm my time and place as a woman. I just don't know anymore. And I most certainly don't want to wake up to feelings like I have for you, then go through a crash and burn when the relationship dissolves because I can't be everything you want, and need. The idea of that scares me to death. I've been denied so much—so many things that my heart holds most dear. I know how selfish and narcissistic that sounds, but my feelings are my feelings, and I can't escape them, no matter how hard I try." She hung her head, returning to the couch.

Jeremy joined her.

"I'm so sorry for backing off from everything, and everyone, today. But can you possibly understand how Daveny and Kiara's announcement cut through my heart? How being around your family affected me?"

He studied her for a moment before answering. "Yes, Monica, I can. But the only way you're going to get to the other side of this situation is by grabbing hold of some semblance of faith, and trust. Learn to let go of what God is denying you, and focus instead on everything He's given you!"

She'd been down this road before, and she was ready. "Really?" She fired back. "What has He given me? I'm empty! I'm literally and figuratively empty! How can that appeal to you—in the long term? Once the passion and excitement is replaced by the day-to-day, how will you be able to be happy with a woman who can't give you a family? A woman who can't give you a child, and the legacy you've admitted to building your life for?"

"Thanks for shortchanging me, Monica. Thanks a lot."

"Jeremy, listen to what I'm *saying*! Be *realistic*! This is as much about how inadequate I feel as it is about my feelings for you!"

"OK, then let me be realistic." He stood and turned to her. He met her hot and confrontational posture straight on. "In fact, here's a healthy dose of realism for you: do you think you're not benefiting every single child at Sunny Horizons? What about the girls who dance for you? What about them? Don't any of them count in the balance?"

Monica gaped. "Well there we go. Problem solved!"

"Monica, stop it!"

"No, *you* stop it! First of all, the answer to my problems is *not* that simple. Secondly, even the point of view you just expressed doesn't answer what I'm unable to bring to a relationship, to a family life, with you or anyone else over the long term."

"So your answer is to give up? Really? That's so not like the woman I've gotten to know, and admire."

"It's not giving up, it's being realistic." Monica tried to steady her breathing; she leaned forward and cradled her head in her hands. "I've been operated on by scalpels and lasers, spent portions of the month flat on my back, endured tests and needles, been treated with drugs and still endured the pain. At the end of the road the truth is this: I'm not meant to have a family. I've had to find a way to accept that."

"Monica, you're one of the strongest women I've ever met. You're good hearted and intelligent—smart enough to recognize stubbornness! You're suffering from tunnel vision."

"Tunnel vision." She shook her head. "I guess that's how you'd see it. I suppose it's easy to downplay what I feel, and the emptiness that goes along with it." Then, since they were at the point of no return anyhow, she admitted to the worst of her doubts and fears. "I feel like I was marked as unworthy. Less of a woman."

He studied her in silence for a long, tense moment. "You couldn't be more wrong."

She shook her head, making an exasperated noise. She looked up in time to see Jeremy squeeze the bridge of his nose.

"You know, I could talk until I'm blue in the face, but you won't realize the truth of what I'm saying until you find a way to take a long, hard look at the life you really have in front of you versus the life you're clinging to despite everything God's showing you!"

"Once again, Jeremy, you're using platitudes to simplify what I feel—and I'm here to tell you, it just doesn't work! It sounds great in theory, sure, but that philosophy has failed me miserably." Almost immediately, she regretted those snapping words, and her waspish tone.

Her attitude didn't seem to deter him in the least, though. Jeremy possessed the ability to recognize pain versus anger. Further, he cared—cared enough to endure the sword slice of her self-doubts. So when he took a deep breath, and returned to her side at the couch, Monica welcomed his touch—the way he held her shoulders fast, but with tenderness.

And he urged, "*Please* don't make this your life's deal breaker. You're better than that. You're an exquisite, remarkable woman. And you have too many gifts to offer this world, and the children in it, to let this beat you, or close you down. Anything less is a waste."

The words slipped past her defensive walls and struck home, giving her a lot to think about. Jeremy continued. "One last thing to consider, Monica – and I want you to understand this fact with complete clarity: passion and fire may cool, but they never disappear. My *feelings* for you won't disappear. If you're waiting for that to happen—expecting it to happen because of infertility—then you'll end up disappointed. I told you at *Polonia*, I'm a man of action. I'm about resolving things—good and bad—by being present to the people I care about. I don't disappear. I don't vanish in the face of what I do, or don't, receive in this life. My blessings come from God—and you're just that to me,

Monica Kittelski. You're precious. To me. To God. Accept that fact. Deal with it."

His tough-minded declaration stirred her senses. Her blood sang, pounding in her ears. Tears poured down her cheeks, a sudden and unstoppable flood of release and longing. "I'm scared, and I *hate* being scared. I blew it today, and I know it. I didn't mean to. Honest. Thing is, I don't know how to move ahead without screwing up, JB. And I do *not* want to screw this up." The resumption of his nickname came easy just now.

He relaxed his shoulders a bit and took her hands in his. "I told you before, I'm not good with the words, with putting emotions forward," he said quietly. "But I know who is. Would you please, for me, talk this over with Ken? I promise you he'll provide objective advice. He's been through heartbreaks that are different from yours, but just as powerful, and he's a remarkable man. I trust him completely, and he will *not* pressure you. You don't have to claim God. Not yet, if you're not ready and able—but give a try to *listening* to God. I believe in His providence with all my heart, Monica. Pour your heart out, and I promise, in His hands, you'll be safe. You'll be cared for. Would you do that? For me?"

"For us?" she asked with a shaky voice and a trembling that was probably easy for him to see, given her tight stance.

"For us."

"I can only try."

His eyes dimmed. "Trying is fine, Monica, but you can't bolt in the face of what you've been denied, like you did today. That worries me a lot more than whether or not you can have kids. Get a handle on that part of your battle, OK? More than a mother to my children, I want a woman who will stand by my side—no matter *what*—knowing our strength, and provision, will come from Christ, and that in that faith will come goodness. Lean on Him, Jellybean, or your troubles will only intensify. You've been bearing the load on your own for way too long. You need, and deserve, His grace. It's perfect, and it's faultless, no matter what your outward circumstances appear. The time-worn cliché is so very true: when we can't, God can. Will you talk to Ken?"

She deflected her gaze, but slowly—very slowly—she nodded.

11

"I'm not saying I don't like Monica, JB. That's not my point at all!"

"That's not the way it seems to me right now, Mom."

Just days after Sunday dinner with his parents, Jeremy found himself the subject of a motherly debriefing. She knew he usually spent Tuesdays and Thursdays at the offices of Edwards Construction in a grudging concession to company bureaucracy, so she paid him a visit, the subject matter of said visit, his girlfriend.

His mother sat across from his desk in the utilitarian office he occupied. Just down the hall was a second office for the bookkeeper, Paula Cromwell, and out front sat the receptionist and Jane-of-all-trades, Allison Moynah. The duo comprised his corporate team, and they were housed in a small business office along Jefferson Avenue.

He stretched back in his chair, doing his best to absorb the crux of her comments without becoming angry, or defensive. "So can you clarify what *are* you saying, Mom? Because what should be a pleasant get-together is starting to feel more like an inquisition."

When his mom had called Monday and asked to meet, Jeremy had embraced the opportunity. Now he wasn't as enthusiastic. Tension crept through the muscles of his shoulders. His fingertips twitched with a pen; he clicked and tapped it while he sat, and waited.

His mother temporarily embraced the silence, then continued. "JB, she's nice enough, I suppose, and certainly she's as attractive as can be, but I don't know, she seems remote. Shuttered. She's very guarded. It's like she was uncomfortable for some reason. I guess I'm surprised she holds such strong appeal to a family man like you when all she wanted to do all day was hide."

That comment struck a chord. All he could think of, all he could see in his mind's eye was Monica's defeat, her sadness and the futility she experienced. She was lost right now, and he cared for her. Therefore, abandonment was not an option. He wanted to stand up for her. "Mom, trust me when I say there are circumstances that can cause even the most wonderful person to stumble, and hold back."

Her eyes sharpened. "And this family knows that better than most, JB—especially after what Collin, and all of us, endured after Lance was killed."

Jeremy sighed, sipping from the mug of coffee before him. Elise's ginger tea steamed nearby, thus far untouched. More and more he realized this visit wasn't about catching up, it was about probing. "True, Mom, and I appreciate your protectiveness. But show some compassion as well. Show her some leeway and understanding. She has a few things she's working out." He couldn't bring himself to be as open and blunt with his mother as Monica had been with him. Not yet. Not when quicksand shifted and pulled all around.

"All right, all right—but still, I just don't know

what to make of her."

"Meaning?"

She leaned back, crossing her legs and finally sipping from her mug. "For example, she loves kids, but this past weekend, she wanted nothing to do with them. She owns a daycare center, for heaven's sake, but we had to force her to play a few simple board games with the kids, and join in the soccer game."

Jeremy went stiff. His mom made valid points. Her honest, though blunt observations were on the mark, but they only served to stir his disquiet, and increase his understanding of the undercurrents that had affected Monica's mood that day. So, once more, he stepped forward to be a buffer. "Daveny and Collin are excellent judges of character, and so am I. Trust in that, OK?" After a calming pause, Jeremy felt better. Shifting aside a half-unrolled set of blueprints, he retrieved a stack of job files and made ready to dive back into paperwork. And he bluffed just a bit. "As to avoidance, maybe she was looking forward to a little adult company and conversation. Remember, she's with kids almost twenty-four seven. She may have wanted, and needed, a bit of a breather from the pitter-patter, know what I mean?"

"Yes, to a degree, but I think there's more to it. You've said you're talking about it. Working it through. If that's the case, then I'm happy. I promise I'll leave my overly protective fingers out of the mix. I don't mean to be so rough on her, or you, but I worry about my kids. It's wired into my DNA. Always has been, always will be. If she has your heart, then she'll have mine as well. No question."

She hadn't been thrown off the scent, but her final words were just what he expected, and hoped, from his mother. A twisted knot of anxiety and tension loosened its grip from the base of his neck. Jeremy reached across the desk and squeezed her hand. "Thanks."

"You're very much like your father. You're quiet about your emotions, but you carry them deep, and your feelings are strong. I'm only speaking up because I don't want to see you get hurt."

Jeremy took a quick mental walk through the past few days. Monica had stepped forward, albeit tentatively. After all, she had spoken freely, and frankly, about her condition. She had taken custody of Ken's phone number on a promise to connect with Woodland's pastor. From there, Jeremy toyed with the idea of including her in this weekend's services as well and decided it would be a good idea to extend an invitation.

Inviting her to Woodland on Sunday would establish a point of comfort for Monica with the church and its atmosphere before she met with Ken. It would also show his family, once again, his intent and seriousness. He wanted Monica to find God's mercy. He wanted her to feel acceptance. Within the embrace of Woodland Church, she might make a way to God, to being affirmed.

His mother leaned forward setting aside her tea in a smooth, deliberate way. Her sea-green eyes narrowed just a bit, but she smiled. "She means a great deal to you."

"Yes." No need to embellish. For a millisecond he considered the emptiness Monica felt. The insecurity. It tore him apart inside. Jeremy refused to add to her sense of pain and insecurity. This relationship merited solid footing and every fighting chance.

Indeed, she meant that much.

"I see it all in your eyes," his mother said quietly. She left it at that, giving his arm a gentle pat.

Jeremy played it close to the vest, and kept it to himself that he intended to take her to church on Sunday. He also kept quiet about his intention to invite her to Rebecca's wedding. Despite well-meaning, motherly intrusion, Elise Edwards knew her children well. She was right when she said he didn't play cavalier with his emotions. He wanted to establish firm footing with Monica. Nothing else mattered.

❧

Jeremy had to admit, he felt out of place.

It was Wednesday night. About a half-dozen women were gathered outside the doorway of the Saint Clair Shores Community Center. They looked inside, bragging proudly about their daughters, who currently practiced ballet. He belonged here like a square peg in a round hole.

Hanging back, he watched the class taking place inside, smiling while he watched Monica spin, stretch, and form her arms into a perfect arc above her head.

"Monica is so good with the girls. I wonder if she has any kids of her own."

The comment came from one of the moms who peered inside, and it won Jeremy's attention.

"I'm not sure," a second parent answered. "I wonder if she's married. She doesn't wear a wedding ring." A pause followed that remark. "One thing is for sure," she added, "if Monica weren't so nice, I'd hate her."

A third woman chuckled. "I know what you

mean. No woman should have blonde hair, blue eyes, and that much grace. It's disgusting. Just watch her."

That's exactly what Jeremy did. Throughout the last few minutes of class, Monica coached the little girls along, performing the ballet routine along with them. Each lift of her arms, each dip and sway, was executed with a smoothness that could never be taught. Fluid grace like hers was innate, and it textured each of her movements, even beyond the dance floor.

The song came to an end, and she concluded class for the week. Monica looked toward the doorway. After she delivered a smile and a wave, the waiting parents entered the room. Still chatting amiably, adults laid claim to their young dancers who charged forward eagerly after bidding Monica good night.

When the noise and activity died down, Jeremy slipped inside. Monica's back was to him as she stashed one set of CDs and retrieved another. She picked up a water bottle and drank deep, which left Jeremy with a definite sensual vibration. When she patted a towel against her neck and shoulders, he stepped up. He hid his hands, and a treat, behind his back.

"Hey, Miss Monica." His playful call caused her to freeze for a moment, then she turned, her eyes alight with happiness and affection. Jeremy smiled and gave her a slow wink. A bit closer now, he moved his hands from their hiding position, revealing that he held a single, long-stemmed pink rose. Attached to the stem, via a white, curled ribbon was a small bag of jellybeans. "For the teacher."

Monica accepted with a blush that almost perfectly matched the hue of the flower. "Thanks, JB."

Just like that, he found himself the willing target of

her large, luminous eyes. A wisp of golden hair slid over the hollow in her shoulder. Jeremy watched its trail, mesmerized. Following an hour of dance instruction, her skin glowed, radiant with health.

"You were quite the topic of conversation out in the hallway." He itched to reach up and twirl that silky curl of hair around his finger. "The moms out there are about ready to start a fan club."

Monica laughed. "Stop it!"

"I'm serious. Rumor has it they're headed out to get t-shirts printed up." Her second round of laughter played like music, tickling his senses. "They love you."

"They're just a really nice group. They seem to appreciate what I do with the girls."

"The moms aren't the only ones who are captivated." That caused Monica to look away shyly, which left Jeremy all the more eager to heighten her awareness. "I watched you just now. You're as graceful in body as you are in spirit."

As hoped, the flush ripened, and she turned away, kneeling. She placed the rose and candy gently next to her tote. Still, Monica was Monica, and when she stood, she quickly recovered her playful *élan*. "And how sweet are you—coming all the way out here just to tell me that, and deliver a treat? What's the occasion?"

"I have a proposal to make." He'd created the opening he wanted. "How do you stand on the topic of church?"

Monica gave him an inquiring look. "I like church just fine. Why?"

A pony-tailed young lady with big brown eyes and peaches-and-cream skin interrupted them. The little girl dashed up and hugged Monica's legs. "Bye,

Miss Monica. See you tomorrow at school. Thank you for helping me practice today."

He watched Monica quite literally dissolve under the youngster's loving regard. She ran her fingertips against the straight, silky strands of the girl's chestnut colored hair and she hugged the child right back. "It's my absolute pleasure, Jessica. I'm so proud of the progress you've made! See you tomorrow."

Wearing a great smile, Jessica ran off. Following a brief look into Monica's eyes, Jeremy tracked the girl's progress to the outside hallway where her mother waited. The mom gave Monica a wave along with a tired, but happy smile. "That wouldn't happen to be the pair you were talking about at dinner the other night?

Monica kept an eye on the pair and nodded. "Yeah, sorry for being so scant on the details when we talked, but I always try to be careful when it comes to confidentiality issues."

Jeremy took her hand and swung it loosely. "Relationships mean intimacy. Intimacy means revelation—and the situation was bothering you. I won't compromise that show of trust, Monica. It's part of growing together."

She stretched up on tip-toe and kissed Jeremy's cheek; her eyes came alive with tender affection. "I appreciate that, because it's hard to keep lines from blurring when you…ah…"

Jeremy chuckled at her stutter. "Develop into a couple?"

She blushed and moistened her lips. But then, she nodded. "To answer your question a bit more directly, that's Jessica and Caroline Dempsey, and I think they're going to be OK. I really do."

"Good. She looks like a precious little girl."

"She is, but I'm sorry for the interruption."

"Not a problem at all."

Monica's focus centered in, and she tilted her head. "You were asking me about church."

"Yes. I was wondering—do you think you could join me for services at Woodland this Sunday?"

Her eyes went a bit wide. She tilted her head and leaned back a bit "I, ah…JB, really…I appreciate you including me. That's so thoughtful, I enjoy church and everything. I'm a little worried, though, and…and it's your family, and I'm just not sure…Would it be right? Would I fit in, and…"

He pressed a fingertip against her lips to still her speed talking, warmed by the fact that he now recognized the nervous habit. He waited a moment for her to be still. "One step at a time, Jellybean," he murmured. "One brick at a time."

Her shoulders sagged. Her eyes went soft, and plaintive. "But I'm embarrassed."

"About what?"

"About facing your family again. They probably don't even like me much, and I can't honestly say I blame them."

"Don't fear that road; walk down it instead. My family is about care, and love. They get protective, and intrusive, yes, but they're also very quick to forgive, and ask forgiveness in return. They care. They don't understand all your battles yet, but they know what happened this weekend isn't about them, or how you feel about them. I promise you that."

"How do you know, JB? How can you be so sure?"

"Because I already talked it over with my mom."

Monica's mouth opened and closed.

He chuckled. "We don't let things fester or go unquestioned, and unresolved. The Edwards clan moves forward. And, my mom is as tough as they come, but she knows, without question now, how important you are to me. That's what's called a deal breaker."

Jeremy looked down and took hold of her hand, oddly touched by the sight of their fingertips entwined. His flesh, slightly darker, seemed such a striking contrast to her fair, creamy skin. "We're scrappy and affectionate and we take no prisoners. Kinda like a certain exquisite lady I'm quite fond of who teaches little girls about grace and beautiful movement, and teaches kids about the rules of school, and life. Know what I mean?"

He could see her reaction in the shallow fall of her breathing, the wide, questing expression on her face as the words he spoke hit home. The pink leotard she wore was snug, but discreet, with a slight, scooped neckline. Her ensemble included a short matching skirt of rippling silk that floated around her legs with each move she made, each breath of air.

"You were wrong, JB, when you said you aren't any good with words. You keep showing me how gifted you are in that regard." She nibbled her lower lip. He longed to reach out and stroke the corner of her mouth until she relaxed.

"Thanks, Jellybean."

"I made the call yesterday. To Pastor Ken. I'm seeing him next week, on Tuesday, after work. I want you to know that. I did it because you're important to me, too."

Hope performed a vigorous dance through his blood stream. She was hesitant—he recognized that clearly—but she looked up at him in eagerness for approval. Jeremy was so happy she had made that difficult first step, and he wanted to help make that forward motion as easy on her as possible. "Then it seems to me like timing is everything. If you can come with me on Sunday, you'll get to see what Woodland's all about. Maybe spending some time at church, seeing Ken and the family again, will help you feel a lot better about things, and more comfortable when you meet with him."

"I'm sure it will." She fidgeted with the ends of the satin tie of her skirt, which was fashioned into a bow at her waist. "I'd like to go with you."

The moment was broken by the arrival of her second class of dance students, this group slightly older than the last. The girls filtered into the room, full of noisy greetings and laughter. Jeremy stepped away, but kept hold of her hand for as long as he could. He released her at last. "Bye, Jellybean."

She watched after him for a moment. "Call me later?"

Jeremy thought about that for a second or two. "I'll do you one better. Can I tempt you with dessert after class?"

"Cold Stone ice cream?" she requested expectantly.

Jeremy just grinned, and arched a brow. "I'll take that as a yes. Class is done at eight?"

"Yep. I'll meet you there."

Jeremy left the room and closed the door quietly as Monica began class.

"I'm impressed." Jeremy stared at Monica with wide eyes.

Monica sat back comfortably in the curved back, metal chair of the small table they shared inside the ice cream shop. She smiled victoriously because her paper cup, formerly overflowing with an order of chocolate peanut butter, was now empty. "Two scoops goes down *so* well after a ballet session."

"Let me follow you home. Make sure you get in OK."

"What?"

"You heard me."

"JB, I'm a capable, intelligent woman who's gone home alone thousands of times. I'll be fine."

"But it's dark, and it's cold. Call me old-fashioned. I want to see you home." More to the point, he wanted a pitch-black night to surround them, full of the promise of snow; and he wanted kisses—dewy, warm, soul-saturating, provocative goodnight kisses.

Monica picked up the cup and spooned out the very last remnants of her gourmet ice cream treat. She licked the utensil clean, her gaze narrow when she looked up at him once more. "Are you sure you're not a closet chauvinist?"

"Positive. Now, indulge me."

"It's out of your way."

"By two whole miles. How will I *ever* find a way to justify the fossil fuel emissions?"

Monica burst out laughing. "Oh man—and this game is over. You win."

"Besides, think of the convenience. I'll be able to help you carry in all that equipment from class. Now. Are you done, or are you going to go after that last little dribble of chocolate right there on the side of the cup—"

"Shut up," she admonished through giggles, diverting her gaze as she went after that last little dribble of chocolate right there on the side of the cup.

They left the shop hand in hand, strolling slowly to their parked cars. After following Monica home, he walked her to the door, carrying the stereo and duffle bag.

"I've decided. You're not a closet chauvinist. Rather, you're openly chivalrous," Monica set aside her ballet class supplies.

The beckoning warmth of her eyes, the curve of her lips, were his undoing.

Jeremy moved slowly, but with purpose. He took hold of her hands as he pressed forward, pinning them next to her head when he landed her back against the wall of the porch. The rough feel of brick against his hands, the chill, the scent of burning wood and snow to come, combined into a heady sensation and atmosphere.

He dipped his head and her warmth, her scent, swirled through him. Jeremy's resistance snapped. He claimed her mouth with delicious desire, devouring her every answering response. Against his chest, he could have sworn he felt the thundering of her heart— or perhaps it was his own. The connection worked magic, ignited fire, provoked his senses. He bent to its power, then fell headlong before he even knew what hit.

This was possession, soul-deep and irrevocable. The realization glided through him. He gave a throaty sound, releasing her hands so his fingertips could take a dive through her now loosened hair. Monica sank heavily against the wall, and he flattened his hands against cold, gritty brick. The effort somehow tethered him to reality. Just barely.

She sighed as she took hold of his arms and continued to kiss him senseless. His body formed a cover against hers, like a perfect, well-honed shield. With a last sound of wrangled desire, JB stepped back. His breathing was shallow. "Take out your keys." He almost growled the words, needing to put some distance between them before his senses overtook his rationale.

"Huh?" Her eyes were glazed and heavy.

He traced her jaw with a fingertip. "Take out your keys. I want to make sure you get in before I leave." He looked her straight in the eye, knowing his battles were visible. Still, he maintained restraint. "I need to leave."

Only then did he realize Monica's purse now resided on the ground at her feet. It had slid off her shoulder, unnoticed. Before she could move, JB bent smoothly and retrieved it for her, handing it over— though he kept a safe measure of physical distance between them.

"Ah—thanks." Her voice, of smoothest whiskey, stirred a warm throb of life, a shivering echo of their touch, their kiss.

"Inside," he directed once more, his own voice husky, and abrupt. The only thing that kept him from stepping over a moral boundary was his inbred belief system, and the pure sense of reverence he felt toward her.

"Inside," she murmured in agreement, fumbling for her keys. It took two tries, but the key found home in her doorknob. Inside, Toby went nuts. She swung the door wide, clicking on a nearby light switch. The dog bounded forward, jumping, grunting, wagging his tail. Light, sound and Monica's exuberant pet helped dissipate a few more of Jeremy's mental fog curls. He made quick work of greeting his new four-legged friend, and set the remainder of Monica's gear inside the entryway.

When he walked down the porch steps, Monica looked back at him and said softly, "See ya.'"

He turned, intending to give a wave. *Tempting. So tempting.* Instead, Jeremy buried his hands deep in the pockets of his leather jacket to keep himself in check.

"You knock me out, Jellybean," he murmured. "You absolutely knock me out. See ya.'"

12

Sunday morning, Jeremy walked through the doors of Woodland Church hand in hand with Monica. He edged them toward the etched glass doors to the sanctuary, which were presently flung open to welcome one and all to ten o'clock services. Jeremy was stopped repeatedly by people he knew, but he didn't mind. It gave him the chance to mix and mingle with Monica at his side, and introduce her to his place of worship.

They moved through the entrance and down the main aisle to join his family. Jeremy was about to slide into the pew, next to his mother, but Monica restrained him by taking hold of his arm. She moved smoothly ahead, claiming that spot instead. Following a deliberate glance into Jeremy's eyes, Monica sat.

"Good morning, Elise," she said. "How are you?" She leaned forward to make eye contact with his father as well. "Hi, Ben. It's good to see you again."

Genuine and welcoming, Monica possessed top-notch intuition. Jeremy warmed on the inside, proud of her. Monica seemed eager that any residual discomfort from last weekend vanished, and her efforts didn't go unnoticed. His mother didn't bubble over, like usual, or offer one of her automatic hugs, but she smiled and handed Monica a hymnal and a brief discussion ensued regarding the rundown of the day's readings and order of service.

It was a positive start, and Jeremy telegraphed that recognition into physicality, placing his arm along the back of the pew, keeping a connected, protective touch on Monica's shoulder.

Afterwards, they hung back to spend some time talking with family members and friends. Ken was deluged with departing parishioners, so one-on-one time with the pastor seemed out of the question for the time being—especially when one church member, an elderly lady who was speaking with Ken intently, ended up being led to his office after services. Looked like Ken's help was required elsewhere today.

Jeremy didn't mind much, however. Monica had made an entrée into his life at Woodland with genuine comfort. Hope bloomed.

After church, it was time to bond with his brothers. He dropped Monica at her place, made a mad dash home to change clothes. He'd soon be on his way to Ford Field for a Detroit Lion's football game.

Monica's introduction to Woodland was a success, however a new realization dawned. What got lost in translation of late was his own reaction to falling so hard, and so fast, for a woman who would never be able to carry a child. His child. *Their* child.

Was it crazy to think so far ahead? The practical side of his nature said yes, but his heart screamed no—loud and clear.

Definitely a topic for discussion with his most trusted confidantes—his brothers.

A short time later, he and his brothers were on the road, headed into downtown Detroit. And it didn't take long for those trusted confidantes to gang up on him. In fact, the tag team event began almost immediately.

"So, bro," Marty began, "you hearing the call of the ball and chain? You getting ready to take that fateful plunge?"

From the rear seat, Jeremy looked at his watch. "Wow, Marty. That only took three minutes. Coll, you had even money on five minutes. I had greater faith in his lack of restraint and pegged that question coming in at seven minutes after pick-up."

Riding shotgun, Collin turned to look over his shoulder. His grin went devilish. "Sorry, JB, but I'm with Marty on this one. Next thing you know, you'll be strolling the aisles of some high-end department store with one of those radar guns, electro-registering for flatware and china patterns. It's a sad day, really. The end of a legend."

Jeremy openly gaped at Collin, the one he had expected to be his champion. "Way to perform a stand up, Coll. Let's hope the Lions defensive line shows more skill than you."

"Touchy, touchy," Marty quipped. "Might as well give in, JB. Monica's great. Steph said she's real nice. She enjoyed spending time with her."

That was good to hear. "Thanks. Mom's a bit of a tougher nut to crack on that count, though. I think she came away a little disappointed. And concerned. Her expectations were different than what Monica showed last weekend. Especially with the kids."

By intent, the sentence dangled, creating a means by which to seek their counsel on the issue of children, and family. Marty was shrewd, and perceptive, too. He picked up on the undercurrent with ease. "I kinda noticed that. In the backyard, during that soccer scrimmage."

Collin nodded. "St. Antoine Street garage is coming up."

Their conversation on hold now, Marty pulled up to the gate of the parking structure and swiped a ticket from the dispenser. From there, walking into Ford Field was akin to facing a blitzkrieg of sound, sensation and excitement. The crowd hummed, speakers blared music with a pounding beat that synched with digital ads and crowd-sparking prompts that formed a never-ending circle of lights and color across the mid-section of the stadium.

After stocking up on food and drinks, they took their seats and settled in. They sent up a unison roar of support at kick-off when the Lions took possession and performed a decent, 30-yard return. After a while, the game evolved into a back-and-forth rhythm that enabled Jeremy to join his brothers in simply stretching back, downing some junk food, and chatting.

The Lions and Packers were locked in a three-three tie at the end of the first quarter. Jeremy put out a test comment as he surveyed the cheering crowd that surrounded them. "This is the best. And I love watching the families."

"We gotta train 'em young to appreciate the joys and agonies of pro football in Detroit," Collin answered, tossing back a handful of popcorn and propping his feet against the chair in front of him.

"Pro?" Marty shot back. "You sure about that?"

Jeremy's eyes narrowed. "The Lions are hanging tough. Have faith." He bit into his hotdog and chewed, pondering for a bit. "Have you ever thought about what your life would be like without kids?"

If surprised by the question, Marty and Collin didn't show it.

"Nope. Once you have them, you can't remember a time when they weren't a part of your life," Marty said.

"They change everything, for sure," Collin added.

Jeremy's intensity increased by small degrees. "Yeah, but"—he stopped watching the game and instead, regarded his brothers—"what if you weren't able to have them? What if Stephanie couldn't have conceived? What if Daveny were infertile? Would it have made a difference to you? You know, in your relationship?"

Marty and Collin exchanged a look, then gave Jeremy their complete attention. Collin leaned in. "It would have been a tough thing to consider, I have to say that, but I also have to say nothing would change the love I feel for Daveny. It's that powerful a thing."

"Same here. I can't imagine my life without Steph. But it would have taken some serious help to overcome. Some serious prayer time and heart-to-heart."

"Tell me about it," Jeremy muttered, trying to keep track of the action on the field. Players, uniforms, downs all became a blur.

"What are you saying, JB?" Collin asked. "What's up? Does this have to do with Monica, somehow?"

Jeremy speared his brother with a look. Come clean? Protect their privacy as a couple? He wasn't quite sure what to do, but these were his brothers, his allies. "Monica can't have kids. She can't conceive."

Despite the noise level of the game, a stillness settled between the threesome. Glances were exchanged as Jeremy's revelation was absorbed.

"So, that's what these questions are all about." Marty's eyebrows lifted, and he blew out a sigh. "Gotta say, that's a tough one, JB. What's the issue? Why can't she have kids?"

"Ever hear of endometriosis?"

Compassion glimmered through Marty's eyes. Collin frowned.

"She's had it for years. It's serious enough that she'll never be able to have kids of her own." He filled them in with a bit of background.

When he was through, Marty seemed to check in with Collin. "Listen up, JB," Marty began. "You want some input from my end? Stick by her. She's good for you. I've never seen you look at a woman with love in your eyes. You've never let your heart go. Not completely. Now you have. You've got Monica, and you're happy. I could tell that as soon as I saw the two of you together on Sunday."

A bomb blast could have taken place at mid-field and Jeremy wouldn't have noticed. His focus latched onto Marty and stayed put.

"All I'll add is that you can't let her condition stand in the way," Collin put in. "Not if she's the one. If you do, you'll lose the woman you're meant to be with."

The Lions must have done something great on the field, because the crowd sent up a yell that resounded through the stadium. When the cheering abated, Jeremy admitted, "I don't know if I can take it, guys. I want a family. I want kids. I want a houseful of noise and love like we grew up in. With Monica I'd have to give up that dream."

Collin paused, then looked Jeremy straight in the eyes. "And Monica?"

Jeremy stared at him blankly.

Collin sighed, and shook his head. "What about

Monica? What about *her* dreams? You've told us just now how important kids are to her, and I see her day after day at Sunny Horizons. I can tell how much she loves them. This isn't just your dream, JB. It's hers, too."

"Yeah, you're right." Jeremy's reply came out tinged by heat because Collin's observation placed him smack-dab between love and heart-felt wishes. "Her needs, my needs, they're tough to reconcile, all things considered, know what I mean? That's my problem!"

"You bet I know what you mean," Marty said. "And we're on your side—but maybe what the two of you need to do is see all the alternatives available—all the opportunities you have to pursue a family outside of traditional, natural means."

"Adoption," Jeremy said.

"Adoption," Collin and Marty answered.

Jeremy pursed his lips and looked, unseeing, at the carpet of green field before him. He focused enough to recognize the Lions now led by a field goal. So that had been the cause of ruckus just a bit ago. "I hate to even raise the issue. She's emotionally and physically exhausted. To be honest, I think she's done trying to deal with family issues. Instead, she's pouring her energy into the daycare center and her dance classes at the community center."

Collin leaned forward on his knees. His attention centered on the field, but his eyes were cloudy, distant. "I can understand that method of coping. She's trying to convince herself she's fulfilled. That everything is OK in her life. I used to practice that kind of evasion about Lance, until Daveny, and God's plan, entered my life and turned it completely around. Maybe that's the role you're meant to play in Monica's life, bro. A catalyst. A lifeline, as well as a partner."

Marty took it from there. "I'll bottom line it for ya,' JB. Do you love Monica enough to forego the single life, *and* family? She's unable to have kids. If she's dead set against adoption once you guys talk it over, you'll need to make that decision."

Marty's observation was on the mark. Jeremy swigged back some soda and crunched some popcorn. "I can't help how I feel. I want a family. I've worked hard to build Edwards Construction into a source of provision, a company I can maybe pass on to my kids someday, or at least see to their security as they grow up. That's part of what drives me. Part of what I am."

Collin gave him a sharp look. "Fair enough. But don't sacrifice your heart for that. If you do, you'll end up miserable. Provision, and legacies, are great, but they won't fill that empty spot you're talking about."

"But—"

"But *nothing*," Marty chimed in. "You may not be able to have it both ways—Monica and a family, too. Figure out what you want, sort it out and build from there. Time will win her trust. Your support—and it can't waver—will do the rest."

A course to follow. Back to basics.

Marty started to pay attention to the action on the field. He sent up a happy whoop that drew them all back into the game. "First down, baby!"

Collin and JB exchanged smirks.

"Don't fall into the trap, Marty. Remember, it's the Lions." Collin slapped Marty on the shoulder.

Marty looked at Collin with a determined glint in his eye. "And remember, like JB said, hope springs eternal."

࿔

At home that night, Jeremy's restless mind refused to calm. He changed into sweats, tried to unwind. Instead, he paced.

In the end, he stood before golden, slowly-dying embers in his fireplace, studying a lineup of photographs along the mantle. He reached out, picking up one of the framed pictures. This particular shot featured the entire Edwards family; it had been taken by a professional photographer last year. Methodically he traced several of the images, thinking how important each person was to him.

Adoption. Jeremy was of the mind that if Monica were comfortable with that idea, she would have floated it by now. Adoption, an obvious means to the end of having, and raising, a family, had never been mentioned.

So, the biggest question looming involved his own ability, or inability, to reconcile himself to the possibility of being a family of two—him, and Monica.

He had witnessed Monica with children both at her daycare center, and at the dance classes. Now, he felt nothing but a yearning that bordered on jealousy. Over time, she would be able to dote on children. Knowing her condition, she had wisely made them fundamental to her life. She could pour loving energy into their care. How was he supposed to make that adjustment, and find fulfillment? This was all so new to him still, and such a surprising—unexpected—twist of heart.

He paid particular attention to the images of his nieces and nephews. He had always enjoyed spoiling them. If his relationship with Monica continued and grew, his siblings' children would become even more precious; they might help fill the void in his heart.

But it won't be the same.

One by one, different scenarios came to mind: teaching a little boy how to swing a bat, playing catch, helping a little girl color with crayons, or fly high on a swing. He thought of school days, dances, dating and milestone moments like first days of school, driving a car, graduation. Weddings.

Jeremy replaced the picture and rubbed his eyes with a tired sigh. Nieces and nephews were wonderful, but they weren't *his*. He couldn't raise them, or watch them grow each day. He couldn't be the constant they relied upon when they had problems, or when they wanted to share a victory.

But then, like a circle, his thoughts returned to Monica. He couldn't sacrifice his love for her. Not even for children.

I need to adjust, he told himself. *I may have to find a way to be fulfilled without children. And if that's the case, I'll cope somehow. She means that much.*

13

What in the world am I doing here?

Monica sat in a comfortably appointed reception area at Woodland Church. The appealing aroma of fresh-brewed coffee drifted in the air, tempting her to indulge in a cup from the nearby counter-top service. Warm lamplight bathed gently worn wooden end tables that were positioned next to a couch and the easy chair where she sat.

Jeremy *is what you're doing here,* came the annoyingly perceptive reply of her inner voice. *And that should tell you something important.*

She toyed with a couple of magazines that were placed on the coffee table in front of her. *Parenthood.* Oh, sure. *Family Circle.* Naturally. There were even a few copies of *Highlights,* for the kids and a pair of big, colorful Bible books. In nervous repetition, she kept glancing at a closed door bearing a gleaming brass nameplate.

Kenneth Lucerne, Pastor

She gathered a deep breath. It didn't help. She twisted a simple sterling ring round and round her right middle finger.

Girl, you're such a coward! Seriously! This is just a conversation, not an inquisition!

For days after she'd taken Ken's number from Jeremy, she'd studied the small sheet of paper until she knew the sequence by rote, but making the appointment proved to be a challenge. She had picked up the phone—even dialed a couple of times—but promptly hung up before the call connected.

Why did she need God? It's not as though He could change any of the circumstances in her life. Plus, not even a gifted, well-meaning member of the clergy could wave a magic wand and make her infertility go away—or grace her with the children she longed for.

Still, for Jeremy, she had stiffened her resolve and made the jump. After all, what could it hurt?

A click and a soft *whoosh* filled the air. The door to Ken's office came open, and Monica snapped alert, standing up fast. Nerves prickled hot along her arms.

Ken entered the room with a powerful vibration of warmth and a smile that almost set her at ease. "Monica, hi."

"Hi, Ken." She winced. "*Pastor* Ken."

"Ken works for me just fine. Come on in." He gave her extended hand a squeeze when she approached, and gestured to the interior of his office. "Have a seat." He closed the door and crossed to the chair behind his desk. "I'm so glad to see you. Actually, our meeting today aside, I intended to give you a call, unless Kiara already beat me to the punch. We're eager to check out Sunny Horizons. It sounds like a terrific facility."

Monica relaxed. What a nice thing to hear—especially when she considered that Kiara would be a protective first-time mother, and Monica didn't feel like she had made much of a winning first impression on any of the Edwards clan. "Please stop by any time. You don't even need an appointment for a walk-through. My policy is strictly open door. I'd love to show you both around."

"Then we'll do it. Thanks. I admire what you do, Monica. I meant it when I said it's a special gift you share to be so engaged in the lives of children."

Straight away his words cut to the very core of what was taking place in her heart, but he didn't know that, and she needed a few more minutes of assimilation before taking any kind of emotional dive—even with someone as welcoming as Ken Lucerne.

"Let me return the compliment. I enjoyed my introduction to Woodland this past weekend. The services were wonderful."

"I'm happy you were here. Sorry I didn't have a chance to talk to you afterwards. I feel bad about that."

"Don't even worry about it. You were kind of busy." Busy? The man had been corralled by parishioners, and he had focused exclusively on each one. Most of them simply wanted to reach out, extend a hand, an encouraging word, or share a story. A few had talked to him somewhat intently, and he had nodded, held a hand, offered himself as a source of support.

She had enjoyed the ebb and flow of the Sunday gathering, the connection of the people in this faith community. It had felt good to become familiar with the heartbeat of Woodland before attempting this meeting with its pastor.

"I hope we'll be welcoming you again soon." After that, Ken rolled his eyes, and he laughed. "That wasn't about pressure, by the way. Honest."

Monica laughed, and relaxed completely, because he was disarmingly genuine, and sincere. "You don't even need to say the words. No pressure taken at all."

"Good. I'm glad." Ken leaned forward, and settled

his folded hands on top of the desk. "What can I do for you, Monica? What's on your mind today?"

The question was gently framed—curious and nothing more. Still, it stopped her like hitting a brick wall at the speed of Mach 3. Comfort and ease sailed away, replaced by an onset of the trembles. Monica looked into the patient stillness of Ken's eyes and shifted restlessly.

How to begin? Where?

While Ken waited, and gave her space to move forward, Monica could think of only one thing to do. Talk. Come clean. The idea of unburdening suddenly felt right; it would be OK.

Once she reached that decision, the emotional wall burst. "I guess you might say I'm here because I'm angry." She gave a small, sheepish laugh. "Not a very positive way to begin, I suppose, but that hits the worst of it."

"No, Monica. The worst of it isn't that you're angry. The worst of it is whatever creates and feeds that anger. Do you want to talk about that? What's going on?"

Just like that, Ken earned her admiration. This man wouldn't be fooled by coy witticisms. She couldn't help but respect the way he called her out, yet at the same time encouraged her. Ken was easy. Most of all, there was no sense of awkwardness. He seemed not the least bit distressed or dissuaded by her confused attitude.

Like Elise had been. Silence built, and re-fed her tension.

"What happened, Monica?" Ken gently urged.

"I…" She picked up a nearby crystal paperweight. Cube shaped, it was heavy, and prismatic. As she toyed with the piece, its squared ridges and laser cuts captured the desk light and set off rainbows of color. "I had to tell Jeremy that, if our relationship continues, he's going to end up making a sacrifice he never would have banked on."

"What sacrifice is that?"

Monica barely registered the question. She heard the words, but her thoughts spun ahead. Giving them voice became paramount. "It's not something he can control, and it's not even something I can control. It's like this…curse…this inadequacy I've had shoved into my life, and I hate it, and it makes me angry." Her voice rose a bit, and her words, at the end, had begun to rush. She slowed herself. And breathed out.

"What, Monica? What is it?"

The summons was quiet. Monica continued to still herself, muscle by muscle, breath by breath. She looked up at him. "I worry about the fact that the one thing Jeremy probably wants most is something I can't give him. A family."

Ken blinked hard. He opened his mouth, as though to speak, then closed it. He seemed to gather himself. "You can't have children."

"No. No, I can't."

"Oh, Monica—I'm so sorry. Not just for that, but, I can't help thinking about what you must have gone through when Kiara and Daveny announced their pregnancies."

Monica set aside the paperweight with care, and she sighed. "Please don't. On that count, I'm the one who's sorry, Ken. I reacted poorly. I came off seeming rude. I didn't mean to, but that entire day was like enduring a marathon for which I'd never trained." As best she could, she provided him with an overview of that Sunday dinner from her point of view, ending with the fact that at its conclusion, she had informed Jeremy of her condition.

"In so many ways, I lashed out at him afterward, and I know it. The thing is, I didn't know how to stop. Maybe I was testing him, seeing if he'd duck and run. Half hoping he would, maybe. Terrified of what I'd do if he did."

"Why do you think you feel the way you do?"

"Because I'd rather lose him than hurt him." That stilled their conversation for a moment.

"Cut him loose and you *would* hurt him, Monica. Have you considered that?" Ken let her ingest that, regarding her in thoughtful silence. "On the other side of the table, maybe you felt safe enough with him to release yourself a little," he said at length. "Actually, the same thing probably holds true with Elise. You may not know her well, but you recognize her heart, and the love she puts into all of the most important aspects of her life. Especially her children. Those are ties that bind. They're strong and deep. Certainly strong enough to withstand the process of helping someone find their way."

"But she shouldn't have to feel that kind of negativity toward me. I should be a better person than that, and I know it, but I couldn't avoid what I felt. I couldn't make any of the pain disappear, or even diminish. Then, I felt so embarrassed facing Elise again at church."

"Why?"

Monica lifted her hands. "Isn't it obvious?" Ken had been at the family dinner, after all. "I was standoffish, and she saw right through me. Furthermore, I knew my behavior troubled her, but I couldn't seem to draw myself into...into..." Silence fell, oppressive. Hot.

"Into everything you feel you lack, but want more than anything else?"

In reply to those quiet words, Monica nodded and sank against the back of the chair in resignation. "You just nailed it."

"I realize I'm asking the obvious here, something you've probably already given a lot of thought to, but I'm going to ask anyway. What about adoption?"

How could she even begin to express the tumult of emotion that went along with that seemingly innocuous word? All of a sudden, the meeting became difficult again. "I'm afraid of adoption."

"I can't even imagine how intimidating that process would be."

Monica shook her head. "No. I mean, yes. Yes, it's intimidating to go through the process of adoption, but no, that's not the point. Not for me." Silence stretched. "Sure, there's the fear of not meeting the requirements, and of course there's that constant sense of scrutiny and having outsiders dive so deep, and so thoroughly, into your life—past, present and future."

"You get big points for honesty." His praise, his kind smile, drew her gaze to his, and she calmed. But the silence returned. Ken waited for a bit before speaking. "Care to fill me in on the rest of the story?"

"You want to know the truth? It's not very Christian. Part of me knows that, and knows my reasons are wrong, but..."

Ken waited in steady regard, not stepping in. Rather, he watched patiently while Monica felt like squirming. She wasn't proud of what she was about to say, but she'd come this far. She refused to waste the opportunity. "I'm afraid I won't feel the same way about an adopted child that I would for my own, natural child. Isn't that awful?"

"No. It's not so much awful as it is a natural means of questioning yourself. I do think it bears some analysis, though, and prayer time. You don't even need to speak, or perform a litany of needs. Just listen. God speaks in the silence. He'll direct that yearning you feel, and answer all your questions. Just give up this restlessness and clinging to the 'have not.' Let yourself surrender and go still instead. You need to come to terms."

That made sense, but there was a bit more simmering beneath the surface. "The other thing is, I figure why bother? What'll it all come to anyhow? Maybe the message God has been trying to send me throughout the course of my life is that I'm not *meant* to be a mother. Why should I put myself through an additional roller coaster of family issues—with all that anxiety and stress? Know what it's like? It's like I'm just not supposed to have a family, no matter what." She shrugged and looked down, trying to squelch a blooming sense of shame. "It's like I'm not good enough."

"And if you believe that to be the case, I have some advice. Take a long, hard look at how you live your life."

Monica's brows pulled together as she pondered those words.

"Think about what you bring to the children at Sunny Horizons. That's a form of motherhood times the number of students who cross that threshold every single day. Secondly, look at the self-esteem and encouragement you provide those little girls who dance for you every week."

She looked up at him, still puzzling. "But…really? That's just…that's what I do. That's what my life involves." She shrugged. "I made it that way because of emptiness!"

"I don't quite see it that way. I believe you made it that way in answer to a *calling*, Monica. In the life you've been given, you're not just touching two or three or six kids in a blood-linked family. Instead, God's given you a much larger platform. Instead of limiting you, He's expanding the wishes of your heart. Can you can find a way to embrace that fact and stop fighting against what you feel you've been denied?

"It seems to me like you're trying to fit your life into your own set of expectations, rather than taking a different point of view and realizing your prayers have been answered. Look at what you can do beyond being a child's mother by blood. Look at the gifts you give each day, to literally hundreds of kids. Do you think God hasn't heard your longing, and answered it? Not in the square peg to round hole manner you're letting defeat you, but in a broader, more powerful stroke of His brush?"

Jeremy had said much the same thing. Not since her counseling sessions some two years ago had she come so close to confronting the issues, and emotions, involved with infertility. Was God truly at work in this situation? Could she find His hand and hold it fast? "I'm so afraid of botching things up." The admonition came more easily that she'd thought it would. "Jeremy. He means so much to me, and I want to make him as happy as he makes me. I'm afraid of letting him down. I don't want to ruin something that's so good."

"Monica, you've used the word 'afraid' so often

during the course of this conversation. Think about that. You're carrying too much of the weight. Your feelings run deep, understandably. However, I believe the people who care about you will understand and cope with the issues you're facing. Most likely, what they wouldn't be able to handle is you shutting down—or stepping away. Don't be afraid to fight, or rail. Get mad. Release the hurt you feel. But after that? Get square with the life God means for you to live. The blessings you find, I guarantee, will outweigh the losses, if you let yourself move forward into a new perspective. You'll also end up much happier, and in a much better place."

Monica smiled and gave a short, punctuating laugh. "Boy. JB was right about you."

He looked at her in confusion.

"You're good, Ken. You're good at listening, and you're very perceptive."

He dipped his head and shrugged, but she sensed his appreciation.

"When I made this appointment, I didn't believe I'd ever find my way to being open and frank, and comfortable. But I am. Thank you."

His eyes crinkled at the corners just a bit when he smiled at her. "I'll return the favor. Thank you for allowing me your confidence and for letting me get to know you better. What I see happening with you and Jeremy is like watching God unfold a plan, and that affirms my faith. I *always* love that."

The idea of God Himself unfolding a plan that included her and Jeremy, left her feeling humbled, and filled her heart. She stood, and they shook hands across Ken's desk. "I'll be back this Sunday. I'm really looking forward to it."

Ken walked her to the door, which he opened. "That would be great, Monica. I look forward to seeing you."

14

Lunchtime neared, and the door buzzer to Sunny Horizons sounded. From her spot in the pre-K room, Monica heard Deborah greet a visitor, and then she promptly tuned out so she could focus on the kids who stood near. Positioned around a table dotted by oversized papers and paint pallets, about a half-dozen students wore smocks; each wielded a brush to create their own vision of Thanksgiving.

In the week since her meeting with Ken, her optimism crested at a near all-time high. She had seen Jeremy a couple of times since then—for dinner one night, for a chick-flick the next—but only with her sworn promise to view the latest action-adventure movie for their next outing. She had happily conceded the point.

Monica figured it was a point of mutual consent by which, for the time being, they let the topic of infertility rest and focused instead on the process of building their relationship. The memory left her smiling as chatter flowed, and paintbrushes swished earthy, autumn colors across cream-colored paper.

Outside the room, in the lobby of the center, a rapidly escalating conversation drew Monica away from introspection and child play.

"Get out of my way!" a male voice shouted.

That thunderous demand caused the children

around her to go unnaturally still. As one, the assemblage of children turned to Monica in question. Brows furrowed, she walked briskly through the room and yanked opened the door leading to the main room. There she nearly collided with a large, burly man wearing a belligerent expression. Dressed in a business suit, his eyes sparked; his mouth was a tight, hostile line. She closed the door behind her, inserting herself as an added barrier between the man and the children inside. "I'm Monica Kittelski, the director of this facility. Can I help you?" Her words were gracious; her tone wasn't.

"So you're the next one in line? Are you going to try to kick me out, too? I'm Jessica Carter's father. Her *father!* I want to see her. I need to take her home, and as her father, I have the right to—"

Monica pointed to the hallway on her right. "Wait for me in my office and I'll be happy to discuss this matter with you. At the moment, your tone is frightening the children, and I want that to stop." He didn't go down the hall. Instead he moved toward Monica. The hard glint in his eyes and ominous stance made it clear he had every intention of bullying his way inside the toddler room.

"I'm not following you anywhere! And if you don't like my tone, that's too bad! Give. Me. My. Child." He stalked forward until he was right in her face. "Now."

Monica stood firm, arms crossed against her chest. Her eyes didn't waver from his. "Deb, feel free to call the police if he takes another step toward me."

"Gladly, Monica." A quick glance revealed Deb already had her cell phone in hand, ready to dial.

Defeated, but huffing and grumbling beneath his

breath, David Carter turned abruptly and stalked down the hallway.

"I've got your back and I'll stick close." Deb's quiet assurance helped Monica steel herself for battle.

"Thanks."

Monica entered her office with a stride that was deliberately confident. She closed the door, but not completely.

"It's David, correct?" He didn't even reply. Sitting behind her desk, she withdrew the enrollment forms Caroline Dempsey had filled out. For show, she scanned the release authorization form, already knowing what she'd find. "I'm sorry, Mr. Carter, your name isn't on the list of people who are permitted to remove Jessica from my care."

"Take your forms and toss 'em in the garbage, *director*. I want my daughter!"

"Mr. Carter, I don't care who you are. I expect to be treated in a civilized manner." She paused, wanting to add weight to her next words. "I can't turn Jessica over unless you're on this list or I'd be held legally liable."

He cursed vehemently. In a fit of violence, he swiped his arm across Monica's desk, clearing it in one fell swoop. She jumped back and gasped as a pencil holder, files, souvenirs from the kids, all hit the floor in a crashing symphony of sound. The crystal bowl full of jellybeans toppled to the ground as well. Candy bounced along the tile, clattering like keystrokes on a computer until all that was left behind was a heavy, tense silence.

He stalked around the desk; the menacing approach of his tall, somewhat paunchy form was more than enough to prompt Monica to move away and pull her cell phone from the pocket of her blazer.

"Either you give me my kid," he barked, "or I'll take her by force. You have no right to keep me from Jessica!" He toppled her chair, and it collided with the edge of the credenza behind it, causing items stored there to fall and clatter...including her porcelain ballerina.

Stunned, Monica realized she had to move fast, or she'd be the next object of his wrath. She inched toward the safety of the doorway, activating her phone, already punching in a nine, and a one. "Mr. Carter, leave, or I have no choice but to call the police. I've already dialed all but one digit for 911." He gaped at her. His surprise gave her time to open the door. At that point, Deborah practically stumbled across the threshold, her hand on the knob, her cell phone at the ready as well. This, Monica decided, would end promptly. "I said leave. You're disrupting my daycare center, and I want you out of here right now."

"I'll be back," he growled. "Mark my words. Carrie will not walk off with our daughter along with everything else in my life."

Monica didn't even blink. Deborah stood at her side, her eyes narrow, her jaw set. When David Carter left, he slammed the door so hard the windows rattled.

"Deborah, I'm going to call Caroline. Meanwhile, please direct the staff to be alert, and make sure Jessica isn't upset."

"She had early lunch today, so she was outside playing. I'll keep the teachers from talking, and I'll make certain Jessica is unaware of what happened until Caroline can step in."

Monica gave her friend and colleague a wavering smile. Damage control instigated. "Thank you."

"Are you OK?" Deborah finally asked.

"Fine. I just need to take care of my office."

Hot, debilitating rage—*pure* rage—bubbled, rose, then overflowed. The first order of business: pick up the glittering pieces of broken crystal before the kids could get hurt. Monica snatched a broom and dustpan from the nearby storage closet and swept up debris. With a frustrated growl, she heaved the pieces hard, smashing them into the bottom of her steel trash can.

Instant contrition followed, melting her into a puddle of-of nothing.

In physical response, she sank backwards against the side of her desk then slid down slowly, until she was seated, a weakened heap on the floor. She rested her head on her up-drawn knees, barely able to react to the soft crescendo of a nearby whistle that filled the air.

"Nice arm you have there, Jellybean. I had no idea."

Monica shuddered out a sigh. The tips of a pair of slightly worn, brown-leather work boots came into her line of vision, along with the bottom edge of a pair of faded blue jeans.

Jeremy touched her shoulder. "Deb gave me a thumbnail sketch about what happened. It's over, Monica. Come here."

She looked up, silent. He held out a hand, a beseeching look in his eyes. Reluctantly she took hold. She felt damaged. Angry and bitter. Bleak.

Jeremy tugged her to standing. He took the connection a step further and pulled her in snugly, nesting her body against his. Warmth enveloped her. A heartbeat, strong and steady, sounded assurance beneath her cheek. The hard strength of his body became a haven.

"It's OK now."

She dissolved. She rested her head against his chest and breathed deep. The essence of him entered her system in a soothing stream that eased her troubled spirit and settled strong in her heart. His hands rested loose, yet protective, around her. His body aligned perfectly to hers.

That was too dangerous an enticement to a spirit that thirsted for everything he could offer—and everything she *couldn't*. Life was so *unfair!*

Monica stepped away, dropping to her knees to begin scooping up papers, and knick-knacks—like a treasured monkey and elephant combo a class of kids had made for her years ago when they had learned about papier-mâché. Her glance took in the remains of her credenza, and she couldn't help feeling grateful that, though toppled, her porcelain ballerina had survived.

But there were the jellybeans to contend with—currently a rainbow colored booby-trap to the feet that had bounced all over the floor. Tears burned, but she blinked and swallowed, stubbornly refusing delivery. This wasn't her problem, after all; it was David's.

Well, sort of.

Thing was, she was ticked off. In the extreme. So, while she cleaned up, she began to spew and vent, knowing full well that if she didn't, she'd simply burst. "I swear, some people should *not* be allowed the blessing—the flat-out *miracle*—of a child."

"The miracle of a child."

Jeremy's quiet repetition of her declaration caused Monica to pause in the midst of her increasingly frantic organizational frenzy. "Yes," she barked back, stopping just long enough to look into his calm, deep brown eyes. Her arms were now laden by displaced art pieces: a couple of stuffed animals, pictures, a stack of paperwork she'd now have to re-sort. *Oh…!* She dumped the entire stash on the ground; it was too heavy. *Everything* was too heavy for her right now.

She sank into the chair behind her desk, the one JB had righted for her without her even realizing it until now.

"Talk to me." His firm, but gentle demand caused her to exhale a shaky breath; in surrender, she let her head loll back against the comforting, familiar contours of well-worn leather.

"There's nothing to say, JB. Look around you. My office speaks for itself, and Deb gave you the basics. David Carter came in and trashed the place because I wouldn't let him take his child—when he doesn't have permission to do so! The man is a monster. Calculating, manipulative, and he's putting an innocent, unknowing child at the dead center of a divorce target. It's so infuriating to me. Unfathomable. People putting a child into the middle of emotional nastiness—I hate it!"

"And you're allowed. I can't understand his methods, or his actions, either; but I feel your anger at what he's done, Monica."

She went weak. "Please? Call me Jellybean," she whispered sadly.

Jeremy chuckled softly and stepped behind her. He rested his hands on her shoulders and automatically his thumbs pressed into tight, knotted muscles, working them free. His fingertips moved against shoulders held too taut; under his ministrations, Monica felt herself go lax.

Her eyes fluttered closed, and in a second moment

of surrender, she simply let herself rest, content in his care. Until she bounded forward in her chair, eyes wide, remembering herself. "Oh my goodness. Lunch! Leo's Coney Island."

"Which is kind of why I showed up in the first place," he teased lightly. He turned her chair slightly and smiled into her eyes, smoothing a hand against her cheek in assurance.

"Thank God you did."

"Already done."

Monica laughed, turning back and reclining once more. She slid her hands against his. "You're good for me, JB. So good. I only wish I could return the favor." Her words were as serious as could be.

15

It was difficult, but Jeremy forced himself to let Monica's comment rest. Still, for the rest of the day, the residue of it roughed against his spirit like sandpaper. Since their lunch date could only last for an hour, he focused on lightening her mood. He strove to help her work past the dark cloud of confrontation so she could move through the rest of her day at Sunny Horizons.

Before leaving her at the center that afternoon, however, he'd offered to cook dinner for her at her place. And he had a plan brewing. On the way to Monica's that night, he stopped at the local grocery store and paid a visit to the butcher counter.

When she opened her front door a short time later, he offered up a few sacks of groceries, which she accepted with a smile. Jeremy also carried a small package wrapped in heavy, white paper. As he intended, that part of the delivery put a puzzled look on Monica's face. Toby, meanwhile, sniffed and started wagging his tail so hard his entire body shimmied. The dog made low-rolling noises, hopping around their legs when Monica led the way inside. In the kitchen, Jeremy kissed her cheek and chuckled. "I once read that the way to win a woman's heart is through her dog. I'm about to find out if that statement is true."

"Oh, really?"

"Yep."

Monica waited, and watched, while Jeremy unwrapped the package to reveal a large, fresh steak bone. "Can I hand it over?" Even he could hear the hope in his tone.

Judging by Monica's soft eyes and large smile, her heart had indeed been won. "If you don't, he'll probably maul you. Don't let those innocent, velvety brown eyes of his fool you. He's a chocolate lab on the outside, but inside, he's a beast."

"Sure he is." Truthfully, Jeremy couldn't wait to spoil him.

Toby seemed to sense something was afoot, because he whined and bumped up against Monica's body. Then, he changed course and head-butted Jeremy's hand in a playful bid for attention when Jeremy took just a bit too long to surrender the treat. Victorious at last, with the bone clenched in his mouth, Toby trotted into the living room and promptly flopped into place directly in front of the couch. His throaty noises and teeth clicks left Jeremy laughing. "I miss having a dog. I haven't had a dog since I was in high school."

Monica began to unpack dinner supplies. "He's my buddy. I sure do love having him to come home to."

"I'll bet." Jeremy stole another look into the living room. The spot where Toby rested, right next to the coffee table at the left end of the couch, seemed like his natural "spot" in the house. Jeremy could easily picture him in that exact position, right next to Monica's feet, as she curled up each night. Her unconditional companion. She needed that. Her entire spirit yearned for connection. He took in the woman before him. Bursting with spirit and life, it seemed such an injustice that she would never carry a child, and nurture it from conception to birth, and each day of her life thereafter.

He squeezed his eyes shut, shoring up his strength of will. There *were* options. Would she—*could* she—see that?

"You picked up some nice pork chops, JB." Her observation hit him like an alarm buzzer going off. "These'll taste great with a little light breading and some stir-fried veggies, don't you think?"

Jeremy blinked free of his thoughts and found his way into an easy smile. He stroked her shoulder in passing. "Sounds great to me. I figure after we season them up, and put them in the oven, we can take a walk with Toby while they cook." He pulled out some jasmine rice from the paper sack. "We can have this, too."

"Perfect. It's one of my favorites." Her eyes danced with affectionate mischief. "You get Toby a bone, *and* offer up a walk? He's never going to want you to leave."

Jackpot, he thought. Like a conspirator, Jeremy moved close. He nuzzled her cheek, then leaned in. "You've happened upon my ulterior motive," he whispered.

Monica's answering laugh launched his heart.

Minutes later, the meat was cooking, and Jeremy helped Monica slide into her coat. As soon as she jangled Toby's leash, he bounded out of the living room and scrabbled across the tile in the kitchen, meeting them at the back door in a headlong rush.

While Jeremy laughed and grabbed a nearby plastic bag, Monica clipped the leash into place. Toby yipped gleefully while Monica stroked the dog's thick, glossy coat, cooing at him as his exuberance propelled him into hip-hops and dancing circles.

"Toby," she beseeched, "you're going to knock us over! Behave!"

Monica hardly exaggerated. Pinned into a confined space, the three of them were forced to tuck together quite cozily. Jeremy slipped a stray slice of hair beneath the wool cap Monica had just pulled on. "I don't mind." Being pinned against her warm, giving body, even in total innocence, was heaven.

"You don't mind?" Monica sounded a bit breathless. "The six months of traction you'll endure once you tumble down my basement stairs doesn't intimidate you?"

Jeremy just grinned, opening the door so they could leave. Cold air buffeted him immediately, and when he looked over at Monica, he noticed the way her cheeks almost instantly brightened in color.

He laced his fingers through hers, sliding their joined hands into the pocket of his coat. Monica sidled up next to him, leaving no doubt she enjoyed the connection. She stepped that much closer, their steps smooth and syncopated.

A comfortable rhythm in place, a bracing wind at their backs, Jeremy shrugged deep into his coat, and ventured forward. "I want you to do me a favor."

"What would that be?"

"That last comment of yours. At school. Do you remember it?"

Monica drew in the leash just a bit to keep Toby on the sidewalk. She avoided Jeremy's eyes, but she lifted her chin, and he could have sworn she went tight. "Yeah. I remember."

"Well, I want you to explain it to me, because here's the thing: in case you didn't get the memo, you *are* good for me. Why don't you see that?"

Nestled within the thick, wool lining of his coat pocket, her hand went taut in his, so Jeremy stroked her hand with his thumb until the tension eased. Monica finally turned his way and arched a brow, as if waiting on him to draw the obvious conclusion. *Family. Kids.* Inwardly Jeremy sighed, but he drew on his patience, and waited.

Toby sniffed at bushes; he pawed at a few dirt piles and trotted along. His presence, and the motion of walking, lent a calming distraction to the moment. And at last, Monica came forward as well. "It's the story of my life lately. You were actually on my mind all morning, and I felt so good. After talking to Ken, I had a lot to think about, sure, but for the first time I felt *good*. You know, to-the-bone good. I actually allowed myself the luxury of contentment."

"So far, I like where this is headed."

"I did, too. But then, like clockwork, in walked reality. *My* reality. What David Carter did only served to send me crashing down to earth like a meteor."

"Because he has a child, and you don't."

"Not *don't*. *Never will*. He's been blessed in such a precious way, and doesn't even realize it!" Her frustration bubbled between them like a tangible thing. She picked up after Toby and their walk resumed. "I want to ask you a question."

"OK."

"About adoption."

Jeremy couldn't help looking at her in surprise. Just like that, as prepared as he was to initiate a heart-to-heart conversation about that very topic, Monica came forward on her own. She seemed ready, too, which left Jeremy oddly assured. He slowed his steps, but didn't stop. He tilted his head her way only to find her gaze already latched on him, direct and faultless, sparkling in the overhead light of a street lamp.

"Ask me anything," he said.

"When I met with Ken, he asked me how I felt about adoption. To be honest, and fair, it's not something you and I had a chance to even touch on when I told you about my condition."

"One step, one brick, at a time," he reminded gently.

Monica nodded; her lips even quirked upward a touch, but somberness colored her dimly lit features. Somberness and fear. A sharp ache lanced his heart, a longing to take those two emotions and erase them completely from her heart, and her mind.

"It's a pretty logical, reasonable jump to move from infertility to adoption," Monica said. "When I was diagnosed, adoption was the first thing the doctor talked to me about. He gave me all kinds of advice about adoption as the means to having a family of my own someday, and he encouraged counseling, to get me through the aftershocks of dealing with my condition."

Jeremy nodded, keeping the walk moving slow and steady. He kept his hold tight on her hand as well. "What was your reaction to the idea? Then and now?"

Monica shrugged. "Honestly, back then, the word adoption hit me like a blue fog. It was a word, thrown in among thousands of other words that swirled around me without really sinking in. I couldn't focus on it or anything else, really. The only thing I came away with was the fact that I'd never have children."

"By blood," Jeremy clarified, again keeping his voice deliberately gentle.

Monica sighed. "Yeah, I know. And—adoption is great. I don't have a problem with adoption."

Oh, yes she did. Jeremy heard the word "but" dangling at the end of that sentence as clearly as he felt the first, tentative tingles of snowflakes brushing and melting against his face. "Monica, let me in. Play this thing out so I'll know what you're feeling." *If you don't, we won't stand a chance. I'll have no idea how to reach you.*

The words remained trapped in his throat, but he had the feeling she sensed them anyhow. Her reply confirmed that fact.

"You want the reality, right? Not the candy-coated, public-consumption version."

"Always."

She gave Toby's leash a gentle, guiding tug, turning back toward her house. "Let's go back."

The topic dropped while they prepared dinner, and sat down to eat. Jeremy waited her out, wanting Monica to be the one to take the initiative. They sat across from each other at the dining table in Monica's kitchen; they chatted and relaxed, but toward the end of the meal, Jeremy could only hope his endurance would be vindicated. He craved even a small measure of resolution between them.

"I meant it when I said adoption is great." Monica returned to their critical topic and Jeremy took a deep, relieved breath at her attempt to come forward. "It *is* an answer. For some people. Most people, I suppose. In my case, I'm just not so sure about it."

That statement astounded Jeremy, and this time he couldn't filter, or cushion his words. He got up to pour them both a cup of freshly-brewed coffee. "How can that be? Monica, you'd be perfect."

The surrounding atmosphere featured soft

candlelight coming from tall tapers set in crystal holders at the middle of the table. She had also extended the effort of serving their meal on china of simple, almost translucent white that featured a subtle floral pattern along its edges. The meal was meant to be enticing and intimate.

Now, tension seeped in like an unwelcome blast of cold air. Monica's back went straight. She lifted a linen napkin from her lap and dabbed her mouth. After delivering the coffee, he resettled across from her and longed to reach for her hands. Almost immediately, she had wrapped her fingers snug around the warmth of her mug which rested atop the table for the moment. Slowly, gently he eased them away; that accomplished, he held them firm. Monica swallowed, her eyes downcast.

"Trust me," he whispered. "*Please*, trust me."

Monica's chest rose and fell on a shuddering sigh. "I can't help wondering…"

"About what?"

"About…well…would they truly be mine? Would that bond, that mysterious, irreplaceable bond that happens between a mother and a child, ever come to be? To my way of thinking, that's a connection that can only happen through blood, right? Like your family has. It comes about through the process of carrying an infant from that first second, that first cell burst of creation. A tiny, miraculous being from a communion of body and spirit. From the soul of you and the one you love. That's how I see it, and that's why it means so much to me. I don't see or understand how adoption can come close to that."

She spoke fast, the first sign of letting nerves get the better of her. Jeremy let that truth run its course, and perhaps empty itself into his care.

She seemed unaware of his calm, steady regard. "Then, there's the idea of being given a child to raise through adoption. Well, I can't help thinking…and I cringe at this one because a part of me knows it's irrational and everything else…but what if I get angry at my child, or something goes wrong—an accident, a careless blunder? What about when we make mistakes as parents? What if someone steps in and takes our child away?"

Resigned, out of steam, she slumped her shoulders. She moved a hand from his and lifted her mug, but set it back down without taking a drink. "So, you see? All in all, I'm nothing more than a mixed-up mess about kids."

"Jellybean, you're *emotional* about kids. Big difference. My entrée into your life, then meeting and mixing with my family, hasn't made the issue any easier for you to sort out."

Tears coated her eyes like a shimmering mist. "Jeremy, please don't say that. Meeting you and everything that's come along with it, means so much to me. I'm just—confused. And I'm sorry for that, but it can't be helped. How can I make you happy?"

Heightened emotion tinged her cheeks with red, testimony to the degree of her pain. Now cognizant of how deeply Monica had been scarred, Jeremy watched her with a constricted heart.

He stood and stepped around the table. A glance at her hands told him how tense she had become. Each of her ten fingers had been wound in tight, her rigid posture a fortress raised against attack.

Cautious, Jeremy knelt in front of her chair. He reached up a fingertip and lifted a stray tear away from her cheek. He brought the droplet to his lips and drank it in then cupped her face, all the while transfixed by her turbulent eyes.

He murmured. "Monica Kittelski, you sweet, beautiful woman. What battles you've fought. I don't ever want to negate your feelings. I only wish I could answer the most important questions of all: How come a remarkable woman like you, with so much to offer, can't have children? Why has fate been so unfair? I don't understand it. I never will. The only thing I can do is stand next to you. The only thing I can do is try to reassure you with the love I feel. But I want you to think about something."

"What?" she rasped, looking tired, but she didn't back away, and she maintained their physical, and visual connection.

That lifted his hopes.

"It's true, and unchangeable, that you've been cheated in a big way when it comes to children. But maybe because of that, you've been given the chance to shower love and respect and attention on the kids you work with every day. I've said it before, I know, but you're giving them so much—so many things they need in order to survive. The end result is this: You make a difference. You care. That's motherhood, whether by blood or not."

She studied him for a moment. "Ken said almost exactly the same thing. I heard similar advice in counseling years ago, but JB, something inside me just refuses to absorb it. On one level, I realize that makes no sense, and it chokes off something inside of me, but that's how I feel. I can't get past it. I wish I could!"

Monica blinked fast and hard. She turned away, and he realized at once that she was trying to avoid the emotions cresting over her. Jeremy moved close and took hold of her shoulder. "Stop turning away from me and turn *toward* me instead."

She rested steady and gave him the trust of going still, and listening, despite tears that rolled fat and slow down her cheeks when she faced him once again. "Monica, you have *got* to stop boxing with God."

He maintained eye contact to emphasize his next point. He took hold of her hands, kissing the backs and squeezing them tight. "I don't doubt your stamina, and your strength, but you'll never outlast God, and you certainly can't outrun Him. Look at what's in front of you. Look at your blessings."

Her turbulent eyes delivered the message, as did her silence: she was trying—but with minimal success.

16

In the week that followed, Monica worked hard to make sense of herself.

The dinner date with Jeremy helped her outlook tremendously. It was like he knew her needs clearly; he strived to help her find a sense of equilibrium while her heart spun like a top, bouncing, skittering, bobbling until it rolled into some form of smooth and consistent orbit.

She sought answers just as desperately as Jeremy. That fact alone lent a balm to her stormy soul because it reinforced their mutual depth of feeling. God was moving in her spirit—Ken's council and Jeremy's steadfast support His lightning rod.

Over the next few weekends, she attended church at Woodland with Jeremy and the entire Edwards family. Doing so reinforced a strengthening spirit, and stirred within her a need to do something else— something she hadn't comfortably done in years, almost since her youth.

Pray.

Each night when she first climbed into bed, Monica grew accustomed to the habit of tucking beneath the blankets, clicking off the light, and giving herself over to intensive, from-the-soul prayer sessions with God. Recalling Ken's words helped. No wordy petitions were necessary. Sometimes thoughts and pleas spun through her mind. Other times she simply closed her eyes, sank into her spirit, laid silent and listened.

And she didn't just pray for herself, for answers to the questions she held in her heart. She prayed for her students, and their families—Jessica, Caroline and David in particular. She also prayed for acceptance and a comfortable, more welcoming place within the heart of Jeremy's family—especially with regard to Elise. She even found herself praying, almost automatically, for Woodland Church, Ken Lucerne, and the faith family with whom she became increasingly involved. Woodland possessed a spirit of unity, of loving community that not only drew her in, but became a home to her searching spirit.

Then, into that mystical stillness, worked a song of pure gratitude that left her feeling more centered, and at peace, than she could ever recall. Miraculous voices from the heavens, burning bushes, none of that happened for her; she continued to wonder about where she was meant to go with Jeremy, and how they would handle a mutual desire for family life, but at the same time, she embraced his love, and his every attempt at understanding.

This process of growing taught her patience. Every time doubts set in—every time she felt like her physical emptiness would ultimately let him down—he drew closer, and his intimacy with her spirit only increased. The sessions left her feeling calmer, more receptive and open.

Like God unfolding a plan.

The memory of Ken's words came to her as she drove to Wednesday ballet class with Jessica. She parked her vehicle in front of the community center, smiling at the little girl who rode in the passenger seat. Jessica Carter was fast becoming one of Monica's best dance students. She was committed to learning the dance she'd be performing in the recital a month from now.

"I'll help with your bag, Miss Monica, OK?"

"Sure, Jess. Thank you so much!"

Jessica beamed, flourishing under the positive affection of the adults and kids around her. Today, as usual, Monica allowed for extra time before class started so they could set up, and practice. So, while Monica performed some warm-up stretches, the music for Jessica's performance played and her protégée went to work rehearsing.

Monica watched, and observed, "Your turn was right on the mark, and you ended in first position just like a champ, Jess. You're learning fast."

Jessica relaxed from her graceful pose and bounded toward Monica. "Am I caught up, Miss Monica? I want to be caught up with the other girls. I want to be in the Christmas recital."

"You know as much as they do. You just need to keep practicing. You're very graceful; I'm impressed. The recital will be no problem for you."

Jessica looked at her with happy pride. "I want to dance again, OK?"

"You bet."

Monica reset the CD and pressed play, prepared to coach Jessica's performance once more.

This kind of interaction is what Monica lived for. She was amazed at the little girl's determination. She discovered, during each week's drive to class, that Jessica was a non-stop chatterbox about ballet. Monica had already taught her the five basic ballet positions, and Jessica practiced the steps repeatedly, watching Monica's every move.

For now, Monica gave up stretching and joined her student at the center of the room. They executed the dance piece in tandem with about fifteen minutes left until class formally began.

"Watch your arms," Monica said, pleased when her eager pupil curved them above her head with a beautiful sense of timing and grace. "Good girl! That looks wonderful!" A new part of the recital song began, so Monica continued to prompt Jessica along and perform the routine.

Movement in Monica's peripheral vision drew her attention to the entrance of the room. With quiet footsteps, seeming reluctant to interrupt, in came Caroline Dempsey.

And David Carter.

David fidgeted and shifted. Any semblance of his previous arrogance and hostility was gone. Jessica's back was to the door, but when she caught sight of Monica's expression, she spun, and charged toward her parents. Caroline knelt, and opened her arms to the delighted youngster.

"Did you see me? Did you see me?" Jessica's attention bounced from her mother to her father, her eyes shining and happy. So innocent.

Caroline looked at Monica over the top of Jessica's head. "I'm sorry. We don't mean to interrupt."

Monica couldn't find her voice yet. David Carter gave her a long, unreadable look. He seemed a far sight from the explosive man who had trashed her office, but she had no idea what to expect. He gave Jessica's shoulder a squeeze then crossed the small, open space toward Monica. She fought against the urge to recoil.

But then elements of his approach sunk in—his hesitant footsteps, the apologetic expression on his face. He extended his hand in a tentative gesture. "I owe you a lot more than an apology, but for now that's all I have to give."

Monica felt lightheaded. What was going on here? She accepted David's handshake with a nod, waiting, not knowing what she should say, or do. What on earth had happened?

"I can only explain it to you the way I tried to explain it to Carrie. I was at the end of my rope when I came to your center. I had received the final divorce papers that morning, and everything hit me, and caught up with me all at once. The only thing I could think about was seeing Jessica. All I wanted to do was hold my daughter. Being denied the ability to see her..." The sentence dangled, with no need for elaboration. "Ms. Kittelski, you may not believe me when I say this, but I'm not prone to violence. I never meant for my behavior to–to–well—turn so frightening. You bore the brunt of it, and I'm truly sorry about that. If I can make monetary amends, I will."

Still thoroughly confused, Monica felt a dawning gratitude. Obviously, a momentous shift had taken place within the family relationship that revolved around Jessica. For now, that was more than enough.

"Don't worry about the money," Monica replied quietly. "And as long as you have your focus where it should be, I'm more than happy to accept your apology."

Caroline stepped up, her arm around Jessica's shoulder. "I know the timing is terrible, but we're here because David and I are going to take Jessica out to dinner tonight. He's leaving on a business trip in the morning, or I wouldn't interfere with her ballet schedule. We wanted a bit of time together. You know. As a family." She paused. "Will that be a problem?"

Monica waved that concern aside. "Don't even think about it. As you just saw, Jessica is doing great, and she knows the choreography better than I could hope. Go, and enjoy dinner together."

A few students began trickling in. Before leaving, as David and Jessica left to retrieve Jessica's backpack and ballet duffle, Caroline looked into Monica's eyes with a happy smile. "I'll fill you in when I drop her off in the morning."

Monica couldn't resist giving her arm a squeeze. "Your smile says it all."

"Yeah. I'll bet it does. Thanks for your understanding. You really are one in a million."

A warm flush skimmed upward against her neck and cheeks. "See you tomorrow."

She watched them leave, the two struggling, but hopeful parents with the little girl held between them, their hands linked into a solid unit.

Her heart nearly overflowed with joy—a joy that was tempered only by an acute sense of longing.

❧❧

Monica had known Caroline Dempsey less than a few months, but the change in her was remarkable. Reconciliation—coupled with forgiveness—left the woman stronger now; ready to take on the world.

The next morning, Caroline sat in the chair next to Monica's desk at Sunny Horizons, pausing for a few minutes to talk before heading off to work. They shared a cup of coffee, and Caroline began to relay the events that had transpired yesterday. "After what happened at your office, David knew he crossed the line. I was all set to take him down after the way he behaved. I was even ready to threaten him with an outright claim to full custody. Even a restraining order. I was that afraid."

Monica leaned back in her seat, still amazed. "What do you think turned him around? Do you think it was the divorce decree, like he said?"

"I think so." She shrugged. "I didn't even have to make the first move, Monica. We talked on the phone just a few hours after he showed up here—right after you called and told me what happened." They sipped from their mugs; the tantalizing scent of coffee wafted through the air. For some reason, the aroma sent Monica reeling backward, to Woodland, and her meeting with Ken. The earth continued to shift beneath her feet, yet she felt oddly grounded—anchored by...she wanted to say the hand of God.

Caroline continued. "We ended up meeting for dinner at an old-fashioned, mom-and-pop restaurant near where I'm living now. We're not reconciling or anything, but we *are* going to work harder to make sure our divorce remains civil. We have to. After all, we both want to be part of Jessica's life—a *good* part of Jessica's life—and we don't want our problems to become hers."

"Caroline, I only wish everyone were as level-headed."

She shook her head. "Oh, trust me, I have my moments. I mean, I won't be able to trust him completely until he earns it, that's for sure. Still, he apologized. Imagine that! He said he won't interfere with Jessica anymore, because he doesn't want to lose all contact with her."

That was a relief. Monica stood, raising a blind to let in the day's first rays of sunlight while Caroline continued. "I want to believe him, but I'm being careful. I have to, for Jessie's sake."

"I think that's smart."

"I may be going on blind faith, but I've decided to give him the benefit of a doubt. If he breaks his promise, I won't hesitate, so let me know if he bothers you again, Monica. For now, though, I want to try to help him turn a corner. Maybe it'll help smooth out the remnants of our divorce and give us the chance to move on."

"I think it shows a lot of compassion on your part, and some hoped for maturity on his."

"The way I see it, I have to try. We owe Jessica that much."

Faith. Benefit of a doubt.

The words swept through Monica's mind for long moments after Caroline left.

17

He needed to operate from a position of knowledge. At least, that's what Jeremy kept telling himself. Today he was in the office, ostensibly to see to year-end reports, upcoming budgets, and the continuing development of project prospects for the spring season to come.

Today, however, there was more to the story. *Much* more.

Like the two sides of a freshly minted coin, he wanted to explore every possibility, every potential loss—and gain—held deep within the situation he faced with Monica.

Monica. She slid around him, and through him, a cloud of enticement. His brothers' observations at the Lion's game were right on the mark. He was in love. Now, resolving and claiming that fact took priority in his life.

On side one of the coin, Jeremy pictured a family—kids. The vision forced him to analyze the means by which to embrace a life without that link to blood, to tradition and a lasting legacy. On the other side of the coin came a love that would make that sacrifice worthwhile. Monica's verve, her tenderness and playful spirit, engaged him completely.

One side or the other. Heads or tails.

Oddly enough, considering this necessary

reevaluation of his life didn't leave Jeremy with a heavy heart, or a sense of denial. Instead, his mind and heart moved toward resolution; he wanted only to make a way through. He'd swing the hammer, and drive the nail; somehow, a sturdy and comfortable conclusion could be created. For everyone.

He cleared his throat and straightened his back. Rolling his chair close to the desk, he clicked onto the Internet, pulled up a search engine, and typed in three fateful words: *Adoption Agencies Michigan*.

His pulse went erratic. The heat index climbed within the confines of his office. Just beyond the threshold he watched his receptionist, Allison, pass by carrying a stack of file folders in one hand and a lunch sack in the other. She glanced into his office with a warm smile. Jeremy's fingertips twitched on the keyboard. He almost feared she might know what he was doing, and start asking questions, exerting curious, well-meaning pressure. But, of course, that was irrational. She was clueless, yet he was already a wreck.

So this is how it feels, he thought, *when you take that first, fateful step off the edge—the weird quake at the pit of your stomach, the shiver of uncertainty, the hopes, and the fears. This is life-altering huge. Just exploring possibilities feels monumental. How would it feel to be doing this for real?*

The questions and sensations circuited his mind, yet here he was, no more than an outsider looking in. At this point, he wasn't even signing up for anything— he was simply on the hunt for information—processes and procedures—an enlightening degree of background. He wanted to be informed. That's all.

Right?

His conscience, and God's spirit, didn't answer him back right away, so he scrolled, and hummed at some of the agency names he drew his cursor across. *Bethany Christian Services*. That sounded promising. He clicked the hyperlink, and began to wander through the website that opened. The rest of the world promptly faded away.

…Thousands of young women and men choose to make an adoption plan for their unborn children…

…any number of reasons why, but what remains consistent is that they want the very best for their children, and feel adoption can provide it. Bethany has been bringing families together through infant adoption with tremendous success for the better part of a century…

…birth parents relinquish their rights voluntarily, and completely…

…the majority of birth parents meet with the prospective adoptive parents and attain some level of openness in their adoption, even after placement…

That nugget of information caused Jeremy's hand to go still on the mouse. His brows rose. He understood Monica's fears a bit more clearly now, even after just a cursory glance through the information. What if the birth parent, for whatever reason, simply didn't feel a connection with the prospective couple? How crushing would that be, especially since that level of meeting wouldn't come until well into the adoptive process? Still, that degree of openness provided for a commendable and dignified means by which to assure everyone involved. Though difficult in some ways, a pre-adoption meeting with the birth parents made emotional sense, so he found himself in favor of it.

Aside from the potential to be chopped at the knees, that is.

Jeremy climbed deeper and deeper into web-based information gathering, satisfying his questions on one level, opening up all new ones at the same time. He took notes on a nearby legal pad, jotting observations, facts and statistics. After the better part of an hour, he returned to the Bethany site. There he even spent a few minutes watching a video that featured a family telling their adoption story. Intent, Jeremy listened, hanging on every word. There was a happy ending, sure—but what about the times when hopes were dashed? What about the heartbroken birth parents surrendering the life they had helped create? How much strength would that take—to sacrifice a God-given piece of yourself for the opportunity to give a child a better life?

Through it all, Jeremy came back to one fundamental truth: he couldn't blame Monica for being confused, and heart-protective, when it came to an issue that was so important, and, through no one's fault whatsoever, seemed riddled with the chance for heartbreak.

In her case, even *more* heartbreak. All of it centered on family.

Following a heavy sigh, Jeremy stretched, inching his chair backward a few degrees while he pondered. He spun the chair, looking out the window at a line of typically slow-moving lunch-hour traffic. The motion of the cars soothed him almost to the point of hypnosis. And he continued to ponder.

There might even be a third side to this mysterious relationship coin—one he hadn't considered fully until after the football game with Collin and Marty. That third side of the equation included the faces of his nieces and nephews. That particular silver piece encircled his extended family, and the love he felt for them.

But, even with their precious faces in mind, Jeremy couldn't deny the fact that he wanted to know more about the process of adoption. He couldn't help imagining the prospect of welcoming into his heart, and life, the presence of a child who simply couldn't exist in happiness, and security, with its birth parent.

A pair of soft, slender arms slid slowly around his neck, accompanied by the subtle aroma of jasmine and lily. After a bit of a jump he smiled, automatically closing his eyes and going still so he could simply saturate himself with Monica's presence. Her chin came to rest on his shoulder, and she kissed his cheek. "Hi there, handsome," she said softly.

Jeremy took hold of her hands. "Hi there, back." He swiveled his chair around, half-tempted to topple her onto his lap and enjoy a brief, warm snuggle, or perhaps a restrained necking session...

That's when his breath caught. On the screen before him was the adoption site. To his right, a notepad full of information about adoption. In a hurry, but as smoothly as possible, Jeremy flipped over the sheets of paper and clicked the exit toggle to his internet connection.

"Hey, Uncle Jeremy?"

The summons caused Monica to start with visible guilt; she quickly worked free of his grasp. Jeremy stifled a laugh. They were both acting like guilty teenagers. "Yeah, Alex. What's up?"

Ten-year-old Alex Edwards stood before them, carrying a long, cylindrical shipping container. "Mrs. Moynah wanted me to give you this tube. She says the building plans for the Wiltson complex are inside." Apparently nonplussed by Monica's close proximity,

Alex gave her a smile. "Hi, Monica. 'Member me? From dinner?"

Jeremy reclaimed her hand and glanced up at her. "Marty and Steph's oldest," he whispered.

She nodded her recognition. "Absolutely I remember you, Alex. It's great to see you again."

"You, too!"

Monica was dressed in a burgundy wool skirt and a black turtleneck that was cinched at the waist by a thick, black belt. With her patent dress boots, chunky jewelry and upswept hair, she was delicious. Jeremy tore his focus from the lovely blonde at his side and turned to give Alex the benefit of his full attention. "Thanks for the delivery, bud. You can set that on top of the credenza for me."

"Ah, OK. Umm…what's a credenza?" Alex's gaze ping-ponged around the room.

"It's the storage cabinet right behind me."

Jeremy could tell Monica had trouble fighting back laughter at the scene: uncle and nephew, forging a path side by side in the cut-throat, dog-eat-dog world of business and construction.

"I hope you're getting top dollar for your work, Alex," she offered. "I'll bet you've earned it."

The youngster gave her an easy smile. "Oh, I'm here for free. I get to spend the whole day with Uncle Jeremy. It's for school. Isn't that great?"

"It's Take a Kid to Work day," Jeremy elaborated. He handed his nephew a stack of manila folders and a pile of purchase orders. "Alex, there are purchase orders for each one of these job files. Can you match them up for me and paperclip the PO to the top?"

"Sure." Alex looked at Monica. "Uncle Jeremy says we're going to do a power business lunch at—"

Alex checked his wrist watch. "Twelve-thirty. Hey—that's now. Could Monica come?"

This time she couldn't seem to resist. She burst out laughing, and gave Jeremy a wicked glare. "A power business lunch? What are you teaching Alex about life in the work force?"

"Don't gripe. After all, you're invited. Can you join us?"

"Frankly I wouldn't miss it. Lunch is why I'm here. Count me in, gentlemen."

Gratified, Jeremy stood while Alex set the shipping tube on the credenza.

"Let this be another very important lesson you learn today, Alex," Jeremy explained with supreme authority. "The business world is all about establishing priorities. First, the good stuff. Lunch. Then, the not so good stuff. Paperwork."

Alex cracked up, and so did Monica. "Got it, Uncle Jeremy!"

"Nicely done, young man." He looped one arm around Alex's shoulder, the other around Monica's waist, and they left the office behind.

18

At the restaurant, Monica watched Alex eat, and she gaped, amazed. "I've never, ever seen a ten-year-old polish off so much spaghetti."

Jeremy laughed. "He's been raised on quality. Outside of a homemade meal, Frank's Trattoria is the best. That's why I brought him here. It's a favorite in our family," he answered between bites of chicken primavera.

Monica shook her head in continuing wonder as Alex soaked up red sauce with a slice of bread, and then devoured it. "Well, he's certainly learning how to put a dent in an expense account." She couched her next question with as casual an air as possible, but deliberately averted her eyes. "So I guess Marty and Stephanie weren't able to take him to work?"

Jeremy shrugged, downing his food with as much enthusiasm and gusto as young Alex. "They could have, but he went to Marty's architectural firm last year. Steph's a residential realtor, and she had a couple high-level property tours, so I told them I'd love a turn."

Monica smiled gently. "I can tell you enjoy it. You're great with him."

Jeremy regarded his nephew with an affectionate look. "I've been looking forward to it, actually. It's fun."

That piece of elaboration was unnecessary. Monica kept her thoughts to herself, but, when she had walked behind Jeremy's desk to announce her arrival, she had seen the webpage left open on his computer monitor and noticed the smooth way he shuffled a stack of papers and a note-filled legal pad. A subtle sense of being "caught" had rippled from Jeremy, but when she didn't make an issue of it, he seemed to relax, and she let the moment pass. She was certain he wanted to keep his explorations a secret. For now, that was fine. After all, Monica faced a similar dilemma. She wasn't at all sure how to respond to her own tumult of emotions about the topic.

Still, avoidance didn't change facts. Family issues built and loomed around them like an oncoming thunderstorm, full of tense expectation, rolling clouds and dangerous, electric undercurrents.

But just like a cloud break, another thought came to mind. As lunch progressed, and she enjoyed their company and interaction, Monica couldn't help but recall her concluding words to Ken Lucerne:

I want to make him as happy as he makes me.

It was just that simple—and just that complicated. Monica toyed with a luncheon portion of lasagna, moving it around on her plate, staring at her food. Sometimes, it felt like getting God to answer a prayer the way she wanted was just this side of impossible. Now, Monica understood why. There was so much more out there, so much love she could hold fast to, if she would open her heart, and her spirit to receive it in faith—and trust.

Watching Jeremy now, realizing the effort he put into ignoring his own call for a family, gave her a lot to think about. He refused to pressure her about her life choices, despite his own depth of feeling. Instead, he attempted to put his nephew at the forefront, exploring the option of becoming even more firmly engrained in the lives of his extended family. His attitude did a miraculous job of tenderizing her spirit, and strengthening the abilities she needed in order to try to move forward in her own way.

Through it all, she became certain of one inescapable fact: she wanted, desperately, to build a life with Jeremy Edwards.

❧

Late the next day, one of the teachers opened the door to the rumpus room. "Monica, you have visitors in the lobby."

"Thanks. I'm on my way." She knew she sounded a bit breathless from the exertion of lifting a toddler in both arms and circling him through the room like an airplane. Playtime interrupted, Monica set the boy down and gave him a pat on the back. Walking out of the rumpus room put her directly in the lobby, and when she saw who her visitors were, her footsteps stuttered. Her nerves awakened, and a subtle, anxious tremor began.

Daveny, Kiara, Ken, and Elise turned in unison. They shook snowflakes from their coats and Ken stamped lightly on the rubber entry mat to knock slush from his shoes.

"Hi there!" Monica stepped up in welcome. "Let me take your coats."

"Do you mind the invasion?" Daveny asked, taking in her surroundings with a smile. "Kiara and I had a slow spell at work, and since she's been so eager to see your facility, we figured there was no time like the present to stop by."

"I don't mind at all."

Elise's encompassing sweep of the room struck Monica as sharp, and keen. "This is nice." She pulled off her leather gloves finger by finger. "Still, it's so difficult. Please don't take it personally—I just wish every mother had a chance to be home with their kids."

Monica understood where Elise was coming from. "I know what you mean, but there isn't much of a choice anymore. Even if both parents don't have to work, and one of them stays home with their child, they end up discovering most kids in kindergarten have extensive daycare, or, at minimum, a year or two of pre-school in their background."

"Makes sense. I'm just glad we can come to a center like yours, where we know the owner, and have built-in trust, and respect."

That unexpected piece of praise from Jeremy's mom brought Monica to a stilling pause. "Thank you, Elise. I really appreciate hearing that."

Kiara, who had been wandering, stopped to turn and give them a grin. "She's as protective as any mother would be."

"And I don't blame her at all. Daveny, let me get Jeffrey. He'll be so happy to see you. After that, Ken and Kiara, I'll be happy to show you around."

Moments later, following a stop in the pre-K room, Monica returned, hand in hand with Jeffrey. He let out a happy shout and broke into a run the instant he saw his mother crouch down and open her arms wide in welcome. Daveny and her son settled at a nearby table and began to make good use of the nearby coloring books and a coffee tin full of crayons.

They made the most beautiful picture, Monica thought, fighting back an onslaught of wistfulness that bordered on envy. Two chestnut heads, close together, quietly chatting, filling the pages before them with vibrant colors. Monica closed her eyes, breathed deep, and rebuked the inflow of negativity, focusing instead on the blessing of a tender-hearted mother at play with her child, and nothing more.

After all, a convicting voice inside her said, *what good is envy when you know you could have something just as rewarding. If you let yourself.*

"For now, Ken and I are leaning toward enrolling for childcare once our baby is around six months old or so." Kiara's words ended Monica's bout of introspection.

Ken nodded. "We've both done a lot of figuring, to see how long we can stay home and focus on just being parents."

"After that, I plan on working part-time in the office, part-time at home."

"We can definitely help you out." Monica took the lead from there. " Come on over to the nursery area and I'll show you what we offer." She began their tour at the infant section of her facility where there were cribs, playpens, and a two-to-one teacher-to-baby ratio. There were foam rubber balls, colorful, plastic blocks and a spacious main area with cushioned flooring, and mat games. There were bouncy chairs as well, one of which was occupied by a cooing baby who held hands with the staffer who was seated, cross-legged, nearby. "Also, I can be flexible about scheduling, as long as I have a little notice to plan for staffing."

"Meaning?" Ken had lifted a large, sturdy picture book, but set it aside to focus on Monica.

They continued walking and he kept a protective hand near Kiara's back as she moved forward, taking everything in. Her stomach, Monica now saw, had rounded pleasantly, and a loose-fitting silk blouse flowed around her growing midsection. Monica closed her eyes for a moment, braced against an onslaught of imagined sensations and pleasures: a child's movement within an ever-expanding womb, the roll and thud of a baby's movement. Witnessing pregnancy didn't normally hit her so hard; this time, though, she couldn't escape the alienation she felt. These people comprised Jeremy's world, and occupied his heart. Therefore, all she longed to give him, left her aching.

Discussing Sunny Horizons and focusing on work lent her a needed lifeline. "Well, for example, if meetings come up, where you know you need to shift daycare from one day to another, I can be accommodating. I only need a few days' notice to be sure there's adequate staffing."

Kiara nodded. Her hair was fashioned into an elegant French braid. The style drew emphasis to high cheekbones and creamy skin, leaving wide green eyes the focal point of her features. "That makes sense."

Monica continued to fill in details while they walked. "My infant area is somewhat smaller than the toddler and pre-K program, but we have half a dozen children we care for who are at least six weeks old to eighteen months."

"Hmm." Elise followed them, exploring right along with Kiara and Ken, who conversed quietly, smiling and pointing out items of interest.

Jeremy's mom stepped up to Monica's side. "I see now why Collin speaks so highly of the work you do. Taking care of this many children is quite a challenge.

You have a beautiful facility, Monica."

On nervous automatic, Monica tucked an errant wave of hair behind her ear. She wanted so much to win this woman's good grace and favor. This was Jeremy's mother, a guiding, loving force in his life. Elise was unmistakably sincere, but she searched for assurance as well. She chronicled the most important aspects of Monica's life for two main reasons—the love and protection of her son.

"Thank you very much for the compliment. This center has been wonderful for me. So are the children. I'd miss them terribly if they weren't a part of my life." That comment escaped without a filter. It reached deeper than Monica had truly intended. Elise, however, seemed to bypass the deeper layers. When she laughed lightly, Monica released a relieved breath.

"You'd miss them? Even on snow-bound days like this? They must be hard to handle when they get cabin fever."

Refocused, Monica smiled as well. "True, but you learn to divert and entertain."

"You seem to be a natural."

A drawing of sunshine and rainbows caught her eye; for the time being, Monica turned away from its symbolism. And she opted to leave Elise's comment alone.

Since Ken and Kiara continued to explore, Elise stayed near Monica. "Jeremy tells me you're coming to Becky's wedding in a couple of weeks."

"I accepted his invitation, yes. It sounds like it will be a beautiful event. I haven't been to the west side of Michigan in years, and Jeremy's excited for his cousin, and her fiancé. I'm really looking forward to meeting them."

She was speed talking, and increasingly nervous—and her curiosity was piqued. Why had Elise brought it up? Was she troubled by it? Monica wanted to wince. Instead, she slowed her breathing, and stopped short, wishing she felt more comfortable with Jeremy's mom.

Elise's gaze softened. "Monica, you're trying too hard. Relax. You hold Jeremy's heart, and I know it, so I'll tell you what I've already told him. If that's the case, then you hold my heart as well. And I'm sincere about that."

Monica couldn't find the words she wanted, and needed, to let Elise know how much that statement meant. Her mind spun, but into the vortex came the sound of a loud cry from the next room over. Snapping to, Monica nearly jogged to the rumpus room. There a small group had already gathered around an injured child. "What happened?" She asked the closest teacher.

"Jason and Lindsay were in a bit of a disagreement about who got to play with that big, metal dump truck. They were tussling back and forth with it. When Jason let it go, Lindsay lost her footing and when she fell, the toy truck hit her head."

The teacher made ready to help, but Monica shook her head. "Go ahead and help watch the others. Calm the kids down. I'll take care of Lindsay."

Lindsay continued to cry, hugging her knees to her chest as she rubbed her forehead and rocked back and forth. Monica gathered the little girl onto her lap, holding her close until the tears slowed. There was a small gash on Lindsay's forehead that would require cleaning, some antiseptic and a bandage, but nothing more, thank goodness. She'd be fine.

"You're OK, honey," Monica cooed softly, rubbing Lindsay's back, continuing to cradle her. In silence they rested. Lindsay's sobs lessened to hiccups, and she clung to Monica's neck, her tears warm as they trickled against Monica's skin. Lindsay's breathing eventually evened out, and she closed her eyes with a sigh, just the signs Monica was waiting for. "Let's go back to my office. I'll clean you up and make things good as new. Then, you can come back and play."

"I hate that truck now. I don't want it anymore!"

"For now, I don't blame you, honey, but let's see how you feel once you're back on your feet."

Lindsay sniffled. She looked up at Monica with watery eyes, but an authentic, grateful smile. "M'kay. Thank you, Miss Monica. I'sorry. An' I'sorry to Jason, too."

Monica gave her little student a snuggle. "You're a brave girl, Linds, and I'm proud of you for being sorry about what happened. When we're done, let's have you and Jason apologize to each other. C'mon, sweetie."

They stood and held hands, preparing to move toward the hallway leading to Monica's office. Suddenly she realized she had completely ignored her visitors. All four of them now stood in the rumpus room, watching. In passing, she gave them an apologetic look. "I'm so sorry. I'll be right back."

Ken and Kiara exchanged glances, and knowing smiles. "Actually," Kiara said, "I think we just saw everything we need. Where do we sign up?"

Monica fell victim to a heated flush of shyness and pleasure, but what set her heart soaring even more than Ken and Kiara's show of confidence was the impressed, tender expression presently worn by Elise Edwards.

19

Swags of white netting stretched like curved arms across the length of the ceiling. Clear twinkle lights illuminated the great room of the Baxter Morgan Bed and Breakfast with a creamy glow. Music pumped through the air, sometimes fast and driving, sometimes slow and romantic. The atmosphere was perfect for the wedding reception of Steve Richards and Rebecca Tomblin Richards and the party was in full swing.

Watching the newly married couple dance made Jeremy smile. He held a flute of champagne; best man and maid of honor had just offered their toasts. He stood near the family table, and a pleasing rhythm surrounded him punctuated by chatter, flashbulbs, laughter, music and dishware chiming and clattering as attendees finished eating wedding cake. Swaying a bit, tapping her fingertips on the back of a chair, Monica stood close by, watching the proceedings with a happy look in her eyes.

Jeremy's hand came to rest against the small of her back, and before she could even turn, he wrapped an arm around her waist and tucked in close. She leaned back with a contented sigh, which he could hear despite the party atmosphere. Among many things, he loved her natural, effortless affection, the connected intimacy she created with nothing more than a well-timed caress, or a meaningful look.

At a loss for the moment, Jeremy caught his breath, then leaned in close to her ear. "You seem like a lady who might enjoy a turn on the dance floor."

"You prowling for volunteers, JB?" she teased.

"Actually, I'm quite selective."

The music shifted from fast to slow. Jeremy edged her away from the table. "I'm stealing her for a bit. We're going to dance," he called over his shoulder to his parents and siblings.

She followed his lead, and he ached for the feel of her arms around his neck, the synergy of sharing a tender dance in time to a lush ballad. Jeremy drew her neatly into the circle of his arms. He nuzzled her cheek and Monica slipped her fingertips beneath his hairline, then against the skin of his neck. Jeremy closed his eyes. "Nice."

"Very," she whispered back, settling into the well-executed moves of their dance. She relaxed against him and seemed to drift into the moment, which suited Jeremy just fine. Her natural grace carried him away, lending smooth connection to their movements.

"When the song ends, do you feel like taking a break for air out in the lobby?"

Monica tilted her head to look into his eyes. "Not a minute before, though." They shared a laugh. "Actually, I'd love it. Once I checked into my room and changed for the wedding, I didn't have much time left to explore the place. It seems beautiful."

Jeremy leaned in to skim his lips against her throat. He couldn't get enough of her scent and the satiny texture of her skin. Giving a restrained sigh, he dotted her cheeks with slow, deliberate kisses, nuzzling as they swayed. Monica settled against him; her trusting surrender amplified his determination to remain noble, despite the silken temptation of her lips, the smoke of her deep blue eyes.

Pulling apart at the end of the song left behind an exquisite promise of all that Jeremy knew would come to life between them in the years and decades to come. But that was just it. Life. Life was an issue in need of direct confrontation. He prayed for finesse in what he was about to do, and the guiding stroke of God's hand. God had brought them together. Now, Jeremy relied on Him to keep them together, fulfilled, and united as a couple.

"Let's head to the lobby. There's a sitting area."

Monica fanned her face, shooting him a saucy grin. "Good idea. I'm about to overheat. Maybe because of my date?"

Jeremy loved her playful spark, but longed for seriousness, for open hearts and a bit more vulnerability. So, he held her gaze steady and drew her forward. He detected her answering shiver in the subtle tremble of her fingertips.

"Come here, Jellybean," he beckoned quietly. Enticingly.

Tingles woke up along his skin, transferring, he imagined, directly to her. He turned toward the entrance of the room and led the way through a set of glass double doors. Monica, meanwhile, went shy. The closer they came to the bright lights of the outer reception area, Jeremy noticed her skin's heightened color. She toyed with the slim strap of the evening bag presently secured on her shoulder.

People walked in and out of the entrance of the bed and breakfast, which left the lobby temperature refreshing and cool. Wanting to be attentive, before Monica could even voice the need, Jeremy removed his suit jacket and settled it smoothly across shoulders left bare by a blue satin dress he had admired all evening. He drew her close once the garment was in place.

"Hard to believe there are just a few weeks until the recital," she offered, more timid than he would have expected. That was OK by Jeremy. Being off balance would leave less time for defenses, and those walls she sculpted and nurtured.

"Christmas is coming fast," he agreed.

"You still planning to be there? At the recital?"

"Am I still invited?" he joked.

"Of course." She laughed, a light, happy sound. She seemed to have regained her mental footing. Monica linked her arm through his.

They sat on a couch, in a lobby devoid of crowds. A picture window overlooked Lake Michigan not far beyond; though at the moment, only shore lights interrupted the rich black view. As carefully as possible, he tried to foster intimacy—physical closeness, eye-to-eye connection, linked hands, a light caress.

"This has been a great night," he said softly. Monica's luminous eyes were more than enough to shut off the world around them. No longer did he hear the underlying beat of music from the nearby great room. No longer did he see people floating about, mingling, taking breathers. "And from it, I want you take just one thing, Monica."

She waited, her posture still, anticipatory.

"I'm yours. I'm not going anywhere, no matter what. I have every intention of celebrating a day like this with you. I have every intention of marrying you."

Tears sprang to her eyes. Even though he half-expected them, the evidence of her overwhelmed and tender reaction undid him. "In spite of everything I'm not?"

Those words undid him even further. "Because of everything you *are*. Because of the *love* I feel. I'll deal. *We* will deal. But ask yourself something. From the gut. Are you happy as you are right now? Because if you're happy, I'll be happy."

"I think the answer to that question is pretty clear in the way I live my life. I have enough kids to literally fill a school. The question for me is, will *you* be happy without a family?"

As she waited on his answer, her body went taut. A sharp, squeeze hit his heart when he decided his answer, but really, the choice was no longer his. The decision had been made when he'd fallen in love with her.

"Yes, I will. If I'm being given a chance to spend my life with you, that would be enough to make me happy. Do you want to know why?" Monica nipped at her lower lip and nodded. Jeremy stroked a fingertip against her jaw, trailed it against her throat, then her chin. "Do you remember our kiss? When I saw you home?"

Monica swallowed. "Pretty tough moment to forget."

"You referred to me as chivalrous."

"You are."

"Maybe, yeah. But the reason I walked away that night, the only thing that made it possible for me to back away from you, is the reverence I feel about what we've found together."

"Reverence."

He liked the way she let the word roll off her tongue—slow and savoring. "Yes, reverence. You inspire that deep of an emotion in me. You fulfill and capture a part of me that leaves me in awe. It's a feeling I've never experienced before, and never will again. I'm that certain of you. Of us.

"And whether we were destined to have a dozen kids or none at all, that truth is never, ever going to change." He leaned in and claimed her lips. He coaxed, enticed and captured, drawing her gently forward by a tug against the lapels of his jacket.

"I love you, Monica," he whispered against her mouth. "No matter what. Don't forget that, and don't ever, ever doubt it."

❧❦

Monica dealt with the after-effects of a sleepless night, of revelations from Jeremy that knocked her senseless, even now, hours after the fact.

She packed to leave, but her gaze strayed to the nearby window, and its gorgeous view of Lake Michigan. Before heading to church with the rest of the Edwards family, she wanted to indulge one last whim before leaving this gorgeous location. Brisk winter winds or not, she wanted to take a quick walk along the shoreline.

A short time later, she was bundled into a knit cap, thick gloves and a calf-length coat of royal blue wool, traversing the golden beach. Frothy gray water coated the sand, leaving dark marks and indentations as it pushed inland, then receded. Whitecaps rolled forward, ebbing and flowing, as timeless as a heartbeat.

Jeremy's words played through her mind, tempting her to give up her fears, once and for all, in order to cling tightly to a man, and a love, that made her whole for the first time in her life. When Jeremy was nearby, the emptiness in her spirit vanished. Doubts crowding her mind, fled. But when she was alone, the demons seeped into cracks and crevices, where fear and misgiving could bloom large, and flourish.

"Good morning, Monica." She nearly stumbled in surprise at the unexpected greeting.

"Hi, Elise. I see you're willing to brave hypothermia, as well." Monica smiled, but the gesture felt hesitant on her lips.

"I still like Lake Saint Clair the best," Elise remarked. "Although, it's not nearly as impressive." For a few minutes, they walked the beach, buffeted by cold wind, but swept into a majestic view. "Did you enjoy the wedding?"

"Very much."

You know, I have the feeling this might be you and Jeremy before too long."

I'd like to be that lucky, and leave him fulfilled.

"Do you think you could do me a favor?" Elise asked.

"I'll sure try. What's that?"

"Well, we've tap danced around it a bit recently, and the tour of the daycare center ended before I could really speak to you at length...and sort a few things out."

Monica watched Jeremy's mother, encouraging her with a nod.

"I'm hoping you might tell me what lies beneath."

"What lies beneath?" Monica's curiosity built.

"Well, I know we've talked about the day we gathered for dinner, and I've seen how you relate so beautifully, and so openly, to the kids at Sunny Horizons. It's impressive." Elise lifted a shoulder and offered a self-deprecating smile. "I know we've moved past any kind of misconceptions between us, but visiting the center left me wondering what caused it in the first place. If you don't mind my asking, that is…"

Monica sucked in a breath, taken by surprise. There was no acrimony or conviction in Elise's tone, only a request for mutual understanding. Therefore, Monica was completely unsure how to proceed and respond.

Elise gave her a warm, tender smile. "I'm famous for being blunt, so, like I said, please proceed only if you feel comfortable. You're just—you're like a mystery to me. A mystery that involves one of the most precious people in my life, my son."

Monica finally understood Elise's continuing sense of displacement. She didn't know. Jeremy's mom had no idea about Monica's battle with endometriosis. "He never told you, did he?"

"Jeremy?"

Monica nodded in reply.

"Tell me what?"

In an effort to protect their relationship, to guard its development at a very vulnerable, and critical moment, Jeremy had kept her condition a private matter so they might sort out their own feelings and plans before trying to bring family, and all of its attached emotions, into the mix. It was an inherently protective move on Jeremy's part. One that Monica couldn't help admiring. Maybe openness, now, would pave a smoother road for her, and Elise.

"I think it's the answer to those questions you have about me." Chilling winds swept across the water, skimming over the sand, blowing hard through empty tree branches that chattered above them. "I'm unable to have children, Elise. I want them more than anything—but it's just not meant to happen."

Elise stopped walking. Her eyes went wide. "Oh, Monica. That's tragic. Someone with your gifts, and heart? I'm so sorry." Elise reached out and gave her hand a tight squeeze.

"Thank you." Monica didn't know what else to say.

Elise lifted her chin, gathering her poise. "I wish I had known. I certainly would have been more understanding about the issues you faced during dinner that weekend. It must have been awful for you."

"By the same token, I should have been more rational, but it was like a perfect storm coming over me. Please don't worry about it. I'm sorry if I gave you the feeling I don't appreciate all that you did that day—and all that you mean to Jeremy."

"Thank you, but I can't help worrying. Especially about matters that concern my son, and the woman he's fallen in love with."

"How would you feel about that, Elise? If you watched him marry a woman who couldn't have children?"

"I've said it before. If Jeremy's happy, I'll be happy."

Monica quelled the urge to squirm under such a direct and blunt declaration. Instead, she forced herself to relax. "Your family is such a blessing. I envy you their love, and numbers."

"I thank God for each and every one of them, each and every day."

Monica smiled, and nodded. "I would, too. Believe me." Conversation lapsed into the rhythmic, thundering beat of lake waves. "You know, I used to make wild deals with God when I was going through diagnosis. I'd promise him perfection itself if I could only hold a tiny baby in my arms and call it my own, care for it and raise it. To this day I don't think there's much I wouldn't do to have even a cranky, sick child of my own to take care of."

"I can imagine."

"I'd gladly give up a few nights sleep, rush to the doctor or make a midnight run to the pharmacy. I'd willingly sacrifice my time to teach a child to tie their shoes, or ride a two-wheeler. I would have made a good mother. Parenthood is something I'd find hard to take for granted. But then, reality comes crashing in."

"That's where you're wrong." Elise's eyes had reddened, a visible testimony that she shared Monica's pain and sense of injustice. "You could be a fantastic mother, a mother to a very lucky child. Think of what you could do for a child who was born to a woman unable or unwilling to care for it—a child who needs someone like you the most. Is there any better way to become a parent? Blood is blood, but adoption is the means to that same family end as far as I'm concerned, especially for a person like you who has so much love to give."

"I appreciate the support you're giving. I really do, but—"

"No *but*. Don't take the love and needs you feel and push them into remission, or act like they don't exist. That would be a horrible waste of your heart."

"I care about Jeremy so much, but I don't know what to do anymore. We've discussed the issue several times. I give him tremendous credit for being head-on about this. It's awkward, to begin with, and it only gets worse when you know the things you need to discuss are going to make you feel, and seem, less of a woman."

"You feel like you're less of a woman because of infertility?"

Monica nodded. "Without question. I'm less. I'm less than he deserves, less than you'd probably hope for or expect for your son, and beyond that, I can't escape the feeling that, on the whole, I'm just—" Monica shrugged. "Empty."

Their footsteps slowed to a stop. Elise buried her hands in the pockets of her wool coat. For a time she studied Monica, occasionally closing her eyes to take a breath of the water-spiced air. "The only expectation, the only hope, I have for my son is his love and contentment. Whether that brings me twenty grandkids, or none, it's all I care about. You understand that, right?"

"Without question. Your family is beautiful, Elise. I felt...I *feel*...honored to be included as a part of it."

Elise smiled, and moved a few steps forward to link her arm with Monica's. "Thank you. That means a lot."

"I hate that I got off on bad footing with you. And I wish I could be different. For him. I'd love nothing more than to give him the life he envisions."

They resumed walking. Connected. "Well, I'm beginning to understand the battles you've fought. I consider it an honor that you've opened up to me, and I appreciate it. You weren't what I expected, but that's OK. I *get* that now. Revised perceptions and expectations are a blessing." Elise stopped. In posture

and gaze, she squared off. "Still, like I said, Monica—
there are options."

Options. Everything seemed so simple when
placed within the context of that one simple word.
Even so, the idea struck like hammer blows against her
heart. Monica lifted her face, praying the wind would
dry her tears before they fell. "Adoption again."

"Monica, I'm not trying to pressure you, I'm just
talking aloud. I haven't gone through the anguish you
have, so my perspective is different. So is my
objectivity."

The point hit its mark. Monica knew that Jeremy,
with his vigor and love, would make an ideal father.
How could she have failed to see that fact above
everything else? Monica felt selfish, as though she had
fallen victim to self-defeating fears.

"Elise, I'm a strong-minded, happy individual."

"We definitely have that in common."

Following a shared smile, they turned back toward
the bed and breakfast. "I honestly don't walk around
feeling sorry for myself," Monica said. "Doing so is a
waste of time. I need to trust God. He led me to Jeremy
for a reason. I need to trust that Jeremy and I can work
this out together."

"Sounds to me like a wonderful solution, and
plan."

"Still, there sure are days, and times, when trouble
creeps up on you. Sorry you witnessed mine."

"Understandable emotions, but in real life, you've
got to let yourself move on, and embrace a new form of
happiness." Elise sighed heavily. "For you, it's the
kids. For me, it's watching parades, or any kind of civic
military function. To this day, I get such a wicked,
burning pain in my heart when I see those gleaming,

proud lineups of police officers, or fire fighters, and realize Lance, my firstborn, should have been standing right there among them. With *us*. The badges, the crisp uniforms, the flag. It crushes me sometimes to the point of leaving me out of breath. We should have been given the grace of celebrating Lance's every victory." Elise blinked and swallowed hard. She sighed. "My pain comes from a different source point, but it's powerful; in that respect, I completely understand how you feel. You're right. It can creep up on you out of nowhere. I guess what I'm saying is it's only natural, so forgive yourself and try harder the next time. I know it's the only way I've survived."

Covering her mouth with a shaky hand, Monica looked into the distance, at the ice swept, silver-gray water that stretched to the horizon. Far in the distance, winter birds swooped through the sky, dotting a cloud-banked sky. "How can this whole situation keep such a strong, and terrible hold on my spirit? Ever since I've started going to church with Jeremy, and all of you, I've paid attention to what I've heard, and learned. I fully intend to take what I feel and keep giving it to God, but sometimes it's like He's just not listening."

"He's listening. But He's causing you to grow as well. Growth spurts sometimes cause pain. Maybe He wants you to let go of all the bitterness, and He won't leave the issue alone until you finally do." Elise shrugged. "Collin, went through much the same thing after Lance's murder, so I know the signs."

"It's familiar, and comfortable in its way, even if it's bad. Is that what you mean?"

Elise chuckled wryly. "The devil you know versus embracing the unknown and all of that. Yes."

Monica tucked her fingers beneath Elise's, and, for the first time ever, comfortably held on tight. "I don't want devils. I want angels. I want Jeremy. I want hope, and a future."

Seeming bolstered by their moves forward as well, Elise took hold of both Monica's hands now. She stopped walking, and looked hard into Monica's eyes. "Then I'm going to speak to you like a daughter right now." Her tone was strident. "Don't fear the pathways God gives you. Even if they're not what you might have expected, they'll be full of blessings. And while you're at it, give yourself some breathing room. Pain hits you. Accept it, roll with it, then move past it. When you've been hurting so badly for so long, your perspective can't help but get skewed. Fight back. It seems to me you have more than enough spunk to accomplish that task."

Monica diverted her eyes and her focus; Elise's words turned over and over in her mind. Walking just ahead of Jeremy's mom, Monica picked up a pair of smooth black rocks and tossed them into the turbulent water. "I just don't know where to take things from here. I need to make tough choices. Life-changing choices. I need to figure out whether or not I have the fortitude to move ahead with adoption, or if I can come to terms with the emotional turmoil involved with family, infertility, and the rollercoaster ride of the adoption process. If I don't, I can't lie, or hide from the fact that there's part of me that feels like I should let Jeremy go. He deserves the chance to fall in love again, and have the family he's always dreamed of."

Elise didn't get overly sentimental or verbose. All she said in conclusion was: "I hear what you're saying, and I understand. I just make three requests: First, pray. Pray for discernment—pray for an answer to the doubts you feel. Second, don't underestimate my son."

Silence followed. Monica paused as they entered the bed and breakfast, its warmth a welcome relief from the elements. She turned to Elise. "What's the third request?"

Elise waited a strategic beat before answering. "Don't underestimate *yourself,* either."

20

Sequins, beads and sparkles were everywhere. Nearly a hundred girls between the ages of four and twelve were gathered in the auditorium of Saint Clair Shores High School, dressed in ornate, colorful costumes, preparing for a dress rehearsal of the annual community center dance recital.

Monica assembled her students into one big group and marked attendance for the session. After that, she gave each girl a typed rundown for their parents so they'd know the order they would dance in at tomorrow night's program. Throughout the space, other dance teachers followed a similar routine.

Noise reverberated off the walls, loud but somehow appealing. Oddly, the constant flood of conversation soothed Monica's nerves and kept her from getting swept away by the tense excitement of the girls. Her youngest dancers, Jessica's class, would be the first to go on stage, so she herded them to the wings to prepare them for a run-through.

Petrified, Jessica clung to Monica's hand as she led them to center stage. "Miss Monica, how will I know where to stand? Will you walk us on stage tomorrow?"

"No, Jess. One of the older dancers will. I've assigned someone to lead you on stage. Don't worry."

Monica made her way down the row of dancers and moved them into position for their song. Jessica looked up, seeming determined despite wide, searching eyes. "I'm not scared. Not even a little."

Before returning to the wings, Monica addressed her students. "I'll be right over here, and you'll be able to see me. I'll prompt you along in case you forget a move."

Once the stage lights brightened, about half the girls forgot her instructions and watched overhead with fascination as the technician played with the dimmer, then practiced illuminating the girls with a spotlight.

The music began, and despite the fact that activity in the auditorium came to a stop and everyone started watching them, Monica's students were un-intimidated and performed their dance beautifully.

Afterward, she looked on with a smile as Jessica ran to her mother.

"Mommy! Did you see me? I did it! I did it!"

Wanting to say hello to Caroline, Monica joined them. "Jessica has been so excited that you're getting to see her dance. That's all I've been hearing about at school lately."

Caroline gave her daughter a tight hug. "She did great, but I had the devil's own time trying to get her hair into a bun." She gave Monica a meaningful look then turned to Jessica, "Daddy's going to be here tomorrow night, too, honey. He's excited to see your performance."

That piece of news warmed Monica like a fireplace in wintertime.

"He'll like it, right, Mommy?"

"Absolutely!" Caroline returned her attention to Monica. "You've been so busy! What an event!"

"Actually, I've got a break for the next fifteen

minutes or so while they stage and place a different class. After that, my second group of girls take the stage, and the frenetic pace picks up all over again. I love it, though."

Stage makeup, pink tutu, sequins and all, Jessica plopped herself onto her mom's lap, still squirming and bubbling. "Isn't Miss Monica the *best* teacher, mommy? I love ballet!"

Monica smiled, savoring Jessica's exuberance. "She's a natural, Caroline. I'll bet she inherited that natural grace of hers right from you."

A strange expression glanced Caroline's features. "Oh, I don't think so."

"I take it you're not a dancer."

"Well…ah…" Caroline paused and gave Monica a peculiar look.

Jessica, meanwhile, caught sight of one of her friends and dashed off. Monica watched as the two little ladies compared costumes and ballet slippers amidst chatter and giggles.

"I guess I didn't ever tell you," Caroline said.

"Tell me what?"

"She's adopted."

Monica's breath grabbed, then exited her body in a soft huff of surprise. She hid that reaction well enough, but knew her eyes had gone wide. The revelation about Jessica's adoption was nothing compared to the way this piece of news hit home with her spirit. Monica felt galvanized, compelled forward.

"I'm sorry I didn't tell you," Caroline apologized.

Monica hadn't yet recovered from the surprise, but she managed to say, "There was really no need. I just assumed—"

"That I'm her natural mother." Caroline shifted a

bit, watching after her daughter. Her *adopted* daughter. Monica didn't merely imagine Caroline's soft glow, her maternal—yes *maternal*—pride and connection toward the little girl. That instinct, that love, was real.

This wasn't the time or place, but there were thousands of questions Monica wanted to ask. Was the grueling process fair? Had the uncertainty worn her out? Had the bond between them been easy to forge? Difficult? How old had Jessica been at the time? An infant? Toddler? Had Caroline experienced that gut-wrenching fear about everything falling apart?

Monica, you've used the word "afraid" so often during the course of this conversation. Let it go.

Crystal clear, the memory of Ken's gentle admonishment swept through Monica's mind. And she obeyed his advice. Because ultimately, the only question that mattered had been answered from the start. Love, potent and unbreakable, had brought them together as a family. The love David Carter and Caroline Dempsey felt for their daughter had even helped make a bitter, contentious divorce more manageable.

Excited, determined, Monica considered everything Caroline had been through recently and realized her own fears and misconceptions about being denied a child, and about adoption in particular, weren't nearly as frightening. Caroline had gone to the mat for her daughter; she had fought hard and faced overwhelming adversity. If Caroline could stand up to emotional challenges like that, then Monica felt certain she could give up her own doubts and look more seriously into the prospect of adoption. In affirmation, another memory played through her mind, Elise's concluding bit of advice from when they walked along the lakeshore together:

Pray for discernment—pray for an answer to the doubts you feel.

Monica had. Fervently. Now, Elise's words caused her to realize that getting God to answer a prayer wasn't at all like pulling teeth. It was, instead, a soft, cooling breeze in the dead of a dry, arid summer.

"This may sound crazy," Caroline continued, "but when David and I started having problems a couple years ago, when he became so bitter and angry, I was half afraid the adoption agency would come back for Jessica and take her away—you know, like maybe we were no longer fit parents. Like we were unworthy."

Enrapt, Monica sank onto the velvet-padded theater seat next to Caroline.

"They didn't, of course, but subconsciously, the thought came to me, and rendered more than a few sleepless nights."

Her heart racing, her attention transfixed, Monica nodded. A craving to know more spurred her on. "I don't blame you for your reaction, Caroline. It would have been mine as well. That must have been an awful time for you."

Caroline smiled, an innate gentleness riding along its surface. "It was, but I survived. And so did Jess. Blood ties are blood ties, no question, but Jessica couldn't be more mine—or mean more to me—than if I had given birth to her myself. To be fair, I believe the same thing holds true for David. If not, he wouldn't be so determined about her, and so emotional."

"If you don't mind my asking, what made you decide to adopt?"

Caroline settled back. "We had no luck trying to conceive on our own. We reached that point where we both had enough of the frustration, and decided to go through fertility testing."

A compatriot. Monica wasn't alone. But in truth, hadn't she known that from the very beginning? Between God's love, and Jeremy's presence how could she have ever doubted it? "Do you mind my asking? What did you find out?"

"That the problem was with David." Caroline sighed, and bowed her head. "To this day, I believe that's what changed him. After he found out the test results, I think he started to feel like a failure. Like he was somehow inferior. All of a sudden, he'd go on these awful rampages. He'd blow up at me over the smallest, most inconsequential things. Adoption solved some of our problems, but David was never the same. I tried to stick it out, but our marriage became unlivable."

When you've been hurting so badly for so long, your perspective can't help but get skewed.

Elise's words came back to Monica, hugely amplified. "I can understand that."

"Oh?" Caroline also seemed to realize she had come up against a soft spot.

There wasn't much time left for them to talk. Near the stage, Monica watched her older aged students begin to assemble. Several launched into practicing their arm lifts and plie's. "There's comfort in knowing you've been through upheaval and still kept fighting— not just for you, but for Jessica, too." From there she gave Caroline a thumbnail sketch of her own history.

"Monica, have faith. It's worth it. Take the chance."

Monica watched Caroline in steady contemplation. The fact that Jessica was adopted shouldn't have swayed her so strongly, but somehow it did. Jessica was a wonderful girl, a charmer whom Monica enjoyed teaching and watching over. Jessica proved that there was a lot to be said for adoption, and the emotional threads that ran through it like connecting fibers.

"Thanks." The current performance came from a group of tap dancers who wound down their number. Monica stood to leave so she could organize her next class. "I've got to go, but I'd love to talk more later, OK?"

"Any time, Monica. You've been a God-send to me."

Just like that, with a soul given over to faith, and a heart given over to love, Monica made a resolution. If Caroline could do it, she could, too.

ॐঔ

When recital practice finished, she went home and retired promptly to the den. There, she booted up the computer and accessed the Internet. She remembered the name of the site Jeremy had scrawled on the top of his legal pad: Bethany Christian Services. Lots of bullet points had followed, so, Monica figured he had discovered a lot of information and seemed comfortable with the site, and its offerings.

Her body went tense with anticipation; she scratched Toby behind the ears when he trotted into the room and sat primly next to her chair. "Lie down, Tobes," she commanded, ruffling his fur one last time before turning away so she could focus, and jot down some notes of her own.

When she was finished with her discovery session, she moused to the top of the web page, where a toggle directed, "Contact Us."

Monica bit her lip. Restlessly she moved her feet, which caused her leg warmer of a chocolate lab to stir and give a brief, soft whine. She clicked the icon and opened up a new window where she could request additional information. She made a couple of typos because her fingers trembled, but in the end, she sent the e-mail. This wasn't a commitment, after all. This wasn't promising anything to herself, or to Jeremy. This was nothing more than a simple information request.

But that piece of logic didn't quell the images that rolled through Monica's mind. While the transmission zipped through cyber-space, she pictured herself and Jeremy, hand in hand with a dainty little girl, or a precocious little boy, swinging the youngster between them. She smelled autumn, and saw them all jumping into a pile of brightly colored leaves, savoring the family bond of a triple hug.

God's spirit moved through her heart, helping her inch her way forward into foreign, but beautiful terrain.

21

Jeremy focused on the crowd that packed the auditorium. He barely registered the large and pressing body count before he felt a persistent tug on the bottom edge of his suit coat.

"Hi, Mr. Edwards."

He had made his way about mid-way through the theater, searching for Monica, and nearly passed Jessica Carter without a second glance. Dressed in a costume of vibrant pink dotted by sequins, wearing stage-level rouge and lipstick, she was nearly unrecognizable.

"Jessica! Hi!" He grinned, because with her hair slicked back into a glimmering bun, with her peaches-and-cream skin heightened by makeup, she looked just like a porcelain doll. "Wow, look at you. I like your costume."

"Thank you ve'y much." Proudly she brushed at the layers of tulle that formed her tutu. Jessica turned to her mom who sat nearby. "Mommy, this is Mr. Edwards. He's Miss Monica's friend."

They shook hands and Caroline gave him a warm smile. "I remember seeing you briefly at the Community Center. It's nice to meet you officially." Jessica's mother gestured toward a subdued man, dressed in a business suit, who sat next to her. "This is Jessica's father, David."

Jeremy received a tentative nod, and a wavering smile from the man. "I'm glad to meet you."

"Likewise. Enjoy the show."

Space in the auditorium was literally standing room only for the recital, which made it hard for Jeremy to spot Monica in the sea of shifting faces. "She's up front by the stage with the other teachers," Caroline said, seeming to read his mind.

"Thanks." Before leaving though, he cast Caroline a warm glance, and received a friendly nod in return. He squatted, then, to be at eye level with Jessica. Affectionately, he tweaked her chin. "Good luck tonight. I can't wait to see you dance."

She beamed. "OK. Bye!"

When he straightened, he spotted Monica. It never failed to astound him that just looking at her gave him a thrill.

Three rows from the front of the stage, she shared a discussion with parents who sat in aisle seats. She leaned an ear toward them, and laughed. Even from a distance, her smile captivated him. In keeping with this dressed-up event, she wore a knit dress of pale pink that rippled around her legs.

Jeremy moved forward but waited until she was finished talking before gaining her attention. When she turned away from the parents, she caught sight of him immediately. Her smile, intimate and loving, dawned instantly. It made his pulse race.

"Hey!" She stepped into his offered hug. "So what do you think of this chaos?"

"It's…chaos. Seems fun, though." He touched her flush-warmed cheek. "And you're in your glory."

"Well, this glory-girl is on her way to the maintenance office. I've got to see if there are any chairs we can use to set up additional seating in the back."

Jeremy scanned the tight press of bodies. "Is it always this crowded?"

"I've been doing this for five years, and it gets bigger every time." She gave him a rueful look. "Who knows what we'll do next year. We've basically outgrown this space."

He followed her to a set of doors that opened to a school hallway. Dance students gathered there as well as in the auditorium. Excited talk and laughter filled the air, and several girls greeted Monica with happy exclamations.

At the maintenance office door, Monica knocked. A uniformed janitor answered and listened while Monica explained the seating shortage.

"I've got some folding chairs back here. Got some folks who can help carry?"

Jeremy quickly volunteered, and Monica took a few chairs herself, recruiting several fathers of her students along the way. In the theater, the chairs went up, and Monica gave Jeremy a grateful smile. "Thanks for the muscle. Meet me right here when the recital is finished. This is where the parents pick up their kids. Once they clear out, I'm free."

He kissed her cheek and smiled. "See you then. Good luck, Jellybean."

She walked away, but Jeremy had begun to understand her nuances so well that he swore he felt a glow coming from her, a vibration of promise.

"The excitement of performance night," he murmured to himself. "That's what it is."

From a standing position at the rear corner of the facility, Jeremy watched the fruits of Monica's efforts. He paid particular attention to Jessica's class, his gaze straying periodically to the third row, left-of-center position where David and Caroline sat and watched their daughter, united even if no longer married.

Pleasing as that distraction was, Jeremy also kept his eye on Monica. Though nearly hidden by the edge of the curtains, tucked into the wings of the stage, she prompted the dancers along until the song ended, to thunderous applause.

She remained backstage along with the other teachers, barely visible as she watched the progress of the recital. When the event concluded, instructors were called on stage, one by one, and awarded a large bouquet of red roses.

Jeremy's applause rose with that of the crowd, and his heart swelled with pride as she stood in the spotlight for a moment and performed a perfect curtsey.

Afterward, since the hallway became packed with people, Jeremy waited at a side door of the auditorium until he noticed Monica looking for him.

He joined her with a smile. "Pandemonium."

"Yeah. I could meet you outside."

"OK. Want me to take you home?"

People moved past, pressing and pushing as they connected with family members, and recital participants. Monica had one student at her side, tugging on her hand, waiting to offer up a gift bag.

Monica shook her head. "I drove. Tell you what—I have an idea." She bent to whisper a few words to her student, most likely a request for her to stand by for a few seconds. Monica then disengaged from the hubbub around her and stepped up to Jeremy's side. "Give me half an hour?" People moved all around her.

"Yeah."

"Then meet me?" A student stepped up, but Monica's focus stayed put on Jeremy.

"Where?" He felt a heated tingle slide up his arms, through his chest. Foreshadowing of something— something monumental.

She looked him straight in the eyes, and the smile she gave him knocked his senses into a delicious, free-spinning orbit. "At Woodland."

ॐ≪

Jeremy arrived first. He knew the church and its sanctuary would still be open. Wednesday night adult fellowship had ended a short time ago, and Ken generally left the church open for an hour or so afterward. What surprised him was that Monica knew they'd be able to meet here as well.

This really was a blessed place. Woodland was a perfect blend of the old and the new. At first glance, it looked like an old-fashioned country church with aged, red brick, stained-glass windows and white shutters. But behind its soaring, red-brick bell tower and double-door entrance stretched a large, modern sanctuary along with a series of buildings for meetings, staff offices, and the activity center where fellowship took place after each week's service.

Lush, rolling land was framed in by old trees, an ice-laden pond, and a walkway that led to Parishioners Bridge. The wooden structure acted as a memorial to Woodland's members, past and present, with hundreds of names inscribed upon its surface. Just beyond the busy hub of Jefferson Avenue crested the shoreline of Lake Saint Clair, empty and soundless for the winter.

Jeremy loved Woodland deeply. The spirit of this church carried into his spirit like a pulse; it had been that way ever since his youth. The fact that Monica felt a growing connectedness to his faith home lightened him all the more. As he wandered toward the entrance, he noticed Monica's car as she pulled into the parking lot and brought the vehicle to a stop right next to his truck.

He didn't wait. Rather, he entered the sanctuary, claiming a pew not far from the front lip of the altar. So many of the important milestones in his life could be catalogued right here in this spot. Family celebrations of baptisms, service group meetings, weddings, deaths. Jeremy's breath caught when an image of Lance came vividly to life—a deep blue uniform, crisply starched and ironed, bedecked by pins and ribbons; a regulation crew cut; a tight, solid build with wide shoulders and features capped off by a mischievous smile and sparkling eyes.

He dipped his head, closed his eyes and offered it all up to Christ in a grateful prayer.

Lance had been slain by a bullet long ago, yet all these years later, Jeremy still ached at the senseless loss. Although he heard Monica's footfalls along the main aisle, he kept his eyes closed, continuing to pray over Lance's departure, and the hole it left within him. Ironic, he decided, that "The Chief," Collin's little boy who was in part named for Lance, had led him to the woman of his dreams.

❦

Monica stood next to the pew where Jeremy sat. She kept a respectful distance, quietly waiting until his eyes came open and he returned to the moment. He turned his head and silently offered his hand.

She promptly accepted the gesture. "You're a million miles away."

"Not anymore."

Monica responded to his saucy reply with a wink. She took him in like the air around her, all spiced by evergreen and bayberry. The energy radiating through her couldn't be denied, or contained. As though it were a talisman, she fingered the large, flat packet she held. She knew full well how deeply its contents could impact them, recognized the world of joyful possibilities its contents could unlock—not just for her, but for the man she loved. Where should she even begin?

"Hi there, by the way," she said at length.

"Back at you. Come here." Using a gentle pull, he drew her onto the pew. "What do you have there? He nodded toward the envelope but Monica placed on the seat beside her. Upside down. For now, protecting its mystery suited her just fine.

She moved close and held Jeremy tight, kissing his cheek slowly. She ignored his question. "Thank you for tonight. For being there for me. I loved seeing you in the audience."

Jeremy nodded, but he kept keying in on the envelope, obviously seeking enlightenment. Monica settled her hand atop the package in an unspoken request that it stay as is for the time being. She leaned back against the pew with a peaceful sigh. "I really do love it here." She studied the empty, echoing space of the church interior. "I should thank you for that as well. For drawing me into a relationship with God, and helping me tune into His truths, and a wonderful church."

"Actually, that's what I was thinking about when you walked up."

Monica tilted her head, her focus centered on Jeremy alone. Her stomach jumped. Tingling sparks ignited her nerves. "Woodland is a place where I can easily make my faith a bigger part of the relationship you and I build together."

Jeremy wound his arm around her shoulders. In his eyes, she saw questions begin to spin and push, but she also noticed the way he set everything aside for the time being. Instead, he kept quiet. Monica, therefore, could unfold as she wished, with no pressure. So, for a time, they simply rested in the serenity of the church. A Christmas tree, toward the right of the altar, was lit by hundreds of tiny, multi-colored lights. A white star graced its topmost branches. The mix of colors from the tree played against the glossy surface of the pew and sparkled in Jeremy's dark eyes. Natural evergreen swags and a pair of matching wreaths dotted the walls; once again she detected the subtle spice of them as she breathed deep—and prepared to open herself in complete love and trust.

"I want to give you an early Christmas present," Monica finally said. She handed him the package, and waited.

Jeremy opened it eagerly, still not seeing the front. From inside he withdrew a thick brochure from Bethany Christian Services along with some printed pages from their website and a few sheets of paper from a notepad which were full of Monica's notes.

His breath caught. He looked at her and she ran her tongue against her lips, watching him right back in a hesitant sense of uncertainty. It was their moment of truth. All that the future might hold, all of her most heartfelt dreams, were about to be confronted. For an instant, doubts tried to ensnare her. Was she being too presumptuous? Had she pushed forward too far? Would he be happy?

"So what you're saying is—" Jeremy didn't complete the sentence. He cleared his throat roughly and blinked hard. When he closed his eyes and took a deep, shaky breath, Monica's every fear, every emotional blockade, and every doubt, evaporated.

"What I'm saying is this: I contacted Bethany Christian Services. I sent them an e-mail, but after work yesterday, I couldn't wait for the information. I made a phone call and asked if I could pick up an information packet in person." Her pulse went wild. Hope set the beat and love flooded her entire universe.

"Before you and I take another step forward," she continued, "before we decide on a future together, and what it can hold, I want you to know something very important." Monica turned to him fully, taking hold of his hands. "I love you." Raw emotion lent texture to the words. "I love you, JB, and I refuse—I *absolutely* refuse—to let anything stand in the way of your happiness. Not even *me*."

"But I *am* happy. Monica, I love you."

He released one of her hands so he could cup her face, and frame it gently. She reveled in the warm, work-roughened stroke of his fingertips. She could scarcely believe the miracle that was unfolding. Droplets of tears built on her lashes and fell. They struck the back of Jeremy's hand when he rested it lightly upon her knee. The moisture glittered like diamonds, like snow beneath a full moon.

"You show me every single day, and in every way imaginable, that you love me." Monica choked back the lump in her throat. "You, and Woodland, have helped me realize how precious I am. You've shown me God's love in so many ways." Her chin quivered, and she lifted a shoulder. "I guess that's been part of my problem all along, until now. Until you. I didn't quite believe God cared about me."

Jeremy moved in haste to interrupt, but Monica held him off by raising a hand. "Oh, I believed in Him, definitely, and truly, but He scared me. I looked at Him as a judge and perfect overseer who weighed right and wrong, catalogued every good deed and every bad. God intimidated me. He walked in unapproachable light, and I was content to cower, and never try to experience His grace in a personal way."

Jeremy remained speechless, and expectant. "After all, really, who am I?" Monica said. "I figured, billions of people on this planet have billions of more problems than I do – and are in much greater need of God's attention than the circumstances of my life. I worshiped Him at a distance. I kept Him remote. I just didn't feel worthy."

The admission caused her skin to burn with heightened emotion. She heard Jeremy's breathing go sharp. "*No*, Monica. *Never*. Please know that."

Tenderly she touched his face. "Then in you came. *You*. You were the answer to all those questions I had for God. You've shown me so much, just in the warm, loving way you live your life. I'm not afraid anymore, of being unworthy, or of loving you, or giving you the life I know we both want. God wrote a message on my heart, Jeremy. He wrote peace, and joy and love on my heart, and every letter of that note is carried in your name. You give me so much. Gratitude doesn't begin to scratch the surface. I'm in awe."

More words, more emotions, tumbled through her soul, but all of them tasted woefully inadequate. So, rather than embellish, she locked eyes with him. The love she found there, the love she hoped he saw in return, was all that was necessary anyhow.

Besides, she'd never get a single word past the lump in her throat.

Monica tilted her head, still connected to him by the touch of her fingertips against his face. "I prayed so long and so hard for the things I wanted," she whispered once she composed herself, "most especially for children. You said it yourself, though. I boxed with God until my perspectives became skewed and I almost lost everything that will bring me real happiness. I didn't realize until now—until you—that my prayers had already been answered. That God had already seen into my heart and provided me with everything I dreamed of—and more."

"He did the same thing for me, Monica, the minute I walked into Sunny Horizons and saw you for the first time. Know that...and believe it...because you've changed me forever."

"I do. Now, I do. But before I could let myself consider this"—she nodded at the packet of information Jeremy had placed next to him—"I had to move past everything I held onto about motherhood and open myself up to other options than having a child naturally. And I needed to realize that there's importance and value to what I do every day at work and at the community center."

Silence filled the air once again. They held hands. Monica rested her head against his shoulder and breathed out in a soft, wavering way. They lingered in Woodland's sanctuary. Jeremy held her close, and they talked. They chatted and planned and dreamed. Much later, they were interrupted by the sound of quiet footfalls, then Ken Lucerne's familiar chuckle. "Hey, guys."

Never looking away from Jeremy, Monica blushed and smiled. "Hey, Pastor Ken."

"Time to close it down. Sorry." Wearing a playful grin, he moved to the altar and unplugged the tree lights, dimming the interior lights as well until the church was bathed in nothing more than a milky, pale glow.

"No problem," Jeremy replied, holding hands with Monica as they stood and prepared to leave.

Monica pulled away. When Ken passed by, she caught hold of his arm and pecked his cheek. "Thank you. Thank you *so* much."

While Jeremy watched them in open puzzlement, Ken looked into Monica's eyes and gave her a knowing smile. "My pleasure. Kiara's waiting, though, so I better hit the road." He glanced at Jeremy, then back at Monica. "Y'know, it's like I always say: there's nothing that affirms my faith more than watching God unfold a plan."

They followed Ken outside. After he slid into his car and drove off, Jeremy stood next to Monica, who made ready to step into her vehicle. "What just happened back there? And how did you know Woodland would be open tonight?"

Monica blinked prettily. "Just a hunch is all." She

lifted to her tiptoes and placed a delicate kiss on his chin.

"A hunch and perhaps the authorization of a certain romance-loving pastor who shall remain nameless."

Monica unlocked her car and opened the door. "Oh, feel free to name him. After all, Ken deserves the recognition."

Jeremy gave her a hug before leaving, then launched into a heated, heady kiss that left Monica hungry on so many levels. "He does indeed, Jellybean."

22

Christmas Eve festivities moved into full swing at the home of Elise and Ben Edwards.

The whole gang attended, including Monica's parents, her younger brother and sister. Seeing everyone together left her with just one thought: *my cup runneth over.*

Jeremy had met her family on a number of occasions, but this was the first time they had all gathered in one spot. After spending the day with Monica's family in Hamtramck, a caravan to Saint Clair Shores took place and everyone now settled at the table of Ben and Elise Edwards for Christmas Eve dessert. Monica couldn't help smiling as she considered the idea that today was but a glimpse of holidays to come.

In the dining room, mini cheesecakes of all varieties, ice cream and coffee concluded the day's festivities. Monica helped clear plates afterwards, working in tandem with her mom, and Elise, Stephanie and Liz, to return the dinner table to some semblance of normalcy. It was a warm, laughter-filled time of sharing.

On her final trip through the dividing doors between the dining room and the kitchen, Jeremy stood and stretched casually. "If you all don't mind, I need to borrow Monica for a minute. We'll be right back."

Naturally, sassy comments and cat-calls accompanied. Jeremy chuckled, shrugging off the jocularity with negligence. Monica just rolled her eyes and grinned while Jeremy took hold of her elbow and led the way out of the dining room. They ended up in the now vacant den of the Edwards' home. Jeremy shut the door, causing Monica to arch a brow. "You're going to ruin my reputation, JB."

"Or save it, one of the two. Have a seat." His lips kept twitching, as though he held back a face-splitting grin by nothing more than a supreme act of will.

"Bossy today, aren't you?"

"Be nice, or no present."

In haste, Monica obeyed, perching with exaggerated perfection upon the edge of the couch cushion. She even added a saccharine sweet smile and wide, innocent eyes to the mix.

Jeremy snorted and rolled his eyes. "As if."

"How rude!"

While they laughed, Jeremy reached behind the couch and pulled out a gift bag. But he didn't hand it over right away. Instead, he sat down as well, and then moved in snug. His kiss slid down her throat in a warm, tingling glide that she welcomed and longed for. His slow-moving touch, against her jaw, then her neck, left her miles away from the celebration at hand. "Merry Christmas, Jellybean."

His breath tickled the inside of her ear when he whispered those magical words. Her head lolled to the side, and a breathy sigh escaped from that achy, quivering spot deep inside. She couldn't keep her eyes open. In fact, she barely found the means by which to stay upright. That was fine, though—a strong, steady pair of arms came around her, and held her fast, drawing her safely home to the haven that was Jeremy Blaise Edwards.

She hardly even realized his intent, but, before she knew it, Monica found herself holding that shimmering, red and green Christmas bag that was flooded by tissue paper of silver and gold. It was heavy, too.

Confused, and brought back to reality, she blinked a few times to clear her vision, and her head. "Ah? What?"

Jeremy stroked her cheek with his thumb. "Ah, that would be a Christmas present. From me. To you."

Her heart sparkled, bursting with joy. He was simply off-the-charts adorable. No other way to put it. He watched her eagerly, peeking inside the bag like a kid as she removed the flood of soft, crinkly paper and set it aside.

Monica uncovered a heavy, dark colored box, hallmarked by the Waterford insignia. Her breath caught, and her gaze lifted to his in the span of time it took for her heart to beat. "Ah?"

"You're becoming redundant."

Monica clucked her tongue at his devilish comment and pulled the lid gently from the top of the box. After carefully peeling back a top layer of cushioning, she nearly burst into tears. From within she gently removed a cut-crystal candy dish chock full of jellybeans. Clear, plastic covering held the candy in place, as well as red curling ribbon.

"Jeremy, this is stunning!"

"I figured you might want a replacement."

The ugliness of the whole confrontation with David Carter seemed so long ago. It had been washed away, cleansed by revised thinking, and a whole new lease on life. Monica speared Jeremy with a look, pushing back laughter, and a grin. "If you think I'm putting a piece of Waterford crystal, your first ever Christmas present to me, on my desk at school where anything could happen to it, you're seriously mistaken. This gets a place of honor."

"First off, I'm Irish, so, what else would I get you but Waterford? Furthermore, your desk at Sunny Horizons *is* a place of honor. It's where we met, and it's where your heart lives."

"Not when I'm next to you," she clarified, slowly swayed by his thought process. She settled the crystal piece on her lap, and pulled the ribbon free. Since the colorful candies were simply too good to resist, she peeled back the securing plastic so she could grab a few.

That's when her diving fingertips came upon an item most definitely not made of sugar.

Monica froze, and her heart rate skyrocketed. "Ah?"

Jeremy, it seemed, could do nothing but laugh with delight at her continuing use of the word "Ah," as well as her reaction to what she pulled from the bed of candies. Her hands trembled. Wide-eyed, for real this time, she stared into his face and fell in love all over again.

"Nothing delights me like catching you off-guard, Monica." He spoke the words softly, with such tender affection her heart flew. He brushed his fingers against hers, taking custody of a breathtaking diamond solitaire set in a slim band of yellow gold. "But you have to answer a question before you get to keep it."

Jeremy didn't go down on one knee. He went

down on both, settling into the space before her, looking up into her eyes while he held her hands gently in his. "Monica," he whispered, for their ears, their hearts alone, "would you do me the *indescribable* honor of becoming my wife?"

She wanted to answer back with her usual display of sass and spark, but her tight throat, her overflowing heart and the love Jeremy showed, all combined to leave her perfectly undone.

She knelt next to him, wrapping her arms around his neck, snuggling into him like a perfectly matched puzzle piece clicking into place and finding home. "Will you do me the indescribable honor of becoming my husband as well?"

She leaned back, giving him a saucy grin through misty, tear-filled eyes. He tilted and wiggled the ring like a temptation. It caught the light and split it into millions of colorful pieces. "I think that could be arranged."

"Ah, the sooner, the better, JB."

"Ah, amen to that!"

With that, as their laughter filled the room, Jeremy slipped the ring into place on the third finger of her left hand. It was a perfect fit.

This was a day of celebrating births—the birth of new hope, the birth of a lifetime commitment made in love, and the birth of a Savior who would see them through it all—good times and bad. So, before leaving the privacy of the den and rejoining the family, they remained kneeling. In unspoken synchronicity, they cuddled together, offering up a prayer of thanks and joyful praise for all they had been given, and all that their lives would embrace.

It was a perfect, blessed moment of communion.

Hearts Key

Hearts Key Dedication

To those who share ministry, and talent, via the
wonderful Christian music I listen to each day. I'm a
fan, and I'm grateful. Also, to high school sweethearts
everywhere who still remember that first flush of
love—and longing.

PROLOGUE

One Year Ago

Amy Samuels shifted an armload of groceries, so she could flex her shoulder muscles. The supermarket was just a few blocks away, and she walked there whenever she could. She needed the exercise to clear her mind, and ease stress.

The front door of her home stood open; she frowned, going tense. Seeing her husband's car parked in the driveway triggered an immediate, instinctive sense of disquiet.

Mark's home. In the middle of the day. Why?

The manufacturing company he worked for was in the midst of a big job, providing parts for the next generation of SUV's. He was busy, and she didn't expect him to be home until late tonight. To be honest, Amy had been looking forward to his absence and the inner peace she knew it would bring.

Why wasn't Mark at work?

She walked inside, trying without success to ignore the sound of slamming cupboards coming from the kitchen. Wouldn't you just know it? The line of fire was exactly where she needed to deposit her stash of groceries.

All of a sudden, glassware clanged and banged, coming dangerously close to crashing. Amy steeled herself for battle.

"Mark? Mark, where's Pyper?"

His answer was an unintelligible, guttural sound.

Alarms sounded in Amy's mind, making her heart pound. "Marcey from next door was sitting with her while I shopped. What happened to Marcey?"

Braving it up, Amy crossed through the living room, taking stock. Her footsteps came to an abrupt halt. On an end table by the couch rested an open, well-sampled bottle of whiskey. Positioned right next to it she spied a tumbler, coated by dripping beads of condensation. Inside the glass were traces of gold liquid and a pool of melting ice. *So,* Amy seethed, *Mark had come home, and imbibed in the hard stuff. Nice.*

She wilted, but continued on to the kitchen. How long had the booze been out in the open? They had a rule about no whiskey in the house. What was a bottle of high-proof alcohol doing within potential reach of their four-year-old daughter?

In that instant a flashpoint occurred. Resignation and sadness morphed into rage. His reckless disregard for the safety of their daughter added fuel to her mood. "Mark!"

Mark Samuels stepped into the threshold, planting his feet firmly while he braced against the archway between the living room and kitchen. He wobbled a bit, but the stance said it all: drunken belligerence. "Back off on the sanctimonious vocals, Amy! I'm not in the mood! I'm not taking any of your crap! I mean it!"

She was so used to this. Instance by instance, Amy became immune to his menacing tone; it bore no impact or dissuasion. Calmly she moved past him and set her groceries aside on the small kitchen table. Then, she returned to the living room and picked up the bottle and glass. The new food could sit and rot for all she cared. Amy pushed past him on her way back to the kitchen where she planned to dispose of both the whiskey and the glass.

"Back off?" She stepped up to the sink but turned to glower at her husband. "Back off when you're home early from work, guzzling liquor? Where's my daughter?"

"*Our* daughter," he amended harshly, "is in her room. She's being punished. She wasn't listening and refused to do what I told her to do, so I sent her to her room until dinner."

Amy stopped short. Dinner wouldn't be ready for a couple of hours. On this humid, stifling summer day, being jailed in her room would be terrible for Pyper. Their home wasn't air conditioned, and there wouldn't be much for the four-year-old to do. Toys, games, and furnishings were sparse. In fact, it was a miracle they maintained possession of their home, considering the heavy debt load they carried and Mark's sporadic income.

She became aware once more of the bottle and glass she held. "After I toss this out, I'm telling her she's free to leave her room."

"Oh, no you're not." Mark swore liberally as he stalked in close. Looking him straight in the eye, Amy poured the remaining whiskey down the drain and threw the glass into the sink so hard it shattered.

"I see. So you think *that's* how it is." Vindictiveness shone in Marks' eyes. "That's just *fine*."

He staggered to the small china hutch tucked into a corner of the kitchen. Crafted of maple, it was well worn, a beloved heirloom from Amy's grandmother. They had inherited the piece a couple years ago. Mark yanked open the doors. With sloppy motions he reached inside. He grabbed stacks of dishes from inside and just let them fall.

Irreplaceable, depression-era glass and Rosenthal china smashed to the floor. "We even yet? Want s'more?"

Amy ran, pulling on Mark's arm in an attempt to get him away from the cabinet. But he was a big man, solid muscle; when she came near, he shook her off easily, sending her to the floor in a sprawl. She righted herself quickly, stumbling against the refrigerator.

"Stop it! Stop! *Please* stop!" Helpless, she could do nothing but watch while Mark swiped at an artfully arranged display of wine goblets. Soon they were reduced to nothing more than sparkling shards that decorated the hardwood floor.

Amy cried out, thinking of the beautiful memories held within those few precious mementos from her past: the family dinners, holiday celebrations, happy laughter. Her china was sacrosanct, one of the few things she refused to pawn in order to support her family.

The china and…

Mark spied her camera, a simple digital unit that was her lifeline to sanity. A part of what augmented her income as a receptionist for a fitness center in Sterling Heights, Michigan. Her heart lurched. *No*, she screamed in silence. *Please, no! I have a freelance assignment this weekend!*

The inner plea came just seconds too late.

He hefted the small, silver unit, which gleamed and still looked like new even two years after purchase because Amy pampered and cared for it. Photography was her release, her joy…and Mark was about to destroy it!

He threw the camera against the wall; it burst apart on impact and Amy cried out, sinking against the counter.

"I got fire—laid off today." He continued to storm through the kitchen. "Stupid idiots in charge of that stinkin' factory don't know their left hand from their right." He spun toward her. "So if you push me now, I'll push you right back. If you get in my way, I'll take you right out of it!"

Amy didn't doubt that fact for a minute. However, she hadn't missed the slipup Mark made between being fired and being laid off. Her husband was defeating himself. Again. He was taking her right down with him. Again. Gambling, booze, and spotty work attendance had combined to do him in. Again. Amy scraped the very bottom of her heart, trying desperately to find even the tiniest piece of hope for her relationship with Mark. The effort was answered only in an emptiness that stole her joy, and ever increasing fears for herself and Pyper.

She wished for surcease, but all the wishing in the world wouldn't make the nightmare of living with Mark go away. Not this time. Amy knew she alone had the power to make a final move and end this abuse and insane pattern of living—not just for her sake, but for Pyper's as well.

Mark ranted on. "I lose my job, and I'm not gonna be able to get another one any time soon living in this Godforsaken place." Amy winced at his curse. Although she no longer attended church regularly, like she used to—back in happier, more innocent times— the use of God's name in vain scalded a place in her spirit and returned her to who, and what, she used to be.

He kept on raging. "I don't want griping from you, Amy. If I want a drink after work, not you or anyone else is gonna stop me! You have a choice. Clean up this mess and deal with it, or get out of my sight!"

Frozen with terror, Amy stared as he kicked furniture, trashed cupboards, and systematically destroyed the kitchen. Then, something in her mind snapped. She couldn't hold back the cry of angry frustration that bubbled up from her chest. Now, every-day dishes joined the pile of chaos. She barely dodged being hit by the plate her husband threw.

This is insanity, she thought. *No one should have to live this way.*

"If it weren't for your drinking and gambling, we might make it! If you'd discipline yourself to live a normal life, you'd be able to function at work and keep a job! Instead you'd rather hock everything we own, right down to your soul, for a night of poker, or a night of drinking so you can go numb!" She pulled him away from the cupboard; anger-driven adrenaline made her strong. "It's easier that way, isn't it? Well not for me! I'm sick of it! I'm sick of being trashed— literally and emotionally! I'm sick of living in debt! I'm sick of being heartbroken! Most of all I'm sick to death and tired of not giving Pyper the life she deserves. You need *help*—"

"Get out!" Mark pounced on her like a rabid animal, shoving her against the kitchen counter so hard that an explosion of pain shot up her back and spine, and she lost her breath. An instant later, the back of his hand crossed her face with such impact she saw red haze and had to fight off nausea. "I said *get out*!"

Amy refused to give in. For Pyper's sake, she had

to persevere. She squirmed away from his grasp. This marriage was finished. With that realization came a degree of resolution that lent her additional strength.

"Fine. I'll leave. But not without my daughter. She is *not* staying with you."

In that instant, all the anger left his face. She watched as her words sank in. Only then did Amy realize her mistake. She had exposed her greatest vulnerability. Pyper. Mark remained just lucid enough to connect the emotional dots and play an ace.

"Get out of here if that's what you want—but you don't get Pyper. She's *mine*."

Her heart endured a shower of spears. How could she possibly leave without Pyper? She had to get to her daughter! Amy would never, ever leave without her.

She stared at her husband, her vision blurred by tears. She had to find a way to Pyper. Backing slowly away, she noticed the way he moved toward her, bullying her into the living room. He wore a gloating expression, moving her slowly, and inexorably, to the front door.

"Go ahead. Just try to get her. *Try* it."

He deliberately blocked the hallway that led to the two bedrooms of their home. Amy could hear Pyper crying now, and that left her frantic. She wanted to scream—crumple up and wail.

God, please, please, give me strength! Send me help!

There came no instant answer, no miraculous flash.

"My things," she objected weakly. Her belongings were all she could think of that might get her past him and into the hallway of rooms to grab Pyper.

Mark stood solid, his posture unyielding. He advanced her a few more steps toward the front door, and away from Pyper. "Get 'em later. If they're still around."

Finally, as though he could tolerate her no longer, Mark shoved her onto the front porch and slammed the door shut. The dead bolt banged into place with added emphasis. Panic swept through her body and quickly overwhelmed. She had no purse. No keys. No cell phone. No money. She had nothing but the shorts, t-shirt and tennis shoes she wore.

And she didn't have Pyper.

Desperate, her breath exiting in a heaving, labored effort, Amy looked toward the front windows of the house. Fear kept her from thinking clearly, yet she had to figure out a way to get Pyper away from Mark.

Not giving herself time to reconsider, she climbed through a hedge of thigh-high evergreen shrubs that surrounded their house. Her clothes were no protection against the long, stabbing needles. The window to Pyper's bedroom was open. The sound of her daughter moving around inside only increased her obsession to get her free as she worked her way through the bushes as quietly and as quickly as possible.

Standing on tiptoe, Amy looked inside. The expression of bleak, hopeless fear on Pyper's face prodded her on.

"Pyper...Pyper Marie..." She didn't want to speak too loud for fear of alerting Mark. "Come to the window, sweetheart. It's OK. Come here to Mama."

Shaking, her wide eyes brimming with tears, Pyper inched her way to the window. "Mama, get me! I scared! Get me now! *Please*!"

Fat tears rolled down Pyper's plump, red cheeks. A thick, curling tumble of blonde hair fell to her waist.

Dressed in a tank top, shorts and flip-flops, the vision of her daughter consumed Amy, and spurred her on.

"Hush, baby! Hush! I'm not leaving you! I'm not going anywhere without you." Scanning the window line, Amy thought out loud. "I've got to open the screen." There wasn't much a four-year-old could do to help, but as she spoke, Amy spotted a tiny hole in the netting of the screen that she might be able to use to pry the screen off and pull it free. She worked fast, jimmying the protective cover relentlessly, making the tear larger and larger.

Soon she ripped away the piece of finely-woven metal.

Sweat beaded her face. Nerve-inspired heat nearly sent her world into a tailspin. But in that instant, Pyper reached out for her, and Amy grabbed onto her for all she was worth. Her control firmly in check, Amy dragged Pyper through the window.

Freedom. Blessed, precious freedom. But for how long?

They ran down the street and headed toward a nearby convenience store. The life she chose with Mark had left Amy alienated from her family, from friends, and everyone else she had held dear just five short years ago. The only thing she knew she could do now was place a collect phone call to the most welcoming place she had ever known, and fall into the arms of a God she hardly believed in any longer.

As she prayed a prodigal might return to the sanctuary of Woodland Church, she dialed operator assistance. "Please tell Pastor Ken Lucerne that this is a collect call, from Amy Maxwell," she said when the woman came on the line. Her voice shook. She knew Pastor Ken wouldn't recognize her married name of

Samuels. Everyone at Woodland had known her as Amy Maxwell—the bubbly and sparkling life of the party, the leader of the youth group. Once upon a time, she'd been the girl most likely to succeed and take the world by storm.

Oh, how far I've fallen, she thought on a choking sob.

The call rang through and she waited, tightly clutching Pyper, praying insane, ridiculous prayers of promise and petition that Mark wouldn't spot her. That safety might be hers and Pyper's once more. Somehow. Some way.

"Ken Lucerne," came a warm, deep voice.

Amy nearly went faint with relief while the operator informed him of the collect call. She clung tight to Pyper; she clung tight to the edge of the plastic encasement of the public phone, cradling the receiver against her shoulder. Tears fell free, and she trembled.

"Yes, I'll accept the charges." The operator clicked off and Ken took it from there. "Amy, honey, what's the matter? Are you OK?"

She could barely talk she was shaking so bad. His tender concern allowed her the luxury of a complete, and much-needed internal collapse. "Pastor Ken, can you please…can you help me? I'm in such a huge mess, and you're the only one I could think of to help. I'm so sorry to bother you, I just…I…"

"Where are you?"

She didn't answer the question. "I don't know how long I can stay here. He might find me, and Pyper, and that'll be the end…of everything! I—"

"Sweetheart, rest easy. Where are you? I'll come get you." Though he interrupted, his voice was so reassuring. A calm in the storm.

"I'm at Robtell's Quick Mart on Groesbeck."

There was the slightest of pauses. "I can be there in ten minutes, fifteen tops. Are you in any kind of danger?"

"I just don't know anymore, Pastor Ken. I don't know anything right now. All I know is I'm scared! I need help!"

"Stay right there, Amy. I'm on my way."

Ken hung up abruptly, and she found she could actually breathe again. Pyper clung to her neck, burying her face in Amy's neck, shaking with tears. "Baby, I'm so, so sorry for putting you through this." She pushed through the doorway to the store. It was cool inside; that helped. There was also a deep, empty window ledge where Amy sank down and waited in an obscurity she embraced. Slowly she uncoiled, knowing she would need some aspirin for the pain that echoed through her back and her face. She rested her head against the cool plate glass and drew in deep, steadying breaths.

It's over, Mark. From this day on you are no longer a part of our lives, and neither is this horrible, sickening fear. Not once after this nightmare passes will I allow myself to look back.

Marianne Evans

1

Present Day

"Mr. Brock, we're pulling in at Woodland. You all set? Ready to go?"

"And then some." Tyler Brock moved to a nearby window next to Anthony, their driver. "Hey, Anthony? How long have we been on tour together?"

"Almost three years, sir. Why?"

Even as they spoke, the enormous tour bus swung into the parking lot of Woodland Church. The first landmark of Tyler's arrival home was the familiar, beautiful brick bell tower, topped by a gleaming, simple cross. The sight filled him with warmth. He smiled. Opposite the church crested the pristine, diamond-tipped waters of Lake Saint Clair.

"Well I'm just wonderin'. D'you think it might be possible for you to call me Tyler?"

Anthony chuckled. "No, sir. Sorry."

"Glad we got that settled." Tyler spared him a wry look.

The chauffer shook his head and grinned. "Likewise, Mr. Brock."

Theirs was an age-old back and forth. Tyler gave up the battle and instead looked outside the rectangular window as Anthony navigated the vehicle to a slow, shimmying stop. Tyler took note of familiar

526

surroundings. Michigan. Saint Clair Shores. Woodland Church. *Home.*

He really had been gone too long.

Excitement filled him, dancing across his nerve endings like a live wire. A crowd of people converged on the bus and the equipment semi that followed close behind.

The first face he saw belonged to Ken Lucerne. The pastor of Woodland Church stood at the front of the gathering of about a hundred or so people. Rimming the crowd were members of the local news media. Kiara, Ken's wife, stood next to him. The happiness that expanded in Tyler's chest increased.

He knew the drill. He had lived it repeatedly over the last four, almost five, years. But never here. Never at the heart of where he had been raised, and never at Woodland, his faith-home since birth.

He prepared to exit the bus. "Thanks for the smooth ride, Tony. As ever."

"Pleasure, as ever. Have a great concert, Mr. Brock."

In passing, before he trotted down the bus steps, Tyler gave Tony's shoulder an affectionate clap, and they traded nods. The rest of his team—both musical and technical—gathered up and prepared to walk out with him.

The doors whooshed open, unfolding into a world of smiling faces, camera lights, cheers, colorful poster-board signs, and desperate calls for his attention. The instant his feet hit the asphalt, the focus was on him, and it was chaos.

"Tyler! Tyler we love you!"

"Tyler, over here, please."

"Can you look this way?"

"How does it feel to be back in Michigan?"

"How long will you be here?"

"Tyler! Can we have an autograph? Please?"

"Can you comment on the addition of a second show tomorrow night, since this one sold out in hours?"

Tyler walked smoothly through the din—the strobes of cameras, the video floodlights, the shouts and jostling. He went straight to Pastor Ken, his mentor in so many ways. He had to weave through clusters of young ladies who carried glitter-covered signs, and wore bright, hopeful smiles. He had to dodge a few other bodies along the way, but he made it.

Suddenly he was seventeen years old all over again—shy but eager—hoping desperately to take on the world, and his dreams…

"Hey, Pastor Ken." Tyler found himself instantly enfolded in a hug that he returned with equal force and conviction.

"It's so good to see you again, son."

Tyler didn't allow the hubbub to decrease meaning. He paused to look right into Ken's eyes with heartfelt emphasis. "You too. You look great."

Ken groaned in a self-deprecating manner, drawing Kiara close to his side. The gesture made Tyler feel good. They were such a great pair. A team in love and in life. "Well, there's a bit of fresh gray around the temples these days, but I blame that on our little Annie. Wait until you meet her. She's a pistol."

"And I happen to like that subtle touch of silver," Kiara said before she, too, hugged Tyler close. "I've missed you!"

A spring breeze, sweetened by an undercurrent of

fresh flowers, lifted Kiara's long, straight hair. She gave Tyler a smile sparkling with delight and so beautiful—just like her. "How are you doing with the youth group?" he asked. "I hear you're the director now."

"Great...and we're growing! I love it. In fact, about twenty members are waiting inside for the meet and greet. You good with that?"

"Absolutely. Lead the way."

"We figured the kids would appreciate that you were such a vital part of Woodland's youth ministry years ago," Ken continued, "and give the S.T.A.G.E. group some added impact. After the meet and greet, you'll have time for a sound check, and a bite to eat before the concert."

"Perfect."

S.T.A.G.E. The acronym for Woodland's youth group left Tyler swept through by nostalgia. *Super Teen Angels Go Evangelize.* By God's grace alone, he had been given the opportunity to heed that call. As they moved toward Woodland's activity center, Tyler paused, signing CD covers, photos, and posters for whoever happened to be closest.

"Today and tonight are crazy." Ken gave Tyler a look that bordered on apologetic. "I promise tomorrow will be much quieter. Dinner, at our place, with you and your family. If you're game."

"You better believe it. Thanks!"

"Do you ever get used to this...this...frenzy?" Kiara viewed the assemblage with wide, disbelieving eyes.

Before answering, Tyler paused just long enough for a quick photo-op with a doe-eyed fan who wore an earnest, dazzled expression.

"Sort of, but never completely." He lifted a

shoulder. "What matters most is the fact that I get to share my music, and my own kind of ministry. That's all I ever wanted."

"I remember." The corner of Kiara's mouth curved. She arched a brow. Tyler didn't need a roadmap to recognize that her thoughts had gone back in time, to a mission trip to Pennsylvania during which they had all grown to know, and love, one another.

He remembered as well. That's why—despite Ken and Kiara, despite the media frenzy and solid press of fans—Tyler searched for one face. One person. Despite the five years that had gone by, there was no way he'd miss the one he sought. None at all.

Amy Maxwell.

Would she be here? Was she even still around the Shores? What was she doing now? He was too shy to be obvious about his interest and ask. Ken would have unlocked the answers to those questions better than anyone else. A more active, engaged pastor Tyler had never come across in his life.

But he wanted the matters of his heart to unfold on their own. He trusted God to reveal her—or not— according to His intent.

Nonetheless, Tyler couldn't help hoping. Was she the same compelling, beautiful girl of his memory? He really hoped God's will was to have their paths intersect once more. In large part, she was the reason why he had come back to Woodland in the first place.

"We've only got about an hour and a half for the meet and greet," Ken said. "We've given everyone the rules, but once these kids see you, the excitement is going to be difficult to contain. They're going to be all over you. Timetables might fly out the window."

"No worries, I'm used to it. It'll be OK. If we have

to shorten the sound check to make sure everyone is taken care of, that's not a huge deal. The tech crew is setting up as we speak, and they're the best. They know what they're doing."

Inside the activity center, multi-colored streamers, balloons, and music notes in shimmering silver and gold foil hung from the ceiling. A couple dozen teens and their parents milled about—after completing a meal, judging by the used plastic dishware on the tables and stuffed into trashcans. Others sat on metal folding chairs surrounding long, tables.

Spontaneous applause erupted, along with a chorus of cheers and greetings. Tyler waved and walked toward a podium at the far end of the room. A sense of honor and awe worked through him. It never failed to humble Tyler that the message, and impact, of his music ignited this kind of response, this kind of loyalty and affection.

"Hey, everybody! Thanks… thanks." He waited for the noise to diminish. "I appreciate you coming out tonight." He gestured both to stem the additional applause and to encourage folks to return to their seats. "Of course I want you to know how much I appreciate your support of the new album, and your encouragement. It truly does keep me, and the rest of my team, motivated to do our best both for you, and for the glory of the God we serve."

Applause broke out once again. While Tyler waited, he scanned the room, taking in faces and smiles and affection. A doorway at the rear of the room came open just far enough to admit a stealthy, sheepish-looking newcomer.

Tallish, and slender—almost too slender—she entered the room. Long, blonde hair fashioned into a utilitarian braid, trailed in a thick line down her back. Large, blue eyes, more guarded, a bit more tired than he recalled, completed the picture. A white Oxford shirt, sleeves rolled up to her elbows, revealed petite arms. Tucked into a pair of low-slung blue jeans cinched by a thick leather belt, the shirt modestly accentuated a shapely figure. She slid the neck strap of her camera into place as she took a fast sweep of the room.

She looked right at him and Tyler's throat went dry. It only took a heartbeat, a breath really, and Amy Maxwell reentered his life.

But the hesitance he detected was shocking. The Amy Maxwell who lived in the memories of his heart was the epitome of self-assurance and spunk.

Just one thing kept him from stumbling: a hard-won sense of perseverance and smooth polish. "Beyond the music, beyond any kind of acclaim people might offer, I consider this a ministry. My music is something I feel honor-bound to share with believers and non-believers alike in a spirit of love, hope, and faith. Look at tonight, for example. The good works you're supporting through the Macomb County Shelter are for the benefit of everyone—no matter what their situation, life circumstance, or faith. I'm proud to be just a small part of that endeavor, and support Woodland Church as we do our best to bring Christ to the world. Thanks for joining me on this journey, folks. I hope you enjoy the concert, and I'm looking forward to meeting you one-on-one."

The concluding words shot a circuit of electricity through the orderly, but expectant, assembly. Tyler, meanwhile, barely managed to cohesively finish his introductory speech.

Amy kept her distance. She tucked into a corner and alternated between fiddling nervously with her camera and stealing glances at him every now and again. How odd was that? How come the bubbly, take-charge girl he remembered from high school now acted like a timid fan? The irony of such a thing almost made him laugh out loud. Tables surely hadn't turned *that* much. Sure, he was building a career as a Christian music artist, but just one look at Amy Maxwell and he instantly fell back to the days of being a shy, gangly boy who wanted nothing more than to spend time with the sweetest, and most popular girl at Saint Clair Shores High School.

A growing press of people forced Tyler to snap to proper attention. Meet-and-greets were one of his favorite parts of being on tour, but this hour-long window of sharing with his fans tended to be fast-paced and excluded any focus but the people who came up to meet him. In many instances, they had waited hours to simply shake his hand, or get a picture, or an autograph. As such, Tyler refused to shortchange a single soul.

After all, Amy was here—with a camera, no less. That didn't surprise him much. She had been the official photographer on the mission trip to Pennsylvania years ago. And now, she was headed his way.

Still, she approached slowly. She didn't make direct eye contact for any appreciable amount of time. Instead, she focused on Ken and Kiara who stood nearby and ushered the group into a reception line.

Just like in high school, Tyler's heart reacted to Amy's presence by skipping into an impassioned form of overdrive. Just like in high school, he experienced that bittersweet yearning for a woman who captivated him…yearning, and that inexhaustible heat of longing.

But the nearer she moved, the more Tyler realized she didn't just *act* different, she *looked* different, too—as though she carried an enormous weight. Oh, she was as beautiful as ever, and her eyes, when she dared look his way, seemed as clear and as vibrant a shade of blue as he remembered, but she seemed drained. Her posture and movements, formerly brimming with confidence, now spoke of being browbeaten and cautious in the extreme.

Sad.

Something had robbed Amy of the joyful spirit she had possessed, the spirit that had drawn in, and touched, everyone who came into contact with her. To so deeply impact a person of such strength, it had to have been something harsh. She looked like a changed woman.

Why?

2

Now more than ever Amy sought refuge behind the filter of a camera lens. Viewing the world from the safety of a photographer's eye created distance, an emotional and physical buffer that enabled her to create the pictures of her heart often without having to engage in the deeper aspects of what she saw and cataloged. Far safer that way, she knew. Far less a chance of getting hurt.

That is, until the moment she walked into the Woodland Church Activity Center and began her commission as the evening's photographer.

"Amazing," she murmured, dazzled somewhat by the atmosphere, but even more so by the man who stood at the center of the festivities.

Tyler Brock had come a long way since the last time she'd seen him. He was now a polished, confident man. That recognition hit Amy right between the curves of her tender, broken heart and set butterflies free.

Instant infatuation. She knew the symptoms, and infatuation was the last thing she needed. Additionally, infatuation with an acclaimed Christian music star? *Yeah.* Like every other woman on the planet.

For now, she needed to release past history and get to work. She was here for the youth group members who had been given the opportunity to meet Tyler Brock, nothing more.

When Amy walked up, Kiara waved to garner everyone's attention. "Before we begin, let me take you through the way things will work. First of all, you're in line, by family, to have an opportunity to share a few words with Tyler, get an autograph, and a picture." Kiara turned to Amy.

Amy took a nerve-stilling breath, which didn't work in the least toward calming her nerves.

Kiara smiled and gave a nod. "In an effort to give you each the most time allowed with Tyler and to keep the line moving forward at a fair pace for everyone else, no cameras are allowed. Instead, to capture the moment, Amy Matthews will be taking pictures for you, and they'll be posted tomorrow morning on the Woodland Church website where you'll be able to download them for free."

Ken stepped up to the table where Tyler stood and handed him a can of pop. Sure enough, it was Vernors. She remembered how much Tyler loved the Michigan-made ginger ale.

Tyler sat casually on the edge of the table, his legs dangling while he watched and waited. After popping the lid of the can and downing a long sip, he settled the beverage next to him. The vision of this more developed version of the high school friend she had cared for, was dramatic.

"Amy and Tyler have the common history of being members of STAGE, just like you. In fact, they attended a mission trip to Pennsylvania years ago. They know and understand where you're coming from, because they've both been there."

"You used to hang out with Tyler?" the first girl in

line piped up. "Boy, are you lucky."

Amy blushed and Tyler laughed while Ken and Kiara gracefully covered that ebullient comment. There was no chance to speak with Tyler directly, of course, so instead she focused on her mental walk-through of who Tyler had once been versus the man he had become.

To say Tyler Brock had come of age, to say he had outgrown the cocoon of quiet, gawky but straightforward teenager, was gross understatement.

Kiara gave Amy a nod, letting her know her job had begun. Camera at the ready, Amy stepped up and began framing shots, clicking away while Tyler welcomed his fans. He filled her lens, in more than just a literal way. Tyler was sculpted beautifully, and handsome. He wore his hair just a touch long in back, but combed away from his face in well-styled waves of light brown. Jeans and an un-tucked, deep green shirt emphasized his hazel eyes.

Which were presently focused on her.

Or, her camera, to be more precise. Amy broke loose from her thoughts and realized the family standing near Tyler waited on her. She executed a nicely framed shot of them as they concluded their visit with Tyler.

When she lowered her camera, Tyler's attention remained fixed on her, and he gave her a private, quirked smile. Amy felt the power of it clear down to the farthest, most aching regions of her heart. She lowered her gaze and sighed, double-checking her equipment, fiddling unnecessarily with calibrations. The past came calling once more, eating away at her resolve to think of nothing else but her photography duties.

Once upon a time, Tyler had perched his heart on his sleeve, with an arrow that pointed straight at her. Meanwhile, she had taken him in as a friend, with authentic care, yet blithely took him for granted. Now, times and tables hadn't just turned between them, they had spun wildly out of control.

In response to that recognition, Amy steeled her spine and became resolute, lifting her camera with newfound determination to move past emotional folly. The next group stepped forward. Throughout the remainder of the greeting session, she melted to the sidelines, tucked away by design from direct interactions.

I'm not being a coward, she told herself. *I'm not letting this whole unsettling reunion thing set me off balance. I'm simply being unobtrusive, like any good photographer.*

Still, one truth remained in place, no matter what her rebuttals. The camera remained her guard. It opened up a wonderful opportunity to focus on Tyler and re-familiarize herself with him, yet at the same time, kept her safely distant and protected. The best of both worlds.

❦

Woodland Church featured two-tier seating, and an altar that was raised a step. There, tour crews had set up overhead lights, sound equipment, and instruments. The concert kicked off without a hitch.

Amy continued to chronicle Tyler's visit, moving fluidly through the venue to capture a variety of shots: crowd responses, multi-colored lights playing across surfaces of the stage, the faces of the audience, Tyler and his band.

Whenever she paused to take in the scene and view the world around her in the context of a potential photograph, a twitch of loss and unpleasant emotion speared her heart—especially when Tyler interacted with his back-up singers.

And then he introduced his duet partner, Rebecca Graham—brought her center stage and kissed her cheek. They shared on on-stage sass and connection that was eloquent. It Amy froze in place.

Rebecca's sparkling, genuine smile, her easy grace and charm on stage—particularly with Tyler—sent a bead of regret across Amy's skin. She could have had that with Tyler. Camaraderie. Companionship. Instead, she'd let him go.

Tyler and Rebecca drew up stools and placed them side-by-side. The spotlight tunneled in and focused on the two of them alone while the rest of the houselights went dim.

Amy fell into the scene, her camera forgotten.

Microphone in hand and at the ready, Rebecca perched gracefully on her stool, her lace skirt of peach and her sparkling tank top accentuated by a gauzy over-shirt of stark white. Fiery red hair shimmered in wavy curls that fell to her shoulders. She slid it aside while she waited. That's when Amy fell victim to a nasty shock. An unpleasant stab agitated her already prickly nervous system. The taut sense of disquiet she fought? It wasn't just regret. It stemmed from jealousy. Plain and simple. This was a gorgeous woman who spent long hours at Tyler's side, and that bugged Amy.

As if that reaction made any degree of sense.

Meanwhile, Rebecca waited, as appealing as an angel, watching Tyler as his fingers strummed an acoustic guitar in a melody that began to take shape.

"I want to tell you the story of Amazing Grace," he said quietly, in a hushed, moving tone that held the entire crowed enthralled. "Now, I'm not talking about the traditional, time-honored hymn we all love." Music rolled through the church, slow and haunting. "Rather, this is the story of a woman. A woman named Grace. What makes her amazing? Her journey of faith. Amazing Grace travels the badlands spoken of so eloquently in Psalm 23, but through love, and the grace of God, she emerges on the other side. She's amazing because she never gives up on her faith, on her God. Therein she finds her hope. Her redemption. Her *grace*."

The song began in earnest—a stirring duet that emphasized just how skilled, and syncopated, Tyler and Rebecca were as performers.

Or perhaps even more.

Trembling, trying to maintain focus, and distance, Amy lifted her camera, but she just couldn't click the shutter. She nipped at the inside of her cheek and lowered the lens. Tears stung her eyes as the words of the song—of heartache, surrender to pain, a renewal of faith, hope and love—took root in her heart and left her moved yet so desperately at a loss in her own life.

The audience was captivated, strung together on pearls of music and harmony. Words and notes drew them in. Moments later, Amazing Grace concluded— pitch perfect and on a blended note that echoed through the facility for long moments afterward. Following an awed silence, applause erupted; the crowd moved to its feet in unison.

Tyler joined hands with Rebecca and lifted them high, turning toward her to give her a moment in the spotlight. He kissed the back of her hand and they shared a telling look before separating. When moisture spattered against the top of her camera, Amy came abruptly alert and steeled her emotions. She brushed away her tears, giving herself a hard internal shake.

That's when a gentle nudge came from behind. Then an arm slid around her waist. "You OK, Amy?" Pastor Ken asked.

She took a deep breath, but the effort ended on a none-too-graceful hiccup. She cleared her throat to cover that display of weakness. "I'm OK."

"Kiara noticed your reaction. She wanted me to lend some support if you need it."

Amy's shoulders relaxed a bit beneath the strength of his hold. She hung her head and fingered her camera. Ken and Kiara were two of the most gentle-hearted, caring people she had ever known. They had taken her in for a time and helped her land on her feet. Thank God.

"I'll be fine...the song just hit me."

"And Tyler's hitting you, too?" There was a trace of knowing in his tone. "I remember the connection you two shared back when."

"In different times, yes. He was always a great friend." Amy lifted her chin and found just enough steady resolve to reply with a bit of her former spirit and pluck. "He's doing great, isn't he? I'm really proud of him."

"You know what? You should tell him that. I'm sure he'd appreciate it."

Amy shrugged casually, but realized she had walked right into that one.

"Do it tomorrow at dinner. We'd love to have you and Pyper join us for a small get-together Kiara and I are hosting to welcome him home. Can you make it?"

Amy's gaze lobbed from the stage, to Ken, to Kiara, back to Tyler, then Rebecca.

Torture. Dinner with Tyler and the crew would only serve to magnify the chasm between her life and his. The changes. Further attempts at a connection would only end up breaking her heart, and increase awareness of everything her life lacked—and all it could have been under different, and better-chosen, circumstances.

"I'll think about it." Amy gave him a wan smile and lifted her camera once again. She started taking pictures, and Ken moved slowly away, but she could tell she remained on his radar screen. And Kiara's.

That was a blessing, and a burden. She hated the idea of others continually having to mentor her, care for her, and feel compelled to intervene. But by the same token? Thank *God* they were there, and in her corner. And Pyper's as well.

֍

When the concert ended, a few authorized guests and Woodland VIP's gathered in a cordoned off area for a backstage visit at the activity center. Then and there Amy decided it was time to give Tyler a proper greeting. After all, her emotional issues were hers alone. At a minimum she owed their past a gesture of support.

The noise level was intimidating as a celebration of the show kicked off, but it didn't take long for Amy to find Tyler; the crowd ebbed and flowed around him like a tide. He stood comfortably amidst it all, his arm looped around his mom's waist, his father nearby as well. The image made Amy smile. Mr. and Mrs. Brock radiated familial pride, and judging by the way she kept her sparkling eyes and happy smile trained upon her son, Mrs. Brock—LuAnne, Amy recalled—was delighted to have Tyler back home again, if only for a couple of days. According to Ken, he'd be staying with them tonight and tomorrow. Back home again.

If only it were that easy.

Amy took a deep breath. It was time to move forward, and act like the friend she had always been. She made progress toward approaching Tyler, watching as he shook hands with members of his crew and received enthusiastic hugs of support. Then in came Rebecca. He saw her immediately and grinned while she made a dash for his ready embrace. She gave a happy shout as he lifted her up, and spun her in a full circle.

"You were great," she enthused, her voice touched by the cadence of the south. "Honestly, what a show!"

"Inspired, wasn't it, Becs? It feels so good to be home!"

Rebecca pecked both his cheeks and smiled into his eyes. Amy's heart sank. His dynamic backup singer then greeted others around them and dissolved into the crowd of tour staffers. Amy winced, battling off turmoil, self-doubt, and inadequacy.

It was a battle she lost.

In that instant, her mature, straightforward intentions vaporized. Hiking up her purse and camera strap, Amy kept a tight hold on them both as she turned to leave. She took a few steps toward the exit. She'd beg off tomorrow's dinner, and bid this entire, world-rocking episode farewell. In the morning, everything would be back to normal. In the morning, she could—"Seriously?"

Amy froze at the sound of the smooth and deep voice that carried with it just a touch of the South. She closed her eyes, and she trembled. Bad.

"You were seriously gonna leave without sayin' hello to me?"

She couldn't pull in a proper breath. Her heart skittered wildly. Red-hot heat crawled up the skin of her neck and ignited her cheeks, melting and burning in one fell swoop.

Bravely she turned around, her lips pressed tight, though she fought through it all to offer a tentative smile. "Hey, Tyler."

It was the best she could manage. His eyes were unspeakably gentle and tender. His attitude of warmth so typical of the Tyler she had known, once upon a life. Amy welcomed that fact, and at the same time, she was swept away by just looking at him.

"Hey, Amy," he greeted softly. His smile bloomed when he took her hands. A beat later, he drew her in for a long, tight hug that left her aching. He felt so hard, and strong. So wonderful. A lump formed fast in her throat—a bit of mourning, she supposed, for all she missed.

"I, ah, didn't want to interfere or anything." As soon as the words crossed her lips, she realized how lame they sounded.

Tyler kissed her cheek, and Amy went a bit dizzy. A bit weak at the knees. "You couldn't interfere if you wanted to." He leaned back and drew a fingertip against her chin; he looked deep into her eyes. "I've missed you."

3

The last thing on earth Tyler wanted to do was step away from Amy, and this much-longed-for moment of reunion. Despite the tumult of activity taking place around them, he experienced the certainty of a connecting rod between them. It was as if they were isolated as a single unit despite the blur and rush of the activity center.

Just as he was ready to speak to her again, the double doors of the facility pushed open once more. A pair of little tornados, dressed in the guise of angelic-looking young girls, burst onto the scene with enough combined power to break the spell. One of them, a pixie with an ocean of long, curly blonde hair, bee-lined to Amy and grabbed her legs.

"Mommy! Mommy, I'm so excited! Annie says I get to have dinner with her tomorrow at her house, and we had fun with Miss Monica and all the other kids! We played house and we played games, and we colored pictures while you concert-ed!"

The words came out rapid-fire, bubbling with excitement. On a fast track, his mind processed the words: Mommy—that would be Amy. Annie—that would be Ken and Kiara's daughter, the one Pastor Ken had described as a pistol. Dinner—tomorrow night at Ken and Kiara's.

But his thoughts bounced back repeatedly to just

one word in that laundry list of information. *Mommy.*
Amy was a mother.

*Did you think she had gone into seclusion, Brock?
Come on. She always possessed tremendous allure and
magnetism. Remember that all-star athlete from high school
she went to homecoming with right after the mission trip to
Pennsy? What was his name? Samuels something. He was
the 'King of the School,' and even* he *fell all over himself to
be with Amy Maxwell. In fact, they were all but engaged
when you saw the writing on the wall and chucked
everything in Michigan to head south, to the only dream you
had left to pursue: Music.*

That brought him back around again. *Maxwell.* If
she was married, why did she still go by the last name
of Maxwell? Amy had always been independent, and a
strong-minded person in their youth, but she hardly fit
the type who'd refuse a man's name in marriage.

New realities, new questions, crashed in while
Amy whisked her daughter upward with a happy
exclamation then pulled her in tight, holding her in her
arms as snug as a caterpillar in a cocoon. Her eyes,
however, were a reflection of hesitance. "Pyper, this is
Tyler Brock. He's a friend of mine, and the one who
sang for everyone tonight. Can you say hello?"

Pyper was a mini-Amy. The child was shy, but
possessed a sparkling personality that instantly
touched his soul. Pyper leaned back against Amy,
however, keeping distant from him; still, she was
polite, and so sweet looking. She thrust out her little
hand with formality. "Hello, Mr. Tyler."

Tyler took hold of her hand, careful not to impose
himself beyond a simple grasp and squeeze. He looked
into the child's sea-colored eyes and smiled widely.
"Pyper, it's an honor. I'm so glad to meet you."

She didn't respond. Instead, her brows pulled together, and she remained glued to Amy, searching him thoroughly.

Tyler was undeterred. "Did I hear something about pictures you made?"

Pyper nodded, and her hair shimmered and bounced.

"I'd sure love to see them."

Silence strode in. In his periphery, he saw Amy's gaze lift to his in surprise. Meanwhile, a second bout of shyness came over Pyper. She snugged a bit closer to Amy's neck, looking at him with hesitation. Then, she leaned back and blinked at Amy. "Can Annie come, too?"

In unison, Tyler and Amy glanced toward Ken and Kiara's daughter. As expected, she stood next to her parents, chatting with Kiara while Ken conversed with members of Tyler's family.

"OK, you can go see if she wants to join us."

Pyper crawled from Amy's embrace and scrabbled for the ground. "Annie! Annie, c'mere!"

They were alone once more. People seemed to sense, and respect, his focus on Amy; therefore, he was given a bit of a berth. His heart pounded hard and fast. "Wow. Your daughter is absolutely phenomenal."

"Thanks. She warms up, but...well..."

"It takes time?"

Amy nodded. "Especially around men. I don't want you to take it personally or anything."

Especially around men? That comment begged even more questions, so did Amy's guarded, timid posture. But this was not the time or place. Instead, wanting only for her to be comfortable with him, Tyler deflected. "I'm the reformed shy-guy, as you know better than anyone else. So, I can relate."

Amy's gaze lifted to his, and Tyler saw what he wanted—a heavy downgrade in her discomfort. She even smiled. "A lack of shyness isn't the only change."

"Oh?"

She nodded. "The accent, for example."

She had always known how to catch him by surprise. She glanced at him with the sassy light in her eyes that he remembered best, the one that even now caused a pulse rush. He took in her playful expression and heat blanketed his system. "A bit of one, yeah. I suppose five years in Nashville is bound to rub off on a person. As for losing my shyness, well, life didn't give me much of a choice in that regard."

The girls bounded up, hand in hand. Now that she had strength-enforcing support, Pyper pointed toward the hallway outside. "Come on, Mr. Tyler. We wanna show you now!"

He found himself led away from the activity center. It still amazed him. Amy. A mother. He tried to check for a wedding ring, but couldn't get a good look at the third finger of her left hand.

Pyper and Annie entered a brightly lit classroom where a petite, blonde-haired lady reassembled the space; she turned to greet them with a smile. "Hey, Pyp! Hey, Annie! What's going…" The woman's gaze rested on Tyler and she stopped short, her mouth hanging open. Her eyes went wide. "…on…?"

Tyler stifled a laugh. He was becoming used to fan recognition as his career progressed, but still, the reactions left him humbled.

Amy chuckled, and the sound tickled Tyler's ears. "Monica Edwards, meet Tyler Brock." Amy faced Monica again. "Pyper mentioned something about drawings the kids made while you conducted the nursery tonight. We wanted to catch a glimpse of their handiwork."

"Oh, yeah. Mm-hmm—" Monica didn't even blink. Instead she stared at Tyler, and the word *dazed* crossed his mind as a descriptive.

Annie stepped up, wielding a pair of pictures. "This is my house, and this is my church. See how I did the bell tower? Plus, mommy planted lots of pretty flowers for spring at our house. See?"

After Tyler checked them over and doled out appropriate praise, Pyper came to the fore and spoke, presenting her own creations. "This is church, too. It's like Annie's 'cause we go to church together and everything 'cause we're bestest friends. And this is mountains. I heard about them in school from Miss Monica. I *love* mountains."

Mountains. Tyler focused on that aspect of the drawing he studied and admired, realizing he might be able to use it to build a comfort zone for Amy's daughter. "Know what, Pyper? I live near mountains. You can see them from my house. Ever hear of the Smoky Mountains?"

Now that she was his sole focus, Pyper's shyness returned with a vengeance. She ducked her head. When she reclaimed her pictures, she kept her gaze on the floor while she fiddled with the papers. She scuffed the tip of her sandal against the tile at her feet.

Tyler focused on Monica Edwards, giving her a smile. She had regrouped following his arrival and struck him as the warm and engaging type. Besides, he wanted to give Pyper some breathing room. "You're a teacher?"

"I sure am. I own and operate the daycare center

where Annie and Pyper spend their days."

"And Sunny Horizons is also where I work during the winter and school months." Amy stepped forward, giving Monica's arm an affectionate squeeze. "She's a godsend."

What about spring and summer? Tyler wondered. *What do you do then?* He remained consumed by curiosity, and a desire to know everything possible about this new, matured version of Amy Maxwell.

Monica huffed out a teasing laugh. "Oh, you're just being biased. I'd take you full time, but winter and fall are the only points in the calendar year when I can pry you away from Jeremy. I'm going to finish cleaning this up. Tyler, it was great to meet you."

Jeremy? Calendar? Pry her away from what? Was Jeremy Amy's husband? Questions continued to spin in an assault of sorts. Nothing added up yet, but his heart begged for answers. "It's good to meet you, too. And thanks for handling the nursery tonight. What a huge help for the families."

"It was my pleasure…" She hesitated. "Although, it sure would be an excellent consolation prize if…"

Tyler heard Amy snicker, and once again, his heart flipped at the happy sound. In fact, he turned to her automatically, just in time to see her lift her camera and arch a brow. "Would you like a picture?" she asked Monica.

"You don't have to ask me twice!" In haste, Monica stepped up to Tyler's side amidst a round of laughter. She peered up at him apologetically. "I also brought my copy of your new CD. Do you think you'd mind… ah…"

He didn't need a compass. "I'd love to sign it for you." Charmed, Tyler set out to reassure. "It's the least

I can do after all your help tonight."

The photo-op was interrupted when a man entered the room, hand in hand with twin children, a boy and a girl, who appeared to be of Asian descent. "Hi, JB!" Amy's greeting was addressed to the adult, but then she bent to tweak the boy and girl on their noses. "Sam and Katie, how are you?"

"Ready for home, I think." JB laughed, and the sound was deep and rich—as though it was something he did often. He stepped up to Monica and gave her a kiss—then a rueful grin. "I think they're finished with church, Monica. They had a bit too much fun with some fruit juice that cost us a big stack of napkins."

Monica cringed, but she giggled, too. "They were angels in here during the concert. I asked Lisa to take them to you so I could clean up; I'm nearly finished." JB, who had a strong, tough build, easily hefted the children. Monica stepped close. "Were you guys good for Daddy while Mommy was away?"

In perfect unison, the kids turned wide, innocent eyes on their mother and nodded emphatically. Monica took their hands in hers and placed kisses on both chubby fists.

Amy gave a formal introduction to Monica's husband, Jeremy Edwards, and some of Tyler's panic dissipated. "I think we need to make this photo a family affair. Why don't we have Amy take a shot of all of us?" he offered.

Monica looked at him with adoration in her eyes. "Know what? You're even sweeter than I thought you'd be. Thanks!"

Monica's heartfelt gratitude warmed him. In a moment of praise, Tyler gave silent thanks to God for being able to live out such an enormous life blessing.

Then, in deference to the picture, his eyes focused on Amy.

❧

As he followed Amy back to the main assembly room, Tyler's cell phone vibrated in the front pocket of his jeans. Since Amy walked ahead with Pyper and Annie in tow, he slid it free and flipped it open. One missed call—and a text— from an increasingly familiar phone number. Since a text message would be quicker to deal with than a direct phone call, Tyler opted to open that rather than check his voicemail.

Hope the Woodland concert was all u hoped. We need 2 talk when ur back in TN. Urgent – 4 ur good – n I admit it – mine 2. KR

Tyler shook his head. Often, when assaulted by frustrations—and mounting anxiety—he had to battle back the desire to bite off a mild curse. This was just such a moment. He took an extra second to scroll through calls he had received during the past few weeks. A large chunk of the electronic demands came from the author of his latest text. This very powerful, deliberately persuasive person tempted Tyler with an offer most artists would beg to claim. Not Tyler, though. Instead, he fought temptation by simply refusing delivery.

But time was running out on that particular option.

"You all set?" With Pyper in her arms, Amy turned to face him, her brows drawn. Tyler snapped to attention, now realizing she had stopped at the threshold of the activity center. The facility had grown considerably quieter as people left Woodland. His fingertips moved restlessly against the phone while Amy puzzled over his delay.

He fixed a smile into place. "Absolutely. Sorry. Just a bit distracted by a piece of business I need to take care of once the tour is finished."

The explanation sufficed; in fact, the way Amy looked at him, he could read how impressed she was, and he wanted to sigh. He wanted to tell her that it wasn't as awe-inspiring as people thought. It was tough sometimes, holding on to faith and your principles, especially in the entertainment industry.

For now, though, he kept quiet and found relief in the fact that he had dodged another round of electronic prodding from a troubling suitor.

With Amy at his side, Tyler met up with his tour mates and began making the rounds to say goodnight. Dave Wells, his tour manager and closest friend, joined their circle. In typical fashion, Dave wasted no time on preamble. He jiggled his own cell phone from his fingertips. "Rossiter is on the hunt for you, Tyler. Again. And again...and again..." For dramatic effect Dave's voice trailed off and his lips twitched into a wry curve.

Tyler scowled. "Wait a sec. Now he's tracking me through *you*?"

Dave offered a good-natured shrug. "So it would seem."

"Sorry for that." Tyler firmed his lips, noticing the exchange held Amy's full attention. He gathered in a stilling breath, uncertain about having her witness the pressures he had to endure.

"Not a problem. Sometimes running interference is part of my job. But, you know, maybe if you just *talk* to him?"

"I will." Tyler knew he sounded harsh. "When I'm ready. Kellen Rossiter is pushing, and he knows it. I don't like being pushed. Not about my career." Tyler let a sharp, punctuating pause follow his declaration. "Maybe my silence will clue him in that he's being annoying."

Dave's brows lifted. He pursed his lips and slid his fingertips into the front pockets of his jeans. "It's also flattering. Don't kid yourself into thinking you're not impressed by his attention, Tyler." Delivering a final, pointed look, Dave rocked back on his heels then walked away.

Tyler closed his eyes and flexed his jaw.

Amy remained a silent, though increasingly curious, observer. At length, she gave him an encouraging look. "OK. That was interesting."

"Just a business fire to deal with; that's all."

"Oh? Can I ask what's going on? Who's this Rossiter person?"

In an instant, everything faded from his world but Amy. He saw them as they used to be back in high school, best of friends, sitting side-by-side on the well-worn couch of his parent's family room after school, sharing their latest problems—or dreams. Oh, how he missed that connection.

But now wasn't the time to dive deep.

Tyler stiffened his stance, wishing like crazy he could just pour out his heart to her

But this wasn't the place.

Exhaustion crept through his system, coloring his attitudes about everything, even Kellen Rossiter. *Especially* Kellen Rossiter. Post-performance adrenaline leaked out of him like sand particles, depleting his energy by the second. For now, it would be best to turn in for the night and try to come out fresh after some rest.

"It's a long story. Hey, will you be around tomorrow?" He didn't mean to sound quite so eager, but there was no way he could mask his feelings.

"I've been invited to Pastor Ken's for dinner. But I'm just not sure about going...I mean..."

She attempted to shrug the idea aside, but, tired or not, Tyler operated on high alert when it came to Amy; it was time to dispel her doubts as quickly as possible. "Please come. I really want to catch up with you."

He wouldn't beg; he kept his voice steady. Following the pattern of their past history, he simply laid out the call of his heart and then let her, and God, decide what was meant to be. Noble, sure; but on the inside, just like in high school, he quaked. Amy was his most vivid, stirring crush, the first love he'd never forgotten nor entirely released. To do so, he had discovered, was impossible. For as long as he was in Michigan, he wanted to spend as much time with her as possible.

"Are you sure?" Her words were so quietly spoken he nearly missed them. Now Tyler puzzled. He stared into her eyes, letting her see the questions he held there. "Why would you even need to ask me that? Of course I'm sure."

He stepped in close and glided his hand against her arm. He couldn't get over the changes in her, especially the diminished spirit and verve. Dinner plans were fine enough, but dinner would provide only a couple of hours together.

Earlier that evening, just before Tyler spotted Amy getting ready to leave, Pastor Ken had invited Tyler and his parents to a day of boating and swimming on

Lake Saint Clair. Ken and Kiara had recently purchased a pontoon boat. Since the day promised to be gorgeous, and overly warm, the idea of a relaxing cruise, free of outside distractions, became the agreed to itinerary for tomorrow afternoon.

Tyler kept quiet on that count for the time being. An idyllic plan swirled into place with a reviving power that pushed back a bit of his exhaustion. As seconds ticked by, his idea developed substance, and fast, strong roots. Before leaving Woodland and going home with his folks tonight, he'd float the idea of including Amy and Pyper. He imagined Ken would be happy to have them join the party.

Thoughts of professional pressures, and hard decisions to come once his tour concluded, vanished in the face of being with Amy again. They'd have a bit of uninterrupted, one-on-one time. They'd have an opportunity to swim, lay out in the sun, and talk. *Really* talk. Throw dinner into the mix and they'd end up with the full day together.

After that, reality would set in. But for now, if Ken agreed to the plan and Amy accepted, they'd have tomorrow.

4

The last thing Amy wanted to do was sleep.

It was close to midnight when she pushed gently and quietly through the door of her second-floor apartment; Pyper was sound asleep, a heavy but pleasant weight in Amy's arms. She moved as gingerly as possible, not wanting to disturb her daughter.

They had stayed too late at Woodland, but any excuse she could find to spend a few extra minutes with Tyler left her feeling like a fairytale princess doing battle against the fade of a magical spell. *Tyler.* Amy's lips curved. Something deep in the core of her body melted without resistance. The reaction couldn't be helped because it was so incredibly good to see him again.

She tiptoed toward Pyper's room, making her way through the darkened house by rote. Once there, she pulled back the blankets and laid her daughter on the bed. She unbuckled and prepared to remove Pyper's sandals. One shoe was off, and she was working on the second when Pyper tossed a bit, and gave a breathy, unintelligible sound.

Amy stopped just long enough to brush a hand against her daughter's satiny curls. She marveled at the serenity reflected on Pyper's face. A degree of love washed through her so powerfully it left Amy's chest to ache. For a moment, she simply adored her slumbering child. She gave thanks once more that Pyper had become her miracle, born from the tragedy of her marriage. "I already love you to the depths of my soul, little girl. How is it possible I keep loving you more and more every day?"

Pyper rustled, but never fully roused, nor opened her eyes. "Mommy," she whispered contentedly.

With that, she snuggled in deep, and Amy finished bedtime preparations, certain Pyper was now lost to the world until sunrise ushered in a new day. "If only I could rest as easy."

She kissed Pyper's forehead then exited the room. In passing, she clicked on the living room lights. She was at loose ends. She had a lot to think about, but couldn't bring herself to focus on a single thing except the image of Tyler Brock. She looked around her simply furnished living room; there was a used but still lovely and comfortable sofa, a wooden rocker she'd found at a garage sale, end tables and mismatched but pretty brass lamps. She couldn't stay focused, or relaxed, and she knew precisely why.

She knew what she wanted to do, but…

"Bad idea," she chastised herself, perching her hands on her hips. "Memory Lane needs to shut down for a little while."

As usual, though, her heart overruled her head. She crossed through the open, spacious layout of her apartment to a storage closet located at the end of the hallway near the bedrooms. There, from the second shelf, she pulled down one of two photo albums. Every possession that pre-dated her marriage to Mark was gone now. Not that there had been much to begin with. Still, she was a memory box kind of girl. Always she had stashed away odds and ends from her life and its milestones; she had treasured them with a heart that was inherently sentimental. Now, everything was history, relegated to memory alone.

Except for this gift from Kiara.

She reached to the shelf above and grabbed a thick, cozy afghan her mom had given her a few months ago and then made her way back to the living room.

She curled up on the couch, tucking her feet beneath the warm blanket while she settled in. Slowly she opened the cover of the album. The first thing she came upon was the birthday card that had accompanied the gift. Amy flipped it open, already feeling the sting and build-up of tears. She could practically quote its inscription from memory:

Amy:

On this day especially, allow yourself to remember. Remember who you are, and who you long most to become. You're a remarkable lady destined for remarkable things.

"For I know the plans I have for you," declares the Lord. "Plans to prosper you and not to harm you; plans to give you hope, and a future." Jeremiah 29:11

I know you've missed having this memento—among many other things. I hope you enjoy it. It's a replication of all the photos you gave me and Ken after the mission trip to Appalachia. They're the work of your hands, the mission through your loving eyes. I hope it helps you recognize the fact that you possess such a beautiful servant's heart.

Love you, Miss Thing. Kiara

Amy bit her lips to stop their trembling; her throat

was tight, and she brushed her fingertips beneath her lashes. She turned the pages gently, smiling now as image after image worked through her spirit like a cascade.

Memories crested in, her tired mind just lax enough, and vulnerable enough, to let them have their way with her.

The shot of a group campfire was beautiful, full of oranges, reds, and yellows. Sparks floated toward the sky as Tyler led the group in a song on his beloved guitar. In the picture, she sat to his right; her old fried Carlie Jamison sat to his left, on a thick, downed log in front of the fire pit. This was one of the few pictures Amy was in, because David Parker had insisted on finally getting her in a shot.

"It's tough being the photographer," he had said. "You never seem to be part of the action. Go on. Get in there and join the group."

Amy smiled, stroking the plastic cover of the photo as she noted the way Tyler was lost to whatever song he played. She was leaning forward to watch him, a friendly smile on her face. Carlie, on the other hand, watched him in an open adoration that had gone unnoticed by Tyler.

Similar to Tyler, almost perfectly suited to him in fact, Carlie had no problem at all leaving her heart bare. Amy recalled the whispered conversation they had shared in their bunkhouse after that campfire.

"He's awesome, Amy. I don't know why you'd ever push him aside." The two of them had squeezed onto Amy's narrow cot. Beneath the blankets they hid a flashlight's illumination and whisper-chatted. Carlie harrumphed. "I wish he weren't so hooked on you. If he weren't, he'd realize you're not interested, and focus outside of that crush of his. I mean, like, the two of you aren't ever meant to go anywhere, right? Then, he just might discover someone else who could be just as good."

Amy couldn't disagree. "I hear you. I know what you mean. It's just...I can't help it, C. It's not that I don't like Tyler. In a way, I'm flattered by the way he always thinks of me, and sticks close. I'm not trying to string him along or anything, but he always treats me so good. I know he likes me. And I'd be stupid not to like him back—as a friend and all—but I just can't stop thinking about Mark Samuels! I swear, he wires me like no other! He's *so* incredible! I can't believe someone as popular and awesome as him is interested in me! Tyler's great and all, but Mark is...like..." With wide eyes and a waving gesture that ruffled their covers, Amy encompassed the very air, the very universe around them. The two of them burst into giggles.

"OK, then do me a favor."

Amy giggled again, and they squiggled for a bit of extra room; the beam from the flashlight slid erratically across the light-dousing blanket. "Anything for you, C."

"Will you let me sit by him on the way home?"

They burst into a fit of full-fledged laughter that stirred the restful breathing patterns of their bunkmates, chaperone Kiara Jordan included, but they toned it down promptly and cricket sound, leaf chatter and undisturbed night air, returned.

"That's a deal. Enjoy."

The echo of those words took the edge of a scalpel deep and sure to Amy's heart, causing her mind to scream: *God help me.* Her heart began a heavy thud.

How blithely she had given away solid gold while grasping instead for the seduction of sparkling, but meaningless, glitter dust.

Oh, Mark had been interested all right, just as Amy hoped. In fact, he had asked her to the homecoming dance less than a week after her return from Pennsylvania. For a time, Carlie and Tyler had ended up going together as well, once Tyler got the message loud and clear that Amy's heart was held firmly by the school's basketball team captain and most popular star. Their senior year went somewhat cold as a result, and as soon as graduation hit, their paths split into completely opposite directions.

Almost immediately, Tyler left Michigan, opting to spread his wings and stay with his aunt and uncle in Nashville. Before departing, he told his friends—Amy just barely included—that he was on his way to Tennessee to make a mark in the only arena that mattered to him from a professional standpoint. Music.

Amy had continued her heady, electric relationship with Mark. Passion in all its forms ruled her world, blinding her to the consequences of being reckless and emotionally intoxicated. They saw one another constantly, feeding off the irresistible pull of physical desire. Still, somehow, Amy had never believed an unplanned pregnancy would happen to her—the queen of the school—nor to Mark, its undisputed king. They made love, surrendering completely to the pull of their minds, and their bodies, repeatedly savoring every new connection they discovered.

Until the moment Amy found out she was carrying his child.

But even then, she clung to the absolute belief in

happy endings. Certainly, theirs was a critical error in judgment. Yet by God's grace alone, Amy held to Pyper's conception and birth as her life's greatest blessing.

She knew once they married, they would be happy. As a couple, and a family, they would make a way together. But it hadn't turned out that way. Amy's chin quivered as she continued to page through the photo album. How could she have *ever* been so naïve?

She flipped through a few more pages, and a wavering smile replaced tears as she studied a photograph of Kiara kneeling in the front yard of the home they had renovated, with two of its four occupants: twins Amber and Alyssa Kidwell.

Amy's gaze moved to the colorful beaded bracelet Kiara had on her wrist. Amber had made it for Kiara's and Alyssa had created an identical bracelet for Amy — a thank you to two of the people who, by virtue of elbow grease and donated time, made their mother's life a bit easier and more civilized. The two little girls had shown maturity far beyond their years when they recognized the change in their circumstances, and their mother's outlook that had been brought about by the help of the Woodland team.

Alyssa had lovingly placed the piece on Amy's wrist and Amy had refused to remove it for long months afterward. When she did take it off, she had tucked it safely away, never wanting to forget the love behind its creation.

Amy's gaze strayed to her empty right wrist, and she got choked up all over again. The bracelet was gone, left behind in her desperate escape from abuses both physical and mental. Amy blew out a breath, wishing she could will the bracelet, and the innocence of that missionary period, back into existence.

She sniffed back tears. This trip down memory lane was making her an emotional wreck, but what a sweet, loving memory the photo stirred, as well.

Amy had been just as much an emotional wreck after Alyssa gave her the bracelet. The gesture was so selfless, so poignant. Amy had found it necessary to break away from the home rebuilding crew for a few minutes so she could regroup.

She closed her eyes and tipped her head upward, remembering how perfect the cobalt sky had been on that day. Ever-moving tree branches towered high above. Studiously she kept her back to the house, not wanting anyone to see her tears, though she knew her shoulders trembled. From behind, the crackle and snap of dry groundcover signaled oncoming footsteps.

"Hey, Amy. I wanted to check on you."

Something within her went soft and perfectly still when she realized it was Tyler. Rich and low, his voice possessed the power to caress her soul. She'd closed her eyes, letting herself privately savor his arrival, and his obvious, caring concern.

"I can leave if you don't want to be disturbed, which I'm pretty sure is the case. I wanted to make sure you were OK. If I'm bugging you or anything, I'll go. Really, no harm, no foul."

He barely got the words out. In a blind move, unwilling and unable to consider anything else but the sanctuary he offered, Amy spun and tumbled into him. As though mysteriously prepared for just such a reaction, Tyler took her in smoothly and held on tight, rubbing her back as they swayed, and buried their faces against each other's shoulders. Despite the morning's work, he smelled of appealing, musky spice, and his warmth radiated through her, dispelling the chill of the battle she recognized two small girls had to face each day as impoverished children. The slow glide of his caress across her shoulders soothed Amy's ache of sadness.

So, she sank into the moment, and let it go on. She tucked into him in an alignment that felt a lot better than it ever should have.

"Thank you," she whispered at last. But she continued to rest against him, taking in his strength. "You know what, Tyler? You deserve…"

Oh, Lord, she thought in a panic, *where is this sentence coming from, and where will it lead us?* Amy didn't lift her head from its comfortable resting spot against Tyler's shoulder, but her eyes popped open, and went wide.

"Yeah?" He pulled back just far enough to study her face. He tracked his fingers through wisps of hair that had floated from her loose ponytail. He didn't seek her eyes, or look at her with eager hope, or a giddy sense of expectation. Instead, he focused on the path of his hand, which moved now to her shoulder, and stayed in a gentle hold.

"Oh, nothing." She stammered the words, staring at him, stunned by this unexpected wash of longing.

He looked down, obviously deflated by her response; but he didn't make an issue of her stumble. He didn't let any sense of awkwardness remain. Instead, he grinned. "I see. So, I deserve….*nothing*?"

The tightness in Amy's chest eased; tension and the fear of hurting someone so dear to her evaporated as Tyler delivered the tease and then looked her straight in the eyes. "You deserve a lot more than nothing," she said. "C'mon. You know that. You deserve everything good. That's what I was going to say."

They remained together, his arms snug around her waist, her hands resting on his shoulders. But briefly, Tyler's gaze focused on the stand of trees around them, then the twigs and leaf clutter on the ground. "Yeah. Maybe."

"Try *totally*." Even if she refused to become romantic about Tyler Brock, he was special, a treasured friend, and he needed to know that. "Besides, I found out something."

"What's that?"

"Remember the game we played on the drive down here from Michigan? You had to compare me to a box of crayons, and you said I was colorful, like a rainbow. I had to compare you to a rubber band and I said you were musical, like a rubber band when you pull it tight and pluck it."

Tyler chuckled lightly, and she could have sworn he blushed a little bit, too. "Yeah, so?"

Suddenly she was desperate; she needed to assure him of his place in her heart, even if it wasn't the place he wanted most to occupy. She stroked her fingertips along his smooth jaw, and let herself bask in the open, honest beauty of his hazel eyes, if only for a moment.

"*So* what I found out is this: you don't need to be pulled tight in order to make music, Tyler. You do it naturally. Literally. You're really just a great, great person. Thanks for always being there for me. I notice it, and it means a lot."

He watched her for a time. Then, Tyler inched closer—just a trace—almost as if he couldn't help himself. Amy lost her breath, caught between the fear of what might come next and the wish and the hope that he'd close that brief space of air between them and take her on a long, free-fall of a dizzying kiss.

Her lips went dry, but lax. Her entire body tingled. His head dipped just a bit lower, and Amy's hold on his shoulders tightened in expectation. The tingle morphed into a deep-seated ache. His eyes focused on hers, intense, mature in feeling and awareness far beyond that of a seventeen-year-old.

Tyler displayed such tenderness, and soul-deep emotion that she nearly stepped into the unfamiliar terrain of reevaluating and leaving behind everything her budding heart yearned for and wanted most to grasp.

In this moment, she caught a promise of all she somehow knew, deep inside, Tyler Brock would one day become. It was a glimpse so powerful it tempted her heart into uncharted territory, because all the signs of a potent, ordained emotion were right there in front of her.

She almost skimmed her hands upward against his neck, almost trailed her fingertips through the slightly dampened ends of his hair; she almost drew him down of her own accord. Somehow, she knew he'd taste wonderful. Somehow, she knew he would guard and treasure her heart.

In the end, though, *almost* carried no weight and the moment passed.

Following a lengthy silence, intensity diminished. Expelling a quiet sigh, Tyler froze. His tongue coursed his lips, which drew her fascination and focus. He continued to hold her, and they studied each other's eyes. He remained comfortably in place, his arms still a welcome, promising circle against her waist. Amy flushed shyly, lowering her gaze, unprepared for this influx of heady, magnetic feeling toward Tyler Brock of all people.

Like a fool, she had stepped back. Instead of casting aside her preconceived notions, she took possession of his hand in a casual, friendly manner, and they returned to the front yard of Casey Kidwell's home to resume their assigned landscaping detail.

Amy blinked hard, still able to recall the warm, somewhat work-roughened texture of his hand in hers. She re-found her focus, and the present moment, but not without the sharp ache of regret.

"You opted for arrogant, troubled, and controlling instead of gracious, loving, and tender-spirited." Her murmured chastisement cut the silence of the empty living room. In a resolute motion, she closed the album and set it aside. "Way to go, Maxwell."

Yep, this pretty much clinched it. There was no way she'd ever be able to sleep tonight.

She straightened abruptly as it occurred to her she needed to take care of uploading the concert pictures. That would give her something productive to do. After all, first thing in the morning, members of the standing-room-only audience would be clamoring for the concert and meet-and-greet photos. She padded to the entryway of her apartment, where she had dumped her purse and equipment bags in deference to putting Pyper to bed. She pulled out the camera and went to her bedroom, where she sat down at a small desk, before a glowing computer monitor.

She booted up, extracted a USB cord from the drawer and connected her camera to the terminal. During the next few hours, she downloaded and labeled photos, setting up a page at the Woodland Church website to commemorate Tyler's concert.

Joy welled up as she worked. Image after image clicked through her increasingly relaxed and sleepy mind, soaking into her thirst-driven heart with each moment she spent creating the concert page. She went a bit unsteady when one particularly striking photo filled her monitor. This one was a solo shot of Tyler, centered perfectly in the frame and backlit by multi-colored stage lights. Such a handsome man. The number of hits on the Woodland site was going to be astronomical tomorrow.

Tomorrow. What should she do about tomorrow? Giving a moan, too tired to properly consider what to do about Ken and Tyler's dinner invitation, Amy checked her email before shutting down her computer.

Five unanswered e-mails from the top was a note from Pastor Ken's address with a subject line that read: *Life's Too Short.*

Puzzled, Amy clicked it open.

Hey, Amy –

I think I can speak on behalf of everyone who attended Tyler's concert, and the meet-and-greet, in saying thanks for all your hard work tonight. I can't wait to see the pictures.

As a reward for your efforts, but mostly because we enjoy you both so much, please bring Pyper and join Kiara and me, and the Brock family, for a day of boating and relaxation on Lake Saint Clair. You've really earned it, and since life is too short to waste a single day of beautiful, late-spring weather in Michigan, I hope you say yes. After all, this is the least we can do.

Let me know as soon as you can. We're trying to plan a lunch menu for the boat trip, and don't forget about dinner afterwards. We'd meet up at our house at around 11 o'clock and take off from there.

God bless, and thanks again, Amy. You're a godsend ~

Ken

Amy stared at the missive; she clicked on the reply toggle because she knew she had to respond quickly. Then, she sat stymied, unable to construct anything. *The Brock family.* Tyler would be there. She wasn't committing to just dinner with him, but an entire day of boating fun. More opportunities to…what? Reconnect? And what about his duet partner? Sure, when they'd spoken after the concert, Tyler had acted as though Amy was the only woman in the world. But what about Rebecca? Amy drummed restless fingertips against the keyboard, waiting for words to form. Naturally, the idea of spending a gorgeous Saturday boating along the pristine waters of Lake Saint Clair held tremendous appeal. Pyper, of course, would go nuts at the prospect of spending a day with Annie. She couldn't say no, and frankly, she didn't want to.

But at the moment, her heart was a tangled mess.

Not allowing herself a chance to second-guess, Amy typed out an acceptance, thanking Ken for thinking of her and Pyper. She clicked send. There was no future in this interlude with Tyler, of course, but she wanted to see him again, and spend the day with him. Owning up to that realization helped her understand how miserable she'd feel if she denied herself this last bit of time with him. For old time's sake.

She rubbed at her increasingly heavy, gritty eyes. It was almost three o'clock in the morning. "It's already tomorrow," she murmured, extinguishing her desk light and turning off her monitor. She climbed into bed shortly thereafter, equally divided between excitement and melancholy.

The day ahead would have to fill her up for a long, lonely time to come.

5

Tyler rolled out of bed, thoroughly refreshed and energized. It felt so good to be home. Smells from the kitchen prompted a smile. Certain things were a weekend tradition, like the aroma of fresh brewed coffee, the added smell and sizzling sound of cooking bacon and sausage, dish clatter, and muffled conversations as his mom and dad prepared a batch of fluffy scrambled eggs. He closed his eyes and breathed it all in. Riding just beneath the surface of those scents was the subtle spice of onion and green pepper; there was probably cheese in the mix as well.

"*Mmm* is it good to be home," he murmured, pulling on a t-shirt and sweatpants so he could indulge in his morning necessity: a large, strong hit of coffee.

Yawning, he left his bedroom behind, following the siren call of delicious food. He worked his fingers through the waves of his hair as he entered the kitchen. Staying in his old room, at his parent's home in the Shores, filled him with déjà vu—but in the best sense of the word. He smiled at the vignette he came upon at the stove. Side by side, his mom and dad moved in synchronization, buttering toast, cooking eggs. His bare feet didn't make a sound on the tile. He sneaked up behind his mom and gave her a playful poke. "Morning."

She jumped, letting out a yelp of shock. She

whapped at his arm; his dad just laughed.

Tyler, grabbed a bistro-size mug from the nearby dish cabinet and filled it. He tipped his head back to check the digital clock on the stove. Nine o'clock. A prickle of anticipation went live inside him. Two hours. Just two short hours and perhaps he'd be seeing Amy again...

"We made bacon and sausage. They're keeping warm in the oven." His dad turned to offer a nod, and he arched a questioning brow, forcing Tyler away from his thoughts. Temporarily. "You in for a few of each?"

"You bet." He wondered if Amy had accepted the invitation Ken promised to send. Had she seen it yet? He looked at his mom, setting an arm around her shoulders for a second. It felt good to be back in the care of his folks for a couple of days. "Can I help you at all?"

"Nope. We're ready. Have a seat and we'll eat."

He ignored her request to sit and instead fell into his old habit of grabbing a pot holder so he could help pull dishes out of the oven and carry them to the table. The gesture, he noticed, left his mom to smile nostalgically, her eyes to grow a bit glittery. He delivered the food, then pecked her cheek when he passed, returning to the kitchenette with his cup of coffee now in hand. "I sure have missed you guys."

"I know the feeling," his mom said. "Now sit."

"Yes ma'am."

The meal was a glimpse of heaven, his favorite, plus he hadn't eaten in—Tyler tried to figure out the hours and failed. A long time, anyway. In ravenous quiet, he devoured breakfast, his energy and attention on the rise.

"I noticed you touched base with Amy Maxwell

last night." His mom offered a plate of still-warm toast, and Tyler helped himself. Her comment caused his focus to zoom in and stay put. "I'm so glad she's back at Woodland. She's always been so sweet, and her daughter is such a cutie-pie. We see them at church all the time now, but she was gone for a while."

Parents as informants. Tyler nearly grinned, but stifled the reaction. Why hadn't that thought occurred to him as an option to find out more about Amy?

"Back at Woodland?" Tyler spread a napkin across his lap and leaned forward. "Did she leave town or something? Where'd she go?" Waiting, he chewed on some toast.

His dad gave a light shrug. "Oh, she stayed local, but stopped coming to church after she got married. Kinda lost touch with the Woodland crew. Last thing I would have expected, since she was so active in the church and all." Tyler swallowed some coffee, waiting to hear more, wondering if his folks realized he was now riveted. "Who was it she married?"

"Mark Samuels," Tyler's mom answered. "You might remember him, Tyler. He graduated with you, right?"

Tyler nodded, but closed his eyes briefly, absorbing that piece of news. Not that it surprised him much. "Are they still married? She's going by the name Maxwell, after all."

His parents exchanged uncomfortable looks. "No," Mom replied. "They're divorced. He's in South Carolina now, I think. Isn't that what Amy told us a while back?"

"Yep." Tyler's dad finished up his meal by spreading a bit of strawberry jam on the remainder of his toast. "I don't know anything about what caused the divorce, though. All I know is that Amy used to be as effervescent as a fresh serving of soda pop. Now she's real quiet. Reserved, you know? Hesitant."

The exact same traits Tyler had noticed last night. "She sure wasn't that way back when I knew her. She put the confident in confidence."

His parents chuckled at the comment, but sadness layered the sound; Tyler understood the reaction, because Amy *had* changed. Life had walked in on her and delivered an obvious blow. He wanted to know more. She had always been a faithful, God-loving girl. She had always found joy in helping others, and building her faith by sharing her time, talents—and even her convictions—with those around her.

"She works the spring and summer seasons at a construction company here in town." His dad stretched back and rested his hands on his stomach. "Edwards Construction. She's the office manager over there. Her boss, Jeremy Edwards, is a good guy. I know him from Woodland. His brother, Collin was your English teacher senior year, wasn't he?"

Collin Edwards, Jeremy Edwards. Connections fell into place. "He sure was. A great one, too. I liked him a lot."

Tyler's mom nodded. "And I've always liked JB. He and his wife Monica really helped Amy out when she came back to Woodland. During off-peak times in construction, Amy works at the daycare center and school that Monica owns. It's where Pyper goes. Sunny Horizons, I think it's called."

Tyler took in every nugget of information, storing each morsel carefully.

In a fond tone of voice, his mother continued. "I remember when you and Amy would hang out together after school, or before and after youth group meetings." She sighed. "If only things were different. She sure could use a good man like you in her life. I think she's afraid to reach out again. I have the feeling she was hurt, badly, but no one wants to intrude, or open up an old wound. Know what I mean?"

Tyler added that perception to the growing list of items he wanted to explore about Amy. He leaned back in the whaler chair he occupied. Discreetly he looked to the left and checked the stove clock once more. Almost ten o'clock. Would eleven o'clock *ever* get here?

"Need any help packing for our day on the boat?" Tyler offered his services to his mom, wanting to lend assistance, but also eager to burn off any amount of excess time that he could.

"Sure. Can you bring up the cooler from the basement and clean it out? My offering for the outing is veggies and cheese, plus some chips. There's also some pop in the fridge that we'll bring along. There are ice blocks in the freezer we can use to keep it all cold if you want to fish them out for me."

"Done."

Tyler took his dishes to the sink and rinsed them off. For a few moments, he stood at the kitchen sink and finished off his coffee. Gazing out the window, he absorbed the details of a good-sized backyard dotted by a couple of sturdy old maples. This is where he had grown up, where he felt most like himself. It was, unquestionably, home. Five years in Nashville hadn't changed that truth.

He smiled. The sky was a perfect blue, uninterrupted by even the tiniest cloud; the temperatures inched upward by the second. It was going to be warm—almost hot—and humid.

He fulfilled his mom's requests—which took him to ten-twenty.

Issuing a sigh, Tyler decided to take a shower. It would feel good to clean up, even though he'd just be diving into the waters of Lake Saint Clair before too long. Besides, he freely admitted to himself, he wanted to look good for Amy—and showering would eat up some more of the clock.

In his bedroom, Tyler pulled out a pair of swim trunks, a polo shirt and some toiletries from his suitcase. Preoccupied with thoughts of Amy, he was on his way to the bathroom when his phone chirped to life. He picked it up without a second thought. "Hello?"

"Well, it took me almost a half hour, but I finally got through to the Woodland website. I think they've reached their bandwidth. The pictures are great. The concert looks like it was amazing."

Tyler's pulse went into overdrive, and he swallowed hard. He had completely forgotten to check caller ID—a testimony to just how relaxed and distracted he had become since returning home. "Hey, Kellen."

Kellen Rossiter's low, appealing chuckle crossed the airwaves. "Good morning, Tyler."

Tyler paid pleasantries no mind. "The concert was good. I'm headed out in a bit though. Want to spend some time with my family before I have to hit the road again. What's up?" Unimpressed. Succinct and to the point. His words and tone presented just the image Tyler wanted to portray, even if his hands shook a bit.

"Then I won't keep you, but I've been trying here, Tyler. As I think you know."

"Yeah. By any means necessary."

Again came a rich, smooth laugh. "Don't expect me to apologize for that. All I want is a meeting, once you're back in Nashville. Tour's over in two weeks. When that happens, let's sit down, and talk, and find out if there's any reason for this cat and mouse game of ours to continue."

Kellen was relentless, and savvy. The man knew Tyler's schedule and everything. Tyler was annoyed on one level but, as Dave had correctly observed last night, he was extremely flattered as well.

"OK. Talk to Jess. She'll set you up." Tyler referred to his personal assistant, Jessica Farbare.

"I know she will, and I would have done that already, but I don't want to waste my time. Or yours. Before I set anything up, I want to know the answer to one question."

"Which is?"

A muffled sigh crossed their connection. "Are you interested in hearing what I have to say? I'm not sure how hard I can, or should, keep pushing. You've been doing an outstanding job of avoiding me. Frankly, I'm not used to that."

Tyler breathed, considered, thought and thought…and thought.

Kellen made a point. He wasn't a man people in his position typically avoided, under any circumstance. For good reason. Tyler pushed back the fear—fear for his soul, his convictions, and the entire pathway of his professional life.

"Brock, to a degree I understand where your uncertainty is coming from." Kellen's words were even and un-accusing. "I just want you to hear me out. No one's putting a gun to your head. I simply want you to listen to what I have to say." Silence passed. "Bottom line. Are you interested in taking a meeting or not?"

Kellen was forthright, yet ready to cut and run at this point—not that Tyler blamed him. As suspected, avoidance had run its course. If he didn't meet with Kellen, he'd regret it. Admitting to that truth, however, reeked of compromise. Potentially *dangerous* compromise.

Nonetheless, he had to be honest—with Kellen, and with himself. From there, he would trust God to move His purpose, and His grace, through whatever decisions might need to follow. With flutters erupting through his body, Tyler answered the question. "I'm interested. In a *meeting*. I'll listen to what you have to say, that's all I promise right now. Set it up with Jess and I'll be there."

"Fair enough, and thanks. Rest assured, she's my very next call."

Tyler didn't doubt it. Kellen Rossiter was on a mission—but would that mission best serve Tyler, and his career? Only God could answer that question, and Tyler was counting on His intervention and grace to do what was right.

Disengaged from the call, Tyler expelled a shaky breath. Well. So much for a day of escapism. Now Tyler was wired. Adrenaline pulsed through his veins; so did the thrill of possibilities and everything that might happen as the result of his music. Kellen's comments about the Woodland website left him intrigued. Tyler glanced at his laptop, which was open and humming. His computer rested atop a dark wood desk that had stood sentinel beneath his bedroom window for years. Since he had time to spare, he logged on, intending to explore. He was anxious to review Amy's photographic handiwork.

It took him a while. Kellen wasn't kidding about slow log-in times and spotty access. Were that many people logging on to review the chronicle of his concert? Really?

His brows pulled together. Tyler clicked, waited, clicked, propped his elbows on the surface of the desk and waited some more. He rubbed his stubbled jaw as the hourglass spun and lingered. At last, he made his way onto the "Welcome Home Tyler Brock" page and smiled with genuine amazement at what he found. Amy had captured it all. Picture after picture spoke not just of a concert, but a faith-filled event, full of life, energy and a family of fans that had been in his corner since his victory on *Opry Bound*.

Lord, what a ride that televised talent search had proven to be. The appearance had marked the dawn of his career.

Never had he expected to find his way onto a countrified version of American Idol, but, he had quickly run out of options. Fresh out of high school he had hit the Nashville pavement hard, knocking on the doors of every record label, talent agency, and musical connection he could think of in order to establish his dream. Fading fast one particularly hot and humid afternoon, he wandered through the doorway of Notes of Spirit, Inc., a talent agency that drew him in by virtue of its name alone. The agent he spoke with that day had forsaken representation in the face of a lack of experience—the story of Tyler's life thus far—but he had been encouraging. Tyler left the agency with an application in hand to join thousands upon thousands of hopefuls auditioning for next season's edition of *Opry Bound*—a CMT series that searched for the next, best country music star.

Tyler had been nervous, but figured: Why not leave this opportunity—like everything else in his life—to the hand of God? After all, this kind of opportunity is exactly what he had prayed for upon leaving Michigan and moving in with his aunt, RuthAnne Newman. God opened up the pathway; Tyler simply trusted enough to follow the call.

He plowed through week after grueling, draining week as the field narrowed. Performances led to evaluations, then rounds of fan voting and the agony of watching other talented, multi-faceted performers, many of whom became dear friends—like Rebecca Graham—get voted off.

But Tyler's music, his message, had a twist that seemed to intrigue the judges and audience members alike. Rather than performing pure country, or a combination of pop/country rock, Tyler focused on the music that spoke to him the strongest. His performances centered on contemporary Christian music that rolled straight out of his heart into the famed rafters of the Grand Ole Opry Theater.

At the end of it all, he had emerged victorious.

On a professional level, his life rocketed forward after the show results. He found himself the featured artist on thousands of Christian radio stations across North America. He made high-priced, glossy videos; he toured, and his name recognition began pulling in audiences at bigger and bigger venues. Last year culminated in Dove Awards for songwriting, and record of the year for the anthem that fast became his trademark, the duet he performed with Rebecca: *Amazing Grace*.

It sent a shiver down his spine that the mood and lyrics of the song seemed to somehow reflect the life and times of the one he missed most since leaving Michigan, the one who, even now, completed a piece of his heart: Amy Maxwell.

Clicking through the pictures, Tyler sensed Amy's spirit behind each photograph. And he yearned— yearned to know her all over again, in the here and now.

6

"Mommy, there's Annie! There's Annie!" Pyper yanked hard on Amy's hand. They moved forward, leaving their car in the driveway of Ken and Kiara's home. In tandem, they walked toward the front porch. The door rested open. Annie's light brunette head popped in and out of view as she bounded through the entryway inside and peeked out the door window, watching after them, and waving emphatically.

All of a sudden, Annie was swooped up into the arms of Tyler Brock. He swung her high while she giggled and squealed. That was enough of an image to stop both Amy and Pyper in their tracks.

She glanced at Pyper. A half-scared, half-resentful expression clouded her daughter's features. Pyper's hold on Amy's hand tightened and she looked up, her brows pulled tight, her eyes stormy. "Mr. Tyler is comin'? I didn't know Mr. Tyler was comin.'"

"Pyper, he's a good friend to Pastor Ken, to Miss Kiara and me, too." Amy dropped a beach bag and a small cooler at their feet and then knelt so she could be eye-to-eye with her daughter. "It'll be OK."

Pyper's down-turned lips and doubting eyes broke Amy's heart.

"He's nice? You promise?"

"Very nice. I *do* promise. You remember that from last night, don't you? Plus, you'll be so busy having fun with Annie you won't even have to worry about him."

The furrow between Pyper's eyes didn't ease. She looked toward the doorway, where Tyler and Annie waited—a cheerful picture that contrasted starkly against Pyper's dubious mood. Pyper rolled her lips inward, pressing them tight between her teeth, not moving forward quite yet.

Episodes like this battered Amy's soul. On the outside, her daughter looked the quintessence of little girl innocence. She wore a pair of white terry cloth shorts over the lower half of her orange and yellow polka dot swimsuit. Upon purchase, Pyper exclaimed she loved the swimsuit because it included a thick, matching headband that presently held her bevy of hair in place. Sunglasses were perched atop her daughter's head because Amy had a pair, too, and wore them just the same way. Pyper appeared every inch the picture of girlish charm, until she had to go face-to-face with a grownup man she didn't know. When that happened, she faded like a flower without water.

"OK." Pyper steeled her shoulders and firmed her jaw. "I'sorry, Mommy. I'll go. C'mon."

Heaviness pervaded Amy's spirit. Pyper didn't say the words because she was reassured. Body language and the false bravery that illuminated Pyper's eyes left Amy to realize Pyper offered the assurance only to please her mother. That made the moment twice as sweet, but ten times as heartbreaking.

Before re-gathering their gear, Amy leaned in to kiss Pyper's cheek. "I love you, snug-a-bug."

Pyper's wide, uncertain gaze touched hers. "Me, too."

Amy led the way to the front door. Pyper kept a tight hold on Amy's hand until Annie pushed open the screen door and yanked Pyper inside.

"You're here! Finally, you're here! We waited and waited!" Annie bounced, chirping with glee. "Mommy, Daddy, let's go!"

"Good morning, ladies. How are you doing?" Tyler's warm greeting encompassed Amy, but seemed to be directed mostly toward Pyper. Annie's presence certainly helped. In the company of her friend, Pyper assumed her more typical, sweet personality. She ran after Annie with gusto, but bypassed Tyler with nothing more than a short glance and a barely audible hello.

Amy's gaze met Tyler's, and she gave him a reassuring smile as she stepped inside and set her supplies on the ground. Once she straightened, she found herself wrapped in a hug from Tyler.

He was warm; his heartbeat next to hers was sure and steady. Hugging came as naturally to Tyler as breathing—she recalled that now. She used to be the same way, until life pulled a shutter over her emotions. The connection, while wonderful, also set her nerve endings on edge with an awakening sizzle.

"I'm so glad you came." His breath skimmed against the skin of her neck. He pulled back and took custody of her bags then gave Amy a directing nod toward the kitchen where, she assumed, food packing took place.

"I want gummi bears." Annie knelt on a nearby chair so she could oversee proceedings and help supervise her parents' efforts.

"Me too!" Pyper danced from foot to foot, peeking around Ken and Kiara, who stood at the counter, stashing foodstuffs. "An' don't forget cheese curls! I *love* the cheese curls!"

"Gotcha covered, kiddo," Ken gave Pyper a wink and Annie's hair a brief tousle when she left her chair and made a dash to stand by her friend.

In the meantime, Tyler gave Amy a look of mock offense at Pyper's food choices. Amy stared right back and shrugged. "She inherited my junk food gene. You're surprised about that?"

Tyler's easy laugh filled the room, causing Ken and Kiara to turn and greet Amy's arrival with a round of hugs.

But Amy's focus was all on Tyler. Dressed in loose swim trunks and a polo shirt of light blue, he moved through the kitchen, hefting a couple of grocery sacks and a cooler Kiara pointed to at the corner of the kitchen.

Ken clapped his hands together, eyeing the little girls like a conspirator. "Let's say we pack up the car and get outta here! Ready to hit the water?"

The enthused squeals of two delighted five-year-old girls was his answer.

∂∘∞

"Here's a good spot. Let's drop anchor." Ken steered the boat slowly toward the shoreline—close, but far enough out that it felt to Amy as if they had a spot in the lake all to themselves. "According to the depth gauge, it's just over five feet. Should be perfect for swimming."

The engine came to rest and the boat began to float in a peaceful wake as the guys anchored the pontoon into place. Pyper and Annie, both safely secured in their float vests, sat next to Kiara and Mrs. Brock. The little girls started to squirm in their seats, chattering happily, as seagulls spun and cawed up above. A push of humid air crossed through the open space of the boat. Pyper and Annie shucked their shorts and shoes, which became a colorful heap on one of the padded benches. Amy and Tyler followed their lead, making ready to dive into the lake.

Amy joined the guys at the rear of the boat; Ken passed by, giving her a smile and a friendly squeeze on the arm when he made his way back to the pilot's chair. Ken was followed by Tyler's dad, who made passing remarks about a spiffy-looking powerboat that zoomed past. She sat down on the almost water level metal bench, hanging on to the nearby access ladder, and then made the critical error of dipping her foot into the water.

She promptly pulled free, shocked laughter bubbling up from her chest. "Cold! Ice cold! I am *not* swimming! *No* way!"

"*Way.*" Tyler sidled through the narrow space behind her and sat down. "If I'm goin' in, you're goin' in." He gave her a goading look. "And I'm definitely goin' in." They were side by side, shoulder to shoulder. Amy stole a glance his way and found him already tilted toward her, his eyes focused on her face, his lips turned upward just slightly. "Count of three. Then we jump."

Amy's eyes went wide with horror. "You're insane!"

"One."

"Tyler! No!"

"Two."

Her nerve endings sparkled, alive and

anticipating. Amy found her fingers suddenly and firmly entwined with his. "It's way too cold!"

"Three!"

Next thing she knew, she was pulled into the water as Tyler dove in. A mighty splash bubbled through the water. Cold surrounded her, but quickly went to temperate against her skin as she absorbed the shock.

A strong, warm arm slid around her waist, lifted her up then drew her in. Sputtering, shaking her hair back, Amy dragged her arm along the surface of the water, blanketing Tyler with a drenching arc. "You rat!"

But he wasn't finished yet. His hold tightened and before she could even scream, he lifted her up like a catapult, launching Amy through the water and above its surface before she crashed into the water once more, feeling like she had taken a brief, explosive ride through paradise.

But she refused Tyler the leverage of knowing how much she enjoyed his antics. Laughing on the inside, she emerged from the water and gave him a fierce glare. Tyler laughed at her and arched a brow in temptation. "Wanna go again?"

She found no way to refuse the smile that burst across her features. Moving through the water, she swam toward him. "Oh, yeah!"

For a few abandoned moments, they romped like kids. Sunlight sprinkled diamond dust along the rippling surface of the lake. The air around them warmed just as perfectly as the water cooled. Before long, Amy noticed Pyper approach the back of the pontoon. Pyper watched after them and Amy gave Tyler a quick look before swimming toward her daughter.

"Hey, Pyp." At the boat's access ladder, Amy dipped her head beneath the surface and quickly slicked back her hair.

After Kiara stepped up briefly to release the door lock, Pyper scrabbled to a sitting position on the rear deck, swinging her legs and stretching them downward until her pink-painted toenails brushed against the surface of the water. She kept her balance by holding on to the ladder rail while she studied Amy and Tyler. "That looks like fun."

Amy giggled. "It is. You want to come in and swim with us?"

Pyper regardedTyler for a long, intent moment. Slowly she nodded. "Mmm-hmm. Annie's gonna come in, too, though. With her mommy and daddy. But not for a few minutes."

The response was extremely tentative, but it was a "yes." Amy hoped to build on that; she wanted to make this confection of a day a joy for her daughter. The water surged and rippled next to Amy as Tyler approached.

He floated next to Amy, but smiled at Pyper. "Come on in and I'll give you a toss too, if you want, and if your mama says it's OK."

Pyper looked down, and then back up again. "It'd be OK. I got my vest on an' everything."

"It's cold when you first get in. After that, it's fantastic!" Amy backed away just far enough from the boat to give Pyper some room to jump. Then she held her arms open wide, waiting.

Pyper squiggled to a stand. She crouched, scrunching up her face as she launched forward. The splash drenched Amy, and left glittering drops to pour down Tyler's neck, shoulders and chest. Amy couldn't look away. Despite the chilly water, her body went warm; longing grew into a desire that sparked and sizzled against her senses.

When Pyper bobbed back up into Amy's arms, she squealed with shock and glee. "It's cold, it's cold, it's cold!"

"Wanna get out?" Tyler asked with a laugh.

"Nuh-uh!" Pyper started to paddle, suspended in place by her life jacket. She kicked, and sprayed even more water. She laughed. "I'm not even cold anymore. Wait 'til Annie jumps in. She'll be so scared! But I did it! She will too. I'll make sure. I'll make sure she knows it's OK." She kept paddling and kicking. "I wanna fly. Throw me, Mommy, throw me! Like Mr. Tyler did with you!"

Amy took a deep breath, and sent up a fast prayer. "You know, Tyler does throws a lot better than me. He's stronger."

"OK." Pyper's hesitance took the back seat—for a second, anyway. She turned back, looking at Tyler with wide, questioning eyes. "You won't scare me real bad, right?"

"Nope. I won't."

Her lips rolled inward. She nipped at them. Amy recognized how hard Pyper struggled to reach out in trust toward a man. *Help her, Lord. Please. Not every man is like Mark. Please. Help her to see that…*

"You *really* sure?"

Tyler's eyes went intent as he swam in, and took hold of Pyper at the waist, just below the chunky line of her day-glow float vest. "Sugar beet, I guarantee you this: I'll sink to the bottom before I let anything bad happen t'ya. Deal?"

Amy's lips trembled. Tears sprang to life, blurring the sight of Pyper relaxing completely and giving Tyler an expectant nod, a tenuous smile. Then, up she flew. A mighty splash blanketed them with water. Tyler swam toward Pyper. When she broke the surface, she howled with laughter. She scrubbed a hand over her dripping face and rubbed her nose. Then, Pyper speared Tyler with a teasing look. "That's silly, you know."

"What?" Tyler asked.

"Sayin' you'll sink to the bottom of the lake." Her features split into a wide smile, and her giggles danced across the air, carrying straight through to Amy's heart. "That's just *silly*, Mr. Tyler!" She doggie paddled and kicked across the distance between them. Not shy at all now, she grabbed on to Tyler's shoulders. "Again!"

Annie evidently had caught wind of the action in the water, and would not be denied her share of the fun. She fussed urgently with the rail latch of the pontoon. "Mommy, Mommy, my vest is on and everything! I wanna jump in! Le' me get throwed, too!"

Kiara barely made it to the back end of the pontoon before Annie freed the latch and made fast tracks to the boat's edge. She didn't look left or right. She didn't even flinch. Instead, she dived straight in.

Kiara chuckled, starting to remove her t-shirt and shorts. "I'll be right there! You may need some reinforcement."

Tyler's eyes tagged Amy's in a form of panic. "Kiara's not kiddin'. What have I unleashed?"

Amy didn't respond to the playful rejoinder. She was too choked up. He must have caught sight of the look on her face, the residue of her reaction to his interplay with Pyper. Tyler's puzzled gaze touched on hers, but then Annie paddled close, and the moment passed. Amy watched while he threw the girls and splashed through the water with them.

Kiara slipped into the water, issuing a brief exclamation of ice-water shock. Then, a pair of bright orange noodle-shaped floats splashed into place right next to Tyler and Amy. In unison they looked back toward the boat where Ken stood, watching them with somewhat of a knowing smile. "I thought those might come in handy if you want to just float, and catch your breath for a bit. Imagine the news flash if I allowed Christian music's hottest rising star to drown."

Tyler just groaned at that, but Amy's heart went full. Ken was right. Tyler had accomplished so much, and still seemed to remain true to himself. She was incredibly proud of him. They horsed around with the girls for a while longer, and then floated about in a boisterous game of Marco Polo.

Tyler swam up behind Amy and circled. He moved in close and looked into her eyes. Water, like silk, slid against her skin in a supple caress. Beneath the surface, their legs bumped from time to time as they dog-paddled, lost to one another.

"Guys," Kiara said over her shoulder, swimming for the access ladder, "I'm headed back to the boat to get lunch going."

"Wanna take a break?" Tyler asked Amy. "We could lay out and soak in some sun."

Amy nodded; after last night's marathon session and today's activities, she was pleasantly extended, both physically and emotionally. Her gaze tracked to the two fish-like five year olds who romped nearby. "You may have some trouble convincing Nemo-I and

Nemo-II over there to leave the water behind."

"Yeah? Watch me." Following a sassy wink, he faced the girls. "What's that, Amy? Kiara busted into the cheese curls and gummi bears? I say we better grab some before they're all gone."

Amy grinned, enjoying the way the two girls began a furious paddle to the boat. She gave Tyler a firm nod of respect. "Oh, man. You are *good*."

The girls climbed out first, with guiding support from Amy and Tyler. Tyler followed, but once Amy started up the ladder, he reached down, offering his hand to assist. She paused for an instant, already knowing his touch, the secure feel of his fingertips locked around her hand, would stir an electric echo through her insides. Looking at him now, she could barely recall his shy demeanor, his quiet ways. Those traits had evaporated; confidence and charisma now claimed their place. Some things, however, remind solid—his openheartedness, his faith, and a penetrating honesty in the way he engaged people.

Giving herself an internal shake, she accepted the gesture and absorbed the warmth that spread through her body. She stepped onto the rear of the pontoon and thanked him quietly. After they toweled off, Amy moved to join the others who occupied benches along the sides of the boat. She shook out her towel and prepared to lay it on an open space of the boat's floor.

Tyler took her by surprise when he claimed her towel and draped it over his shoulder. He had a smooth, supple chest. His shoulders and arms were well muscled and traced by lines of sinew that flexed as he moved.

Amy realized she ached; her longing built from the chest on out, radiating a slow, steady pulse of need.

"Let's go over here; it's a little quieter."

More private, remained unspoken. He retraced their steps to the rear of the boat. Everyone else began exploring food offerings, and Ken turned on the radio. Melodic, contemporary Christian selections filled the air. For Amy, everything faded to indistinguishable background noise. Her entire being zeroed in on Tyler Brock and stayed put. He laid out their beach towels. He stretched out promptly and sighed with delight. That was more than enough of an incentive for her to do the same.

Warmth seeped through the cotton towel from the metal flooring below, soothing her water-chilled body. She heaved a happy sigh, too. Ken had retracted the overhead canopy, so a clear sky, dotted by the spin and dip of birds stretched to the horizon. In a drowse, she closed her eyes.

"Delicious," Amy murmured unintentionally.

Tyler chuckled, the sound low and rumbling. She smiled in response, simply because it was such an appealing reaction to her verdict. They rested on their backs, side-by-side.

"Absolutely."

Waves lapped against the sides of the pontoon, a gentle punctuation mark of noise. The sound of nearby boats and muffled conversations, music and commercials, surrounded them for a moment.

"Can I make an observation?" Tyler asked.

"Sure."

"Well..." Their hands rested just a hairsbreadth apart. Tyler closed that distance and Amy nearly started when his fingertips slid softly, lightly against hers. Her eyes remained closed, but her body tingled. "You've always been beautiful. No question. But this.

Who you are now? You've grown into a truly breathtaking woman, Amy. And you've raised a spectacular little girl."

His subtle caress came to an end, but his touch continued when he covered her hand with his and let the connection linger. For the second time in less than a half hour, Amy was overwhelmed, instantly overcome by being treated so lovingly.

"Thanks." She spoke against a tight throat.

"So beyond that, here's what else I know."

Amy smiled to herself, drifting, relaxing. That new, subtle flavor of the south that now laced his words did something molten and liquid to her insides. "I know you work for a construction company and a school."

"Yep." She cleared her throat, deflecting her reactions as best she could. "I wish you could get to know JB. You two would really hit it off. He's a gem. And his wife, Monica, who you also met last night, is the one who owns the school where I work. She has a state-certified kindergarten program at her daycare center, Sunny Horizons. Annie and Pyper both go there."

"Sounds like an ideal setup."

Amy nodded, absorbing once more the absolute beauty of God's grace. "I couldn't possibly be more grateful. When I—" *Crashed,* she wanted to say, *when I made a fallen daughter's return to Woodland, JB, Monica, Ken and Kiara stepped forward with support that was both emotional and intrinsic.* Tyler, she realized at a quick, hand-shaded glance to her left, waited for more. "When I needed work, Ken gave me a referral to Jeremy's company. It was the start of summer, and Edwards Construction had a lot of work to handle.

Plus, his office manager resigned when she had a baby. Thing is, the job was only full-time work for half the year."

Tyler nodded, turning toward her now, leaning on his elbow so he could look down at her—and block the sun from her eyes. Amy unshielded her eyes and blinked, realizing the openness she longed to give him, the trust.

Much like Pyper, in a way.

"That's when Monica stepped in and offered me an assistant position at her daycare center. I work with the toddlers during the school year, fall to early spring. So it works out great. I get to be with Pyper more often that way."

Tyler's smile grew. "I think that's completely awesome."

Amy laughed, easing up the internal tension levels a bit. "Yeah. Me too."

Ken had tuned the radio to WMUZ, the Christian station in Detroit. A Britt Nicole song, Hanging On, drifted through the air. "And what else I know—" his voice was a slow and gentle leading. Amy knew at once this conversation was headed places. Big places. "—is that you ended up marrying Mark Samuels."

She had no excuse to hide her eyes. Tyler's position next to her blocked the blinding orb of the sun. Still, she reached for her sunglasses, and cleared her throat again as she did so. Tyler took hold of her wrist to still the motion before she could follow through. In emphasis, he slipped his thumb against her skittering pulse point in a light, but deliberate stroke.

"Don't put up a guard, Amy. Relax." The stroke continued, lulling. Assuring somehow. "Just talk to me."

She watched him, Tyler Brock, shadowed and framed against a pure blue sky. She refused to go tense and bitter with memory; she refused her past that kind of subtle victory.

And so, she confessed to the worst of it. "I divorced him, too. Best to get that out in the open, I suppose."

"My folks told me as much. I'm so sorry, Amy. I don't care how many years have passed, I know who you are, and I know for certain that kind of decision did *not* come easily to you. What happened, honey?"

The earnest question, the naturally delivered endearment, coasted into her blood stream and stirred up an emotional flood. Instantly she was carried away, her heart delivered to a place where she could reveal herself, and not fear for the consequences.

Patient and steady, he waited, watching her. She lay prone, oddly relaxed in contradiction to the increased tempo of her blood. She needed to see how close Pyper might be, and determine if she was within hearing distance. Amy lifted just far enough to see that her daughter was happily occupied by the companionship of the Brocks, who were presently being charmed out of a sandwich and some grapes.

Assured, Amy laid back down, tilting her gaze toward Tyler. "He..." Amy took in a breath. Like ripping off a sticky bandage, she came clean all at once, in a quiet, defeated voice. "He abused me, Tyler. Physically and mentally. And he took out a lot of his anger on Pyper, too. He'd startle her with unexpected, unwarranted spankings, he'd scream at her to be quiet whenever she cried, and he'd yell at the both of us for no good reason. Everything he did just seemed to scare her all the more. He couldn't hold a job, so his frustration grew by the day—and so did his use of alcohol as a way of escaping it all. When he started hitting me, I left." She shook her head. "And when I say I left, I mean there's absolutely nothing left of my old life. He saw to that quickly and efficiently."

She was so carried away by the admission, so wrapped up in the pain of a past she fought to move past every day of her life, she didn't realize until then that Tyler regarded her with steel-like eyes and a clenched jaw. Automatically Amy reached up, wanting to apologize for upsetting him. She stroked his chin and shook her head, whispering, "Hey…hey…I'm sorry…"

Tyler flinched. "Stop." He closed his eyes, taking deep breaths. "You mean to say he physically hurt you? Physically harmed you and Pyper?"

All Amy could summon was silence, and a nod.

"Gimme a sec."

Tyler seemed to lose his battle with control. He growled out a sound and sat up abruptly. A startling beam of sunlight crossed against Amy's face. She shaded her eyes. Tense seconds swirled past, so she reached for her sunglasses and slid them on. Moving into a sitting position, she slowly drew up her legs then encircled them with her arms. She rested her chin on her knees, watching him. Waiting, protectively sinking in upon herself.

"I can't even find it within myself to pray for him right now," Tyler whispered tightly, looking out across the water. In the face of his desolate, troubled admission, Amy ignored a round of laughter that came from their cruise mates, the song switched from Britt Nicole to a Point of Grace classic.

"No. Not right now. But you will. It took me a

while, too." When tense silence lengthened, she began to worry. "Tyler, talk to me. Please? What are you thinking?"

"That Mark Samuels doesn't deserve one precious second of the time God gave him with you, and that wonderful little girl."

Typical Tyler Brock. He was never, ever afraid to speak his heart. That was the beauty of him. Just like the words and melodies of his music, he laid it all out there and withheld nothing. Oh, how she admired that bravery of spirit.

Once, she had been the same way, but she had never been smart when it came to matters of the heart. Instead, she had opted to keep Tyler playfully enamored, a friend but nothing more while she chased after the bigger, better deal. Well, woe unto her. "I paid the price for being star-struck by the popular guy, the guy everyone admired. In theory, he was Mr. Right. In practice he turned into Mr. Devastation." She pursed her lips, and looked at her daughter. "And you've seen how hard it is on Pyper when it comes to adult men. It leaves me sick at myself sometimes."

Tyler leaned in and captured her chin gently in his hand. He looked intently into her eyes. "Don't ever, *ever* take responsibility for a man abusing you and your daughter, Amy. You've pulled sunshine out of the rain. Do you understand that?"

The words were kindly spoken, tender in a way, but she heard the reinforcing steel that went along with them. The force of his conviction unsealed a chamber of her heart where fear and loneliness had been caged for far too long. Set free at last, their power diminished as they performed a fast and final dance through her soul.

Through it all, though, Amy wondered where she could, where she *should* she go now.

7

The party moved to Ken and Kiara's lovingly maintained ranch-style house, and continued into the early evening, when everyone gathered around the dining table and shared memories, laughter, and a wonderful, grilled surf-and-turf meal of steak and shrimp kabobs. After dinner, Tyler wandered through the house during meal clean up and found himself in the family room. He trailed his fingers against the entertainment unit. Currently the stereo played quietly. Music was as much a fixture within the Lucerne's home as it had been on the boat that afternoon.

A song change on the radio left him rearing back, and blinking hard. "Hey, Ken?" he called toward the kitchen, "is that WMUZ you're listening to?"

"Nope. Should be WNIC. They play some great jazzy after-hours music."

Puzzled, Tyler moved slowly to the kitchen, feeling dazed. "You sure?"

Ken entered from the kitchen, nodding but looking confused by Tyler's questions. "I think so. Feel free to check it. Why?"

WMUZ was Detroit's Christian music station. WNIC played mostly adult contemporary selections, a few oldies, and a variety of soft rock. Tyler opened the cabinet door and checked the radio dial. Sure enough, it was WNIC. "'Cause they're playin' my song. Right now. They're playin' *Amazing Grace*. C'mere and listen!"

Ken's eyes went wide as he tuned in and made the connection. Meanwhile, Tyler watched Kiara spin away from the sink, where she stood with Amy, cleaning dishes. Ken's wife did a quick boogie dance and joined Amy in an excited shout. His parents, he noticed, rose from the kitchenette. As one, everyone charged for the family room..

Like the fans they were, his family and friends started cheering, and they all danced like adorable fools. That's when a word, and a feeling, crested over Tyler with the impact of a tidal wave. *Crossover.*

In more ways than one, is that what was going on here? Would a crossover circle around not just his music, but his life as well? Was he poised at the precipice of soul-deep compromise? Desperation clutched at Tyler's chest. He did *not* want to compromise.

But the plan, and the momentum, just might be out of his control—happening to him whether he wanted it to or not, whether he was prepared for it or not. His stomach clenched and shivers worked through him from head to toe.

"Is this from when you concerted at church, Mr. Tyler?" Pyper asked the question as she sashayed with Annie and the song continued.

"No, sugar beet, this is a recording I did in a studio."

"It's cool!" Annie exclaimed.

"It's the *best!*" Kiara rushed forward to give him a tight hug. "Tyler, 'NIC! Can you imagine? This is fantastic!"

"It's just as great when it plays on 'MUZ," he answered. Still, his hands trembled. Still, his heart reacted with a thundering, excited beat.

At the end of the song, the DJ came on. "That was *Amazing Grace*, performed by Detroit's own Tyler Brock who's home this weekend for a benefit concert at Woodland Church in Saint Clair Shores. We can see now why this young man is taking Christian music by storm. Congratulations, Tyler, and welcome home."

The DJ's send-off inspired a second round of enthusiastic chatter in the Lucerne home. Once his fan club retreated to the kitchen, he caught Amy's eye and tilted his head toward the doorway of the family room that led outside. He looked at her expectantly, and she nodded, picking up on the cue. The girls had run off to play in Annie's room; the Lucernes and his parents chatted companionably in the kitchen.

Amy mouthed, "Let's go."

Sliding glass doors led to the back yard and a spacious patio. Thanks to Kiara's talents, the back yard of the Lucerne's home was a haven of tranquility, a showpiece of her landscaping skills and a sharp eye for all things beautiful. A series of ground lights illuminated a cobbled pathway that curved along the perimeter of the yard. Just now, the lengthening shadows of early evening painted their surroundings.

The peace and quiet enveloped his troubled mind. It helped that Amy reached for his hand and held it while they began to walk. He wondered if she realized the gesture had come to her automatically.

"If hearing *Amazing Grace* that way doesn't give you an adrenaline rush, I don't know *what* will."

"Aw, it's not as big a thing as you might think." Tyler bent and plucked a pair of pale pink hyacinth from the bevy of colorful blooms that ran alongside the bricks. "I'm in Detroit. That's all. Someone at 'NIC found out about Woodland and decided to play the song is all. Not a huge deal."

A soft, cooling breeze skirted past. The early night air sang with cricket noise. He handed the flowers to Amy and she smiled, lifting them to her nose. Her hair, now loose from the ponytail she had worn all day, fluttered across her face as she breathed deep. Tyler watched her in fascination. He didn't need to be close to smell the sweet, rich aroma. A blanket of hyacinth framed in slightly taller snapdragons then well-shaped evergreen shrubs. Lilac trees dotted the fence line, and periodically the combination of scents carried through the yard, intoxicating and bursting with spring's renewal.

Despite the blows of life, Amy remained stunningly beautiful. Sure, she had gone for comfort and ease for their day on the water—wearing a simple shorts and t-shirt combo. The lavender colored one-piece swimsuit she had worn was discreet and basic as well, but none of that mattered. Even in flip flops and ultra-casual attire, she left him breathless.

Being near her, all he could think of was new life. New opportunity. The parallels caused Tyler to re-center as they continued their stroll. Between the airplay on WNIC, and Kellen Rossiter's heated pursuit, he was a lot more nervous about the way things were going than he wanted to let on. He needed to pull back a bit; he needed to think things through. Most of all, he needed to pray.

Amy interrupted his introspection. "Mainstream airplay is a huge deal, Tyler, and you deserve it." He was grateful for her loyalty, and pride, but she didn't understand the constant battle he fought to remain true to his principles when the call of celebrity, with all of its advantages, and all of its pitfalls, grew by the day. She twirled the flower stems gently. "You should tell Rebecca. I'm sure she'll be thrilled to hear the news."

That comment thoroughly diverted him from his anxieties. Tyler used his hold on her hand to turn her toward him. "Is there something you'd like to ask me about her, Amy?" When she didn't answer, when instead she watched him with wide, searching eyes, he reached up to brush his knuckles against her cheek. Sure enough, they were warm as toast. That made him smile, and gave him the courage to push a little. "C'mon. Ask me."

She shrugged in a negligent way, but her eyes betrayed her. Big time. That's probably why she looked away. "I think she's amazing. And she's very gifted. You two seem to get along really well."

Affection for Rebecca rose to the surface of Tyler's feelings, but that affection paled in comparison to what he held in his heart for Amy. Nothing had ever come close, and he somehow knew nothing else ever would. "Yes. We sure do. Now, Amy...*ask me.*"

She sighed, her brows furrowed. "Whatever the answer is, it wouldn't make a difference." He swore he heard tinges of regret woven through those whispered words. "I mean, you and I, we...we're friends, we're *great* friends, but...it's not like I have a hold...or like you owe me anything..."

The blurred edges of a relationship with this revised, grown-up version of Amy Maxwell gained new resolution. Her display of hesitant interest, an interest she couldn't seem to fight or deny, made his heart take flight. He slid his thumb lightly against the back of her hand. "You're stammering. Please, just ask me what you want to know."

Her soft sigh cut the stillness of the night that drew in around them like a blanket. "Is she…are you two…involved? Are you together in a romantic way?"

"No, honey. Not at all. If I were, I wouldn't have been on a boat with you all day, hanging on every last second we have together."

He watched her downplay the smile, stifle the sparkle that lit her eyes, but they were there, and they sang to him as perfectly as a well-crafted melody. Tyler leaned down. Before kissing Amy's cheek, he let his lips brushed against her jaw line, whisper against her neck. She smelled of an alluring spice, and vanilla.

"You two were on *Opry Bound* together." Her voice faltered, but she was obviously going for some semblance of control here. "You were competitors. That had to be hard."

He ignored her unsteady breathing pattern, and they resumed their meandering walk. "Yes, we were, but we were always friends, too. We connected from the start. It honestly broke me up when she got voted off. She was then, and is now, one of the few people who will ever understand how crazy and wonderful and difficult that whole period was. She's one of my closest friends as the result. But that's as far as it goes. For either one of us."

Something he'd said left Amy grinning like the young girl he remembered from high school, leaving him to puzzle as they nearly completed a circuit of Ken and Kiara's backyard.

"I have a confession to make," she said.

"Oh, yeah? It's good for the soul, you know."

"Ha, ha."

"What's the confession? I'm intrigued."

She shot him a bashful look. "Well. I dialed my fingers off voting for you when you were on *Opry Bound*."

"Really? You did?"

"Of course. I couldn't get over it. The sensation you created is something most people can only dream about."

Tyler ignored that, and instead focused on the revelation. "Who knows, Amy? You just might have been the difference. You might have been the one who put me over the top."

She stopped and turned to look deep into his eyes. "No, Tyler. You did that all by yourself."

Her simple, yet powerful degree of conviction left him silent for a time. She still didn't realize. She *had* been the difference. All that he pushed himself to achieve had begun on a mission trip to Pennsylvania years ago, with Amy at his side, a childhood friend he loved with wistfulness and an absolute, unabated longing. It was then that he had known for certain how his life would evolve: The power of his mission he would give to God—through music. The key to his heart, he would give only to Amy.

"You've always been there. Always. Don't ever doubt it."

Amy's lips twitched into a smile, and she sidled him a narrow-eyed glance. "Here's what else I know about you, beyond that well-deserved victory on *Opry Bound*. Most of it comes from CMT, but..." The way she parroted his words from their time on the boat made him smile. The crack about CMT made him laugh outright. "You have someone hot on your trail by the name of Kellen Rossiter. What's his deal? Who's

Kellen Rossiter?"

This was an unexpected turn in the direction of their conversation. It circled Tyler back to anxieties and the professional circumstances he had to resolve, with the fate of his career in the balance. "Rossiter's annoying."

"And flattering?"

Tyler huffed out a sound that didn't agree or disagree, but he forced himself to relax. He gave her a sidelong look. "Yeah. Admitting it makes me feel weak, but, yeah. I'm flattered by his attention. Dave Wells has me fully convicted on that count. Kellen is one of the biggest agents in the music industry. His roster is absolute A-List."

Amy paused. "And he's looking for you."

Tyler shrugged. "He got wind of the statistics for the new album and he's intrigued, that's all."

"Sure, because high-powered agents track every potential client, via any means necessary, when they're simply *intrigued*."

Tyler attempted to stifle a laugh, but in the end, he couldn't resist. They continued to walk, nearing the patio. "Sometimes, you're still a piece of sass, Amy."

"Sometimes? C'mon. What's the story? It seems to have you bugged. Why?"

"It's not that I'm bugged; it's that I'm afraid. He wants to represent me. Word I get from his numerous voicemails, e-mails, Facebook messages, Tweets, you name it..." This time it was Amy who burst out laughing. "...is that he's got his eye on me as a crossover artist."

That stopped her short once more, right at the lip of the patio. "Wow. It makes sense, but still. Wow."

Tyler wasn't as impressed. Not yet, anyway. "At

the sacrifice of the work I do for God, yeah. Wow." He eyed the large, padded chairs that were placed around a glass table, not wanting the moment to conclude. He'd do anything to stretch out the gift of this time with her, but she was probably tired, and… "You ready to go back in?"

She looked his way for a moment. "Not necessarily."

The grin he gave her was returned full-force, and they sat down.

"How would you be sacrificing the work you're doing for God by signing on with Kellen Rossiter?"

Tyler looked at thin, wispy clouds drifting across the light of a half-moon. Darkness increased by the second, adding an intimacy to the atmosphere. "Kellen is driven, and he's not afraid to push. If I sign on with him, I'll be pushed. I'm not sure how I feel about that. I don't want to get in over my head with a person who may not have all my best interests at heart. My life, my music, is a lot more than just making money and gaining audience exposure, know what I mean?"

Amy nodded. "In fact, I'd expect nothing less coming from you." She let a pause slip by. "But maybe Dave is right. Maybe you should at least talk to him. There's no harm in that."

"Yeah, you're right." Fast vanishing sunlight painted golden rays against the mauve, blue and pink colors of the sky. "I've already come to the conclusion that I'll regret it if I don't. It's just that I don't want to be led into the land of temptation. I'm meeting with him when I get back to Nashville, once the tour craziness is over with."

Amy studied him in silence for a moment. "Well, I know who and what you are. You'd never compromise. Not when it comes to the way you live your life."

A breeze rustled the leaves. She slumped comfortably, and closed her eyes as she rested her head against the back of the chair. "This place has the best vibe. I always feel at peace when I'm here. Content. Wish I always felt that way."

Tyler leaned forward, bracing his elbows on his knees while he watched her and absorbed. "Sounds like you've spent some time here." Her eyes remained closed, but her body went taut. Tyler instantly regretted the comment. "Sorry. I didn't mean to make you uncomfortable."

"No problem. It's tough. On one hand, I don't know what I'd do without Ken and Kiara. When I left Mark, I had nothing, Tyler. Literally nothing. I had the clothes on my back, and Pyper, which is all that mattered anyhow. Ken and Kiara let me stay here for a few months, until I found work, and was able to get an apartment and start a life of my own again."

"And on the other hand?"

She sighed, still never opening her eyes. She spoke in a low, quiet voice. "On the other hand I wish I hadn't made such stupid mistakes. I wish I hadn't needed to rely on them in the first place."

"What about your family? Your mom and dad?"

Amy turned her head, and at last looked at him. There was an ocean of pain in her eyes.

Tyler's brows pulled together.

"It's taken a while to find our way back."

A rift. Between Amy and her parents. Tyler remembered them—loving and devout, caring. Her statement earned his full attention. "They knew Mark was wrong for me. I wish I had listened to them. They were against our marriage from the get go, but when the pregnancy happened, there was no going back. We became alienated. Mark never wanted to be with them, so my visits became less and less frequent. Taking care of Pyper, protecting her, took every ounce of energy, every minute of time I had. They didn't give up exactly, they simply stepped back, and waited, and hoped. We're better now."

"But it wasn't the ending they hoped for you."

"Nope. Not at all. Emotionally, it was easier to crash here than with my parents. They wanted me, and Pyper, of course, but this was better. In all things, God works His good, right?"

Tyler didn't hesitate. "Yes."

He reached across the space between them and caressed her arm. At first, she seemed mesmerized by the play of his hand against her arm, so he kept his touch purposefully soft. Enticing. She stared, lost and dreamy, then her gaze lifted to his in transparent fascination.

That's when it happened. The epiphany.

The events of the day combined into a sudden and startling display; a stunning recognition hit him over the head, and slipped clean through to his heart. *He had an advantage here.* Loving emotion radiated from the one woman he had always wanted the most. He saw the longing in her eyes. He detected the faint trembling of her hands, the intense, heightened awareness that flowed between them—heated and electric.

But he'd be foolish if he didn't also recognize her fear, and the scars she carried from a failed marriage and the remnants of a broken heart trying hard to mend. No way would he move forward without extreme caution, and tender purpose.

Amy sat up. She stood more quickly than he would have expected, as though she were a bit nervous. "I should probably get Pyper home. I'm sure the excitement of the past few days is going to catch up with her before too long. I'll see you at services tomorrow, though. Ken tells me you'll be singing."

Tyler nodded and stood as well. Darkness moved in, deepening the shadows, draining away the day. That recognition stirred a heavy sadness. The end of their time together on his brief visit to Michigan inched inexorably closer, punctuated by his recognition of Amy's interest.

Maybe there was a way they could get together again, this time for longer than a weekend. In fact, he thought he knew just the way to make it happen. First, though, a couple weeks would have to pass in separation, to finish the tour. After that, he needed to resituate himself back home in Nashville and plan out his next steps—professionally, and now personally as well.

But for every night between now and then, he'd wonder if absence, however brief he intended it to be, would make her wounded but opening heart, grow even fonder.

8

Amy had never enjoyed services more. Naturally, Tyler's guest appearance had people crammed into every available space. Amy fell into the happiness of the service, rejoicing in the opportunity to absorb God's presence via prayer, Ken's preaching and Tyler's amazing music.

Afterwards, when she looked through the entry doors of the church, that euphoria and positivity took a nosedive. There, lined up outside the activity center, the tour buses waited, a convoy that would take Tyler back to his life on the road, and, ultimately, his home in Tennessee. Far from Michigan. Far from her. She bit her lower lip.

Suddenly, the beauty of yesterday's time together seemed like years ago.

"Mommy." Pyper tugged on her hand and Amy swallowed, blinking hard in an attempt to readjust herself.

"Yeah, sweetie?" She looked down, only to find Pyper regarding her intently. With concern.

"You gonnna cry?"

"No, Pyp. I'm fine."

"Mm'kay. You look sad." Amy could tell Pyper was nibbling on the inside of her cheek. "I thought maybe sayin' g'bye to Mr. Tyler might make you sad." Pyper peered toward Tyler who stood near the entrance of the church, surrounded by people. She was cautious, but something else rippled through Pyper's mood. Beneath the uncertainty, Amy sensed her daughter's affection, and longing to reach out. "We pro'bly should go see him, huh? Annie's over there with her mommy and daddy and everything."

Amy looked toward the swarm of people who engulfed Tyler. There was no way she'd get anywhere near him without a bulldozer. But she had to see him one last time. She needed to say goodbye, and thank him for giving her, and Pyper, such a sweet pair of days.

She stayed put, watching, and after a time, their eyes met. Amy gave him a tremulous smile but kept her distance for the time being. Tyler stood in place, his focus trained on her; his smile dawned. In short order, he did his best to politely disengage, nudging Ken and whispering. Ken glanced Amy's way and nodded, becoming a gentle buffer who interrupted conversations and redirected attention so Tyler could execute a smooth escape. They made a good team.

Amy caught his directing nod toward the rear corridor of the Narthex, near Ken's office. He took off promptly. Walking toward the group, Amy tagged up her daughter with Annie. "Would you mind keeping an eye on Pyper for just a few minutes?" she asked Kiara.

Kiara offered an understanding nod when Amy's gaze betrayed her, straying toward the doorway of Ken's office. Tyler had just gone inside. "Take your time," Kiara said in a tender voice.

Amy looked at her friend, feeling exposed. Uncertainty left her trembling. "I'll be right back."

Kiara smiled knowingly and ended their

conversation by turning to a parishioner who waited nearby.

Amy didn't think her walk down that straight stretch of a hallway would ever end.

She entered Ken's office and closed the door, not turning toward Tyler right away. What could be said, after all? Where could they realistically go from here, except to the land of farewell?

For the moment, she faced the door, clutching the cool, metal knob. A stirring of air alerted Amy to Tyler's approach. His hands came to rest on her shoulders. The motion was light, yet possessive in the best sense of the word. The warmth of his touch caused her to go still, close her eyes, and breathe deep. She folded her arms across her midsection; the moment lengthened and surrounded her completely.

"I hate to leave." His voice, the words, performed a tender caress. "There's still so much I want to say, and so much more I want to know."

"I feel the same way."

A weighted silence slid by, and at last she turned, facing Tyler, facing the inevitable. She relaxed her hold on herself, but her hands remained in tight fists at her sides. *Why?* she wanted to scream. *Why isn't my life ever easy? Why can't we be saying hello instead of goodbye?* She believed, believed absolutely, in the overriding goodness of God's plans. But at times like this, she sure did puzzle over what He could possibly be thinking.

Tyler studied her face, and stepped close, almost as though wanting to shield and protect her. She tipped her head back and looked into his eyes, not caring if he saw how much this moment hurt her, how much she cared, how much she now wished life had provided for a different outcome between the two of them.

Tyler regarded her steadily. "Give me your cell phone a sec."

Something in his features, that familiar warmth coupled with newfound intimacy, a compelling magnetism, made her catch her breath. She reached into her purse, and handed it over.

The intensity of the moment didn't end when he broke eye contact long enough to work his way into her list of contacts and start clicking keys. Her skin went warm as she waited, watching long, lean thumbs press and move. He paused, glanced at her in a considering way and then continued. When he finished, he snapped the phone shut and handed it over. He didn't release the device until her fingertips met up against his.

"I've added my phone...and my e-mail. Please use them, Amy. Please?" Amy trembled. His leaving stabbed through her spirit; she floundered, reality crashing in against wishes, and longing.

Valiantly, she shoved back the onslaught. "Turn around."

"Huh?"

"Turn around." Once he complied, she dropped her cell into its pocket and pulled a piece of paper and a pen from the depths of her oversized purse. Using his back as a surface, she began to write.

Tyler chuckled, and the sound let tingles loose against her skin. "This is so high school."

Amy stopped writing just long enough to peek at him around his shoulder. "High school was fun."

"Some of the time, yeah." He sidled her a look and his lips curved upward.

Finished, she gave him the small slip containing

her e-mail and cell number. "I'm not techno-savvy enough to enter in my contact information as fast as you just did, but I want to stay connected too, Tyler. Really."

With slow, careful motions, he folded the paper and slipped it neatly into the breast pocket of his shirt. "Amy?"

"Yeah?"

He looked at her intently for a moment. "This isn't high school. Not anymore."

He drew her in tight for a resistance-melting hug. *Tell me about it, Tyler. Tell me about it.* She let her world go soft. Her eyes fluttered closed, and for the first time in years, Amy remembered what it felt like to possess a yearning, loving heart that still believed in happily-ever-after, that still trusted, and still held fast to love's beauty and grace.

Tyler took both her hands in his. He stepped so close she could absorb his warmth. Placing their joined hands on his chest, he rested his forehead against hers.

Never, ever in her life—even in the throes of her crazy-mad longings for Mark Samuels—had Amy craved a kiss so badly. He was leaving. She just wanted a small, simple taste of him before he left.

In fact, that need overwhelmed her, transforming into tears that rolled slowly down her face as he leaned in, as she tilted toward him, ready. Waiting. But rather than claim her mouth, he slowly and tenderly brushed away her tears away with the slow glide of his cheek against hers. "Amy, I've dreamed of this moment for way too long. I don't want our first kiss to be a kiss goodbye."

The words rocked her world. She forced herself to focus, and look into his eyes. There she found the truth.

This moment, their reunion, was too precious to compromise. "I don't either," she admitted softly, hanging her head, weak with longing. "But we may never see…"

Tyler backed up and shook his head even harder. He lifted her chin and looked deep into her eyes, halting her words. He drew the pad of his thumb slowly, slowly against the line of her lower lip, and he blinked heavily. Then, his fingertips slipped beneath her tear-spiked lashes. "Yes, we will see each other again. I'm going to be bugging you."

"I give you permission," she answered, and she meant it…with all her heart.

"I want you to bug me back, OK? And, we'll see each other again soon. Count on it."

He was emphatic. Somehow, in the face of his sincerity, she found the tiniest measure of hope. It was thin and delicate but strong enough to help her hang on. And let him go.

So she nodded, and they held hands as Tyler opened the office door and they walked to the lobby. There, chaos reigned. Everyone at Woodland had lagged behind to wish Tyler and his crew a bon voyage. Beyond the now-open doors, the tour buses revved, belching diesel exhaust, engines rumbling. Doors squeaked as the drivers swung them open and tour members climbed aboard.

"Where will you be tonight?" Crazy, but she wanted to know, to have a connection to his whereabouts.

"Grand Rapids tonight, then Chicago for a few days afterward. Then we hit Columbus, Pittsburgh, and wrap up in Nashville."

Amy watched Pyper break away from Kiara and

Annie. Pyper stepped up slowly, taking Amy's hand, but her focus belonged to Tyler. "G'bye, Mr. Tyler," she said quietly. "Thank you for throwing me so good in the water."

"It was absolutely my pleasure." He crouched down, to Pyper's eye level. She backed away just slightly, tucking next to Amy's legs. Still, she smiled at him shyly. "I hope I see you again real soon, sugar beet."

Her smile went wider and she nodded, giving a soft giggle. "Sugar beet," she repeated, and giggled again. "I'm a sugar beet?"

Tyler gave her arm a gentle squeeze. "Yep. You're sweet, just like a sugar beet."

She gave a little wave. "Bye."

Tyler tweaked her nose lightly, and stroked her cheek. "See you soon."

Now, he focused on Amy. "Remember. We're gonna stay connected."

"I promise to reach out, if you do, too. I don't want to lose you."

"You won't, Amy. You *won't*."

She fought against tears once more, already aching with the pain of missing him. Pretty much a ridiculous reaction, Amy thought, since they had been reunited for less than forty-eight hours. Tyler's rock-solid embrace trembled a bit, but he held her tight and sure. Amy sighed, an involuntary reaction to breathing in the subtle aroma of his earthy, appealing cologne, savoring the way his arms felt, locked securely around her waist.

She wanted to believe him. He lifted a hand to her cheek, stroked it as though revering a treasure. Fire lit her skin, blooming through her body, a fire stoked by the sureness of being in his arms, sharing with him, simply being with him.

But her mind worked in direct contradiction to her heart, warning her, sounding off alarm bells and raising flags.

He's Tennessee; you're Michigan. He's a celebrity; you're barely on your feet again. You've devoutly guarded your heart from further harm, yet you fall for him so easily. This is absolutely crazy.

In the end, all of her arguments did nothing to alter one key truth: being with Tyler again felt good. And right.

9

"Pyper, you got a package in the mail." And it was postmarked Tennessee. That made Amy's lips curve.

"I did? What is it, Mommy?" Pyper bounded from her room, where she and Lucy Robbins, a friend from down the street, were playing with fashion dolls.

"D'no, honey. I think it's from Tyler."

Pyper's eyes went wide, her smile large and just a little shy. "Really?" She took the thick, insulated envelope in eager hands and plunked her bottom down on the couch so she could tear into it. Lucy came out of Pyper's bedroom, drawn by the commotion.

Amy thumbed through the rest of the Saturday offerings. A glossy set of advertisements, a pair of bills—nothing nearly as exciting as Pyper's delivery.

"Wow!" Upon hearing Pyper's happy shout, Amy set the mail on the living room end table and joined her daughter on the couch.

"What is it?" Lucy asked, crowding her friend to see what Pyper uncovered.

"Color books, and a big picture book, too—with mountains! An' he sent me playing cards and stickers, too!"

Amy grinned. Tyler had sent Pyper all kinds of stuff native to Tennessee. A thick coloring book was all about Nashville, and another one about the Smoky Mountains. The third item was a hardback, coffee table book with pictures and information about the state. On the cover of that one, Amy noticed a bright blue sticky note.

Pyper turned to Lucy, a happy set to her features. "This is from Mr. Tyler. He's a friend of me and my mommy, and he's a really good singer. He's on the radio and stuff, and he throws real good in the water, too." Pyper ended her litany of Tyler's traits just long enough to point to the sticky note. "Mommy, what's this?"

Upon it was scrawled the words, *Amy, Open me. ASAP.*

Puzzled, and intrigued, Amy took custody of the book. "I think that one's for me, snug-a-bug."

"Mm'kay." Enthused, Pyper scooped up her prizes and grabbed Lucy's hand; she was flushed with pleasure, and that tickled the sides of Amy's heart. "C'mon, Lucy. You can color in them with me."

Off they charged. Left in peace, Amy opened the book. Inside the front cover, she found a folded sheet of letter-sized paper that she opened promptly.

Her breath caught. Her jaw dropped open and she launched from the couch, scrambling to grab her cell phone. She scrolled fast for Tyler's name.

When he answered, there was no greeting, no preamble, just the sound of his soft, musical laughter. "Le'me guess. You just got the mail."

Amy's laughter bubbled over. "Yes, I did."

"And? So? You in?" His eager excitement rolled through the connection.

"Tyler! You can't even be *halfway* serious about this."

"D'ya wanna bet?" His teasing tones went serious. "I know my proposal may be tough to execute, with your work schedule and all, but I'm missin' you. I really want to try to get together, sooner rather than later if you can swing it…"

His words trailed off and he waited. Amy let herself fall into the moment, and breathe. The printed sheet she held detailed a one-week trip, for her and Pyper, to Tennessee. The itinerary, coordinated by a travel agency in Franklin, was marked "Draft" with travel dates yet to be determined.

"Nothing is set in stone. You can pick whatever dates you want, but nothing changes the intent. I want you and Pyper to take a taste of my life here in Tennessee."

Amy couldn't begin to wrap her head around the idea, or summon a proper response without careful thought and consideration. After all, this involved Pyper as well.

"It's all on the up-and-up. Let me know when you're coming and my aunt will stay with us for the week. Call her a chaperone of sorts. All I know is this: I want you and Pyper here, as soon as you can manage. I miss my girls."

His girls. Amy braced herself against futility, thinking, *Oh, Tyler, if only.*

Still, the sound of his voice wrapped around her, and she savored its inflections and rich, deep warmth. His love saturated her, fed her craving heart with miraculous, life-giving food that came to her spirit as nothing less than a benediction from God. "I wish…"

"What? What do you wish?"

"I wish I could just let go, and say yes, but I'm afraid. I'm afraid for what the end of this whole thing would mean, for me, and for Pyper. I can't afford to be risky with my life, and my emotions, or Pyper will pay the price just as dearly as me."

He sighed, but not out of anger, or disappointment. Amy knew that at once. "I know, but don't deny me the pleasure of being able to do things for you. There's so much inside of me I want to give you."

"Can you give me a day or two to think this over, and see what I can do?"

"I'll give you even more if you need it. Like I said, the dates are flexible, the idea is a constant."

She allowed a tender laugh at that. "Understood, and appreciated—on both counts. Tyler, this is amazing, please don't think I'm hesitating to be coy, or difficult, or—"

"Amy, don't diminish how well I know you by even saying such a thing. I understand exactly where you're coming from. And let me reassure you again—my aunt would stay with us when you and Pyper come to visit. This isn't untoward; it's about giving ourselves a chance to build on something. Something special. So, think it over and let me know when...not *if*...you can make it out here, OK?"

Safe enough, and fair enough. Nothing would give her more pleasure than spending time with Tyler again, and he was going to such effort to make sure she was cared for on every level.

For the first time in five dry, stagnant years, Amy actually recognized herself as being precious. God had to be at work, bringing Tyler back into her life.

Amy stroked the phone, tucking it almost lovingly against her cheek. He was at the other end. He was present and faithful to the promises he had made before leaving Michigan. They had both made sure to reestablish their old ties, and in the week and a half since his departure, they had e-mailed, shared text updates, and chatted on the phone regularly.

"OK. Let me check in at work and see how quickly I can get away from Edwards Construction. I'm not going to kid you, it may be a little dicey. It's spring into summer, work is ramping up. I don't want to pull the rug out from under JB."

"I understand completely. Keep me posted."

"Deal. I will. And Tyler?

"Yeah, honey?"

"Thank you. Thank you for making Pyper so happy, and for being so wonderful, to both of us."

"That comes to me as easy as breathing, Amy. See you," he concluded with emphasis.

She smiled, her heart tripping with expectation, and a dangerous level of hope. "See you," she replied softly, but with equal conviction.

She ended the call and stared straight ahead, seeing nothing whatsoever, as the ramifications set in. Her mind began to spin with plans and ideas. From here, there were only two places Amy could think of to turn: first prayer, and then Kiara.

❧⟡❧

"Why, Kiara? Why am I being so completely reckless? Don't you think I'm being reckless?"

After Sunday services the next day, Amy visited with her friend in the Youth Formation offices at Woodland Church.

Amy leaned against the arm of the chair, cradling her head. "Do you have any idea how often I've thought of Pennsylvania?"

"I'll bet. Tyler's return kind of brought it all back,

didn't it?"

Amy chose to let that observation, and its double entendre, go. "I remember, back then, when you told me to pay more attention to the man who treated me well rather than the one who would rule the basketball courts, and the court of popularity."

They sat next to each other at a small, round conference table. Kiara nodded, and Amy could have even sworn she heard her sigh softly. "I remember that conversation, too. You've always been so bright and positive and magnetic. You draw people in by virtue of your beauty—inside and out. At the time, you couldn't help how you felt—about both of them."

"You're being way too easy on me."

"No, I understand exactly where you're coming from, and what led you to the choices you've made."

Amy sighed, her heart aching when she looked at her friend. "I never, ever should have refused that piece of wisdom, Kiara. You came by your knowledge through hard knocks. I should have paid better attention and learned from you. It would have saved me so much grief and regret. I made a mess of my life. I'm ashamed of what I let happen, and all my stupid decisions."

In a gesture of compassion, and understanding, Kiara reached across the tabletop and rested her hand on top of Amy's. "Whoa back a second, and slow down. Don't take the brunt of the hit, here. You weren't the one who abused, you were the victim. And when you're young, it's so hard to absorb the larger truth—that life always plays the equalizer. After all, look at the difference between Mark and Tyler now that high school and teen influences are past." Kiara leaned forward. "That said, I want you to remember one other very important fact. God uses everything for the good. Everything. After all, if you had made different choices, you wouldn't have Pyper. Right?"

The statement stopped Amy's self-centered thought pattern like a brick wall. The shock of Kiara's words sank in deep and rippled through her system. "Ye…yeah…"

"*Yeah.* God, my darling girl, is now giving you an open door. Offering up a second chance. You're being directed toward a new road to explore with someone who's adored you from the moment he met you. And isn't it ironic? The quiet, shy boy you knew back then has evolved into a handsome, charismatic, talented man. He's become the kind of man you probably always dreamed of being with as the popular young girl who was the life of the party back in high school. The boy you knew needs to be reconciled to the man he is now. Because I tell you true, Tyler Brock is as swept away by you now as he ever was in high school." Kiara arched a brow in challenge and provocation. "Think you can handle that, Miss Thing?"

Amy nibbled her lower lip. She fingered the worn edges of her bible, the well cared for, but much used black leather book her current focal point. Just before seeing Kiara, she had touched base with her boss, Jeremy Edwards, letting him know she might need to take a week off in the very near future. He had seemed interested, and even agreeable; Amy promised to let him know more about it on Monday morning.

For now, it seemed, all signs pointed to Tennessee.

Foot traffic and chatter faded the longer they sat together. Parishioners left Woodland. Soon, Ken would probably stop by, looking for his wife. The idea made Amy sigh wistfully on the inside, longing for a life that featured the love, and devotion, of a wonderful man. Still, everything remained uncertain. "And after the week is finished? What about then? The facts remain. He's a celebrity; I'm most definitely not. His life, is far from mine, and then there's the whole uprooting thing."

Kiara puzzled. "Uprooting thing?"

"Um-Hmm. Let's play the fantasy card for a moment. We have a great time together. We decide to build a future together. That future, for Tyler, won't be in Michigan. His home is down south now, and as for me, well, during the past year, I've done nothing but drag myself, and Pyper, all over creation in an attempt to rebuild our lives. We're getting back on track again. I don't want to ruin that progress by yanking both of us away from everything we know, and everything that's familiar."

Kiara's lips curved into a grin, then blossomed into a smile. "Know what this reminds me of?"

"What?"

"The story of Ruth and Boaz. Honestly, the book of Ruth is my favorite. It's full of such upheaval, yet so much tender loving mercy and romantic devotion."

The point struck Amy's soul like a well-aimed arrow. She tilted her head, wondering where Kiara was headed with that comment.

"You make valid points about abandoning the life you've known here in Detroit. But in the end, the answers you're looking for depend on you and Tyler. Listen to what I have to say, Amy, and think about it. Take it deeply to heart. Faith is a risk. Faith always requires trust. Faith requires vulnerability and absolute belief that, despite everything, God leads you to goodness. I honestly and truly believe Tyler has reentered your life for a reason. As part of a plan. Figure out where to take it, and I think happiness will follow. Just like Ruth and Boaz. It won't be easy, but it'll be so worth it."

Amy went flush, prickly and expectant. She realized, for the first time in years, that there was happiness, and joy, to be found, if she could just let go and embrace it. Could she? Could she trust herself again, like she used to in her youth?

"All I know is I want to try," Amy swallowed hard, banishing the tightness in her throat. "I'm so sick of this hole in my chest. It hurts so much."

"Then fill it up. Fill it up by recognizing God's grace, by recognizing the love you feel. It's the only way that hole you're talking about will ever get repaired."

10

Amy held fast to Pyper's hand as they skittered down the jet way to their waiting plane. Pyper glowed with excitement, pulling hard on Amy's arm. They entered the cabin, welcomed by a lovely female flight attendant who gave Pyper a wink. "Welcome aboard. Enjoy your flight to Nashville."

Amy's heart raced.

Pyper beamed. "Mommy, this is so cool! I can't wait to fly! I'm so *excited*!"

Tyler had purchased first class tickets, so their seats were close to the nose of the plane. Pyper shimmied her arms free of her backpack, which was stuffed full of necessities like the coloring books Tyler had provided, a couple of stuffed animals, some crayons of course, and a pair of her newer fashion dolls, complete with clothing changes. She claimed her seat, right next to the window, instantly fascinated by the arrival of the luggage trolley. Amy buckled in, already grateful for the wide, comfortable seats. While she pushed a canvas tote into the storage space in front of her feet, Pyper likewise stowed her backpack. Pyper tucked her hands beneath her thighs as she swung her legs back and forth. Her smile burst across her face like a heavenly light. She wore a simple, flowered sundress and sandals, her hair a wavy cloud of deep blonde around her face and shoulders. Amy had opted for white capris, and an aqua blouse, worn open over a white silk shell. Her belt was a converted scarf full of pastel swirls. Yes, she admitted to herself, she had fussed for Tyler.

"When will we be there?"

"In a couple of hours."

"But you said it'll be weird—that the time changes."

"Yep. Nashville is an hour behind Michigan. It's nine o'clock here, but it's only eight o'clock where Tyler lives. We arrive in Nashville at 9:40."

Pyper visually puzzled, then shrugged. "Weird."

Pyper's energy and overflow of exuberance only fed Amy's nervous, but happy outlook about the trip to come.

A male flight attendant, dressed in a crisp blue uniform stopped by their seats. "Would you like something to drink, ladies?"

Pyper shrank back a bit, nesting as close to Amy as she could in a body-warmed request for reinforcement. Amy smiled at her daughter, tucking an arm around her. "Want some orange juice?"

Pyper looked into her eyes and nodded. "Orange juice for two, please."

The man returned a short time later with a treat for Pyper. He had mixed a bit of sparkling tonic water with Pyper's juice and added a maraschino cherry that floated on top. "This is a specialty of our airline. We're asking our most special passengers to try it. Can you tell me what you think?"

Blinking, still ducking by Amy's side, Pyper accepted the ice-filled plastic tumbler and took a sip. She smacked her lips and her eyes went wide. "It's awesome!"

"I'm so glad you like it. Here's another treat for being our official beverage sampler today. It makes you an honorary part of our crew." He handed Pyper a plastic-wrapped set of wings.

"Thank you ve'y much." Pyper tilted her head and fluttered her lashes at the attendant.

"You're more than welcome. Enjoy your flight!"

"Mm'kay. I will." He started to walk away. Pyper leaned forward, tracking him. "An' if you want any other drinks tested, I'll do it for you."

Amy stifled a charmed laugh, diverting her reaction by kissing the top of Pyper's head. Their flight steward grinned as well.

Minutes later, they were soaring, and Amy couldn't stop thinking about what awaited her at the other end of this voyage. Kiara's comments about Ruth and Boaz had stuck with her, working through her with a resounding sense of God's promise when it comes to love. She had read through the Book of Ruth twice since their conversation, renewed by the tender shoots of Ruth's hope and unshakable faith, by Boaz's demonstrative affection, his compassion and protection.

The Book of Ruth, with its message of love and an intimate mercy, spoke to a chamber in her soul that remained, since her divorce, in desperate need. Even now, as she embraced the comfort of a deluxe flight, as she slid deeper into Tyler's care with every mile that passed, a tingling quiver went wild in her belly; a dance of sparks lit her senses. Her entire body went flush, radiant at the mere thought of the one who was already giving her, and Pyper, a world full of blessings.

❦

Hand-in-hand with Pyper, Amy made her way through the airport and down an escalator towards the baggage claim where Tyler had agreed to meet them. She found the turnstile for their flight and while she waited for the conveyor belt to begin churning, she punched in the auto-dial connection to Tyler's cell phone.

"Baggage claim five, right?" he said instead of the standard hello.

Amy laughed. A flood of goose bumps danced against her skin, building her sense of anticipation. "Tyler Brock, ladies and gentlemen. He's not just a talented musician. He's also psychic." The rumble of his laughter made her so happy. "Are you here yet?"

"Close."

An instant later, the slightly roughened touch of a man's fingertips slid against her hand from behind, slowly removing the cell phone from her grasp and disengaging the call.

Amy spun, delight filling her as Tyler performed a quick and tempting nuzzle against her neck. "Welcome to Nashville," he murmured into her ear.

He wore a pair of faded blue jeans and a nondescript blue sweatshirt. A baseball cap was turned backwards, sunglasses dangled from his fingertips. He may have been attempting to blend and sink beneath notice, but Amy's heart beat erratically. She looked up at him and smiled, her emotions exposed to the core. Tyler slid an arm around her waist and gave her a squeeze, but then he let go so he could squat down and say hello to Pyper.

"How's my sugar beet?" He didn't reach out or

pull her toward him. Instead, he kept his distance and simply smiled into her eyes.

"I fine," she answered quietly, holding tightly to Amy's side. "How're you?"

Tyler's smile only grew. "I'm doing a whole lot better now that you and your mommy are here to visit. My aunt, RuthAnne, can't wait to meet you. She's already planning a lunch spread. You hungry?"

Pyper took a small inch toward being receptive. "Sorta. I helped the people on the plane test out how good their soda drinks were."

"Amazing!"

Chuckling, Amy stroked a hand against Pyper's hair. "I think taking her maiden voyage in first class spoiled her for anything less." Amy gave her daughter's shoulder a gentle squeeze. "Can you show Tyler your wings?"

"Mmm-hmm. Here." She stayed glued to Amy's side, but rifled through the pocket of her dress and found what she was after. Tyler admired the plastic toy wings she handed over that bore the logo of the airline.

An alarm sounded and a few seconds later, the rotator belt of the baggage conveyor came to life. Not long after, their two suitcases were in Tyler's hands, and he led the way to an adjoining parking garage. "I'm right over here."

Tyler pointed his key fob. After a chirp of the security system and a brief flash of the rear lights, Amy realized which car was his, and her eyes went wide. It was a fire engine red Ford Mustang.

Convertible.

Even Pyper was awestruck. "Mr. Tyler, that's a really cool car!"

"Oh, Pyper, you're a Detroit girl. You know better

than anyone that this isn't a mere car. This is a work of art on wheels."

Pyper burst out laughing. "That's not true! It doesn't even got a picture frame!"

"Know what? You're right, it doesn't, especially when I open up the roof. You guys game for some wind in your hair, and some sunshine?"

"Yeah!" Amy and Pyper answered in unison.

Tyler stowed luggage, then joined them next to the car. Amy's eyes went wide when she saw that he carried a booster seat. "You honestly thought of a booster seat? I'm officially amazed…I have to admit, I was a little worried, but of course, I didn't even think of it until we had boarded the plane."

Tyler went about setting up the child restraint in the back seat. "I'd love to take credit, but this is all RuthAnne. She has grandkids, and knew enough to let me know I'd need it. She had an extra one she's letting me borrow for the week."

Being in the care of an inherently thoughtful man caused Amy's delight to bubble and flow, for she had nearly forgotten what such a thing was like. Her gaze locked with Tyler's, and she hoped her eyes reflected her appreciation.

Once they were settled, he retracted the top of the vehicle. At the first stoplight outside of the airport, he draped a wrist over the steering wheel and turned toward her. "You look fantastic. I'm so glad you're here."

"Me, too."

He leaned in. She watched him do so with wide eyes, trembling with the expectation of his mouth gliding against hers. She imagined his textures, and flavors. But then Tyler paused, and chuckled softly.

His breath skimmed warm against her skin when he tilted her head slightly and gave her cheek a tender nuzzle, just like he had in baggage claim. She tilted her head, turned, beset by the sweetest cloud of wanting...seeking his lips...but Tyler moved smoothly away, a grin lighting his eyes. . "More on that later," he murmured.

The light went green, but she wanted his kiss, literally ached for it. Shaking her head, Amy worked free of languor and focused on the road ahead. Once they cleared out of Nashville, heading south on I-65, they sped through rolling land dotted by large trees and crowned by expansive homes.

Half an hour later, Tyler pulled down a gravel road that curved through a thick stand of sycamore and magnolia trees. At the end came her first view of his home.

It was a farmhouse of deep yellow with large windows that shone in the sun. A wide, wrap-around porch framed in the lower level. Towering old trees stood sentinel. Dark green evergreen shrubs, a variety of brightly colored flowers and ground covering phlox in pink, white, and purple completed the welcoming landscape. A few of the large windows, she now noticed, were edged by stained glass squares that captured the light as they drove up. The overall effect was an invitation to homey comfort with the added touch of southern charm and warmth.

Tyler slowed the car and pulled close to a set of wooden stairs that led to the front door. This was exactly the kind of place she had imagined for him. When he parked, Amy turned, and found him already watching her.

"Tyler, this is gorgeous."

"I like it, too!" Pyper looked around eagerly, already itching to explore, Amy could tell.

They filed out of the car; as they unloaded the trunk, the front door came open and a tall, attractive woman of middle age stepped onto the porch, smiling a greeting.

"Hey, RuthAnne." Tyler paused to give her a wave.

"There y'all are!" RuthAnne Newman was slim and lean, her gray hair fashioned into a loose bunch at the nape of her neck. "So, I finally get to meet Amy and Pyper! Come on in! Y'hungry?"

"I am!" Pyper drew up the straps of her backpack while Amy took custody of her tote and purse. Tyler claimed their luggage and carried it inside.

"Then let's eat! How was your flight?"

There wasn't a formal or stuffy vibration to be found here. Amy liked RuthAnne instantly, drawn by the older woman's sweet graciousness. Simple jeans and a t-shirt added to RuthAnne's aura of comfortable appeal. In the kitchen, serving platters filled with deli meats, cheeses, and bread, a platter of fruit and a bowl of chips, plates and utensils and a tall, crystal pitcher full of lemonade were laid out.

Amy's mouth watered. Pyper looked at RuthAnne with the sweetest expression on her face. "Thank you for this."

"Oh!" RuthAnne seemed genuinely touched. "Well you are a peach, aren't ya?"

Pyper giggled. "No. I'm a sugar beet. That's what Tyler says."

No *Mr.* Tyler this time. Amy sent Tyler a knowing look, but kept quiet. Tyler, however, smiled widely. Another slow, sure, step forward as formalities vanished. But Pyper had yet to truly relax around him, and completely let down her guard.

Time, Amy thought to herself. *Time and stabilizing influences will have to work out Pyper's fears.*

"The thanks go double for me, RuthAnne," Amy said. "This looks wonderful."

"I'm happy to do it. Tyler's been awfully excited about you finally gettin' here."

Tyler cleared his throat and shuffled in a manner that touched Amy's heart.

After lunch, Tyler took them on a tour of the house. A great room stretched across the bulk of the lower level. It was elegant—just leaning toward formal—but that formality was tempered nicely by country-style touches like a large wreath of dried wild flowers that decorated the space above the fireplace, brass lamps with simple white shades, braided area rugs, and an overstuffed sofa and loveseat. A nearby rocker, with a brimming brass magazine rack to its left, was comfortably padded and draped by a crocheted afghan.

Next came a large den/music room, where Amy spied his music awards, and a framed platinum record for his latest release. Pride and awe tickled her fingertips as she lightly stroked the surface. A grand piano and half dozen guitars were stationed throughout. A stack of blank sheet music rested atop the piano bench. On the instrument's music stand were additional pages. These sheets featured filled in staves complete with hand-written notes, and what looked like lyrics in progress. An image of Tyler at work in this space came to life in Amy's mind. What was he working on? What would come next? She longed to step up, and explore, but instead followed the lead of their host.

Upstairs, Tyler showed them to their rooms. At their first stop, he allowed Pyper to walk in first. "Pyper, you get your choice. Do you want to stay with your mama here in this room, or do you want to see the room I thought you might enjoy?"

She looked a bit doubtful. "Can I...like...sorta wait and see?"

"Sure you can," Tyler assured.

Amy's room featured a king-sized sleigh bed with a quilted down comforter of white that looked like a cloud. Sunshine yellow walls were sponge painted with dabs of blue, and crank-style windows were wide open to the gorgeous summer day.

Pyper's room came next. It featured a four-poster bed with tied-back netting. A cherry wood desk filled space beneath the open window with curtains that rippled in a soft breeze. "This is so pretty!" Pyper walked in, and gasped.

"I hoped you'd like it. And even if you don't sleep here, there're some things I got for you to play with, and you're free to hang out here any time."

Pyper shuffled through the room, taking note of a fresh stack of coloring books, a supply of blank paper, and an open box of markers. Small puzzle boxes dotted the top of a long dresser and there was also a large plastic ball and a mesh bag that held a pail, a trowel, a spade and a pair of small, flowered gardening gloves.

"I always wanted to play with flowers." Pyper lifted up the tools and looked them over.

"I sure could use your help with that." Tyler stepped up and explored the gardening bag along with Pyper. "I've got yard work to do now that I'm all done with the tour."

She turned to him. "Maybe…could I stay with my mommy tonight, and then see about being here after?"

"Sugar beet, you can do whatever you want."

They finished settling in, and then Tyler took them for a walk. Amy discovered he owned quite a spread of land, bordered by white wooden rail fences. There was simply no way to stay closed up and tense in such a perfect setting, which, Amy imagined, was precisely why he purchased it.

That evening, Amy tucked in her exhausted daughter. Pyper had been existing on excess adrenaline for hours. After prayers, and a promise to join her shortly, Amy left the bedroom behind, but not before cracking open the door slightly so the room would be bathed in the pale illumination of the hall light.

She returned downstairs. In passing, she noted Tyler was on the telephone in the landing, and he gave her an apologetic look during a pause in the conversation. Amy just smiled at him and gave him a wink. In the living room, RuthAnne rocked peaceably, watching a game showon television as she cross-stitched.

The domesticity appealed to Amy, as did the quiet, homey comfort of being in Tyler's home. Strolling toward the entryway, she pushed open the screen door and decided to enjoy the front porch.

A pair of cylindrical hanging lamps poured buttery, yellow light across comfortably worn floorboards. Amy sat on the thick padded cushions of a swing that was suspended from the porch ceiling by sturdy metal chains. Wicker chairs and tables were positioned close by, and hurricane lamps dotted the window ledges and tables. There was a box of matches within reach, so Amy lit them and settled back to enjoy the flickering glow.

After an early start this morning, and the stress of making sure everything was set for the trip, she felt a bit rumpled, but being with Tyler again reinvigorated her spirit. She leaned her head back and closed her eyes. For a soothing length of time, she absorbed the scent of spring-kissed air, the caress of the soft, warm breeze that glossed her skin. Incrementally her body unwound and relaxed.

"Hey there."

Amy turned, watching Tyler set a mug of tea on the wicker table next to her. "Hey there yourself." She delivered a sheepish grin. "I think I've discovered my favorite part of your house. This is a wonderful spot. "

"It's my favorite, too."

Tyler sat next to her, propping a booted foot against the edge of the large wicker table positioned before them. Pushing slightly, he set the swing into a slow, lulling motion. The black bowl of a sky was sprinkled with stars, lit by a half-moon. The only interruption in the view came from rolling mountain peaks, the valley lights curving upward against the ridge basin.

"Sorry about the call. I didn't mean to be rude."

"Don't even worry about it. Is everything all right?"

"Fine." Something strange rode beneath the surface of that too-fast reply. "So is my sugar beet all tucked in?"

"She is. Happily exhausted, too. Just like me."

"Good. On both counts."

Amy kept quiet for a time, but remained watchful, savoring the joyful nuance of being in this moment, with Tyler, on such a beautiful night. Since Tyler kept them in motion, she drew up her legs and wrapped her arms around them, tucking against the side of the swing so she faced him. "You're a busy man. Even in the off-tour season. Was it an important call?"

He stretched his arm across the back of the swing and stroked her cheek with his knuckles, giving her a smile. "Amy, know what I love about this? It feels like only five minutes ago that I hugged you goodbye after the mission trip to Pennsylvania, or said goodbye to you a couple weeks ago in Detroit. It's like we're just now picking up the threads of a conversation that never ended. I wish you knew how much I love that aspect of our relationship."

She went warm, and smiled at him brightly. "I know what you mean. Now answer the question."

They swung, and Tyler paused a moment, seeming to take a few beats of time to form his words. Amy studied his profile.

"I'm planning to take y'all to Rutledge Falls and Fall Creek tomorrow, but I've got an eight o'clock meeting in town to contend with first. Our Tennessee tour will be my reward for enduring it."

"Town meaning Nashville?"

"Kellen Rossiter. I was going to meet with him last week, but I ended up having to reschedule. That was him on the phone. He wants to meet for breakfast beforehand. Kind of an informal pre-meeting to make things a bit more personal and friendly."

Tyler sighed heavily, and all at once, Amy came aware of the reasons behind his nervous, unsettled attitude. He was still worried about the potential for selling out. Crossing over mounted monumental pressures upon him.

"I swear. The most difficult thing to contend with

is the whole atmosphere of the entertainment industry. I love making music. I love sharing God's truth through the songs I sing. I truly do. Nothing else compares to it."

"Because it's your calling." Giving a nod, she reached for her tea to take a sip. Mint flavor swirled, and burst on her tongue.

"True enough, but the people I see every day? They're not my crowd. I hate that terrible sense of aggression and the self-centeredness of the entertainment industry. And, not to belabor the point, since we already hashed it out back in Detroit, but I just can't get a bead on this guy. I admit that's got me nervous. I can usually gauge people pretty well. Not this time. This time, I'm confused, and I'm still not sure where God means for me to go with the opportunities Kellen is presenting."

"You never had an agent?" That surprised Amy. Somehow she assumed they would have beaten a pathway to Tyler's doorway.

"I never needed one. When I won *Opry Bound*, I had plenty of offers, but I had a guaranteed contract with Exclamation Point Records. They took good care of me on album number one, and gave me lots of room to create on record number two, so I didn't see a need. But, maybe now the time is right to sign on with some representation. Not out of greed, or a need for *more*, but to insure I'm making the most of the opportunities I'm being given."

"Opportunities you've *earned*," she amended tenderly. "And part of the purpose of performing, and sharing your gift is to gain exposure to more people. There's no shame in that, Tyler."

"No, there isn't, on the surface, anyway. I do want

to grow as an artist, and help more people discover the message in my music." Tyler seemed to think about that for a moment.

"Pray."

That single stronghold of a word drew his gaze to hers, but Amy could still see a hint of hesitation in his eyes. "I don't mean for that to be a pat, simplistic answer to what you're going through," she said. "I believe it's the only way you'll find your way through, and keep on track with what God wants for you."

"I agree. Completely. I *have* been praying. Trouble is, the confusion doesn't go away. God knows, from the depths of my heart, I don't want to mess this up, but I just can't figure out what to do yet. I'm not feeling the answers yet. I'm not sure of God's pathway right now."

"Then you're not supposed to. God knows what you're up against. He'll give you the discernment you need, the comfort you're looking for, but for now he's obviously telling you to rest in faith, and trust Him."

"I know. I'm trying. But the world I'm pulling closer to? I'm not going to lie to you, Amy, it scares me."

"And that's understandable. Plus, Kellen Rossiter is so much a part of that whole scene you're probably not sure of his motives, and if they'll serve you well."

"That sums it up." They shared a smile, and Amy drank a bit more of her tea. She wrapped her fingers around the warm mug and savored the spicy aroma of the rising steam. "I don't want to fall into a guitar-string style of faith and morality."

Amy couldn't help it. The analogy caused her to bubble up with laughter. "Excuse me? A guitar-string style morality?"

"Yeah. You know. Variable. Conforming to our needs instead of God's plan." He held up an imaginary air guitar, pretending to fiddle with it. "Oh, I like this a lot. I think I'll tighten it up a little here. Hmm...don't like that so much. It's hard, and doesn't feel so good. No problem. I'll just loosen up that next string and make it all work." Tyler shrugged, resuming their swinging motion by pushing gently against the table. "It's all about making things what you want them to be, forcing them into place by stubborn will and pride instead of paying attention to God's overall symphony. Know what I mean?"

Boy, did she. Amy nodded. "Leaning on our own understanding."

"Exactly." Tyler didn't hide his unease at the idea. "Biggest pitfall there is, especially in the entertainment industry. People start reading, and believing, their own press releases, and start thinking they know better than God. Or, worse yet, think they're on a par with God. It's such an easy trap to fall into. I'm trying to avoid it, but—"

"But then along comes an amazing opportunity to minister in an even bigger way and move forward with what you love. Music."

"Yeah."

"Starting tomorrow."

Tyler chuckled, but the sound lacked any degree of humor. "Starting tomorrow."

On impulse, she reached out and gave his fingertips a tight, reassuring squeeze meant to convey her support and faith in his strength of spirit.

God, she prayed in silence, *thank you. Thank you for this wonderful, Christ-centered man whose mission in life is to spread your love. Please. Please, dear Lord. Take care of him for me. With my past history, with the abuse and horrors I've endured, I still don't see a future for us as a couple. I feel like I'd bring him down. I'd never survive the glare of a public spotlight, and either would Pyper. I can't yank my daughter into a whole new life at this tender point in her development. But, all that aside, he's precious. Guard him. Be with him tomorrow.*

11

At just after seven the next morning, Tyler left his home. Amy, Pyper and Aunt RuthAnne were sound asleep within. He, on the other hand, had barely closed his eyes all night. Tension slid through him. Nervous anxiety thumped at his spirit, giving him too much energy, too many things to think about.

Purposely early, he made his way into the heart of Nashville and parked on 5th Avenue, not far from their chosen restaurant: 417 Union. The block or two he needed to walk would do him good, and hopefully help him settle before the meeting. He was shown to a booth positioned toward the front of the restaurant. It was then that Tyler rested his fidgeting hands, closed his eyes, bowed his head, and repeatedly prayed a simple, three-word petition: *Discernment, Lord. Please.*

Tyler heard the door squeak open. Footsteps sounded. Reflex left him wanting to lift his head to see who entered the restaurant. He rebuked the reaction, but his prayers drifted to silence.

"Good morning, Mr. Rossiter. How are you?" When Tyler heard the greeting, he sucked in a deep, smooth breath, still diverting his eyes, forcing anxiety to take a back seat to God's prompting and direction.

"I'm great, Janie, thank you."

"Your party is here, and seated."

"I see him. Thanks again."

"My pleasure."

The simple exchange of pleasantries finally roused Tyler. With a restored sense of calm, he greeted Kellen's approach. "You're a regular here."

Kellen took the seat across from Tyler and gave a laugh. "Guilty. This place roped me in a couple years ago with their prime rib hash."

Tyler winced. "Something about the word 'hash'…."

Kellen laughed again. "Give their French toast platter a try. It runs a close second."

They perused menus for a few moments while their waitress introduced herself and delivered iced water. Tyler desperately needed his morning coffee fix, so he ordered that promptly. Kellen went for a tall orange juice.

"I meant to ask you," Kellen began, spreading a white linen napkin across his lap. "You going to the Exclamation Point party on Friday?"

Tyler nodded. He wondered if Amy would be interested in attending his record label's annual publicity push. They could make a full, fun evening of it. Otherwise, he'd make an appearance, and return home as soon as possible. Nothing superseded Amy and Pyper's visit. "Yeah. I plan to be there."

"Good. Me, too."

"You seem to be making more and more inroads with Christian artists."

"Let's just say I'm *trying*." A pointed look was tempered by the curve of his lips.

Tyler shook his head, bemused. While they made small talk, and placed a food order, he studied the agent, still trying hard to figure him out.

As a person, Kellen presented an appealing

package, Tyler had to give him that. Kellen was of average height and build—nothing too extraordinary there. He was handsome, but that wasn't extraordinary either. What defined Kellen Rossiter was something intangible, and it radiated straight through his eyes, his carriage, and demeanor. In a word, that intangible quality had a name: magnetism.

He was easy, and friendly.

So far.

Kellen wore a gray silk suit, a crisp white dress shirt, and a deep blue tie that added a splash of color to the ensemble. Tyler would have felt a bit underdressed, since he wore simple black slacks paired with a loose fitting polo shirt, but Kellen was all about business, and since this was the start of his day, the attire was to be expected.

Tyler ticked off the seconds until he could reclaim his peace of mind, and enjoy spending more of his time with Amy. Once this breakfast and the meeting to follow was concluded he'd rest a lot easier. First things first, though; he needed to give Kellen Rossiter his full attention, and do so with an open heart, and mind.

About mid-way through a delicious and hearty meal—during which Kellen's recommendations were accepted and enjoyed—the hostess checked in at their table. "How is everything, Mr. Rossiter?"

"Very good, as always. Thanks."

She smiled at Tyler. "I wanted to say that I'm glad to see you here, Mr. Brock. I'm Janie Field, the hostess here, and I'm a big fan of your music. Congratulations on its success."

That took Tyler by pleasant and unexpected surprise. He gave her a friendly smile. "Thank you very much. I appreciate you saying that."

"You're welcome, and keep it up. Enjoy your meal, and if you need anything, just let us know."

Tyler watched her leave, still flushed by a thrill that never diminished when he came upon people who enjoyed, and were influenced by, his music. He gave Kellen a quick glance before digging in again. "They sure do take good care of you here, Kellen."

Kellen continued to eat, but his lips twitched, as though he could barely contain a chuckle. "Humility is such a rare treat to find in my neck of the woods, Tyler. Thanks for that. Janie came over here to meet you, not cater to me. Trust me on that."

Tyler shrugged it off. "Mm-hmm."

They finished breakfast; Kellen leaned back after sliding a credit card into the padded bill holder. "Shall we continue this at my office?"

Nerves came back with a wicked force. "Sure. Thanks for breakfast. It was great."

The bill was taken, and settled. "Glad to do it, Tyler. C'mon. We can walk from here."

❧❧

Once again, the walk helped. Motion cleared his head. By the time they reached the high-rise office building, Tyler had offered up final prayers for calm, and God's answers. By the time they walked into the elevator, and Kellen directed them to the twentieth floor, Tyler felt emotionally and physically prepared for whatever might come.

The doors opened upon an impressive suite, but he had expected no less. In Kellen's office, Tyler's gaze trailed to a pair of unframed abstract paintings that decorated the wall. He wandered across the threshold, continuing to look around. A glass-topped desk, trimmed in mahogany, was accented by a leather chair that looked plush and comfortable. The chair resided at a slight tilt before a panoramic view of downtown Nashville framed by floor-to-ceiling windows. A thick, cream area rug, bordered and slashed by deep burgundy, silenced their footfalls, and he now noticed an inlayed beverage service, bookshelves illuminated by recessed lights. A pair of leather chairs were positioned in front of the desk. Tyler sank into one, trying not to be obvious about the way he clutched the arms of the chair. Kellen sat behind his desk and thumbed fast through a small stack of messages.

OK, OK, I get the message—this is the big leagues, Tyler thought.

Kellen tossed the paper slips aside and stretched back a bit, giving Tyler a smile. "Let's get down to it, huh?"

Tyler nodded, and leaned back as well.

"Obviously I want to represent you. My idea is this: you're a phenomenal Christian artist. But the inherent problem with contemporary Christian music, as I see it, is a lack of mainstream exposure. The music's good, but the artists aren't getting the push they need to be heard by more listeners." Kellen shrugged. "Some artists, in my view, have the chops to bust through that barrier and cross over. Obviously you're here because I believe you're that caliber performer. I want your professional growth to match the potential I see in every one of your recordings."

Tyler didn't answer right away. Instead, he studied the man before him and constructed a figurative blockade against any kind of pride, or selfish pleasure that declaration might inspire. Only then did he weigh in. "Likewise I'm sure I don't need to build a ladder to the doubts I have. The doubts have nothing to do with you, per se, or your intentions, per se. I'm honestly flattered to be here. My fears come in at the exact point where I might be expected to give up parts of who and what I am in order to satisfy the 'greater PR good.'"

Kellen seemed about to speak, but Tyler continued on. "Furthermore, what about the people I work with? What about Dave, and Rebecca, and the team who've seen me through everything, right from the start? I don't want wholesale changes just because I sign on with an A-List agent."

Throughout Tyler's turn at bat, Kellen's lips tightened into a firm line. He sighed. "You're still not getting it, Tyler, and that puzzles me. I'm not about changes; I'm about enhancements to a package I already believe in wholeheartedly. I believe so much that I've already taken a bit of initiative. Let me show you something." Kellen slid open a desk drawer to his right and extracted a stapled set of papers. He held them out. "Give this a look."

Puzzled, Tyler took custody. "OK."

Kellen rose. "Can I get you some water?"

"Sure, that'd be great. Thanks."

Kellen went to the beverage service. While ice chinked into glasses and water splashed, Tyler looked at the information Kellen provided. What he found was a playlist—dated two weeks ago—for WNIC radio in Detroit. Over the span of two days, *Amazing Grace* was highlighted six times.

Tyler blinked. "You did this? You set up 'NIC to play *Amazing Grace*?"

Kellen looked over his shoulder, his gaze tagging

Tyler's. He shrugged, waiting.

"You did this, while I was back home in Detroit, performing at Woodland?"

"I thought it would be a good idea to deliver a bump to your exposure while you were home."

"But you had no right to do that! I'm not your client!"

Kellen was nonplussed by Tyler's agitated retort. "I made a phone call, that's all. Consider it a freebie. My only intent was for your song to get added airplay, and, yeah, for you to catch a glimpse of what I can do for you. If you walk away from the gesture, no harm done, but the facts remain." He gestured toward the papers. "It worked. It worked because your music is *good*, Tyler."

"Actually, I heard it when I was at my pastor's house." Tyler studied the play list again, and he couldn't quell the wash of disappointment. The exciting moment he had shared with his family and friends dimmed now, as though a slight "cheat" had taken place to give his song a push. Or had it? Was he being overly defensive with regard to a harmless, helpful act on Kellen's part? Tides were sweeping him onto a new mission field, whether he welcomed it or not. "It's just…I thought the song had received air play on its own merits."

Kellen returned from the bar service and shot him a hard look. "It did." He approached his desk carrying two crystal glasses. He handed one to Tyler and resumed his seat. "The song, the music, *the message*, it's all based on merit, and it's all *you*. I just touched base with a connection—reached out to the programming director at WNIC and put you on his radar. Tyler, that's what I *do*."

Tyler sighed, and he couldn't stifle a nervous, uncomfortable shift.

"You know, you might want to get over yourself a little bit." Kellen bit off the words. "I'm not the devil in this scenario, and if you want to know the truth, I think that's part of what's got you so riled up and unsettled right now. It's also part of why you've been avoiding me. You're running scared from opportunity."

"Nice job of salesmanship." But talk about finding himself *convicted*.

"I don't sugar coat." Kellen paused strategically. "And I didn't get where I'm at by being a pussycat." He leaned forward against the desk; his eyes went narrow. "I'm tenacious and relentless about going after whatever will serve me and my clients for the best. I'm not asking you to give up who and what you are. That'd spell disaster. I'm not asking you to spew expletives on stage in front of hundreds and thousands of zoned-out fans. That stuff turns my gut as much as it does yours."

"I don't sugar coat either, so let me be just as frank."

Kellen gestured openly and sat back in his chair. "Please. That's what today's all about."

"No matter what you want from me, expect from me, or try to accomplish with regard to my career, my symbol is a cross. It'll never be a bar chart in some media popularity poll. You'll end up asking me to compromise. You'll end up asking me to move just far enough away from a Christian message to dilute my mission. For the sake of sales and exposure. It's not worth it."

"Wrong. I'm asking you to loosen the reins just enough to reach more people. People who need what you offer. I want to help you spread your message on a larger stage. Isn't that why you perform? Isn't that why you've created that Christian message to begin with? To reach people?"

Tyler had no ready rebuttal to that piece of analysis. Kellen nodded slowly, his eyes unflinching. "A large number of Christian artists have remained true to their message of faith and Christianity, but at the same time they moved forward into mainstream markets. I play hardball, but I have convictions, too. My convictions lead me to the belief that your time is here. You possess exactly the degree of talent, charisma, and message to swing open a powerful door. Take it to the next level, Brock. You've got the will to make that happen? You ready? If you are, I'll make it come to be."

"That's where you're wrong. *God* will make it come to be, not you." Tyler fought against two diametrically opposed forces in his nature: Ambition versus mission. Passion for music versus passion for God. He had to fight hard to make sure he remained true to himself, and his faith. "I won't move forward without God, and who and what He brings to my music. That's my final answer."

Kellen leaned back, steepling his fingertips, tapping them lightly against his lips. "I respect that. But I also believe you can do both. In fact, maybe that's why God has put me into your pathway. Think about it."

Kellen's challenge left Tyler off center. Would this extraordinary offer mean serving two masters? Dividing his heart and loyalty? In the heat of this charged, electric exchange, he didn't know the answer. He needed prayer time. *Serious* prayer time.

That, Tyler promptly recognized, was God's answer, wafting through his heart, providing that needed certainty of course.

"I'm not sure yet, Kellen. Until I am, and I'll let you know my answer either way, give me some time to think about this, and pray about it. In *peace.*"

Kellen's lips curved. Admiration shone from his jet-colored eyes. "Fair enough, Brock. Fair enough."

The man was a tiger. Tyler had to give him credit for that, and part of him recognized clearly that Kellen Rossiter would be a formidable champion—if black and white could ever be comfortably reconciled.

As those thoughts crested through Tyler's mind, Kellen ropened the desk drawer and removed a Bible. Tyler could tell instantly the item was no prop. The spine featured numerous, deep creases. The cover was worn and a bit frayed at the edges.

Kellen handed it over. "Look it over for a second," he invited quietly.

Tyler paged through the thin, onionskin pages with reverence. It was full of penned notations, highlights of verses, all of it in various shades, but all of it in one person's handwriting. On the front page, the Bible was inscribed to Kellen, from his parents, with a confirmation date inscribed just beneath.

"I'm not trying to sway you with religion," Kellen continued. "That's not how I operate. My faith isn't something I use as a bargaining chip. But in this case, I want to demonstrate commonality." He gestured toward the black-leather volume. "I can't share this with many of the people I come into contact with. It's just not built into the nature of this business. But when I come upon an artist like you, when I see your message, and recognize its impact, I get hungry. On your behalf, and on God's behalf."

Stunned, Tyler lifted his eyes briefly. Kellen regarded him in steady silence. Tyler continued to turn pages, and he ended up in Proverbs. Though he didn't really believe in playing "Bible Roulette" he didn't think and ended up at Proverbs 3:5-6 by mere happenstance:

Trust in the Lord with all your heart, and lean not on your own understanding; in all your ways acknowledge him, and he will make your paths straight.

Last night's conversation with Amy played through his mind. In regard to their relationship, in regard to Kellen Rossiter, in regard to his career, no words from God could have struck his soul with richer impact.

12

Amy came awake in slow, pleasant degrees, her body lulled by soft breezes that circled in through an open window, her mind soothed by the steady crescendo of bird-song. She stretched, issuing a quiet, happy sigh.

And then she got whapped on the forehead.

The contact came from her daughter's stray hand when a still sleeping Pyper tossed from her back to her side. Amy winced, and rubbed her head, but she squelched a pained sound because Pyper resettled instantly, softly cooing while she snuggled into the depths of her pillow. Amy re-tucked the blankets around Pyper's body, then kissed her cheek.

She rolled out of bed and prepped herself for the day as fast as she could. She was eager to find out if Tyler had returned from Nashville and what he was up to. The intimacy of sharing with one another last night had happened so naturally, with such ease. It had been perfect to while away a beautiful evening side by side with Tyler, lulled to contentment by the steady motion of a creaky porch swing, tucked together perfectly.

But she knew today's meeting with Kellen Rossiter rested heavy on his mind, and she wanted to know its outcome.

Amy's slumber had been completely serene; her world unblemished by mixed-up dreams, taut muscles and the anxieties that bore down on her day in and day out, even at rest. It was part of being a single mom, and draining though it might be, Amy wouldn't trade an instant of Pyper's life, and finding happiness for them both outside of the horrors Mark had inflicted. So, this morning she had slept in way too late. Following the call of fresh-brewed coffee, she walked down the staircase, making her way to the kitchen. The area was vacated, although a set of breakfast dishes were rinsed and stacked in the sink, most likely by RuthAnne. A flutter of disappointment moved through her at missing Tyler's aunt. Amy looked around, now noticing something that caused confusion, and then a smile. The kitchenette featured two settings of cheery, orange stoneware placed with care upon thick, dark blue placemats. Silverware and linen napkins were stationed nearby. An envelope rested atop one of the plates, bearing her name in Tyler's increasingly familiar handwriting.

She tore into it like a Christmas present.

Amy (and Pyper, too!) ~ Bacon and eggs are warm and waiting in the oven, courtesy of RuthAnne. She'll be back around 10, 10:30. She's indulging her weekly produce market fix. I'm out front when you're done, so no worries. Wake up slow, and enjoy. ~ Tyler

Amy nipped her lower lip, trying so hard to fight that lovely dissolving surrender to the belief that this could become real—and permanent—in her life.

She poured herself a mug of coffee and set it on the table. Next she found a hot pad hanging on a wall hook, and slid a serving platter full of scrambled eggs, bacon, and toast, from inside the oven. She trailed her fingertips along the arched back of the whaler's chair, lost in thought as she dished food then sat, preparing to dig in, and re-read Tyler's note, just because it made her feel…treasured.

She filled an empty and grateful tummy, with Tyler's note her accompaniment. The gesture got her to thinking. She really needed to put together something for him to commemorate his recent visit to Woodland. She should create something special, like an album of the best pictures she had taken at the concert. Or maybe something even more immediate, like—

"Mornin'!"

RuthAnne entered the kitchen through its side door, delivering a happy nod as she hefted a stash of bags onto the counter with a thud. She began to unpack groceries, and Amy stood to help. Her arrival couldn't have been more perfectly timed. It synced right up to the idea Amy had brewing.

"Good morning, RuthAnne. How was the market?"

"Excellent selections, I tell you. Sit down and finish eating! I've got this."

"I'm done. No problem." There were all kinds of fragrant, fresh vegetables, some cantaloupe, a watermelon, and a couple packs of blueberries. Amy stored what items she could, then turned to Tyler's aunt. "Hey, RuthAnne, do you happen to know what Tyler's favorite dinner is?"

RuthAnne paused and thought about it for a moment. "I make a chicken stew that he always seems to love."

"Would you mind showing me how to make it? Sometime in the next day or two I'd like to treat him to something special, if it's not a family secret or anything."

"Oh, it's no such thing. I'd be happy to share it

with you." RuthAnne continued to put away the food. "We'd need some chicken breasts—maybe we could make a run to the store and pick them up. We'd have to prep it in the morning and let it stew for the rest of the day."

"Thank you! I think that'd be wonderful."

"Y'all are off to the falls today, right?"

"Yes, we are. And I guess Tyler's out front."

RuthAnne nodded, and she grinned. "Waiting."

Lifted by the prospect, Amy retrieved her dishes from the table and gave them a rinse before setting them in the dishwasher. After that, she exited the house through the front door, and when she looked around the porch, found nothing but empty seats and extinguished hurricane lamps on wicker tables. The memory of sharing this space, the flickering candlelight, with Tyler seeped into her soul and left happiness in its wake.

Trotting down the few steps leading to the front yard, she found him, almost hidden from view as he knelt by the flowerbeds, hard at work weeding. For a few unguarded moments, Amy savored the sight. "Well if this doesn't bring back some memories."

He looked up, the late-morning sun glimmering in his dark blond hair. His skin was richly tanned, his arms sinewy and strong as he continued to yank away traces of overgrowth. He wore a pair of faded cut-offs and a white t-shirt that did odd, fluttery things to her insides. "So get on down here and help. We always made a great team."

"Glad I just ate a hearty breakfast." She shot him a teasing look, and then knelt next to him on the thick pad where he paused for a few seconds. "I loved the note, too. So far, the entire morning has me feeling quite pampered." She pulled away some scrub grass and weeds. "Well, until now, that is."

"Mission accomplished then. Until now, that is."

They worked at weeding for a bit, but then Amy couldn't wait any longer. Curiosity was eating her alive. "So…how'd it go?"

Tyler shook his head, but didn't miss a beat in his landscaping detail. "I'm working myself senseless—after a sleepless night, and following a very intense meeting—because it fills me with equal parts fear and thrill to realize I'm just about ready to sign on with him."

Wow. Amy settled back on her haunches, ignoring the overgrowth for a minute. "Really."

"Really."

"So you're ready to make the decision, but you're not completely content."

"Truth to tell, I probably won't be content until we strike an agreement and start to actually move forward. Part of me is blown away by him; he's a really impressive guy. And, in basic terms, I trust his intent. But there's this other part of me that's scared of the whole rug-being-ripped-out-from-under-me thing."

She looked into Tyler's eyes. A world of long-standing friendship and knowing, was revealed in their depths.

"That's why we pray." They spoke the words in a perfect unison that left Amy wistful for the ease of their youth.

Tyler touched her cheek with the tip of a clean finger. "God truly knows how much I miss those youth group days when we'd gather in a circle, talk about our troubles just like we are right now, and end on that very claim."

"I feel the same way. It was so simple then."

"To a degree." A pause followed, ripe with an underscore of tender emotion. "Where's Pyper?"

Amy chuckled. "Still sleeping. Hey, do I have a bruise on my forehead?"

Tyler studied her. "No. Why?"

"Good. I was worried there for a second. She walloped me a good one just before I got out of bed."

"Restless sleeper?"

"Yeah. Always has been."

Tyler shook his head and his wry grin had her curious.

"What's that look all about?"

"You. You're the opposite of a restless sleeper. I remember the trip home from Pennsylvania. You executed a none-too-subtle seating arrangement that put me between you and Carlie. Remember?"

Amy pulled dandelions and more overgrowth from the soil around the bushes. "She wanted to sit by you. I was being a good and gracious friend."

"But I was caught in the middle. You fell asleep on my shoulder about a half hour after we started home. My arm went to sleep and my whole right side basically went stiff because I didn't want to move. You snuggled in like a cat takin' a nap."

A delicious sensation of weakness seeped through Amy's insides. "I don't even remember that."

"Well, honey, you were asleep at the time."

Tyler's expression made Amy laugh though she felt suddenly shy. Infinitely warm.

"Frankly, I would have taken a lightning bolt before I moved and disturbed you and made you move away. I loved it."

Amy picked up their refuse piles and stuffed them

into a nearby recycle bag. That was the thing about Tyler. He'd never, ever, take a loved one for granted, or fail to see to their comfort. "I swear, Tyler, I didn't deserve you then, and I question why you think I deserve you now." Awash in high emotion, in dreams of all that could have been, Amy leaned in and kissed his cheek, wishing for so much more from this man. "I sure am glad to be with you, though. Truly."

He turned, and his gaze roved over her like a slow-moving caress. "Ditto."

"Mommy? Wh're you?"

The summons jarred them apart just when Amy had hoped for a bit more—like that kiss she had been aching for. Through the open front door, she saw Pyper slow-step down the stairway, holding tight to the built-in banister. Pyper rubbed her eyes and yawned big.

"I'm right here, snug-a-bug. C'mon out to the porch."

"Mm'kay."

Tyler watched Pyper's progress and grinned. "She's got every one of your cutest mannerisms, Amy."

"Mm-hmm. Including a wicked right hook."

"I'll keep that in mind. Morning, Pyper," Tyler called out. "You ready to go for a hike, and see a big, beautiful waterfall?"

"Mm-hmm. Hi, Tyler." She pushed open the screen door and padded across the porch in her bare feet. A long, cotton nightgown rippled around her ankles in the breeze. Her hair was an adorable, uncombed tangle; her eyes sleep coated, but slowly coming alive.

"Did you sleep well?" he asked.

"Mm-hmm. I'm hungry." Right on cue, probably

hearing their voices, out came RuthAnne with the place setting full of food that had been saved for Pyper. A tumbler of milk completed the meal. "Thank you, Ruthie." Pyper dazzled RuthAnne with a smile, then looked at Amy. "Las' night, when we said g'night, she said I could call her Ruthie."

The adults exchanged smiles, and Pyper sat down on one of the big, padded wicker chairs; setting her plate on the table in front of it, she dug in.

"Mommy, can I help with my diggin' tools Tyler got me?" She asked the question while munching a mouth full of toast and bacon.

"Tell you what. Your mama and I are gonna call it quits on the gardening for now, so we can all go have fun. Wanna give me some help tomorrow morning?"

Pyper downed some milk that left a white mustache on her upper lip. "Mm-hmm. I want to."

"Great. I appreciate that." Tyler stretched his back, then stood and trotted up the stairs. "I'm gonna change real quick, then we can head out. I want to show you some of the places I love here in Tennessee."

Pyper didn't say anything when he passed, but she watched him with careful intensity. When he was gone, Pyper returned to her breakfast. "He's bein' real fun, Mommy. Like when we were at home."

The words were kind, the tone, though, was just this side of doubtful. Amy figured it out. Pyper was waiting for Tyler to betray that fledgling bit of trust and growing connection. How could that be helped, after all? How could Pyper continue to refuse such a consistent, tenderhearted man?

Again, an answer came to Amy, whispering through her soul like an answer from God. *Time. Give it time.*

❧

"Do you like waterfalls, Pyper?" Tyler asked. They were just over an hour outside of Franklin, the top down on his Mustang, the warm air, blue sky, and sunshine filling Amy's senses.

"I never saw one up close before." From her spot in the back seat, Pyper watched the world zip by. Amy noticed the way her daughter took everything in: the hills, the horses, the farms and homes, the cows that made her exclaim and giggle.

Tyler turned off a hilly, two-lane highway that snaked through an unspoiled, quiet area. He parked in front of a simple metal barricade, next to a hand-lettered sign that read: *Rutledge Falls*. "Well, let's take care of that right now. Follow me, ladies."

The tumble and crash of water echoed around them as they scrabbled down a narrow gravel and grass pathway. They clung to sturdy tree trunks and stepped carefully over the stones and bramble that covered the uneven terrain. After descending as far as they could, Pyper stopped in her tracks and tugged hard on Amy's hand. "Mommy! Look at it! Look at it!"

Their hike ended at a stunning view of a four-tiered, sixty-foot cascade of mountain water that sang through the air like ancient music. The sparkling flow tumbled and sprayed into a wide pool far below that rippled with life. Tyler held Amy's other hand; the three-way connection left her elated as they stood on a wide rock ledge, watching the never-ending cascade. "I know! Isn't it gorgeous?"

"I remember once, a few years ago, they filmed a movie out here," Tyler informed. "There were film crews swarming this place just like the ants on that ant hill over there." He pointed at a nearby mound of earth teeming with insects and Pyper propped her hands on her knees, bending promptly to investigate.

Tyler continued. "I remember watching the movie afterwards. The scene they filmed here was all about this group of kids having a fun day in the summertime, diving into that pool of water down there by swinging on ropes, and—"

"Oh, now you've done it," Amy muttered in a teasing way, already knowing what was coming as the result of Tyler's added detail about Rutledge Falls.

First came a squeal that launched a family of birds from a nearby tree with flapping wing noise and irritated squawks. "I wanna rope swing! I wanna rope swing! Where are they? Can I go? Can I swing? Mommy, did we bring my floaty vest?"

Amy laughed. "Way to step into that one, Tyler."

Pyper bounced around, searching desperately for a rope swing, and the means by which to get to the base of the waterfall far below. "I had no idea," he muttered back. Tyler blinked hard, and then addressed Pyper. "There's no rope to swing on, sugar beet. Sorry. They only did that for the movie, with cranes and hoists and stuff. To be honest, it's a tough proposition for even trained hikers to get to the bottom."

Pyper frowned, but wandered to the edge of the outcropping, looking down at the bubbling, gurgling water. Wearing a slight frown, she studied the waterfall, then its emerald colored reservoir, with longing. "What a bummer."

Tyler gave Amy a sardonic look. "See what Hollywood does? Builds things up and then dashes 'em against stones."

Amy giggled at that verdict.

He refocused on Pyper. "The next place we're going to, Fall Creek Falls, has a beautiful waterfall, too, and that one we can actually see from the bottom."

Appeased, Pyper's excitement returned. "Cool!"

"Nice save." Amy whispered the compliment, more than happy to keep her hand snug in his.

"I'm learning on the fly."

❧

Fall Creek Falls was everything Tyler promised: lush, unspoiled and radiant with life. When they reached the base of the falls, Amy edged her rucksack off her shoulder and unzipped it in a hurry, not wanting the inspiration or the play of light and color to escape her. She lifted out her camera and slid the strap into place, beginning to chronicle the nature display. Water burst, tumbled and spilled. The sweet aroma of brightly colored flowers combined pleasingly with the heavier musk of damp earth. Rocks, sun, and field unified into a view that left her breathless. Crouching, she framed a gorgeous shot of Pyper, who stood in ankle-deep grass surrounded by a sea of bell-shaped purple flowers that were nestled into the body of thick, green leaves. Water glistened and flashed, the spray shooting off rainbows as it tumbled over gleaming black ledges of Chattanooga shale.

In sun-drenched profile, Pyper's hair tossed softly in the wind, her eyes cast upward in wonder as she studied the waterfall. The sky was a perfect, stark blue above her; thick, leaf-laden tree branches textured the shot.

Amy clicked away, losing herself, moving from

spot to spot to capture moments, freeze memories and images into a place she could revisit over and over again. Creating shot after shot, she couldn't stop smiling. Photography was such a joy. Photography filled a calling in her soul and lifted her up.

The meadow was a riot of colorful wildflowers and Pyper set about playing in the middle of it all. Amy crouched low once more, framing. Not satisfied, she laid flat on her stomach, capturing images of her daughter as Pyper stripped off her sandals and dipped her feet in the pool of water that crested nearby. Then, Amy laid on her back and lifted up just a bit, executing a shot of Tyler, who stood not far away, enjoying Pyper's playful antics as well. His tall, lean frame blocked the sun from invading the picture. The overall effect was like rays of light bursting to life all around his darkened silhouette.

She lowered her camera slowly, consumed by him. Suddenly, all she could think about was capturing him somehow; she wanted to retain the perfect beauty of this time together to help comfort her in the empty days to come. Without him. After all, this idyllic week would have to come to an end...and that thought caused her throat to swell tight with a sharp stab of pain.

Tyler squatted, taking in their surroundings with a contented expression. He brushed his open hand against the carpet of purple flowers. She couldn't quell her response to the image; she lifted the camera and reeled off a few more pictures. He turned his head, to look at her, and his quirk of a smile left her aching to capture it forever. She fought against being so blatant about photographing him, but in the end, she couldn't resist. The shots came to life in digital form, touching her heart as surely as the touch of his hand in hers.

Tyler joined her, offering up a trio of the tiny purple flowers she had been admiring. "You seem to be in your element."

Amy accepted them happily, and tilted her head to look into his eyes. "Thanks for these. And, believe me, I'm thinking the same thing."

"Good." The emphasis he placed on that word made heat flow to her cheeks in a subtle reaction of pleasure. His focus remained relentless, intent, and compelling. Amy sniffed at the blooms, enjoying the sweet, delicate perfume. "They're Virginia bluebells."

"They're gorgeous." In secret, Amy tingled, already planning to add these tiny flowers to the hyacinths he had given her back in Michigan, the ones which were now pressed carefully into the pages of her Pennsylvania mission photo album.

"Now, I want you to do me a favor."

"OK."

Tyler slid a fingertip beneath the thick strap of the camera. He lifted it up and over Amy's head, taking possession. "Look at everything again. Take it in. Only, this time, without the filter, without the buffer of a lens. With nothing but the gratitude and joy I've seen in your eyes all morning. Take it in, Amy. It's God's gift."

Dumfounded, she considered his request, and then, she obeyed. Propping back on her hands, she settled comfortably. Utterly at rest, Amy took in the scent of damp earth, the rough texture of twigs contrasted against the softness of the green leaves of ground cover that pressed against her palm. The petals and deep green leaves burst into life all around. Water crashed. Birds cawed. Subtle moisture, an after-spray from the waterfall, touched her cheeks, her neck, and arms left bare by a sleeveless blouse. Still, Amy couldn't help but think of her surroundings in terms of pictures, framing shot after gorgeous shot in her mind. Memories. Each image was a memory she didn't want to lose to the elusive, swirling fog of time. And distance.

Nevertheless, a thrill of delight worked through her. Pure happiness took over with as much power as the waterfall that formed a down rush just a few yards away. Tyler was right. This was truly God's gift.

So, she revealed herself in response to the exercise he imposed. "It's not that I don't *see* my world, or appreciate it when I'm taking pictures."

Seated next to her, Tyler pulled up a leg and crooked an arm around it. He nodded in agreement, waiting on more.

"Maybe it's protective—a bit of a hiding place— but overall, it's just that pictures are precious to me. They forever capture a moment that can never, ever be replicated. They're tangible pieces of the lives we've lived."

A life Mark had destroyed with a sledgehammer. Amy refused to dwell on that fact for long, though. After all, she had Pyper. Always, always her beloved daughter.

Amy closed her eyes, face lifted to the sun. "I know it sounds selfish and even a bit simplistic, and maybe it's not even a good way of coping, but something about my photography helps me grasp anew the fact that I won't ever be left that desolate again, that abandoned."

"Perfectly natural, human reaction. Just remember one very vital component to those emotions you're feeling."

"What's that?"

"You've never, ever been abandoned. Not by God most especially, and not by the friends and family God placed in your pathway—and Pyper's."

Amy heard the familiar sound of shutter clicks, and the subtle crunch of Tyler's feet as he moved quietly around her, taking pictures. Amy's revelry ended. She looked up at him with a smile not meant for the camera, or pictures, but instead reflecting sheer gratitude for the words he had spoken.

"Hey, Pyper," Tyler called, "c'mere to your mama."

Pyper nodded and ran to where Amy sat. Spontaneously she threw her arms around Amy's neck. Cheek to cheek they looked at Tyler with wide happy smiles as he clicked his own series of shots.

But Amy knew the picture she wanted the most, and she was determined not to let the moment pass without the acknowledgment of something precious and special that she wanted to be able to call upon forevermore. "Wait. I've got a timer setting, and a mini tripod. Let's do a shot of the three of us."

Amy set up the camera on a nearby tree stump and she blocked out a fun shot of the three of them laying on their stomachs, looking up at the camera. They lined up—Tyler, then Amy, then Pyper with their chins propped on their hands. The timer counted down, and Tyler's words came back to her, hugely magnified by the wants of her heart:

You've never, ever been abandoned. Not by God most especially, and not by the friends and family God placed in your pathway—and Pyper's.

The truth of that statement resounded through her

spirit for long hours after their return home from Fall Creek Falls.

13

Tyler kept Pyper in his peripheral vision while he worked in the yard. She played with the bag of gardening toys he'd picked up for her last week at a local dime store—for all of fifteen minutes. Then, she'd returned to the house and came back to their spot in the yard, carrying the sparkly kickball he had also acquired for her visit.

At present, she blasted the ball through the yard, chased it, then let loose with follow-up kicks, and giggles. Amy was out grocery shopping with RuthAnne, and so far, Pyper had seemed pretty comfortable to be left alone with him. It helped, though, that Amy promised to be gone only for a short time—a half hour to forty-five minutes at the most. It also helped that Pyper had something to do, outside, in wide-open spaces.

Tyler's bit of yard maintenance was nearly finished, and he loved the results. Yeah, the work was a pain, but no arguing with the polished up results. Pyper went on a mad dash again and Tyler watched, enjoying her increased abandon and childish delight.

He started to dispose of the weeds; that's when Pyper jerked violently in mid-stride to chase the ball. Then, she went perfectly still. She didn't shout; she didn't make a sound. She tumbled to a sitting position, drew up her legs tight and began to rock back and forth. Her eyes sparkled with moisture. Tyler stopped what he was doing, watching as she trembled and rubbed her left leg, her eyes wide with shock, and what he could only assume was some form of pain.

"Sugar beet? You OK?" He started toward her, but she winced away from his approach. Tyler froze. He knelt to her level, soft grass cushioning his knees. He was puzzled, but game to try reaching out to her. "What happened, honey?"

Her eyes brimmed. Tears trickled over, and her chin quaked. She didn't look at him. Instead, she stared at her leg where he noticed an angry, blooming welt of red. "I won't cry." The trembles increased. "I promise. I won't. I'll be very, very quiet." She whispered the mantra to herself, not Tyler, still clutching at her leg, curling in on herself.

The poor thing had been stung on the leg by a bee, and she trembled more from fear than pain, backing away from him in meek retreat. Tyler didn't need extra reasons to detest the emotional havoc Mark Samuels had wreaked, but this one skyrocketed to the top of his list.

"Pyper, can you let me help?"

"No. S'okay. I'm fine."

Once more, the words were a whisper. She was leagues away from fine, and he knew it. She remained tightly crouched, the angry-looking bite her only focus. Soft hiccups and choked sobs accompanied Pyper's now rolling tears.

Tyler remained squatted and steady, respecting her appointed measure of distance. Likely the freshly injected venom sang hot through her calf. He tried once more. "I can help, Pyper. I can make the pain go away. Please trust me. I'd be happy to help take care of you."

She looked up at him hesitantly, through glittering, watery eyes. "Mommy's not here, an' it really, really hurts. I'll be good if you help me, Tyler. I promise I will. You won't have to be mad at me like Daddy. I won't cry or make sad noises." She eyed the bee sting and rocked back and forth. "I'll be very, very quiet," she whispered.

Rage simmered deep in his blood, rage toward a man he'd gladly throttle—but he knew that reaction was instinctive, rather than Christian. Pyper was the only one who mattered right now, and Tyler determined to use this episode to show Pyper a different pattern of male behavior.

He moved closer, taking his time. "Did you get stung by a bee?" he asked gently.

Pyper dissolved. She nodded emphatically, reached up for him and held on tight, sobbing against him. "I got stunged!"

"Honey, I'm so sorry. I've been stung many times before, and it hurts so bad. I understand just how you feel. You don't have to hold back around me. I don't mind tears, and I don't mind sad noises. Honest."

For a long, soothing moment, he just held her tight, right there in the cool, damp grass, cradling her close, rocking just a bit. Pyper rested, content and at ease, relaxing in steady increments. Once she calmed, he took her hand in his and helped her to stand.

"Come on, Pyper. I've got a lotion that will cool the pain away, and we can get the stinger out. Once we do you'll feel lots better."

Despite wobbly legs, she followed him, keeping her hand tucked in his. She looked up at him with a mix of expectation, hope, and uncertainty. *Lord,* he petitioned with urgency, *let me handle this right. Help me assure this precious little girl, and help me show her Your loving care.*

"Let's go to the bathroom." He directed her inside. "I've got cotton balls and calamine lotion that'll fix you up just fine."

Pyper nodded. She sat on the commode and after retrieving a few necessities from the medicine cabinet, Tyler knelt in front of her, lifting her leg by the calf. "You're one brave young lady." He pushed up the hem of her Capri-style jeans. She went taut watching him uncap the calamine lotion and tip the bottle until a dab of it colored the cotton ball. He stopped, and looked deliberately into her wide, scared eyes. "It's going to feel cold. That's all."

She rolled her lips in and winced as he applied the medication, but then she relaxed, and stared at her leg in wonder. "It's sorta like a ice cube. It's workin' I think."

The harder part was coming. "I need to try to get the stinger out. While I do that, know what we can do?"

"What?"

"Sing a song. What's your favorite?"

She shrugged. Her hair tossed against her shoulders with the motion. "What do you like to sing when you're scared?" Her question was spoken in a tentative voice, as though she didn't want to be irritating, or weak. *God,* he prayed, *this little girl is such an angel.*

While they talked, and decided to sing their A-B-C's, Tyler kept her attention away from the fact that he squeezed the red welt; that he gently worked at the tip of the stinger's exposed end until it slid free. She flinched at one point, when he had to squeeze her skin pretty tight, but at least he didn't end up needing to use tweezers. Just seeing the instrument might have terrified her. He applied another dab of calamine to the wound, wanting to soothe and heal anything he had freshly exposed. A Band-aid later, she was ready for action once again.

"I wanna see it," Pyper said, taking him by complete surprise.

"See what, sugar beet?"

"The stinger thingy."

He had set it on the sink for the time being, intending to wipe things down and toss it into the trash once Pyper was taken care of. He gave her a grin, because she looked a whole lot braver and happy now that they had achieved crisis containment. "Really? You do?"

"Mm-hmm."

Tyler slid the miniscule black stinger into the palm of his hand and held it out for her inspection. In fact, they both bent over it. Tyler imagined they looked like a pair of scientists on the brink of some world-altering discovery.

"Sheesh," she muttered.

"Sheesh what?"

"Sheesh that stupid tiny thing hurt me. How'd it *do* that?"

They left the bathroom behind, and Tyler launched into a child-friendly dissertation on bee stings and venom. Without any encouragement on Tyler's part, Pyper slipped her hand into his and looked up at him with a beauteous smile.

Music played through his heart with a joy that was absolute. That's probably what inspired another idea.

"Know what I want to do now?"

"What's that, Tyler?" She was openly and completely adoring now. Tyler wanted to rejoice— laugh, shout and dance.

"I want to teach you the most fun song ever to be played on the piano."

"Really?" Her steps stalled. Her eyes went big, like clear blue saucers. "You'd let me actually play your piano? Touch the keys 'n stuff? I'd be so, so careful!"

"Sure I would. Piano's need to be respected, but they need to be played, too. After all, that's the only way they make music."

"An'…an' you'd let me?" Her hero worship was now blatant.

"Come on over here, sugar beet. I'm gonna teach you how to play Chopsticks."

"I love that song!"

Happy moments passed—with plunked piano keys, laughter and the two of them cuddled side by side on the bench of Tyler's piano. She was pretty good, too, at catching on to rhythms and melodies. Focused and determined, this bright little girl picked up on Tyler's instructions with ease.

Soon enough, activity in the entryway of the great room caught Tyler's attention. That's when he saw Amy come through the door, grocery sacks in tow, watching the vignette from a spot just to their right. RuthAnne followed close behind. Amy stood there for a moment, cataloguing the scene, and the look on her face touched Tyler's heart. Surprise, disbelief, love—for Pyper, and for him—it was all right there in her cobalt eyes.

"Hey, baby," she addressed Pyper, setting the sacks on the floor at her feet. "You enjoying a piano lesson from Tyler?"

Music forgotten, Pyper charged into her mother's waiting arms. "I got stunged, Mommy!" She backed away just far enough to hold out her leg and point at the bandage. "An' he had to give me special lotion, and we looked at the stinger, and we sang, and then he taught me piano music. Chopsticks. He says it's the best song ever for the piano, and I think he's totally, totally right."

Not once did Tyler relinquish his visual hold on Amy. RuthAnne moved past, off to the kitchen with her own stash of food, but Amy riveted him. "I treated it with some calamine to take away the sting. It's a little swollen, but I don't think she's allergic or anything. She's been a champ. I'm real proud of her."

Pyper just glowed, her smile bouncing from him, to Amy, as she swayed happily from side to side.

Amy remained still, looking at Tyler. RuthAnne, seeming to realize the groceries Amy carried in weren't about to walk into the kitchen by themselves, lifted them up and slipped quietly away once more. Tyler noticed all this on one level, but on another, he couldn't help but wonder about one very important thing. He wished he knew what Amy was thinking. And he could only pray it was something positive, because at the moment, she looked shell-shocked.

☙❧

Tyler kept his thoughts to himself until later. That evening, he peeked through the front screen door and discovered Amy relaxing on the porch, swinging gently in her favorite seat as night rode in. A night filled by the sparkling dance of fireflies.

He left his warmly lit home behind, taking quiet steps onto the porch just in time to watch Amy stretch her arms over her head, pulling her body into a long, languorous line. She crossed her ankles as she leaned back against the plush cushions of the swing once more and issued a happy sigh. She, too, watched the lighting bug display. The insects floated throughout the yard, sparking and fading, sparking and fading.

Tyler settled next to her carefully, not wanting to disturb her, yet at the same time wanting to be close. "You seem rested. Relaxed."

Amy looked at him with a soft curve to her lips that swept against his senses. "I have to tell you, I haven't felt this good in over a year. I feel..." she stumbled over word choices. "I feel..." She came up dry again.

"Safe?"

"Yeah. That's part of it."

"Content?"

Her skin went flush with a rise in color he detected even under the bath of yellow-gold light from the hanging light above them. "You could say that, too."

He chuckled lightly and settled his arm along the back of the swing. Nudging the wooden floorboards at his feet, Tyler set the swing into motion.

"It's just that, my life is kind of a sun up 'til sundown marathon session. Being able to rest feels really good."

He watched her intently, prompting her without words.

"I'm not complaining. Not in the least. If I didn't have the marathon session, I wouldn't have Pyp. She gives me so much joy that I couldn't, and wouldn't, trade a single teardrop or a single exhausted moment with her."

Amy closed her eyes and breathed in deep. The rise and fall of her chest told him clearly that she soaked up this moment and captured it in her system. He longed for that for her. He wanted God's love, and peace to flow and soothe— thereby healing an ages-old wound.

But Tyler didn't press; he was content to let her rest, and savor the silence. He knew her well enough— and trusted the strength of their relationship enough— to allow her to unwind and reveal herself at her own pace.

For the time being, Tyler tipped his head back and relaxed into the evening as well, smiling to himself as the realization occurred that she wasn't the only one basking in contentment right now.

The screen door squeaked and banged. Small, fast-moving feet padded across the porch, disappearing into the soft grass just beyond the porch. Next to him, Amy chuckled. She didn't even open her eyes. "This has got to be a small taste of heaven."

Tyler rejoiced in the way she simply surrendered herself, and her daughter, to a gorgeous spring night in the south.

"Mommy! Mommy, look!" Pyper's none-too-subtle summons jarred Amy to attention, but she smiled at the reason for the interruption.

Tyler followed her line of sight. Pyper had spotted the darting, flashing fireflies.

Excitement gone, Pyper suddenly went unnaturally still. She turned toward them fast, brows knit tight. Her alarm was plain to see, despite the lengthening shadows and the encroaching darkness of night. "Are they good bugs or bad bugs?"

"Those are good bugs, Pyper. They're fireflies, and they won't sting you," Tyler reassured her. Down here, we call 'em lightning bugs, too. They just light up, and float around and play. In fact, they're a lot like *you*, sugar beet."

Relaxed now, Pyper giggled. She held her arms wide, playing and dashing, trying to touch the insects. Framed in the rippling grass of the dusk-shadowed yard; her face shone as brightly as the bevy of lighting bugs that floated through the air all around her.

"I've got a mason jar or two." Tyler made ready to stand. "Want to catch yourself a couple of 'em?"

Pyper stopped on a dime. "Oh, no, Tyler. *No*." She shook her head, blonde curls shaking and bouncing.

The answer took Tyler by surprise. "Why's that?"

"'Cause then they wouldn't be happy anymore." Her face was so sad. So empathetic. "I just want to watch them. Right here." For emphasis she pointed at the yard in a gesture of hard punctuation. "This is where they belong. They're so pretty! I love them!"

"Know what? You're absolutely right." Tyler leaned close, curved his arm around Amy's shoulders. "Do you have *any* idea at all what a wonderful child you've raised?"

Following a lengthy look into his eyes—one he took in with deliberate, steady calm— Amy was the one who toed the floorboards to initiate a gentle swinging motion. Tyler enjoyed the gentle sway, the comfortable squeak of the chunky metal chains.

"Thanks. She owns my heart." Her voice was husky. "We're a team—it's me and her taking on the world, that's for sure." She took a breath and turned toward him. "And thanks for the way you stepped in and helped Pyper this morning. That *episode* was tough on her, in a number of ways. You scored a big round of points in the trust department, and that means the world to me."

"She was scared to death." And so different from Pyper in the here and now. Presently she squealed with delight and raced across the grounds, oblivious to everything but innocence and the joy to be found in nature.

"More of how you might react than the bee sting."

"I could tell." That statement left them at a small impasse before Tyler moved forward. "It shook you up, too. Beyond her getting stung."

"Yeah, it did." She closed her eyes; tipped her head back. Her rough tone belied the depth of her feelings. "I wish I could play you a movie from the day I left Mark. I keep thinking about it." She spoke quietly—resigned, it seemed. "I want to explain; I want you to know. It's just not an easy thing to verbalize."

Pyper trooped up the stairs, breathing heavy. She flounced into place on the swing—right between them. "I'm gettin' tired."

"You want to go inside?" Amy asked.

Pyper shrugged. "Ruthie is watchin' TV, I think. I hear her favorite game show." Pyper's eyes lit up. "She's teaching me how to crochet!" She launched from the swing. "I'm gonna go in and practice. See ya'!"

In a blaze of motion punctuated by bouncing blonde curls, Pyper pulled open the screen door and ran inside.

For a moment, Tyler went with the silence. After a while, though, he resumed their conversation, unable to fathom the nightmare Amy, and Pyper, had lived through. "I'm gonna be real direct right now." He waited, searching her face until he was sure he had her acceptance.

Amy nodded hesitantly.

He reached down just far enough to stroke her shoulder, lightly, repeatedly. "What did he do to you? Don't sugar coat it. Don't hide from it, or push it aside. I want to know you again, Amy. All of you. The good stuff and the bad."

Words didn't come; instead, she bowed her head. Her shoulders shook, and it took mere seconds for him to realize she was crying. Breaking down, in fact. Tyler gave her space to shatter, and absorb the unspoken support of his touch, while she reassembled. She drew up her knees and tucked against the side of the swing—like she had the other night. She wiped her cheeks with her hands. Her hair slid against the back of his hand, silky and soft. Lavender scent, the last traces of her perfume, lifted to him.

Instinctively he longed to ease her reaction by offering comfort. But he didn't. Something told him she needed this, desperately.

"Today brought everything back," she said, her voice shaky, her eyes distanced by memories. "It was sunny, and humid and hot. And I carried groceries." She didn't look at him. Instead, she rested her cheek on her knees and stared out at the yard and the sky. Tears glittered, rolling occasionally against her hand, and knees, but she swiped at them. "I came home from the store and he was there. Drunk out of his mind and a bottle of whiskey left open in our living room right next to the ice-filled tumbler he was using. Nice, huh?"

Tyler braced himself. "Where was Pyper?"

"In her room. Being punished by Mark for some random, meaningless reason so she'd be out of his way. She was trapped and terrified in a stuffy, hot bedroom so he could drink, and let his temper build. He had just lost his job so he was in a bad place to begin with, but I reached my breaking point. I just didn't care anymore. I fought against him in ways I never had before. It was like a reflex. Instinct."

He kept his touch rhythmic, his presence steady and open. On the inside, however, he absolutely raged.

"That day, he turned the full brunt of his fury on me. For the first time ever, I shoved right back. Oh, he'd always demean me, and make me feel worthless, but this time, it was physical, and horrible beyond anything I had ever gone through before. He shoved me, he destroyed our kitchen; he shattered a camera he knew I needed for a freelance photography job that weekend. I had dumped out his whiskey. I threw the tumbler in the sink so hard it shattered. That's when he struck me across the face. A blinding backhand. He shoved me again, this time against the edge of a counter so hard I saw stars. He was big, and strong, and he pushed me around like a rag doll when I said I was leaving."

"But Amy, thank God you did. You obviously weren't safe around him any longer."

"True." She drew in a deep breath. "But you see, the leaving was fine by him. The day I left, all he cared about was keeping me away from Pyper. Because he could. Because he knew I was out of my mind with worry and fear for her. Because he was stronger. At one point, he deliberately blocked me from Pyper's room. When he was finished toying with me, he just pushed me out the front door of our home and dead-bolted it."

Without a thing to her name. Tyler's stomach

clenched. He was sickened, but for the sake of Amy's chance at openness and healing, he swallowed back the bile. "You got her, though. How?"

Only then did she turn her head to look at him. She sniffled and blinked tiredly. "I pulled her out of her bedroom window after I tore the screen away."

The queasiness threatened to overwhelm.

She moistened her lips, and she sighed. "I left Pyper alone with him too often, and that was wrong. I see that now. But, I was so eager to embrace anything, like my freelance work, that would keep me away from him. He married me out of pity because I was pregnant, and at first he was tolerant. But after a while, even that token piece of emotion vanished. Bitterness grew, and instead of love, a sense of injustice filled him up."

She began to cry again; for the second time, Tyler didn't halt the flow. He wanted her to let go of a gut-wrenching past.

"Mark never looked at Pyper and saw our gorgeous, precocious little girl. Instead, he saw obligation and an unwanted commitment that came along way too soon in his picture-perfect life. Our marriage and Pyper's arrival crimped his ambitions, and his dreams, without any kind of warning."

"Making love is a warning, Amy. He can't plead ignorance on that count."

"And neither can I."

Tyler had to cede the point, much as it tore him up inside to think of her with anyone else but him. Still, he hadn't meant for the statement to hurt her.

"That's why I stayed with him for so long. I was in it right along with him, but I believed everything would work out. That happiness would happen."

"Amy." He spoke her name like a command. As intended, the tone re-centered her focus. "The big difference here—and I hope you listen to me carefully when I say this—is that no matter what the circumstance, you honored your marriage as best you could, and while he neglected Pyper, you never, ever did. Don't buy into the whole he-got-mad-at-me-for-getting-pregnant argument. It doesn't wash, honey. If he realized what he had, if he took care of the treasures he was given—namely you and Pyper—there's no way on earth he could be so filled with anger and bitterness, unplanned pregnancy or not."

Her gaze trained on his. "I feel like a failure, Tyler. I failed at the most important relationship we're called to create."

"Are you taking responsibility for what Mark did to you? And to Pyper? Because if you are, you need to adjust your thinking. Seriously."

Her lips curved; she gave him a wry look. "That's almost exactly what Kiara said to me before I left." She shrugged, and blew out a puff of air. "The statement rings with truth, but somehow, no matter how hard I try, it refuses to sink into my mind, and my heart."

He couldn't stand being distant from her any longer. Tyler slid his arm against her shoulders and drew her to his side, nuzzling her hair, savoring its silky texture against his cheek, and lips. "Keep trying. Like everyone else, you're a beautiful work in progress."

"I *wanted* it to work. It was *supposed* to work. It *should* have worked. What does it say to my level of commitment that I walked away?"

"That you had to maintain your welfare, and that of your daughter."

"To a degree, sure. But, how could I ever expect a man to have faith in me, and believe in my Christian convictions? Could you ever trust me, Tyler? *Really* trust me?"

He paused, and looked her straight in the eyes. "I already do."

Amy cleared her throat and shifted, relaxing against him completely. The feel of her body next to his became the completion of a season in his life that would forever revolve around Amy Maxwell. Darkness deepened, drawing in around them like a cocoon, seeping into the atmosphere with a sense of velvet intimacy. Tyler stretched his legs, nudging the swing again to maintain their motion.

Amy took in a deep, stilling breath. "You know what I keep thinking, ever since the concert? I keep thinking about how much I wish I had made different choices; that I had been smart enough to realize your worth instead of focusing on Mark with all the narrow-eyed, single-mindedness I possessed back then. Now I feel broken. I feel like such a failure...not just for the divorce, but for not seeing people as they really are. I relied on my own perceptions, and images. That was *such* a huge mistake. You and Mark are a perfect case in point. Look at what I could have had with you."

With that, the words were finally out in the open, heartbreaking, but a fissured pathway to everything that might be re-found. The words provided hope, in a chipped, but sturdy bottle. Tyler reached for her hand and held it tight. "I have a better idea. Don't look at what you could have had. Look at where you're at now. Let's look at the chance we're being given. After all, that's the whole reason I asked you to come here. And keep something else in mind."

She searched his eyes. "What's that?"

He thought about Pyper, and the breakthroughs he had made with Amy's daughter today. "Sometimes it takes the pain of a bee sting to bring about a world full of change, and a heart that's finally ready for happiness."

14

Slowly, Amy climbed the stairs to her bedroom; Pyper had just disappeared into the bathroom to change into her pajamas and brush her teeth. Amy's mind still spun at Tyler's words. All day he had laid out tantalizing breadcrumbs of come-toward-me emotions she found impossible to refuse. Since high school, his heart had belonged to her alone. Over the span of five long years apart, his feelings remained steadfast and true. Meanwhile, Amy's had taken time to emerge. It was a tentative process, but no less definite.

Sometimes it takes the pain of a bee sting to bring about a heart ready for happiness.

Do you have any idea at all what a wonderful child you've raised?

Tyler's words soaked into her soul and found rich, nourishing soil. Under his influence, her heart moved dangerously close to a complete meltdown. She gave over to him—unable to help it—and furthermore, she didn't even want to stem the tide.

A heavy gust of wind whistled through the window, billowing the curtains, smelling vaguely of rain. Amy turned, glancing outside. A late-night thunderstorm had been forecast, but up to now, the weather had held. A rumble of thunder sounded in the distance.

Amy waited for her turn in the bathroom, pulling out lightweight fleece pajamas and preparing supplies. Her mind refused to rest as she hunted for a hairbrush, her toothbrush and some face cleanser. An ache of wanting pierced her heart. She closed her eyes and saw nothing but Tyler. The ache uncurled through her chest, prompting a mix of love and reverence toward the image now held in her heart of a man who was a devoted, tender Christian full of a giving spirit. She kept her eyes closed, going still as his handsome features swirled into even richer clarity, drawing her further into a world she hadn't dared to hope for, or dream of, until now.

She could almost taste him—feel him—in the escalating wind that moved through the room. Rolls of thunder rumbled, echoing upward through the valley in a somber vibration that literally moved against the house. Amy sat on the bed and promptly sank against its plush surface, stretching out while she continued to do battle against old demons while trying so hard to embrace new angels.

The bedroom door banged open, and Pyper entered the room at a run, charging toward the bed with happy gusto.

"Mama, I heard thunder! We're gonna have a storm! And I get to not be scared 'cause you'll be with me!"

Was it just Amy's imagination, or was Pyper picking up a southern twang after less than a week? The thought left her to grin while she grabbed for her daughter. "You bet I will. Come here, snug-a-bug."

Amy pulled her squirmy, giggling daughter onto the down comforter of the bed. They laid side by side, cushioned by feathery softness, both of them happy, for the time being, to simply look into one another's eyes and rest in contentment. Amy's mind slowly eased as rain came down in a soft downpour that played like a lullaby to her soul.

Yes, this whole contentment thing was contagious. It was addictive. Beautiful and beneficial. For the first time in ages, Pyper looked and acted as innocent and carefree as any five-year-old should. That fact applied a necessary balm to the long-standing scar across Amy's spirit.

All of a sudden, Pyper smiled big, and cupped her hand against Amy's cheek in a way that she always did when she simply wanted to connect and touch her mother, heart to heart. Her other hand was presently tucked beneath her chin.

"You like Tyler, huh, Mommy?"

"Yes. Yes I do."

The smile grew even bigger. "A really lot?" Pyper's eyes twinkled, alive with playful mischief—and the first signs of a little girl beginning to recognize matters of the heart. No sense hiding from the most important person in her life. That was another life-lesson Amy had learned the hard way.

"Yeah, Pyper. A really lot."

Pyper blinked a few times, her long, inky lashes fluttering a bit tiredly over eyes of palest, most luminous blue. "Me, too, Mommy." Pyper yawned, her eyes closing as she moved in close. Amy wrapped her arms tight around her daughter who drifted promptly to sleep.

Conversely, Amy came to life. Despite every doubt and fear, her heart began to race, beating in time to an influx of battered but stalwart hope.

❧⧉

Pyper was down for the count, oblivious to the continuous strobes of lightning and the aftershocks of crackling energy that rippled through the air. Rain intensified; the rooftop drumbeat a strong and steady pound. Amy glanced at the bedside clock and groaned softly when she registered the time. At just after midnight, she was nowhere near the realm of sleep. The hissing voices of doubt kept crowding in.

Old demons, or new angels—what's it going to be, Maxwell?

Tyler deserves better than the damaged spirit you present, doesn't he? And what about Pyper? Amy, you can't possibly consider *pulling her into yet another new version of life, in a place that will remove her from everything, and everyone, that's familiar. Get a grip on this situation before it runs you over!*

Then, a new thought crept in, pushing more disruptive ripples against her psyche: she hadn't heard from Mark in ages—not since the divorce—but perhaps all it would take to make a desperate man reemerge is finding out his ex-wife and daughter were now an important part of Tyler Brock's life. A media push of interest and excitement, especially if they emerged as a couple, would put her past under intense scrutiny. Not only would her battles with abuse and an alcoholic husband come to the fore, they would be broadcast everywhere. How would that affect Pyper? What if Mark picked up on the idea of trying to stake an exploitive claim on their daughter?

That's why we pray.

The simple phrase she had exchanged with Tyler rolled through her troubled mind. Amy tried hard to find the words; all that came was a sense of devastation. A reconciliation of her life with Tyler's refused to materialize, no matter how hard she petitioned God.

There was just no way to remain in this idyllic world and relationship. No way at all.

Giving up on sleep that refused to come, Amy slipped out of bed as carefully as possible. She padded across the floor and looked outside for a moment, wondering what she could do to doze off and leave all that negativity behind.

She had never tried the warm-milk antidote, but decided to give it a go. She moved with light steps down the darkened stairwell, tip-toeing her way to the kitchen. By now, she was familiar enough with the layout to pull open a lower cabinet door and fish out a small saucepan. Next, she lifted a jug of milk from the refrigerator and poured.

Amy lit the burner beneath the pan.

"Storm keeping ya up?"

She gasped and nearly upended the saucepan. She turned fast, instantly nervous, and took a hard swallow at the vision before her. Sleep-tousled hair, a rumpled, plain white t-shirt and black sweats were an absurdly adorable combination on Tyler. He yawned, walking into the kitchen nonplussed…and barefoot.

Amy's muscles went tight; need slid into place with unraveling speed and efficiency. She fumbled with the cap of the milk jug and cleared her throat when she brushed slowly past Tyler to return it to the fridge. But then, his arrival, and what might be behind it, prompted her to put her sensual cravings into simmer mode rather than boil. "Are you having trouble sleeping, too? Would you like me to make you some?"

Tyler gave a small shake of his head. "Nah. Thanks, though. You OK?"

"Yeah. Just a little restless I guess. Couldn't quite settle for some reason."

"My fault, maybe? I didn't mean to rip open your heart tonight. You comfortable enough?"

His earnestness touched her heart, and made her smile when she looked into his eyes. They struck her as being a touch sleep dusted. And he was so cute…

The simmering ratcheted upward again. "I'm fine, don't worry. Sorry if I woke you."

"No problem. I've been sleeping light the last few days." He moved to the spot next to her and peeked into the pot where bubbles began to lift upward and pop.

"Thinking about Kellen's representation offer? Your work?"

He shrugged. "Partly. Mostly it's just…" He shrugged again and the t-shirt bunched and flexed around his shoulders, which were broad and perfectly toned. Amy drifted into that image as he paused. How easily she could imagine the feel of his warm skin, the texture of downy hair and sinew. "Mostly it's you and Pyper. Having the two of you here."

Amy centered back on the conversation in a hurry. "Oh?"

"It's a good thing—a very good thing—but it's–it's complicated."

"How so?" His comments took her aback. Now she wanted answers.

He moved in close enough to rest a hand against her arm and give it a squeeze. "It's important to me. It's like a picture of everything I've wanted for so long.

But it's going to be over within a few days. I don't want it to be. Please—tell me it won't be."

Amy took a breath, lost in his eyes as a breaking point came and went, dealt with by nothing more than the power of her heart.

She found enough courage to remain close to him. "I don't want it to be, either," she whispered. "You didn't want our first kiss to be a kiss goodbye." *It's not goodbye. Not yet.* Amy trembled. "Kiss me, Tyler."

She saw his surprise. Wishing on a hundred dreams, she looked at him with wide, but steady eyes. Waiting.

"This isn't casual for me, Amy. Never has been. Never could be. You understand that, right?"

His warning didn't trouble her at all. Slowly she nodded. Her world blurred at the edges with a delicious warmth and dizziness, with feathers going wild against her senses. "That's why I want it so much. If you do, too, that is…"

Tyler breathed out. He lowered his head until his forehead rested against hers. "Only since I was seventeen years old."

He slid his hand against her neck; not once did his eyes leave hers. Amy took strength from that. He cupped her face so gently, with such soft, reverent care that her eyes fluttered closed, and she sighed. Tyler's lips skimmed softly against her neck, her cheeks, her chin, in a smooth, tantalizing glide. His caress tickled her skin. He continued to nuzzle and seek, and Amy gave a pleasured, almost desperate sound. She could think only of his kiss—*their* kiss.

"Remember," he murmured against her now trembling, waiting mouth, "you asked."

He claimed her lips fully, exploring her in touch

and taste as his fingers slid down her arm. The modest covering of her long sleeved pajama top didn't diminish the warmth, or the tingling. Tyler pulled her snug against him as the kiss continued, blooming amidst a love that had been denied for far too long.

Amy sank against him and gave over to the moment. His lips were supple, sweetly flavored. Desire sang through her bloodstream, but she trusted him implicitly. The truth that she rested within the circle of his arms, her entire universe reduced to Tyler and the dimly illuminated kitchen—their two hearts beating an erratic tattoo—left Amy to soar.

Out of necessity, the moment ended way too quickly. Incrementally Tyler tempered the kiss, reducing the long and lush exploration to soft, sweet repeats of a connection that stirred heat and longing into a heady flow.

Finally, he leaned back, casting her a long look. "That…was *well* worth the wait."

She blushed furiously and looked down, toeing at a seam in the ceramic floor. But suddenly, up rose the Amy of old. She looked into Tyler's eyes head on. "We came close. Once."

Tyler grinned, but the gesture was touched by sadness, and a haunting sense of loss. "Most terrifying sixty-or-so seconds of my life."

She didn't buy into the humor. Instead, she used a soft touch to stroke his chin, then his jaw. "I'm so sorry."

He shook his head, combing his fingers very gently, very slowly through the loose strands of her hair. "For what?"

"For making you doubt that your love, your show of affection, wouldn't be accepted. I wanted you to kiss me that day. Did you know that? Did you sense how much I needed everything you offered? Mostly I'm sorry for all the time I wasted. For how stupid I was in not seeing the truth—that the best thing in the world was right in front of me."

"Honey, do *not* go back down that road, OK?" He leaned a hip against the counter and slid his hand against her arm lightly, automatically. He closed the distance between them once more to nuzzle her cheek for a moment and give her a kiss with a sigh before backing up, and looking her straight in the eyes. "There's one thing I know to be true in my heart: God's timing is perfect. If we'd tried this all those years ago, it may have ended differently. It might not have worked. We weren't the same people back then."

But he was. He truly was the same caring, wide-open person she had always known. Amy glided her fingers through the fall of his hair. "Not much change took place in your case," she murmured. "You were good to the core then, and you've stayed that way."

In the instant that followed, Tyler's eyes clouded, darkening with his own inner turmoil. Amy turned off the heat on the burner and poured milk into a mug to take with her to bed. She knew the pattern of his thoughts without benefit of words. He was in his own quandary—this one of a professional nature, and it required resolution before too long. Tyler Brock, one of the straightest, most forthcoming people she knew, faced heavy temptation—a pathway to mega-success, mega-exposure and perhaps a mega-loss of his soul.

Or not…depending…

After caressing his cheek, Amy lifted up on tiptoe and kissed him once more, taking her time with the gesture. The ready way he answered the summons and held her caused a pulse rush.

"G'night, Tyler," she finally whispered. Regret layered her tone. An intense need had built ever since he entered the kitchen, a need that would only know surcease when she belonged to him in fullness and a mutual, life-giving commitment. Tears stung her eyes.

As if such a thing could ever even happen.

15

The next morning, Tyler rose from bed following a long, invigorating stretch. Outside the bedroom window, a view of the distant mountains greeted him. He looked out, over the curving bowl of a verdant green valley presently blanketed by a thick layer of ghostly white fog. The view never failed to take his breath away. Air-cooled vapors blanketed the base of the mountains, swirling upward and dissipating beneath the rays of a golden sun just rising above the peaks.

After a quick shower, he changed into shorts and a polo shirt. He jogged down the stairs, drawn by an unexpected smell: cooking meat. It seemed RuthAnne was already active in the kitchen. God love her and bless her, he thought with a sincere sense of devotion.

Upon entering the kitchen, however, he came upon a surprise. Dressed in shorts and a t-shirt that were covered by an apron, Amy stood at the stove, fussing over a couple of pots. His heart pumped; a thick, heady thrill worked through him at the natural way she moved through his home, and his life.

She greeted him with a distracted, adorably frazzled glance. Tyler moved in on her from behind and lifted the lid of the largest pot. Steam curled upward, as did the tantalizing aroma of simmering chicken and seasoned sauce. He breathed in appreciatively. "RuthAnne's been busy this morning."

"No. I have." Amy took advantage of his lid retrieval to dump in an array of fresh vegetables—carrots, celery, green pepper, onion, corn, and cubed potatoes.

"Really? This is her classic. How'd you get her to give you the recipe?"

Amy spooned broth over the meat and veggies. She stirred slowly. "I love RuthAnne. She's great, and very generous."

Tyler replaced the lid and Amy set the now-empty strainer in the sink. "I wanted to do something special for you. To say thank you for everything you've done for us. When I explained, she surrendered the recipe."

Her subdued mood troubled him. Amy toweled off her hands and untied the apron she wore so she could pull it over her head and hang it on a nearby wall peg. He thought about her comments from last night and adrenaline spiked through his system, performing a dance that prickled against his arms and rang in his ears. He walked over to the counter and slid a knife from the wooden holder. Armed, he diced up a few more vegetables, preparing cauliflower and broccoli by separating the heads and rinsing them in the strainer.

"Pyper and I have been having a great time with you, Tyler," Amy continued. "To be honest, I don't remember ever feeling as happy and just...good...as I have during the times I've spent with you lately." She lifted the lid again and resumed stirring, occupying herself with unnecessary business. Tyler carried his prepped vegetables to the pot and slid them in while trying not to let his imagination get the best of him. But then, Amy gave a sad sigh. "I don't want to lose this."

"Then we won't." His answer contained a calculated force of conviction and finality. After last night, he didn't want her thinking about goodbye. Not yet. There was still time enough left on the clock to convince her that a conclusion to this week together would—and should—be nothing but temporary. So, he moved ahead with his own thoughts and ideas. "Did you happen to bring anything kinda dressy?" he asked in an offhand manner.

Amy went to the sink and began cleaning dishes. "I brought a dress and a pair of heels. Why?"

"That'll be fine."

She tilted her head, and gave him an expectant look. "Fine for what?"

"Well, see, my record label is throwing a promotional party tomorrow night." Tyler let pleasure run free through his system. He couldn't resist the idea of attending a glitzy function with Amy at his side. He crossed behind her and whisked a baby carrot from the extras that were stacked on a nearby cutting board. "Want to come? It's going to be at the Grand Ballroom of the Hermitage Hotel."

Amy's most immediate response was wide eyes.

"I'd love for you to be there with me. You'll get to see some of my band mates again, and you'll also meet Kellen Rossiter."

"Really?" That piqued her interested, but he detected her disquiet as well. Unless Tyler misread the slight furrow to her brow, and the hesitance in her eyes, Amy seemed a touch intimidated by the idea.

"Kellen will be recruiting. I'm sure I can line up RuthAnne to take care of Pyper for us so we can indulge in a five-star meal beforehand, then some necessary schmoozing and networking. And on

Saturday—"

Amy laughed. "I see there's no rest for the wicked in your world. Is that the point you're trying to make?"

Tyler sighed dramatically. "On Saturday," he tried again, "you and Pyper can spend some time at the recording studio with me. After the way she enjoyed playing on the piano, I think Pyper will go nuts for it, actually."

"No question about that. Sounds like fun."

"I'm putting together a couple of new songs I wrote that I think will be part of the next release. I want to get some preliminary recordings down. The studios are in downtown Nashville, so after we record, we can play tourist."

Amy shook her head, obviously still overwhelmed, but less taut in the shoulders; her answering smile appeared genuine. "OK, I'm officially impressed."

"No need to be. It's just a job."

"Yeah. OK." She spared him a wry look on her way to recheck the bubbling pot.

Tyler grabbed an extra celery stick this time and crunched away. He arched a brow. "So are you in?"

Amy lifted her hands in mock surrender. "Ah…sure. Why not?"

She stepped close. Tyler reached out easily and drew her into the circle of his arms, which tucked neatly around her waist. He rested his cheek against her hair and gave an inner sigh of delight. "Thanks. I'm actually looking forward to it now."

∼∾

The sounds of a creaking floorboard and carpet-cushioned footsteps at the top of the stairs drew Tyler's attention. Paused in the landing, he stood before a picture mirror where he adjusted the knot and fall of a silk tie. He looked up, and could do nothing but stare.

Amy gave him a fast, hesitant look, and then walked slowly down the staircase. She was a vision in delicate, pale blue lace. Lined beneath by fluid, darker satin, the v-necked, knee-length dress moved like it was a part of her. The color drew his focus to her fair, creamy skin, her large blue eyes.

The overall impact left his throat dry and knocked him straight back to those enchanted moments in high school when he had imagined sharing just such a moment with her. Now, like then, his knees went weak.

"I, umm, I hired a driver for tonight. A limo. It's out front. It'll be easier that way." He was babbling. He nearly burst out laughing at the crazy thought that crossed his mind: he somehow felt like he should have gotten her a corsage.

He saw her intimidation return when she tilted her head, and looked up at him almost plaintively. Tyler thought, once more, about the badlands she had traveled in their years apart and the changes life's imprint had left on her formerly free, confident spirit.

"A limo? That's deluxe."

Tyler took her hands in his and gave her arms a gentle shake. "Nah, it's not deluxe, just easier to navigate. There's going to be a lot of traffic out front of The Hermitage." He looked deliberately into her eyes, and did his best to telegraph assurance through a smile. "You OK?"

She nodded, but the gesture was too fast, and she looked away.

"Do me a favor—relax. Relax and enjoy being treated well. Sometimes it's OK to be the belle of the ball, and to me, that's what you'll always be. I want you to have fun tonight."

He touched her cheek to punctuate that statement. Amy had pinned up her hair; a number of tiny, sparkling clips held it in place. Blonde curls swirled and danced around her neck, making him want to reach up—just for a second or two—and twist a satiny strand around his fingertip to enjoy the texture.

Amy smoothed her fingers beneath the lapel of his suit coat. "You look great, by the way."

"Yeah? Thanks, because you wrote the book. I'm just tryin' to keep pace."

Pink color bloomed through her cheeks. Amy glanced into the great room just beyond. There, Pyper was on her stomach, scissor-kicking her legs and watching television. RuthAnne sat in a rocking chair and worked on her cross-stitch pattern that was gradually taking the form of a flower-filled meadow. Once Tyler realized Amy was comfortable and satisfied by the homey scene they would leave behind, he offered his arm. "Are you ready?"

Amy nodded, taking hold and letting him lead the way.

❧⋅❦

Exclamation Point Records had pulled out all the stops for tonight's networking event. Tyler kept a guiding hand on Amy's waist as they joined the crowd that milled through the wide-open space of the Grand Ballroom. During the span of his five years in Nashville, Tyler had never visited the Hermitage

Hotel. The Nashville landmark was impeccable—the definition of elegance and old-world influence. Not a bad underscore to the idea of promoting a Christian music label to the agents, producers, and performers who would help the company grow.

Directing their progress toward the spot where Dave and Rebecca stood, Tyler left Amy in their care while he went to the bar to pick up a pair of soft drinks. He entered the line. While he waited, he nodded at a few people he knew; he smiled into the lenses of a few cameras that flashed and popped. The ballroom was lush and extravagant, featuring ornate ceilings with deep, textured coves punctuated by dark, walnut paneling. Elaborately framed paintings accented the walls.

The line moved forward, and he centered on the people around him once more. That's when he realized Kellen Rossiter stood just ahead, at the head of the queue.

The bartender greeted Kellen with a courteous smile. "What can I get for you, sir?"

"Two tonics with lime, please."

Tumblers were filled promptly. Tyler waited just behind him, but moved close enough to enter Kellen's field of vision and give him a questioning look. "Not a drinker?"

Kellen shrugged. "If I drank at even half the events I'm forced to attend, I'd be out of control, so, I don't drink at all. I like to keep a clear head."

Tyler couldn't help but smile. "Impressive."

"No. Necessary."

"Mm-hmm" Tyler ordered two colas—one for him, one for Amy—but he longed for the snappy spice of his favorite—ginger ale.

Kellen took a generous sip of his beverage, eyeing the crowd. "Nicely done, by the way. Your girlfriend? She's stunning."

"Nothing gets past you, Rossiter," he jabbed lightly, giving his would-be agent a territorial grin. "And keep your distance."

"No problem. I'd never interfere in your potential happiness as a well-grounded Christian recording artist. Given the chance, I could sell the idea of a solidly committed and caring singer by the mile. It's an appealing image. Besides, my wife wouldn't approve."

Tyler was about to take a sip of his drink, but stopped midway. Kellen. Married. The fact added a new dimension to the man. When Kellen lifted his glass again and drank, Tyler considered the second tumbler and took note of the wide, gold wedding band, noticing the ring for the first time. "Is she here?"

"In the same circle as your girlfriend, as a matter of fact. Right over there." Kellen gestured and Tyler took note of a beautiful, petite-framed woman dressed in jewel green. She had softly waved, auburn hair, gentle curves, and the face of an angel.

"Nicely done yourself, Rossiter."

"I'm keenly aware of the fact. Come on over and meet her. Juliet's heard a lot about you. Besides, I'd like to meet this famous photographer and blast from the past of yours."

Tyler gaped. "Honestly. How do you *know* all this stuff?"

Kellen's smile was hard to refuse. "I'm good at my job. I connect dots, do some research, and *voila*...a picture comes to life."

Tyler chuckled. This guy was unique to his experience. *Very* unique. "You never give up, do you?"

"Nope."

They joined their group just in time to hear Dave filling Amy in on the history of the hotel. "...yeah— even presidents come here. Kennedy, Roosevelt, Wilson and Nixon—they've all slept at The Hermitage. Plus, from Al Jolson to Al Capone, all kinds of celebs have stayed here, too."

Tyler stepped into the circle of his friends. "Jolson and Capone. That kinda covers the spectrum of human endeavor, now doesn't it?"

"For better, and for worse." Dave greeted the newcomer to their group with a quirked grin and an arched brow. "Kellen. It's good to see you. I've already decided your wife here doesn't deserve you. You lucked out in the marriage department."

Juliet Rossiter swatted at Dave's arm, but wore a large smile. "Stop it!"

"Tell me something I don't know. It's good to see you, too, Dave. Juliet, here you go, love." He handed his wife her drink, which she accepted with a smile that moved straight from her eyes and into Kellen's. Something in the natural, easy intimacy of their interaction left Tyler compelled, and intrigued.

"Dave's not just a world-class tour manager. He's a history geek, too," Tyler spoke, recapturing the conversation at hand.

"Which is why I love Nashville so much, hot-shot."

Tyler handed Amy her drink. "Amy, meet Kellen Rossiter. Kellen, this is Amy Maxwell."

"Great to meet you, Amy."

"And Amy, Kellen is truly my better half," Juliet interjected, her green eyes sparkling when she looked up at her husband. "I was telling Amy how much I wish I had an eye for imagery and photography like she does. What a wonderful gift."

Amy received Kellen's handshake. "And obviously I'm enjoying getting to know your wife. I understand she's a native to Nashville, like Dave."

Kellen tucked into Juliet's side in an automatic way, wrapping an arm around her waist. "Meanwhile, I followed my heart to the south from California. I'm a Los Angeles transplant."

Paul Jacobs, president of Exclamation Point Records took his position behind a podium on a dais at the front of the room. Conversations came to a standstill. Opening remarks prompted people to move to their seats, each of which were identified by name cards crafted in calligraphy. Gift bags prompted Tyler to lean close to Amy's ear. "Enjoy the swag. I remember at last year's event there was a pretty nice selection of treats."

Kellen and Juliet settled in across from them. Dave and Rebecca arrived as well and sat down. Expansive and oval-shaped, the table they shared featured rose-hued linens, simple bone china, crystal goblets and silver flatware. Tyler took in the details and atmosphere but sat back to listen as formal proceedings began. His attention alternated between Amy, who watched with an expression of subdued awe, and Kellen, who kept his eyes trained on the dais and his arm draped loosely along the back of Juliet's chair.

The agent managed to make his interest known, while at the same time maintaining a comfortable distance.

Media members swarmed at the beginning of the program, snapping pictures at a fast clip. Tyler noticed that Amy tracked the progress of the reporters. She looked bewildered by the degree of attention. As people moved through the room, a number of producers, back-up singers, technicians, and label execs from Exclamation Point stopped by to pay Tyler a quick, though discreet greeting.

Amy leaned close. "I feel like Alice falling down the rabbit hole."

Tyler regarded her intently. The comment didn't resonate with humor. He could tell by her reserved, closed-off posture that she honestly felt like she had entered an alternate universe.

Disquiet over Amy and confusion over Kellen, built as the evening progressed.

∂∞∞

A couple hours later, his thoughts tumbling, Tyler left the fading party behind. He walked into the lobby, waiting for Amy to return from a visit to the restroom. Kellen had made only one overture about representation all night—that joke at the bar about selling Tyler via commitment to a happy relationship. Kellen didn't push; he hadn't hovered. Tyler appreciated those facts, but at the same time, came away perplexed, wondering about the agent's lack of pressure.

Then there was Amy's reaction to the evening. The mood he sensed from her wasn't at all reassuring. She had been warm; she engaged easily when spoken to, but beyond that, she kept to herself, cataloguing the events of the evening in a manner Tyler could only describe as shuttered. He intended to ask her about that.

Beyond the glass doors of the hotel entrance, he

spied a lineup of limousines. A few stray photographers milled about. The glamour of the hotel lobby drew his focus. Italian marble floors, a vaulted ceiling created of stained glass and overstuffed, luxurious furniture all vied for his attention, drawing him into a world he could most definitely admire, but never dive in to with complete abandon. The whole evening had affected him that way. A night of glitz and glamour was one thing; living in the constant glare of a spotlight was quite another, which was a new point to ponder.

As the thought evolved, a conversation nearby earned his interest; one of the voices he heard belonged to Kellen Rossiter.

"Rossie. You're headed out, too?"

Kellen's laugh reached Tyler. Only, the laugh didn't seem warm, or overly humorous. "I hate being called Rossie, which you know full well, Clay."

"Why else do you think I'd use it? You know how it goes—agent to agent nothing delights me like needling the competition."

Tyler stayed out of range for the time being and watched the proceedings. Kellen stood near the entrance of the lobby, chatting with a short, pudgy man who presently chewed on an unlit cigar. In vague terms, Tyler remembered him from the party. Kellen kept an eye on both the ladies' room and the line of cars outside. Waiting for his wife, Tyler assumed. If he recalled correctly, as the party disbursed, Juliet had headed out with Amy.

"Juliet's getting tired and there's no need to overstay my welcome."

"Suppose not, especially since you seem to have achieved your agenda for the night: charming Tyler

Brock. Everybody knows you're after him in a big way. Seems you've made inroads. Have you clinched the deal yet?"

"What *deal*?" Though smooth in tone, Kellen's voice carried with it a slice of tension that spelled danger to Tyler's ears.

"The deal to add Tyler to your client list." Clay's reply was unapologetic and blunt.

"I'd love to represent him, but he's not an agenda item. I came here to check up on Exclamation Point's progress. The label is up and coming. Great portfolio of talent."

Tyler still kept to the side, and away from their immediate notice; his brows pulled together. Kellen's discretion and tact won Tyler's appreciation—especially when Clay continued to push.

"A great portfolio of talent that includes Tyler Brock, right?"

"Yeah. So?"

The simple two-word response resounded with a steely warning. Tyler waited, expectant and on edge.

"Well, I guess I'm just a little curious is all. I mean, why are you hinging yourself on Bible-belt performers, Rossiter?"

"Because the music is good, and the message is even better. Since that equals a win/win situation, sure I'm exploring the genre. What about that equation doesn't make sense to you?"

Kellen's tone was casual, but once again Tyler sensed something just beneath. Something battle-ready and challenging that he could appreciate, and completely relate to.

"Hey, easy on there. Don't be so defensive, I—"

"I'm not being defensive. You're the one who

asked. I'm just straightening out a misguided perception."

Kellen's companion shrugged in a show of magnanimous tolerance. "Whatever, whatever. It's not a bad idea, really, to practice inclusiveness, especially when it comes to the Christian sect."

Tyler bristled at the demeaning comment. He made ready to step forward, and make his presence known.

"What I'm doing isn't about a *sect*." Kellen answered sharply. "I believe in the music, and the artists I'm coming to know."

The words stopped Tyler from interrupting. His footsteps stuttered to a stall.

Again came a shrug from the other guy, this one dismissive. "Gotta give you credit. You've always been ahead of the curve when it comes to pushing trends and pulling in the talent to do it. You've always known what buttons to push, but I have the feeling this will be your first stumble. After all, squeaky clean and righteous? Not sure how great that'll sell these days. Too bland. Not enough intensity and drive to draw in that young, sexy demographic we're all fighting to win."

Kellen's rumbling chuckle drifted through the lobby. "Well, to me, the idea of eternity is pretty intense, and can offer that *demographic* plenty of drive when given the right platform. I'm ready to give Christian music, and its more promising artists, the push they deserve."

Absorbed by the scene, Tyler shook his head and gave a soft snort when he watched Clay sneer in a placating, completely insincere manner. "Good luck with that. Well, there's my car. See you later."

Kellen didn't reply, continuing to wait for Juliet. That's when Tyler finally re-found his footing. He crossed the lobby in a few short strides. "Kellen."

If perturbed by the previous exchange, Kellen didn't show it. He offered a warm smile and a nod. "Hey, Tyler."

Kellen, he now noticed, carried two gift bags, his and Juliet's. Since Tyler did the same for himself and Amy, they shared a grin and looked in the direction of the restrooms.

"Amy and Juliet really hit it off," Tyler said.

"They did. It was a fun night. I'll make sure I say as much to Paul."

"Nice name drop," Tyler teased.

Kellen, still being Kellen, was on the job. Paul was the president of Exclamation Point Records.

Kellen's features went stormy. "You know? Sometimes it's a battle to even try to do what I dream of. I wonder if you understand that. I'm not *after* anything. It's just that I see tremendous potential in you and the other artists here at Exclamation Point. I see potential in the music you create. A potential I'd like to encourage. Paul's a friend, that's all, so I intend to thank him for a nice evening."

Though taken aback by Kellen's strident response, Tyler understood the undercurrent. Kellen's mood obviously stemmed from residual steam that had built up following the previous exchange. "You know what, Kellen? I get that now. I really do." Tyler took note of the skeptical expression Kellen wore, and went serious in a hurry. "That's why I'd like to invite you to a recording session Saturday morning. After that, let's plan to talk for a bit."

Kellen went still, then he nodded, studying Tyler

with knitted brows and narrowed eyes. "I'll be there, but why the generosity?"

"Because you recognize a genre, not a *sect*. Because you recognize the message in the music. I appreciate that." Tyler waited a beat, watching realization dawn in Kellen's eyes. He gave Kellen a knowing grin.

The women joined them, and Tyler tucked his hand into Amy's as she bid the Rossiters goodnight. "Juliet, it was a pleasure to meet you. Kellen, the session is set up for Saturday morning at eleven o'clock. Studio B."

"I'll see you then."

16

Surprisingly enough, it was the swag bag that re-released a floodgate of doubts for Amy. Especially the 14 Karat gold bracelet she had discovered inside, tucked into a black velvet jeweler's box placed artfully amidst sparkling tissue paper. Also included were a myriad of high-end goodies like designer label cosmetics and generous gift cards to apparel stores she normally wouldn't tempt herself by going near, let alone actually patronize. The bracelet now decorated her wrist. Amy touched the simple, shimmering cross that dangled from the chain; it captured the morning sunlight that poured in through a nearby window. She slouched at the small dining table in Tyler's kitchen, lost in thought.

Where is this really headed? Is this nothing more than a week-long voyage down a primrose path leading to a mirage?

Amy's entire being repelled the idea, even as practical logic snaked its way into existence all over again, pushing hard against each of her newfound joys and a tenuous hope for what the future could hold.

Following last night's "A-List" style celebration for Exclamation Point Records, the prospect of media speculation, and a spotlight being shined on the stains of her past, continued to gain traction. Tyler was making headway into both Christian and mainstream recording markets. That was tremendous. And much deserved. But, what would fans, and media members, think of him being involved with a divorcee who coped with life as a single working mom following the end of a marriage marred by both physical abuse and alcoholism? Worse than that, what would the glare of a spotlight mean for an unsuspecting innocent like Pyper?

Additionally, thoughts of Mark crept into the corners of her heart. Would he catch wind of her relationship? Would he reemerge and exert pressure on her, via Pyper, in order to manipulate or extort? Certainly in such a case Tyler would step in, ever a source of strength and support. But Amy didn't want him to have to contend with such an event. He didn't deserve additional pressure and concerns about his image, his work—and his heart.

Gossip-laden headlines—based upon fact or fiction—would not bode well for Tyler and his forward momentum. Plus, constant scrutiny, and the idea of tarnishing Tyler's life in any way, gave Amy a lot to consider.

She didn't doubt Tyler's depth of emotion. To do so was impossible. Nor did she question her own veracity of spirit. How could she? Guided by heartfelt sincerity and tenderness, Tyler drew them into the loving circle of his life with an expert's precision. But those facts didn't keep her from having to face a colder, harder truth: life with Tyler Brock would take her, and Pyper, far from the stability of the life they had worked so hard to build back in Michigan.

The Ruth and Boaz analogy Amy had embraced just one short week ago didn't seem to make nearly as much sense any longer. Why? Because the story of Ruth and Boaz didn't feature the life of a child—a child who desperately needed a solid and comfortable foundation.

Here, in Tennessee, they were happy, certainly, but upheaval was upheaval. Together, she and Pyper had struggled through so much life change that additional uprooting wasn't a viable option. Especially when coupled with the intrusive speculation of tabloids and the thousands of media outlets clambering for details on the lives of celebrities—the racier and more controversial, the better. Several aspects of her relationship with Tyler would feed that quest.

Amy groaned aloud and balled her breakfast napkin into a tight wad of paper. Would a relationship be in Tyler's best interests? He might think so. In return, she might long for just such a connection. In reality, however, "Tyler and Amy" would be a sticky, scrutinized model. Most likely, the situation would turn ugly for all three of them. That was a circumstance Amy couldn't accept, nor in any way reconcile.

Fantasies involving Tyler and a picture-perfect life now struck her as impossible.

So, with forty-eight hours left on the clock in Franklin, Amy arose from her seat in the kitchen to a tune of growing discord and sadness. She took her dishes to the sink and rinsed them, weakened at the shoulders by sullen thoughts and an ache of tiredness that filled her soul.

Falling asleep last night had been a solitary experience; before the record label event, Pyper had proudly announced she wanted to give *her* room a try. Amy recognized the decision had much to do with the plethora of goodies stored there, and the gauzy netting of the canopy bed, which simply begged for a little girl to curl up beneath its protection and dream of glorious fairytales. Solitude proved a double-edged sword for Amy—peaceful, certainly, but echoing with the thoughts and doubts that churned through her mind.

At breakfast this morning, RuthAnne had joined them, and the meal struck Amy like the precious pieces of a family unit. Determinedly she rebuked that thought as fast as it arose, although outwardly she remained as warm and upbeat as possible.

Now, with everyone disbursed into the call of the day ahead, she stewed while she stored dishes in the washer.

Presently, Tyler showered and dressed. Amy, Tyler, and Pyper had decided to spend today at a slow pace and keep close to home so Pyper could play, and the adults could simply relax. The interlude was soothing, but Amy remained unsettled. Her emptiness correlated directly to a lack of confidence she couldn't quell, or ignore. Not when all of the arrows in her life pointed away from the truest call of her heart.

For dinner, they went to Puckett's, a Tennessee institution with standard American fare, live music, and a country-style atmosphere that roused the embers of her doused mood. After praying over their meal, Tyler dug in. "Tomorrow's recording session will probably take a couple of hours." Tyler helped himself to a stash of fries then bit into his hamburger. "Are you sure you don't mind coming along? I really want you with me, so you can see how everything comes together, but it might be a little boring."

The question cut into her thoughts, which had strayed once again. Amy gave herself an internal shake, drawn back to the appealing hubbub of dining out at a restaurant full of happy energy. Conversations swirled, glassware and dinner utensils chinked and clanged, footsteps creaked against worn wooden floor planks. Pyper swung her legs, errantly connecting with Amy's calf from time to time. Pyper was lost to the atmosphere of Puckett's, happily absorbing the crowd and some well-played banjo music.

"I can't wait to hear what you're working on. It'll be anything but boring." Amy smiled at him and forced herself into a more proper, upbeat demeanor. She propped her elbows on the tall, window-side table where they sat. Bathed by the golden light of late afternoon sunset, people milled through the streets, enjoying a gorgeous summer evening. She let the beauty of the scene seep into her soul.

Pyper chewed on her grilled cheese sandwich and looked up at Tyler with wide, pleading eyes. "Me, too? Can we sing together too, Tyler? Please?"

Amy cringed, preparing to interject at once, but before she could speak, Tyler rested his hand on top of hers and gave a warning squeeze that kept Amy silent for the time being.

"I need to record a couple songs with my group, but I'll see what we can arrange. Maybe we can lay down a track of you and me playin' Chopsticks."

Pyper gasped. "And singing our ABC's, too? We're really good at that."

He laughed and tweaked her nose. "We sure are, sugar beet. I think that's doable."

She nodded hard. "And know what else? I decided something. Something important."

Amy braced herself for just about anything. "What's that?"

"I'm gonna be a singer when I grow up. Just like Tyler."

The statement worked right past every defense Amy possessed. And stirred up a world full of emotions: good and bad.

❧

On their way out of the restaurant, Pyper weaved through a cluster of customers who had just arrived at Puckett's. Amy watched after her daughter while Pyper charged toward the window display of a toy store they had passed on their way into downtown Franklin. Pyper leaned against the cement sill of the shop, looking inside with dreamy eyes.

"Pyper has certainly taken a major-league turn when it comes to you, Tyler. I'm glad for that." The automatic way he reached for her hand warmed Amy's heart despite the cold of her misgivings.

"I am, too. She's happy, don't you think? Confident."

"Yes. Definitely."

They meandered toward Pyper, down the length of a wide sidewalk dotted by ornate wrought iron street lamps, but then, Tyler's subtle tug on her hand brought Amy to a stop. "You know? The same can be said for her mom." His firm tone, the openness of his clear, hazel eyes, jammed any form of reply deep in her throat, right behind a thick swell of emotion.

She took a deep breath and swallowed. Removing her hand from his, she moved a few steps ahead. "I suppose so."

Pointedly Tyler stayed in place. When Amy attempted to venture forward once more, he held his ground. "Really? Is that all you're going to say?"

"What more do you want?" She wondered if the

words even registered over traffic noise and the chatter of passersby. She kept her lips from trembling by pressing them together.

"I want everything, Amy."

His intensity left her wanting distraction, so she looked toward her daughter. Pyper chatted with a little girl who joined her in admiring the toys that were framed in by a glass window. Happily occupied, they watched a twirling ballerina, admired a fully trimmed dollhouse and a chugging train. Amy resumed their stroll.

"What are you saying, Tyler? Seriously? That you want to marry me?"

"It's not an official proposal, no. Not yet. That moment will be much more precious, I promise you that. But ultimately, marriage is my intent, Amy. You wouldn't be here otherwise, and I think there's a big part of you that already knows that." He paused, letting her ingest that fact. "Why else would I bring you into my home, let you into the deepest parts of my life? I'm not casual when it comes to my heart, and I'm not cavalier about how I treat people. You know that better than anybody."

She shook her head slowly, meekly retreating from everything he offered. It was like a beautiful dream— therefore, it was also terrifying. "You can't possibly be serious." She swallowed, and her breathing went shallow. "Tyler, be rational. If you count Detroit, we've been together again for a week, and a handful of days."

"Is that all, Amy? Really?" His voice was deliberately soft. "You know? You might be the one who needs to be a little more rational right now."

"Don't you understand that I've just now begun to find myself again? After five long, horrible years? I'm starting to make my way back to a place where I can rebuild my life, but I don't know what can happen from here. Honestly. Look down the road and ask yourself if it'll work. Ask yourself if what you and I have is real, or if you're looking for nostalgia, and feelings, and a person you remember in far too idyllic a way, I'm not her anymore. And—"

He drew their steps to a close, capturing both her hands and holding her still. They stood in the middle of the Main Street sidewalk, in the rapidly darkening downtown. He cupped her face gently between his hands, brushing his thumbs against her cheeks. "Don't be afraid. Please. For *both* our sakes." His gaze traveled to Pyper, who bounded just ahead, this time captivated by another window display, this one full of sparkling crystal sculptures. "We're going to discuss this—at length—before you leave. For now, I make only one request. It's a plea from the depths of my heart."

Amy felt choked up, overly emotional. She gazed at him, vulnerable and helpless to everything she felt.

"For *all* our sakes, stop being afraid."

Let go. That was the underlying message, and she received it clearly, but not without a constricting dose of trepidation as well.

இ×௯

When honesty is missing from your world, keep shining the truth.

When compassion is missing from your world, keep reaching out.

When love is missing from your world, keep showering love.

That's the only way to live true justice.

Because someone – somewhere – is:
Drowning in hate, drowning in fear, losing hope.

So never give up, and never give in –
Fight the fight you know you need to win.
Reflect what this world needs –
True justice.

Piano music flowed to a conclusion, fading into a silence that left the assemblage in the control booth awed. "Wow. Where did *that* come from?" Kellen Rossiter spoke for them all.

The ballad was a perfect blend of loving emotion laced by Christian value and dedication. Amy still tingled, awash in the moment. She wanted to answer the question by saying: *from the depths of an open, giving heart.* Kellen concluded the matter on his own. "The man has undeniable soul."

"Yeah, he does." Amy stood next to the powerhouse of an agent, who struck her as handsome, confident and smooth. "Know what I hope?"

Kellen waited on her.

"I hope and pray that nothing—and no one—ever tries to take it away from him."

Kellen's initial reaction was nothing more than a sidelong glance, accompanied by a quiet sigh. He absorbed her pointed look with grace, but not without a fight. A fire lit in his eyes. "Is it so hard to believe that I might have one, too?"

Amy shrugged, staring straight back. He didn't intimidate her. Not in the least. What did she have to lose? Not nearly as much as Tyler, and she wanted some form of assurance that he would be all right facing the glories—and tribulations—of widespread fame.

Once she was gone.

Kellen shook his head, looking back at Tyler who remained seated at the piano, studying music sheets with Rebecca. "In my own way, I'm trying to help evangelize, Amy. Whether you see that fact, and accept it, isn't up to me." His gaze returned to her, hardened by traces of hurt. "Tax collectors were the parasites of Jesus' day, so I can easily relate to Matthew's gospel. By living in a world of sin, he brought those who most needed Christ to the hem of His robe."

Startled, she folded her arms across her chest and watched the man. He looked back at Tyler, a smile just starting to reclaim his features. So, he was a Christian. Immersed in a world of glitz, materialism, fame, ambition and a never-ending quest for "more." Yet at the same time, he pushed for Christian artists. Pushed *hard*, in fact, if his courting of Tyler was any indication.

"Then don't hide a light as effective as yours under a bushel basket, Kellen. That's the other lesson Matthew learned. Be forthright about your faith, and you'll accomplish miracles. You'll help feed hungry souls out there."

He nodded toward Tyler, who stood from the piano and stretched, smiling and joking with his crew. Tyler seemed buoyed by the results of the session. "I like to think I already do." Kellen stepped out of the booth and slipped in to the recording area. "Hey, Tyler. Question for you."

"What's that?"

"The song you just sang, *True Justice*. Did it feel at all like a compromise?"

Tyler shrugged. Amy watched through the

glassed-in sound booth as he regarded Kellen in a puzzled way. "No."

Kellen extended his hand. "Then welcome to preaching in the mainstream. It's going to be a hit."

Tyler accepted the gesture then listened intently when Kellen continued. "Depending on what you come up with next, I easily see that as single number one. Single number two? Let's push a bit more into your Christian roots, something upbeat and unapologetic about bringing God—and God's grace—into the texture the song. I know you can do it, and do it without the feel of preaching—kinda like *Amazing Grace*. A song like that would make a great second release, and maintain the message you've always presented."

Slowly, *very* slowly, Tyler's expectant smile bloomed. "I can get behind that scenario."

Pyper sat next to the soundboard, twisting her chair back and forth. Holding her beloved fashion dolls on her lap, she bobbed her head and swayed the dolls in a dancing motion as she hummed the refrain of *True Justice*. Amy watched after her daughter who remained happily occupied. Pyper had been an angel during the session. As a treat, she had been given permission to record a CD of music with Tyler. A rousing rendition of Chopsticks and the ABC song were now preserved forever.

Amy's throat went full and tight. *Lord,* please *help me. How can I—how can we—leave this world behind tomorrow morning? I don't want to, but I don't see any other choice.*

Tears pricked and stung at the corners of her eyes. Telltale moisture built against her lashes, so she ducked her head to flick the droplets away with a fingertip.

"Mama, why are you crying?"

Amy sniffed quietly, grateful to be ignored by the others for the time being. "It's OK, Pyp. I'm just happy for Tyler is all. Very happy."

Appeased, Pyper straightened and gave a nod. "Me, too."

In a way, Amy wasn't fibbing to her daughter. Tyler was going to have an amazing, fulfilled life. Why did that realization leave her with such a sharp stab of pain?

The only answer she could come up with was love. And its impending loss.

17

Returning home from the studio, Tyler gave Amy some space. Now, however, it was time to confront the issues she had raised at dinner the other night about being uprooted, and finding a life in Tennessee. Without question, he needed to know where she stood before they parted in the morning.

After checking in with RuthAnne, Tyler walked into the kitchen while Pyper and Amy trotted upstairs. There, he assumed Amy would freshen up and Pyper would settle into her bedroom with its treasure trove of toys…and the freshly minted CD of her recording debut.

Tyler smiled at the memory of sitting next to Pyper on the piano bench in the studio and having more fun than he'd had in years doing what most people in his business might refer to as "goofing off." The joy in Pyper's eyes, the determination and enthusiasm she put into the music, told a completely different story than mere goofing off. This was life at its richest and most blessed.

Following a brief, closed-door meeting with Kellen Rossiter at the studio offices of Exclamation Point Records, Tyler let everything else drift away except Amy. They had spent the remainder of the day in Nashville, grabbing dinner at The Palm restaurant. Now, it was time to unearth the reasons for her recent preoccupation and establish a pathway for what would come next.

Lifting a glass pitcher from inside the refrigerator, Tyler poured two tall glasses of sweet tea. He walked out to the porch, already knowing Amy would gravitate there soon, to soak in the beauty of her final evening in Tennessee.

The unending cadence of cricket chirps and insect song placed him at rest. The air was stirred by soft, warm breezes; once again, the yard came alive with the sparkle of lightning bugs. He felt a wash of bittersweet pleasure when he considered the fact that, forevermore, lightning bugs would bring to mind the way Pyper had danced and twirled through his yard, and the way quiet southern nights had led to heart-to-heart conversations with the woman he loved—and always would.

He deposited Amy's glass on the table to the right of the porch swing, his on the table to the left. He sank onto the thick cushions, and waited for her. Only a few minutes passed before the screen door came open with a squeak. He turned in time to see Amy register the beverage offering and give him an appreciative smile.

"Thanks."

"Pleasure."

She joined him, and took a sip.

"Pyper settled in?"

"Yes. All she keeps talking about is being in the recording studio. You just might have created a protégée."

Tyler chuckled low in his throat. "Good. You see, it's all a part of my great, grand plan."

"Your great, grand plan?"

"Mm-hmm. My plan to keep you here."

Her expression went uncertain. Tense. Tyler leaned forward on his knees and looked directly into her eyes. Amy's lips quivered. She broke from their visual connection and leaned back. "I should have known…"

Tyler picked up on the subtle show of distance, and respected it, taking a drink of his tea. "Known what, honey?"

"I should have known how hard it would be to say goodbye." Her voice shook against those whispered words. "This is putting me through a wringer. What I feel for you? It's tearing me up inside. For my sake, and for Pyper's as well, I *really* should have seen that coming."

"Seems to me the answer is pretty simple." He reached out and brushed his thumb against the back of her hand where it rested on the cushion between them. Amy glanced away. "Don't leave. Not permanently, anyway." Tyler wanted to see her eyes, but when she had dipped her head, the fall of her hair hid her face. Undeterred, he slid a fingertip against her cheek, then slowly tucked her hair over her shoulder.

She finally lifted her gaze. Turbulence rolled off her in waves. She straightened and gave him a tight, brave smile. "I leave on Sunday morning, and by Monday morning you'll officially be represented by Kellen Rossiter. I still can't get over it. Obviously your meeting today went well, huh?"

So, he thought, *she wants to ignore a painful topic.* In compromise, Tyler decided to sidestep. For now, anyway. He leaned on his knees again, and stared knowingly into her eyes, silently agreeing to her conversation shift. "Yeah, it's official. His office is drafting an agreement. What do you think of him?"

Amy curled up her legs and turned toward him. "I think you'll end up being good for each other. He seems to have a lot of substance—once you work past the flash and polish."

The answer pleased him; it mirrored his own assumptions. Her answer validated the risk he knew he was taking. "Thanks."

She looked puzzled. "For what?"

"For being my sounding board. For being someone I can open up to and trust. You know me; you know what I'm all about. That's comforting in the face of uncertainty."

Amy gave his arm a squeeze, and she smiled. "I understand where you're coming from. Being at a crossroads is never easy."

"True enough. This episode has taught me to stop fighting and start reaching out instead. Are you finding that to be true as well?"

She went stiff. The smile all but faded. "My. What a pointed question."

In deliberate contradiction, Tyler leaned back and forced himself to relax. "Don't expect me to avoid what God's trying to show me. Especially when it comes to you."

"OK then, you want the truth?"

"Always."

Amy firmed her jaw. She pushed herself forward and looked at him intently. "Your pathway can't include me, or Pyper. How could it? How could we uproot ourselves and blend into something new, someplace different?"

Tyler didn't allow that verdict to fluster him. "Quite easily. In fact, we just discussed the recipe. Stop fighting and reach out. I'm not Mark, and I never will be."

His conviction was authentic. Absolute.

Amy's eyes flickered but her posture stayed tight. "I know that, Tyler, and that's not even my point." He opened his mouth to continue, but Amy sliced her hand through the air to stop him. "My point is this: Beyond the enormous life change that would happen logistically, there's an emotional aspect to it as well. I can see the tabloid headlines right now"—She snorted. Then, in dramatic fashion, Amy put up air quotes and assumed an announcer's voice—"Christian rock phenom, Tyler Brock enters into a romantic relationship with a divorced single mother who's apparently on the mend and looking for love following the end of a marriage marred by alcohol abuse and domestic violence." She sank back against the side of the porch swing. "Do you really think your fans, and the media members who cover you and help shape your career are going to let that one slip by? I don't. How many of your fans are fundamentalist who frown on divorce? And what will happen when the find out my"—more air quotes—"'spiral into an abusive marriage' was caused by my philandering pre-marital sex?"

Tyler gasped. "Do you realize how badly that demeans what we feel for each other?"

"Tyler, it's not meant to demean. It's meant to be realistic! And then there's Mark! What if he reemerges, and tries to pressure you, or me, about Pyper? What if he exploits you, and me, for money, or some other form of support, in exchange for keeping away from me, and Pyper? These are legitimate concerns, Tyler. These are things we need to consider.

"My life is in Michigan. My *reality* is in Michigan.

It's what I know. It's what I've learned to handle, and it's what kept me, and Pyper, alive during the past year. Meanwhile, your life is here. Your career is here, and it's headed to wonderful places. Uprooting Pyper, uprooting myself, from everything that's familiar all over again and placing ourselves smack-dab in the middle of a harsh spotlight isn't a smart option right now—on a number of levels."

The peace of the evening evaporated like the day's humidity. Tyler stood abruptly from the swing. His steps turned into pacing. "Amy, do you think my life hasn't featured upheaval, and change, and challenge?"

"Of course it has, but—"

"No buts." His sharp interjection caused her to flinch, and Tyler winced. He hadn't meant to scare her, but he needed to get out how he felt. The clock was ticking away the last moments of their week together, and nothing was as important right now as giving voice to his heart. "I came to Tennessee with nothing but faith, and a dream. I gambled on Opry Bound with nothing but the sure knowledge that God would be in control of whatever happens. Now I'm facing an even more daunting circumstance—the danger that accompanies mass exposure and everything that goes along with it."

She blinked, folding her arms against her midsection. "Which is part of the point I'm trying to make. Don't you see? I won't be an asset to that part of your life. I'd do you more harm than good."

"*What?*" Tyler spun on his heel and gaped at her. The exclamation hung in the air, tethered by strings of shock and disbelief. Across the space of the porch that now separated them a boiling edginess grew, but Tyler fought back anger as best he could. She didn't need anger. She needed clarity and understanding—and so did he. "Where is all this coming from, Amy? And is this why you were so remote last night?"

She nodded. "Yes, it is. I have to admit, the media gave me a lot to think about when it comes to privacy, and when it comes to what would be best for me and Pyper, and for you, and your career."

He could only stare at her, aghast. "You're serious about this."

"How could I not be?"

"Do you honestly expect me to validate that question with a response? Silence stretched, then transformed into palpable tension. "Yes, there are frustrations when I'm—" he shrugged, at a loss. But then, the words came, in a heartbroken torrent. "I know there are times when I'm on display. When I'm catalogued, and even handled to a degree. But never has it compromised my privacy. Nor would I allow it to compromise yours and Pyper's. And as far as your ex-husband is concerned—" Tyler's tone had turned fierce, his eyes went narrow and angry. "—just let him *try* to interfere with what you and I have together. Just let him *try!* Frankly, I'd love to take him on!"

"That's not within your power to say, Tyler, especially once your fame increases. And you can't stand there and tell me it wouldn't matter!"

"Oh, yes I can." He forced himself to remain calm, but as they faced off, he clutched the edge of the porch railing so hard his fingers hurt. "You matter. Pyper matters. The rest is details, Amy. Insignificant details."

"Insignificant to you. Not to me. To me it's about a sordid divorce. It's about abuse. It's about a degree of alcoholism that ended up devastating not only me, but my daughter as well. My past isn't something I want, or need, to have magnified. A relationship with you would put all of us under intense scrutiny, especially as you gain more and more exposure. And don't discount Mark coming back hunting for money, or Pyper!"

"If that's truly how you feel, then I'll walk away from the career." He spoke with measured calm because he meant the words. With all his heart. "I don't need any of it. What I want is what's been missing in my heart without you, Amy."

"Tyler, that's ridiculous! Please! Listen to me!"

"No, *you* listen to *me*. What I want most in this world is what I've found ever since we reconnected at Woodland. Unless I'm grossly mistaken, you feel the exact same way. When will you learn to trust my feelings enough to just let go, and believe? When will you finally allow this relationship to be everything it was meant to be?"

A tapestry of dreams wove neatly into place: long days and sweet nights with Amy and Pyper, and even more kids down the road. There'd be Christmases, Easter celebrations, music that would fill his house and his heart, tours in the summer, family-friendly life and more than enough love to fill out the remainder of the year. The pictures his heart drew were of a happy, beautiful future—*with Amy*.

"What about all the mistakes I've made?" She eased back against the swing, almost as if she were sinking away from the truth. "What about privacy and protecting Pyper? I pored over everything this morning, and I just can't find the answers."

"You don't need to. What you need to do is stop looking for safety nets, or for assurances and guarantees. There's no such a thing. It won't happen.

Life gives us nothing but God's will and grace, and that's *enough*. You used to know that to the depths of your soul." Tyler took in a fortifying breath. "Nothing will change what life gave either of us, honey. I know Mark left you with a broken heart, but even in your marriage, God stayed with you, and with Pyper. He gave you goodness. Find your way back to that truth and maybe—just maybe—you'll find enough faith to love again."

Her eyes went wide with a kind of marveling wonder. He sensed her longing. In a spot of her heart where he alone was granted entry, he sensed Amy's most strident wishes.

Tyler pushed on. "Life is about change, Amy. We're not meant to remain stationary. I believe God always, *always* meets us where we are in life and can work anything for the good. In the storm of your marriage, your daughter came to life. In the storm of your divorce, God can—and will—continue to work His goodness, love and mercy. Nothing will ever change God, and his absolute goodness, his absolute love for us, because God *alone* is set in stone."

He ignored her glittering tears, her imminent breakdown. He needed her to understand her precious worth, and her hold on his spirit. Desperation poured through his veins, and Tyler hammered his point home. "God shows us pathways—for everything. That encompasses the good and the bad. Evolution is about following His call and that's what life is all about. Live again, Amy. If you don't, you're going to regret it. The loss will be yours. *Again.* Are you willing to accept that?"

"Tyler—" She choked, her eyes wide with desperation and a spirit-deep thirst he only recognized because he felt it so keenly himself.

"No. Hear me out. You're grasping at straws. You're clutching at anything that will justify walking away. Well, you need to ask yourself if walking away from me will save you from heartache." He waited, set his hands on his hips. The words hung in their air, framing the ultimate question that stood between them. His heart teetered precariously when silence held sway.

"Will walking away make you happy? If that's the case, then so be it. I've shown you everything I am, but if that's the case, all I can do now is let you. And yeah, like the fool that I am, I'll keep prayin' you find a way back. I'll keep faith that you'll eventually recognize the connection—the thread our lives have always carried to each other. That's what I'm clinging to, Amy. Not fear. But the decision is yours."

18

Tyler stopped short at the threshold of Amy's room the next morning. He intended to speak with her privately, before they rejoined Pyper downstairs. Next to the bed, Amy's suitcase stood ready, packed and zipped closed.

He hated it.

Not because she was leaving. Leaving he could tolerate. He had expected nothing else at the end of the week. What sliced through him right now was the finality. Unresolved and uncertain, his relationship with Amy was taking an exit right now that he couldn't begin to bear.

She stood at the window, holding back the curtain with her hand, surveying the sprawl of the valley and mountains. Tyler shut out the image of the extended metal pull handle of her luggage and made a decision. He wouldn't let her go without giving her something to think about. And miss.

Without a word, deliberately catching her unprepared, not allowing her a single second to realize his intent and lay out a defense, he pulled her in by the waist and didn't stop until she was pinned against him. His mouth covered hers, his kiss capturing her startled exclamation of surprise and swallowing it up with his own sigh of desire, and surrender.

She melted into him, raking shaky fingertips

through his hair. He clung to her, fed her, adored her, doing his best to seep into the very core of her system until she knew no escape and no other pathway but the one that led to his love.

His fingers dove in as well, combing through her hair, dislodging a satin hair tie. Her hair drifted free around his hands. The familiar smell of his brand of shampoo in her hair, now a fragrant part of the thick, silky strands, caused his muscles to clench with a longing as familiar as his own name, and it broke his aching heart.

They shared so much, yet she could walk away?

The kiss remained intense and heated, spiraling nearly out of control. He barely maintained the wherewithal to pull back and step away from her, refusing the temptation of claiming her definitively, with all the love in his heart.

His body was taut, strung as tight as a wire on one of his six-strings. His breathing was ragged. In slight vindication, though, he realized she suffered as well. So he reigned in his strength and determination. "Amy, think about us. Think about everything you're turning from. I'll be here. I always have been. I feel like it's a huge part of God's plan for me. Know why? Because no other woman comes close to you. I guess it's His will that I let you go again, so I'll do my best to make music my life. I can say this without reservation or anger because I believe in God's promise. He promises that when you love someone well, and when that love is returned, that love will last a lifetime. I look at you, and I know you feel as strongly as I do. I let you go before. I'll let you go again if it'll help you recognize that truth and find your way back to me."

Finished, not letting himself absorb the sheen of

tears that glossed her eyes, or her trembling, kiss-swelled lips and staccato breathing, he took custody of her luggage and carried it downstairs.

Saying goodbye to Pyper was almost as hard.

She was one unhappy young lady, if her flushed face and watery eyes were any indication. When he joined her in the entryway, she slipped off her backpack and charged for him in open trust and love. Tyler took her in, lifting her up and squeezing tight.

He inhaled her sweet scent and feathered his fingers tenderly through her hair. "Miss you already, sugar beet."

"I want to see you soon again," she whispered, her voice shaky.

Convoluted grammar and all, Tyler's heart swelled at the words. "Me, too. But until then, I'll be in touch with you, Pyper." He leaned back, tucking wisps of hair away from her damp, red cheeks. "And here's an idea. I want you to do me a favor."

"What?"

"Every time you see a firefly, I want you to think of me. And I promise, I'll do the same for you."

She nodded, but her chin quivered badly. Tears rolled down her face, and she tucked into his neck and shoulder like a missing puzzle piece. She shook with tears she obviously tried, and failed, to keep silent. Tyler kept rubbing her back, swaying a bit to give them both some semblance of comfort.

For now, though, the airport called. And with every prayer of his heart, he held fast to the belief that releasing his two beautiful doves would ultimately lead them all home, and bring them together once more.

19

For the second day in a row, Amy had a pounding headache.

She'd been back on the job at Edwards Construction for less than a week; the summer schedule for JB's construction company was at an all-time high. She was grateful for busy, fast-passing days. That way, there was far less time to consider the enormous hole in her spirit.

She found herself reliving the parting, that final kiss with Tyler, over and over again. The emotions, the textures and tastes combined to overwhelm her at the most random points during the day. She'd be in the midst of job setups and staffing, service proposals, invoicing—then, in an instant the present world would slip away.

The kiss provided such an exquisite memory—the sensations as real to her now as they were then. She'd lose herself so completely and so willingly to her daydreams, that even her breathing, her heart rate, would react. But then, the return to reality and the recognition of her loss would end her revelry on a note of intense sadness.

Hence the headaches.

Tonight, at least, she had chores at home with which to contend. Pyper dabbled with a spelling game on the computer for a time while Amy retrieved a load of freshly dried laundry from the basement of their apartment unit. Amy had finally started on the photo album for Tyler—the one chronicling his concert at Woodland. After all, it wasn't as if they couldn't remain connected and enjoy each other. Amy figured delivery of the gift might do the job of telegraphing that hope.

For now, however, silence stretched between them, and her heart instantly betrayed the truth that her head couldn't quite grasp yet—she loved him. She ached for him. Friendship, sadly, would never be enough.

The thought plagued her as she returned to her apartment, clothes basket in tow, and went to her bedroom where she intended to sort and fold. Coming upon Pyper caused Amy to stop abruptly, and set aside the laundry basket on the floor next to her bed.

Bathed by the grayish blue illumination of the computer screen, Pyper's entire face looked crumpled. Her lips quaked. Fat tears rolled down her cheeks as she regarded a photograph displayed on the monitor. Tyler. Amy silently cursed herself. She had left the folder of pictures from the Woodland concert open on her task bar. Pyper had apparently clicked away from her game and discovered the readily-available images.

Amy bit the inside of her cheek, going immediately to her shaken daughter. She scooped Pyper up and held on fast. "What's the matter, snug-a-bug?" But she had a feeling she already knew.

"I jus'…I jus' miss him, Mommy. I miss Tyler."

Precisely as she thought. Amy became buried by the weight of that admission. Pyper had come so far—and now, once again, Amy knew she had let her daughter down.

"I can't help it! I wish Tyler was my daddy, and I wish I could see him all the time, and that he could be with me, and you, all the time."

Oh, Lord, help me. Help me now. I can't possibly make it through this without You.

Amy's throbbing head pulsed with a fresh onslaught of pain as she carried Pyper a few feet. In a deliberately playful little tumble, they toppled to the bed, and snuggled up side by side, face to face. Just like they had in Nashville. At Tyler's.

This time it was Amy who reached out and cupped Pyper's cheek. Pyper, in turn, rubbed a soft fingertip against the tight furrow on Amy's forehead.

"I'm so sorry for how sad you feel." Silence followed Amy's apology. "I've messed up a lot, Pyper, but I don't want to hurt you again. Not ever."

Pyper frowned, her eyes still sparkling. "You don't hurt me. You love me. You love me best."

"Oh, honey, you bet I do. The only one who loves you better than me is Jesus. But, still, I wanted better things for you than what you've gotten. I want you to be happy, and to know you're safe, and have a good home, and most of all I want you to know that you're precious, and loved."

Pyper looked into Amy's eyes, her lips rolled inward, pressed between her teeth. The signal was clear—she was emotional, and she was unsettled. But in contradiction to that, she kept a light touch moving against Amy's forehead. Thankfully, Pyper's touch helped ease the relentless band of pressure. Bit by bit, Pyper's eyes dried of tears.

"I know you love me, Mommy, and you made us safe."

"Yeah, but then we had to stay with Ken and

Kiara. We bounced around a lot, didn't we, Pyp?"

"Mm-hmm. They were nice to us. And Annie? She's my bestest friend because we take care of each other and love each other." Pyper blinked her eyes, and smiled. "I think Ken and Kiara and Annie are my family. Like Grandma and Grandpa Maxwell."

A theme developed, swirling slowly into place, but Amy couldn't quite grasp it yet…

"Then I brought you here."

Pyper nodded, and her smile curved larger. "This is *our* house. An' you're not scared of nothin' anymore. You smile. And you and me? We're the *best*. We've got happy."

We've got happy. Amy closed her eyes and took a gulp, thinking, *God, thank you.*

But her daughter wasn't finished yet. Pyper's brows pulled together, and she frowned as tears built once more. "Know what though? You and me never smiled more than when we were with Tyler. I love Tennessee, and I miss him, Mommy. Do you miss him, too? Do you want to see him again? Soon?"

That's when a stunning realization took place. The theme she caught traces of earlier circled to completion and a sharp focus. Not once as Amy poured her heart free, and Pyper examined their lives together, had Pyper reacted in the negative. Pyper transformed every nightmare in their lives into loving kindness, safety, and a fresh, happy life. Together.

We've got happy.

Yes, the past left Pyper sorting through trust and safety issues with adult men, but she worked past them—just like she worked past all the challenges of their life together. Pyper knew the horrors, of course, but she didn't cling to them. By the grace of God alone, she had let them go and continued to embrace each movement forward with hope. Pyper's outlook stayed trained on blessings instead of darkness. Exactly how Amy would want it.

Amy, meanwhile, had worked so hard to make that come to be, she had hardly been aware of, nor acknowledged, the impact of God's hand and the true depth of God's healing, loving power.

With her heart in her throat, she decided to answer Pyper's question, then pose one of her own. "I miss him so very, very much, Pyper. But in order for us to be with Tyler, we'd have to make a whole new bunch of big changes. We'd have to move to Tennessee. It would be far away from everyone and everything we know."

Pyper nodded, and she thought about that for a moment, her lips pursed softly. "Everything 'cept Tyler. And us."

"What about our family?"

"Well. Can they fly like I did? Can we see them that way a lot of times?"

Tyler, Amy imagined, would probably insist on it. "That's a distinct possibility."

Amy's concluding comment caused Pyper to smile, and glow. Amy's heart raced wildly. Energy built so hard and so fast Amy wanted to leap out of bed and start running—clear south to Tennessee. A dam burst free in her heart and love rode in on the energy spill. The right decisions became clearer and clearer, persistent to the point of being undeniable.

We've got happy.

Maybe not yet, Amy thought. Not completely, anyhow—but perhaps soon enough...

৵৽

"Kiara…I…" Amy had stalled long enough, and she knew it. She steadied herself. "I need to ask a huge favor."

Amy knelt next to Kiara in the Lucerne's back yard. Together they weeded, not because Kiara had asked, but because Amy had volunteered. It helped Kiara, but it helped Amy as well. Ever since last night, ever since *The Decision*, she had energy to excessive degrees, and she had never, ever been as happy, nor as terrified.

The thoughts crested; not until they receded did she realize Kiara had leaned back on her heels and was watching her. Waiting, and intrigued.

"What's up, Miss Thing?" They shared a smile at the ages-old nickname, but a swell of emotion colored Amy's world. She chewed her lower lip and went back to work pulling away weeds. Kiara, however, didn't continue with their work. "Amy? What's up?"

"Well…I…" Amy focused on their weeding session like a woman on a mission, not meeting Kiara's eyes. "You see…my folks are going to be out of town this coming weekend, and…and…I need to go to Tennessee."

Now Kiara stripped off her gardening gloves and switched from kneeling to sitting cross-legged. "Tennessee."

Amy nodded, and she surrendered the pretense of working. She sat next to Kiara and leaned back, propping against her hands. "I've got a lot to tell you."

Amy launched into a detailed overview of the past week, especially the conversation with Pyper. Kiara listened, silent and intent while Amy let her emotions pour free, especially her growing realization that a life without Tyler wasn't a life lived happily, or in completeness with the call of her heart. Apart from him, she felt apart from God's plan for her life.

"With Mark, I fell in love with an image more than a man. With Tyler, I love the *person*, the boy he was, and the man he's become."

Kiara just nodded, wearing a wise, but non-condemning expression.

"You said it best when he came back into town and you told me to reconcile the boy I knew with the man Tyler is now. I have. Without question. At his core, he was always the one for me. My life and my heart synchronize with him so beautifully. I've been given the most incredible luxury imaginable—the gift of a second chance with the man I should have been with from the start. I'm not turning my back on that again. I can't. To do so is making me miserable."

"OK." Kiara's eyes went wide, and they were misty, but she smiled, and seemed just a touch nostalgic, as though she was already letting Amy go. "You know what I have to ask, right? Just to be a proper big-sister-type person."

Amy laughed. She was already two steps ahead. Reaching into the pocket of her shorts, she pulled out a folded piece of paper and opened it up. "Here witnesseth my reservations at the Country Inn and Suites Hotel in Franklin."

Kiara started to laugh, too.

"Not because I can't be trusted, but because I want you to know exactly where to reach me if anything should come up with Pyper."

"Naturally." Kiara let out a soft sound and pulled Amy in for a long, tight hug. "Oh, Amy...I wonder if you realize how much I'm going to miss you."

"Kiara, c'mon. It's just for the weekend!"

Kiara pulled back. Now the moisture spilled over into a few teardrops that skimmed her cheeks. "Sure it is, Miss Thing. Sure it is."

19

Tyler fiddled restlessly with his cell phone. He held it in his hand and immediately began to drum his fingertips against the side of the device. He paid a visit to his list of contacts and started to scroll until the last name *Maxwell* was highlighted.

She was right there. A simple key click and they'd be connected. He'd hear her voice. Just the idea set his heart racing, his blood pumping.

He backed out of contacts in a hurry, expelling a frustrated groan. The decision had to be hers. But a full week of silence left him less and less able to maintain an even-headed, confident spirit.

He nearly pocketed the unit, but it sprang to life with a vibration, then a chime of melodic bells. It was a ring tone he had assigned to just one person in his far-reaching phone book.

Amy.

He bobbled the phone in his eagerness to activate the connection and see what was going on. What he found wasn't a phone call, but a one-word text message.

Faith.

"What?" Tyler spoke aloud, to the empty quiet of his living room. Was her message sent by mistake? Must be, because it made no sense at all.

This warranted a call. Perfect excuse, Tyler

figured. She had sent the text after all. If it was in error, then she could explain, and maybe talking would open up an avenue to something deeper.

Seconds later, Amy's chimes sounded again. Another text. Another single word.

Opens.

Tyler shook his head, puzzling at the message on the display screen. He wasn't about to try to figure out what was going on. Instead, he called Amy promptly. Four interminable rings later, he got to hear her voice—in recorded form, anyhow.

Hi, you've reached the voicemail for Amy Maxwell. Sorry I missed you, so leave me a message. I'll get back to you. Thanks!

In acute terms, Tyler learned that even in electronic format, the sound of Amy's voice had the power to do him in. He missed her that much. He realized he was hanging on the line, filling up her voicemail with nothing more than dead air so he spoke up in a hurry. "Amy, it's me. Got a couple weird texts and wanted to be sure you're OK, or what it, what they, you know, what you mean." He was reduced to stammering. Tyler rolled his eyes at himself. "Anyway, call me when you get this. Miss you. A lot."

The quietly spoken endnote left him to sigh as he disengaged.

The sound of tires crunching on the gravel drive out front of his home barely registered with Tyler, especially since at that precise moment a third text from Amy rolled in. What in the world was she doing?

Doors.

The doorbell rang and Tyler groaned for a second time. He was so not in the mood for company right now. He strode to the front door, redialing Amy as he yanked it open with an impatient, bothered tug.

Tyler stared, mouth open, phone to his ear. Amy stood before him, the woman he had longed for day in day out, smiling and as glorious as an angel.

Amy held her phone in her hand, and her smile quivered as tears sprang to her eyes. Moisture beaded and glittered on her lashes like diamonds before tracking slowly from the corners of her luminous blue eyes.

"Faith opens doors, Tyler," came her greeting.

He could hardly breathe.

ॐ

"Where's Pyper?"

It was the first question that popped into his head and by her smile alone, Tyler knew Amy appreciated that particular consideration.

"She's enjoying a weekend with Annie, and Ken and Kiara."

Tyler still hadn't found center, but that didn't bother him in the least. "Weekend. You're here." He wasn't making much sense, just trying to absorb.

"I'm only here until Sunday. I took the first flight I could after work today and booked the last flight home on Sunday night." She shuffled a bit, seeming, for the first time, a bit uncertain. "That is, if you don't mind."

Mind? Was she insane?

While he stared, Amy looked past his shoulder. "Ah, do you think I could come in, or…"

She burst out laughing, and Tyler joined in. The sound of it filled him like he most beautiful music. Before he let her cross the threshold, he yanked her into his arms and lifted her up, carrying her to the entryway where he spun her in circles.

This was too good to be true! Too blessed for belief!

She was *here*. She was *home*. And she was *his*.

Finally.

It only got better. "I had to see you," she whispered as she flew in his arms. "I had to let you know…know that…that…"

He didn't need roadmaps. He needed Amy. He set her down then pulled her in for a kiss that left them both out of breath and silent with awe.

"I hope you keep selling a lot of records, because my daughter is going to cost you a fortune in family airfare."

"Well, honey, since in the times to come I'd love for her to become *our* daughter, all I can say to that is: bring it on!"

❧

He made sure he kept his word.

In the months that followed, while summer gave way to the cool breezes and leaf-fire of autumn, Tyler arranged for Amy and Pyper to visit Tennessee as often as possible. Weekends spent together became precious bookends to weeks full of work on the new album, tour plans and preparations, and a relationship with Kellen Rossiter that increased his confidence as each day passed.

September was on the wane when, on a blustery Saturday night, he took them to dinner at The Franklin Chop House, a favorite haunt of theirs. Private booths, intimate atmosphere and delicious food were a perfect combination that allowed them to relax together in peace and anonymity.

Since it was Saturday night, Amy gave voice to her usual weekend-concluding sentiment. "I hate to leave." Tyler kept quiet for the moment and simply watched her instead. Candlelight flickered, shimmering against the curls of her upswept hair as she tilted her head. Her eyes roamed the restaurant and its patrons. "The more time that goes by, the more Tennessee feels like home to me."

Pyper, he noticed, kept watching her mother. The keen-eyed girl sat next to Amy and didn't say a word, but there was expectancy to her appearance. Hope.

That made Tyler smile. "Know what? I forgot something in the car. I'll be right back."

Amy nodded, and opened up the menu to explore dinner options with Pyper. When he passed by, Tyler planted a kiss on Amy's cheek, then Pyper's forehead. His reward? Twin smiles as bright as the twinkle lights that framed in the restaurant ceiling and booth windows.

He returned just a minute or two later, a crackling plastic bag from a local drug store swinging from his hand. He made a ceremonious production out of settling it in the middle of the table. Shocked expressions registered on Amy and Pyper's faces. The waitress approached with her pad in hand. Tyler smiled at her, but shook his head slightly. "Thanks, but can we have a minute here?"

"Absolutely. Y'all just let me know when you're ready."

Amy ignored the exchange. "What's this?"

Tyler stretched back against the padded bench seat and grinned. "Guess there's only one way to find out." With a wave of his hand, he invited her to explore the offering.

"Is it for Mommy?"

"Mmm…actually, sugar beet, it's for all of us."

Pyper bounced in her seat. "Cool! C'mon, Mama, what is it, what is it?"

Amy snickered under her breath and Tyler covered a laugh by coughing. Lately, Pyper seemed determined to pick up a southern twang. She vacillated, currently, between Mommy and Mama, which both Amy and Tyler thought was hilarious. She'd even busted out a "y'all" for the first time yesterday.

Amy unsealed the bag, and her quizzical expression only intensified when she pulled out a good old-fashioned box of sixty-four crayons—secured by a pair of rubber bands.

"This looks like it's for me, Tyler," Pyper said.

"Nope. Not quite. Just wait while your mama opens it."

Amy spread out her hands in surrender, but she smiled. Oh, how she smiled. "I get it. I'm the crayons. You're the rubber bands. Cute reminder of the mission trip to Pennsylvania. But seriously—what's going on?"

Tyler straightened and slid the box toward the place setting in front of him. "Let me explain." He pulled off the rubber bands and knotted them together. After that, he opened the box of crayons so that a vivid, colorful display could be seen and enjoyed. He then settled the offering in front of Amy. "Yes, the rubber bands are me, and I'm connected to you, my lady of rainbow colors and vivid beauty. Kinda like this." Demonstrating, he stretched the slender piece of tan rubber toward Amy. "Here. Take hold. And Pyper, you have a very important job. Make sure she holds on real tight and doesn't let it go no matter what, OK?"

"Mm'kay, Tyler. I will!"

Fascinated, squirming with anticipation, Pyper monitored Amy's hold on the rubber band with the utmost care.

Quick as lightning he removed an item from the pocket of his slacks and hooked it onto the rubber band. He set it gliding along the taut connector where it ended up bumping against Amy's fingers. Pyper gasped. Amy let out a shocked exclamation that nearly caused her to drop her hold on the rubber band, until Pyper yelped. "Hang on, Mama! Hang on tight!"

"Yeah, Amy. Hang on tight," Tyler reiterated tenderly, smiling wide as Amy's stunned eyes touched on his.

Dangling between them, resting against her hand, was a brilliant cut solitaire diamond set in platinum. It sparkled in the dim lighting of the restaurant like wildfire.

"T..T..Tyler..."

"Mommy, it's the prettiest ring ever in the world!"

Tyler gave the little girl a moment to settle. "I can't think of a more perfect moment to ask you to be my wife, Amy. I want Pyper to be my daughter. I want you to grow old with me. I want to build a family with you. You're my best friend, and my soul mate. But beyond anything else, with God's grace and hand, I promise I'll love you forever."

Amy remained silent and overcome, the fingertips of her free hand pressed against her trembling lips. Pyper squiggled, seeming to fight the urge to cut in. In the end, though, the task proved too great. Pyper let out an urgent sound. "Mama, please say yes. Please? *Please?*"

Amy burst out laughing through an onslaught of tears that flowed down her cheeks. Her hold on the rubber band was so shaky it trembled between them, making the ring dance a bit. Tyler moved his hand toward hers, relaxing the tension on the rubber band. He took possession of the ring, and held tight to Amy's left hand. He arched a brow, waiting.

"Yes! Of course my answer is yes!"

Pyper clapped and let out a shout that drew a bit of attention from nearby guests of the restaurant. Tyler stood just far enough to stretch across the length of the table and kiss Amy's lips. They were moist and giving, salted by her tears. He uncurled her ring finger and slid the ring into place. While Amy and Pyper studied its flash and sparkle, Tyler kissed Amy's cheek. "Didn't I promise you this moment would be precious?"

She nodded. "And you've always, always kept your promises. I love you, Tyler. You've made every one of my dreams come true."

"Well, there's a lot more to come, honey. Just wait and see."

Thank you

We appreciate you reading this White Rose Publishing title. For other inspirational stories, please visit our on-line bookstore at www.pelicanbookgroup.com.

For questions or more information, contact us at customer@pelicanbookgroup.com.

White Rose Publishing
Where Faith is the Cornerstone of Love™
an imprint of Pelican Book Group
www.PelicanBookGroup.com

Connect with Us
www.facebook.com/Pelicanbookgroup
www.twitter.com/pelicanbookgrp

To receive news and specials, subscribe to our bulletin
http://pelink.us/bulletin

May God's glory shine through
this inspirational work of fiction.

AMDG

You Can Help!

At Pelican Book Group it is our mission to entertain readers with fiction that uplifts the Gospel. It is our privilege to spend time with you awhile as you read our stories.

We believe you can help us to bring Christ into the lives of people across the globe. And you don't have to open your wallet or even leave your house!

Here are 3 simple things you can do to help us bring illuminating fiction™ to people everywhere.

1) If you enjoyed this book, write a positive review. Post it at online retailers and websites where readers gather. And share your review with us at reviews@pelicanbookgroup.com (this does give us permission to reprint your review in whole or in part.)

2) If you enjoyed this book, recommend it to a friend in person, at a book club or on social media.

3) If you have suggestions on how we can improve or expand our selection, let us know. We value your opinion. Use the contact form on our web site or e-mail us at customer@pelicanbookgroup.com

God Can Help!

Are you in need? The Almighty can do great things for you. Holy is His Name! He has mercy in every generation. He can lift up the lowly and accomplish all things. Reach out today.

Do not fear: I am with you; do not be anxious: I am your God. I will strengthen you, I will help you, I will uphold you with my victorious right hand.
~Isaiah 41:10 (NAB)

We pray daily, and we especially pray for everyone connected to Pelican Book Group—that includes you! If you have a specific need, we welcome the opportunity to pray for you. Share your needs or praise reports at http://pelink.us/pray4us

Free Book Offer

We're looking for booklovers like you to partner with us! Join our team of influencers today and receive at least one free eBook per month. Maybe more!

For more information
Visit http://pelicanbookgroup.com/booklovers